Golden Trail

Discover other titles by Kristen Ashley at:
www.kristenashley.net

Commune with Kristen at:
www.facebook.com/kristenashleybooks
Twitter: KristenAshley68

Golden Trail

Kristen Ashley

Copyright © 2015 by Kristen Ashley
First ebook edition: July 6, 2011
Latest ebook edition: February, 25 2015
First print edition: April, 2015

ISBN: 0692410287
ISBN-13: 9780692410288

Prologue

Fluid

Layne opened his eyes and saw dim light in an unfamiliar room. Groggy, he sensed movement and turned his head to the left.

Rocky was sitting there. Her head bowed, dark hair with fashionable (but fake) streaks of blonde pulled back in a ponytail, but that heavy fall at the front that wouldn't fasten back, as usual, covered one eye.

What the fuck?

His eyes moved beyond her to the walls then they kept scanning and he saw the monitors, the drips and cords.

He was in a hospital bed.

Shit, I've been shot.

He closed his eyes, feeling heavy fatigue and not much else. It wasn't like he just woke up. It was like he hadn't slept for a year.

When he heard rustling, he forced his eyes open again and saw Rocky move, adjusting in her chair, putting an elbow to the arm, her jaw in her palm, her fingers curling around her cheek. Her head was up now and her face was flawlessly made up, also as usual. Perfection. He hated it. When they were living together years ago she would put on makeup to go to class, to go out dancing, to go get a meal, but it was light. If she wasn't going anywhere, or nowhere special, she didn't bother. He preferred it that way.

Her eyes skimmed over him and shot back, fastening on his.

"Layne?" she asked, her voice quiet.

"The boys," Layne said, his voice scratchy and hoarse.

She stood, the movement liquid, the way she always moved—full body or just lifting a finger to point at something.

Fluid.

Her chair was so close standing brought her right next to the bed.

"They were here with Gabrielle. Dad took them home," she whispered, looked to his chest, her eyes lifting again to his. "How are you feeling?"

"They okay?" He was still talking about his sons.

"You're okay," she told him. "It'll take a while but the doctors say you'll be fine so…they're okay."

The exhaustion was nearly overwhelming and the last person on earth, outside of Gabby, who he'd want in his hospital room or anywhere near him, was Raquel Merrick Astley. He'd rather go to sleep and wake up when she was gone but he struggled against the sleep that wanted to take him because he had to know.

"What do the docs say?"

"You'll be fine. They hit you in the thigh, gut, shoulder," she answered. "The gut was the bad one, but they stitched you up."

He took three. Now he remembered, he took three. He felt each one.

He wanted to ask if it was her husband that worked on him.

He didn't ask that, instead he asked, "How long am I gonna be in here?"

"Awhile," she evaded.

"What's awhile?" he pressed.

"Not too long. At most, two weeks."

Fuck, he didn't have any insurance. *Fuck.*

"Where's Merry?" he asked.

"At the station, he's coming later," Rocky answered.

His eyes closed because he couldn't keep them open anymore, but he forced them back open.

"He safe?" Layne knew he could ask her that. Rocky and Merry were close. Merry told Rocky everything. She did the same with her brother. They looked out for each other. They kept each other's secrets. She'd know.

"Yes, far as he can tell, you kept him clean."

Thank God, Layne thought and his eyes closed again.

Then he asked, "What're you doin' here?"

"Shh, Layne, just rest," she whispered.

He forced his eyes open and to focus on her. "What're you doin' here?" he repeated, now his voice sounded scratchy, hoarse and as tired as he felt.

He watched her face change, her eyelids descended to half-mast, her mouth got soft.

Layne stared.

Fuck, he remembered that look. She used to look at him like that a lot and always it came unexpected no matter how often she did it. While they were watching TV, across the room at a party, but mostly across a table from him—any table. At her dad's. At a restaurant. At their apartment. He'd feel her looking at him and catch her eyes, see that look on her face and know his life was beautiful.

He hadn't seen that look in eighteen years.

She leaned in, lifting a hand and placing it gently against his cheek.

"Rest, Layne," she repeated quietly.

His eyes slid closed and he wanted to tell her to get the fuck out. He wanted to tell her to go to hell. He didn't want her near his sons, near him. They lived in the same town again but that was as close as he wanted to get. Her brother had been a family member, who, after Layne came back, turned into an old acquaintance then a loose colleague, and finally, a friend. Her father the same, without the loose colleague part. But a year back in town and she hadn't re-entered his life and he took pains to keep it that way.

As these thoughts drifted through the weariness, he felt her hand slide down his cheek to his neck.

Then, fuck him, he could fucking swear he felt that heavy, soft fall of hair slide along his cheek, his temple and he smelled her perfume, expensive, elusive, then he felt her lips brush his.

Jesus.

By the time he forced his eyes back open, her lips were gone, her hand was gone, but the scent of her perfume remained. With effort he turned his head to the side and saw the door close behind her.

Then his eyelids closed and sleep took him.

One

DREAMS

She rolled him then her mouth was on him, her tongue, her hair trailing down his chest. She nipped his side with her teeth, sexy, hot. Christ, she'd devour him if she could.

He hauled her up and rolled her back, his lips taking hers, his tongue shafting into her mouth. He fucking loved the way she let him kiss her, let him take, did nothing but give. It was contradictory to the way she fucked him, a tussle, a battle for supremacy.

Not, of course, when he made love to her, that was different.

But now, they were fucking.

Both her hands slid down his back to his ass, fingers curling in. He could feel her nails, all the while she arched her back, pressing into him. She wanted it, he knew it and his cock was so fucking hard, aching, if he didn't give it to her soon, he'd come on her belly.

His hand moved down her body, between her legs, down the inside of one thigh pushing it open and his hips moved between.

Her mouth broke from his, lips sliding across his cheek to his ear.

"Yes, Layne, come inside," Rocky rasped.

1

Layne's eyes opened.

He was on his stomach, in his bed and his cock was rock hard. Aching.

He rolled to his back.

"Christ," he muttered into the darkened room.

He lifted his palms to his forehead and pressed in.

Every night, every night for six weeks since he saw her in his hospital room, he had these dreams. Always sex, hot sex, wild sex, and not what they had eighteen years ago. These weren't memories. She wasn't twenty and he wasn't twenty-four. They'd had hot, wild sex back then, the best, the fucking best he ever had, by a mile. But, in the dreams, she was who she is now and the same with him. And the sex was better.

Far better.

Out of this fucking world.

He stared at the ceiling, concentrating on bringing his body under control.

Layne didn't understand these dreams. He hadn't even seen her since that night. He'd seen her brother Merry and father Dave dozens of times, but not Raquel. He hadn't talked to or asked Merry or Dave about Rocky's visit either. After days slid into weeks and she didn't show, he'd actually tried to convince himself he'd been hallucinating. Especially after seeing that look, smelling her perfume so close, feeling the touch of her hand, her hair, her lips.

But he knew he wasn't hallucinating.

He rolled out of bed and got up, walked to the bathroom, took a piss, washed his hands, splashed water on his face and then brushed his teeth as he stared at his torso in the mirror.

The wounds were fading. Still red, the violence of a bullet tearing though flesh still visible. Three inches down from the middle of his right shoulder and another at his upper gut. His pajama bottoms hid the wound to his right thigh. They joined the stab wound he got in his right side in San Antonio and the deep graze wounds from the shrapnel he took to the left hip and side of his thigh after that car bomb went off in LA.

He bent his neck and spit, rinsed and wiped his mouth with a towel he took from and threw back to the counter before he raised his head and looked into his eyes in the mirror.

"I need a new fuckin' job," he told himself.

Then his head cocked and he listened.

Nothing.

He walked into the bedroom, his eyes at the drawn curtains, seeing weak light coming around the sides through the slit in the middle. His eyes went to his alarm clock.

Six thirty.

He listened again.

"Fuck," he bit out and strode fast from his room, a huge master suite that had a bedroom that held his king-sized bed, a low dresser and another narrower, higher dresser on which he'd put a flat-screen TV. If he wanted, he could put a chair and couch in there, which he didn't, so there was tons of empty space making the room seem cavernous.

This led to a master bath that had a double sink, a huge mirror in front of it, acres of counter space between the sinks, cabinets underneath separated by a space where the woman of the house—if there was one, which there wasn't—could put a bench and have a dressing table. Behind the sinks, a room with the toilet, giving privacy—to the left, if you were facing it. Across from that, a shower stall big enough to fit two. In between and up two carpeted steps, a huge, oval sunken tub. Beyond the bathroom was an enormous walk-in closet nearly as big as the bedroom.

Layne threw open one of the double doors that led out to the large open area at the top of the stairs that held his weight bench, weights, a treadmill, a wall filled with in-built shelves, cabinets and a desk unit under the wide window where his computer was, a beat up swivel chair in front of it.

He walked through the room and to one of the doors at the opposite side of the stairs. He knocked loud, twice. His hand went to the handle, he pressed down and pushed in. Swinging his torso into the dark room, he saw his youngest son Tripp dead asleep in bed.

"Tripp, up, shower," he ordered, his voice loud.

Tripp's body moved, rolled. "Wha'?"

"Up, boy, shower. You're late. You gotta get to school," Layne told his son.

"Right," Tripp mumbled and rolled back to his stomach.

3

"Now, Tripp," Layne demanded, pushed the door all the way open and walked down the hall to the next door.

He knocked twice again and opened the door. There was movement immediately but this was Jasper's dog, Blondie, a way-too-friendly yellow lab. She jumped from Jasper's bed and moseyed to the door, her body swaying with the force of her wagging tail. His son, however, didn't move.

Blondie skirted him and then stopped, her body close. She wanted out.

The room smelled like teenage boy and dog. Not a great combination.

"Jasper, get up. Time to get ready for school," Layne called, again loud. Jasper didn't move.

"Jas, get up," Layne said louder.

Jasper's body moved, only slightly, but he didn't make a sound.

"You're up, showered and downstairs in fifteen minutes. Get me?" Layne informed him, pushed open the door and flipped on the bright overhead light as added incentive.

Tripp was a big fan of the snooze button but Tripp would get up. Tripp would do what he was told.

Jasper would not. Jasper was not a big fan of getting up. He was even less a fan of school. And he was even less a fan of his old man and especially his old man telling him to do something. He was supposed to set his alarm and wake his brother if Tripp wasn't up. He never did because he never set his alarm, and when Layne started doing it, Jasper turned it off just to get under Layne's skin. This was their everyday dance when his boys were with him and it never failed to piss Layne off.

Layne turned from the door and walked down the stairs, Blondie so close to his side she nearly tripped him.

She was shaking with excitement. This was her favorite part of the day. She got to go outside, which she loved, then she got to come inside to food and all her boys together at the same time, something she didn't get very often, or not as often as she liked.

Gabby hated dogs, but she bought Blondie for Jasper two weeks before Layne moved home. She did this to be a bitch because she *was* a bitch and because she hated Layne more than she hated dogs. Three weeks later, when he was home and they'd established the joint custody schedule, she declared that Blondie was to stay at Layne's no matter what.

4

So Tanner Layne was home for the first time in twelve years and he had an active, excitable, yellow lab puppy on his hands as well as two sons who barely knew him and one of them could barely stand the sight of him. Not to mention Rocky breathing the same airspace, albeit ten miles away, that was still too damned close.

His life, never great, or it hadn't been great for eighteen years, had turned to complete shit.

He walked through the vast open space that was the kitchen and the living room to the sliding glass door that led to the backyard. He bent, yanked the steel pole out of the rails, straightened and unlatched the door. He reached out an arm, pulled down the door to the security panel, punched in the code, slapped the door back up and then slid the sliding glass door open for Blondie to go outside. She didn't hesitate, she raced right through.

Layne slid the door closed, flipped the switch to the kitchen lights, turned and surveyed the bottom floor of his house.

For twelve years, he'd had nothing but apartments and condos. Sometimes his apartments were small, even studios. Sometimes they were large or townhomes. Some were shit, some were palaces. All of them were crash pads.

Now, to his right was the kitchen. In the far corner, countertops and cabinets at a right angle around the door to the big pantry and utility room that led to the garage. A huge triangular island with the points cut off was in the middle of the kitchen, stools in front of it on the outside. An enormous space for a dining room table by the big window, a space Layne hadn't filled. He ate standing up or sitting in front of the TV. His boys ate at the stools, in their rooms, on the fly or sitting in front of the TV.

To his left, the living room, enormous console of cabinets and shelves into which he'd fit an equally enormous, big screen TV. Two reclining chairs at either end of a big deep seated couch, enough tables around where you could set your beer or bag of chips so you didn't have to reach very far to get to it. There was a low wall and a column beyond which there was nothing but open space. Dead space. He'd never figured out what to do with it. If it didn't store food, have a couch and TV, a weight bench or a bed, he had no use for it. So, like the dining area, it was empty.

There was a toilet and sink under the stairs, the rest of the downstairs was taken up by a two-car garage that jutted out at the front of the house.

Layne stared at it, his gaze moving right, left, then right again.

How the fuck he ended up in a three-bedroom house in a development with other three and four-bedroom houses, all painted one of four colors, each, one of limited floor plans, and with an HOA that made the Nazi party look like a bunch of pansies so pretty much the whole fucking development looked the same, he didn't know. Hell, when he'd first moved there, more than once on his way home he'd gotten lost in the acres of houses that all looked the same and he had a highly tuned sense of direction.

Well, he thought, *at least the fucker's paid for.*

He walked into the kitchen, straight to the coffeepot. He pulled out the filter, the grounds from yesterday in it, used and soggy. He dumped them in the open trash can that was so overflowing he had to shove the trash down first so the grounds wouldn't drip out.

It was Jasper's week to take out the trash so of course the trash hadn't been taken out.

He went back to the coffeepot, grabbed the glass carafe and yanked it out, going to the sink. It, too, was overflowing.

Layne sifted through the schedule in his mind. Last night, it was Tripp's turn to cook, Jasper's turn to do the dishes. Therefore, the dishes weren't done.

Layne sighed as he rinsed out the filter and the carafe and heard the shower go on upstairs. Then he filled the carafe with water, went back to the pot and made coffee. He'd just flipped the switch when the doorbell went.

His eyes went to the clock on the microwave over the stove. Six thirty-six. Who was at his door as six thirty-six?

He moved through the house, silent on bare feet. He went to the big picture window in the empty space at the front of his house. He had blinds there, they were partially closed. He turned the bar at the side so they were open and looked to the door.

His eyes narrowed as his blood turned to acid.

Rocky was standing out there. Her hair was pulled back in a pony-tail, that fall draping down the side at her temple, tucked behind her ear. She was wearing a pale pink blouse that fit her middle like a glove, drawing your attention to her ribs and tits, and it had little poofy sleeves. She was also wearing a mushroom colored skirt that hit her at the tops of her knees and fit tight. Skintight. So skintight it cupped her ass and was snug across her hips and down her thighs. And last she was wearing pink pumps, a thin strap rounding her heel, the heels of the shoes high and pencil thin. The whole package slick, polished and unbelievably fucking sexy.

What the fuck was she doing there?

She lifted a hand, finger pointed toward the doorbell and he moved to the door. The doorbell sounded just as he opened it and stood looking down at her through the glass in his storm door.

The bell ceased and she stood there, looking up at him, her makeup perfect, pink at her eyes, her cheeks, her lips glossed. Her hair was sleek, shiny, thick. He wondered if she hired someone to come every morning to do her hair and makeup. She could. She had the money for it.

"Raquel, what are you—?"

He stopped speaking when her hand went to the handle. She turned it and opened the door, coming right through. He had to step out of her way as she swiftly skirted him and moved into his house, her high heels making dull sounds as they thudded across his wood floors.

She stopped five feet in and turned. Her eyes went to his first, they dropped down to his bare chest, he saw a flinch she couldn't hide and he opened his mouth to speak.

She got there before him.

Her eyes coming back to his, she asked, "How are you, Layne?"

"Fit," he answered tersely. "Now, what're you—?"

He stopped speaking when they both heard Blondie whine and scratch at the glass. Raquel twisted her torso so fast, her ponytail flipped around so its length shot over her shoulder.

She turned back slower, that hank of dark hair still resting against her light blouse.

Her eyebrows were up.

"Is that Jasper's dog?" she asked.

"Yes. Now Raqu—"

7

Again, he didn't finish. She turned, moving quickly through his house, her heels sounding against his floor, dull on the wood, turning sharper when she hit tile, her ass swaying as she went.

Layne watched.

Rocky could strut. She didn't do anything else. Her movements fluid, her ass generous, she could strut like no woman he'd ever seen, even the ones who practiced.

Rocky didn't have to practice. She was a natural.

Before he could move, she had the sliding glass door open and Blondie bounded in.

He moved then because Blondie was in ecstasy. She loved her boys. The only thing she loved more was company. She was jumping all over Rocky's fancy-ass outfit.

"Down," Layne growled, and Blondie's head jerked to him. She whined then she dropped down, removing her paws from Rocky's blouse.

Rocky dropped down too. In a low squat, ass to heels, knees to chest, her skirt stretched to the danger zone, delineating every inch of flesh on her ass and thighs.

She was rubbing Blondie's head and neck at the same time craning her own to avoid Blondie's lashing tongue.

"Who's a beautiful girl?" she cooed at Blondie and Blondie replied by tagging the length of Rocky's jaw with her tongue.

Raquel laughed, the sound hitting him like a bullet to the gut.

Worse.

And he knew just how much fucking pain that could cause.

At his end, he clipped, "Raquel, what are you doing here?"

He sounded annoyed because he meant to and he *was*.

Her head came around, tilted back to look up at him and she muttered, "Right." She gave Blondie one last rub and straightened, turning to him. "Leg of lamb," she finished ridiculously.

"What?" Layne asked.

"Leg of lamb," she repeated. "Dad won one in a poker game."

Jesus, only Dave would accept a leg of lamb as a bet in a poker game. All three Merricks were nuts in their own way. Or, they had been, eighteen years ago. He had no idea if Rocky was still a nut but he knew Dave and Merry were.

Layne gave slight shakes of his head then asked, "So?"

"He asked me to find a recipe. He's never cooked a leg of lamb. I haven't either but I found one. It's Greek. He wants you and the boys to come over for dinner tonight." She stopped and he didn't speak, so she went on, "It's a big leg of lamb."

She was, essentially, asking him to a dinner she was cooking.

Layne wondered if he was hallucinating again. Maybe he was in a coma and the last six weeks, and those dreams, were all some coma-induced fantasy.

No, if he was having a fantasy, Jasper would have been jolted out of being an asshole kid when his father took three bullets instead of becoming more of an asshole kid.

It was then Layne noticed Blondie was staring at him, need in her eyes. She wanted to get fed.

Layne turned and headed to the pantry.

Raquel spoke to his back. "We're thinking six thirty. The boys'll be done with football practice then, they can get home and showered. But we can do later if you want."

He didn't speak. He went into the pantry, nabbed a can of dog food and came out. He heard the shower had gone off so he walked to the foot of the stairs, ignoring the fact that Rocky was now standing at the island, hand light on the counter, hip resting against the side.

He yelled up the stairs, "Tripp, if your brother isn't up, get him up. I want to hear the shower. Two minutes."

"Right, Dad," Tripp yelled back down.

Layne headed to the dog bowl wondering how he could get out of leg of lamb. He picked up the bowl and Blondie crowded him, shaking with excitement. He lifted the tab, pulled the lid off the can, reaching to yank a clean spoon out of the dish drainer. He gouged into the food and was about to plop it into the bowl when he heard Rocky speak.

"What are you doing?"

He twisted his torso to look at her. His eyes went to her face. Her eyes were on the dog bowl.

"Feeding the dog," Layne pointed out the obvious.

Her gaze lifted to his and she looked disgusted.

Then she moved. Pushing away from the counter, she came at him. She got close as he watched and didn't move.

She grabbed the bowl and went to the sink, explaining softly, "Even puppies need clean dishes."

He felt his mouth get tight and it got tighter when she dug into the sink and he saw her pink-tipped fingernails. Perfectly manicured, the nails not long and sharp but shortish and squared off, looking classy, stylish, yet she didn't hesitate in digging through dirty dishes. She found a dishcloth and turned on the water to rinse it out.

"Raquel—" he started, but her head turned to him.

"The shower isn't on, Layne," she said quietly.

He cocked his head to the side and listened.

It wasn't.

Fuck.

He watched as she rinsed out the cloth, dropped it into the bowl and reached for the dishwashing liquid at the back of the sink. Then he put down the dog food.

She wanted to clean Blondie's bowl? He'd let her. Blondie didn't give a fuck. He looked down at his son's dog seeing he was wrong. She did give a fuck. A clean bowl meant an unnecessary delay in breakfast.

Layne sighed then he moved away and walked up the stairs to see Tripp coming out of his brother's bedroom. He was wearing jeans and nothing else, his hair wet and spiking out everywhere. Layne had no idea if this was the style he was going with that day or if it was just wet and spiking out everywhere. Tripp changed hairstyles like women changed shoes.

"He doesn't want to get up," Tripp told his dad.

"Finish getting ready, pal. I'll get him," Layne told his son and walked to Jasper's room.

Jasper had gotten up, Layne knew, but he'd gone back to bed. Layne knew this because the overhead light was out.

He walked to Jasper's dresser and tagged his son's car keys. When he'd turned sixteen the year before, Layne had given him a 2007 Dodge Charger, red, with a black racing stripe and spoiler. It was a sweet ride. It had bought Layne forty-eight hours of Jasper liking him.

"Jasper, you're up and in the shower in two minutes or I call school, say you're sick, then call Coach and say you feel so shit, you can't play Friday's game." Then he left the room and made certain he jiggled the keys as he walked out.

Layne went to his own room, tossed the keys on his dresser, opened a drawer and grabbed a gray t-shirt. He pulled it on and down over his blue with burgundy stripes pajama bottoms. Melody had bought those for him last Christmas, along with three other pairs. Said, since his sons were living with him, he needed to sleep in something other than nothing, which was how he usually slept.

Melody.

He hadn't thought of her in weeks.

Now, he thought of her. He thought of giving her a call. If Layne gave her a call, she'd take vacation and come to town. Melody was in town, Layne wouldn't have sex dreams about Rocky. Melody might not be as good as Rocky had been, or as good as Rocky was in those dreams, but she was far from bad.

He grabbed Jasper's car keys and was relieved to hear the shower going as he went back downstairs. When he got to the kitchen, Blondie's face was in her bowl and Rocky was leaning against a counter, one arm wrapped around her middle, the elbow of the other arm resting on her wrist, a coffee cup held up.

He stopped dead and stared at her.

"You should keep your mugs over the coffeepot," she informed him. "Makes more sense not to have to walk across the kitchen to get a mug."

He felt his eyes narrow.

He was about to ask if she was shitting him, coming to his house first thing in the morning, asking him and his sons to dinner, feeding his dog, helping herself to coffee and telling him where to keep his mugs but he didn't get the chance. Her arms moved, she twisted to grab a mug and then she twisted back to hand it to him.

"Still black with two sugars?" she asked, but her eyes didn't meet his.

He ignored the coffee she held out.

11

"What the fuck are you doin' here, Raquel?" he asked, voice low and angry.

Her eyes finally met his.

"Dad wants you to come to dinner," she answered.

"Dave can call me himself," Layne pointed out.

"I told him I'd pop by on the way to work," she replied.

"On the way to work?" Layne bit out.

He lived in a middle-class development on the west edges of the 'burg. She lived in a six-bedroom mini-mansion by a manmade lake in a development that included a nine-hole golf course with driving range and putting green, a clubhouse with restaurant, bar and party rooms as well as a full gym and indoor-outdoor swimming pool in a definitely upper-class development on the north edge of town. She was a teacher at Jasper and Tripp's school, which was *in* town. Layne's house was *not* on her way to work.

"Yes," she answered.

Layne opened his mouth to tell her to get the fuck out and maybe to shove that leg of lamb straight up her ass, when Tripp spoke.

"Mrs. Astley?"

She tore her eyes from his face, leaned forward and looked around Layne.

Then she smiled.

Another shot to the gut.

"Hey, Tripp," she greeted.

"What are you doin' here?" Tripp asked, and Layne turned to look at his son.

If Tripp didn't have Layne's body—long legs and torso, wide shoulders, the power not developed in either due to his being fourteen—Layne would have asked Gabby for a DNA test.

Tripp had sandy blond hair (now darkened because he filled it with gunk to style it and make it spike out all over his head, which apparently was his 'do for the day) and blue eyes.

Gabby didn't have blonde hair and blue eyes and neither did anyone in her or Layne's family…that he knew. Tripp had a bit of Gabby in the face but the rest of him, Layne had no fucking clue where it came from. Layne wouldn't doubt Gabby would step out on him, but as Tripp grew older, there was no denying Layne gave Tripp his body.

It didn't matter because he loved the kid. This was because Tripp was lovable. He'd always been a good kid. Once or twice a week, always, Tripp called—from the time the kid could pick up the phone and dial, the whole time Layne lived away. They'd talk, or Tripp would. The kid could talk for ten. Whenever Layne came home for a visit, from when he was little to when he got older, the minute Tripp saw Layne he'd dash to him, throw his arms around him and give him a tight hug. When he got older he tried to make the dash cooler, but there was no mistaking he was happy to see his dad.

He felt pressure and heat at his abs and looked down to see Raquel was pressing the coffee mug there. Automatically he took it and looked to her. She was close, close enough for him to smell her perfume.

"Inviting you to dinner," she answered Tripp's question. "Dad has a leg of lamb."

Layne looked to Tripp. Tripp was staring at Rocky like she was a movie star, pink in his cheeks, eyes dazzled.

Layne looked back at Raquel then at Tripp, who still hadn't torn his eyes away from her.

Fuck. She was an English Lit teacher at his school and he had the hots for her.

He would. She was fucking gorgeous. She wore those skirts, those shirts and those heels to school every day, probably every boy went home and jacked off, thinking about her.

Even his son.

Fuck.

"Tripp, breakfast," Layne ordered.

Tripp blinked, looked at his dad, then he moved forward and toward the pantry.

"A leg of lamb?" Tripp asked as he moved.

Rocky headed back to the island, her heels clicking on the tiles as she went. To put distance between them, Layne headed to the sink.

"A leg of lamb," she replied.

"I've never had a leg of lamb." Tripp could be heard from the pantry, although not seen.

"You're in for a treat. Greek night. Homemade pita. Homemade tzatziki sauce. You'll love it."

Tripp came out of the pantry with a box of cereal.

"Cool," he said, smiling at Rocky. "Uncle Dave a good cook?" he asked when he made it to the cupboard to pull down a bowl.

"I'm cooking," Rocky informed him.

He was still smiling at her when he put the bowl and cereal down at the island and headed to the fridge.

"*You* a good cook?" he asked.

"I've had no complaints," she answered, smiling back at him.

She wouldn't. She had been a fucking great cook. Eighteen years of practice, especially not cooking on a budget, she was probably a master chef.

Layne felt his jaw get tight again as he saw Raquel's eyes fall to the box of sugary cereal and her smile faded into a frown.

"Tripp, you should have oatmeal or something," she advised as Tripp hit the island with the milk. "Sustained energy. That cereal will burn out halfway through first period."

"That's okay. I always get a candy bar from the vending machines between first and second period," he told her and her eyes shot to Layne, communicating, clearly, that he should do something about his son's lack of nutrition.

That's when he'd had enough.

That was also when he was interrupted yet again in doing something about it.

"Hey, Mrs. Astley," Jasper said, and he saw Rocky start to turn then his eyes went to Jasper.

Now Jasper was undoubtedly his son. Dark hair, dark eyes, olive skin that looked tan even in the dead of winter. He had Layne's body too, but at seventeen, and dedicated to football, as well as being a stud and therefore at Layne's weight equipment more than Layne was, he was ripped. He was nearly Layne's height at six feet two whereas Tripp was still growing and he hadn't broken six feet yet, but he would.

Jasper was slowly pulling down a t-shirt as he stood at the edge of the kitchen counter. This was so Rocky could get a good look at his chest and six pack.

Layne's eyes rolled to the ceiling.

His firstborn son was also cocky. Further, he was already sexually active. Layne knew it and supplied condoms because his efforts at discussing sex with Jasper had been unsuccessful and eventually volatile. So he bought condoms and put them in Jasper's nightstand as well as slid packets in his wallet. He knew Jasper was active because the boxes were opened with condoms missing and his wallet was almost always empty of stash. Jasper had no girlfriend—a serial dater, working his way through his school and the rest of the schools in the county.

Jasper knew he was a good-looking kid with a sculpted, teenage-boy body and he wanted his thirty-eight-year-old English Lit teacher to know it too.

The minute his son pulled his shirt down, Layne put his teeth to his lip, his tongue to his teeth and gave a sharp, low whistle. Jasper's head swung to him and Layne tossed his car keys to him. With quick reflexes, Jasper caught them.

"Breakfast, Jas," Layne ordered.

"We're going to Uncle Dave's tonight," Tripp announced, shoveling cereal into his mouth. "Mrs. Astley is cooking."

Jasper tossed his keys by the coffeepot and went to the cupboard to get a bowl.

"Awesome," Jasper replied, turning to the island with his bowl. "Merry gonna be there?"

"Yes, Jasper, a family affair," Rocky answered, and Jasper gave her a grin so she grinned back.

A family affair.

A fucking family affair.

Fuck *her*.

Layne was done and he moved.

"Eat," he growled as he strode behind his sons at the counter with Rocky.

He made it to her, grabbed her bicep in his hand, yanked her coffee cup out of her other hand and slammed it on the island. Then he pulled her toward the door.

"Layne," she said softly.

"Shut the fuck up," he snarled, but quietly.

She tried to twist her bicep out of his hand and he let her, but only to run his hand down her arm until it caught hers. He dragged her through his front door, the storm door, down the walk and straight to her car in the drive.

She drove a sporty, black Mercedes coupe that probably cost a third of what he paid for his house.

Jesus Christ.

He walked to the driver's side of the car and yanked it opened, using her hand to maneuver her around and in. When he had her back between the door and the car, he moved in, pinning her there.

She tipped her head back.

"Layne," she whispered.

"He don't do it for you?" Layne asked low.

She blinked then asked back, "What?"

"Jarrod," he snarled her husband's name, watched her wince and thought that was telling. "He don't do it for you? Don't make you burn? Don't make you come so hard you stop breathing? Think to go slumming, find a way to get off?"

"Layne!" she hissed, her entire body getting visibly tight.

"We were good, baby, you remember. So good, I'm surprised it took you a year to make that play." He jerked his head to the house.

"I'm not making a play!" She was angry. He could tell by the fire in her eyes, the line of her body and the way she spoke.

And he didn't give a fuck.

He ignored her. "But I'm not interested. You want, I can shop around for you. Bet a lot of boys in this 'burg would jump at a shot at you."

"I was just asking you to dinner," she snapped.

"Bullshit," he clipped back.

"I don't believe you."

"I'm not twenty-four, Roc. Not a man to be led around by his dick anymore. Had eighteen years to learn how to be the one who does the fucking, not the one who gets fucked."

Her body jerked then locked but not before he saw pain carve a path through her features before they blanked.

She took a breath in through her nose, so big it expanded her chest. Then she asked, "What can I tell Dad?"

Rocky, he couldn't tolerate. Dave and Merry were another story. This meant he was wrong, she'd fucked him.

Again.

"We'll be there. Six thirty," he growled.

"Brilliant," she bit out and then whirled so fast in the small space he'd given her, her shoulder brushed roughly against his chest and her ponytail slid across his neck, but she didn't stop moving.

She folded herself into the car and didn't hesitate to reach out to the door handle. He moved out of the way just in time to miss getting hit when she slammed the door. She hit the ignition and backed out too fast, yanking the steering wheel at the end of the drive. Then her expensive, high performance vehicle shot forward and he lost sight of her in seconds.

He stared after her for longer than their entire conversation in the drive lasted. Then he sucked in breath to calm his frayed temper and walked into the house.

"What was that?" Jasper asked the minute he hit the kitchen.

"Nothin'," Layne answered.

"That wasn't nothin'. You were pissed..." he hesitated, his eyes sharp on his dad, "at *Mrs. Astley.*"

His last two words were said disbelievingly. Like wealthy, polished, sexy, high school English Lit teacher, wife of the Chief of Surgery at a big hospital in Indianapolis, charity-working, pillar of the community Raquel Merrick Astley was a step away from the 'burg's own Princess Diana.

He stared at his son and noted Tripp was also watching him.

Then he made a decision.

"A long time ago, before your mom, we were together. We lived together. It was good. Then it went bad. Very bad. I'm not a big fan of Mrs. Astley."

"No shit?" Tripp asked, and Layne looked at his younger son.

"No shit," he answered.

"Wow," Tripp whispered.

"How'd it go bad?" Jasper asked, and Layne's eyes went to him.

"Maybe, you still care, in about five years I'll tell you," Layne answered.

17

Jasper studied his father and then, miracle of miracles, he let it go.

"We goin' to Uncle Dave's tonight to eat her cookin'?" he asked.

"Yeah," Layne answered.

"That'll be interesting," Jasper muttered.

Layne's anger dissipated and he grinned. It was too bad Jasper spent so much time honing his asshole teenage-kid act. When he wasn't doing that, he was smart and damned funny.

"Yep, it'll be interesting," Layne agreed. "Now, you guys hafta get to school. And Jasper, I want you to take the trash out before you go."

The asshole teenage kid came back in a flash.

Still, he took the trash out before he went.

After they were gone, in the house alone, Layne let Blondie out to roam the yard while he showered and dressed to get ready to go into the office. He was on his way through the kitchen from the sliding glass door when he saw her mug sitting on the counter, the impression of her lower lip in pink gloss on the side.

Layne stopped and stared at it.

Then he decided to do the dishes before he took a shower.

Two

My Sister Goes the Distance

*L*ayne sat at his desk in his office and stared at his bank balance on the computer.

Six weeks ago, it was healthy. A year ago, before he bought the house, furnished it and bought his son a car, it was very healthy.

Now, after taking the gargantuan hit of paying his hospital bills, it was not.

He'd lived tight. Not much to spend money on, his biggest expense was child support, which Gabby, on a strict schedule of every three years, went to her attorneys to jack up. He never fought her. He just gave her the money. She was a bitch but she loved her kids and she worked hard as the manager of the checkout clerks at the grocery store. She wasn't rolling in it and wanted her sons to have a good life. So Layne did his part to help her give it to them.

He heard the warning beep. Someone had tripped the sensor, which meant someone was coming up. His eyes moved to the video screen on the shelf to his left and he saw Gabby walking up the steps.

Layne had offices over Mimi's Coffee Shop in town. They consisted of his office, a reception and a small room beside the front door with a counter, a coffeepot on the counter (not that he used it, he wanted coffee, he went to Mimi's), a sink, a microwave also on the counter and a half-fridge under it. There was a small bathroom—toilet and sink. There was also a big storage room off his office where he kept his equipment.

He watched as Gabby made it to the top and turned to the door and he realized that it wasn't just a shit day, it was a super shit day.

He stood and was leaning against the doorjamb to his office when she walked in.

"Tanner," she snapped when her eyes hit him and he shook his head. He hadn't even said hello and she was snapping at him.

"Good to see you, Gabby," he replied, and her eyes narrowed at his hard to miss sarcasm.

It was not good to see her. It was never good to see her. His ex-wife was a bitch.

At first, he knew she had reason. When Rocky broke it off with him, not even a week later, he'd been out, he'd been drunk and he'd hooked up with Gabby. She had dark hair, like Rocky, but also dark brown eyes, not like Rocky. Rocky's eyes were deep blue. Nevertheless, he'd fucked Gabby because she reminded him of Rocky. It had been a one night stand. That was, until two and a half months later when she hunted him down and informed him she was pregnant, it was his and she was keeping the baby. She also informed him they were getting married.

He did not want to do this mainly because, when he wasn't drunk, he didn't like her. Also because he didn't believe the kid was his. Everyone knew Gabrielle Weil got around.

When she had it, though, even as an infant, Layne took one look at his son and knew.

So he did right by Jasper and married Jasper's mother.

It was the second stupidest thing he'd done in his life, outside getting hooked up with Rocky.

Gabby was far from stupid, though. She knew he was hung up on Rocky and this made their marriage unpleasant, to say the least. Layne tried. God's honest truth, he did. She wasn't Rocky, that was true, but he had to give it to her. He couldn't imagine being tied to a woman who was hung up on another man, knowing she was thinking about him when you fucked her.

But he'd wanted to be a good dad. He didn't have a father, his father took off within weeks of him being born, and he didn't want his son to grow up like that. That was the primary reason he'd married her.

But no matter how he tried to make their marriage good and worked to bury the bitterness of losing Raquel, Gabby sensed it under the surface and she made life a living hell. He was close to breaking it off with her when she fell pregnant with Tripp. They hadn't had sex in months and she knew he was pulling away. That was why he woke up with her mouth latched to his cock, his cock hard under her working him and he'd fucked her. If Tripp hadn't come out of that, he'd think it was the third stupidest thing he'd done in his life. But he couldn't imagine life without Tripp.

He'd lasted nearly two more years before he split.

"We need to talk," she told him, coming into the reception area.

"All right," Layne agreed, having learned it was better to let her say what she had to say and move on than try to fight it. She wasn't only a bitch, she could get mean and the mean could turn nasty. His day started with Rocky and would end with a dinner she'd cooked that he'd have to eat with her and his kids there. He didn't need Gabby to turn nasty.

She stared at him a second, then looked beyond him into his office. Her face turned hard when she realized he wasn't going to ask her to come in, take a seat, offer a cup of coffee.

"I need you to take the boys next week," she announced.

Layne sighed.

The reason he was home was because she'd hooked up with Stew Baranski.

When Tripp told him that, Layne's blood ran cold. Stew Baranski was a total asshole. He'd always been an asshole. Fuck, the guy could teach classes on how to be a total and complete asshole. He didn't want that guy around his kids, but when he'd called and shared this with Gabby, she'd lost her fucking mind. Then she'd ranted about how she'd taken care of his kids for twelve years and now that she had something good in her life (that was a joke, Stew being anything good was a freaking joke), he was trying to screw it up for her. She continued to rant about how she gave everything up for her boys while he did whatever the fuck he wanted.

He had to admit, she wasn't entirely wrong.

21

But it was clear she was past bitter straight to hostile and it was also clear she wasn't giving up Stew. She'd dated, he knew this, but she hadn't had a long-term relationship in a while. She'd let herself go after Tripp, in a huge way, and no longer bore any resemblance to the attractive, built woman she was in her twenties. She was hanging onto Stew, a last ditch effort to end a lonely life of single parenthood.

It was either let Stew Baranski turn his sons into assholes, or be an asshole to them, or both, or come home.

He came home.

And since he did, he often doubled up his weeks so Stew and Gabby could do whatever Stew and Gabby did that they needed his sons clear of it. Layne didn't want to know. He also didn't argue. She was right. She'd borne the brunt of raising his kids. It was his turn to kick in.

"Fine," he replied. "You need to come into the office to tell me that?"

"Nope," she shook her head once. "Needed to come in to tell you I need five hundred dollars."

Layne did a slow blink. "Come again?"

"Need five hundred dollars," she repeated.

"Gabby, this may have escaped you but circumstances are changed. I got joint custody and your support was reduced because of it. You get what you get and that's *all* you get."

He watched her straighten her shoulders. "I need five hundred dollars, Tanner."

"Is this something for the boys?" he asked.

"Yes," she answered.

"What?"

She looked over his shoulder. The bitch was lying.

"What?" he repeated.

Her eyes came back to his. "Jasper and Tripp need stuff for school."

"What do they need?"

"Stuff," she answered. "Clothes and shit."

They did not need clothes and shit. He knew this because he handed them both wads of cash about two days after he got out of the hospital so they could go back to school shopping. Both his boys were kitted out with trendy gear like rock stars.

"I think they're covered," Layne replied.

"Yeah, with stuff they keep at your house. They don't have as much at my place."

"Well, since they're at my house most of the time, that works. Don't you think?"

Her face started to get red, not with embarrassment, with anger. "Oh, I get it. Dad's the cool one, gets his son a hot rod, fills their closets with designer clothes. They go to Mom's and they've got shit."

"It isn't like they don't have bags. They want their stuff, they can take it with them to your place."

"You *want* them to go back and forth like vagabonds?"

Layne sucked in breath and sought patience.

Then he reminded her, "Stew's livin' with you, Gabby, your expenses are lowered and you still get money from me. You wanna get them clothes, get 'em."

"I work at Kroger, Tanner. I'm not a shit hot PI who charges a hundred and fifty dollars an hour plus expenses."

"You've worked at Kroger for fifteen years, Gabby. You're a manager and you had to disclose your income the last time you took me to court. You are far from hurting."

This was true, except the part about him learning this when she'd had to disclose it the last time she took him to court. He'd checked up on her regularly. He'd known for years exactly what she was paid, what she spent her money on and what she spent his money on.

"Jesus, why do you make me jump through hoops like this when it's for *our* boys?" she snapped, her voice rising.

That pissed him off.

"I have never, not once, Gabrielle, made you jump through hoops when it's for our boys. Not...fucking...*once* and you fucking know it."

She snapped her mouth shut. She knew it.

"And you're standin' there lyin' to me. You got trouble? You tell me, I'll help you out. But do not walk into my office and hand me a load of shit and expect me to pay you to do it."

"I'm not lying," she retorted.

"Bullshit, Gabby. You think in my line of work I can't spot a liar? I didn't learn that quick, I'd be dead."

Her flush suffused her face. She knew he'd pegged her.

"Now, why do you need five hundred dollars?" he continued.

"I don't," she returned.

"You asked for it not five minutes ago."

"Stew does," she bit off, her eyes sliding away from him.

Layne felt his body get tight.

Then he stated in a quiet voice, "You are fucking shitting me."

Her eyes shot back to him. "He's in a jam."

Layne pushed away from the door and crossed his arms on his chest. "Don't give a fuck Stew Baranski is in a jam."

"If he's in a jam, *I'm* in a jam."

Layne's brows drew together. "You in danger?"

"No," she hissed, pissed as all hell she had to tell him what she had to tell him. "Things are just tight. I might not be able to make the mortgage."

Layne sucked in another breath and his head dropped back so he could look at the ceiling.

He made a decision and looked back at his ex-wife.

"I told you—" he started.

"Don't!" she clipped, her voice again rising.

"I told you not to let that asshole in your life. You did," Layne went on.

"He's my man. I love him," she shot back.

"Your choice and because of that, he's your problem."

"I miss the mortgage, I could lose my house!"

"They don't foreclose for months, Gabby. Tell him to get his shit together and figure it out. I'm not getting involved."

"He's in deep, Layne. He's trying to sort it out but it'll take time. I can't lose the house in the meantime."

"What I don't get is how the house is on the line. You got enough money to—"

"I've been helping him out."

Layne studied her. Then he asked, "How bad is this?"

"Bad."

That wasn't a good answer.

"How bad and how long's it been goin' on?" he pressed.

She stared at him and didn't answer. That meant awhile.

Then she said, "I lose the house, Jas and Tripp—"

"Then you're lucky I'm home, Gabby. Means the boys are good, always got a bed with me."

"I can't believe you!" she yelled.

He dropped his arms and walked to her. While doing it, he tried to find Gabrielle Weil in her bitter face, now twisted with anger. She hadn't been a knockout but she had been very pretty. She carried an extra fifty pounds now, at least, and she didn't carry it like she was comfortable with it. Her hair was now dyed and looked that way. She should have left it to turn gray. Her mother's hair was thick and gray and attractive. She worked it, Gabby could have too. The skin on Gabby's face was slack because she didn't take care of it, bags under her eyes, probably from not sleeping or being pissed off at Layne and the world for nearly two decades.

He stopped in front of her and tipped his head down to look at her.

Softly, he said, "I told you not to get hooked up with that guy. I told you he'd bring you trouble. Stew is no good. He treated you right, I'd be happy to eat my words. But I get from this that he's been fuckin' around and he's involved you in it and that is one way a man doesn't treat a woman right."

"You'd know how not to treat a woman right, Tanner," she shot back.

"Don't go there, Gabby. I took care of you. I took care of our house. I took care of our boys. I worked my ass off to make a life for our family. We weren't a love match and you knew it and you wanted my ring on your finger anyway. I gave it to you and did the best I could. It wasn't good enough. You gave a little, even the barest fucking inch, we coulda made a go of it. You didn't. You can blame me but we both know that's bullshit. That's on you and *this* is on you. I don't want any part of this. You made a decision a decade and a half ago to hold on to something when you shoulda let it go and you fucked up your life. You made a decision two years ago to hold on to something you shoulda let go and it's happening again. I'm not getting dragged into this. I start, it won't stop for me either and I'm not down with that. You go home, you talk to that asshole and you tell him to get his shit together and you don't come here again and hand me this bullshit. Am I clear?"

25

"You are so full of shit," she hissed.

"Yeah?" he asked, "How?"

"I gave," she informed him.

"Yeah, you gave. You gave me attitude for five fuckin' years."

"My husband was lusting after another woman!"

Fuck!

He wished he had a dollar for every time she brought up Raquel. He'd have a much healthier bank balance if he did.

"That's the something you shoulda let go," he told her.

"Yeah, how would I do that, Tanner? How?"

"You cared about what we were tryin' to build, you woulda found a way to let her go, like I did."

The second time that day he watched a woman's body jerk. He knew he had her. She knew he'd done the best he could with the hand he'd been dealt. She knew he wouldn't step out on her, even if Rocky had come back. Gabby had his ring on her finger, their sons under their roof, so she had him. She couldn't fight that corner. She tried, way too often, and she never won.

"This was a waste of my time," Gabby gave in acidly.

"Yeah, it was," Layne agreed.

"Thanks for all your help," she spat, turning.

"Happy to oblige," he muttered, also turning.

"And you think Stew is an asshole," she mumbled, opening the door.

Layne sighed.

He heard the door close behind her.

Then he walked into his office, logged out of his bank account and started to investigate Stewart Baranski's finances.

Dave Merrick opened his front door and Layne, Jasper and Tripp were assaulted with a scent that could only be what heaven smelled like.

"That smells great!" Tripp shouted and bolted in, nearly bowling Dave over as he kept shouting his greeting, "Hey, Uncle Dave!" as he ran down the hall to the kitchen in the back.

Dave had turned to watch and he turned back, smiling.

"Hey, Uncle Dave," Jasper repeated his brother's words, socked Dave in the shoulder and followed Tripp, much slower, playing it cool, not wanting Mrs. Astley to know he couldn't wait to see her.

"Jas," Dave replied. He stepped from the door, keeping one hand on it, his other outstretched, inviting Layne in. "Tanner, good to see you, son."

Layne took his hand, squeezed and got a squeeze back.

Dave Merrick was still a good-looking man at sixty-three, tall, lean, fit. He only limped when he got tired and he only brought out the cane when it was raining and the wet got in his bones, making his old wounds ache.

A long time ago, Dave had been married to a woman named Cecilia, the town beauty. Layne remembered her and exactly what she looked like, which was a lot like what Rocky looked like now.

And he remembered he'd never seen her not smiling.

He also remembered the day he'd heard she'd been murdered on the same night Dave had been shot five times.

He further remembered going to her funeral with his mother and everyone else in town, standing across the casket and watching Raquel the whole time as she sat in her seat, her eyes not moving from the casket, not once, her skin pale, blue shadows under her eyes, her face perfectly blank. He had only known of her then, he hadn't really known her. She was already beyond pretty. But she was fourteen, he was eighteen and he was out of her league. It wouldn't be for three years when he'd run into her and decide to make his move.

He let Dave's hand go and moved into the house, pausing to wait for Dave to close the door. When he first got back and renewed his relationship with Dave and Merry, coming to that house messed with his head. Too many memories there. Now, he and his boys had been there so many times, it didn't faze him.

Except for that night and the fact that Rocky was somewhere in that house. She was never there when they were there.

"How's things, Tanner?" Dave asked, coming to his side as they made their way slowly down the hall by the stairs.

"Could be better," Layne answered honestly. Dave was a friend, Dave had known him a long time and Dave used to be a cop, three reasons not to lie. One way or the other, he'd know.

Dave was silent for a beat before he said, "We'll talk later."

Layne nodded and they hit ground zero on the smell.

Merry was standing at a counter, wielding an electric knife. Tripp had his head in the fridge. Jasper had settled on a stool at the counter.

Raquel was nowhere in sight.

"Yo, Tanner," Merry called with a grin over his shoulder.

"Merry," Layne replied.

Garrett Merrick looked like a male replica of his sister, but taller and definitely masculine. Same dark hair (without the fake streaks), same deep blue eyes.

Merry's nickname was apt. He was a good ole boy. Always had been. He was such a good ole boy he made an art out of it.

"Dad, you want something to drink?" Tripp asked.

"Beer, pal," Layne answered.

"Where's Mrs. Astley?" Jasper asked, looking around while trying not to look like he was looking around.

"Went home about two minutes ago, buddy. Headache," Merry answered Jasper, and Layne's eyes went to his friend.

She didn't have a headache. After the way he spoke to her that morning, she had an intense desire not to be in his presence.

He told himself that worked for him when he knew he felt guilt that he could see all around, and *smell*, how hard she'd worked and she'd blown out of there before she could enjoy it.

Then again, she could also have a headache.

"Bummer," Tripp muttered and handed him a beer before he took a can of pop to his brother and cracked open his own.

"Yeah, I've tasted this shit," Merry put in, lifting his hand, a slab of meat between his fingers. "Bummer. This stuff is the freaking *bomb*." Then he tossed the meat into his mouth.

"Awesome, I'm starved," Tripp replied.

"She get headaches a lot?"

That came out of Layne's mouth before he could stop it and both Merry and Dave looked at him. For over a year, anytime the three of them were together, Rocky had been the elephant in the room. This was the first indication Layne had given that he was aware of its presence.

But she'd suffered headaches when he was with her, migraines. Pain so extreme he couldn't touch her. He couldn't even be in the same room walking around. The barest hint of noise, light, anything, increased her agony. He hated having to leave her to battle it alone but he had no choice. Nothing worked. She tried everything. It didn't happen often, thankfully he could count on one hand how often it happened when she was with him, but he remembered every last one.

"Not really," Merry answered and Dave looked at Layne's sons.

"Boys, grab bowls of whatever you see and take them to the dining room. Roc set the table. Sit your butts down when you get in there. Grub's up, we should eat," Dave said and the boys, unlike at home, moved quickly to do as ordered.

"How do you do that?" Layne asked jokingly when the kids left the room.

"Years of practice," Dave answered, a smile lighting his blue eyes.

Then, completely unable to control it, Layne looked at Merry and said, "She gonna make it home?"

Merry dumped another load of lamb on a platter and looked at Layne. "What?"

"If it's a migraine, she'll have trouble making it home. She used to get sick," Layne told his friend something he already knew.

Those were the only times she let him touch her when she had a headache, when she was puking in the bathroom. He'd hold her hair back and press a cold washcloth to her neck while she did it. When she was done, she'd wait for him to rinse the cloth and she'd sit on her ass on the floor, head tilted up to him, eyes hazy with pain and she'd let him wipe her face and mouth.

Merry studied him then said, "She doesn't have far to go."

Dave lived about five minutes from Layne. Merry lived about two minutes from Dave. Rocky lived at least fifteen minutes from all of them. Rush hour traffic, even in the 'burg, could get rough and it was still rush hour and would be for another half an hour. That could mean a twenty-five minute ride home, if not longer.

"Rush hour, Merry," Layne said.

Merry's head tipped to the side but his eyes slid to his dad. He only answered when he was looking directly at Layne again.

"She's stayin' with me, big man," he said quietly.

Oh fuck. This didn't sound good.

"Come again?" he asked, and he wondered why the fuck he did. But he did.

"Left him, Tanner," Dave said, moving forward to grab the platter as Merry unplugged the knife. "She did it over two months ago."

"No joke?" Layne asked, this time he knew why it came out of his mouth. He was shocked. Jarrod and Raquel Astley were pillars of that community. Rock solid.

"No joke," Dave answered.

"And no joke that fuckwad moved his latest piece right in before Roc's side of the bed was even cold," Merry added, his tone low but trembling. He was pissed.

Layne felt his body freeze.

The he repeated, "Come again?"

"We'll talk about it later," Dave said.

"We'll talk about it now," Layne replied. "He's moved another woman in?"

Merry turned away from the counter, wiping his hands on a dish towel.

"Been steerin' clear of this, big man, but you have to have heard," Merry said.

He hadn't heard. Everyone he knew in that town knew he and Rocky had had a thing. No one said boo about her to him.

"Heard what?" Layne asked.

"Fucked around on her all the time," Merry informed him. "Far's I can tell, since about a week after they said 'I do.' Nailed every nurse in his hospital. Every nurse's aide. Every decent looking patient, probably."

"You are *shitting* me," Layne whispered.

He could not believe this mainly because it was unbelievable. Not once, not even once had he considered stepping out on Rocky when he was with her.

He didn't have to. She was great in bed, she loved sex, she was good at it and she wanted it often. Her appetite was so healthy, she'd nearly killed him but it was a death he didn't mind dying.

Outside of bed she was affectionate, attentive, funny and almost always in a good mood, unless she had a headache, was stressed about a test she had to take or they were fighting about something, which they did a lot, which meant they could make up a lot. She could cook. She kept a clean house. Even working as a waitress on the weekends and going to school full-time, she still took care of him in every way there was to take care of a man and she took care of their apartment, their bills, the food, their lives. Except for paying the rent and utilities, taking out the trash and helping her do the dishes every once in a while, Layne hadn't had to lift a finger.

Who would step out on something like *that*?

"She's already filed," Dave said and finished before walking away with the platter. "She's through."

Layne watched Dave disappear into the dining room then he turned to Merry.

"She okay?" he asked.

"Nope," Merry answered. "She had no clue. Whole town's talkin' about it, have been for years and she's the putz. She found out, moved out and he moved his new girl in. She's twenty-three. Spittin' image of Roc fifteen years ago. She's also a cheerleader for the Pacers." Merry got closer and his voice dipped lower. "She's a freakin' Pacemate, big man. That dick's got courtside season tickets and has for the last ten years. If shackin' up with some hottie almost half your age who dances on court at halftime isn't in your face, nothing is. So, no, she's *not* okay."

Layne did not know much about Jarrod Astley. He knew he was from Indianapolis, Broad Ripple. He knew he was nine years older than Rocky. He knew he was Chief of Surgery at Presbyterian in Indianapolis and supposedly a hotshot since he'd been Chief of Surgery for five years, which made him young when he earned the post. He'd seen the man, not often, a few times around town. He was good-looking enough, in a stick up his ass kind of way. He struck Layne as ice cold, which Layne thought didn't work with Rocky, who was anything but cold.

Now, he knew the man was just a plain fool.

"Jesus," Layne muttered, tilting his head to the side and looking at the floor.

He was wondering, again, why she'd come to his house that morning.

He was also wondering why she'd come to his hospital room, looked at him the way she did, touched him, put her mouth to his.

Rebound or something else?

"Tanner," Merry called, and Layne looked at him.

"Let's eat," Layne said and watched as Merry's eyes flashed then his face closed off, not giving away anything.

Then he smiled huge—a cover—grabbed a basket that had something wrapped in a clean dish towel and he replied, "Fuckin' A, bubba."

Layne inhaled from the cigarette, took it from his lips and exhaled.

He had one smoke a day, after dinner with a beer, or if the day had been shit, a whisky. Since quitting ten years ago, he only had the one a day.

Unless the day was *really* shit.

He looked to Merry as Merry exhaled. Merry didn't have one smoke a day. He had a lot more.

They were both standing outside, but Dave, not smoking, was sitting on a garden chair. The boys were in the house watching some movie on TV.

"So Stew's fucked her over?" Dave asked.

Layne had told them about Gabby's problem.

"Yeah," Layne answered.

"Can't say I'm surprised," Dave muttered.

"That'd be because it isn't surprising," Layne muttered back.

"I'll keep my ear to the ground, big man, but, with Stew, it could be anything," Merry told him.

"It's bad shit, she's in danger, I gotta know," Layne said to Merry.

"What'd you get on your searches?" Dave asked.

"He's maxed out," Layne answered. "Overdrawn at the bank, credit cards over the limit, hasn't paid any bills in over six months, debt collectors circling, his truck has been shopped out for repo. She's been holdin' on, but the last three months she's struggled. Utilities are only two months out but I figure she pays them so she won't get shut off. She was always current, always paid on time and the last six months, she's been juggling, payin' late, fallin' short, payin' minimum payments instead of payin' the full amount. Now, outside the utilities, she isn't payin' at all. She didn't often carry debt, except around Christmas. She's been inchin' up, but, last two months, she's shot up and she's also maxed. They've both been declined for new cards, him twice in the last month and she's tried taking out three."

"That's not good," Merry mumbled.

"Nope," Layne agreed. "She makes decent money and never lived beyond her means. We bought that house together sixteen years ago. Her mortgage is low. He lost his job, which he hasn't, she could take him on. She'd feel the hit but she can do it. This kinda shit, he owes someone. Gambling. Betting. Something."

"I'll ask around," Dave offered.

"It would be appreciated," Layne replied.

Merry crushed his butt in the ashtray on the outdoor table and twisted his head to his dad.

"Got a date, Dad," he said, and Layne smiled.

Merry was Jasper except forty years old. He'd been married once, for six years. Before and since, he played the field as often as he could. Like his sister, young, he'd been an exceptionally good-looking and age hadn't touched it. In fact, it seemed to enhance it so Merry's field was wide and varied.

Layne's smile died when Dave got up from his chair and headed into the house, muttering, "I'll leave you to it."

Layne took one last drag and then crushed out his cigarette on the exhale, knowing now this invitation to dinner was more than a family get-together.

Layne watched Dave close the back door then he locked his eyes on Merry.

"What?" he asked instantly.

"You know we gotta talk, it's been six weeks," Merry replied quietly, his eyes on his dad's dark backyard.

"Yeah, we'll talk but not now. I took a hit—"

He didn't finish when Merry's eyes sliced to him and he growled, "Yeah, you took a hit."

He was talking about Layne getting shot.

"I didn't mean that kinda hit, Merry. The hospital bills wiped me out. It kills to say it but I can't focus on that right now. I gotta take cases that pay."

"You're off on this one," Merry declared, and Layne felt his neck muscles contract.

"No, Garrett, I'm not," he said softly.

"Yeah, Tanner, you are," Merry shot back. "You've been blown."

"You can't work it," Layne pointed out.

"I won't be. Rocky is," Merry returned.

Every muscle in Layne's body contracted.

"What?" he whispered.

"She's gonna cozy up to Rutledge, get in on the inside," Merry shared.

Layne's fingers curled into fists and he turned fully to face his friend. It took a lot out of him, but he didn't grab his collar and shake some sense into him—or beat it into him—both of which he'd prefer to do.

"Are you fucking *insane*?" Layne asked.

"She's all over it," Merry retorted.

Layne sucked in a breath and it made a sound like a hiss.

Then he looked at the yard.

She would. Rocky would. She'd be all over it.

He now had proof that Raquel was just as nuts as ever and her brother surpassed her by a long fucking shot.

"She doesn't know what she's doing," Layne pointed out.

"We're talking. She's learning. She's good," Merry replied.

He looked back at his friend. "News flash, man. I took three because of this shit six weeks ago and I know what I'm doin'. You want that to happen to your sister?"

Merry leaned into Layne and he saw it in his face. It wasn't stark, he was trying to control it, but it was there.

Fear.

"It was her idea," he whispered.

"Fuck me," Layne whispered back, and it hit him.

She knew. Merry told her everything. She knew there was a dirty cop in the department. She knew it was Rutledge. She knew Merry couldn't work it so he farmed it out to Layne. She knew Layne got too close and Rutledge got tweaked and Layne got ambushed. And, it was worthwhile to repeat, she knew there was a dirty copy in the department.

And she knew her father's partner twenty-four years ago was a dirty cop. She knew that her father knew it. She knew that her father was working at proving it and he got close. And she knew because she'd heard the break-in. She'd heard her mother's shouts, the partner's replies. She'd called 911 then she'd heard the shots and she only stayed alive because she was smart enough to hide and the partner had to get out before he could find her because the sirens were approaching. Before the cops could stop her, she saw her mother's dead, bloody body in the front entry of this same fucking house. And she knew her father had been hit the same night and left for dead, but by a miracle, he'd survived. Dave hadn't made his wife's funeral because he was in a hospital room with a tube down his throat. Merry and Rocky had gone with their grandparents. He also knew she'd testified at the hearing.

And Layne knew this because she'd told him, in the dark of night, in their bed, her body pressed to his, hers trembling like she was freezing to death.

And Layne knew one last thing.

Raquel Merrick Astley would do anything to take down a dirty cop.

"I can't talk her out of it, man." Merry was still whispering.

"You should have never told her, Merry. *Jesus!*" he exploded. "What was in your fuckin' head?"

"She…Tanner…*fuck*," Merry hissed. "When you got shot…fuck…let's just say, Roc was not good. She kept at me, wanted to know what you were workin'. And, big man, you know, *you know*, when Rocky keeps at you, you got no choice but to talk. Fuck, more than once in my career I wished I had her in an interrogation room with me. She's the master."

He knew this. She wanted to know something, she was a dog with a bone. And not just any dog, a vicious pit bull. She never let anything go. Hell, their first Christmas together, she knew every last present he gave her before she opened them. He'd learned to go shopping last minute on

Christmas Eve or the day before her birthday and then come home and keep her occupied in a multitude of ways where she couldn't use her mouth to speak and he'd had to do it for as long as he could so she'd be exhausted or she'd always know what gifts he'd bought her.

He'd thought it was kind of cute and he definitely liked the exhausting her part.

Now he did not find it cute.

Merry interrupted his thoughts.

"Did you hear me, Tanner? She was not good when you—"

Layne cut him off, his mind on other things, namely keeping Raquel Merrick Astley alive until her next birthday.

"I'll talk to her," he declared.

"Oh boy," Merry muttered, rocking back on his heels and looking to the heavens.

Layne ignored him. "She start this gig?"

"Not yet," Merry answered.

"What's her plan?"

"You're not gonna get it outta her head," Merry warned.

"What's her plan, Merry?"

Merry pulled in a breath then blew it out. Then he said, "She's gonna reel him in."

"Come again?"

"She's gonna get on his radar, hopin' he'll be interested, which I know he will. Then she's gonna get him to ask her out and get close."

Layne felt the leg of lamb, cooked with rosemary and garlic and served with roasted potatoes, homemade tzatziki sauce and fresh, still hot from the oven, homemade pita bread followed with homemade baklava smothered in a sugary honey, roil in his stomach.

"She intends to sleep with him?" he whispered.

Merry gave him an unhappy look.

Then he said, "We're talkin' Rocky here, brother. My sister goes the distance."

"Fuck," Layne was still whispering. "*Fuck!*" he repeated, *not* in a whisper.

"You talk to her, she's gonna be pissed...*at me*," Merry informed him.

"I'll take that chance," Layne snarled.

"Fuck, now *you're* pissed at me," Merry muttered, studying him.

"Believe it, brother," Layne clipped. "You should have nipped this in the bud."

Merry threw his arms out. "This is Rocky!" He took a step closer to Layne. "We been skirtin' this awhile, Tanner, but here we are. It's over, long over, but we all know shit's so fucked up between you two, it isn't ever gonna get sorted. We also know shit's so wound up between you, there'll always be a connection. No." His hand came up almost in Layne's face, close enough for Layne to snap his mouth shut, not close enough for Layne to feel the need to take a swing, "Do not bullshit me. There's shit you don't know and I'm not gonna tell you, but let's just say the last eighteen years you aren't the only one been lickin' those wounds, keepin' 'em fresh."

Another shot to the gut. This one bounced around, tearing through a variety of organs.

"You are shitting me, Merry. *She* walked out on *me*," Layne ground out.

"I'm not goin' there," Merry shot back.

"You brought it up," Layne bit off.

"I'm just sayin', you are not comin' at this in a position of *not* bein' in the know of what I'm dealin' with here. Roc gets somethin' in her head, nothin's gonna shake it out and you and I both know it. The other part of this is, even with that, you aren't in the position to do dick about it."

"You wanna bet?" Layne asked quietly.

"Yeah, I'll bet. Tell me somethin', brother, she went all out tonight, why isn't she here?"

Layne straightened and didn't answer, which he knew, fuck him, *was* the answer.

"Yeah, that's what I thought. She wanted to be in on our little chat." Merry indicated the two of them with a hand jerking back and forth. "Tonight was her idea. Dad didn't win a fuckin' leg of lamb in a poker game, for fuck's sake. *Rocky* bought it. She isn't stupid enough to think she can head into this without as much firepower at her back as she can get. She went to your house, proverbial olive branch, and you shoved it up her ass. I get that right, brother?" Merry asked cuttingly.

Layne didn't answer this time because he was grinding his teeth.

"You're blown," Merry stated. "You got two sons, an ex-wife shacked up with the town asshole and three bullets for your troubles. Rutledge knows you took your shot, he nearly took your life makin' his warning for you to back off, so I reckon, since you're still breathin', he figures he's got nothin' to fear from you. He can only guess I gave you the intel. You're close with every cop in that department, half of us you worked with when you served."

"Yeah, but I'm closest to you and Colt," Layne reminded him.

"And?"

"And because of that, he'll make Rocky in about a second," Layne bit out.

"Yeah, and Rocky knows that. What Rutledge doesn't know is that I'm close to my sister and I talk to her. Not a lotta cops share shit like this with their sister. Wife, maybe. Their sister? No freaking way."

"That is, if their sister didn't hear their mother get murdered by a dirty cop in their own damned house," Layne reminded him and watched Merry flinch. "He'll make her."

Merry recovered quickly. "She's not dumb, Tanner. She'll play it smart."

"He'll make her," Layne repeated.

"He won't make her, man. Shit, he's got someone in that department on his ass. Because he felt the heat from you, he doesn't know if it's me, Colt, Sully or Haines. He's too busy tryin' to figure out which one of us *made him* to even think about makin' Rocky."

Layne was done with this conversation.

"I'm gonna talk to her," he stated.

Merry was done too.

"Suit yourself, but one thing. I got here tonight and she was in her head. Roc goes into her head for only one reason, and that's when she's got her feelings hurt. I know it isn't her fuckwad husband because she won't even speak to him except through an attorney and she tells me all about that shit. My guess is, whatever went down this morning between you and her, you scored a direct hit. I love you, man, you know it. Sucked losin' you when you two disintegrated and I'm fuckin' thrilled to have you back. But I love her a fuckuva lot more than you, and I find out she's in her head because you can't let go of something that happened *eighteen years ago* and still feel like gettin' your licks in, you got me to worry about. You get me?"

"Like I said, Garrett, I'll talk to her," Layne gritted from between his teeth.

"Yeah," Merry replied, watching him closely. "I know you will. I know from this conversation that you got her best interests at heart too, no matter that other shit. You just gotta know that she's not in a good space right now. She's the town chump, sleepin' on her brother's couch and knowin' dirt is sittin' at a desk next to her brother, that same dirt ordered a hit on her ex-boyfriend. She's exposed, Tanner, vulnerable. I do not get a good feelin' about you havin' a chat with her when she's this way and the only reason I'll allow it is because I trust you. Don't fuck that up."

Layne knew Merry loved his sister, more than anyone on this earth, but he was done.

"One more word, Merry," Layne said softly. "You know me better than that shit. One more word, I'm gonna take it personal."

"Any other time, I'd know she could fight her corner—"

"This morning, I didn't know she'd left Astley and I didn't know any of this shit. You also know what happened between us and you know what it did to me. Cut me some fuckin' slack."

"Yeah," Merry said quietly. His face had changed. It had gone soft, but his eyes had grown intense. "Yeah, brother. I know what it did to you." He paused, leaned in and his voice dropped even quieter. "I know what happened too, I know more than you, brother. I know *why* it happened so maybe you'll cut *Roc* some slack."

Layne felt his body freeze again, but before he could say a word, Merry finished.

"Got a date."

He reached down, nabbed his smokes off the table and walked into the house.

Layne grabbed his smokes too and shook one out.

Today was a two cigarette day.

Absolutely.

Three

WHITE HAT

*A*t two o'clock that morning, Layne stood outside Merry's condo door and knocked, loudly.

He'd gone home. He'd made certain the boys had their homework done and he'd gone to bed. He was going to sleep on it, think on it, consider his strategies after he fucked things up so royally that morning with Raquel.

Then he couldn't get it out of his head. None of it. Her husband fucking around on her. Her sleeping on her brother's couch for two months. Her going in to do whatever the hell she was going to do to find dirt on Rutledge. But mostly whatever the hell she was going to do to get Rutledge to trust her.

So he got up, got dressed, got in his truck and went to Merry's.

Merry's car wasn't in the lot. He was sleeping elsewhere that night, as usual.

Rocky's Mercedes was there.

When she didn't answer, he knocked louder.

He heard her at the door before he saw her, hopefully checking the peephole. Then the outside light came on and the door opened. She was standing there, and with one look at her the breath went clean out of him.

First, because she was wearing a big t-shirt. She'd worn big t-shirts to bed, his, when they were living together (and before, she'd confiscated several while they were dating).

This one was a blue Indianapolis Colts tee and he knew it wasn't Jarrod Astley's because the man was taller than her, but slim, and she swam in it.

If he'd thought about it, he'd have guessed she'd graduate to silk, satin and lace. She had not.

Something about this hit him and it hit him hard.

Second, because she had her hair down. He hadn't seen much of her the last year he was home, but it wasn't exactly a bustling city they lived in. He saw her—at Mimi's, at Frank's, coming out of Reggie's with a pizza, at the grocery store. She always had her hair up in a ponytail, a twist, a clip, a bun. Now it was down and it was longer than he expected. Longer even than when they were together. Long and thick and tousled around her face, over her shoulders, down her chest.

Christ. Gorgeous.

"Is everything all right?" she asked, her voice sounding funny, scared, and he knew she was worried about Merry.

He took advantage of that fear. Instead of answering straight away, like she had that morning, he walked right through her. But he stopped close, closed the door and locked it before he moved into the condo and saw the bed pulled out of the couch, the covers mussed. Merry had a multitude of beds he could choose to sleep in. He should let Rocky have his.

Once he successfully gained entry, he turned to her. "If you're worried about Merry, he's fine. He's probably a lot more than fine just about now."

She stared at him unblinking then she turned to the door. Finally she looked back at him.

"What time is it?" she asked.

"Why'd you come to the hospital?" he asked back and watched her body lock. There was only one lamp lit in the living room, but he saw it lock to statue-still as the confusion and sleep swept out of her face and she went on alert.

"Sorry?"

"When I was shot, why'd you come to the hospital?"

She straightened her shoulders. This took effort, he could tell, but she did it. It also took time. Just a bit of it but enough for her to come up with a believable lie.

"You were at Jarrod's hospital and I just happened to be—"

He cut her off. "Bullshit, Roc, you left Jarrod two months ago."

He watched her lips thin and she glared at him.

Then she whispered, "Merry," and he knew he'd thrown Merry right under the bus. He also didn't care.

"Why'd you come to the hospital?" he repeated.

"Why are you here?" she asked.

"Answer me, Rocky."

She crossed her arms on her chest. "Go home, Layne."

"Okay, you don't wanna answer that." He shrugged, took a step toward her and stopped. "Then why'd you come by this morning?"

"I think you ate the reason why tonight," she answered.

"Bullshit again, Raquel. You know Merry and I talked tonight."

"Yes, well," she threw a hand out and then crossed it right back on her chest, "I had an alternate reason for coming to your house this morning. After your fond farewell, however, I decided I no longer have that reason."

He took another step toward her and she held her ground, but her eyes flashed their warning and he stopped.

"We should talk about that," he said softly.

"Oh no. No we shouldn't. I think you said enough this morning."

"Rocky, you showed up out of the blue, stormed into my house, fed my dog, made me a cup of coffee, gave my boy advice on what to have for breakfast and I haven't spoken to you in eighteen years except groggy in a hospital bed after being shot three times," he reminded her.

"Yes, I can see that's reasonable, now that you explain it. I can see why you'd speak to me that way considering I…" she leaned in and finished on a hiss, "*made you a cup of coffee.*"

"You're bullshitting me again," he told her. "You get what I'm sayin' to you."

She shook her head and repeated, "Go home, Layne."

"We gotta put this behind us, for your dad and your brother."

"I tried to do that this morning. It didn't work. Once bitten, twice shy. I think the avoiding each other tactic is a better strategy. Let's go back to that."

"You didn't try to do that this morning, Rocky. You came by, olive branch extended, but only so you could soften me up for the blows you'd deliver later."

Her upper body jerked back. "What?"

"Rutledge?"

She looked away but when her eyes came back to him they were narrowed. In that second she'd braced for attack *and* she'd dug in. He knew it.

"That's none of your business."

"That wasn't what Merry told me tonight. He told me you were looking for firepower."

"Yes, but like I said, after our chat by my car, I'm no longer looking for that. Not from you."

"And who's gonna take your back in this crusade, Roc? 'Cause trust me, sweetcheeks, you go in without backup, you are gonna be fucked."

Her face turned to marble before her lips moved. "I'll be fine."

"You'll be fucked."

She leaned in again. "I'll be *fine.*"

"Lotsa reasons a dirty cop goes dirty. But unlike a criminal, he's got more reasons not to get caught. He gets caught, he loses everything. He loses face. He loses family. He loses respect. He loses his badge. He loses his career and he goes to a place he does not wanna go. Boys in prison, they don't like cops. He's either dead or he'll wanna be. That means a dirty cop who hasn't made all he needs to break away clean and disappear is gonna get antsy when he feels heat. And by antsy, I mean *desperate.*"

When she replied, she did it quickly and quietly. "I know that."

"I know you know that which makes me wonder, your dad uses a cane when it rains but is reminded every day when he wakes up alone, why you'd put that shit out there for him to experience again."

He heard her suck in breath.

Merry told him to go easy on her but he had no intention of doing that. Too much was at stake.

"Carson Fisher was dead three days after he was sent down," he reminded her.

"Layne—"

"Shiv to the gut. They didn't twist it. They yanked it straight through him, straight through his heart. He bled out about a second after he hit the ground."

"Be quiet," she whispered.

Layne wasn't quiet. "Your mom went down so he could avoid that."

"Be *quiet*," she whispered louder.

"Your dad went down for the same reason."

"Stop it, Layne."

"*I* went down six weeks ago for the same fuckin' reason, Rocky."

Her arms uncrossed, she leaned forward sharply and she yelled, "*Stop it, Layne!*"

"Merry doesn't want you out there with Rutledge and I figure your dad doesn't know about this. But if he did, he wouldn't want you out there either."

"You forget, Layne, that Dad knew exactly what you're telling me and he still stayed on Fisher," she shot back.

"True enough, but he had no idea he was puttin' more than his ass on the line. You asked him now, I bet he'd tell you he'd stand down."

"Then you don't know my father very well," she returned.

He had to admit, she was probably right about that. She was also wrong about it.

"He fucked up," Layne told her.

"He did not. He did the right thing. Shit like that happens to cops every day. He knew the score, so did Mom."

"You sure about that?"

"Absolutely."

"Got yourself all talked into it then," he noted.

"Go to hell, Layne."

"Sweetcheeks, your dad thought Cecilia or you were in danger, he would have done things differently."

"He wouldn't stand down."

"No, but he would have made you safe."

She tossed her hair then said, "You're right. That's a good idea, Layne. I'll let Dad in on this. He won't like it. It'll probably piss him off. But, like Merry, and you, he won't stop me but at least he'll be in the know and he can do what he wants with that knowledge."

"Merry's right. You're smart. None of us can out you, which means none of us can stop you. You got us all cornered."

She didn't reply, just stood there and glared at him.

"Problem with that is, if I remember the story right, your dad talked to your mom. The deal was, something happened to him, she took what he left her to the cops. That's why, after Fisher dropped your dad, he went for your mom."

He watched her face get pale as she swallowed but she didn't speak or lose the fire in her eyes.

"Now, it's the other way around," Layne continued. "See, he's guessin' now, which boy enlightened me. He can't be sure and he can't ask questions. So he's off-balance. But he makes you, he knows Merry's made him. So he drops you then goes after Merry. Maybe your dad. Maybe me too."

Rocky remained silent.

Layne went on, "I was in surgery, then unconscious. Tell me, Roc, what were Tripp and Jasper like when you saw them at the hospital?"

She spoke then. She whispered, "Shut up, Layne."

"You recognize the look in their eyes?"

"Shut up."

"See that somewhere? The mirror, maybe?"

"Go to hell!" she shouted and whirled. Her hair flying out behind her, she stomped to the door, unlocked it and yanked it open. Standing there holding it, she turned back to him. "Get out."

He walked right up to her, wrenched the door out of her hand and slammed it. Then he moved into her. She retreated and he backed her up until she was against the wall and he kept going until their bodies touched. He caged her in, one hand flat against the wall at her waist, the other one at her shoulder.

She put her hands on his chest and she put pressure there.

"Step back!" she demanded.

"All that worth it to you? You think your mom would be proud?"

She stared in his eyes and she did this awhile.

Then she answered softly, "Yes."

He felt his brows shoot up. "Yes?"

"Where's Daddy going?" she asked in a high-pitched, fake little girl voice. Then she went on to answer her own question in her normal voice. "Out to get the bad guys, baby. Your daddy wears the white hat, makes the world safe for all the mommies' precious babies…" Her hand slid up his chest, his neck, to rest curled around his jaw. "Just like you."

Jesus. Cecilia said that to her, touched her like that.

Jesus.

"Roc," he whispered.

"She was proud of him."

"Rocky."

"She was proud of what he did."

"Roc—"

"He goes to work, every day, sits down by Colt, Mike, Sully, Sean… *Merry*. He sits down and puts on the white hat and pretends he's a good guy. Those boys, they face danger every day. They get to wear the white hats. He doesn't get to do that, Layne."

"He'll go down," Layne assured her. "Give Merry and me time to regroup."

"You're exposed."

"Give us time to regroup."

"There *isn't* time."

"There is."

"This *spreads*," she told him the truth. "One goes down, others will follow. If they don't, a dirty cop taints the whole team. Word gets out—"

"Let Merry and I get our bearings."

"No."

"*Fuck, Rocky!*" he exploded, pounding his palm against the wall by her shoulder. "You have no fuckin' clue what you're doin'. Merry's already swung his ass out on this one and you know what happened to me. We need to cool it. You're putting the entire operation in jeopardy."

She again fell silent and did it apparently forgetting she still had her hands on him.

He didn't forget. Both of them burned right into his skin.

He didn't say a word.

They went into stare down and he realized he'd forgotten this. When she left him, he'd glorified every memory of her. He'd forgotten she could be unbelievably fucking stubborn and he'd forgotten just how incredibly *annoying* that was.

Back in the day, he had several outs to a stare down with Rocky. The one he used most frequently was to tickle her. His second top runner was to kiss her. Once, he'd been so pissed, he'd caught her up in his arms, walked to the couch, turned her over his knee and spanked her.

The first two he enjoyed, and if he stuck with it, which he always did, she eventually did too. The last served to piss her off to such an extreme, she attacked him, which eventually ended with them doing something a whole lot different than fighting. Something they also both enjoyed. It had been the best sex they'd ever had. To the point where it gave him option four, when they were in stare down, to break it, he'd ask if she needed a spanking. The memory cut through the stubborn, her breath would start getting heavy just thinking about it, and *she'd* end up kissing *him*.

He didn't have any of those options open to him now, she wasn't backing down and he had to get her hands off him or he'd put his on her.

"Merry's out on a date, Roc, I think it's safe you use his bed," Layne remarked, pushed away from the wall, walked to the door and tugged it open, turning to her to see she was still pressed against the wall where he left her. "Lock this after me," he ordered then he walked out, slamming the door behind him.

Four

ROBIN HOOD

"*L*ayne," she begged.

Layne sucked her nipple sharply into his mouth.

"Layne," she repeated on a moan.

He lifted his head and looked toward hers. It was pressed back into the pillows, her neck arched.

"You promised," he murmured.

Her head came up and her eyes came to him, unfocused. Christ, she was turned on. It was written all over her face.

He felt his rock hard cock start aching.

Then he put his mouth to her, trailing his lips down her belly. He stopped and kissed her right above the dark triangle of hair between her legs.

She lifted her knees and dropped them to the sides, offering herself to him.

Fuck, but he loved her.

He settled between her legs and slid his finger lightly through her wetness.

Her hips bucked then her body moved with agitation.

"Layne," she said again.

He looked up at her and she was staring at him, need stark on her face. Her hands were clenching the slats in the headboard, what she'd promised.

48

Layne got to touch, to taste, to lick, to suck and she held on to the head-board—no matter what.

"You promised, baby," he reminded her again, using his finger to retrace its path.

A low sound came from her throat and her head fell back.

Layne grinned.

Then he looked down at her, opened her with his fingers and used his tongue to do the same thing he'd done with his finger.

Her hips surged up. His mouth closed over her, he pulled deep and then growled with satisfaction against her when he heard and felt her come.

Layne's eyes opened.

He was on his stomach and his cock was hard. Again. And aching. Again.

He rolled to his back, muttering, "Christ."

He stared at the ceiling. It felt like he'd been asleep for two minutes, which was about as long as he actually had been asleep since he'd spent most of his night thinking about Rocky, some of it arguing with her, and the rest of it pissed at her.

Even so, he still had a dream. All of them were different, some hotter than others, but only by shades and degrees.

This one, however, was the best so far.

He put the dream out of his head when he heard the boys' shower going. He turned and looked at the clock. Six twenty-seven and they were up on their own, or at least one of them was. A miracle.

He gave himself a minute to get his body under control then he got up, went to the bathroom, did his thing, went to his dresser, grabbed a tee, tugged it on and left his room. He checked Tripp's room first. Light on, bed unmade, clothes and shit everywhere, Tripp not there. The shower was still on so he walked down the hall to Jasper's room and found it the same as Tripp's. Light on, room a mess, Jasper not there.

He walked down the stairs and halfway down saw Blondie outside, panting against the glass, body swinging side to side, tail whipping around.

He walked directly to the sliding glass door, but turned to see Tripp was emptying the dishwasher. Another miracle.

"Hey, pal," Layne greeted.

Tripp looked at him and smiled. "Hey, Dad."

"Is that Tripp?" Layne asked, sliding open the door. Blondie shot in and began instantly to dance around him. Once the dog was clear of the door, he threw it to.

"What?" Tripp asked back as Layne walked to the coffeepot.

"You Tripp?" Layne repeated.

"Well…" Tripp stared at him, a funny look on his face. "Yeah."

Layne pulled the filter out of the coffeemaker. "You sure? See, the real Tripp doesn't unload the dishwasher unless I've asked him ten times. I remember askin' you to do it last night but that was only once. I got nine more to go."

Tripp's comically confused face split into a smile and he muttered, "Shut up, Dad," before he turned back to the dishwasher.

"You feed Blondie?" Layne asked, but he knew Tripp hadn't because Blondie was dancing between both him and his son, unsure which one of them was going to end her enforced fast. If she'd been fed, she'd pick one or the other to bug.

"Not yet. Just got downstairs. She's only been out a few minutes." Tripp answered.

"I'll get her after I make coffee. You get breakfast after you finish with that."

"Okay," Tripp agreed and shoved some plates into a cupboard.

Layne made the coffee and started to feed Blondie but stopped when he was about to plop the food in the dirty bowl. He stared at the bowl a second then cleaned it before he fed his son's dog. By the time he set down the bowl, Blondie was beside herself and Layne added a trip to the garden center to his day's agenda to buy her more bowls so they could put them in the dishwasher and she didn't have her breakfast delayed.

Layne had a cup of coffee in his hand, his hips against the counter by the sink and Tripp was sitting at the island spooning up cereal when Jasper showed. He let his oldest son get his cereal and sit by his brother before he moved to stand in front of them at the island.

"Spoke to your mom yesterday. She wants you guys to stay with me next week."

Tripp had been looking at him while he talked, and when he finished, his head dropped down to look at the milk in his bowl. Jasper had been looking at him too, but his head didn't drop down. Layne watched anger flash through his features before he looked away and Layne saw a muscle tick in his cheek.

This was another reason why he knew they were his boys. They'd pegged Stew before Layne even moved home. They didn't like him and they didn't like spending time with him. But more, they didn't like him with their mom.

Gabby might be a bitch to Layne but she loved her kids and they loved her. For this reason, Layne knew they were torn. After they spent time with her and Stew, when he got them back, they were both tense to the point of wired and it took a couple of days for them to settle in. Even not liking Layne, Jasper obviously liked him more than Stew because he relaxed when he was at Layne's house. Then they'd go back and it'd happen all over again.

This caused Layne concern, but neither of them had shared and he felt it important to let them deal with it how they saw fit. They needed him, they needed to man up and ask. Until then, it was up to them to cope.

They were torn because he knew they preferred to be at Layne's house because Stew wasn't there. But they didn't want to be away from their mom because Stew was there. If Stew wasn't there, he wondered how they'd be. Tripp probably would take it in stride. Jasper would probably be more of an asshole.

"That cool with you guys?" Layne asked, and they both looked at him.

"Yeah," Tripp answered.

"Whatever," Jasper muttered.

That was the best he was going to get from Jas and he'd take it.

Then Jasper decided to take his anger out on Layne and Layne knew this because Jasper stated, "Mrs. Astley is thirty-eight years old."

This was a bizarre statement leading into unknown territory, but considering he was referring to Raquel at all, Layne braced.

"Yeah," Layne confirmed. "How'd you know that?"

"Kids know everything about Mrs. Astley," Jasper answered.

Layne bet they did.

"You were twenty-five when Mom had me," Jasper went on.

Layne studied his son and prompted, "Your point, Jas?"

"You said you lived with her before Mom," Jasper replied.

Layne kept his eyes locked to his boy.

Layne had made the decision when he moved home that he would treat his sons, mostly, like men. Neither of them were kids anymore, not really, and both of them were smart. They had to learn how to be men from somewhere and Stew sure as fuck wouldn't teach them how to be good ones. So Layne was going to do it.

Therefore, he was straight with them, at all times, at all costs. They had to learn how to deal with whatever life threw at them and no one could tell you how to do that. You had to learn by experience.

Neither of them had asked about him getting shot, not yet. He was going to let them sort what they had to sort in their heads and then he was going to share more about who he was and what he did. That time was getting ripe, he knew it.

Therefore, Layne nodded to Jasper. "I did."

Jasper got that look in his eye, the one he got when he was going to be more of an asshole teenage kid than usual, and Layne braced again.

"You like jailbait?"

"Jas," Tripp muttered. He wasn't a big fan of his brother's asshole teenage kid act either.

Jasper turned to his brother and defended himself. "She's four years younger than Dad. They lived together before Mom, she was, like, a teenager, dude."

Layne held on to his patience and studied his sons.

Then he made a decision.

"Don't move, I'll be back," Layne ordered and walked out of the kitchen, up the stairs and to his desk. He pulled out a drawer, rifled through it and found the big manila envelope. He opened it, his fingers sifting through the pictures. He found the one he was looking for, pulled it out and walked back to his sons.

He resumed his place opposite them at the island and tossed the picture down in front of them. It skidded and Tripp's hand shot out to stop it.

He brushed it with his finger, twirling it so it was right side up to him and Jasper.

In it was a picture of Rocky. She was wearing jeans shorts, a tight pink t-shirt, her hair was down and around her shoulders and she was sitting on a high, cement wall next to a statue of a lion. They were at Purdue, her and Dave and Layne. She was seventeen and scouting universities, she'd later be accepted at Purdue as well as five other schools. She wanted to go to Purdue, but she got hooked up with Layne and made the decision to stay closer to home so she'd picked Butler. Layne felt no guilt about this. Butler wasn't sloppy seconds by a long shot.

Layne had always loved that picture. She'd been smiling. It was a little smile but the dimple in her right cheek had popped out. At seventeen, she'd made it to far beyond pretty, her sitting there, in her tight pink t-shirt, that smile on her face, young, the promise of a good life ahead of her. It was captivating both in person and in the photo. That smile, that t-shirt, her long legs exposed by her jeans shorts, ankles crossed, the promise on her face, it all defined why he'd fallen in love with her. He'd known her three weeks and in that instant, when he snapped that photo, he remembered looking through the lens and he'd lost his heart, or more to the point, he'd given it to her.

"That was taken about three weeks after we started going out. She was seventeen," Layne told his boys.

"Wow. She's pretty," Tripp mumbled and his head came up to look at his dad. "But she's prettier now."

He wasn't wrong.

"Seventeen?" Jasper asked, his tone biting. "That's sick, you were twenty-one."

Jasper wasn't wrong either. Twenty and twenty-four was okay. Nineteen and twenty-three was still good. Anything below that, the guy in his twenties, the girl in her teens, was frowned upon in that 'burg.

But he didn't give a fuck then, and thinking about it for the first time in over a decade, he didn't give a fuck now.

"Look at her Jas," Layne urged quietly, and Jasper held his eyes, Jasper's belligerent. Then he looked down at the photo.

"It's safe to say, her brother and dad weren't all fired up that she caught my eye," Layne continued. "She was in high school. I'd graduated Ball State and was at the academy. The first six months I was with her, every date we had happened at her dad's house. He wouldn't even let me put her in my car. He got to know me and that changed. We moved in together a month after she graduated from high school and we lived together for two years."

He knew Jasper would do the math, he already did. Layne's son was far from dumb.

Layne carried on, "She went to Butler. She'd drive into Indy every day to go to class, worked at Frank's as a waitress on the weekends. I worked for the 'burg's PD."

Jasper looked from the photo to him and Layne went on.

"You see her?"

"Yeah, I see her," Jasper replied.

"Three weeks before that photo was taken, I saw her. Took one look at her and I knew. She was it. I didn't care if she was seventeen. She was it. You want something bad enough, you know it's right, you know it'll be worth the wait. So I waited and I was right. Rocky was worth it. Until you two came along, she was the best thing that happened to me in my whole goddamned life."

Tripp was staring at him, his mouth had dropped open. Jasper was shielding his response.

"Look at that picture, Jasper, and tell me that girl wasn't worth the wait," Layne said quietly.

Jasper licked his lips and then sucked them between his teeth.

Layne waited.

Then Jasper showed him that he had broken through.

"I know it because she's the coolest teacher in school," Jasper informed him.

"Yeah?" Layne asked, curious, even though he told himself he did not want to know.

"Yeah," Tripp put in. "She's like that *Dead Poets Society* dude except a lady. She even shows that movie in her class. Kids are always hearing that she's gettin' into trouble with the principal because of something she's done. Half the time, they aren't even in the classroom but doin' all sorts of shit all over the school. You get in her class, you got so many field trips, it's awesome. I hope I get her. She even lets kids read *comic strips* for *credit*."

Yes, another indication that Rocky was a nut.

"You have her yet?" Layne asked Jasper.

"Had her when I was a sophomore and she was awesome, so I'm takin' Advanced English Lit next semester. I hope I get her because Mr. Halsey is a moron," Jasper replied.

Layne hoped he got Rocky too. Jesus, Halsey had been there when Layne had been at that school. He must be a hundred years old.

Jasper cut into his thoughts. "If she was the best thing that happened to you, how'd it go bad?"

Layne answered without hesitation. "She left me. She didn't say why. One day it was good, really good. The next day she was gone. Everything that was hers was out and she was gone. She didn't talk to me, she didn't explain it. We weren't fighting. It wasn't turning bad, and you know when that happens even though sometimes you don't admit it when it's happening. But it wasn't. It was good one day and she was gone the next. I reckon she had her reasons but the right thing to do was share them. She never did that. To this day, I have no clue why it ended. All I know is that it did. Whatever happened I might not have been able to fix, but after what we had, she should have showed me the respect of tellin' me where it went wrong."

"Did you ask?" Jasper asked.

"Yep, about a hundred times, on the phone, when she didn't hang up on me. Showin' up at her dad's house, at her school, at Frank's. She shut me out. Eventually, I had to man up and move on. So I did."

"To Mom," Tripp guessed.

"To your mom," Layne confirmed.

"But Mom wasn't the best thing to happen to you," Jasper noted, his eyes locked on Layne and Layne gave it to him straight.

"No, Jas, she wasn't. She's a great mom and a good woman but she was not a good wife."

Jasper surprised the hell out of him when he nodded.

Then, always sharp, Jasper noted, "Word is, Mrs. Astley is gettin' a divorce."

"Word is correct," Layne affirmed.

"She want you back?" Jasper asked, clearly having spent some time considering why Rocky was there yesterday morning.

"No," Layne answered.

"So why was she here?" Tripp put in, also clearly having thought about Rocky's visit.

When Layne answered, he did it honestly but he didn't do it fully.

"Her brother is a good friend, so's her dad. She and I are connected. We've been tryin' to avoid each other but me gettin' shot made that less easy for her to do. We're workin' shit out."

"You gonna go for it?" Jasper asked.

"Can't tell the future, Jas. If I could, we'd be livin' in Rio and you'd each have your own jet," Layne answered, hoping to inject humor into the discussion, which already not the most comfortable, was getting even less so, and Tripp laughed.

Jasper's lips twitched and he shook his head.

"You should go for it," Tripp suggested, and Layne's surprised eyes cut to his younger son.

"Tripp, don't, pal. Okay? Whatever happens, happens. But Rocky and me, we may sort it out so she'll be over at her dad's when Dave has a barbeque but she won't be ironing your boxers."

Tripp kept his eyes on his old man then he nodded and whispered, "Right," but, fuck him, Layne still saw hope there.

Deciding their conversation was done, Layne indicated their bowls with a dip of his head. "Get those in the dishwasher, get your books, get to school."

Tripp moved instantly. Jasper stayed where he was and studied Layne for a while before he followed his brother.

Layne timed his next for when Tripp was in the garage heading to Jasper's Charger and Jasper was almost at the utility room door.

"Jas, a second," Layne called. Jasper stopped, looked at him and Layne got closer. "You're stayin' with me next week but when you talk to your mom and when you go home, I want you to keep your eyes and ears open."

Jasper's body went tight as did his face. "Why?"

"Don't know, not yet, but I need you to be my ears with your mom."

Jasper's eyes narrowed, not in anger at Layne, but in understanding. "Stew?"

Layne nodded and gave his son the truth. "He's an asshole. I don't like him with your mom. She's got her sister in town, friends, and she's also got you, your brother and me. Of all of those, all she's really got to look out for her is you, your brother and me. We gotta look out for her. I'm gettin' a bad vibe and I want you to keep sharp. You hear anything or even feel anything, you tell me. Yeah?"

Jasper stayed silent and stared at Layne for a long time. Then something lit in his eyes. Something Layne hadn't seen since Jasper was a little kid. Something Layne missed like he'd been breathing half the amount of oxygen any other human needed and the other half just came whooshing into his lungs.

Then he muttered, "Yeah, okay, Dad."

Layne wanted to touch him. Christ, his hand itched to curl around Jasper's neck but he checked it.

"Do me a favor and keep this conversation from Tripp. Right now, you and me are workin' this. We need Tripp, I'll let you know."

Jasper nodded.

Layne jerked his head to the door. "Go to school."

"Can't do it, Drew. Wish I could but I gotta focus on shit that pays," Layne told Drew Mangold.

He was at the station because he wanted to talk to Colt, Sully and Mike about Stew.

He'd been to the station a couple of times since he'd been released from the hospital but Rutledge had not been there any of those times.

Rutledge was there now. Layne had locked eyes with him as he'd walked up the stairs ten minutes ago. He'd buried the burn seeing that asshole ignited inside him. Then he'd tipped up his chin, lifted a hand and gave him a flick of two fingers. Rutledge had visibly tensed when he'd seen Layne, but his face went slack when Layne greeted him like he always did if he was at the station when Layne walked up the stairs.

Layne knew a lot of the men in that department. Most of them he knew well. Some of them had worn a uniform at the same time Layne had.

Rutledge was not one of those men. He hadn't been around for very long and most of what Layne knew about him was that he was dirty so he didn't want to know much more. Unfortunately, since he was dirty, Layne had to investigate him so Layne knew Rutledge a lot more than he wanted to, and none of what he knew was any good.

Layne couldn't begin to guess what was going on in Rutledge's mind after Layne behaved like normal. He could think it was indication that Layne had learned his lesson and backed down. He could wonder if he'd been wrong about what he suspected Layne was doing before he told whoever was pulling his strings to order the hit thus wondering if he acted rashly. He could be considering both, or something else. Layne hoped he was considering both. They needed him off-balance and guessing not only the extent of their knowledge and who held it, but also what they'd do next.

Colt, Sully and Mike weren't there and Drew had corralled him to tell him about some weird shit that was happening at the Christian Church. Drew wasn't wrong. It didn't sound good, but Layne couldn't look into it.

About two days after Layne came home and set up shop over Mimi's, Merry punted him a case. Something the cops couldn't stick their noses into and something that the interested party couldn't pay a private detective for, especially not at Layne's rates.

It wasn't a big deal, doing some searches, printing out credit history, it took him ten minutes. But he'd done it, he'd done it gratis and he shouldn't have. It was the beginning of what Merry called Layne's "Robin Hood Caseload." Merry regularly punted shit he knew needed looking into, people he knew who needed help—all of them unable to pay for it—and Layne took them on and took care of their shit. The problem was, shit like that spreads, so Sully and Sean jumped on the bandwagon. Then Drew.

The only ones who didn't do it were Harrison Rutledge, Alec Colton and Mike Haines.

Rutledge didn't because he didn't know Layne and because he didn't give a shit if someone was in trouble and needed help.

Layne figured Colt and Haines knew it was happening and didn't interfere, but they also didn't participate. What Layne didn't know was if it was because they disagreed with him doing it or they didn't want to take advantage of a friendship.

Gabby didn't lie, he charged top dollar because he gave quick, efficient, confidential service on any matter you could possibly need a private investigator for. He'd traveled a lot, had an extensive and varied set of skills and people all over the country knew of him or had worked with him. He came highly recommended. Because of that, his reputation had preceded him and he had clients even before he'd located office space.

Most of his clients came from Indianapolis, which meant most of his work was there. He had some clients from the 'burg, but they lived in developments like where Rocky used to live.

With a healthy bank balance and money coming in, this meant he could carry a Robin Hood Caseload. Being out of work for five weeks and his nest egg depleted, this meant he needed to focus.

This sucked, especially after what Drew told him about what he suspected was happening at the church.

"Seriously, man, this is what I think it is, and I got a bad feeling it is, then..." Drew was trying to persuade him but Drew trailed off when his eyes went over Layne's shoulder and his face grew distracted.

Layne turned to see what caught his attention but he heard her heels on the floor before he saw her.

Rocky was walking across the room.

Strike that, Rocky was *strutting* across the room wearing a skirt much like yesterday's, this one the color of cranberries, just as tight, but there was a sexy slit up the front so you saw a hint of her inner thigh every other stride she took. She had on a black blouse, this one almost see-through, a black camisole under it and it fit her perfectly, too perfectly, like yesterday's blouse. She also had on a pair of shoes the color of her skirt, the leather shiny, the heel high and thin, no strap this time and they were the absolute definition of fuck-me shoes. Her hair was twisted in a complicated knot at the nape of her neck and she had a little leather purse that matched her shoes on a short strap that tucked it under her pit.

She strutted through the room smiling, giving little waves to men she knew and also giving absolutely no indication that she knew all the men watching her—and every man in that room was watching her—was struggling to control his dick getting hard.

She rounded Merry's desk and Layne watched, with no small amount of irritation, as she stood there looking at it for a moment as if searching for something. Then she found it, reached for a piece of paper and pen and leaned over, ass in the air, skirt stretched tight across it—*and* her hips *and* upper thighs, leaving nothing to the imagination—and she started scribbling.

Layne tore his eyes off Rocky and looked at the desk next to Merry's, separated by a three-foot aisle, where Rutledge was sitting, his eyes glued to Rocky's ass.

Fuck!

In the second she'd bent over, she'd cast her net, and even with Merry one of the prime suspects of who'd pegged Rutledge as dirty and sicced Layne on him, Rutledge wasn't struggling even a little bit against the net.

Layne looked back at Raquel and saw she'd turned her head toward Rutledge and then she straightened. She smiled at Rutledge and moved toward him.

The instant she did, Layne made a decision.

"We'll finish later," Layne told Drew on a mutter, and he strode, fast and with purpose, right to Rocky.

She had her back to him and didn't hear him coming, was intent on what she was doing or intended to ignore him having no idea what he was about to do.

He heard her saying, "...not answering his phone so it'd be a big help if you could tell him..." when he got up close. Without hesitation, he swung his arm back, hand open, and then smacked her lightly, but the sound carried, right on the ass.

Her body jolted and she whirled as he said loudly, "Sweetcheeks."

He looked down at her stunned face, wrapped an arm tight around her neck and yanked her right into his body. Again without hesitation, his head came down and his lips hit hers, hard, where he kissed her, just as hard. Then his head came up and he tried to ignore her soft body pressed to him, her tits crushed against him, the scent of her perfume and the fact that the vibe in the room had electrified.

He also tried to ignore the fact that her face showed she was openly struggling against being dazed and being really, *really* pissed.

"What you doin' here, baby?" he asked before she could speak.

She blinked.

Then she asked back, "What?"

His arm around her neck tightened and she was forced to press closer. His other hand hit her waist and slid around to the small of her back, pulling her even closer.

"You didn't tell me you were comin' to the station," he informed her.

"I—" she started, belatedly struggling by pushing her neck against his arm.

Before she could say another word, he looked at Rutledge.

"Best thing that happened to me, gettin' shot, man. I *cannot tell you.*" He grinned at Rutledge as Rutledge's mouth dropped right open, Rocky's body turned to stone and then he looked back down at Rocky, who was now glaring at him, her eyes full of fire. "Reunited me with Roc," he muttered to her then looked back at Rutledge. "Take another three bullets if I knew that was what I was gonna get." He kept grinning. "Luckily I didn't have to." He again looked at Rocky and asked softly, "Did I, baby?"

"You—" she began, her eyes sparking, beyond pissed and he dipped his head again and brushed his mouth on hers.

He lifted his head and saw the fire in her eyes was muted and she had fallen silent.

He looked back at Rutledge. "Never know what life's gonna bring. Lyin' there, blood oozin' out of me, thinkin' that's the end, and weeks later, I find out it's actually the beginning. You get what I mean?"

Rutledge kept staring at him, seemingly frozen, then his eyes darted back and forth between Rocky and Layne and he nodded.

"Holy fuck." Layne heard muttered and he looked beyond Rutledge to see Sully had arrived, coming up the back stairs. He was standing just beyond Rutledge's desk and he was staring at Rocky and Layne.

"Yo, Sul," Layne greeted and Sully's body jerked. Then *his* eyes darted between Rocky and Layne.

They finally stopped before he gave himself a seizure and he greeted back, "Layne, buddy, Rocky, um…hey."

Rocky moved in his arms like she was trying to turn toward Sully but his arms locked tighter and she was interrupted when they heard Colt coming.

"Yeah, Feb, honey, do me a favor and…" Layne heard and his eyes moved to see Colt walking toward Sully, his attention diverted. He was on the phone with his wife, February.

Colt's head turned, he caught sight of Rocky and Layne and stopped so abruptly he looked like he'd hit a wall.

Layne stifled a laugh.

Rocky's body got even tighter in his arms.

"Shit, Feb, I'll call you back," Colt muttered into his phone and immediately disengaged, his eyes never leaving Rocky and Layne. "Tanner, hey, what's up?"

"Came to talk to you and Sul, but Roc showed so now I'm gonna take my woman for a coffee. I'll come back. You gonna be around?" Layne answered.

"Your woman?" Sully whispered but Colt didn't speak. His brows shot up and his eyes shot to Rocky.

"Yeah," Layne answered Sully like a kid would say, *Duh.* "You gonna be around in an hour?"

"Um…sure," Sully replied.

"Great, be back," Layne said and then he nodded to Colt then to Rutledge and he turned Rocky toward the stairs.

She yanked her neck out of his hold on the stairs but surprisingly didn't pull her hand from his when he captured it. She stayed stiff but silent and unresisting as they walked out of the station and down the two blocks to Mimi's Coffee Shop.

He knew she was pissed but he didn't know the intensity of it until they hit Mimi's and he started to stop them but she tugged his hand and kept walking.

Layne wanted her in Mimi's. Mimi's was a public place where he had the possibility of keeping her under control.

Rocky, however, had no intention whatsoever of going to Mimi's, and unless he wanted to drag her in there kicking and screaming, he had no choice but to follow.

She didn't go far. She stopped outside the door to his office, the brass plaque next to it saying "Tanner Layne Investigations," yanked her hand from his and lifted her other hand. Her eyes cut to him and they were scorching. Opened palmed, she slapped the door and then jerked her head at the knob.

He watched her thinking he'd forgotten this too. Though, seeing her face he wondered how the fuck he did. She didn't get pissed often but when she did, she got *pissed*. Sometimes, he'd be pissed too, because they were fighting. But if he wasn't pissed, and she was, he invariably made her *more* pissed because she was cute as hell when she was angry and he didn't shy away from informing her of that fact.

Like now.

"Jesus, Roc, forgot how cute you get when you're pissed."

Her eyes narrowed and her shoulders jerked.

"Open the door, Layne," she bit off.

He grinned, turned to the door, pulled his keys out of his pocket and unlocked it. He opened it, swung his torso in and punched in the code to the alarm.

He was still doing this as she was on the move. He felt her push the door open wider and he felt her move in behind him. Then he heard her heels hit the steps. He moved in, the door closing behind him, and stopped at the bottom so he could watch her ass as she climbed the stairs. When she got to the top, turned, looked down at him while she crossed her arms on her chest, he figured he probably better move.

He jogged up the steps, unlocked that door, walked to the alarm panel and punched in that code too. She walked in behind him and again he could hear her heels on the wood floors. He heard her stop and slam something down on the receptionist's desk that no receptionist sat at, probably her purse, and he turned to her.

She stood several feet inside the room, facing him, and he could feel the heat from her eyes even at a distance.

"Roc—" he started, but she moved.

Coming right at him, she did it smart, not making her intention clear until the last second so he almost didn't deflect the punch she threw. But he got his hand up. His forearm catching her wrist, he pushed it back. Using the momentum of her arm and his strength, he whirled her so her back was to his front at the same time he captured her arm and wrapped it around her belly.

She yanked back her other elbow and caught him in the ribs hard enough to make him grunt at the shaft of pain through his midsection before he caught that wrist too and wrapped it around with her other arm.

That was when she lifted a knee and he knew he'd either have a high, thin heel in his shin or his foot and he didn't hanker after either so he bent sharply backward, taking her off her feet.

She let out a strangled, angry cry and twisted in his arms, but he kept hold of her, righted himself and swung her lower body to the side as he took two strides to his couch.

He was sitting and he'd maneuvered her in his lap when she pressed back, her hips and legs flying up to power kick out of his arms, but he went down with her and rolled over her so she was on her back on the couch and he was on top of her.

He gave her some of his weight, tangled his legs with hers to incapacitate them and caught her wrists, which were at his chest, her hands shoving up, and he pulled them out from between them and pressed them into the couch at the sides of her head. This gave her his full weight. He knew he was heavy but he was making a point.

She got his point so she switched to verbal battle. "Get off me!"

"Not until you calm down."

Her eyes caught his, her back arched, and she hissed, "Get...*off*...me!"

"Calm down, Raquel."

"*Fuck you, Layne!*" she screamed.

Layne went silent. He rarely heard much from Mimi's downstairs, but then again, people weren't usually screaming at the top of their lungs while ordering coffee.

She stayed silent, too, for five very long seconds.

Then she accused, "You're crushing me."

"And I'll keep doin' it, sweetcheeks, until I know you won't take another swing at me."

"Stop calling me sweetcheeks," she hissed.

He put his face in hers and whispered, "Rocky, you got two sets of cheeks. One of them has one dimple, the other has two, and you gotta know I remember both bein' *sweet*."

He'd meant to shock her or at least knock her off guard.

He did neither.

"I don't *believe* you!"

"Rocky—"

"You are *unbelievable*!" she repeated with a slight amendment.

His hands tightened on her wrists. "Listen to me—"

"No!" she cut him off. "No way, you jerk. Get off me!"

"*Listen!*" he barked in her face, she fell silent and stared up at him. "You stop and think for a second, what just happened was good."

"Oh yeah? Which part? You walking all over my plan? You *slapping* my *ass* where *my brother works*? Or you freaking out Colt and Sully, which means Merry and Dad'll hear about this if they haven't already?"

"None of those. The part where Rutledge, who thinks he knows what's goin' on, now isn't so damned sure."

That shut her up for a second before she asked, "What?"

"You order a hit on a man, six weeks later, he isn't gonna tell you he's thrilled he got bullets drilled into him and he'd take more."

That shut her up too, and this time she didn't speak. And she didn't speak long enough for Layne to realize this wasn't just good, it was *good*. Because now they had Rutledge guessing and instead of Merry, Dave and Layne being cornered and forced to watch while Rocky did whatever the hell she intended to do, Layne had her cornered and she had to do whatever the hell he *told* her to do.

It would keep her safe. She could make friends with Rutledge and he'd never suspect she was up to something and it was unlikely he'd share anything that would put Rocky into danger. And it would keep *him* safe because, while Rutledge was trying to figure out what, if anything, Layne or Merry were doing, Rocky would deflect attention so Layne could do what he needed to do. And lastly, it would mean Rocky would feel she was doing something when she actually wasn't doing much of anything except innocently providing cover.

So he made a decision.

"We're gonna work this," he informed her.

"Work what?"

"You and me and Rutledge."

Her eyes grew big and her lips parted.

Fuck it all, that was cute as hell too.

Then she repeated, "You and me and Rutledge?"

"Only thing less likely than a man tellin' the man who ordered him to be whacked about his newfound joy at bein' reunited with his ex is that man's woman doin' it too."

Her wide eyes narrowed. "We are *not* reunited."

"Rutledge doesn't know that."

"This is—"

"You cozy up to Rutledge a different way. I'm at that station all the time. Merry works there. You start hangin' there, with Merry or with me. You strike up a friendship with him. You start to confide in him. You convince him all you know is he's a cop; you're a cop's daughter and sister. You convince him that to you, he's in the family. You confide in him, no way he's gonna think Merry's his man. Hell, he'll start wondering if I was as close as I was. I was investigating who got to him, whose payroll he's on. I feed you what to say, we can turn his mind off us thinkin' he's dirty to us just lookin' into his boss and havin' no clue he's got ties. You can also turn his mind onto the fact that I'm not doin' that anymore."

"But you'll be doing it," she surmised.

"Yeah, but I won't go in hard. I'll go in easy."

She stared at him and he knew he hadn't convinced her.

So he kept at it. "Same plan, Roc, except with this one, you don't have to put yourself out there."

"I have no problem putting myself out there," she returned.

"Yeah? You can let a dirty cop stick his tongue down your throat?"

She was a cool customer, when she wasn't taking a swing at him, but he saw her cringe before her eyes shot over his shoulder.

Until he saw her cringe, he couldn't be sure she wouldn't have done it.

Now he knew she couldn't have done it.

"Yeah," he said softly. "I suspected that's where your plan would go south."

He let her wrists go and her hands went directly to his chest where she put pressure, just not much.

"I would have done it," she declared, and he had to hand it to her, she did it with only a hint of obvious bullshit.

"I believe you," he lied and made it clear he was lying.

"It would have been gross, but I would have done it," she reiterated.

Layne grinned. "Rocky, you'd get squeamish seein' blood on your finger if you gave yourself a paper cut. Don't think you'd be able to convince Rutledge you had the hots for him if you puked into his mouth when he stuck his tongue in yours."

"I wouldn't have puked in his mouth," she snapped.

"Okay, so I don't think you'd convince him you had the hots for him if you puked on his shoes after he stuck his tongue in your mouth."

Her face paled and she hissed, "Stop talking about him sticking his tongue in my mouth."

It took a lot for Layne to choke back his laughter, but he did it by asking, "Sweetcheeks, if you can't even talk about it, tell me again how were you gonna pull off this grand scheme of yours?"

"Shut up, Layne," she whispered irately and he knew he had her.

"Just sayin'," he whispered back, smiling at her.

Finally remembering where she was, her hands put more pressure on his chest.

"Get off me," she demanded.

"Sure," he replied. "Once I know we got a deal."

"Well yes, now that you've pointed out how gross it would be to… whatever, then obviously your plan is better than my plan, so fine." She bit out that last word. "We've got a deal."

"Good, then you're comin' over for dinner tonight."

He had no idea he was going to say it until he said it, but once he'd said it he liked the idea. Maybe too much.

"What?" she whispered.

Layne looked at her and, fuck him, it was out there so he had to go with it.

"You're comin' over for dinner tonight," he repeated.

"But…why?"

"'Cause they might be tailing me, watchin' me." That was a lie. They weren't. He'd know. They thought he'd backed off. Taking three bullets had a way of doing that with most men. Layne, however, wasn't most men. But the look on her face made him know she bought it, she didn't like it and she was even scared of it, which made him feel guilt but he had no choice but to use it. "And 'cause I owe you a dinner."

"You owe me a dinner?"

"You fed me and my boys last night, sweetcheeks."

"But—"

"Though you aren't getting leg of lamb. Probably Hamburger Helper."

"Hamburger Helper?" she repeated on a breath. She wasn't keeping up. Finally he had her off guard and he needed to use that too.

So he went on, "And you're goin' to the game with me tomorrow."

She blinked and kept using that breathy voice. "I'm going to the game with you tomorrow?"

"Yeah," he replied. "Though, Rocky, you gotta know I hang with the boys and I watch my sons play ball so you'll have to hang with the boys too." He smiled at her. "Gotta say, though, I figure they won't mind."

"But…um…everyone in town goes to the game."

"Yeah," he agreed.

"So that means everyone will see us," she informed him.

"Sweetcheeks, Sully saw us. Colt saw us. Half a dozen other people saw us and Betsy was at the reception desk when we walked out hand in hand. She was probably on the phone with one of her kids or grandkids before the doors even closed. You don't think that shit's not already flyin' through the 'burg?"

Her face got even paler and her eyes grew unfocused in a way that didn't sit right with Layne.

When she didn't speak and her eyes stayed distant, he called, "Roc?"

Her eyes focused on his and she whispered one word.

"Jarrod."

He felt something sweep through him. An emotion that he didn't quite get, but one he liked, and it rushed through him strong, leaving a golden trail.

"Bonus, baby," he whispered, and he felt her body relax beneath him.

"You know," she said softly.

She meant about Astley's new piece.

"I know," he confirmed.

"Even if he's got...even with her there, he won't like this, Layne," she informed him.

"Good," he replied without hesitation.

She started to look uncomfortable and her body tensed. "Layne—"

"The whole town's gonna know."

He thought she'd like that, getting her own back against her asshole husband, getting in his face by moving on, publicly, to an old flame after only two months separation.

"But—"

"You done with him?" Layne asked, and her face grew sharp.

"Obviously." Her voice was sharp too.

"Then what do you care?"

Her eyes narrowed. "What about Jasper, Tripp...Gabrielle?"

Shit.

He hadn't thought of that.

He looked over head.

"Layne," she called, and he looked back at her.

"The boys'll be in on it."

Her body went so solid, when it did it, it bucked. "They can't—"

"Not everything, Roc, just enough. They'll be cool and they'll keep their mouths shut. They're good kids."

"I don't think—"

"They'll be cool."

"And Gabrielle?"

He stared at her face and it hit him that she was hiding something. Looking closer, he saw it was pain.

What the fuck?

"Rocky—" he started to ask.

"She *won't* be cool." Her voice was inching toward anger, using that as a shield for the pain she was failing to hide behind her eyes. "She's your wife."

Definitely anger. Each word came out clipped.

But what she said made him angry too, enough to forget what he read in her eyes.

"Hasn't been that in a long time, sweetcheeks," he clipped back.

"But—"

"Don't worry about Gabrielle."

"Layne, I'm not sure."

"You got five seconds to give me a better idea."

She glared at him and he saw her mind working.

He counted to five.

Then he gave her ten.

Then he declared, "No? Then the deal's done."

"Layne—"

He jackknifed off her but grabbed her hand and yanked her to her feet in front of him.

"Mimi's," he stated. "Coffee."

"Layne."

"Coffee, sweetcheeks."

She tugged at her hand but he dragged her to the door.

"Layne!"

He turned and pulled her hand so she fell into his body.

She tipped her head back and looked at him.

"Coffee."

She glared. Then she did it some more. They went into stare down and he held it intent to do it for as long as it took.

She read that and gave in first.

"All right," she snapped. "Coffee. But I need my purse."

He turned in order to hide his grin, opened the door, muttered, "No you don't, sweetcheeks, I'm buyin'," and he took Rocky to Mimi's.

Five

IMAGINATION IS A POWERFUL THING

*L*ayne made sure he was home when his boys got home because Rocky was showing at six o'clock. He wanted enough time to tell them what he had to tell them and not enough time for them to have any to think on it.

They came in with hair wet from their after-practice showers and workout bags with their backpacks slung over their shoulders.

Laundry time.

Layne hated laundry. Luckily, his boys both primped as only high school boys did. They felt it a moral imperative to look good at all times and therefore not wear reeking clothes. And since their old man didn't do laundry until it was either that or go shopping for new clothes (shopping something Layne hated worse than laundry), they did their own.

"Bags down boys, we gotta talk," he announced.

"Hey!" Tripp shouted, dropping his bags in the middle of the kitchen and petting an excited Blondie, who was giving them a welcome home as if they'd been at sea for twelve months rather than at school for ten hours, at the same time he reached a hand to some groceries on the counter that Layne had not yet put away. "You got oatmeal!" Tripp finished, waving a box.

Layne grinned at him. "Sustained energy, pal."

Tripp grinned back.

"Shit, Dad, why'd you buy Blondie five bowls?" Jasper asked. He'd dumped his bags too and he was fiddling with the stack of bowls Layne bought Blondie before he went grocery shopping.

"Blondie's dish goes in the dishwasher every night. She gets a new one in the morning," Layne explained and both boys turned to him.

"What?" Jasper asked then asked another question before Layne could answer, "Why?"

"She just does." Layne blew it off. "Now sit."

Tripp and Jasper looked at each other. Then they sat at the island.

When they did, Layne moved to stand across from them. Then he laid it out for them and he didn't pretty it up.

"I talked with Rocky today and found out there's another reason why she came over yesterday," he declared, and both their faces went from mildly baffled direct to openly curious. Layne continued, "I told you that me gettin' shot tweaked somethin' in Rocky and I wasn't wrong. Now, there's things I can't fully explain to you, not now, maybe when this is done, but in the meantime, because of what happened to me, me and Rocky are gonna pretend we're an item."

"What?" Jasper shouted.

"That's so cool!" Tripp yelled, that hope Layne had seen that morning washing full-on through his face.

Layne couldn't focus on Tripp's hope that Layne would hook up with his ex-flame who happened to be the school's coolest teacher. He had to focus on Jasper, whose reactions were usually more hostile and even volatile.

Therefore, Layne's eyes locked on Jas. "Calm down, Jas."

"What the fuck, Dad? She's a teacher. *At my school!*" Jasper was still shouting and now he was in a squat, heels to the bar at the bottom of the stool, ready to go ballistic.

"I said, calm down, boy," Layne ordered low.

Jasper stared at him. He knew Layne's tone, a tone he didn't use with him often but he used it when he meant it and Jasper knew what he meant. So he moved his ass back to his seat. When he settled, Layne carried on.

"I was workin' a case when that happened. I got too close too soon. Now, Rocky and me have made a deal and she's workin' the case with me."

"You're workin' a case with *a teacher*?" Jasper snarled, settled but still unhappy.

"Yeah, Jas, it's safe for her because I'll make it so and she's returning the favor because," his voice dipped quiet, "as you can tell, bud, it became not-so-safe for me. She's gonna provide cover. The thing is, not just the people we want to think we're together are gonna see us together. Everyone's gonna see it. Rocky was worried you two would get confused and I told her not to worry about my boys. I'm always straight with you and I told her you were good kids. You'd sit on it, play it out with us and keep us both safe. Now, I know you aren't my biggest fan, Jas." Layne kept his eyes locked on his son. "But I also know down to my gut you won't make me a liar."

That muscle ticked in his oldest son's cheek but Jas didn't say anything.

Correctly, Layne read that as agreement.

He decided to sweeten the pot.

"There's another reason I'm doin' this," he told them. "Her husband is a jackass and he's stepped out on her and, the story goes, he's been doin' it throughout their marriage. She barely got her foot out of the door before he moved another woman in. The whole town knew about him cheating on her, but Rocky was clueless. She's not handling that well."

Jasper's eyebrows shot up and he asked, "No shit?"

"No shit," Layne replied.

"What? He blind?" Tripp asked.

"No, just stupid," Layne answered.

"Has to be. Yeesh," Tripp muttered.

Layne grinned at him and continued, "Rocky doesn't know this part but I'm gonna be in his face with this and I need you two to be good with that. You get me?"

Tripp didn't get him. He stared at his old man, confused.

Jasper got him. He stared at his old man, blank, then his eyes lit with what was in them that morning before he smiled and when he smiled, he did it slow.

Layne smiled back at him.

"What?" Tripp asked, looking back and forth between his brother and father.

Jasper held Layne's eyes and didn't look away.

"*What?*" Tripp repeated and Jasper finally looked to his brother.

"I'll explain it later," he muttered.

"Later is good since she's gonna be here in five minutes for dinner," Layne told them, and Jasper's eyes swung back to his dad.

"She is?" Tripp asked eagerly.

"She is, pal," Layne answered. "Get your gear sorted and books up to your room. Whose night is it to cook?"

"*I'm* not cookin' for Mrs. Astley!" Tripp shouted, not eager anymore, he was freaked out. "She makes, like, gourmet stuff! She even cooks her own bread!"

"I'll cook," Jasper, cocky as ever, grinned at his brother. "I'm the bomb in the kitchen."

"Dude, you burn a TV dinner in the microwave," Tripp told Jasper.

"I was on the phone with one of my babes," Jasper returned. "Learn from the master, Tripp-o-matic, babes need undivided attention. You get me?"

It hit Layne that Jasper ended his statement with Layne's words of not five minutes before. Maybe Jasper wasn't completely immune to his influence after all. Though, he wasn't certain he was down with where Jasper was taking it.

"*Keira Winters* needs your undivided attention, you mean," Tripp retorted and looked to Layne. "Jasper's got the hots for the prettiest girl in school and she's also the only one who doesn't know he exists."

The muscles in Layne's neck contracted and his eyes sliced to his older boy.

"Keira Winters, Joe Callahan's stepdaughter?" Layne asked.

"One in the same, Dad," Tripp answered for Jasper. "Jasper's hot on the trail of the Lone Wolf's hottie stepdaughter, and getting nowhere, I'll add."

Oh fuck. This was not good. Jasper went through girls like water. He was cocky. He was confident. He was assertive. And he expected to get him some. Jasper did not need an angry Joe Callahan on his ass and Layne didn't need an angry Joe Callahan on his hands.

Cal was a friend and he was a good guy. But everyone in that town knew he'd bonded with his new wife's stepdaughters, and by that, Layne meant he'd *bonded*. Layne already slept with a gun under his pillow, mainly because people in about twenty-seven states wanted him dead. In that 'burg, he slept with it under his pillow because he figured fathers county-wide wanted his son dead. Cal would not be like any other father who went berserk because some hotshot football star got in their daughter's pants. Cal would go commando on Jasper's ass.

"Tripp, sort out your gear and take Jas's with you, I need another word with him," Layne ordered.

"Dad, his gear stinks like all get out," Tripp complained, and Layne's eyes cut to him.

"Do it, pal."

Tripp stared at him. Then he slunk off, grabbed all four bags from the floor and trudged them up the stairs.

Layne looked at Jasper and the second time that night, he laid it out. "Lay off Keira Winters."

"What?" Jasper whispered, the good, warm, golden light flashing out of his eyes, the warning, red, volatile asshole teenage kid one taking its place.

Layne shook his head and leaned toward him, settling on his forearms. "You like her, Jas, go for it. You wanna get in her pants, lay off."

Jasper started to make a move off his stool, muttering, "This is none of your fuckin'—"

"Her father was murdered," Layne cut in. Jasper's body jerked and he froze on the stool. "Her uncle, the same. Her mother was kidnapped, her stepdad too. She almost lost her entire family, Jas. A girl like that, you handle with care. Yeah?"

"You think I'm a dawg," Jasper whispered, disappointment he couldn't hide scoring through his features.

Quietly, Layne replied, "Bud, you go through more condoms than the offensive line of the Colts after a win."

Jasper locked eyes with Layne and kept them locked long enough for Layne to get it without Jasper having to say it.

"You know about her family," Layne stated.

"Everyone does," Jasper returned.

"You like her," Layne concluded.

It took some time but he finally dredged it up, and when he did, Jasper grunted, "Yeah."

Layne smiled at him and straightened off his arms, saying, "Then good luck, bud."

Released, Jasper made a break for it, muttering, "Whatever."

Layne watched his boy move from the room and it hit him that from the minute he lost his virginity at fifteen to Cindy Stanley, a junior with a great rack and a broken home and a need to get whatever attention she could no matter what form it came in, he'd been like Jasper. No steady girl. No one special. The field wide and open and he'd played it. His mother called it "gathering lipstick" (though she did this while muttering and shaking her head) and she was not wrong.

Until Rocky.

He found himself wondering what Keira Winters was like when he heard a car on the street.

His eyes went to the clock and then he walked to the window in the front room, saw Rocky swinging her Merc into his drive. He went straight to the door and out of it.

As he strode down his walk toward her car, he looked across the cul-de-sac of which he was on the southern edge of the curve. Natalie Ulrich lived on the northern edge of the curve. Natalie Ulrich never parked her car in her garage so it was now in her drive. Natalie Ulrich had a huge fucking mouth and ran it as often as she could. And Natalie Ulrich was a surgical nurse at Presbyterian.

She might have missed Layne backing Rocky into her car the morning before. She might not see what Layne was going to do now.

Then again she might.

And if she did, yesterday was all over Presbyterian Hospital and what he was going to do right now would be all over the hospital, and town, before his head hit the pillow.

His eyes moved to Rocky who'd rounded the trunk of her car and met him where the drive met his walk. She'd changed out of her tight skirt and high-heeled shoes and now she was wearing tight jeans, a light, also tight, sweater and a pair of high-heeled sandals.

Layne stood smack in her way, so she stopped and tilted her head back to look at him.

"Is everything—?" she started, but he lifted both his hands to curl around her jaws and he pulled her up to her toes. Her body instantly got tight. "Layne, what—?"

She didn't finish because he dropped his head to kiss her like he did that afternoon. He did it hard, but this time, he did it long. Long enough for her fingers to curve around the sides of his waist and he pulled her close enough and high enough for her to lose balance so her chest was resting against his.

Her lips tasted like mint and he released her when the urge to find out if her mouth tasted the same threatened to overpower him.

He released her mouth but he didn't release her jaw and he kept her close with his two hands there.

"What on—?"

"Natalie Ulrich ever work with your dickwad ex?" Layne whispered and saw her face pale. She misunderstood him. Natalie wasn't hard on the eyes. "Sweetcheeks," he kept whispering, "she lives across the street and the woman has a big mouth."

He kept her where she was but his eyes slid to Natalie's house. He was right. He could see her silhouette in the front window.

Fucking brilliant.

Layne looked back at Rocky and finished, "And she's watchin'."

"She is?" Rocky whispered back, her fingers flexing into his waist.

"Yeah, can't see her well but I'm pretty sure she's got her phone glued to her ear."

"Oh boy," Rocky was still whispering.

Layne grinned and didn't move.

When this lasted awhile, Rocky asked, "Are we going to stand out here all night and pretend we're kissing?"

"Maybe," Layne replied.

"That would be bad since I'm starving," she returned.

"No, Roc, *that* would be bad because you're about to enter a testosterone zone and no one in that house has the first clue how to cook."

"Then I'll cook," she offered and his hands slid down her neck to her shoulders and then around her back and he pulled her closer.

"Nope, you cooked last night. We had a huddle before you arrived and Jas has decided he's going to amaze you with his culinary brilliance."

He watched her eyebrows go up. "You had a huddle?"

"Yeah." His arms gave her a squeeze. He dropped one, slid the other one to her shoulders, moved to her side and walked them forward. "They've been briefed."

She slid her arm around his waist and turned her head to the side, tilting it up to look at him and he felt the soft hair of her ponytail glide across his forearm at her shoulders. "They okay with, um…everything?"

Layne nodded. "They're good."

She looked to the house as they took the two steps to the small, white fenced, cement front porch and whispered, "Okay."

She didn't sound okay. She sounded tentative and scared as hell.

He pushed her forward, opened the storm door and held it over her head as he shoved the front door open and she preceded him.

"Hey, Mrs. Astley!" Tripp shouted, sliding across the wood floors on his tube socks with his greeting, and Layne decided that lessons in cool were definitely in order for his younger son.

"Hey, Tripp," Raquel replied and then was hit dead on with a frontal assault from Blondie that rocked her back on one of her slim high heels.

"Down, Blondie," Layne ordered, closing and locking the door. Blondie ignored him for the first time in her life, pawing at Rocky's fancy-ass sweater and aiming repeated lashing of her tongue on Rocky's neck like Rocky's perfume was eau du bacon. "Tripp, get her off Roc."

"Blondie! Come here, girl, come on!" Tripp called, slapping his thighs and Blondie's head jerked back and forth between Tripp and Rocky in excited indecision as to who was her favorite person in the world. It didn't take her long to decide on Tripp, and she shoved off Rocky and ran at Tripp who tackled her and wrestled her to the rug in the living room.

"Hey, Mrs. Astley," Jasper said, and Layne's eyes went to where he was standing, leaning against the wall, arms crossed on his chest, foot crossed at the ankle, face set in a look of amused indifference.

Layne wished Tripp wasn't wrestling with the dog and instead was paying attention to his brother because Jasper, unlike Tripp, was the master of cool.

"Hey, Jasper," Rocky replied. "I hear you're cooking for me tonight."

"Pasta bake," Jasper returned.

"Pasta bake? What's that?" Tripp called from the floor in the living room while still wrestling with the dog.

"I don't know," Jasper answered. "I'm gonna make it up as I go along."

"Great," Layne muttered and then his world collapsed.

It did this because Rocky's head twisted to look over her shoulder, her ponytail flying, and she smiled at him. Directly at him. Her eyes hitting his and her dimple hitting her cheek.

He could kiss her, hold her in his arms, pin her to the wall, lie on top of her on a couch and have a conversation, and he felt it and knew he liked it but he could take it.

He couldn't take that smile aimed at him. That smile that twenty-one years ago promised a beautiful life and then three years later it reneged without any explanation.

It was then he realized he hadn't fully thought through this plan.

Before he recovered, she turned back to Jasper and said, "I don't know, it sounds good to me and I'm so hungry, I could gnaw off my own arm."

"I bet Jas's pasta bake will at least taste better than your arm," Tripp noted.

"Shut up, Tripp," Jasper returned and looked at Layne. "You want a beer, Dad?"

Layne stopped staring at the back of Rocky's head and looked at his boy.

"Yeah, Jas," he replied.

"You want one, Mrs. Astley?" Jasper asked.

It was then Layne got a good look at her sweater. He avoided shopping like the plague but he reckoned just her sweater cost more than every stitch of clothing he and his boys were wearing. It came to him that when he was at the grocery store, he probably should have bought her wine, or alternately a two hundred and fifty dollar bottle of champagne.

"Beer sounds good but I'll get it," she answered Jasper, her heels clicking on the tiles as she moved into the kitchen.

Layne followed her and rounded the corner right when her head came out of the fridge. She had two bottles between her fingers and she handed both to him.

"Can you do mine? Those twist tops hurt my hand," she said quietly.

"I can do it!" Tripp offered loudly and Layne heard thundering, tube-sock covered feet.

"I think I got it, pal," Layne said, twisting off the caps and flicking both into the garbage before he handed Raquel her beer. "Get your brother a soda to keep him hydrated while he slaves at the stove."

"Gotcha," Tripp grinned and pushed through Layne and Rocky to get to the fridge.

She shifted out of Tripp's way. Layne looked toward Jasper, who was standing in the middle of the kitchen surveying the scene exuding ice cold teenage football hotshot badass cool.

"Jas, you gonna pull together this pasta bake or what?" Layne prompted.

"I'm on it," Jasper muttered and headed to the pantry.

Layne got close to Rocky and touched the small of her back with his hand. She was lost in thought even though she was looking right at him, so when his fingers hit her, she jumped and her head tipped further back.

"Have a seat at the island, Roc," he invited.

"Right," she whispered and moved to the island.

She took a seat. Layne leaned against the end closest to her stool. Tripp leaned forward on the island in front of her with his own soda and Jasper re-entered the room with his arms filled with a variety of groceries.

"So, Mrs. Astley—" Tripp started but she interrupted him.

"How about, if we're not in a building with lockers in it, you call me Rocky?" she suggested. "That work for you?"

"Cool!" Tripp shouted. "And since you and Dad are gonna be an item, can I tell my friends I call you Rocky when I'm not in a building with lockers in it?"

"Tripp." Layne used a warning tone.

"Dude, you don't have to tell them shit," Jasper advised, standing at the stove and dumping pasta in water. "They ask questions, you just say, 'Dad says I'm not allowed to talk about that,' or, 'we had a family meeting and we decided not to talk about home time.' That way, they have no clue what's goin' on and they make everything up in their head. That's way better."

Seriously, if it ever was in question, Layne knew for certain in that moment Jasper was definitely his son.

80

Rocky laughed before she agreed with Jasper. "You're right, Jasper, imagination is a powerful thing."

Jasper threw Rocky an arrogant grin and then ordered, "Tripp, dude, get me a package of hamburger."

"Gotcha," Tripp said and rushed to the fridge.

Tripp got Jasper the hamburger meat while Jas pulled out another pan and Rocky and Layne sipped at their beers. Then Tripp returned to the island while Jasper opened the meat and dumped it in the pan, turning on the burner.

Then Tripp looked at Raquel, he grinned, then looked over his shoulder at his brother.

"So, Jas," he called. "Since we got a hot chick here, you should ask for advice on how to get Keira Winters to go out on a date with you."

Oh fuck.

Jasper turned slowly from the stove. Ice cold badass gone, he was pissed.

Layne moved quickly, which was good since Jasper lunged, shouting, "You *dick*!"

Layne got in between them, lifting up a hand which caught Jasper dead in the chest.

"Stand down, Jas," Layne warned.

Jasper strained against Layne's hand, his eyes locked on his brother, his arms reaching for him, and he repeated, "You *dick*!"

"Bud, cool it," Layne ordered.

"I'm just sayin'!" Tripp shouted back, sounding upset and confused. His comment was innocent and Layne decided that lessons on being cool in a variety of ways were at the top of the agenda for their breakfast conversation the next morning. "Mrs. As—I mean, Rocky's pretty. She should know how pretty girls think."

"Shut…*up*, Tripp!" Jasper shouted, still straining.

"Jasper," Rocky called softly in a way that all three Layne men turned their attention to her and Layne felt Jasper's body go still. "Keira Winters stands outside my door with her friend Heather between second and third period every day."

She stopped talking but her eyes stayed on Jasper.

"I know," Jasper grunted, those two words forced.

"Do you know why?" Rocky asked, and Layne didn't look away from her but Jasper must have shaken his head because she kept talking and she did it even more softly. "Because you walk by my classroom every day between second and third period."

The power of Jasper's body left Layne's hand when he moved back an inch.

Rocky carried on, "They talk. I've heard them and…well, we girls don't tell each other's secrets but…" She hesitated and Layne watched her face change. It was almost the look she used to give him, without her eyes going half-mast, but they got warm and her mouth got soft and she whispered, "I think the best way to get Keira Winters to go out with you is just *ask*."

Then she smiled at his son, giving him her dimple, her eyes warm, and it took effort but Layne forced his gaze from her and he looked at Jasper.

Jasper was staring at Raquel with a version of the expression he'd given his old man twice that day. It wasn't the same but it was nearly as golden. Then Layne watched Jasper smile back at her.

And Layne knew Jasper loved him, once. He knew when Jasper was a little kid that he and his son had a bond that Layne broke when he divorced Jasper's mom and took off, only seeing his kids a couple of times a year when he'd come home or they'd come to wherever he was to visit. And he knew Jasper felt abandoned and betrayed. He just didn't know how to heal that or if he ever would.

So he knew Jasper didn't want much to do with his old man. But seeing him standing there with that golden look of hope in his eyes about a girl he liked, Layne didn't care.

His hand was already in the air so he moved it slightly and curled his fingers around Jasper's neck, giving him a firm squeeze. Jasper's eyes moved to him, that golden hope shone on Layne in that moment and Layne didn't want to lose it and he knew it would be lost when Jasper came back to himself. So Layne quickly gave him another squeeze then a gentle shove, released him and turned away.

Therefore, he missed the fact that the golden hope had changed, gone deeper as Jasper's eyes stayed on his dad's back as his father walked away.

And since he was watching his feet hit the floor, he missed Rocky's eyes go half-mast and her mouth staying soft as she watched him walk away from his son.

⌒

He felt her mouth touch his then slide to his jaw, up his jaw and to his ear.

Then Rocky whispered, "Wake up, baby."

⌒

Layne heard those words in his head at the same time he heard dog tags in the room and his eyes opened.

He was at an angle on the couch, slouched, his feet on the coffee table. The TV was on but low, some sports talk show. There were lamps lit, not many of them.

He looked to the left to see Rocky, her sandals on the floor, curled barefoot in the armchair, knees up and lying on the armrest, head twisted and resting on the pillowed back of the reclined chair. She was asleep.

"Dad," Jasper called quietly and Layne looked up to see his son standing beside him looking down. "Tripp's already upstairs. You cool?"

"Yeah, Jas," Layne replied, straightening in the couch. "You goin' up?"

"Yeah."

"Turn out the lights, yeah?"

Jasper looked across the room at Rocky then back at Layne. "All right, Dad."

"'Night, bud."

"'Night."

Jasper walked away. Blondie came forward and butted his knee with her nose so Layne bent to her, giving her head and neck a rubdown while the lights went out one by one. When they were in darkness outside of a light coming down the stairs, he pushed her off and she got the hint, jogging after Jasper up the stairs.

Layne put his elbows to his knees and turned his head to Rocky.

Pasta bake had been a hit. It was just hamburger meat, spaghetti sauce and penne mixed together, dumped into a dish, smothered in mozzarella and baked, but it was still good. This was mainly because it was smothered in a ton of mozzarella about which Jasper had stated confidently, "Cheese makes everything awesome."

They'd eaten in front of the TV watching sitcoms, which Rocky had laughed through, once so hard she had to curl her arms around her stomach and lean forward, tears streaming from her eyes. They'd graduated to a gritty cop drama during which Rocky fell asleep, probably having had as much sleep as he did last night. Both Tripp and Jasper had noticed and Layne had given them looks to ignore it and keep quiet.

Then Layne had fallen asleep.

He looked at the time on the DVD player, just after eleven o'clock.

He looked back at Rocky.

Then he made a decision.

He walked to her and slid an arm behind her knees, one at her waist and he lifted her up. He figured she'd wake but her head fell heavy on his shoulder then slid forward so her forehead was pressed to his neck and he remembered then that he should have known she wouldn't wake. If she was out, as in *out* out, Rocky slept like the dead.

And she didn't wake until he bent to put her in his bed.

"Layne?" Her voice was groggy, her head came up and she glanced around.

Then her body went alert.

"What—?" she started, her voice sounding not groggy anymore.

"Shh, Roc," he murmured, setting her seated on the side of his bed.

Her head tipped back to look at him and her palms went into the bed to push herself up. He quickly twisted to turn on the bedside light and just as quickly moved back to her, planting a fist in the bed on both sides of her hips, taking his face close to hers so she reared back.

"You sleep in a bed tonight," he whispered and watched her eyes get wide and her lips part.

Then she whispered back, "I don't think—"

"Your car's in my drive," he told her.

"So?" she asked.

84

"Imagination is a powerful thing, baby," he repeated her words of earlier that night. Before she could protest, he pushed away, went to the dresser, grabbed one of his tees and a pair of pajama bottoms and he went back to her. He dropped his tee in her lap and her head tipped down to look at it as he reached beyond her to nab a pillow.

He turned and walked from the room. Going to the linen closet in the boys' bathroom, he snagged a blanket, turned off the upstairs light and went downstairs to the couch. He tossed down the pillow and blanket, changed to his pajamas and settled into the couch.

He waited for her to come down in order to sneak out and he did this awhile.

She didn't come down.

Then he laid there thinking of Rocky wearing his tee and sleeping in his bed.

Then he muttered, "Christ," turned to his side and, after a while, found sleep.

Six

Nepotism

*L*ayne moved through his closet, pulling out a sweater to yank over his tee to wear to the game.

The last couple of weeks they'd had an Indian summer.

That morning, he'd discovered, fall had hit and it had done it with a vengeance.

That morning, he'd also woken up to a note on the island from Rocky addressed to him and his boys thanking them for dinner with a postscript to Layne saying she'd see him that night. That was all she left, except the vague scent of her perfume in his bedroom and his tee folded on the bed she'd made, a tee which held a not-so-vague hint of her perfume.

He was not happy she'd left like that but he gave her that play. What they were doing wasn't easy on him and he reckoned it was just as difficult for her.

Tripp came down first, as usual, and Layne had taken the opportunity with Jasper not around to give a few pointers to his younger son about being cool, for his sake but mostly for his brother's. He explained that Keira Winters was not just one of Jas's "babes" and that Tripp would be doing his brother a favor if he kept his mouth shut and just let his brother make his moves with *silent* support.

Tripp got it, promised he'd be cool and Layne knew he would. Jasper kept his thoughts and feelings to himself most of the time but Tripp wore his heart on his sleeve. He felt shit for pissing off his brother the night before and he wouldn't do that again, innocently trying to help or not.

The boys went to school and Layne went into the office, checked his e-mail and voicemail, returned them, went through his post and wished he had a receptionist because he did not like to be in the office returning e-mails and voicemails.

He liked to be in the field. If he had to be in the office, he preferred to be doing computer investigations, but even that wasn't his favorite activity. Luckily, the post included a paid invoice, the check relatively substantial, for a job Layne completed prior to getting shot.

A receptionist had been on the cards six weeks ago. Now she was not. It would take a fair few more substantial invoices being paid before an ad in the newspaper was scratched on top of his to-do list.

He made an appointment with a potential client and took an appointment with a client who he'd called the day before to tell him that the job was done. The guy was not thrilled with the results of Layne's investigation, but then no man whose wedding was scheduled for three weeks away liked seeing video of his bride-to-be, high on E, taking it from behind while she sucked someone off at the front.

Then again, his client was a spoiled rich kid who fell for an admittedly gorgeous party girl and thought she'd snap to when offered a life of champagne cocktails and charity receptions with vacations in the Swiss Alps. Clearly, at twenty-one, she wasn't done partying in all the forms that could take.

Spoiled rich kid or not, Layne felt for him as he walked him to his front office door. He loved her, it was plain to see. A future he thought was bright suddenly wasn't so bright anymore, and Layne knew exactly how that felt.

After the client left, he was shutting down the office and trying to decide if he should pay a visit to Stew at work or go into Indy and follow the husband of a woman who was convinced he was fucking around on her during his lunch hour (even though Layne had followed the guy to a variety of restaurants on a variety of occasions, not to mention doing extra time following him home just in case, for the last week and for a month prior to him getting shot, and the guy didn't even look at his waitresses too long) when his cell went.

He nabbed it off his desk, flipped it open and put it to his ear.

"Layne."

"Big man, gonna be at Mimi's in five. Could you use a coffee?" Merry asked in his ear.

"See you there in five," Layne replied.

Five minutes later, Layne had an Americano and Merry's cappuccino and was sitting at the table in Mimi's that had the words "Feb's spot, sit here and die" carved into it. Layne had learned from Mimi months ago that Colt's wife, February, sat at that table a lot prior to hooking back up with Colt and Mimi's kids thought her clientele should be aware of the fact that, if Feb was there, she had a reserved seat.

He'd also met Mimi's kids in the meantime and found Mimi was lucky they only carved the words into the table rather than using a flamethrower to mark the entire wall around it.

Merry came in, eyes on Layne, and made a beeline.

"Hey, Merry," Mimi called from behind the counter.

"Hey, Meems," Merry called back as he arrived at the table and looked down at his mug. "Tanner, buddy, no cookie?"

"You wanna keep gettin' laid, Garrett, you can't get a gut. That cappuccino is skinny. Just lookin' out for you, man."

Merry grinned at him and patted his flat abs before he sat down, muttering, "Good friends like you, hard to find."

He meant that in more than one way and Layne studied him closely.

Merry didn't make him wait for it. "Hear Rocky's got herself a new beau."

"Merry," Layne murmured.

Merry leaned forward and whispered, "Wildfire, big man. It's all over town her Merc didn't leave your drive last night."

Jesus, it was barely eleven o'clock. Fucking hell, but Natalie Ulrich had a big mouth.

"What I wanna know is, in less than twenty-four hours, how do you two go from not acknowledging each other's existence to Roc spending the night at your house?"

"It was more like thirty-four hours," Layne corrected him.

"Whatever, Tanner, how—?"

Layne cut him off. "I was at the station when she made her first play on Rutledge."

Light dawned and Merry sat back on a smile. "Not good timing."

"No," Layne agreed.

"So, you saw the play and decided to deflect it by smacking Raquel Astley's ass in the middle of the bullpen on a Thursday afternoon?" Merry asked.

"Seemed a good way to go," Layne answered and Merry's smile got bigger.

Then he asked, "Now, you wanna tell me how that leads to her car at your house?"

"We chatted. I explained the faults in her plan. She saw my logic. We decided to play Rutledge another way."

"You gonna let me in on that?"

"Yeah," Layne said and didn't make him wait either. He leaned forward and his voice dropped before he explained. "She and I are faking a reconcili..." he started then he went on to tell Merry the entirety of the plan while Merry listened without saying a word.

When Layne was done, Merry stated, "Gotta say, not happy she's involved in this shit at all but at least I like this better than Roc's scheme."

"I do too. An additional benefit is that I'm gonna make it so Astley hears, and sees, if I can manage it, a lot of shit that he's not gonna like. He shoved his piece down Rocky's throat. I'm crawlin' down his."

Merry's smile turned cruel. It was a smile Layne had seen before, not often, but he'd seen it. Merry was a cop and therefore his sense of justice was highly tuned. But Merry was Merry and his personal sense of justice, especially when it came to his sister, was another matter altogether.

Through his smile, Merry whispered, "I'm with you, brother."

"Good," Layne returned. "Then I need you to do two things. One, brief Dave about this shit and two, give me intel on how I can hit Astley the hardest."

"You two don't move in the same social circles, Layne."

"Doesn't mean I can't find ways for him to see me and see me with Rocky."

Merry lifted his chin. "I'll put together what I know, e-mail it to you."

Layne sat back and nodded.

Then he changed the subject. "You got anything on Stew?"

Merry shook his head. "Zilch. Heard you talked to Colt and Sully."

"Yesterday, after I dealt with Rocky. Found out Colt, particularly, is not a big fan of Stew's rather than just generally thinking he's a fuckwad like everyone else does. They're happy to nose around." He lifted his mug and took a swallow before he muttered, "Even so, it's lookin' like I'm gonna hafta give that time."

And it was time he did not have nor could he afford.

"Or, you can let Gabrielle sleep in the bed she made for herself," Merry suggested, and Layne's eyes moved back to him.

"She's my kids' mother."

"I dig that, brother, but—"

"She's my kids' mother, Garrett."

Merry closed his mouth and nodded.

Then he opened it and asked quietly, "You and Roc gonna be able to—?"

Layne interrupted him. "We're fine."

"Big man—"

"We're fine, Merry," Layne repeated firmly.

Merry closed his mouth and nodded again, but he didn't hide the fact that he was far from convinced.

Then he sucked back his cappuccino in one gulp and slammed his mug on the table.

"Got your back, whenever you need it," he said, standing and wiping foam from his mouth.

"I know," Layne replied.

"Later," Merry said on a low, short wave, turned, lifted a chin to Mimi and went out the door.

Then Layne made the decision that, even though he wanted to pay a visit to Stew at work, try a direct approach, if he wanted to keep his sons in oatmeal, he needed to rack up billable hours. And nothing racked up billable hours like a woman who had money to burn and nothing but time on her hands and she used that time to convince herself that her faithful husband was being unfaithful, and no matter what Layne said to her to assure her, she wouldn't believe it.

So Layne headed to Indy to watch a man eat a club sandwich on his own while reading the paper. He broke the tedium of this only slightly by taking photos of that man eating his club sandwich and reading the paper. Then he headed back to the office to run off some invoices and print out the digital photos he took to add to the already fat file at the same time again wishing he had a receptionist.

Now he was moving through his bedroom because it was time to pick up Rocky for the game.

He was making his way through the open room at the top of the stairs when his cell rang. He yanked it from his back pocket and looked at his display that said "Raquel Calling." They'd traded numbers and made plans while at Mimi's the day before.

He took the call and put the phone to his ear. "Layne."

"Hey," Rocky replied.

"Hey," Layne repeated as he walked down the stairs.

"Listen, I have a situation," she told him.

He stopped by the fridge and gave her his full attention.

"What situation?"

"See…" she hesitated, "today hasn't been the greatest. I don't know if I can make the game."

Shit. She was backing out. This could mean cold feet and they'd passed the point where she could have cold feet.

"Roc—"

She cut him off, explaining quickly, "Okay, so, I had to leave your place early because I needed to get my car to the mechanics before school. Nothing is wrong, it just needed a service and Jarrod usually deals with that and he…well, we…anyway, it's been too long. It's four months out on that so I had to do it."

She took a breath and went on.

"It won't be ready until tomorrow so they gave me a loaner, which was cool, but that broke down, if you can believe that. A loaner from a mechanic breaking down."

She took another breath and continued.

"Anyway, Dad had to come get me, which he did, then I had some errands to run, which Dad took me to do. But, you know Dad, he lives for football and he's been the Bulldog's biggest fan for the last four decades. He's tailgating with Ernie and Spike tonight and I got a call from The Brendel. I'm on their waiting list and they had someone move out and I got moved up so I have a viewing, like, right now. Dad dropped me off and the girl who is showing me the apartment said she'd take me back to Merry's. But she just called and said she's going to be late and I can't miss this viewing because if I do someone else might snatch up the apartment—"

"Rocky—"

"And I gotta get off—"

"Roc—"

"Merry's couch or my back is going to—"

"Sweetcheeks, shut up a second," he cut in. She went silent, likely because he figured she was still not a big fan of him calling her sweetcheeks and why he did. "I'll come get you."

"But, she's supposed to be here any minute and she's not here yet, and if I want it, I have to deal with the application and—"

"Rocky, I'll come get you."

"Layne, if you do, you might miss kickoff and I haven't had dinner yet."

"Then I'll buy you a hotdog at the game."

She fell silent and he moved through the kitchen, snatching his keys from the counter as he headed toward the garage.

"You got the code for the gate?"

"Three two three seven," she replied.

"Unit?"

"Unit E, apartment three."

"See you in five," he said, having moved through the utility room and entered the garage.

He was about to take the phone from his ear when he heard her call, "Layne?"

"Yeah?"

"Thanks," she whispered and then he heard the disconnect.

He shoved his phone in his pocket thinking he liked hearing Rocky's quiet voice saying thanks.

He folded himself into his Suburban thinking he was glad she left early that morning because she had to do something and not because she was escaping.

And he pulled out of his garage, down his drive and headed toward The Brendel thinking about The Brendel.

The Brendel was an apartment complex across the road and down the street from Layne's development. He could walk there nearly as fast as he could drive there.

Unlike the middle to upper-middle class housing that surrounded it, it was a luxury apartment complex. Rents were high because the apartments were sweet. So sweet, Layne had seen them on the Internet when he was looking for a place prior to moving home and he'd considered it. But the waiting list was seven to twelve months long, taking into consideration when tenants moved out, which wasn't often, and he didn't have that long to wait. It was easier to find and close on a house than get into The Brendel.

Not including the three-bedroom duplex townhomes, each unit and each of the three apartments in the units were different and all the layouts unusual, built with an eye to quality and style. They were appointed with top-of-the-line everything: appliances, carpeting, washers and dryers, bathroom fixtures. There was a full gym onsite with a clubhouse and an outdoor pool that had an expansive cool deck and an abundance of lounge chairs. The landscaping was effusive and colorful. The complex was gated, they had twenty-four-hour onsite security and each apartment had its own private entrance and alarm. Rents for a two-bedroom unit were double the highest rents found elsewhere in the 'burg.

The Brendel was the hot home destination for trendy, high income twenty and thirty somethings and double-income-no-kids couples.

It was also where Harrison Rutledge lived. Harrison Rutledge, who had a cop's salary, an ex-wife, a kid and a child support payment that meant his wife had gotten herself a very good attorney when she'd dumped his ass. Therefore, his apartment alone tagged him as a dirty cop on the take, which was a stupid mistake, something Layne had found Rutledge was not averse to making. And it was that something that made Layne go in too fast, too hard and get ambushed doing it. He'd thought Rutledge was a fool, he'd gotten cocky and he'd paid for that mistake by getting drilled with three bullets.

He stopped at the gate and punched in the code, his mind moving to wondering how Rocky circumvented the waiting list. It was likely she greased some palms. Viewing an apartment at The Brendel after being on the waiting list for two months or less was a minor miracle.

With the help of well-situated and attractive signage, Layne found unit E and saw a sporty BMW parked in the three undercover parking spots allocated to apartment three, which was up a flight of steps around the corner from the ground floor entrance to apartment two.

He parked, got out, slammed the door, beeped his locks, walked to the unit and up the steps.

He barely knocked before the door was thrown open and a woman with sleek blonde hair and more perfectly applied makeup even than Rocky's, wearing a stylish and obviously expensive business dress, stood in the door. Her head jerked when she saw Layne then she did a head to toe and her face changed.

"Hi, you must be Mrs. Astley's friend," she greeted, putting a slight emphasis on the word "Mrs." as she leaned in giving a much stronger emphasis on the fact—with that one move and after having taken one look at him and having no clue who he was—she was coming on to him.

"Yep," Layne replied, moving into her before she moved out of his way, effectively forcing her out of his way.

He walked into the apartment without saying another word and making it clear he was there for Rocky.

He did this because she was too young for him and Layne had passed the point where he wasted time training the women he took to bed.

He also did this because she appeared to have less body fat than he did and he liked the women he took to bed to be *women* with *women's* bodies. He didn't fuck bags of bones. Hard and pointy didn't feel good. Soft and round was a fuckuva lot better. He knew men who liked that, he just wasn't one of them.

He also did this because he didn't like aggressive women. There were ways for a woman to tell you she was interested without her making the first move. To Layne, a woman who made the first move was struck off instantly, even if he was attracted to her. He made the moves.

And lastly, he did this because her slight emphasis on the word "Mrs." was offensive. Her knowing Rocky for all of five minutes and him for all of one second, she didn't get to remind him of Rocky's marital status.

He stopped and looked around, thinking instantly that the apartment was the shit.

White walls, two-story ceilings and floor to ceiling full-wall windows in the compact, but inviting, living room that also had a classy gas fireplace. He could see his development from the windows, and there was a balcony running the length of the living room that you could get to through double doors with highly-designed, shiny silver handles, doors that were set seamlessly into the windows. A staircase with a closed railing in stucco white. A deep, long state-of-the-art kitchen tucked under the top floor, stainless steel appliances, shining black granite countertops and cool-as-shit lighting. A breakfast nook around the corner by the kitchen set in a semi-circle of windows extending out from the apartment like an enclosed balcony over which was a complicated, modern, multi-light chandelier.

"You like?" the blonde asked from close beside him, but he caught movement at the top of the stairs. He looked up and saw Rocky walking down.

He didn't respond to the blonde but grinned at Rocky. "Hey, sweetcheeks."

She looked down at her feet, a small smile on her face, and shook her head while replying, "Hey, Layne."

"Upstairs pass inspection?" he asked, moving to the foot of the stairs where he stopped and so did she.

She tilted her head back, her eyes slid over his shoulder to tag the blonde's location then back to him where she leaned in and whispered low, "I like it."

He leaned in too and whispered back, "So get it."

Her eyes slid back to his shoulder but not to place the blonde in the room. She was thinking.

"I don't know," she said.

How could she not know? The place was the shit.

Then again, it wasn't a six-bedroom mansion skirting a manmade lake.

He turned to the blonde. "Can you give us a minute?"

"Of course," she smiled and started to move toward the kitchen where she could easily still hear. The place was the shit but it wasn't exactly huge.

"No." He stopped her with one word and her head snapped to look at him. He jerked his head to the door. "A minute."

She looked at the door then at him and her face set in a way that made her less attractive than she very obviously thought she was. But she nodded and headed to the door.

Layne waited until she was out of it to turn back to Rocky.

"What's on your mind?"

She looked up at him and bit her lip. She was thinking still, he could see it behind her eyes, but she was thinking about something else.

"Roc—"

She interrupted him. "Layne, do you know what the rent is on these places?"

"Yeah. I looked into them before moving here. Why?"

She shook her head and sat down on a stair, saying, "I don't know if I can swing it."

He stared at her. She was wearing high-heeled boots, jeans and another, warmer-looking, but no less expensive, fancy-ass sweater, this time with a matching woolly scarf wrapped around her neck. She drove a Mercedes. The huge, suede purse she was plopping down on the stair beside her probably cost more than his refrigerator.

"Rocky—"

"I'm a teacher, Layne," she informed him of something he already knew.

"Yeah, a teacher whose soon-to-be ex is a surgeon who makes six figures."

"*Jarrod* makes six figures. *I* do *not* make six figures."

Layne crouched in front of her. "Rocky, he fucked around on you. He's living with another woman right now. You think this divorce isn't gonna go well for you?"

At his words, she reared back and stared at him, eyes wide.

Then she breathed, "I'm not going to take his money."

He felt his brows shoot up. "Come again?"

"I'm not taking his money."

"Rocky—"

She shook her head. "No, no way."

"Roc—"

She leaned in abruptly, her expression turning sharp. "Fuck *that.*"

He caught her hand and held it firm before shaking it. "Baby, are you insane?"

"No," she snapped, tugging her hand in his, but he held on tighter.

"Sweetcheeks, a guy like that does what he did to a woman like you, I'm not a member of the club but I'm pretty sure it's a chick requirement to take him to the cleaners."

"Layne—"

"You don't do it, other chicks might vote to throw you out of the club."

Her face cracked and she smiled, her dimple coming out, and seeing it, Layne wished he'd kept his mouth shut at the same time he felt like he'd scored a touchdown to win the game in the last seconds of the Super Bowl.

"Well, I wouldn't want to get thrown out of the..." she lifted the only hand she had available to her and made air quotation marks, "chick club."

"Atta girl," he whispered as he smiled, but her face got serious again and her hand dropped.

"I see what you're saying, Layne. But, seriously, you don't know...it hasn't..." She looked over his shoulder then back at him. "I don't want anything from him."

He did not like what her words said. He did not like how they made him feel. But he liked it even less that she had reason to say them.

He ignored this, decided on a different strategy, and advised, "Rocky, you greased some palms to get moved up the waiting list for this place. You shouldn't waste that investment."

Her hand clenched his spasmodically and her eyes narrowed in confusion.

"I didn't grease any palms to get moved up."

He stared at her then told her, "Not sure that's against the law, sweetcheeks, but even if it was, I wouldn't turn you in."

"I guess it isn't, but I still didn't do it."

"Roc, when I was lookin' into this place, the waiting list was minimum seven months."

She nodded. "It still is. I've been on it for nine."

He let her hand go and stood, watching her head tilt back to look up at him as he went.

Then he asked, "What?"

She stood too, bringing her body close in front of his. "I've been on the waiting list for nine months."

That meant she'd been intending to leave her husband for nine months.

"You knew he was fucking around on you?" Layne asked.

She shook her head.

"But you been plannin' on leavin' him for a while."

She nodded her head.

"Why?" he asked.

"Why?" she repeated.

"Yes. Why?"

"Layne, I'm not sure we should—"

"Why?"

"I really don't want to talk about—"

"Why?"

"Layne!"

He leaned in to get his face close to hers. "Why?" he repeated.

"Why do you want to know?" she shot back, amused Rocky gone, annoyed Rocky in her place.

"Because I do," he answered.

"Well it really isn't any of your business."

"Sorry, sweetcheeks, but we got a long road ahead of us. I'm not gonna stumble onto enough evidence to take Rutledge and whoever is pullin' his strings down all bound up and wrapped in shiny paper sitting on my island when I walk downstairs to make coffee tomorrow. This means sharing time, sharing space and sharing our lives and it means doin' it for a while. While we do it, we actually have to *live* those lives and *your* life comes with me pretending to be your man while you're divorcing another one. He made you a chump. Don't make me one even if what we got is sham."

Her head jerked back and she took a step up the stairs.

Then she said softly, "I'm not making you a chump."

"You don't share, you are. I haven't been in on your life for a while, Roc, but you've lived in this 'burg a long time and people know shit. Case in point, my guess would be half the town who are of drinking age know your car was in my drive all night and I can guarantee, due to Tripp thinkin' you're one step down from a rock star, that every single kid in your school knows there's times when he can call you Rocky. But for the last year, I wasn't a prime recipient for gossip about Raquel Astley, so you're gonna have to fill me in."

He noticed she'd started to get pissed while he spoke and when he was done, she didn't hesitate to explain why.

"You know what sucks?" she snapped.

"I know a lotta things that suck," he returned.

"Well, what sucks the most right now for me is when you make sense. *That* sucks."

He couldn't stop himself. She was so fucking hilarious he threw his head back and laughed.

What he did stop himself from doing was yanking her in his arms and laughing in her neck.

When he quit laughing, he focused on her to see she was still glaring.

"You gonna share?" he prompted.

"Yes," she bit off. "But not now. We have a football game to get to."

"You gonna get this apartment?"

"I don't know," she replied irately.

"Sweetcheeks, get the apartment."

"Layne—"

"Do it," he prompted.

"Layne!"

"Your attorneys tell you what you got doesn't allow you to fuck him over so bad he'll reconsider any relationship he ever thinks of starting, you tell me, baby. I'll find enough shit on him to make him move to another state."

She didn't speak. She just stared at him with her lips parted.

When this lasted awhile, he repeated, "Get the apartment."

She stayed silent.

So Layne made a decision.

He left her on the stair and walked to the door.

He opened it and the blonde was on her cell outside.

She whirled to face him and Layne declared, "She'll take it."

⟵⟶

"I can't eat this," Rocky announced quietly, and Layne looked down at her.

They were standing three feet away from the concession stand and he'd just handed her a hotdog and a diet and she was looking like she was either going to heave or bolt.

He knew why she'd lost her appetite.

They'd just walked the length of the field from entrance to concession stand. The game was four minutes in and the 'dogs were already on the board. And still, Rocky and Layne walking into the game with their arms around each other had diverted the attention of the vast majority of eyes in the bleachers and folks standing at the fence around the field. The parents were looking and the kids were looking and they weren't being secretive about it.

They also fielded a variety of greetings from giggling girls pulling up the courage to say at the last minute, "Hey, Mrs. Astley," to full-grown men, some of them married fathers, married fathers of kids who probably sat in Rocky's classroom, giving Rocky the once-over and saying to Layne, "Tanner," in a way that could easily be read as, *nice work, dude.*

If that wasn't enough, Gabby, who always came early so she could sit front row, fifty yard line, had come early so she could sit front row, fifty yard line, and she did this by Stew. That meant Rocky and Layne had to walk right in front of her while she glared fire at them both, her face so hard Layne wouldn't have been surprised if it shattered.

Nevertheless, he'd tipped his head to them both, keeping his arm firm around Rocky's stiff shoulders as her fingers dug into his waist and he greeted, "Gabby, Stew." A greeting which was not returned by either of them. He then guided Rocky right by.

"It's fine," Layne assured her.

"It's not fine," she leaned in and hissed. "Did you see Josie?"

Layne felt his brows draw together. "Josie?"

"Josie, Layne. Josie Brand, now Josie Judd!"

"Chip's wife?" Layne asked.

"Yes," she snapped. "Chip's wife and *my best friend. My best friend* who I *haven't called* to inform that I've reunited with my old boyfriend!"

Jesus, that was all it was?

Layne grinned. "She'll get over it."

She threw her hands up and almost lost the lid of her cup as well as the dog out of the bun. "You obviously do *not* know Josie."

He did. He knew Josie Brand, but as far as he knew he hadn't seen her in over twelve years.

"Sweetcheeks, calm down."

She leaned closer. "If you call me sweetcheeks in front of one of the students—"

Like he had the previous day at the station, he hooked her around the neck and yanked her into his body. Both her hands flew out to the sides to avoid her not very exciting dinner getting crushed. This time, instead of her coming to his side, she was full frontal and that was better. Much better.

He dipped his face close to hers. "Baby, I'm not gonna call you sweetcheeks in front of the students."

"Don't kiss me either," she demanded. "I haven't read my contract for a while but I think it has an express clause that I can't make out with seriously hot private detectives at football games or during any other school activity."

His body went still as his mind tried and failed to sort through how fucking great it felt that she referred to him as a "seriously hot private detective" at the same time he wanted, with no small amount of desperation, to laugh out loud for a long fucking time.

Instead, he joked, "It's good they had the foresight to include that in your contract."

"I'm not being funny, Layne," she warned.

"You're wrong, Raquel," he replied.

At his words, she went smack into stare down which, unfortunately for her, Layne thought was cute.

Therefore, he asked, "Your contract says you can't make out, but does that mean I can't kiss your neck?"

"Yes," she hissed.

"Your forehead?" he went on.

"Yes!" Her voice was rising.

"Your nose?"

"Layne, this is not amusing."

He smiled. "Wrong again, sweetcheeks."

"Two seconds and you'll have ice cold pop over your head," she threatened.

She wouldn't do that. She used to threaten all sorts of wild retribution, but she never did it. Their fights might occasionally get physical but only in good ways. She'd once accidentally squirted his t-shirt with ketchup but only because she was yelling while holding a ketchup bottle at the same time gesticulating. The hilarious look on her face after she'd done it had led to him laughing so hard he nearly split a gut, Rocky doing the same and, shortly after, them fucking on the kitchen table during which he transferred the ketchup on his tee to hers.

This memory had while she was pressed against his front served to sober him, so he dipped his face even closer and whispered, "Everything is gonna be fine, Roc, swear."

She stared into his eyes several long moments before she nodded.

He let her loose from his front but kept his arm around her neck and led her to the boys. These being Colt. Colt's best friend Morrie, who co-owned the local bar, J&J's Saloon, with Colt's wife Feb. Loren Smithfield, the local ladies man who stayed a ladies man even when he was legally bound to only one lady (and he'd been that way three times)—a decent guy on the surface, but underneath pure asshole. Ricky Silvestri, who owned most of the car dealerships in the county and who famously fucked around on his wife so she divorced his ass. He was equally famously still in love with her, trying to win her back and spectacularly not succeeding. That said, Layne thought he was a decent guy who was paying due penance for a very bad mistake. And last, Joe Callahan, Colt's across the street neighbor, a well-known, highly-respected security specialist, a serious badass and the man Layne hoped like hell Jasper didn't piss off when he eventually started dating Cal's stepdaughter.

They approached, the boys giving Rocky smiles, all of them friendly except Smithfield's, which was overt and made Layne expend some effort in trying to stop himself from ramming Smithfield's teeth down his throat, and then they settled at the fence. Rocky started eating her hotdog and his eyes went to the field.

Jasper was a starter and had been since halfway through his freshman season. It was extremely rare for a kid in this 'burg—a haven of all sports but especially football since the team had either gone to, or won, State nine times in the last two decades—to make the varsity team in his freshman year. Jasper did it playing tight end. Now he played tight end offense, line-backer defense. He was being scouted and Layne hoped to all hell someone pulled his boy in on even a partial ride because his grades sure as fuck weren't going to get him into college.

Tripp had surprised him by following in his brother's footsteps. He made varsity too, even though he was a freshman. Layne knew his son was good, had seen him play in junior high and before. He'd always shined so bright the other players didn't exist on the field. But that was always playing with kids his own age. Therefore, Layne thought the high school boys would chew him up.

They didn't. Tripp became everything not Tripp on the football field. Not yet as tall as his brother, but faster, more agile and cold as ice. He was playing wide receiver, and when he was on the field his focus was so intense it was clear the world outside those one hundred yards ceased to exist.

If Tripp bulked out, which he probably would in the next year, he'd have to find a different position. For now, that was where he was which was unfortunate.

Coach Adrian Cosgrove's son was a senior, a wide receiver and not a great one. Tripp hadn't played much because Cosgrove wanted any scouts there to get a look at his boy.

Layne suspected this would be unpopular because whenever Tripp played, it was clear he could run circles around Cosgrove's kid.

The rabid Bulldogs fans who lived and breathed high school football did not care about Cosgrove's kid. They cared about winning and they would not put up with nepotism for long.

Cosgrove further wasn't liked because, since he moved up from assistant coach to take over for the beloved, long-time head coach three years ago, the 'dogs hadn't gone past regionals. He was feeling the heat and nasty rumors about Cosgrove's temper were spreading. Layne didn't know if they were true, and neither Jasper nor Tripp shared, which Layne reckoned was another item for a future agenda for breakfast conversation.

Unfortunately, this all became evident in the second quarter when Cosgrove's son went off the field for a play, he sent Tripp in and then Cosgrove called a passing play. If he wanted his boy to shine, this was an asinine decision because Tripp was damned good, but when he wasn't on the field their passing game was garbage. Even if another receiver was open, every long pass was thrown to Cosgrove's son, who hadn't caught a single toss and had even been intercepted twice. The only passes caught were short shots, nabbed and run by Jasper.

Therefore, when the ball was put in play, Tripp shot forward, got open within seconds and the quarterback, under some pressure, let fly. The ball was thrown high but Tripp jumped at least three feet in the air, arm extended to the maximum, tagged the pass, pulling the fucking thing down with his fingertips. He tucked the ball close, ducked his head, deflected two tackles and ran forty-three yards for a touchdown.

The crowd went berserk, every last one on the purple and white side, including Rocky standing in front of him. With her arms straight in the air, she jumped up and down on her fancy-ass boots, her ponytail swinging wildly right in his face. She was screaming her lungs out without even a freaking hint of the decorum a high school English Literature teacher should display at a school activity.

"That's it, Tripp!" she shouted as Tripp ran off the field right in front of them, jerking down the straps of his chin guard. He heard her and his eyes went to the fence. "You *rock*!" she yelled, pointing at him.

Such was his worship of Rocky, for once, Tripp's intensity slipped. He grinned at her through his faceguard and then he was tagged viciously with a slap upside the helmet that came from the flat of Coach Cosgrove's hand, causing Tripp's head to jerk unnaturally toward his shoulder pad. So hard, Tripp's helmet was ripped clean off his head.

Then Cosgrove shoved Tripp's shoulder pad once, twice, three times and finally Tripp started moving back unable to stand firm under the obvious violence of the blows when Cosgrove went through the fourth, fifth and sixth and then he stopped.

"*Head in the game, Layne!*" Cosgrove bellowed in a voice that carried.

The crowd, seeing this, had quieted and Rocky went statue-still in front of Layne but Layne didn't really notice it. His vision had clouded, his body had locked, his fists had clenched and his mouth had gone dry.

"Tanner," Colt muttered, and Layne could feel him close.

When Rocky heard Colt, she moved, her shoulder brushing his chest as she turned to him, but his eyes were locked on his son standing on the sideline. Tripp was looking at his cleats while Cosgrove stood close, his mouth at Tripp's ear, spittle coming out with the force of his continuing tirade, shouting it an inch from his boy's ear.

"You pay attention *to me* and what's happening on *that field*! I don't care if *the Virgin Mary* appears and is shouting at you. You keep your effin' *head in the game!*"

"Lay off, Coach!"

Layne heard it and knew it came from Gabby but he didn't move a muscle.

"Layne," Rocky whispered and he felt her hands on his abs.

"*Hear me?*" Cosgrove roared.

"Hear you, Coach." Layne heard Tripp reply.

"Good. Bench." Cosgrove jerked a hand at the bench and Tripp didn't hesitate to take a seat. He bent to snatch up his helmet, head bowed. His eyes still to his cleats, he turned his back on the bleachers as fast as he could and sat his ass down.

"Layne, sweetheart," Rocky whispered, and he looked down at her to see her head turned toward Tripp. She must have felt his gaze because it quickly moved back to him.

He stared in her eyes and he tried to find a reason not to jump the fence and rip Cosgrove's head off.

"Layne, dude, you good?" Morrie was close too and he put a hand to Layne's shoulder.

"I wouldn't touch me now," Layne said quietly and Morrie's hand disappeared instantly from his shoulder.

"Morrie asked if you're good, Tanner," Colt said softly.

"Yep," Layne lied.

His friends stayed close and so did Rocky, Rocky doing it by moving to his side, wrapping her arms around him and putting her head to his shoulder.

This felt good. It felt very good. But it didn't strip a single layer off the thick wall of fury fencing him in, and he stayed still, not moving a muscle until halftime when Rocky got his attention by pressing into him.

He looked down at her only after he lost sight of both of his boys when they entered the locker room.

"You want a soda?" she asked quietly.

"Nope," he answered.

"Coffee?"

"No."

"Cocoa?"

"No."

"You okay?" she asked.

"Nope."

"Oh boy," she whispered then he felt her body jolt against his, her arms moved from around him and she stepped away.

He saw her looking around him and he heard Silvestri mutter, "Oh fuck," when he turned around and saw Gabby, Stew trailing, bearing down on him.

"You gonna quit snugglin' with your *girlfriend* long enough to do something about *that*," she jabbed a finger at the field, "Tanner?" She leaned into him antagonistically, "Hunh?"

"Not now, Gabby," Layne murmured.

"Tripp's so damned excited that his dad's bangin' High and Mighty Raquel Astley, *he doesn't have his fuckin' head in the game*!" she screeched.

Before Layne could say a word or find a reason why he shouldn't rip the head off his kids' mom, Rocky spoke.

"I'm sorry," she said immediately. "I shouldn't have—"

"*No, you shouldn't!*" Gabby shrieked.

"I'm thinkin' you need to calm down, woman," Joe Callahan suggested in a way that sounded more like a warning.

"It's okay. It was my fault," Rocky stated.

"Damn straight it was," Gabby snapped.

"No, it wasn't," Layne said, his voice sounding like a rumble and his eyes cut to Gabby. "I'll deal with Cosgrove."

"Oh yeah? How?" Gabby shot back.

"Don't worry about it and don't," he hesitated, searching for control. "Ever," he hesitated again, losing the control he found and searching for it again. "Speak to or about Rocky that way again. Do you hear me?"

"You have *got* to be jokin'!" Gabby shouted. "She's outta her husband's house a month and you're in her pants!"

Layne took a step toward her. Gabby took a step back. Stew, he noted with disgust, took *two* fucking steps back leaving Gabby shifting in the wind. And both Colt and Cal came up to his sides.

"Your situation is precarious, Gabby," he informed her, his voice low. He was aware they had an audience and that audience was listening. "Do not push me. Understand?"

"Go to hell, Tanner!" she yelled.

He turned away from her and walked back to Rocky. Then he slid his arm around her shoulders and pulled her into his side. He felt the tension ebb out of the boys around him and he knew Gabby and Stew had retreated and only then did he tip his head down to see she was staring at the top of the fence and biting her lip.

"Sweetcheeks," he called quietly and watched her head tilt back. When he caught her eyes he noted, "One ex down, one to go. We're halfway there."

She stared at him for a second.

Then she gave him the dimple.

There were a fair amount of people milling about after the game and Layne knew why.

Both Jasper and Tripp were going out for pizza, Jas responsible for getting his brother home so there was only one reason Layne would remain after the game.

Therefore Colt, Morrie and Cal remained too. Rocky's dad, Dave, and his cronies Ernie and Spike were also sticking close.

So did Gabrielle, but Stew was nowhere to be seen.

Some of the crowd was waiting around to see what Layne would do. The rest of them were likely there to give moral support, or perhaps set up the ladder for Layne to climb in order to swing Cosgrove's noose around a stout branch.

The folks in that town liked their football but they also looked after their kids. Cosgrove's abuse of Tripp had been widely witnessed and an unpopular man struggling to keep his footing in that community had not only slipped, he'd come crashing to the ground.

Most of the players had come out when Jasper and Tripp came out together. When they did, Layne saw that Jasper was so close to his brother, he was crowding him, but Tripp didn't notice. His mind was elsewhere. He'd stayed benched the second half and he'd been humiliated in front of his friends, his schoolmates and half the town.

Jasper saw Layne first and he started with surprise, his eyes darted to his mom and then came back to Layne.

Gabby closed in on Tripp.

"You okay, honey?" she asked.

Tripp took a quick step away from her, not wanting to be mothered, not anytime at fourteen years old and especially not then.

"Yeah, Mom," he muttered.

Layne approached but Rocky stayed clear, standing in a huddle with Josie Judd, February Colton, Violet Callahan and Violet's extremely pretty daughter, Keira.

The minute Layne met Keira between the third and fourth quarters when the women had decided that they'd given it enough time, they'd borne down on Rocky and infiltrated the boys long enough to pull Raquel aside for a quick, voices lowered discussion before they all returned and hung out with the men, Layne could see why Jas had been hooked.

He stopped close to Jasper, Tripp and Gabby and said, "Good game, Jas. Tripp, sweet tag and great run, pal."

Tripp tipped his head back just enough to look at his father under his brow and then bent his neck again.

"Great catch, kid," Cal said, coming up to Layne's side. Tripp shrugged, not looking at him then Cal went on. "You Jasper?"

"Yes sir," Jasper replied.

"Layne says you're goin' for pizza," Cal remarked.

"Yeah," Jasper answered.

"Keira wants to go. You think you could get her there, bring her home?"

This was something Keira had finagled during the fourth quarter (giving cause to her hanging out with the adults) through a girl gang ambush of Cal that included her mother, Feb, Josie and Rocky while Cal stood, arms crossed on his chest, his eyes to the heavens. Rocky had not been wrong. Keira Winters definitely liked Jasper and it was evident she was tired of waiting around for him to make his move. Layne knew this because, during her finagling, she and her posse had succeeded in enlisting Cal for the maneuver he'd just delivered.

Tripp's head jerked around to look at his brother, but Jasper looked toward Rocky, Keira and the other women. Then he looked back at Layne.

"Why're you hangin' around, Dad?" he asked.

Layne didn't delay in replying. "Waitin' for Coach."

Tripp's body got tight and Jasper's face got hard before he looked at Tripp then to Cal then to Keira.

Then he yelled, "Hey, Keira, can you wait a sec for pizza?"

"Yeah!" Keira shouted back.

"Cool!" Jasper yelled in return.

"Jas, dude, what're you—?" Tripp began.

Jasper interrupted him, "Waitin' with Dad."

"But—"

"Waitin' with Dad," Jasper said more firmly, and Tripp looked to Layne.

"Dad, it wasn't that—"

"It was, pal."

"But—"

Layne leaned into him and got in his face. "No one puts his hand on my boy. Not like that. Get me?" Tripp looked uncertain and Layne repeated, "Get me?"

Tripp stared him in the eyes, heaved a sigh, nodded once and muttered, "Got you."

Jasper and Tripp stayed close. So did Colt, Morrie, Cal and Gabby as well as the milling crowd. Finally, Cosgrove left the locker rooms.

Layne moved right in. Cosgrove saw him and lifted a hand.

"Don't need this Tanner. Those boys are my boys on the field." And he moved to walk by Layne.

But Layne got in front of him and stopped him with a palm flat on his chest.

Cosgrove looked down at Layne's hand, his face got red and his head shot back. But before he could say a word, Layne removed his hand and spoke.

"You got this weekend to come up with a good excuse to tell the School Board when they investigate the formal complaint I'm lodging first thing Monday morning."

"Those boys are mine on the field," Cosgrove clipped.

"I agree. To coach, to motivate, to teach, to train. I get discipline. What I do not get and will not tolerate is you takin' out your frustration that you will not live your dream through your kid by puttin' your hand on my kid in anger."

Cosgrove's eyes narrowed. "Who do you think—?"

"I think I'm a man who watched another man slap and shove my son with such force, he had no choice but to physically retreat."

"He was padded!"

"Yeah. But I counted, Cosgrove, you hit him *seven* times. *Seven* times for lookin' into the crowd. He just tagged a pass most college kids can't tag, ran over forty yards and you hit him *seven* times for smiling into the crowd."

"*He was padded, Tanner!*" Cosgrove bellowed.

"Good luck with that at the School Board hearing."

"I do not need this shit," Cosgrove muttered and moved to pass him. Layne moved to block him and Cal and Colt flanked him.

Cosgrove looked around the men, all three taller, leaner and fitter than him, and halted.

His eyes narrowed and his voice dropped low. "Don't cross me, Tanner. That same School Board is lookin' for reasons to lose your new girlfriend, and you get in my face, I'm thinkin' I might find some."

Layne pulled in breath to control his anger.

"Maybe we should give him a shovel," Morrie, standing behind Layne, suggested. "It'll make him diggin' that hole he's diggin' a whole lot easier."

Cal chuckled but Layne stared in Cosgrove's eyes.

"You do not wanna take me on," he said quietly. "I'm givin' you good advice, Coach. You do *not* wanna take me on."

Before Cosgrove could reply, Layne turned, saw Jasper was close to Morrie, his eyes on his old man.

"Go get some pizza, bud, yeah?" Layne ordered.

Jasper stared at his dad as he said slowly, "Yeah."

"Good game," Layne muttered, stopped himself from clapping Jasper on the shoulder and walked by him to Tripp who was standing with Gabby.

Tripp he slapped on the shoulder. His fingers curling around, he gave his son a few gentle jerks.

Then he said, "Go have fun, pal."

"Okay, Dad," Tripp whispered, looked at Layne for three beats then peeled off and followed Jasper, who was walking side by side with Keira out of the grounds.

Layne looked around, and still not spotting Stew, he asked Gabby a question he *really* did not want to ask.

"You need a ride home?"

"I'm good," she said softly, and the way she spoke made Layne focus on her. "Wish they had that all their lives, Tanner," she went on, and Layne felt his neck muscles contract before she finished on a whisper. "But it's good they have it now."

Then she hurriedly turned and just as hurriedly walked away.

Morrie clapped him on the back as he walked by. Layne tipped his chin up at Cal and Colt as they made their way past him toward their women and he gave Dave, Ernie and Spike the high sign, which made Dave nod and all of them begin to move away while Rocky approached.

"How'd that go?" she asked, her eyes going beyond him, indicating she was referring to the showdown with Cosgrove.

"I'm not thinkin' good," he replied.

She got close and bumped him with her shoulder.

"Tell me over pizza," she invited. "All this talk about pizza and I'm starved. I think it's my turn to treat."

He looked down at her to see she was talking in a light way but her eyes were intense, studying him and trying to read him without showing she was.

"Sweetcheeks, we got two pizza places in this 'burg and both of 'em will be crawling with kids."

"We'll get Reggie's, take it to Merry's."

That sounded like a plan.

"You're on, but I'm buyin'," he said, turning and throwing an arm around her shoulders, pointing her to the exit.

"It's my turn," she repeated, sliding her arm around his waist.

"Baby, you just put down first and last and a deposit. I'll get pizza."

She walked one foot crossing in front of the other so her weight pressed into him, taking them both off stride and he remembered she'd do that too, all the time, just to horse around when they'd walk close together.

That new bullet scored through his gut, but he was able to handle it when she yielded.

"Okay, Layne, you've convinced me. You're buying."

"Let me get this straight," Rocky started, sitting cross-legged facing him on Merry's couch. "Stew Baranski is screwing over your ex-wife. I'm getting divorced from a cheating asshole. I just took on an apartment that costs about double what I can afford if I have to live on my own salary. Coach Cosgrove, who's a jerk all the time, by the way, not just tonight, has thrown down, threatening to get me fired. You're lodging a formal complaint against him on Monday. And you and I are faking a relationship in order to uncover a dirty cop, who, nearly seven weeks ago, almost got you killed."

Layne, lazing back into the corner of Merry's couch, his feet on the coffee table next to the closed box that contained the remains of a decimated pizza (when Rocky said she was hungry, she did not lie and he made a mental note for the future that a concession stand hotdog would not cover it for Roc), replied, "That's about it, sweetcheeks."

She listed to the side and rested her head on the top of the couch, muttering, "We're fucked."

He grinned. "We'll be fine."

"You keep saying that."

Layne kept grinning. "I keep sayin' that because we'll be fine."

Rocky closed her eyes and sighed.

Layne lifted a leg and nudged her knee with his shin before returning his foot to the coffee table.

Rocky opened her eyes.

"Cosgrove got reason to be cocky?" he asked quietly.

She looked over his head then back at him.

"Let's just say that I don't adhere *entirely* to the School Board approved curriculum."

His grin got bigger as he muttered, "Baby."

She lifted her head from the couch.

"It's boring, Layne, and the kids don't learn shit. If they get Halsey, the ones who want the grades do the work but they don't get anything out of it. The ones who don't care, I kid you not, they *sleep*. They sleep through his class. Literature is art and art is about passion. It's about drive. It's about beauty. How can you slide through a semester of that and not be moved by it?"

Layne watched her and he knew this was dangerous territory. He knew it by the light in her eyes, the passion, the drive, the beauty of it, and he was moved by it. He was moved that even after eighteen years, when she had that same light in her eyes when she was studying to be a teacher, it hadn't dimmed in the slightest.

And he didn't need Rocky to move him that way. She was moving him enough.

Even knowing that, he didn't do a fucking thing about it.

"Do what you do and fuck 'em," Layne advised.

"Easy for you to say," she muttered, reaching out to grab her bottle of beer. She brought it back, took a pull, dropped her hand and her eyes went back to him. "*You* didn't just pay first, last and put down a deposit on a luxury apartment tonight."

"They won't fire you," he assured her.

"No? I've worked for that school for ten years, Layne, and I've been hauled in front of the School Board four times."

"Why?"

"Uptight, ignorant parents pissed about shit they don't understand. Do you know, I had a complaint lodged against me because I make the kids memorize Poe's *Annabel Lee* and some parent thought 'sepulchre' was a sex palace?"

Layne burst out laughing.

"No joke!" she shouted over his laughter. "They thought it was about underage sex!"

Layne forced himself to quit laughing and looked back at her. "How could they think that?"

"*I was a child, and she was a child, in this kingdom by the sea, but we loved with a love that was more than a love—I and my Annabel Lee,*" she quoted.

Those words struck deep, all humor fled, and Layne stared at her as she went on softly.

"It's the most beautiful, bittersweet, sad love poem ever written, Layne. When I first introduce it, I take them to the choir room, which is soundproofed and has no windows. I turn out the lights, light candles and make them put on blindfolds and I recite it to them, shutting out everything and making them hear the words of a man broken when he lost his bride."

She closed her eyes and kept going.

"*But our love it was stronger by far than the love of those who were older than we—of many far wiser than we—and neither the angels in Heaven above, nor the demons down under the sea, can ever dissever my soul from the soul of the beautiful Annabel Lee.*"

She shook her head and opened her eyes.

"Sometimes," she whispered, "even the boys cry. I even get through to the boys. I'm teaching beauty, Layne. How can that have rules?"

"Teach how you teach, Rocky," he said quietly. "You don't like their rules, break 'em."

She stared at him and she did this a long time before something unpleasant passed across her face and she looked to the side, hiding her expression from him.

"Roc," he called.

"You know," she told the wall, her voice quiet. "Jarrod always told me to do what they say, play by their rules. He never got what I was trying to do. He never told me to break the rules." She looked back at him. "Eventually, I quit talking to him about it. It annoyed him that I didn't listen. He knew so much *more* than me."

He knew by her face and the tremor in her voice that this was bigger than her husband cheating on her. This cut deeper than infidelity.

"He knew more than you?" Layne asked.

"Well, yes, of course, Layne." Her tone suddenly held the sharp edge of sarcasm. "He's a *surgeon*. A *medical doctor*. He's nearly a decade older than me *and* he's had at least that much more schooling than me. He's from *the city*, not a cow town. His family lived in *Paris* for three years. He speaks fluent *French*. Of course he'd know more than me."

The bastard made her feel small. Stupid and small.

Christ, but he was going to enjoy getting in that guy's face.

"I take it Jarrod's problem wasn't just that he couldn't keep his dick in his pants, but he wasn't much fun at home either," Layne remarked.

"No," Rocky answered on a whisper, her eyes glued to his. "He wasn't much fun at home."

They both fell silent and held each other's eyes and Layne knew she was thinking the same thing he was thinking.

They had fun at home. Even when they were fighting, they had fun. They were young. They were in love. They had fantastic sex. He made decent money. She had a bright future. They both weren't afraid to work hard. They got along and when they didn't they fought clean. They made each other laugh and life was just fucking good. He had never, not once when they were living together, dreaded going home. When work was done or when he'd be heading home after drinks with the guys or doing an errand, he looked forward to going home to Rocky.

And now he knew she felt the same.

Slowly, his body tensed with expectation, and, fuck him, anticipation, as she began to lean toward him, saying, "Layne—" when they heard a key scrape the lock and she sat back and twisted her neck to look at the door.

Fuck!

His eyes went over the back of the couch to see Merry walk in.

"Sorry," Merry said, closing the door behind him. "Saw your truck, brother, but to get to my bed, I gotta walk through this room." He walked to the dining room table and tossed his keys on it, finishing with, "Hey, Roc."

"Hey, Merry," she replied, and Layne looked at his watch.

It was nearly midnight and he needed to get his ass home. Not just getting the fuck away from a Raquel Astley with passion in her eyes, or pain, but because his sons' curfew was midnight and he needed to make sure they didn't break it.

He lifted his feet off the coffee table and pushed up, muttering, "Gotta go."

Merry was shrugging off his leather jacket. "Don't mind me. I'm wiped. I'm goin' straight to bed."

Layne rounded the couch as he heard Rocky get up. "Gotta be home for the boys."

Merry had wrapped his jacket around the back of a dining room chair and his eyes came to Layne.

"Heard the 'dogs won," he remarked.

"Yep," Layne replied, coming to stand a few feet from Merry.

"They got talent this year," Merry noted.

"Yep," Layne agreed.

Merry's eyes grew sharp. "Heard about Tripp, big man."

"Figured that was makin' the rounds," Layne stated.

Rocky burrowed into her brother's side until he slid an arm around her shoulders and she did this whispering, "It was bad, Merry."

Merry looked down at her upturned face and nodded then looked back at Layne.

"You gonna do somethin' about that?" he asked.

"Formal complaint," Layne answered.

Merry shook his head, mumbling, "That isn't what I'd do."

No. Layne knew that wasn't what Merry would do. Merry had control, just not very much of it.

"There are times, man, when you gotta play it smart. This is one of those times," Layne replied quietly.

Merry's eyes fell to Layne's gut, showing Layne they'd both learned the lesson about playing it smart. He looked back at Layne and nodded.

Then he said, "Welp, gotta hit the hay." He leaned down and kissed the top of his sister's head, and after he did, she tipped her head back and grinned at him. He gave her shoulders a visible squeeze, let her go, walked to Layne, clapped him on the shoulder and walked down the hall, saying, "'Night."

"'Night, Merry," Rocky called.

"Later," Layne said and headed to the door.

Rocky followed him.

Merry had a two-bedroom condo. It wasn't the greatest condo, it wasn't shit. At his age, even after the divorce where he let his ex have the house, he could do better. Then again, he had an Excursion, a speed boat, a Harley, a timeshare in Florida and a taste for expensive whisky. Unlike Rutledge, to have expensive toys on a cop's salary, Merry had to juggle and sometimes, make sacrifices.

Layne opened the door and walked out into the cold. Rocky held the door open then moved to stand with a shoulder against the jamb, the door mostly closed. She'd wedged herself between them and her eyes were looking up at him.

"I'm sorry about Tripp, Layne," she said gently.

"He'll be okay," Layne replied and she nodded.

"Thanks for helping with the apartment," she said.

"Not a problem."

Her eyes slid to the side and he watched her thinking.

He should say goodnight and get the fuck out of there. They didn't need to go where they were heading tonight. They needed to stay focused. Both of them. They had what they had and then it went bad.

That was a long time ago. He couldn't get caught in the memories. The good times then and the way he was finding she was now didn't change the fact that she'd turned her back and walked away and didn't explain why. She'd torn out his heart and shattered his world. He didn't see video of her taking it from the front and back, but that would almost make it better. At least that was a reason.

"Even with all the dramas," she broke into his thoughts, "it was a nice night, Layne."

"Yep," he agreed, finally got smart and drew a line under it. "Later, Roc."

Her face changed and he blocked reading it before she cleared her expression and nodded. "'Night, Layne."

He turned and walked away, hearing the door click behind him and thinking any other night spent like that with any other woman, he would not be walking away. At least not until after breakfast.

But Raquel Merrick Astley was not any other woman.

He jogged down the stairs, walked to his truck and went home to his boys.

Seven

CHARMING

*L*ayne was barely out of the shower, just beginning to towel off, when he heard the doorbell.

"Fuck," he muttered.

He was late. He was taking Rocky to Swank's tonight. He'd been working the new case all day, he got caught up in it and he was late.

With drops of water still on his shoulders and chest, he wrapped the towel around his waist and strode swiftly out of his room and down the stairs. He went straight to the door, opened it, barely looking at her but the storm door was already opening and he smelled her perfume.

He turned, saying, "Runnin' late, Roc, come in and get yourself a beer. I'll be down soon's I can."

Then he headed straight back up the stairs, hearing her heels on his wood floors and not noticing she didn't say a word.

It had been two weeks since they'd put their plan into action and he was playing it smart. This was helped by the fact that her apartment was vacant and she was good to move in right away, so she did. She spent her evenings shopping for shit for her house and Layne was dedicated to the cause of bringing down Rutledge but not so dedicated he'd go shopping.

They spent time together but not much. She was shopping and he was working this case. It wouldn't take him long, but it required time, planning, equipment and a shitload of field work. This was good. He'd been climbing the walls while recuperating. Being back out in the field felt fucking *great*.

The Sunday after their night that ended in pizza, beer and heartfelt conversation, Rocky came over with Merry and they ran the Rutledge case down for her. Then they watched football on TV. Merry left and Rocky stayed so Natalie Ulrich could see her car in his drive and know she was alone with him in his house. The boys came home from doing whatever it was they were doing and he got them down to homework and walked Rocky out to the car. He didn't play make out because that was playing with fire. He just touched his lips to hers, opened the car door for her and stood in his drive watching her drive away. Then he went inside.

They'd had dinner together at Frank's and coffees together at Mimi's. She went to both subsequent Friday games with him, one away, the next one, last night, at home. She went with him but she sat with her dad at the away game, Josie Judd and the girl posse at the home game, hanging with Layne, and, for show, *on* him, only at halftime. He didn't know why she didn't stand with him by the field, if it was because she felt responsible for what happened to Tripp or if she was giving him space. He also didn't ask.

She'd started working Rutledge. She was breaking him in but Layne was too busy to be there so Merry was covering her. She'd gone three times to the station on the pretense she needed to talk to or was meeting Merry. Merry made himself busy with bullshit work so she could wander over to Rutledge and strike up conversations. Only once was Layne close enough to go in and see her in action. When he topped the steps to the bullpen, she was sitting by Rutledge's desk and they were both laughing, though Rutledge was staring at her tits *while* he was laughing.

Seeing that, Layne had walked right up and claimed her, giving Rutledge a cursory greeting and that was when they went to Mimi's for a quick coffee.

Other than that, if they were alone and no eyes were on them, he was friendly but kept his distance. He made it clear the getting to know you again part of their operation was done, they needed to focus and, thank fuck, Raquel read him and went with it, returning the favor.

The problem was, when they weren't alone and eyes were on them, he was forced to be far friendlier and there was not even a hint of distance. Rocky was just as friendly back.

This was extremely bad because it always felt extremely good.

Now, he was taking her to Swank's.

Swank's was Jarrod Astley's favorite restaurant in Indianapolis—intel Layne had learned from Merry's e-mailed report of all things he knew about Astley. Apparently, Rocky took Astley there for his birthday every year and Astley took Rocky there to be seen in the exclusive hotspot as often as he liked, which, even though you couldn't get out of there without spending at least a hundred dollars a head, was *often*.

Layne had made time to swing by the restaurant so he could chat up the hostess. He found out promptly that she knew Dr. Astley. She also knew Dr. Astley had recently made a reservation, she knew the date and she knew the time, and Layne convinced her to share that information with him. He then made a reservation for two, half an hour after Astley was to get there, gave the hostess a fifty and asked her to make certain he was seated close to Astley. After he smiled at her, she promised he would be.

Layne learned from the intel on Astley that getting into his face made it even better he had a time-consuming case, because that fifty he'd slipped the waitress was only the beginning.

Astley made a lot of money, even more than Layne reckoned he did (and Layne knew this because he ran every search and report he could on the doc) and Astley wasn't saving for a rainy day. He lived large. Swank's was named that for a reason. The place was trendy and expensive, and the time Layne visited the hostess, packed. In Indy, it was the place to see and be seen.

Astley also came from money. He wasn't the elite of the elite, but he was from the upper class, albeit the *middle* upper class. He had a trust fund that he didn't dip into much since he didn't have to. He also stood to inherit a whack, even sharing it with a brother and sister, when his mother eventually passed away.

Taking his mind off Astley, Layne stood at the sink in his bathroom, shaved, slapped on aftershave and ran a comb through his hair. Then he went to the closet and pulled clothes off hangers.

Melody lived in LA and she worked retail, a fancy-ass store that, from what Layne had learned from Astley's credit card statements, Jarrod Astley would cream his pants over. Melody liked dressing Layne and she got a great discount, so whenever he saw her she always had bags of shit to give him. Even though he rarely wore what she bought, he didn't throw it away. But most of it had never touched his skin.

He put on a pair of slacks, shrugged on a shirt, buttoned it, grabbed the jacket off a hanger, went to his bedroom and pulled on his socks and boots. He shoved his wallet in the inside pocket of the jacket and shrugged that on as he walked downstairs.

Out of the corner of his eye he saw Rocky sitting at the island as he rounded the corner into the kitchen, tagging his keys and cell off the counter as he walked to the utility room door.

"Ready?" he asked, stopped, turned to her and froze.

"Yeah," she replied, her back to him. She was moving, doing something, he didn't know what, because he couldn't force his mind to think.

Her back was bare. Completely. There were only thin black straps that curled over her shoulders and stopped at the back of her pits and her lower body was hidden by the island, but what he could see of her back, it was completely bare.

And her hair was down. Down in a sleek, gleaming fall that went beyond her shoulder blades, but with her movements, was now gliding around the skin of her back and shoulders.

That skin disappeared when she pulled up a black coat and settled it on her shoulders. Turning to the island, with one hand she pulled the thick length of her hair free of her coat and with the other hand she grabbed a little, shiny, deep purple purse and a deep purple scarf in some slithery material. Then he heard her heels on the tiles.

She rounded the island and he saw her from the front.

The black coat went to her knees but she hadn't buttoned it, and as she moved, the coat went back and showed the entirety of the dress. The top front of the dress was straight above her breasts, the middle loose and partially draping, but at her hips and thighs the dress clung, as in *clung*. It was so formfitting it left nothing to the imagination. And it was short. It wasn't short-short, but it came to just below the tops of her thighs. Her long legs went forever under that skirt. They were bare but looked shiny in a sexy way, and she was wearing purple, spike-heeled sandals with a fuckload of thin straps that were so damned sexy, just looking at those shoes made him start to get hard.

He tore his eyes from the shoes, made the grave mistake of trailing them up her body and seeing that dress again, and then he saw her face. She was arranging the scarf around her neck and her makeup was smoky, in deep grays and purples, heavier than usual, just as perfect…and *hot*, especially with her hair falling around her face and shoulders.

She got close and even her perfume was stronger.

Fuck.

She stopped, her head down and twisting around as she settled her scarf around her neck.

She finished with that, tipped her head back to look at him, tilted it to the side, and said, "Ready."

Yeah, she was ready. Fucking shit, it was going to be a long night.

He turned to the door, opened it and held it for her.

Her perfume assaulted him again as she walked through. He followed her, reaching high to grab the edge of the garage door she opened and preceded him through as he bleeped the locks on his truck. Rocky headed to the passenger side, Layne followed. She climbed up and he saw more leg, her coat falling back as the skirt stretched to the danger zone and she settled in.

He slammed the door and rounded the hood forcing himself to think of kittens.

He got in, buckled in, hit the garage door opener, started the truck, backed out and hit the garage door opener again. They were out of the development and on the road toward Indy when she spoke.

"Went by the station today," she said.

"I know," he replied.

"Rutledge and I are forming a bond," she told him.

"Good," he returned.

"While I was there, Drew caught me."

Shit.

"Rocky—"

He heard the material of her coat slide against the seat as she turned to him.

"He wanted me to talk to you. He told me some weird stuff about the Youth Group at the Christian Church."

"Roc—"

"It doesn't sound good, Layne."

"He told me the same thing and you're right. He's right. It doesn't sound good. But we got enough on our plate."

He heard the material slide again as she turned to look out the windshield.

"I've been hearing things at school too. I can't say I'm surprised at what Drew shared."

Layne made no response.

"I think—" she started.

He glanced at her then back at the road while speaking. "Sweetcheeks, I made a formal complaint about my kids' football coach. They were at their mom's last week, but breakfast conversation the week before included the fact that both my boys are bearing the consequences of that. Not at games, he's not that stupid, considering mine wasn't the only complaint lodged and Gabby's wasn't the only *other* complaint lodged, but during practice."

He heard her suck in breath but kept talking.

"I got a case that's takin' all my time so I haven't been able to give any to whatever is goin' down with Stew."

"That's not good," she muttered.

"No, it isn't," he agreed. "And you're wedging yourself close to Rutledge. You got an apartment to set up. And if Cosgrove is pissed about the complaints and not afraid to take payback outta my boys during practice, then he won't be afraid of fuckin' with the woman he thinks is mine. Summin' up, sweetcheeks, I'll repeat, we got enough on our plate."

She sighed. He waited. She didn't speak. He glanced at her to see she was looking out the side window. She sighed again, this time heavier.

Then she whispered, "All right."

Well thank Christ for that.

Layne drove in silence and Rocky followed his lead. They'd had no more heart-to-hearts after the night of pizza and beer. Raquel didn't share with him about work and told him only what he needed to know about her life. She did this, he reckoned, because this was what he was doing.

However, as they drove, the scent of her perfume filled his cab and the sight of her legs filled his vision. The second was because his eyes were drawn to them no matter how he tried to keep them on the road. It was only filling his mind with visions of those legs bloody and lifeless if he crashed that made him stop.

They were on the Circle when she asked, "Tell me again why we're all gussied up and going out on the town?"

"Point of this, you and me, is to be seen," he reminded her. "We haven't been doin' much of that."

"Yes, Layne." He could tell by the sound of her voice she was looking at him. "But shouldn't we be seen in the 'burg?"

"Lots of people need to see and lots of places to be seen."

"Is there something you're not telling me?"

Yes, there was something he wasn't telling her. She knew they were going to Swank's but had no idea Astley was there and he wasn't going to tell her now.

"Just trust me, Roc. I know what I'm doin'."

There was a beat of silence then another sigh before, "All right."

He turned off the Circle, found Swank's and stopped out front, rounded the hood and handed the keys to the valet, taking a ticket. Rocky waited for him. He put a hand in the small of her back and led her into the restaurant.

The hostess smiled warmly at him and before they even made it to her station, where he could, say, give his name, she announced, "Your table's all ready." Rocky looked at her in surprise then looked at Layne, but the hostess was rounding the station and motioning with an arm to a man standing there. "Your coat."

Layne took Rocky's coat from her and got a good look at the full back of her dress, or, more appropriately, the lack of it. He was right. Completely bare. Straight down to the top of her ass.

Fuck.

She unwrapped her scarf. He took it and handed them off to the man waiting. The man gave Layne another slip of paper to go with the one from the valet, Layne tucked it in his inside jacket pocket and moved behind Rocky as she followed the hostess who was carrying menus.

Layne knew the instant she saw him because she stopped dead and he almost ran into her. He didn't hesitate, put his hand on the skin at the small of her back and pushed her forward.

"Layne—" she started, walking forward because he was pushing her at the same time she was pressing back.

"Let's get to the table, sweetcheeks. I'm fuckin' starved."

He noted as he spoke that the hostess had done well. They were in an alcove that held only two two-top booths, either side, separated by about five feet. Astley and some brunette with her back to the restaurant on one side. An empty booth on the other. Fucking perfect.

"Layne—" Rocky said again, turning to him.

They'd made it to the area that separated the booths and he hooked an arm around her neck and pulled her into his side. She tipped her head back to look at him, her face was pale and her eyes were huge.

"I learned early, baby, not to make you wait to get fed." He touched his mouth to hers. "Do me the same courtesy, yeah?" he asked then looked at the hostess and announced, "My baby likes her food."

"Layne—" Rocky repeated, her body tight as a bow about to snap and the alcove was thick with tension, and not just Rocky's.

"Sit, sweetcheeks." He maneuvered her to the seat facing the restaurant, which was what he'd do in normal circumstances. The woman should always have the best seat and it was better facing the restaurant and being able to see the activity than having your back to the room. He noticed that Astley didn't afford that consideration to his woman. But Layne did it for Rocky, even though the better strategic position was to have his back to the wall, Rocky facing him, which meant Astley would find it difficult not to look at her for, if he turned his head, she'd be in his line of sight.

He pushed her down in her side of the narrow booth thinking for the first time he was glad she was wearing that dress. No man seeing Rocky in that dress could be unaffected by it. Layne wasn't the only proof of that. Every man she passed while walking through the restaurant stared at her while she did it.

He sat down as Rocky leaned forward and hissed, "Layne, listen to—"

He tilted his head back and said to the hostess, "Can you help me out and get me a beer?"

"Absolutely," she replied on a smile, opening a menu and handing it to Rocky who took it automatically. "We have a wide selection. Would you like to see a list?"

"Nope." He smiled at her. "You pick. Only two requirements. American and cold."

She nodded, still smiling, handed him his open menu and looked to Rocky. "Do you know what you'd like to drink?"

"Montepulciano," she said instantly. "A *large* one."

Layne looked down at his menu and grinned.

The hostess took off.

"Layne!" she snapped, her voice bordering on shrill.

"Yeah, baby?" he asked back, not lifting his head from the menu, and before she could say anything, he went on, "You've been here, what's good? I hope the portions aren't crap. I could eat an entire pan of Jas's pasta bake."

"Layne!" she repeated, but Layne felt him before he said a word. Layne looked up and to the side to see Astley standing there. His hair was dark blonde, nearly brown, only hints of gray. His eyes were hazel. He was tall, straight and slim. Layne could tell, even under his expensive suit, the man was fit. But he wasn't fit in a bulky, powerful way. He was fit in an active, healthy way.

"Fuck me," Layne muttered like he was surprised, but he was fighting a grin.

"Charming," Astley replied, giving Layne a look to kill. His eyes sliced to Rocky and he greeted through thinned lips, "Rocky."

"Jarrod," she replied. Her lips weren't thin, they were soft, her face was still pale but with her makeup, her hair, that dress, even with her skin pale, she was a freaking *knockout.*

"It seems we're practically dinner partners," he remarked, edging a bit to the side to indicate his meaning and Layne turned his head to see Merry wasn't wrong. Rocky's double was sitting across from them. She didn't have the blonde streaks in her hair and her hair wasn't as long. She was definitely younger but the poise wasn't there and he knew that even though she was sitting. She also didn't have Rocky's style. He could tell she had a great body, but it was just on the wrong side of too toned and her tits were fake. He knew the last because she was wearing a dress that barely covered them.

Definitely didn't have Rocky's style.

The minute their eyes turned her way, hers shot down to her plate.

"Perhaps you can ask the hostess to seat you at a different table?" Astley suggested, and Layne looked up at him to see the man's gaze turned his way.

He twisted in his seat, looked at the packed restaurant and back to Astley. "I'm not thinkin' that's gonna work, man."

"I'm certain something will open up," Astley pressed.

Layne looked back at Astley's table to see his woman, or more accurately, his girl peeking at them, but she again turned her eyes away when she caught his.

He looked back at Astley. "I'm not feelin' in the mood to wait."

"Layne, maybe we can—" Rocky started.

He cut his eyes to her and she stopped.

"Look at their table, sweetcheeks. They've already been served. They'll be gone soon and we're all adults. It'll be all right."

"I think both Rocky *and* Marissa would be more comfortable—" Astley began, but Layne shoved out of his side of the booth and stood, looking down the three inches he had on the man.

Then he said, "I think Rocky would be more comfortable if you went back to your table and let us enjoy our dinner."

"Layne—" Rocky whispered.

"Sit down," Astley ordered, the pompous-ass dick.

"Go back to your table," Layne returned.

"This is ridiculous," Astley snapped. "We can hardly—"

"You might not be able to eat next to a good woman you fucked over, but we'll be fine if you sit...your *ass*...down at your table."

Astley glared up at him. Layne held his glare and counted. It took four beats for Astley to give up and turn to Rocky.

"As our attorneys are both enjoying their weekends then I'll have to inform you here that the house will not be vacant tomorrow for you to get your things. I suggest you call your lawyers and they can make arrangements for an alternate date."

Rocky's face got even paler and her eyes shot to Layne.

That fucking *dick*.

"That's okay," Layne stated, sitting back down. "We'll come over while you're there."

Rocky's eyes bugged out of her head.

Layne grabbed his napkin and put it on his lap.

"I'm afraid that doesn't work for me," Astley replied.

Layne kept his gaze steady on Rocky. "Your name on the deed?"

"Yes," she whispered.

He looked at Astley. "Then she doesn't need your permission to go to her own house. If it doesn't work for you, tough. We'll be there at ten o'clock."

"*You* are not welcome in my home," he clipped.

"Well, lucky for *me*, my woman half owns your home and I'm sure she'll welcome me." His eyes went to Rocky. "Won't you, sweetcheeks?"

Slowly, Rocky closed her eyes.

Astley spoke and when he did, he did it quietly, his tone had changed, something threaded through it, something that struck Layne as wrong. But he couldn't figure out what it was and Layne looked up to see he was addressing Rocky.

"You know what this is, Rocky. You know." He shook his head and finished, "I didn't expect this from you."

Then he turned and walked back to his booth, and while he was doing it, he stopped a waiter and said, "We're leaving early. Bring our check to the hostess station."

Astley pulled his girl out of the booth and Layne looked back to Rocky who had her elbow on the table, her fingers lightly touching her lips, her eyes were unfocused and pointed into the restaurant.

"Roc?" he called, her gaze shifted to him and it was troubled. He leaned forward. Reaching out, he grabbed her wrist, pulling her arm down to the table to hold her hand. Then he whispered, "They're leaving. It'll be fine."

"You knew," she whispered back.

He didn't respond.

"You knew," she repeated. "You orchestrated this."

Layne held her eyes and kept his mouth shut.

She looked over his shoulder and pulled her hand from his as a waiter appeared with their drinks. Layne looked to see Astley and his girl were gone.

"Have you had time to look over the menu?" the waiter asked after he set the drinks down. "I'm happy to answer any questions."

"Give us a minute," Layne ordered.

The waiter dipped his head, his hands pressed together in front of him like he was praying and he murmured, "Certainly."

Fucking hell, this place was pretentious.

The waiter took off and Layne looked at Rocky.

"Roc—"

She started nodding and he didn't know why.

Then she said, "This is okay. This is fine." She straightened her shoulders and asked in a falsely bright voice, "It had to happen sooner or later, right?"

"Baby—"

He stopped talking because now she was shaking her head.

Then she said, "No, no, you're right. You were right to do this. You should be in control. It shouldn't be a surprise. Not like with Gabrielle. This is better. It was shorter and there were a lot less witnesses."

"He needs to get some of his own back," Layne told her, and she started nodding again.

"Yes, of course. You're right about that too. And you were right not to tell me. I wouldn't have come."

He sat back in his seat and took a sip of his beer, his eyes on her watching her eyes move anywhere but to him.

He put his beer down and asked, "So, if I'm right, why do I feel like I'm standin' on a sidewalk lookin' at your bloody mangled body after I shoved you under a bus?"

Finally, her eyes darted to him. She stared at him a second before her face cracked and her mouth twitched up into a smile.

"I'm fine," she said softly. "Seriously, you did the right thing. It's over."

"It isn't," he contradicted her. "We gotta go over there tomorrow."

"No. I'll do that. I don't have much to pick up. Just some things I didn't get before because...well, I didn't have a place so I didn't have anywhere to put them. It won't take me long."

"No way in hell I'm lettin' you go over there with him and his girl there, Roc."

"Honestly, Layne, it won't take long."

"Good, then with two of us, it'll take half the time."

She stared at him and Layne could tell she was thinking.

Then she decided, "I'll take Merry."

"Merry's at the lake this weekend."

"Oh right, I forgot." She chewed her lip then said, "Dad'll help."

"Your dad can't lift boxes."

"I'll make them light."

"Sweetcheeks, it's been rainin' three days and the rain isn't supposed to clear until Wednesday. Your dad probably isn't feelin' great about now."

He knew he had her when her eyes started to flash.

"I'll take Josie then." She was beginning to sound desperate.

"I'm going."

"Layne—"

Layne leaned forward. "Why are you so desperate for me not to go?" She opened her mouth to speak but he asked another question. "And what was his parting shot all about?"

She closed her mouth with a snap, her eyes scanned the ceiling, and if she started whistling a tune, he wouldn't have been surprised.

He leaned in further. "Sweetcheeks, you know I'm stubborn and you know I'll get what I want and I'll go at it all night until I get it, so spill. What's goin' on?"

She glared at him.

Then she said, "He knows about you."

Layne nodded. "Yes, I would guess if you spent ten years livin' with a guy you'd share history. So?" Her eyes shifted over his shoulder. "Rocky," he warned.

Her eyes shifted back.

"Let's just say you're a hard act to follow."

Fuck.

Bullet to the gut. Agony.

Layne sat back and changed his mind. "Maybe we should stop talkin' about this."

"Good idea," Rocky agreed instantly, picking up her menu and flipping it open. "So…the steaks are good here but you have to get a sauce on top. They're killer. They turn the steaks into heaven but in meat form. Béarnaise is good.

They also do a pepper sauce that is very tasty, but the béarnaise is way better. And get the sautéed potatoes. They rock. They sauté them in onions, brilliant. Oh! And I had this seared tuna here once. I swear, it melted on my tongue…"

Layne watched her while she blathered and he really didn't want to think it, but he couldn't help but think, even in that getup with her hair around her face, looking glamorous, she was still downright, fucking *cute*.

They were in the truck on the way home and Layne was contemplating the fact that Rocky was right. The béarnaise sauce was really good. As were the sautéed potatoes.

The best part, however, was watching Rocky eat a pile of custard-filled, hot fudge-topped profiteroles. He could swear, after the third bite, she was going to have an orgasm, and watching her, he nearly had one.

He glanced at her to see she was staring out the side window and it came to him that he was wrong. The best part was sitting across from Rocky wearing that dress, her hair down, after she had recovered from the exchange with Astley, was into her second glass of wine and had relaxed. Even with her behind her shields and with his shields up, that didn't make her any less interesting, amusing, exciting, and especially, appealing.

"Layne?" she called into the silent cab.

"Yeah, Roc," he answered.

"Thank you," she said.

"For what?" he asked.

He heard the material of her coat slide against the seat as she turned to him. "I know this is awkward, and weird, and…well, *awkward*. And I know because of my crazy scheme I kind of pushed you into this whole… um, *situation*. But you're being really nice and you definitely didn't have to go out of your way to arrange that, uh…tête-à-tête with Jarrod. And what you said to him was nice, though, obviously, not nice *for him*, but, I mean, it was nice about me." She paused, sucked in a breath then continued, "You know, being a good woman he fucked over and all, and—"

He cut her off. "Roc?"

"What?"

Golden Trail

"You're welcome."

She went silent before she whispered, "Thanks for, um…you're welcoming me."

He laughed low.

Jesus, she was a nut.

And absolutely no less appealing with her shields up.

He turned into his development and luckily, after living there for over a year, found his house without getting lost.

There was a car on the street parked between his house and the house next door and he hoped to God for the owner's sake that the HOA Nazis weren't out patrolling or someone would receive a testy letter tomorrow.

He hit the garage door opener, slid up the drive beside Rocky's Merc and parked in the garage wondering if she drank whisky. He had whisky and beer in the house and it would be good to sit and end the night with Rocky and a glass of whisky. It wouldn't be smart, but it would be good.

The Charger's spot was empty. The boys were back at his house for the week but out that day and night. Jasper with friends during the day and on a date with Keira that evening. Tripp was hanging with some buds. Having spent the night after the game at one of their houses, he was supposed to spend the day jacking around, going to the mall and being home that evening after they went to a movie.

He switched off the ignition and Rocky had jumped down and rounded the hood by the time he joined her. He opened the door and leaned forward, holding it for her to precede him, and then he walked by her through the utility room and did the same for the kitchen door.

When they both got into the kitchen, he saw the house was dark and he stopped thinking about how to convince Rocky to stay and have a drink. It was early, not even eleven. Tripp was supposed to be home by ten but his curfew wasn't until midnight. Plans may have changed, but if they did, he should have called.

Layne started to reach to switch on the light when they went on, bright and blazing, and he heard shouted, "Surprise, baby!"

Then he looked beyond a rock solid Raquel to see Melody standing in his kitchen wearing high-heeled, black platform sandals and see-through black underwear.

Fuck!

"Ohmigod!" Melody shouted, covering herself with her arms.

"Melody, Christ!" Layne clipped, moving quickly around Rocky and in front of her to block Melody from view. "What the fuck?"

"I...ohmigod!" Melody cried, edging backward toward the couch in the living room.

"Fuck, woman. I got two teenage boys living in this house and you're practically fuckin' naked. Jesus. How the hell did you get in here?"

"Tripp...Tripp let me in then he took off," Melody answered, still edging back. She snatched up a robe off the back of the couch and started pulling it on.

"He took off?" Layne asked.

"He didn't...he didn't tell me you were..." Her eyes shot to Rocky, who still hadn't moved. "I told him I needed alone time with you, that this was a surprise. He called a friend and they...he didn't tell me you were on *a date*."

"No! No, that isn't what this is," Rocky put in and now Layne saw she was on the move, edging along the counter pressed against it as if she wanted the counter, cupboards and then the wall to absorb her. "I'm...I'll be...you two just...I'll be going."

"Roc—" Layne started, and her head snapped toward him but her eyes didn't meet his.

"No, that's okay, Layne. I'll just...just let myself out." She was sliding across the fridge now and looking anywhere but Layne and Melody. "You two just...enjoy your evening. I'll let myself out."

"Rocky." He moved toward her and she started moving quicker. Rounding the fridge, she caught her heel on the lip that separated the tile from the wood and went crashing down, her hand slamming into the wood first, followed by her right hip and thigh.

"Fuck!" he hissed, moving swiftly toward her.

"Ohmigod! Are you okay?" Melody, now wearing her robe, shot forward too.

Rocky waved a hand at them, facing the floor, pushing up, the heavy curtain of her hair obscuring her features.

"I'm okay," she whispered. "I'm good."

Layne bent and put a hand on her hip and one on her bicep but she pulled it violently out of his grip.

"I'm good," she whispered to the floor, pushing forward, dragging her body away from him. She gracefully got up, movements fluid, as only Raquel could do, and gained her feet.

"Did you hurt anything?" Melody asked as Rocky kept her head dipped, much like Tripp did after Cosgrove got through with him, and pulled her jacket together using only two fingers because she was doing this with the hand still clutching her purse.

"No, I'm okay." She was in profile to Layne. She shook her hair back and lifted a hand that he saw was trembling, pulling back the hair on the opposite side to him and tucking it behind her ear. He could see she shot Melody a false smile. "See, just fine. I'll go."

"Roc—" he started, putting his hand on her arm again, but her head turned, slow, the movement liquid. She tipped it back and he caught half a second of her eyes, the bottom edges brimming bright with tears, their depths filled with a pain so stark, his body froze and his chest tightened, squeezing out all his oxygen. She looked to the ground and turned abruptly, breaking contact with his hand.

"Have a good night!" she called and ran, her heels clicking on the wood, to the door.

Layne looked over his shoulder to Melody and growled, "Get dressed."

Then he went after Rocky who was already out the door.

He caught her still opened car door as she folded herself in it, her hand shooting out to the handle. He pushed back as she pulled in.

"Rocky, hang on a second," he said, crouching in the open door.

She kept her eyes glued to the steering wheel. "You should go in."

"Look at me."

"You should..." She took a deep breath and turned to him with a bright, totally fake smile. "Thanks for dinner. It was nice. My treat next time." She looked to the house then back at him before she said softly, "You should go in, Layne. She probably feels like an idiot. You need to talk to her."

"Roc—"

"Go in," she whispered, her voice suddenly trembling so much it was hard to hear in more ways than one. She was losing it. "Layne, please get out of my door and go into the house."

He started to lift a hand to her face saying, "Baby—"

Her head jerked to face forward and her eyes squeezed closed. "Don't! Please, please just *go in*."

He stared at her profile and clenched his teeth. Then he straightened, stepped out of the door and slammed it. She fired up her car and backed out fast, accelerating forward even faster.

He watched until he lost sight of her car then stalked into his house, the look of Rocky, tears and pain in her eyes, burned on his brain. He threw open the storm door, the front door, slammed it and moved through the house, taking the steps two at a time.

Melody was in his bedroom quickly yanking down a t-shirt. He saw her bag on the floor and she couldn't have been there more than two hours and the fucking thing had already exploded. There were two glossy shopping bags from her store lined against the wall.

"You know I was shot nine weeks ago," he bit out.

She didn't look at him when she whispered, "I'm sorry. I'm so sorry."

"That coulda had a different ending, I thought for a second before I walked into this goddamned house that someone might have broken in and I came in armed."

She jerked her head toward him. "Tanner, I'm so sorry. I didn't think."

"No, you didn't. Fuck, even in LA, you pulled that shit, that coulda happened. You know better."

"I know!"

He kept at her. "It coulda been Jas comin' home from his date and gettin' an eyeful."

She shook her head and rushed to her bag, dropping to her knees and shoving things in.

"Things have changed, Melody, from when it was you and me and sun and a population of people with bleached teeth in LA."

"I know, Tanner," she told her bag.

He stared at Melody but all he could see was Rocky.

Fuck! Why couldn't he get that *fucking* look on Rocky's face out of his goddamned head?

She zipped her bag closed and he watched her. Melody was tall, lean, great tits and they were real. Thirty-five. Long, dark hair. Blue eyes. She was also funny and sweet.

Fuck him.

Layne made a decision.

"DeeDee, come here," he said softly, and her head shot back.

"I saw," she whispered.

"What?" he asked.

She shook her head, looked down at her bag, and slowly, she straightened. She had grace, she was in tune with her body, but she wasn't fluid.

She turned to look at him.

"I didn't get it. I didn't understand why you...with me, why you wouldn't..." She shook her head and took in a deep breath then continued, "I looked through your stuff. I found the envelope. I saw the pictures. I know who that woman is."

Layne's anger had ebbed out of him but it came back, slicing through him like a blade.

He didn't speak because he couldn't without yelling.

"Some of them had her name on the back," she whispered. "Rocky."

"That was not cool," he said low.

"I know," she replied quietly then tilted her head to the side. "Are you back with her?"

"No. We're workin' a case together."

"She's a detective?"

"She's a teacher."

She stared at him a second, thrown, then she smiled and it wasn't a happy smile.

"A teacher," she whispered.

"DeeDee—"

"Even with that case with that drug guy who shopped at my store, you didn't let me work it with you and I begged you to let me help."

"That wasn't safe."

"Is this?" she asked, but she knew. She'd called a couple of weeks after he was shot and he'd told her because he figured she'd eventually know. Since he'd left LA, she visited him during her vacations and he definitely didn't wear a shirt the entire time she was there. Even though she couldn't know it was the same case, she sure as fuck knew his work wasn't always a trip through the light fantastic. "You want to be with her," she surmised.

"It isn't like that," he returned.

"Yeah?" She tipped her head again and then pointed to the floor. "A girl knows, Tanner. During that scene, you didn't take your eyes off her. And after it, you went after her. You told me to get dressed then you went after her."

"She just fell to the fuckin' floor, Melody," he reminded her, crossing his arms on his chest.

She stared him in the eyes then she whispered, "You went after her."

"For fuck's sake," he clipped.

She bent double and grabbed the handle to her bag. Lifting it up, she hooked it on her arm and walked to him.

Her hand came up, fingers fiddling with the lapel on his jacket, her eyes watching them.

"I knew this would look good on you," she whispered. "But then, anything would look good on you."

"DeeDee."

"What's in those bags," she jerked her head back to indicate his room, "they're for you."

He uncrossed his arms and both hands went to her waist. "DeeDee," he murmured and her eyes lifted to his as her hand came to his neck.

"I hope you get her back." She was still whispering and Layne's hands got tight on her waist. "In those pictures, you looked happy. Even when you're laughing, you don't look completely happy. But in those pictures…" She stopped and her fingers squeezed his neck. "I hope you get her back and she makes you happy like that again."

Then she pulled away from his hands and walked to the stairs, and when she did, Rocky's face came back into his head.

So Layne stood there and listened to the front door slam.

Then he heard her car door slam.

Then he heard her car driving away.

And he let her go.

Eight

YOU FIT

"*D*o you get it?" Rocky whispered in his ear.

He was on top of her, still inside her, all four of her limbs wrapped tight around him, skin against skin, her body soft underneath him.

"Get what, baby?" he whispered back.

Her limbs squeezed.

"Why I left you?"

Layne's eyes opened.

He was on his stomach in his bed in his dark room.

He rolled to his back, muttering, "Christ."

His back was to the weight bench, feet to the floor. He cocked his elbows, taking the weights down then, on an exhale through his teeth, Layne pushed them up.

Tripp came out of his room and Layne's head turned to the side. He saw his son scratching his ass and shuffling to the bathroom.

"Hey, Dad," he mumbled.

Layne cocked his elbows, "Hey, Tripp," then he pressed the weights up. He heard the bathroom door close.

Showered, shaved, Layne stood at the island watching Tripp sitting opposite him eating his fourth donut, his eyes across the room on the TV. Blondie, Layne knew even though he couldn't see her, was lying at the foot of Tripp's stool licking up powdered sugar residue that fell from Tripp's donut onto the floor.

Layne held his cell to his ear and heard for the third time that morning, "You've reached Rocky's voicemail…leave me a message."

He disconnected and muttered, "Fuck."

Tripp's eyes came to him. "What?"

"Nothin', pal."

Layne looked at the clock over the microwave. It was ten after ten. They were supposed to be at her old place at ten. She was supposed to be at his house at twenty to ten. She had the boxes in the back of her Merc, they were taking the Suburban.

She didn't show.

Layne tagged his keys off the counter and told Tripp, "I gotta get to Rocky's. We gotta do something at her old place. I don't know how long it'll take but I'll be home by the Colts game."

Tripp was still looking at him and asked, "Where's Melody?"

Layne had started to turn to leave. He stopped, looked his son in the eye, and answered, "She's gone, Tripp."

Tripp kept looking at him. Then he asked, "Gone gone?"

"Gone gone," Layne confirmed.

Tripp nodded and murmured, "I liked her."

"I did too, pal."

Tripp nodded again, swallowed and looked at the TV. Then he whispered, "Like Rocky better."

"Tripp—" he started to warn.

Tripp's eyes came fast to him. "I know what it is, but you two fit."

Golden Trail

Layne stared at his son, thrown. "We fit?"

"She does what she believes in too," Tripp explained.

"What?" Layne asked softly.

"All the work you do for people. Dina Kempler's dad, he was a jerk. Her mom couldn't get rid of him, jackin' her around all the time even though they're divorced, and you helped. She told me. She told me her mom found out about you because you helped her mom's friend too. You're practically famous at my school. You don't think kids talk?"

He knew kids talked. He just didn't know Dina Kempler's mom Kim would talk to her daughter about *that*.

"Tripp, don't—"

"Mrs. As—I mean Rocky, she spends a whole week making kids listen to rock music. She says lyrics are poetry. She says some of the greatest storytellers are rock stars. They tried to get her to stop, but she fought and she won and they still listen to music. It's not the same but it is. You know? You fit. Melody sells clothes. Her clothes are sweet and she's nice, but you and Melody, you don't fit."

Layne studied his son knowing his boy was sharp but thinking he'd vastly underestimated him.

But he couldn't have this conversation now. Not that he ever wanted to have it, but he couldn't have it now.

"I gotta get to Rocky, pal," Layne said quietly.

After he said those words, Tripp eyes stayed locked to his.

Then he grinned. "Tell her I said hi."

Yes, he'd vastly underestimated Tripp.

Layne grinned back and headed to the garage.

He was about to pull out when Jasper came tearing through the garage door wearing a wife beater and sweatpants that had been cut off at the knees—what he wore to bed. His hair was a mess, sleep still in his eyes, but his manner seemed urgent.

"Dad!" he shouted, and Layne put the truck in neutral and set the parking brake.

Jasper raced to the passenger side door, climbed up and settled in, slamming the door.

"God! Glad I caught you. I heard the door go up and—"

141

"Jas, I need to get to Rocky's."

Jasper nodded then said, "You were busy with work yesterday and I didn't know how important this was so I didn't want to bug you, but I thought you'd wanna know."

Layne felt his neck muscles contract. "Know what?"

"Know that before Tripp and I took off for the game, some guy came over. He was over for, like, one second. Stew gave him one of those yellow envelopes, the ones with thick paper, but it was small, like a normal envelope and it was stuffed full. The flap was folded in so I couldn't see what was in it, but it was *stuffed full*, Dad."

Shit.

"You get a good look at this guy?"

Jasper nodded again. "You said, if I got a bad vibe, I should tell you and this guy, he was Mr. Bad Vibe."

Fucking shit.

Jasper went on, "Tall, big pot belly, black hair, white dude. He was wearing sunglasses and it was dark, Dad. And he was wearing a lot of gold. Necklaces. A couple of rings. And he had piercings, the top of his left ear, both earlobes and the left side of his bottom lip."

"You ever see him before?" Layne asked.

"Nope," Jasper answered.

"Never, not anywhere?" Layne pushed.

"No, Dad."

Layne nodded. "Good work, bud."

Layne could swear he saw Jasper's chest expand.

Then Jasper asked, "Do you know him?"

Yeah, Layne knew him. He also knew that Stew bet the dogs and obviously wasn't any good at it.

"Yeah," Layne answered.

"Am I right? Is he Mr. Bad Vibe?"

Jas was right. Carlito was Mr. Bad Vibe and it wasn't a good sign a loan shark was showing up at the house to make collections.

"You see this guy again, Jasper, you're invisible. So's your brother."

"What about Mom?"

"Was your mom there?"

"No, she was still at work."

"You tell me if he ever shows and your mother is there, yeah? In fact, you tell me if you ever see him again at all, I don't care where you are."

Jasper nodded. Then he asked, "Will you…" He paused. "Will you take care of it?"

Layne nodded. "Yeah, Jas. I'll take care of it."

"You'll take care of Mom?"

Layne drew breath into his nose. Then he answered, "I'll take care of your mom."

That golden light came into his son's eyes and he whispered, "Thanks, Dad."

Jasper started to turn to the door but Layne caught him by calling his name and Jas turned back. "How was your date with Keira last night?"

Jas was playing it cool. During pizza he'd asked her but waited until the next Saturday to take her out. Last night was their second date. That didn't mean they didn't text each other seven hundred times a day and hang together during pizza after subsequent games, but they met there then Jasper took her home. He was playing it cool, his kid was good.

A slow smile spread on Jasper's face, and watching it widen, Layne knew exactly how the date went.

Then, surprising him, Jasper shared, "She's a nut. She cracks me up. She'll do anything, say anything. But I reckon I gotta keep on my toes. When I say she'll do anything and say anything, she'll do *anything* and say *anything*." Layne knew by the look on his boy's face that this was in no way a bad thing. Jasper's smile changed before he went on, "It's good she hooked up with me. She such a nut, she needs a badass to take her back."

Layne chuckled.

Even at his age, Jasper had serious experience with girls, but Jasper had no idea what he was up against with Keira. Layne hadn't spent a lot of time around Keira Winters but he figured his son was not wrong and therefore Joe Callahan's life was likely a living hell with that teenage spitfire in it. If Cal got it that Jasper was taking his girl's back, Jasper wouldn't have any problems with Cal. Fuck, Cal might even be grateful to share the load.

"When're you goin' out with her again?" Layne asked.

"I thought, if you're cool with it, and Rocky's cool with it, I could ask her over for pasta bake this week, sometime Rocky's here. Keira totally digs Rocky. She thinks she's the bomb. I'd score huge if I made her dinner when Rocky was here."

He *would* score huge with that. The problem was, after what happened last night, Layne wasn't certain Raquel Merrick Astley was even in the country.

Even so, Layne muttered, "I'll have a word with Roc."

"Thanks, Dad."

Then Jasper didn't delay in throwing open the door and jumping out of the truck. But he treated Layne to a half wave before he disappeared into the house.

Layne stared at the door to the garage for a few beats after he lost sight of his son realizing that Jasper just shared, he'd done it without any coaxing or pushing, and he'd done it openly.

Layne drew in breath then smiled as he backed his truck out of the garage.

He drove to Rocky's, punching in the alarm code at the gate hoping they hadn't changed it. They hadn't. He drove to her unit and saw all three parking spots for apartment three were empty. He nevertheless swung into one, exited his SUV, jogged across the pavement and up the steps to her door. He pressed the buzzer and waited. Then he did it again. Then he knocked. No show, he didn't even hear movement in the house.

Slowly, the tranquility he'd felt after his talk with Jasper fading, another less enjoyable feeling invading, he walked back down the steps, pulling his cell out of the back pocket of his jeans.

He called Dave.

"Hello?"

"It's Layne."

"Well, hey there, son," Dave greeted.

"Listen, Dave, Roc and I were supposed to go pick up some shit from her old house. We got our wires crossed. I thought she was meeting me at my place but she didn't show. She's not at her place either. I figure she went over there already and Astley's over there with his girl. Do you have the address?"

There was silence, then, "He's over there?"

Layne bleeped the doors on his truck. "Yeah."

"He was supposed to take off so she could do what she had to do," Dave informed him.

"We ran into him at dinner last night and he decided he didn't want to be so cooperative," Layne explained.

There was more silence, then, quietly, "That guy's a piece of work."

"Yeah, Dave. Do you have the address?" Layne asked as he swung into the driver's seat.

"One three three Greenbriar. The Heritage."

"Got it, thanks," Layne said and disconnected, started up the truck, backed out of his space and headed to The Heritage.

He'd never been to Rocky's place but he'd been to The Heritage. He had a couple of clients who lived there. The development was exclusive, the lots large, the houses huge, the estates spread out. The space of The Heritage was vast, but there weren't a lot of homes in it. One couldn't say that the 'burg didn't have its elite but there weren't that many of them and even fewer who could afford a place on The Heritage. Most of the occupants of The Heritage worked and socialized in Indy, some of them even commuted to Chicago.

Layne didn't have trouble finding one three three Greenbriar. He stopped across the street and looked at Rocky's house. Like Merry said, it was on the manmade lake and it was a monster. He couldn't visualize a Rocky drinking beer, eating pizza, jumping up and down like a crazy woman when Tripp made his touchdown and telling her students rock stars were storytellers living in that behemoth. He could, however, visualize the Rocky of last night with that dress and those shoes living there.

One of the three garage doors was open and a shiny silver Aston Martin was in the bay. Outside in the drive was a yellow Corvette, Marissa's new toy that Layne's searches had shown that Astley had bought for her just over four weeks ago.

Rocky's Mercedes was nowhere to be seen and there were no other cars in the drive or on the street. Layne looked at the clock on his dash to see it wasn't yet eleven. She said what she had to do wouldn't take long but it had to take longer than an hour unless she went early.

He pulled out of The Heritage and went to his offices. Opening them up, he fired up his computer and looked up Chip Judd's address. He wrote it down, shut down his computer, locked down the offices and scanned the street when he went outside. Then he hit Mimi's for a coffee and to check if Rocky was in there.

She wasn't.

He swung by Josie Judd's and saw no Mercedes, not on the street or in the drive. Layne then rolled by Colt's, just in case she went to Feb or Violet.

No Mercedes.

His next stop was Dave's. No Mercedes. Next was Merry's. No Mercedes, not in the lot in front of Merry's place and, gliding through the complex, not anywhere.

Layne swung into a spot in front of Merry's unit and looked up at it. It wasn't really even a condo, the doors opened to the elements. It was an apartment complex, maybe nicer than some, not others. They called them condos because you could purchase the units even though most were rented out by their owners.

Layne sat there thinking that, apparently, during the getting to know you again part of the operation, Layne had not gotten to know Rocky very well. He was out of leads.

Layne leaned forward and pulled out his phone. He scrolled to the second number down from his recent calls file and hit go.

He put the phone to his ear and practiced deep breathing as it rang.

"You've reached Rocky's voicemail...leave me a message."

"You get this, Roc, you call me," Layne growled, disconnected, tossed the phone on the dash and headed home.

Layne lounged on his couch, his cell on the armrest, his finger tapping it.

Surrounding his feet on the coffee table was the detritus of a Sunday at home watching football with his boys. Empty chip bags. A bowl of drying out, spiced, once-melted yellow cheese. Microwave popcorn packets. Empty pop cans and beer bottles. Mostly empty boxes of cookies.

Tripp was upstairs at Layne's computer doing homework.

Jasper was in the armchair at the left of the couch marathon texting Keira, his buds and half the population of Indiana.

It was after six o'clock, night had fallen and Rocky hadn't phoned.

Layne made a decision.

Actually, he made three.

"Jas," Layne called, and Jasper's head came up. "Got things to do. Tomorrow morning, I'll give you money and you and Tripp need to swing by the grocery store after practice."

"For what?" Jasper asked, and Layne's eyes swept the coffee table before going back to his son.

"For everything," he answered and Jas grinned. "Pick this shit up before goin' to bed tonight, yeah?" Layne indicated what shit he meant by dipping his head toward the coffee table.

Jasper sighed then nodded.

"Got another job for you," Layne went on.

"What?" Jasper asked, not belligerent, asshole teenage kid, just resigned, teenage kid. He thought he'd scored more chores but he wasn't shoveling attitude.

Progress.

Layne took his feet off the coffee table, put them on the floor and leaned his elbows into his knees, his eyes never leaving his son. "I need you to get me your mom's work schedule."

Jasper straightened in his chair. "Why?"

Layne told him straight out, "'Cause I got two options with this showdown with Stew. I hit him at work, I got witnesses. I don't give a fuck about that but that shit could get back to your mom. I hit him at home, when your mom is at work, I got no witnesses and it's up to Stew whether he wants to share. I reckon he won't want to share. I'm pickin' option two. I don't know when I'll do it, but it'll help me out knowin' when your mom'll be outta the house."

Jasper stared at him awhile before nodding.

Layne nabbed his phone and pushed up from the couch, muttering, "Sooner the better, bud."

"Right," Jasper replied.

On his feet, Layne looked down at his son. "Be smart about it, yeah? I don't want her cottoning on."

"I'll be smart," Jasper assured and Layne knew he would.

"I gotta go out. I don't know when I'll be back. I'll have my cell, you need anything."

"Okay, Dad."

Layne turned toward the kitchen saying, "Later, bud."

"Later, Dad."

Layne walked to the kitchen shouting up the stairs, "Goin' out, Tripp!"

"Okay, Dad!" Tripp shouted back.

"You help your brother clean up the mess in the living room, got me?"

"Got you!"

Layne grabbed his keys, went to his truck and drove to Rocky's.

The Merc was parked in a spot.

He swung the Suburban in beside it and took his time switching off the ignition, jumping down from the truck and walking up to her apartment. He did this in an effort to control his temper.

Last night had not been good and Rocky had left in a highly emotional state that was worsened by the fact she felt humiliated after taking that fall. Even though it was absolutely not cool she disappeared, there were reasons and Layne knew he needed to handle this situation with care.

He hit her buzzer and waited. It took a while but the door opened two inches. Layne could see Rocky, hair back in a ponytail, through the shiny silver latch that secured the door.

Layne's control on his temper slipped.

"Open the latch, Rocky," he ordered.

"Layne, now's not a good time. I've got papers to grade."

His control slipped further.

"Open the latch," he repeated.

"Really, Layne, I'm being serious. This is going to take all night."

His control slipped even further.

"Open the fuckin' latch, Roc."

"I don't think—"

He lost his hold on his temper.

"Okay, then step back," he demanded.

Through the small space, he saw her eyes widen. "Why?"

"'Cause I don't want you to get hurt when I kick open the goddamned door," he gritted out.

She studied him and he saw she understood instantly now was not the time for a stare down. The door closed and immediately opened. Layne put a hand on it and shoved in, throwing the door to behind him so hard it slammed.

Rocky was retreating. Hair in that goddamned ponytail. Faded jeans hanging low on her hips and clinging in all the right places, a split in the left knee. A tight blue tee with the word "Butler" across the tits. An ace bandage wrapped tight around her right wrist.

The bandage should have served to remind him he should take a minute to calm the fuck down.

It didn't.

He advanced and she kept retreating.

"Layne—" she began, lifting up her bandaged hand.

He cut her off. "We had plans today."

She kept retreating. Layne kept advancing.

"I know but I changed my mind," she told him.

He tilted his head to the side and backed her into her kitchen. "You changed your mind?"

"Yeah, I changed my mind." She hit counter and pressed back.

Layne invaded her space and pressed in, putting a hand on the counter by either side of her waist, he tipped his head forward to look down at her.

"You think to tell me there was a change of plans?"

"I—"

"Maybe pick up one of the four times I called you?"

"Layne, it—"

"Call me back after I left a message?"

"I thought—"

"Where have you been all day?"

Her head jerked. "What?"

"Where have you been all day?"

"I...went somewhere. To think."

"Where?"

"Somewhere, Layne!" she snapped. "Would you please move back?"

"Where…have you been…all day?"

"It's none of your business, Layne. Step back!"

Layne tipped his head deeper and got into her face. "*Where the fuck have you been all day!*" he roared.

"*Step back!*" she shouted.

"Rocky, we're workin' an operation and you do *not* fuckin' *disappear* in the middle of a *fucking operation*!"

"As you can see, I was *fine!*"

"Yeah, but all day, I didn't fuckin' know that!"

"Now you do!"

He returned to his earlier subject. "Where have been all day?"

"Layne—"

"*Tell me, goddammit!*" he shouted.

"*At Mom's grave!*" she shouted back and Layne's body locked. "Step back!"

His voice had quieted when he asked, "You were at your mother's grave?"

"Yes. I go there when I have to think. Now step back."

He didn't step back. He pressed forward.

"And what were you thinkin' about Roc?"

She tossed her head, looked him in the eye and declared, "I'm quitting."

"You're quitting?"

"Yes."

"Quitting what?"

"Our operation."

"You're quitting our operation," Layne repeated.

"Yes," Rocky hissed.

Layne scowled down at her then his eyes went over her shoulder and he stared at the black tiled backsplash.

"Step back," she demanded.

He looked back at her. "You can't quit. You're my cover."

"I can. We both know that's bullshit. You can do your thing without me providing cover."

"Yeah, that was true two weeks ago. Now, since we've started this shit, the whole town's in on it and you're bonding with Rutledge, it isn't true."

"I'm sure we can figure something out."

"You're sure?" he asked.

"Yes, I'm sure," she answered.

"How sure, Roc?"

"*Very* sure, Layne. Now, I asked you, *step back*."

"Tripp says hi."

She went still and stared up at him, her face going pale.

Too pissed at that point to do anything but, Layne pushed it. "And Jasper wants me to talk to you about comin' over when he makes pasta bake for Keira. Apparently, Keira thinks you're the shit. And I know Jas thinks Keira is the shit. He wants to impress her, and he's my boy, I want him to have what he wants."

"Layne," she whispered.

"You got us all in your snare, sweetcheeks. We're bound up in it. You can't cut us loose just because of whatever-the-fuck is goin' on in that head of yours. This time, baby, with my boys in the mix, you can't cut us loose and go your merry fuckin' way because I'm not gonna *let* you cut us loose."

"Layne," she repeated on another whisper.

"You are not quitting. You are not backin' out. I know you're good at that, sweetcheeks, but I gotta disappoint you. This time you're gonna see it through to the bitter fuckin' end."

He pushed away from the counter and went to her fridge. Opening it, he saw two brown bottles of fancy-ass beer. He grabbed one and shut the fridge. He went to the counter and reckoned that she kept her utensils close to the fridge. An area where she'd prepare food, it made more sense not to have to walk far to get what she needed. He opened the drawer and found the bottle opener. He used it, flipped the cap on the counter, tossed the opener in the drawer and closed it with his hip.

Then he turned to her before taking a pull.

She was still pressed against the counter where he left her, her elbows back, the palms of her hands on the counter. Her eyes were on him and he didn't allow himself to process the look on her face.

When he dropped his hand, he said, "You'll need to stock decent beer, baby. Bud, Coors, Miller. Bottles or cans, I don't give a fuck." He lifted his bottle. "This shit sucks."

Then he walked by her and into the living room.

Two weeks and he saw that Raquel had transformed it. He didn't even know you could get furniture that quickly. Couch against the back wall, deep purple color, deep-seated and cushiony, inviting. A chair in a dark gray with a big footrest in front of it, just as inviting. A big, black lacquered, square coffee table, papers spread all around, her kids' work. A big-bowled wineglass, half-filled with red wine and some red pens amongst the papers. Candles here and there, all of them burning, making the place smell like berries.

He walked to some black lacquered shelves next to the fireplace where there were some books and a stereo. He belatedly noticed that music was playing. Rock 'n' roll, but playing soft. He switched off the music, spotted the remote sitting at the base of a stylish lamp on an end table, also black lacquer. He walked to it, nabbed it, turned on the flat screen that was on a stand in the corner and discovered she'd already had cable installed. He found a game and stretched full body on her couch.

It was comfortable, the cushions soft, his body sinking in. Fuck, he could sleep there. He grabbed a big toss pillow patterned in grays, purples and blacks, shoved it behind his head on the armrest and his eyes went to the game.

He was making a point.

Rocky missed his point.

It took her a while but he felt her approach, and even though she wasn't in his line of sight, he felt her presence when she came to stand beside the coffee table.

"Maybe you should go home," she suggested quietly.

"Nope," Layne replied, keeping his eyes on the TV. He took a sip of beer then dropped his hand and rested the bottle on his abs. "Rutledge lives in unit G, apartment one. I didn't look when I drove in, but he's out, he has to drive by your parking spots. He's in, he can see my truck from his front window."

She didn't respond. He heard her move but didn't look at her. Some minutes later, he saw her left hand reach for the glass of wine. His eyes slid to her and he saw her sitting cross-legged on the floor by the coffee table, head down to the papers, a red pen in the fingers of her bandaged hand, her left elbow on the table, wineglass held high.

"What's with the bandage, Rocky?" he asked.

She didn't look up from her papers when she answered, "I'm fine."

"That wasn't what I asked, sweetcheeks."

Her head turned to him and she put down her glass of wine. She wasn't wearing makeup and it sucked, but he couldn't help but think he hadn't seen her looking prettier since he got home.

"It was hurting last night," she answered. "I woke up and my wrist was swollen. I went to the clinic first thing. They did a scan and said it was sprained. They bandaged it and gave me some pain pills. Nothing big. I'm fine."

Then she looked back down at her papers.

Layne looked back at the TV, took another sip of beer and tried not to think of Rocky injuring herself in a desperate attempt to get away from him and Melody, waking up all alone with a swollen wrist, taking herself to the goddamned clinic, again alone, and being in physical pain.

He tried not to think of it but he fucking failed.

Minutes slid by and he heard her say softly, "I'll come over...for Jasper."

Layne kept his eyes on the TV. "Right."

"Just tell me when to be there," she went on.

"You got it."

She fell silent.

More time slid by before she asked, "Have you had dinner?"

"Nope, but I had enough junk food watchin' games with my boys to preserve my body until the end of time."

She hesitated before going on, "Do you want something decent in your stomach?"

His head turned to her. "You're hungry, Roc, eat. But I'm good."

"I'm not hungry," she whispered.

He held her eyes.

She looked to her papers.

Her thick ponytail had fallen forward, over her shoulder, curling around her neck.

Looking at it, Layne had the overwhelming urge to roll off her couch and pull the holder out of that ponytail then pick her up, take her back to her couch and press her body deep into it, under his, then bury his hands in her long hair and, after doing other things to her, burying his cock in *her.*

He didn't want this urge but he had to admit he had it.

He lifted his beer, took another slug then rolled off the couch. He put the beer on an open space free of papers on the table. Her head tilted far back to look at him but he straightened, scanned her place and saw her keys on the counter.

He walked to them, grabbed them, and when he turned toward the door, he saw her torso twisted to look at him.

"I'll be back," he muttered, left the apartment, jogged down the stairs and to his truck. He bleeped it open, went into the passenger side, pulled down the door to the glove compartment and nabbed his smokes. He jogged back, let himself in and walked directly to the balcony doors without looking at her, bending slightly to drop the keys on the table on his way. "I'm havin' a smoke."

He twisted the fancy-ass lock, noting, with some annoyance, that if someone managed to scale the wall to the balcony, not hard with tall trees on either side of it, they could break a window, reach in and open that lock. An exterior door like that should open only with a key. His eyes lifted, checking for security sensors and he saw them on the windows but not on the doors. Asinine mistake and shoddy work. No one would shatter those huge glass plates to breach the apartment. They'd go through the fucking door.

He set this aside to talk to her about later, pushed down the handle and stepped out on the balcony. He pulled the lighter out of his packet of smokes, shook out a cigarette, put it between his lips, cupped his hand around the lighter and fired up.

He slid the lighter back into the packet, set it on the railing, lifted his head and exhaled smoke, scanning her view and wondering what to do next.

One could say he had *not* handled that with care and they were in this for the long haul. He was sensing she definitely got where he was coming from, but something had to give. They couldn't go on like this. Firstly, he needed to know a lot more about her life and he didn't want to know. He did, he admitted, but he also *didn't*. But he had to keep her safe while this shit was going down, and knowing the little he knew about her life, her friends and her schedule, that would be difficult. Secondly, they couldn't work under this cloud. The air had to be cleared and he didn't want to do that either.

He looked from the view to her. She was still looking down at her papers, but she was holding her right wrist in her left hand and doing it gingerly.

Fuck.

She was in pain and she thought his attention was elsewhere. She didn't do that when he was lying on the couch, she did it when he was outside. She was hiding it from him. She didn't want his attention and she didn't want it with the added reminder of how she hurt her wrist.

He looked back to the view. He should give her that play. He knew he should.

But he wasn't going to.

He took another drag and prepared to flick the mostly unsmoked cigarette out into the landscaping when he saw movement.

He stilled, only half a moment, then he brought the cigarette to his lips and took another drag. He kept smoking as he pretended to scan the view, lost in thought, when he saw him. Mostly hidden by a bush on the top swell of a hill, a man with a camera snapping photos.

What the fuck?

Excellent positioning, the hill was high; he was looking right into Rocky's apartment.

Jesus.

Layne finished the cigarette, flicked the butt out into the landscaping and made a decision.

He turned, his eyes going to each side of the windows as he opened the door. She had no blinds.

She was getting blinds.

He entered and her head came up.

"If you're going to smoke, I have ashtrays. You can take one out with you."

He didn't answer and skirted the coffee table.

Her head went back as he got closer.

She kept talking, "I have garden furniture ordered from Violet at the Garden Center. It'll be delivered—"

She stopped speaking when he bent double and put his hands to her pits. Dragging her legs out from under the coffee table, he lifted her to her feet.

"Layne. What—?"

"We're bein' watched," he mumbled right before his head came down and his mouth found hers.

His hands went to her hips and he kissed her, long, hard and closed-mouthed as she held on to his shoulders. Then he turned her. Backing her into the couch, she went down and he went down on top of her.

"Layne," she whispered, her fingers clutching his shoulders.

"Go with it, sweetcheeks, he has a camera," Layne muttered against her lips, ignored her body going stiff under his, he slanted his head and kissed her again.

Her lips tasted like wine and he liked that taste. The longer he kissed her, even without tongue, the softer they got, the stiffness went out of her body and it melted into his. Because of that, he did something on instinct and it was something stupid. Stupid and dangerous.

He touched his tongue to her lips.

They opened instantly.

Heat flooded his blood and that blood rushed to his cock.

His tongue slid between her lips and the show was over. This kiss was real. It was real and it was fucking *great*. She tasted good and she kissed not in the hungry way she kissed when they were together. She kissed like in his dreams, giving, her tongue dancing with his, not dueling, her body relaxed under his, their legs tangling. He gave up her lips to taste her neck as one hand went down and under her shirt then up the soft skin of her back, skin he'd wanted to touch since he saw it last night. His other hand went to the band in her hair, tugged it out and then buried itself in her thick, fucking mane, and after he did this, her hands did much the same.

He wanted her mouth again, took it, and when he did she arched her back, pressing her tits into his chest, her soft hips into his hard ones, and she moaned against his tongue.

He growled against hers.

Then he took the kiss further, made it deeper, wetter, harder, demanding more from her and she gave it.

He felt her nails drag his back and he groaned into her mouth, his lips sliding down her jaw and her head turned so her mouth was at his ear.

"God," she breathed. "I forgot how good you tasted. Tobacco."

At her words, his hand fisted in her hair, he held her head to kiss her again, his other hand moving in, over her ribcage and up, to cup her breast, his thumb rubbing hard against her tight nipple.

Her body jerked, then arched and she whimpered into his mouth.

Fuck, but she was hot.

Too hot.

This was not fucking good.

He tore his mouth from hers, pressed his face into her neck and tried to order his thoughts. This was difficult with her breast in his hand, her body under his and her hand trailing his back.

He rolled to the side, partially off her, his hand leaving her breast to move to her waist, and he said against her neck, "Rocky."

Her hand kept moving for a second then froze.

He gave her a minute, giving the same to himself, and she slid her hand out from his shirt to disappear entirely, her bandaged hand moving from his hair to rest lightly on his neck. She turned her head away.

He lifted his up. "You okay?"

She was looking at the coffee table but she nodded.

"Roc," he called, and she waited a few beats then righted her head to look at him.

Lips pink and bruised, cheeks flushed, but her eyes were blank. He was lying mostly on top of her but she was hiding from him.

He decided to give her that play.

Then he sought to lighten the atmosphere.

"You're a nut, sweetcheeks. Only you would think cigarettes taste good," he joked.

"You smoked when we were together, Layne. You were my first kiss, my first everything. I'm conditioned to think they taste good," she replied, her voice funny in a hard way.

He took that shot to the gut, and while he recovered, she slid out from under him.

He got up on a forearm and watched her grab her wineglass and walk into the kitchen. She went to the bottle of wine opened on the counter and poured more in. She took a sip, her back to him, dropped her hand and stayed where she was.

He pulled in a breath, rolled off the couch and went to her.

She didn't move so he fitted his front into her back and rested a hand on the counter in front of her.

"You gotta put in blinds, sweetcheeks."

"Yes," she agreed quietly.

"You also need to text me the number to the management office of this place. They need to send someone to put in sensors on your doors and change the locks. You've got vulnerability there."

He felt her body stiffen in front of him, and he put the hand not on the counter to her hip. If someone was still watching, they'd think this was a post-make out session, lover's conversation.

"Rocky," he called.

"I'll text you the number."

Layne pulled in breath and his fingers at her hip pressed in.

"We gotta talk about what happened on the couch."

"Not now," she replied instantly.

"Roc—"

"Not now, Layne, I have papers to grade."

He dropped his mouth to her ear. "We got lots of shit to discuss, baby. What just happened, last night—"

She cut him off. "I'm not talking about last night."

"You are. *We* are."

She turned to face him and her head tipped back. "I'm not talking about last night, Layne."

He moved into her, pressing her back into the counter. He took her wine from her hand and put it on the counter. Then he put his hand on her neck.

"The air has to be cleared," he stated quietly.

"No, it doesn't."

"It does, Rocky."

Her eyes narrowed.

"No. It. Does. *Not*," she hissed.

He studied her then he relented. "I'll let that go for now, but only to let you get a pain pill."

"I don't need a pain pill."

"I saw you holdin' your wrist, sweetcheeks."

"I know when I need a pain pill, Layne. I don't need you to tell me."

"You landed hard on it," he reminded her and she surprised him by suddenly coming up on her toes and into his face, her face going tight with anger.

"Yes, *Layne*, I remember," she snapped.

"Then take a goddamned pain pill," he shot back, her anger tipping his.

"God!" she exploded. "Will you leave me alone?"

"No," he returned. "You took all day to be alone."

"Go to hell, Layne," she hissed.

He leaned further into her. "That attitude you're servin' up, sweetcheeks, evidence we need to clear the fuckin' air."

Her shoulders shot straight and she tossed her hair, dislodging his hand so he put it to the counter beside her.

Then she said, "You want the air clear, okay. Here it is, or at least what's bothering me right now. Bothering me enough to serve up my *attitude*," she bit out. "See, last night was not good. You know it. I know it. We don't have to go there. But, even you knowing how *not good* it was, you came here and got in my face. That wasn't nice, you doing that when I know you *know*, but I can take it because I deserve it. Then, on that couch, shit went down and you proved that you haven't changed in eighteen fucking years."

He felt his neck muscles contract and he forced his voice to a whisper when he asked, "What the fuck?"

"You had yourself a leggy brunette last night, baby." Her voice was an insinuation mixed with deep sarcasm. "And as far as I know, she's waiting back at your house and you *still* took what you could get from me on my couch."

"Not that it's any of your goddamned business, Raquel, but Melody left ten minutes after you did."

"I don't really care. You're right. That's none of my business."

"You just threw it in my face, baby."

She blew out some air before she said, "It's not my business, but you should also know I don't believe a word that comes out of your mouth."

"And why the fuck would you not believe me?"

"Because, *Layne*," she ground out. "Jarrod replacing me so fucking quickly wasn't the first time I experienced that, was it? Gabrielle Weil was carrying around your son within *weeks* of me leaving our bed."

Instantly, Layne's back snapped straight and he stepped a foot away from her.

Then he whispered, "What?"

"And she was wearing your ring in less than a year."

His neck muscles weren't just tight, every muscle in his frame had turned solid.

"You are shitting me." He was still whispering in an effort not to shout.

"No," she returned immediately. "I'm not. So don't come off all wounded ego that I broke your heart and left you to lick your wounds because we both know that's not true. You got over me pretty fucking quickly and moved on. You acted to Dad and Merry and everyone like your world was rocked, but it wasn't."

"You left me, Rocky, and after doin' it, you didn't get to tell me where to put my dick."

"You are correct. My point is, you don't get to throw in my face what happened when you don't *understand* what happened and you moved on and got something better out of it."

He lifted a hand to curl his fingers around the back of his neck, staring at her hard and asking, "Are you insane?"

"Jasper has been in my school for three years, Layne, and for a semester in my class *every day*. I've been around kids for a long fucking time. I know a good kid when I see him and I *know* you got something better out of it. Knowing Tripp only upped it."

Fuck him, but she wasn't exactly wrong.

She also wasn't right.

Before he could reply, she finished.

"I'm going to take a bath and you're welcome to finish your game, but you should know, I'm not coming down here again until I know you're

gone. We'll get through this because we have to, but no more of that shit."
She pointed to the couch. "Whoever was out there was probably hired by
Jarrod. What we did to him last night made him angry and he is not nice
when he gets angry, and I'll bet, just about five seconds after he saw us walk
in last night, he decided to play dirtier than he's already been playing. And,
heads up, he's been playing dirty even after putting her in my bed before
there was time to change the sheets. But with our current situation, I'll do
my part, you do yours, and we retreat back to what we've been doing the
last two weeks. That was working. But this," she waved her hand between
them, "is as clear as the air is going to get. You don't like it, tough. You're
just going to have to deal with it."

Then she walked around him, out of the kitchen and kept her head
bent to her feet as she walked up the stairs and landed her last. "Tuesday's
good for me for pasta bake and Keira. I'll be at your house at six."

Then he lost sight of her at the top of the stairs.

Layne kept his hand at his neck, clenching and unclenching, trying to
release the tension in the muscles there as he stared at the top of the stairs.

His eyes fell to her wineglass and he resisted the urge to throw it across
the room.

Then he turned on his boot and stalked out of her apartment, slamming the door when he went.

Nine

PROCEED WITH CAUTION

The next afternoon, Layne sat at his desk and activated his phone. Using his thumb, he typed in, "Management office, The Brendel. Number. Now." Then he sent the text to Rocky.

He clenched his jaw as he turned off the phone.

You were my first kiss, my first everything.

Her words from last night sounded in his head.

He was, even as pretty as she was, he was her first kiss and her first lover. For her eighteenth birthday, he gave her a pair of emerald-cut emerald stud earrings, her birthstone. She'd given him her virginity.

He was her first date, her first kiss, her first boyfriend. She had friends and she was popular at school, but she didn't date, never got close to a boy, until him.

And she let him in immediately. Out of respect for her father, but mostly for her and because of her inexperience, he'd played it cool the first year and he'd taken great pains her first time. He couldn't say he was entirely successful. He could say he made her come before he caused her pain so at least she knew she had something to look forward to.

And she looked forward to it. Christ, it was like breaking a seal then what was held in exploded all over the place.

But she'd never even kissed a guy, until him.

He'd never thought about it, not once, except to thank his stars and consider himself lucky.

Now, he thought, what the fuck was up with *that?*

He flipped and twisted the phone around in his fingers and stared at his desk, jaw clenched, mind filled not just with last night but with a lot of shit. A lot of shit from the last three weeks and a lot of shit from nearly two decades ago, and he only looked up when the security beep sounded.

His eyes went to the monitor and he saw Merry, a white coffee cup in each hand, coming up the stairs.

Answers.

He'd called Merry half an hour ago and told him he wanted a meet, but he didn't tell him why.

Layne was going to get answers and he loved Merry, but if his friend held out on him, after the shit that came out of Rocky's mouth last night, Layne would resort to any means necessary.

He kept flipping his phone around in his fingers as he heard the front door open and close and then he saw Merry coming through the door to his office. He was smiling but he got one look at Layne and his brows went up.

"I'm guessin' you aren't havin' a good day," Merry remarked, walking straight in.

"You'd be guessin' right," Layne agreed.

Merry put Layne's coffee in front of him and sat opposite him, lifting a leg to hook his ankle on his knee.

"Well, join the club, brother. Today is officially shit," he declared before he sucked back some joe.

"You got problems?" Layne asked and Merry nodded.

"But let's get your shit outta the way first. Why'd you call? Somethin' up?"

"A lot of things are up. It sucks I got shot because it delayed me hiring a receptionist. I got so much up I can't fuckin' keep track of it all."

"Break it down for me, brother."

Layne palmed the phone and leaned back in his chair. "Stew's shit is tied to Carlito."

Merry stared at Layne a second then his eyes rolled to the ceiling. "Oh boy."

"Damn straight," Layne said.

Merry's eyes rolled back to Layne. "You know how much he's into him for?"

"I don't know shit. Jasper saw Carlito take a collection *at the house.*"

Merry's face grew dark, his ankle left his knee and he sat forward, putting his coffee cup on Layne's desk. "Tell me you are fuckin' shittin' me."

"I'm not."

Merry looked toward the floor, breathing out, "Motherfucker."

"You know Stew? He play the dogs or is he sittin' a game?"

Merry looked back up. "Dogs. Before Gabby, Stew was at the track every weekend. Since her, I'm guessin' he's at the track every weekend she's workin'."

Layne nodded. "Right."

"I don't need to tell you, a collection at the house—" Merry started.

Layne cut him off. "He's in deep."

"Okay then, I don't need to tell you bein' in deep with Carlito—"

Layne cut him off again. "Isn't fuckin' good."

"That man would break his grandma's fingers if she borrowed a five spot to buy some cat food and didn't pay it back on time," Merry concurred.

"I don't give a fuck about Stew or how deep he is. What I give a fuck about is that this shit is comin' to the house my boys live in and my ex has been workin' her ass off to keep nice for them and that I've been sending money for twelve years to keep over their heads. I want his ass out. I wanna know what he's into Carlito for and why they're gettin' so far behind for so many months, this shit isn't goin' away. Jas says he saw Stew hand over an envelope stuffed full. Where the fuck is he getting that kind of cash, and if he's handin' that shit over, why is the pressure still on?"

"I know it's Carlito, I got some boys I can give calls. I'll run this down for Colt and Sully, Mike and Sean too. We'll see what we can shake out," Merry offered.

"Good," Layne replied.

"Sorry you gotta deal with this shit, brother, but I'm afraid I gotta lay more on you," Merry told him.

Layne stared and didn't say a word. He had other things to talk to Merry about but he'd take whatever Merry had to dish out and move to the important shit later.

So he invited, "Lay it on me."

Merry sat back. "Well, this morning, I got word from a friend, who has a friend who's been hired by Jarrod to investigate you and Rocky."

There it was. Rocky was right.

"Not a surprise, Merry. I saw him taking pictures into Rocky's house when I was there last night. She called it, knew exactly why he was there. The only problem with that shit is he's usin' up money she should get in the divorce settlement with this garbage. He's got a girl who looks like she kissed her teenage years good-bye about a month ago in his bed and Rocky has been outta that house for months. Her bein' with me isn't gonna get him shit."

He watched Merry's lips thin then he said, "She would call it, seein' as I phoned her during her lunch hour to give her the heads up and then I got her to share what she's not been sharin' with anyone but Dad."

That did not sound good. Raquel shared everything with Merry. If she was keeping something from him, it was something bad, as in, something that would make good ole boy Garrett Merrick go ballistic.

"What?" Layne asked.

"Where should I start?" Merry asked back.

"Garrett," Layne said low.

"Okay, first, he's moved their money. *All of it.*"

Layne's back straightened in his chair. "Come again?"

"Drained their joint accounts, bank, investment and liquidated stock portfolios. Opened up new accounts in his name only and deposited the money there."

That didn't come up in his searches.

"When?" Layne bit off.

"Last week. She started buyin' shit for her apartment, he cut her off. Started there, she found out on Saturday when she tried to buy something that he canceled her credit cards. She only has two, but they're also joint and he's canceled them both."

"Fucking shit," Layne ground out.

"Unh-hunh," Merry nodded.

"What the fuck are her attorneys doing?"

"What they can, which isn't much since he's refusing to meet. You know, brother, the wheels of justice don't roll, they grind. Their court date isn't for five and a half months."

"He can't take all the money like that, Merry," Layne clipped.

"He can until the powers that be tell him to give it back," Merry returned.

"You're wrong, Merry. He can't do that. He pulls this shit, Rocky's attorneys can move to have his assets frozen."

"I'm right, Layne, because Dr. Astley isn't just Dr. Astley. Why do you think their court date is buried for five and a half months? She'll be lucky to see that, big man. They'll postpone and delay until she's desperate. He doesn't just make money, he *comes* from it. These boys who got Roc's life in their hands aren't in his pocket, they *grew up together*. They're brothers, brother, like *you* and *me*."

"Goddammit!" Layne exploded, pushing back and out of his chair. Curling his fist around his phone, he turned to the window and stared out at Main Street, his fists to his hips.

"I'm guessin' from that reaction she didn't share with you," Merry noted.

"No, she didn't share," Layne told the window. "She said he was playing dirty, she just didn't say how."

"Now you know."

Layne made a decision and turned to face his friend.

"Names," he growled.

"What?"

"You said he was bangin' every nurse on staff, I want names. I want the name of every woman he even looked at too long since two seconds after he laid eyes on Rocky."

Merry smiled and it was cruel. "Not enough paper in the 'burg for that list, Tanner."

"I'll order a box for you online, have it delivered to your condo."

Merry nodded, still smiling, but the cruelty had gone out and humor had seeped in.

"You might find time to walk across your street," he suggested. "Natalie Ulrich isn't Dr. Astley's biggest fan considering he's not just a dick, he's an arrogant dick, and if he isn't bonin' the nurses, he's givin' them shit. Emma's friends with Natalie and Emma tells me Natalie's in throes of ecstasy that Rocky's Merc is in your drive. Apparently, she's big into romance novels and she's thinkin' one's playin' out on her very own street."

"Natalie just got scratched on the top of my to-do list," Layne muttered and his phone chimed in his hand.

He dropped his head and saw that Rocky had sent him the number. Nothing else, just the digits.

Fuck.

He tossed the phone on his desk, sat back down, looked at Merry and got down to the important shit.

"Remember when I told you everything was fine between me and Roc?" he asked and watched Merry's body get tight right along with his jaw.

"Yeah." The syllable was forced out.

"Well it's not."

Merry closed his eyes and whispered, "I knew it. Fuck."

"I need answers, Merry."

Merry opened his eyes but he might as well have kept them closed because he wasn't giving a thing away.

"Do not shut down on me, brother," Layne warned, his voice low and quiet.

Merry looked him in the eyes and then whispered, "I can't, Tanner."

"You will, Garrett," Layne returned. "Somethin' is *not* right and we can't move forward unless I sort that shit out." Merry shook his head. "I'm not askin' you, I'm tellin' you. I need answers."

"Layne, I can't give you answers." Layne opened his mouth to speak but Merry leaned forward quickly. "I want to, right? Okay? I want to. But, seriously, she would not be pissed if I gave those answers to you. She would be gone. Not gone as in take off and move to Canada gone. Gone *for me*. She'd cut me out, Tanner. No joke. She would cease to exist for me and, big man," he leaned further forward, his eyes glued to Layne's, "you know how that feels."

"She's in pain," Layne informed his friend and Merry's eyes closed again. "Look at me, goddammit." Merry's eyes opened. "I have no clue how to play this and the plays I've been makin' either do not work for her or they don't work for me."

"Only advice I can give is proceed with caution."

"No shit? Thanks for that, buddy, that helps a whole fuckin' lot," Layne clipped.

"You didn't hear me, Tanner," Merry said quietly. "Proceed with caution and the operative word in that is *proceed.*"

Layne felt his chest get tight. "What?"

Merry sat back. "I can't give you more."

"You can and you will."

"Tanner, seriously."

"Yeah, Garrett, seriously."

"I can't—"

Layne leaned forward. "We went out to Swank's Saturday night. I walked into my house with her after, knowin' the biggest fool thing I could do was ask her to stay for a drink at the same time thinkin' about nothin' other than how to get her to stay for a drink. We walk in, the lights go on and we find out a friend of mine from LA was payin' a surprise visit. She's standin' there wearing practically nothing but shoes and a smile. Rocky sees her, she's so fired up to get the fuck out of there, she fell during her run for the door. Went down so hard she sprained her wrist. Before she left, she looked at me, Garrett, she looked at me with pain and tears in her eyes and they weren't from hurting her wrist. That pain...that pain in her eyes shone from her fuckin' soul. I'd get it the next night when I threw her leavin' me in her face and she threw Gabby in mine. I'm tellin' you right now, people do not hold on to this shit. Not for this long. It's like it happened fuckin' yesterday. I understand that pain I saw because I *feel* it every *goddamned time* I *look* at her. It's been eighteen fucking years. That shit is *not* right. There is something I do not know, something that matters. It mattered then and, *brother,* it still matters now."

Merry stared at him and there was pain in his eyes too, Layne saw it, pain for Raquel and pain for Layne.

"All I can tell you, Tanner, is that leaving you broke her."

"Then why the fuck did she leave?"

Losing it, Merry slammed a fist into his armrest. "I can't *tell* you, damn it!"

"Why?"

"I just can't."

"*Why?*" Layne roared.

"*I can't tell you!*" Merry roared back. "But I'll tell you this, leaving you broke her but she did it for a reason, buddy, she did it for a good fuckin' reason. All right? Then you knocked up Gabby and I get that, I'm a man, I get it. Even Dad got it. Rocky did *not*. What was broken, shattered. I watched it. Dad watched it. We couldn't do shit about it. She didn't pick up the pieces, man. She's *never* picked up the pieces."

Merry leaned toward his desk and kept going.

"You wanna know why Jarrod Astley is bein' such a dick?" he asked.

He didn't let Layne answer, he kept talking.

"Because he had heaven in his hands, he knew it, but it was floating just above his reach. It was right there, in his hands, but he couldn't touch it. She never loved him. She picked him *because* he was a dick, she knew he was a dick and she knew she could hold herself clear of that. That didn't mean he didn't want her, but she never gave herself to him. But the fucker didn't try. He did everything wrong because he's an asswipe, that's his problem. He might have been able to get in there if he wasn't such a dick. But he was. He's the type of man who doesn't see his own faults. He blames others and he blames Rocky, and I'll bet my pension, brother, he also blames *you*. No one in this 'burg over fourteen years old doesn't know the Raquel Merrick and Tanner Layne bittersweet love story. With Roc workin' at that school and bein' how she is, that lore is passed on the first day of freshman class. And Astley's had that in his face for more than ten years."

Listening to Merry, Layne's chest was moving like he'd just finished a two hundred yard dash. But even with all he was getting, he was still getting nothing.

He informed Merry of that fact. "All you're givin' me is more questions, Garrett."

"Then find out the answers, Tanner, but the only place you can get them is from Roc and, like I said, *proceed with caution*. But, fuck, man, whatever you do, for your sake and hers, just…fuckin'…*proceed*."

They stared at each other and Layne heard what he was saying.

But he wasn't twenty-four and life wasn't that simple.

"I got two boys who could get caught up in this shit, brother," Layne said softly.

"I hear you," Merry replied, just as softly.

"I put the effort into this, it goes bad, I'm not the only one gets kicked in the teeth."

"I hear you."

"With that reminder, you got different advice?"

Merry shook his head and repeated, "Proceed."

"Shit, man, do you know what you're tellin' me to do?"

Merry held his eyes. Then his face went funny in a way Layne couldn't read, but the only way he saw it was fear.

"I'm givin' you a bonus," he whispered, and Layne felt his chest squeeze as he waited for Merry to go on. "Those wounds she's got, they bleed and they bleed *deep*. Only once did those wounds dry up and that was for three years, twenty-one years ago."

Layne closed his eyes.

He opened them again when Merry spoke and he saw Merry was standing, coffee cup in his hand.

"You heal her again, Tanner, you got my eternal gratitude," he whispered then smiled. It was small and it was shaking. "And I'll throw in my Harley."

Then, without another word, he left Layne's office.

Layne turned his head and, on the monitors, he watched Merry walk down the stairs.

Then he sat back in his chair and rested his head on the back of it to look at the ceiling.

He closed his eyes.

Then he made a decision.

He grabbed his phone and called the management office at The Brendel, identified himself as Rocky's boyfriend and told them to get their security firm to her apartment to set up the sensors and change her locks. They demurred, he convinced them.

He disconnected, scrolled down his phonebook and hit go on Devin Glover, a PI he'd worked a variety of cases on a variety of occasions in a variety of locations.

Dev was long in the tooth. He was a spy during the Cold War. He taught Layne everything he knew that was worth knowing. And he was the best friend Layne had ever had.

When he disconnected from Dev, he texted Rocky. "Sensors will be set up. Contacting you. I'll be there when they do it."

He was in his SUV, navigating his development when his phone chimed.

Rocky's text, "Fine. I'll let you know."

He drove to his house, parked in his drive, but didn't bother with the garage door.

His text back, "My place. Tonight. 6. T is making Hamburger Helper."

He was walking across the cul-de-sac to Natalie's house when he got her quickly returned text.

"Sorry, papers to grade. Tomorrow. Six."

He smiled at the phone, shoved it in his pocket and lifted his fist to knock on Natalie's door.

He checked it because it swung open before he could connect.

"Hey, Tanner." She smiled.

"Natalie." He smiled back. "Got a second?"

She moved back, opening the door.

Layne walked in.

"You set up?" Layne said into the phone.

"Your couch in your office is shit, boy," Dev said back.

"I offered to put you up at a hotel," Layne reminded him.

"Hotel beds are shittier than your couch," he shot back.

Dev would know. He'd slept on enough of them.

"Tomorrow night, at dinner, you meet Rocky, you'll quit your bitchin'," Layne told him. "And once I introduce you to the boys, you can have the couch in the living room."

Dev could be intense, his mood always unpredictable and Layne was working, not around to run interference during an introduction to Jasper and Tripp. He didn't want Dev showing up at the house and doing something, which Dev would do, and freaking out his sons. So he left Mimi the key to his office and gave Dev his security codes.

"She a looker?" Dev asked, his curiosity piqued. Dev was sixty-four years old and still a ladies man.

"You remember Eva?" Layne asked.

Silence for a beat then, with disbelief, "Better?"

"Oh yeah," Layne answered.

"Fuck, boy," Dev muttered then disconnected without a good-bye.

Layne threw his cell on the seat next to him. He'd just sealed the deal on his latest case and he'd been right, it hadn't taken long, less time than he expected. He just had to pull together the file, hand it over, send the invoice and get paid, and he was glad to be rid of it. It was sucking all his time. Billable hours, but with all the stuff raining down on him and Rocky, he needed to be shot of it and was pleased as fuck he was.

The entrance to his development was coming up on his right but he didn't indicate. He'd called Jasper earlier to tell him to set up pasta bake for Keira on Tuesday but they were on their own that night and he'd see them in the morning. He also shared he was spending the night over at Rocky's because her security was shit. Jasper didn't ask questions, but after informing him of this fact, Jasper's voice took on a "you the man" tone.

Layne looked at the clock on his dash. It was after midnight and he reckoned Rocky wouldn't be real fired up to answer her door to him at that hour.

Or, possibly, *any* hour.

But he couldn't give a fuck. He'd sleep on her couch tonight. Tomorrow and for as long as it took, he'd work on getting in her bed.

Or Rocky in his.

And eventually both.

He was just past the entrance to his development and about to flip his indicator light on to take the left into Rocky's complex when he saw a

Mercedes of her make, model and color pull out in front of him, and when his eyes swept the plates, he saw it was hers.

"What the fuck?" he whispered, moved his fingers from the indicator, kept a distance and followed.

His eyes went back to the dash. Twelve oh nine. Where the fuck was she going at twelve oh nine?

He followed her into town. She turned left on Green. He trailed her and drove past her when she turned into the Christian Church parking lot.

"Fuck me," he muttered, now knowing what she was doing out at twelve oh nine. He swung the next left, continuing to mutter, "Rocky, baby, I find you lookin' for trouble, I'm gonna turn you over my knee."

Layne rounded the church and blacked out his headlights as he took the alley and entered the church parking lot from the back. He saw her Merc parked in the far corner under a tree.

At least she'd parked smart, with the tree shrouding her car from light and her vehicle being black, you had to be looking to see it.

He scanned the lot and the church and saw no Rocky.

He parked by her car, unbuckled his seatbelt, leaned to his glove compartment and pulled out a Maglite and a pair of black leather gloves. Then he got out of his car, pulling on his gloves and walking through the parking lot like he, personally, owned the church.

He found the side door slightly ajar. She hadn't left it that way on purpose. The latch hadn't caught when she slipped through.

He opened the door just enough to steal through and stood still, no alarm, no beeps warning him to enter the code. He turned and saw the white of the security box by the door, the panel looking in the dark like it was hanging down. He flipped on his Maglite, shone it on the box, saw the panel was hanging down but didn't see any wires protruding. He traced the door with his Maglite and found the sensors on the door, their wires intact. He leaned into the security box and saw the lighted display saying "unarmed."

How did she disable the alarm?

He moved cautiously through the vestibule outside the sanctuary and remembered coming to this church with his mother. He hadn't been there in years. He also remembered Rocky came to this church with Merry,

Cecilia and Dave. And lastly, he remembered, when Cecilia died, Dave quit bringing the kids.

He kept the Maglite pointed down but forward and made his way through the vestibule, saw it and stopped, flipping off the Maglite.

There was a windowed room but the window was internal, no windows to the outside. Layne tried to remember and he thought it was an office, the windows facing into the vestibule. From it, a dim light shone.

He moved there, around the corner to the opened door and saw Rocky sitting on a desk chair, a file in her lap, her head bowed over it, deep in concentration, her gloved hands moving the papers, a small Maglite between her lips.

He felt at the wall and switched on the light.

She let out a small scream and pushed back, rolling the chair across the small room and slamming against a filing cabinet, her head snapping back, the Maglite falling out of her mouth and clattering to the floor as she stared at him with lips parted, eyes huge.

"Hey, sweetcheeks," he greeted.

"What are you...?" She swallowed, looked out the window into the vestibule then back at him. "What are you doing here!" she hissed.

"Funny, that's what I was gonna ask you."

She flipped the file shut and stood. "Layne, turn out the light!"

"No windows to the outside. No one knows we're in here. No one can see the light and I need it so I can see you when I throw you over my shoulder and," he leaned forward and barked, *"haul your ass outta here!"*

She jumped toward him and lifted a hand. "Keep your voice down!" she whispered.

"Baby, *no one knows we're here.*"

"Okay, so keep your voice down because you're *freaking me out!*"

He leaned back and crossed his arms on his chest. "I know what wouldn't freak you out, Roc. Bein' at home in your bed where you're supposed to fuckin' be."

"Layne—"

"How'd you disable the alarm?" he asked.

"Disable the alarm?" she asked back, looking confused and, fuck him, he was pissed, but he had to admit she looked cute.

"Yeah, Rocky. It's a church but every place has shit to steal. This place has a security system. How'd you bypass it?"

"I punched in the code," she told him.

He stared at her.

Then he repeated, "You punched in the code."

"Well…" she said. "Yeah."

"How'd you get the code?"

"Layne—"

"Are you *not* gettin' that I don't let shit go?" he asked. "How'd you get the code?"

"Well…" she trailed off and looked into the vestibule.

"Raquel," he warned.

Her eyes shot to him. "Okay, well, do you know Sharon Reynolds?"

"Do I need to know her for this story to go faster?"

Her eyes narrowed but she kept talking. "She works in the office here."

"And?" he asked when she didn't go on.

"And, she also works in the office at the school. She's part-time for both."

"Ah," Layne said, his head tipping back and his gaze hitting the ceiling.

"Anyway," Rocky said sharply and Layne's eyes went back to her. "I remembered her complaining once that the pastor is a security freak and changes the alarm codes so often she never remembers them. She comes in every once in a while when no one is around and has to punch them in and she's gotten them wrong so many times and set off the alarm, now she writes them down and keeps them in her wallet."

"Reason one for the pastor to be a security freak and reason one to lose his office lady," Layne noted.

"Layne!" she snapped.

"So, you got the code how?"

"I, um…" She stopped and bit her lip.

"Baby—"

She interrupted him quickly, "When everyone in the office was at lunch, I went to her desk and got into her purse."

"Fuck me," Layne whispered.

"No one saw!" she cried.

"Okay, how'd you get the door open?"

"Shouldn't we be, I don't know, taking pictures of the personnel file or something?" she asked.

He dropped his arms and took a step toward her.

She took a step back, putting her hand up and saying quickly, "Okay." She dropped her hand and explained, "Sharon's always losing her keys. She's famous for it. She leaves them everywhere. It's crazy. So, um…while I was in her purse, I uh…kinda nabbed them."

Layne closed his eyes.

"It's okay," she assured him and he opened his eyes. "She was going on and on this afternoon about how she," Rocky tucked the file under her arm, lifted her hands and did air quotation marks, "*lost* her keys and tomorrow I'll just," she did air quotation marks again, "*find* them."

All right, it was safe to say he was done.

"Rocky, what'd I tell you about this shit?" he asked.

"Layne—"

"Put the file back and get your ass to your car."

"Layne—"

He leaned into her. "Do it or I *carry* your ass to your car."

"I think he's doing something to the girls," she whispered and Layne leaned back.

"Come again?"

She shook her head and stepped forward. "I heard it today, in the bathroom, two freshmen talking through the stalls. One of them is Alexis McGraw. She's a pretty little thing, but about twenty years older than she actually is. She comes to Youth Group here and I heard her bragging about sharing her gum with the Youth Minister."

"So?"

"It had been chewed."

Oh fuck.

"And they didn't use their fingers when they handed it off," Rocky finished.

Damn.

"Could she be lying?" Layne tried but not holding much hope in the attempt.

Rocky took in a breath. "She's older than her years and she's dying to grow up and she's obvious about being impatient for that to happen. So, yes, she could be telling tales, but with that, and the rest of the stuff I'm hearing, I can't sit on this. I also can't start a witch hunt either if it's just a bunch of overenthusiastic kids who really, *really* like Jesus."

Layne studied Rocky while his mind went over what he knew.

That 'burg was in the Bible belt and religion was vital to that community, but that didn't translate to the roster of the Youth Group at the Christian Church that had been skidding by with around ten or fifteen members for the last thirty years adding over fifty new recruits in the last six months, most of them girls.

Fuck.

Layne made a decision, turned to the copier just inside the door and switched it on.

"What are you doing?" Rocky asked.

He turned back to her and held his hand out for the file. "We could take pictures, sweetcheeks, but it'd take forever, the copies would suck and we got a copier right here. Hand me the file and see if they keep attendance records for Youth Group."

She stared at him a second, eyes wide. Then she gave him the dimple. Finally she handed him the file and whirled around, her ponytail flying, and opened a filing cabinet drawer.

⌐⌐⌐

"I don't see anything here," Rocky noted, and Layne looked at the back of her head.

He was sitting on her couch sifting through Youth Group rosters and making note of names and how attendance wasn't inching up, it was shooting up, the vast majority of new recruits female.

Raquel was cross-legged on the floor beside his leg, head bent, the back of her neck exposed, an opened bottle of fancy-ass beer in front of her, and she was reading through the personnel file on TJ Gaines, the Youth Minister.

"You're not gonna see anything, Roc, especially if it's bogus. Not until I run his shit through my systems at the office tomorrow," he told her.

Her neck twisted and her head tilted back to look up at him.

"Do you think we should go back tomorrow night, set up camera surveillance or something?"

Yep, she was cute.

"No, *we* aren't gonna do shit. I run him tomorrow. I find dirt or even that he lied on his application, I turn it over to Merry or Colt or Drew and they run with it."

"That's it?" she asked, sounding disappointed.

He grinned at her and somewhat lied, "Baby, on TV they make my job look exciting. Most of the time it's done either sittin' at a computer or sittin' somewhere else. The action man shit is a stereotype based on total fiction."

Her eyes dropped to his middle and to hide what that said, she quickly turned and grabbed her beer, tipping her head back to take a sip.

When she put it down, she turned back to him and asked, "What if there isn't any dirt?"

"There isn't any dirt, we go deeper."

"Cameras?"

"Cameras are expensive. It'd take forever to set them up and I'd need the feeds to come into the office. I'm not set up to do that and I don't have the cash to get set up. So I'd need recording devices which are bulky, therefore hard to hide, and someone would have to go and collect the DVDs. Each time I go in, I court gettin' caught. I'm good but the law of averages on that kind of operation are never on your side. And, I go that way, I got hours of DVDs to watch, most of the shit on 'em not worth watchin', and I don't have hours to waste."

She turned her body toward him and rested her bent arm on the couch beside him. "So what do we do?"

"Again, *we* don't do shit, sweetcheeks. *I'm* workin' this case because you're worried and what *I'll* do is send in undercover recruits."

Her brows shot up. "Undercover recruits?"

Layne leaned down, reached around and grabbed her ponytail, giving it a gentle tug as he got close to her face. "Jasper or Tripp. I'm thinkin' Tripp. He'd do good at bein' a Jesus Freak. Not to mention, the Youth Group is filled with girls. He'll be all over that."

Tripp would be all over that for the girls, but mostly Tripp would be all over it because his old man asked him to do it *and* Layne would let it slip that it was a favor for Rocky.

Her eyes got bright and she whispered, "That's brilliant."

He let her hair go, handed her the rosters and she took them. "Your job is to look over those rosters and call me tomorrow with Tripp's target."

"His target?"

He nodded. "A girl on those lists," he tipped his head to the papers in her hand, "who's been goin' to Youth Group awhile. Not a new kid, someone who's been around, could have seen things, heard things."

She nodded.

Layne went on, "And she has to be open to Tripp. A shy or plain girl who'll be flattered at attention from a kid on the football team."

She shook her head. "I'm not setting up some girl to—"

He put his finger to her lips and she fell silent but he felt her lips part under his finger as he watched the intensity shift into her eyes.

In about a week, or, hope to God, sooner, he'd kiss her after seeing her eyes get like that.

Now, he took his finger from her lips.

"I'll coach Tripp. He won't leave her high and dry. This is a friendly operation with no collateral damage."

She was still looking at him with that intensity in her eyes when she whispered, "Okay."

"Now, it's late, baby. Go get me a pillow and a blanket and go to bed."

Her back went straight and she asked, "What?"

"Get me a pillow and a blanket. I'm sleepin' on your couch tonight."

She looked at the couch then at him. "Why?"

"Because it's after one in the morning, I'm wiped and you don't have any security sensors on your doors."

She looked at the doors then at him. "But—"

"Go get me a pillow and blanket."

"Layne, you live five minutes away. You could be wiped and still *walk* that far."

"All right, sweetcheeks. I can also walk as far as your bed. You got two choices, get me a pillow and a blanket or I walk upstairs to your bed."

"But—"

"Three seconds."

"Layne!"

"One."

"This is stupid," she hissed.

He started to get up. "Two."

"What about—?"

"Three," he pushed up further, but she shot up, her hands going to his shoulders to press him down.

When his ass was on the couch, she muttered, "I'll go get a pillow and a blanket."

Then she whirled around and ran up the stairs.

Layne watched her ass move as she did.

Ten

YOUR BOYFRIEND IS HOT

*H*e felt her hands on him, her mouth on him, her hair gliding across his chest following her lips.

They trailed up, then along his collarbone and his hands moved to her waist, down to her hips and in, over her ass as her lips went up his neck to his ear.

"You need to get home to your boys, baby," Rocky whispered.

Layne's eyes opened.

He was on his stomach on Rocky's couch.

He rolled to his back and he smiled.

Then he rolled off the couch and stretched, looking out her huge-ass windows, the lights from the parking lot shining in, dawn not close but not far away.

He bent and replaced the back cushions on the couch. He'd been right, he could sleep there and he did, like a log. The seat was wide, especially with the back cushions off, plenty of room. Enough, Rocky could stretch out with him to watch a game. He remembered she loved football, she loved basketball and she loved baseball. It was chick love, it was cute, but there was no denying she liked her sports.

181

He turned to her stairs and went up, his bare feet silent on the steps. He'd taken off his boots, socks and tee and slept in his jeans.

The doors in the hall upstairs were all closed. One blank wall, the wall to the outside, three doors on the inner wall, another one at the wall facing him at the end. One of them had to be a bathroom.

He tried the first and found it was a bedroom. Nothing in it that he could see.

He tried the second and it was a linen closet, mostly empty.

He tried the third and found a bathroom. He used it then washed his hands, splashed water on his face, tagged a hand towel and dried his face, seeing she'd already decorated. Little chrome boxes on a shelf over the toilet, matching chrome soap dispenser and toothbrush holder. Thick towels, a color combo of a bright green and yellow. He was pleased she'd got herself sorted out before that asshole cut off her funds. At least she had what she needed around her while she worried about not being able to make the rent.

He turned off the light, left the bathroom and didn't hesitate when he turned to her door and opened it.

He stopped when he saw her form easily in the queen-sized bed, her curtains open, the lights shining in. Her bedroom was on the third floor, not easy to peer in, but with a man trailing her with a camera, they'd be having a conversation about her keeping her curtains open.

He moved to the bed and halted, staring at her sensing something was wrong. He kept his eyes glued to her as he tried to figure out what it was.

Then it hit him.

Growing up, she'd had a double bed. He knew this because he used to make out with her on it and she'd told him she'd had it as long as she could remember. She slept in the middle of it, on her belly, on a slight slant, one arm pinned by her body, one arm thrown out, one leg hitched at the knee. She wasn't petite but she wasn't a big girl by any stretch of the imagination. Sleeping like that, however, she took up most of the bed.

He knew she slept this way because she had not changed this habit when she'd moved in with Layne. He'd had a queen-sized bed but she did not stick to her side. She slept in the middle and the way she slept meant her arm was thrown over his abs, her hitched leg was resting on his thigh and her head was on his chest or shoulder. He slept on his stomach too. But this position pinned him to his back on the bed, and since Rocky slept like the dead and didn't move all night, that meant he was pinned that way all night.

This left him with two options, he moved her and trained her to sleep on her side or he got used to it.

Layne got used to it.

If memory served, it took two days.

Now she was lying on one side of the bed, closest to the windows, and she was tucked into a ball so her frame was as small as it could be.

He stared at her and he knew she had ten years of that. Ten years of keeping her distance and protecting herself from Astley, even in her sleep.

Layne let the knowledge that she was herself with him, could sleep open and sprawled and close to him and she didn't give Astley that same gift, sweep through him and he felt another golden trail left in its wake. That might make him a dick and it sucked that she had ten years of that, but that trail shimmered through him all the same.

He walked to her side of the bed and sat down. Her hair was dark against her neck and he slid his hand under it, through her hair and against her skin, pulling its heavy weight off her neck and to the back.

She shifted at his touch, legs straightening and her head turned, even in the dim light he could see the movement was fluid.

He knew her eyes had opened when she shot up to an elbow.

"Layne?" Her voice was husky with sleep at the same time openly surprised.

"Gotta get to my boys, baby," he replied. His hand still in her hair, he cupped the back of her head.

"You could have left a note," she told him, her body starting to inch back, but his fingers curled deeper into her hair against her scalp and she stopped.

He ignored her. "You sleep okay?"

"What? Yes." The first was confused. The second was inching close to a snap. "What are you—?"

"Six o'clock for Keira and pasta bake, yeah?"

"Yes, Layne, I remember." She was pressing back against his hand.

"I'll call you when I do the searches on Gaines."

Her head stopped pressing, she kept looking up at him and he knew her mood had changed when she spoke. "Okay, but I can't take calls during class. You may have to leave me a message."

"Then call me when you can. I'll be runnin' him first thing."

"Okay."

"We gotta do it, we'll activate Tripp tonight so you'll need to find time to study those rosters if the searches come up clean."

"Okay," she repeated, this time with a small nod of her head.

"Good idea, baby, to keep your ears open if the kids start talkin' about Youth Group. Report to me what you hear, anything, whether you think it's strange or not."

"I will."

His fingers tensed against her scalp and he muttered, "Good. See you at six."

"See you at six."

"Later, sweetcheeks," he murmured as he dropped his head, hers tipped back as his came down, not to pull away but so she could watch him, and his lips brushed her parted-in-surprise ones. "Be good," he whispered against her mouth. "No covert operations today, yeah?"

"Yeah," she breathed against his lips.

He smiled against hers.

Then he let her go, got up and walked out of her room.

Tripp was sitting on his stool in front of Layne, shoveling down oatmeal that he put four sugars into before nuking. Rocky might be happy about the oatmeal but she probably would frown on the four sugars.

Jasper, not in attendance during the oatmeal discussion, was spooning up sugary cereal while standing at the end of the island.

Layne was standing in front of it, hair still wet from his shower, sipping coffee.

"So," Jasper drawled and Layne's eyes went to him to see his son's were on Layne, "Rocky's lack of security gonna mean she'll need constant vigilance?"

Layne watched his boy's lips twitch.

Jasper was giving him stick.

More progress.

"Likely," Layne muttered against the rim of his mug and took a sip while he watched Jasper's slow smile.

Layne's gaze moved to his younger boy and saw his head bowed. He was grinning into his oatmeal and his shoulders were shaking. Layne watched him struggle to compose his features, his head came up and twisted to his brother.

"Dad takes pride in his work, Jas," he announced. "He's *thorough*."

"Yeah," Jasper replied. "It's good he's so dedicated. No one will guess this whole thing is a big fake."

"Yeah," Tripp agreed. "Heck, I *know* it's a fake and even *I'm* wonderin' if it's a fake."

"I dig you, Tripp-o-matic," Jasper returned.

"Boys," Layne said low, surprised he could make his voice a warning when he was fighting back a chuckle.

Tripp's eyes shot to him then down to his oatmeal, and his shoulders started shaking again before Layne heard him snort.

Jasper didn't hide his amusement. He was flashing an open, huge, white-toothed smile.

It pissed Layne off he had to throw a wet blanket on their mood but he had to so he did.

"What's happening at practice?" Layne asked, the smile fled from Jasper's face and Tripp's shoulders slumped.

"It's smoothin' out," Jasper answered, but Tripp stayed silent.

Layne studied his older boy. "You sure?"

Jasper nodded. "He's still bein' a dick but it isn't as bad as before and they got some chick who comes to practices sometimes and sits there with a notebook. He's totally cool when she's there. Like another coach," Jasper answered and went on sharing. "Kids hate him, Dad, the whole team. Even Seth, his own son. Seth feels shit. Thinks everyone's gonna hate him because they hate his dad. He's not really as bad as he plays in the games. He just knows Tripp's better and he wants the team to win. He fucks up so his dad'll pull him, but Coach just won't."

That was another by-product of the formal complaints. Tripp had seen zero game time. None. And Jas's action had dried up. He was still on the field but never got near the ball unless he was blocking for someone carrying it. The team's morale was so low it was visible. They'd started the season undefeated but lost one, won the next by the skin of their teeth in overtime and the natives were getting restless.

Layne nodded to Jasper and looked at Tripp. "Tripp, you think things are smoothin' out too, pal?"

He heard Tripp suck in breath then he looked at his old man. "He's a dick in the locker room."

Layne stared at his son then his eyes cut to Jasper.

"Yeah," Jasper confirmed. "That chick can't come into the locker room and Coach gets bad. He lays it on me, but mostly he lays it on Tripp."

"How bad?" Layne asked.

"I can take it," Tripp answered and his eyes moved to his younger boy.

"How bad, Tripp?"

Tripp shrugged. "He's a dick, Dad, but I can take it."

Layne looked back at Jasper.

"He can take it," Jasper stated. "But still, it's bad."

Layne clenched his jaw and felt the muscle move in his cheek.

"I can take it, Dad," Tripp repeated on a whisper and Layne caught his eyes. Tripp was looking at him steady, unblinking.

He could take it.

Another indication he was Layne's son.

"You tell me if you can't," Layne ordered.

"Okay," Tripp agreed.

"No shit, Tripp, and no shame in that. Got me?"

Tripp nodded and grinned. "No shit, no shame, got you."

Layne felt his temper ebb and he grinned back. Then he looked between both of them.

"A friend is comin' to stay. He'll be here tonight. Name's Devin Glover. He's an ex-PI. Good, solid guy, he's been around the block and he taught your old man a lot." Both Layne's sons nodded. "He's also a nut," Layne went on and both Layne's sons stared at him. "Total nut. You'll get it when you meet him but, fair warning, the guy's whacked."

"He's not gonna fuck up pasta bake with Keira tonight, is he?" Jasper asked.

"It could happen," Layne answered honestly and Jas's eyes got huge. "I'll be here, bud. I've got your back and, way you describe Keira, sounds like Dev is a member of her club."

Jasper's face lost its worry and warmed. "Yeah, she'll probably think he's a scream. Her long lost grandpa."

Layne smiled at his boy and then said to them both, "School."

Tripp moved quickly, rinsing his bowl and putting it in the dishwasher. Jasper took more than his usual time in getting his shit sorted so Tripp was out the door to the Charger before Jasper was even down the stairs with his books.

Layne would understand when Jasper came up to him and handed him a piece of paper.

"Mom's schedule," he mumbled.

Layne nodded and pocketed the paper. "Good man."

Jasper nodded back and walked to the utility room door. Layne walked his coffee mug to the sink but turned to the door when Jasper called.

"Everyone in school is talking about you and Rocky," he informed Layne.

"That's kind of the point, bud," Layne replied quietly. "You cool with that?"

"Everyone thinks it's the shit, you bein' with her," Jas said instead of answering Layne's question. "Apparently, they all knew about you guys, you know…before," he went on and kept talking when Layne didn't. "Guess they never shared with Tripp and me 'cause we're your sons."

Layne didn't reply. Jasper had something to say and Layne was going to give him the chance to say it.

"Tripp said Melody was here then she was gone," Jasper noted.

Layne kept his gaze steady on his son and stayed silent.

"It's not fake, is it?" Jasper asked softly, and Layne studied his son thinking he had vastly underestimated Jasper too.

"It was, Jas. It isn't anymore."

Jasper nodded.

Layne continued, "She doesn't know that yet, though."

Jasper stared at him then his mouth twitched before, very slowly, it spread into a smile.

Then Jasper shocked the shit out of Layne and walked straight into him. He bumped the side of his chest against his dad's like Layne had seen him doing to his buds.

He stepped away, looking to the floor, mumbling, "Later, Dad."

"Later, bud," Layne returned.

Layne stared at the door for long minutes after it closed. Then Blondie sauntered up to him and sat at his feet, head back, tongue lolling, the invitation to pet her, or preferably give her a rubdown, opened.

He turned and surveyed his house from the kitchen thinking he was beginning to like the place.

He looked down at Blondie and asked, "You wanna go to work with me today?"

She had no idea what he was saying, but she got up on all fours, her body shaking with excitement and she barked.

Layne decided to take that as a yes.

⌣⟶

"Jesus, Mary and Joseph, what the fuck is that?" Devin asked when Layne came through the door to his office. Devin's eyes were on Blondie.

Blondie ran forward and jumped on Devin's wife beater covered chest.

"It's a dog, Dev," Layne answered then ordered Blondie to get down.

Blondie whipped her head toward Layne, whipped it back to Devin, aimed a lash of her tongue at his face, got nothing but air and then jumped down, put her nose to the ground and started her voyage of the discovery of his office.

Devin scowled at her and then looked at Layne. "Jesus, boy, next thing I'll find out is you drive a mini-van."

"That's another reason I called you here all the way from Cleveland, Dev. I wanted you to help me pick the color," Layne returned and Dev rolled his eyes.

Then Devin walked to the reception desk and picked up a white cup of lidded coffee. A Mimi's coffee.

Devin was wearing a pair of dress pants he should have thrown away five years ago, a pair of scuffed shoes and his wife beater. Thick, gray chest hair could be seen out of the top of the wife beater and the shock of white-gray hair on his head looked like he hadn't even run his fingers through it after getting up from the couch. Total bedhead.

"You didn't get me a coffee?" Layne asked, walking into the room.

"What am I, your nanny?" Dev asked back.

Good to know Devin hadn't changed. Layne knew the man would take a bullet for him but he'd give him lip the entire time he was doing it.

"You go to Mimi's in your wife beater?"

Devin moved away from the reception desk to his bag spread open on the couch and Layne moved to the desk, dumping the folder with TJ Gaines's file on it, turned to Dev and leaned back into it.

"Woman runs that joint ain't difficult to look at," Dev muttered rather than answering Layne's question, which did answer Layne's question that, yes, Dev wandered into Mimi's wearing a wife beater like he'd wander up to his own kitchen counter and pour himself a mug of joe.

"Yeah," Layne agreed. "And her husband used to be center on the football team, he's no less solid twenty some years down the line, but his devotion to wife and family, coupled with his gun collection, means you should not go there."

"Can a man pay a woman a compliment?" Devin asked cantankerously and shrugged on a shirt.

"Sure," Layne replied, and Devin buttoned his shirt, his eyes locking on Layne.

"Well, now that we got all the heartwarming reunion shit outta the way, you run off what you got for me. I'm goin' to the po-lice station to take a shower and I'll want it ready when I get back."

It was clear Devin took some time last night to get the lay of the land. He'd never been to the 'burg but he knew where to get coffee and where the police station was, two things Devin Glover was sure to take note of on any assignment.

"Dev, no one knows you at the station," Layne reminded him. "You can't waltz in there and take a shower. You can shower at my house."

"Your house two blocks away?" Dev shot back.

Layne grinned at him. "No."

"Be back," Dev stated, grabbing his coat and hoofing it out the door. Blondie barked at it.

Layne tagged the file and walked into his office, hitting the power button on his computer as he picked up the phone to call the station and tell them a crotchety old man was going to stroll in like he owned the place and take a shower and their best play was to let him. Kath picked up at reception at the station, Dev showed up while Layne was talking to her, and she instantly agreed.

Layne went to his e-mail and found Merry's intel about Astley and he also found that Natalie didn't fuck around. As promised yesterday, she'd sent an e-mail with the names of people at work she thought might be able to help. She added addresses, phone numbers and copious commentary. She even made notes of who she'd already contacted to let them know someone would be calling them, helping out by making cold contacts warm. Checking the e-mail, Layne noted she'd sent it by eight o'clock last night and there were fifteen names on her list, eleven of them she'd already contacted.

Natalie, Layne had discovered yesterday, did *not* like Dr. Jarrod Astley. This e-mail was added proof and indication that she *really* did not like him.

He printed off the e-mails and put them in the file he'd created when he'd done his searches two weeks ago, making notes on the searches of what was probably now bogus due to Astley's recent activities. He needed to start looking into TJ Gaines and he unfortunately didn't have time to re-run Astley's shit.

He'd begun work on Gaines, and was not liking what he was finding, when his cell rang. The display said "Colt Calling."

"Layne," he said after he put it to his ear.

"Hey, Tanner, you busy today?"

"Yeah, but what's up?"

"Merry gave us the rundown on Stew. I got a guy you might wanna talk to."

Layne sat back in his chair. "When?"

"I gotta go with you. He's not fond of strangers," Colt told him.

"Right. When?" Layne repeated.

"How're you fixed to meet me at the station at one?"

"I can do that," Layne replied.

"Got it. See you then."

"Later."

Layne flipped his phone shut and Devin walked in carrying another cup from Mimi's.

"That for me?" Layne asked.

Devin looked him in the eyes and took a sip, this being his answer.

Then he walked to the desk opposite Layne, held out his hand and grunted, "File."

Layne grinned, picked up the Astley file, reached across the desk and gave it to Devin.

Devin weighed it with his hand moving up and down and asked, "How long you been workin' this?"

"Haven't really. There isn't much there."

Devin put his cup down on Layne's desk and opened the file, his eyes skimming the paper on the top. "Rely too much on computers these days," he grumbled.

"It'll get you started."

Devin looked at Layne. "How deep do you wanna bury this guy?"

"So deep he won't remember what oxygen feels like."

Devin studied him. Then he nodded, grabbed his cup and turned to go.

"Dev," Layne called and Devin turned back. "Dinner, my house, be there at five thirty so I can introduce you to the boys and try to talk you into behaving yourself so my girl Rocky and my son's girl Keira don't run screaming into the night."

Devin's eyebrows shot to his hairline. "Only person I can be is me, boy."

"Why don't you try on a different personality for tonight?" Layne suggested.

"Women love me," Devin shot back.

Layne grinned and muttered, "Right."

"You wait and see. I'll have them eatin' outta my hands."

"Just as long as you don't try to do that literally."

Devin grunted. Blondie, standing next to him looking up at him and likely wondering why he wasn't petting her, barked. Devin glared at the dog and then he disappeared.

Layne chuckled and turned back to his computer.

An hour later he'd run through and printed out every scrap of information in TJ Gaines's personnel file twice because he could not believe what he'd found. He'd also made some calls based on info from the file, typed up quick notes and printed those too. He was in Mimi's and Mimi was handing him his Americano when his phone rang.

The display said, "Raquel Calling."

Seeing Rocky's name on his phone, he made a decision, smiled at Meems, turned toward the door and took the call, greeting her with, "Hey, sweetcheeks."

"Hey, Layne. Did you run the searches?"

"Yep."

"Well?" she asked when he said no more.

"You get a break?"

"Sorry?"

"Do you get a break, Rocky?" He walked through the door, gave a quick, sharp whistle and Blondie, waiting outside for him with her nose pressed to Mimi's glass the entire time he was inside, likely wondering if Layne was getting her a seriously gourmet dog treat (Mimi's coffees were great, but her baked goods were so fucking fantastic, Layne wanted to watch Rocky eat one—guaranteed orgasm).

Blondie wagged after him as he headed down the sidewalk to his SUV.

"I wanna talk about what I found face to face," Layne finished.

She was silent. Then she asked, "Did you find something?"

"Do you get a break?" he repeated.

She hesitated then said, "Yes, right now. I have third period free."

"Can I walk right in or do I need to sign in?"

"Layne—"

He cut her off. "Answer me, sweetcheeks."

"I'll meet you outside the office," she told him on a sigh.

"Be there in ten."

He disconnected, shoved his phone in his back pocket, opened the door, Blondie bolted up into the cab and he swung up after her. He was at the school in ten minutes. He left Blondie in the truck with a window cracked and her nose shoved out of it, sniffing at the outside air like she'd never experienced it before. He walked into the school and saw Raquel was standing outside the office, which was right at the entrance.

She was wearing another one of her to-the-knee, tight-and-sexy-as-hell skirts, this one light beige topped with a thin, tight sweater in deep pink with a matching scarf tied around her neck and high-heeled pumps that also matched the pink. Her lips were glossed in a color that looked like raspberries and he wondered if it tasted the same. Her hair was coiled in a twist at the back of her head.

He smiled at her. When he did, her eyes went immediately to the windows of the administration office that faced out to the halls that Layne was certain was filled with colleagues, mostly women, all who were watching avidly. Then she looked back at him and smiled back tentatively, telling him she was at work and he needed to behave himself.

He walked up to her and stopped close. Closer than he should, not as close as he wanted, not close enough to be inappropriate, but definitely close enough to give their audience something to gossip about, and he tipped his head down.

"Hey, Roc."

"Hey," she whispered, staring up at him.

"Can we talk private?" he asked.

She nodded. "We'll go to my classroom."

He followed her down the corridor in front of the office then down the hall of lockers. Four doors in, she turned left, opened the door and he moved in behind her. She closed the door and turned to him as he scanned the room. A narrow window by the door, a row of windows with views out to the front of the school, other than that, privacy.

He wanted to take in more, but she asked, "Well?" so he turned to her then he moved into her space again.

She held her ground and he grinned down at her. She stared up at him and she was off-balance, he could see. So off-balance she didn't even try to hide it. She didn't understand his game.

This was good.

"What did you find?" she prompted.

"The whole thing is a lie," he answered and watched her blink.

Then she breathed, "Sorry?"

"Not one thing he put on his application is the truth. Not even his fuckin' address." Layne moved closer to her and his voice dropped lower. "Not even his name, Rocky."

"Oh my God," she whispered.

"Thomas Jameson 'TJ' Gaines, as far as I can tell, is a Youth Minister at a Baptist Church in a suburb of Chattanooga, Tennessee. He's been employed there for two years and still lives there, or he did last night, when he took his family out to dinner and charged it. So, unless he's discovered a way to clone himself, the man who's Youth Minister at the Christian Church is *not* TJ Gaines."

She was staring up at him, lips parted, eyes huge. Then she swallowed before she asked, "Are you going to give it to Merry?"

"Only one I could probably give it to *is* Merry since we came into the possession of his personnel file by breaking and entering and then stealing confidential documents."

"We didn't break and enter, I had a key," she snapped.

"A key you stole, sweetcheeks," he shot back.

Her teeth instantly sunk into her lip but her eyes were shooting fire. Then she stated, "Merry would run with it and keep us out of it."

Layne shook his head. "We gotta send Tripp in."

"Why?"

"Because, what Drew told me and what you added last night, I had a feeling this was bad. Now I know this is worse. *A lot* worse. Something is going on there and we fucked it up by committing a variety of unlawful acts to come about undeniably damning information. As damning as it is, sweetcheeks, they build a case against this guy, it'll all come crashing down if anyone ever finds out they were tipped from info we acquired and the way we acquired it. That could happen, Roc. So, a kid's gotta report him and that kid's gonna be Tripp, but he has to know what he's reporting. He can't just go to a few Youth Group meetings and cry wolf. If this guy is in there doin' bad shit with those kids, someone says boo, he's gone and they'll never find him. Tripp gets anything, they can investigate in a way where they won't tweak him until they got enough to arrest him. I have a meet with Colt later this morning. I'll give him the heads up Drew punted this case to me and what Tripp's doin' so he can work his end. You see Drew or Merry, you do the same. But what we did no one knows about, yeah?"

She stared at him for three long beats before she muttered, "I hate it when you make sense."

Layne smiled and muttered back, "Baby."

Her irritation fled and her face changed, worry seeping into it. So much, she didn't check herself from leaning closer to him and resting her bandaged hand lightly on his chest. "Layne, we're talking girls here. *Young* girls."

He put his hand to her neck and gave her a squeeze. "I'll coach Tripp, Rocky, and give him the sense of urgency. He'll play it smart but he won't fuck around. You have to have patience. Even if the cops were investigating this, it would take time. Now, we're goin' at it both ways."

"Yes, I understand that, but time—"

Layne interrupted her. "He's doin' bad shit with kids, this guy has gotta go down and stay down, Roc. And, baby," his head dipped so his face was close to hers, "I'm sorry, but that takes time."

She stared into his eyes and then she nodded. She'd agreed but he didn't move out of her space or her face. His fingers tensed on her neck and his eyes dropped to her raspberry lips. His hand on her skin, her hand on his chest, she was so close he could smell her perfume, Layne had the sudden urge to discover if she tasted like raspberries.

"Layne," those lips whispered as his hand at her neck pulled her closer.

"Yeah, baby?" he asked, his mouth nearly on hers.

"What—?"

His mouth captured hers and his tongue darted out to taste her lip gloss. It tasted like fruit, but he didn't know if it was raspberry and he didn't care because her lips parted and Layne didn't waste the opportunity. He slid his tongue inside.

His hand stayed at her neck as his other hand gripped her waist and pulled her body into his. Both her hands went to his shoulders, not to push away, for the fingers to curl in and she held on.

Her head tipped further back and tilted to the side, causing her breasts to press into his chest. That felt good and he wanted more of it.

So he moved his hand along her waist, feeling the fabric of her sweater was soft, not scratchy, and he wrapped his arm around her, pulling her body deeper into his, plastering her softness against him.

Yep, that felt better and Rocky thought so too. He knew this because she made a sweet, little noise in her throat that vibrated against his tongue.

That noise made Layne give a reciprocating one, but his wasn't sweet. It was hungry.

Too hungry, the taste of her, the smell of her perfume, her body pressed against his felt fucking great. His body was reacting and she was at work. This couldn't get out of hand. Not how he wanted it to, not here.

He tore his lips from hers but kept her close with his hand at her neck and arm around her waist.

"Layne," she breathed, and he realized then she'd kissed him back. No complaints, no resistance. Like Sunday night, he'd touched his tongue to her lips and she was his.

This said a lot and all of it was fucking brilliant.

"I got work to do, baby," he whispered.

"What are you…why are you—?" she started to ask, but he touched his mouth to hers once, then again, then he looked in her eyes to see they were slightly unfocused and slightly confused and that look was definitely cute.

"Got shit to do, sweetcheeks. Colt's got a guy who may give me info I need on Stew and I got a file to build on a case I completed last night. I need to get that done so I can get paid."

"Um…okay," she whispered.

His hand at her neck and his arm at her waist gave her a squeeze. "See you tonight."

"Okay," she repeated.

"Later," he muttered and touched his mouth to hers again.

"Okay," she muttered back when he was done, her mutter breathy. "Later."

He smiled down at her, let her go, stepped away from her and her hands dropped from his shoulders. He wiped her berry gloss off his lips with the back of his hand while still smiling.

Then he turned to the door and his timing couldn't have been any fucking better. The bell rang and he opened the door as kids started streaming into the halls. He waited a few beats, looking back at her and finding she was where he left her, staring at him, still seeming unfocused. Then, when the halls were packed with kids, he took a step out, turned back to her, gave her a wink and started to walk down the hall.

A young girl ran into the back of an opened locker right beside him after he took two steps and he caught her by the bicep because the noise of her slamming into the locker was loud and her dazed expression made it look like she was going down.

"You all right?" he asked, and she stared up at him still looking dazed. He bent closer. "Hey, honey, I asked, you all right?"

"Uh…" she stared up at him like she'd never seen another human being before. Then she whispered in a voice so quiet he could barely hear her, "You called me honey."

"Molly," Rocky was there, "did you hurt yourself? Is everything okay?"

The girl tore her gaze from him, blinked at Rocky, and mumbled, "Uh, yeah, Mrs. Astley."

"Her name is Ms. Merrick," Layne told the girl. He heard Rocky suck in breath. He let the girl's arm go and the girl turned her head and blinked up at him.

"Oh, okay." She turned back to Rocky. "Yeah, I'm fine, Ms. Merrick."

Rocky was glaring at him but she spoke to the girl. "That's good, Molly, now you better get to class."

"Right," she muttered, scuttled between them and took off down the hall.

"Hey, Mrs. Astley," a pack of girls called in unison then one of them went on, "Your boyfriend is *hot*." Then all of them burst out in giggles.

"Thank you, Mariah, your opinion is noted," Rocky replied irately, and Layne burst out laughing. When he was done, Rocky was close and she hissed at him, "Don't you have work to do?"

"Yeah, Roc." He grinned at her. "See you tonight."

"See you tonight."

He winked again and she glared. Then she turned, walked back to her room and disappeared inside. It was only two strides but she did it with her strut so Layne took the time to watch. When he was done, he turned, saw two of Jasper's friends, backs against the walls, both of their eyes locked on Layne.

"Hey, Mr. Layne," one of them said in Jasper's "you the man" tone of last night.

"Jamie," Layne nodded and his eyes cut to the other kid, "Mitch."

"Yo, Mr. Layne."

Layne smiled at them and started walking down the hall thinking that his whole play went really, fucking *great*.

Layne met Colt and they took off in Layne's Suburban.

When they did, Layne left Blondie with Sully at the station knowing Jas's dog would love him forever, such was her excitement at being left in a place full of men who liked dogs as well as a variety of corners she could stick her nose into to experience a variety of new and unusual smells.

"Things good?" Colt asked from the passenger seat.

"Workin' on it," Layne answered.

"How's Rocky?" Colt went on.

"Workin' on that too," Layne replied, and Colt chuckled.

"Can't say I wasn't shocked as shit coupla weeks ago," Colt remarked.

"Everyone's shocked as shit, includin' me," Layne told him.

Colt was silent a moment before he asked quietly, his voice openly concerned, "It goin' okay?"

Alec Colton was a good cop, a good man and a good friend. They'd worked together years ago, he'd been that way then and he was that way now. Colt knew Layne before Rocky left him and after. He knew what she meant to him and he knew what it meant she was back.

Therefore, Layne said quietly back, "Path's full of thorns."

Another moment of silence and then Colt replied, "You get to the rose, man, it's unbelievably soft and smells incredibly fuckin' sweet."

It hit Layne then that Colt and Feb had lived their own bittersweet love story in that 'burg. Colt was a few years older than Layne but he'd been at high school with Feb. With Colt best friends with February's brother since he was in kindergarten, Colt had known Feb forever. They'd been solid, unshakable—the couple who hooked up in high school that everyone knew would stick true.

They didn't. Layne had no idea what went down except it wasn't good. Colt had stayed in the 'burg and working with him, Layne knew the loss of Feb, even years after, was a loss that stayed fresh.

Like Layne, Feb had taken off and she'd been gone even longer than Layne. She came back a few years ago and they'd hooked up again when a local guy lost control of what was left of his mind and went on a killing spree in Feb's name. Colt had stepped in to keep her safe and they'd come out of that back together, solid, unshakable, now married with a kid. Whatever tore them apart, they found a way to put it behind them and they made it through.

Reminded of this, Layne could say at that juncture that reminder was really freaking welcome.

"So I take it Feb's good," Layne noted.

"Yeah, man, Feb is good." Colt's words were weighty and Layne didn't try to stop his smile.

Layne drove out of the 'burg, they hit the vast fields that surrounded it and he changed the subject. "Run this down for me."

Colt didn't hesitate. "Guy's name is Ryker. It's happening, he knows about it."

"Informant?"

"He isn't averse to sharing information when he might get somethin' outta it."

Layne glanced at Colt then back at the road. "He the kind of guy I wanna owe a favor?"

"That's the beauty of this, Tanner. Ryker is not a friend of Carlito's and *no one* is a friend of Stew's. I reckon he won't consider it a favor to share what he knows about Stew."

Layne found himself smiling again.

Layne had learned one thing from his father, a man he'd never met—or he hadn't met him at a time where Layne was old enough to form a coherent thought—and that was, you not only didn't shit where you lived, you didn't shit anywhere.

Layne had grown up watching his mother struggle to keep a roof over their heads working as a secretary, going to night school, studying to be an accountant, having no time to do it and even less money, so it took her freaking forever. But she did it and began to make more money, but she always had to work.

Layne was a latchkey kid, she had no choice but to lean on him to help her out by learning how to take care of himself early on, and the minute he could earn, he did what he could to kick in. His aunt and grandparents did as much as they could but they had their own lives to lead.

She was his mom but Layne knew his mother was a looker. He also knew she was a good woman. She was funny. She was sweet. Her family adored her and she had dozens of friends, all of whom she could call close. A man losing out on that, shitting where he lived, turning his back on a good woman and family and never looking back, let the whole world slip through his own fingers.

Layne had fucked up twice and both of them were royally. The first time was out of his control when the condom broke when he was with Gabby, and it was now not debatable that he'd fucked up nailing Gabby in the first place, drunk or not. The second time was when he left his sons and the last year he'd given a lot of headspace to trying to remember why the fuck he did that at all.

Gabby was a bitch and divorcing her made her worse, and Rocky was in that town. Layne had felt tied down, not by his sons, but by the history with Rocky and Gabby that fenced him in. This brought up the urge to get out of that 'burg and roam. There were things he wanted to do, wanted to see and wanted to learn. Things he couldn't learn, see and do in a small town. He'd told Rocky all about this shit when they were together and she was with him all the way because she shared his need to roam, to learn, to see, to do. They had plans, and once she graduated from Butler, they were going to go. They didn't know where, but it would be somewhere.

He found what he was searching for in St. Louis, San Antonio, Reno, Phoenix and LA, but he lost more by leaving what really mattered at home and he'd paid a mighty price for that fuck up.

Nevertheless, he made more friends than enemies along the way, case in point, Devin Glover dropping everything and hitting town after getting a phone call.

Jarrod Astley and Stew Baranski hadn't learned not to shit where they lived, where they worked, wherever they wanted. They didn't care who they screwed over. You couldn't live your life like that and not face retribution eventually.

And it was closing in on Astley and Stew's judgment days.

Layne and Colt hit the even smaller town next to the 'burg, a town right on the outskirts of Indy. It held a raceway, and was a decent place generally, but could get pretty rough when the races were on.

The 'burg had J&J's as its hotspot, no other drinking establishments in town because every one that sprung up failed due to people's loyalty to J&J's. It wasn't the only place to drink. There were restaurants that had bars, but it was the only place people went to meet friends, listen to the jukebox, play a game of pool and tie one on.

This town wasn't the same. They had tons of bars, most of them rough due to their clientele being race groupies or race hangers on. Layne swung into the one Colt informed him they were going to and parked.

He switched off the ignition and turned to Colt. "There a way we need to play this?"

Colt shook his head. "You don't play Ryker. He either likes you or he doesn't. He likes you, he shares. He doesn't, we'll know in about two seconds and then we'll go have lunch."

Layne nodded and they both turned to their doors.

The day was overcast with intermittent rain. Even if there was sun, the light in the bar would be dim, stating openly to its customers that anything goes. You could fuck a race groupie in the corner and not be noticed. You could also make a drug sale or slide a blade into an enemy.

Colt led Layne to a corner table where a man sat alone with his back to the wall and a bottle of beer in front of him on the table. It was cold outside, but the guy was wearing a black tank top stretched across his bulky, ripped torso, with jeans and motorcycle boots, and he wasn't resting with his coat slung on his chair. But he was lounging back in that chair, one of his long, beefy legs straight in front of him, foot resting on its heel, the other leg cocked with foot flat to the ground. He looked relaxed but Layne knew he was alert to anything. He had two sleeves of tattoos running up his arms, full-on wrist to shoulder ink, both sleeves slithering up his thick neck. He was bald, he was ugly and it was easy to read he was not a guy you messed with.

"Ryker," Colt greeted and didn't hesitate before he sat down at Ryker's table.

"This guy a cop?" Ryker asked, his eyes locked on Layne.

Layne took a seat at the same time he held Ryker's eyes.

"Nope," Colt answered.

"Smells like a cop," Ryker commented, and even though Colt was a cop, he did this in a way that stated plainly cops were not his favorite people.

"Used to be one, now he's a PI," Colt replied.

Ryker's eyebrows shot up and he kept his eyes on Layne. "A dick?" That was meant to have two meanings and Layne clenched his teeth.

"What he is, for the purposes of this meet, is Gabrielle Layne's ex-husband," Colt told Ryker.

Ryker's eyes cut to Colt. "Who the fuck is that?"

"Stew Baranski's woman," Colt answered.

Ryker grinned. He knew who she was but he still asked, "Fat bitch?"

"Ryker," Colt said low.

"Dumb bitch." Ryker refused to read the warning.

Layne was done so he entered the conversation.

"She and I have two boys, one of 'em saw Baranski hand off an envelope to Carlito at the house. Gabby tells me Stew has troubles. You know anything about that?"

Ryker's eyes sliced to Layne on the words "two boys" and he waited a beat before he answered, "I know Carlito's a fuckwad."

"I know that too," Layne returned.

"And I know Baranski is an assclown," Ryker went on.

"Yeah, you aren't tellin' me anything I don't know," Layne informed him. "Not here to find out shit I know. I'm here to find out what's goin' on because I'm not a big fan of my boys witnessing Baranski makin' a payment to a loan shark."

Ryker grinned. "That wasn't no payment."

Layne didn't like the sound of that.

"So what was it?" Layne asked.

"Wasn't no payment," Ryker answered.

Layne studied Ryker then looked at Colt.

"Ryker, you got somethin', it'd help Layne out," Colt prompted, and Ryker's eyes went from Colt to Layne.

He examined Layne for a long time before he asked, "Which one?"

"Come again?" Layne asked back.

"Which boy?"

Layne felt the muscles in his neck contract. "Not sure that's relevant, man."

Ryker didn't let it go. "The one that tagged that sweet catch, and after, caught it from that dickhead coach who should have his nuts in a vice? Or the one who can block like that fat bitch pushed him out while he was wearin' shoulder pads?"

Christ, this fucking guy was a Bulldogs fan.

"Jasper," Layne knew at that moment it was safe to say. "My older boy. The one who can block."

"Got quick feet, hasn't seen the ball in two games," Ryker noted. "You doin' somethin' about that?"

"All I can do," Layne replied.

"And what's that?" Ryker pushed.

"The School Board is investigating my complaint," Layne answered, and when he did, Ryker threw back his head and barked out his laughter, something Layne didn't appreciate all that much but he held his tongue.

When he was done, Ryker tipped his chin down and leveled his eyes on Layne. "You give me the word, sport, I might find it in me to convince the coach to let both your boys see the ball. No marker to be paid, I'd give you that for free."

Jesus.

"I like my way of doin' it," Layne told him.

"Scouts not gonna get the full picture. Your older boy's a senior, that motherfucker'll fuck him up."

"I still like my way of doin' it," Layne repeated and it was far more firmly this time.

Ryker watched him awhile then he shrugged.

Layne brought the matter back to hand, saying, "How much is Baranski into Carlito for?"

"Nothin'," Ryker answered immediately and Layne's brows drew together.

"Nothin'?" he reiterated.

"Nope, he *was*, dickhead's shit at the dogs, but he ain't anymore."

Layne felt Colt's eyes on him and he turned to meet his gaze.

Then Colt looked at Ryker. "You wanna fill in that picture?"

Layne looked back at Ryker too and Ryker leaned forward, putting a tattooed arm on the table.

"He got deep with Carlito, so deep he couldn't get out," Ryker shared. "So, instead of Carlito takin' it out on Baranski the normal way, he put Baranski to work. Baranski liked this work so now he's doin' it part-time."

Then he leaned back and stopped talking but Layne knew what he was saying and Layne knew why Gabby asked him to take the boys for extra weeks, even though *she* probably didn't know why. Carlito was undoubtedly a frequent visitor, and even if Gabby wasn't full in the know, she'd read Carlito and wouldn't want the boys around that. And, lastly, Layne was struggling against the urge to hunt down Stew Baranski and beat him bloody.

He won his struggle and sought confirmation. "Stew is Carlito's enforcer?"

Ryker nodded once. "One of 'em, yeah."

There it was. Confirmation.

Fucking *shit*.

"You are shittin' me," Layne whispered, but he knew Ryker wasn't.

Ryker confirmed this too and grinned while doing it. "Nope."

Layne turned his head to Colt. "That asshole's livin' with my boys."

Layne was addressing Colt but Ryker answered, "Yep," and Layne's eyes went back to him.

Then he told Ryker, "Done my homework, Ryker, and Baranski hasn't been payin' bills and neither has my ex."

Ryker shrugged again. "Why would he? He's got a sweet ride. She's fat and she's nothin' to look at, but she keeps him fed. Pays his bills." He grinned again. "Or maybe she doesn't but she tries. She's good cover, all respectable, single mom, two boys." He tipped his head to Colt. "Means even the cops don't know about his leisure activities. Leaves him free to do his job and gives him the opportunity he didn't have before to use his money and his take from Carlito to live his life as he wants to and to keep his other piece sassy. Figure, he got hooked up with your ex because no one else would suck his dick. But lotta women will suck your dick you got the money to pay 'em to do it."

"His other piece?" Colt asked.

"Yep," Ryker answered.

"You know who that is?" Colt pressed.

"Don't know her name but know she ain't no fat bitch, she don't got no kids, she drives an ace ride that Baranski bought her, and also know she takes it up the ass because everyone knows that's the only way Baranski likes it."

Layne swallowed the saliva this statement brewed in his mouth, not needing *that* much information about Gabby's relationship with her fuck-wad boyfriend.

Ryker was grinning at him and then he leaned forward again and his grin disappeared.

"I'll give you an extra bonus because your boys can play ball," he said. "Baranski won't be cryin' in his cornflakes, your ex turns him out. But he'll wring her dry before he gets shot of her. She's diggin' a hole to keep him in her bed, he won't give one...single...shit he leaves her in that hole. You want him outta her bed, wouldn't take but a touch of pressure to get him to go, but that don't mean he won't leave her fucked up the ass and I mean that in a different way. You want him gone, it'll take you about two fuckin' seconds to make that happen. You want him to pay, now that would be more fun *and*, since I'm feelin' generous, I could help you with that too."

"How?" Layne bit out.

"I make it my business to know Carlito's business and I can give you the heads up, he sends Baranski after someone. You're a dick, I bet you got cameras, and if you're a good one, I bet you can make yourself invisible. You take shots of him leanin' on someone—and he has a special flair with that, sport, he's Carlito's top man—what you'll catch him doin' won't be pretty and that's comin' from a man who ain't squeamish at the sight of blood. You can use those shots to lean on *him*. You got evidence, you shove it in his face, make the payoff somethin' that'll get your ex outta her hole and he'll be gone." He sat back and clapped his hands. "Problems solved." He smiled big and his smile made him uglier. "You got a mind to do it, you could even do some ass fuckin' yourself, after he makes that payoff, your ex is good, you hand over those shots to the pigs anyway. Baranski goes down, only people would miss him are Carlito and his piece of ass, and I'm just guessin' here, but I bet neither of 'em will take too long to find replacements."

Layne smiled at him.

Then he said, "I'll give you my number."

Eleven

DARK AND WILD

It was ten to six when Layne turned onto his street and saw Rocky's Mercedes parked, not in the drive, but at the curb behind a white Oldsmobile Cutlass Calais circa 1987.

Dev's ride.

She was early.

Layne was late.

He was late because he'd made the mistake of calling his client who was dedicated to the belief her husband was stepping out on her in an attempt to convince her that her husband was *not* stepping out on her. This should have been a ten minute conversation. It ended up being a forty-five minute conversation during which she'd fired him and informed him that she was hiring someone who would do the job properly. Layne wasn't broken up about this, mainly because she was coming the next day to pay in cash.

He was also late because he stopped at the liquor store. He meant to buy a bottle of red wine for Rocky but ended up purchasing three, and because she hadn't been of age when they were together and he had no fucking clue what she drank (outside red wine and fancy-ass beer, the latter of which he wasn't spending money on on principle), he bought bottles of vodka, rum, gin, tequila as well as margarita mix and two-liters of diet cola and tonic water.

When Layne pulled into his drive, the garage door was up and the Charger was parked inside. Rocky and Dev undoubtedly parked in the street because Layne was coming in and Jasper had to go out to pick up Keira.

He pulled in, jumped down and Blondie jumped down behind him. Layne opened the back door of the SUV and hefted out the three carrier bags. He led the dog into the house and this took effort because Blondie was crowding him in her excitement to get to her boys. So much that they walked into the kitchen together.

Blondie shot forward but Layne stopped dead.

The vacuum was going and this was because Jasper was pushing it around the rug in the living room.

Tripp was also in the living room, a dust rag in one hand, a can of furniture polish in the other, and he was working on the wood of the TV unit.

Rocky was still wearing her work getup, her back to him, standing at an island that was cleared of mail, magazines, papers, used coffee mugs, pop cans, beer bottles and other detritus. It now appeared to be covered in vegetables and at the end was an enormous bouquet of flowers. All the other counters had also been cleared as well as wiped down.

Devin was sitting on a stool opposite Raquel, his fingers curled around a bottle of beer.

When Layne walked in, both Devin and Rocky were laughing.

"Hey, Dad!" Tripp shouted, Jasper's head swung to him, Devin's eyes went to him and Rocky turned toward him, a knife in her hand. Blondie barked and attacked Jasper and the vacuum.

"Have I entered a new dimension?" Layne asked the room, to which Jasper grinned as he gave Blondie a head rub.

"Rocky says girls don't like dirty houses," he shouted over the vacuum then Blondie lost interest in Jas and attacked Tripp.

Jasper grabbed the handle of the vacuum again and started pushing it under the coffee table.

There you go. Rocky was behind this activity.

"She'd know," Layne muttered, his eyes swinging to Rocky and catching her dimple before she turned back to her vegetables.

He walked to the island beside her and dumped his bags next to the vegetables. She had a bowl in front of her already filled with salad leaves, sliced cucumbers, diced tomatoes, strips of yellow bell pepper, and she was working on a carrot.

"Hey, Dev," Layne greeted.

"Boy," Dev greeted back, his eyes slid to Rocky, back to Layne, and he smiled slowly.

Layne had no idea how long Rocky was there, but however long it was, she'd earned Dev's approval.

This didn't surprise Layne. Her dad was a cop, so was her brother and she knew every uniform and plainclothesman in the county—Rocky was Dev's kind of people. Rocky was also a female of the beautiful variety who wore tight skirts, high heels and soft sweaters—that was Dev's kind of people too.

Layne moved into Rocky's back, put a hand to the counter in front of her and discovered one good thing about her wearing her hair up. It left her neck totally exposed. With this opportunity afforded him, he placed a hand on her sweater at her waist, slid it forward to her belly and touched his lips to the skin behind her ear.

He absorbed the minor tremor that slid through her body before it went stiff, and he whispered in her ear, "Hey, baby."

She kept cutting as she whispered back, "Hey, Layne."

"You're early," he noted, and she nodded, her body still stiff, likely because his was pressed the length of her back, from hips to shoulders, and he not only hadn't moved either hand, he also had begun to slide his thumb back and forth across the soft material of her sweater.

"I thought I'd help Jasper impress Keira with his concern over her nutrition," she replied and tossed some of the carrots into the bowl. "Though, not too concerned. I also bought an apple pie and vanilla bean ice cream for dessert."

She hadn't changed because, after work, she'd gone to the store and she'd gone to the store to do something for his boy.

Layne grinned and lifted his face from her neck but didn't move away when he asked, "Flowers?"

"Those're from me. You don't have dinner with the ladies without buyin' 'em flowers," Dev put in and Layne smiled at him.

"Fair warning, sweetcheeks. Dev's a ladies' man," Layne told Rocky.

"He's already impressed that on me," Rocky returned and Layne chuckled.

Then he put his lips back to her ear and invited softly, "You need to get outta those shoes, baby."

"I would," she replied. "If I wasn't scared of what my feet would encounter after doing it."

Layne lifted his head again, still smiling, and called to Tripp, "Finish polishing, pal. Then get that thing that sweeps the floors."

At his words, Rocky twisted her neck and tilted her head back to look up at him. "It's called a *broom*, Layne."

He smiled down at her. "I told you this was a testosterone zone, sweetcheeks. 'Bout the only thing in the house that has a connection to work that doesn't have a plug or use batteries is that polish Tripp's wielding. We got a *thing* that sweeps the floors."

Rocky kept staring up at him after he'd finished speaking, the vacuum had gone off and Layne forced his eyes from hers when he heard Jasper announce, "I'm on that, Dad. Tripp's gonna clean the downstairs bathroom after he finishes with the furniture."

Layne looked to Tripp. He had no idea how his youngest bought that chore but him accepting it gave new meaning to his adoration of Rocky.

"I think I got a gasmask and industrial gloves in the garage, pal. And after you do that, I'll give you five dollars."

Tripp sauntered into the kitchen, Blondie at his heels, muttering, "I think it's worth more like fifty."

Tripp was not wrong.

Both his boys, and the dog, hit the utility room and Layne turned his attention back to the island. He took his hand from Rocky's stomach, nabbed a slice of the carrot she was cutting and tossed it into his mouth.

He was chewing when he asked Dev, "How was your day?"

Devin looked in his eyes and pointedly didn't look at Rocky. "Good."

"How good?" Layne pressed.

"*Real* good."

Layne swallowed, grinned and tagged another carrot he threw in his mouth before he asked Dev, "Oxygen gettin' thin?"

"I already hear someone chokin'," Dev replied.

Layne grabbed another slice of carrot and Rocky said, "As fascinating as you and Devin talking in code is, Layne, you take another carrot, you'll find your hand stuck to the counter with my knife."

Devin chuckled and Layne tossed the carrot into his mouth before he put that hand back to her belly. Her body, which had relaxed, went stiff again, and his mouth went back to her ear. "Baby, I've had four cups of coffee and a breaded tenderloin sandwich today. Aren't you concerned for *my* nutrition?"

Her head turned, his came up, and she looked him in the eyes. "I'm thinking you're healthy enough."

He dipped his face close to hers and whispered, "You have no idea, but you want, later I can show you."

The fire died out of her eyes, the intensity went into them, she stared up at him, totally off-balance and he knew this because she swallowed.

He fought the urge to kiss her as the boys, with dog, re-entered the room carrying new weapons to attack their filthy house and Layne decided to give Raquel a break, moved away from her and toward the bags.

"Tripp, do a good job but do it fast. We gotta have a conversation before Keira gets here," he announced as he emptied the bottles from the bags and he felt all eyes turn to him.

"Jesus, boy, you havin' a teenager over for dinner or you hostin' a rave?" Devin asked as the bottles were unveiled.

"Rocky likes red wine," Layne replied and he felt Rocky's body, already on alert, jerk to solid beside him.

"Yeah, I'm seein' that and then some," Dev muttered.

"What do we have to talk about, Dad?" Tripp called Layne's attention to him.

"Finish in the bathroom, pal, then we'll talk."

Tripp and Jasper both eyed him then Tripp disappeared and Jasper plugged in the thing that electronically sucked shit up from tile and wood floors.

While his boys did this, Dev caught Rocky's attention and they started chatting as Layne put away the bottles of booze and opened one of the reds. He poured her a glass, got himself a beer and then walked back to her to set her glass beside her workspace on the island. Workspace she was clearing now that the gargantuan salad was done.

When her eyes went to the glass then lifted to him, he muttered, "Sorry, sweetcheeks, we don't have any fancy glasses in the house."

"That's okay, they drink it like that in Italy," she replied. Reaching out to grab the small glass, she turned to Dev. "I've never been to Italy, of course, but that's the way they drink it in movies set in Italy and I always thought that was cool." She lifted her glass and reached toward Dev, finishing, "Welcome to the 'burg, Devin."

He clinked his bottle of beer against her glass, sucked back a pull and after swallowing, said, "Dev, darlin'. Pretty girls get to call me Dev."

She smiled at him. "Dev, then."

"You got time tomorrow, you can give me a tour of the 'burg," Dev invited as if he already hadn't scouted out the lay of the land.

"I'd love that but I've got to work," Rocky replied. "But I'll tell you that it'll be worth your while to get up early, go to Hilligoss Bakery and get yourself a donut. I've never been to Italy, or anywhere else really, but I'd put down money on any donut from Hilligoss going up against anything in the world and winning."

"I haven't been to Italy either, but I've been around and Roc isn't lyin'," Layne added.

"Your treat tomorrow then, boy," Dev told him.

"Done in the bathroom!" Trip shouted, rounding the corner and running toward the utility room at the same time juggling an armload of bathroom cleaning stuff.

Layne looked to Jas to see he was also done and winding the cord up. He turned to the back counter, saw Rocky's purse sitting by the coffeemaker, walked to it and dug through it until he found her keys.

Then he turned to Jasper as he heard Rocky start to say, "What are you—?"

"Jas," he called over her. Jasper's head came up and Layne tossed his son the keys, which Jasper nabbed one-handed. "You pull the Charger out then pull Rocky's Merc in the garage."

"Layne—" Rocky began.

Layne talked over her. "Get Dev's keys too, pull the Calais into the drive behind the Merc."

"But—" Rocky tried again.

"You get Keira, you park behind the Suburban. Drop the door after you pull in the Merc," Layne finished.

"Right Dad," Jasper said, carried the sweeper to the utility room and disappeared as Tripp reappeared.

"Layne, you can't—" Rocky started and Layne looked at her.

"HOA isn't big on cars parked on the street overnight."

"Over—" she began again, this time in a whisper.

"HOA?" Dev cut in, sounding disgusted. "Tanner Layne, the boy I proudly watched dodge bullets to enter a house filled with hostiles in order to grab a hostage—a rescue during which he took two boys out with only a half-filled clip in his gun, and he ran out without a nick on him carrying that hostage—is *livin'* in a *place* with a *homeowners' association?*"

Layne heard Rocky suck in breath at the same time he heard Tripp shout, "You did that Dad?"

"Damn straight he did it, boy," Devin growled at Tripp then his eyes cut to Layne. "A dog, an HOA and domestication, three things I did not think I'd ever see attached to *you.*"

"Things change, Dev," Layne replied, acutely aware that, for some reason, Rocky was staring at him and she was *not* doing it the same way Tripp was.

"That sounds cool!" Tripp yelled. "Devin, who were the hostiles? Where was this? When…?"

Layne looked to Rocky while Tripp fired out his questions, and the minute he did her eyes dropped, she turned so he had her profile and her hand lifted so she could take a sip of wine. But she couldn't hide the fact that her face had paled or her hand was trembling.

"It wasn't as dangerous as Dev makes it sound," Layne lied to Tripp in an effort to reassure a visibly shaken Rocky.

It was. It was extremely dangerous and it was a hotshot, bullshit maneuver he'd pulled. He could have been killed and it could have got the hostage killed.

The problem was, the hostage was an eight-year-old, dark-headed boy whose picture reminded him of Jasper. He'd been kidnapped and held hostage for three weeks and Dev had been hired to manage an extraction the

Feds had botched—which meant two parts of the boy had been delivered to his parents, a finger and a toe—and Dev had taken Layne along as backup. It was a part miracle that Layne hadn't been filled with bullets, part excellent cover from Devin.

What Dev wasn't sharing was that he *didn't* watch proudly as Layne did this. What he did was lay into Layne approximately two seconds after Dev took down the last "hostile" and they secured the boy.

"We should wait until Jas gets back so he can hear the story too," Tripp suggested and Layne tore his eyes from Rocky, who at this point had turned her back to him. He looked at his son while walking to Rocky, fitting his front again against her back and leaning both of their bodies into his palm at the edge of the counter.

"Jasper's gotta cook and you gotta grab a pop and take a load off after all your cleaning activity. Rocky and me got somethin' important to talk to you about," Layne said.

Tripp's eyes grew both bright and wary as they looked between Layne and Rocky and he asked, "Really?"

"Really," Layne answered. "Get your pop, pal."

Tripp nodded. He got his pop and sat his ass down as Devin appeared to sip his beer casually, but Layne knew he'd been alerted by Layne's serious tone. Through this, Rocky stood noticeably silent in front of him.

Jasper walked in and Layne stayed close to Rocky even as he turned to Jas.

"You can do the Calais before you go to pick up Keira, bud. I want you to hear this and you need to get your pasta bake show on the road. You wait to cook that shit until after she gets here, she'll miss her curfew, Cal will lose his mind, and I'll have to make sure my gun is loaded."

Jasper grinned and walked into the room asking, "Hear what?" then he put Rocky's keys on the counter by her hand.

When he did, Rocky quietly said, "Thanks Jasper," and Jasper turned his grin to her.

Layne kept her body pinned in just as his son had pinned in her car as he said to Jas, "Just listen, yeah?" and then he turned to Tripp and started to lay it out.

"Got a heads up from a friend on the force and a little while later Rocky shared her concerns about stuff she's hearin' at school. She's got a bad vibe and I've got a bad vibe, and, Tripp, I need you to help us to do something about it."

Tripp's eyes were glued to him and he didn't hesitate in nodding.

"What's the bad vibe?" Jasper asked from behind them.

"It's about the Youth Group at the Christian Church," Layne answered, which he saw made Tripp nod even more enthusiastically.

"Oh yeah, I can see that," Tripp said, and Layne felt Rocky's body stiffen against him as his did the same.

"Me too," Jasper added.

"What can you see?" Layne asked.

"Cult city," Jasper noted. "It's freakin' creepy."

"Totally creepy," Tripp agreed. "Like that pied piper story, except he skipped the mice and went straight to the kids."

Rocky forced him back by turning at the same time twisting her neck and looking up at him.

Layne looked down at her to see she looked even paler and that concern he saw earlier that day was flooding her eyes.

He took his palm from the counter and forced her back to his front with his arms around her, one at her chest, one at her ribs. He gave her a reassuring squeeze and left his arms where they were.

Then he looked at Tripp. "We need you to go in."

Tripp's brows knitted and his head tipped to the side. "Go in?"

"Undercover, pal, I need you to work this case for Rocky and me."

Tripp's brows slowly separated, his face went blank then he smiled huge and bounced once on his stool. "Oh yeah!" he shouted. "I can do that."

"Tripp," Layne said low, "You gotta be cool about this. This is not a gung ho mission. This requires finesse, pal."

Tripp nodded and his voice was quieter when he repeated, "I can do that."

Jasper came to the island, stating, "I can too, and Keira would be all over it."

Layne looked at Jasper. "I'd be open to you doin' it, bud. But Keira, absolutely not."

"Why not?" Jasper returned. "She's up for anything and she's a girl. That guy at the Youth Group, he likes girls."

At this, Rocky's hand came up, her fingers curling around Layne's forearm so tight they almost hurt.

"No to Keira, Jas," Layne replied.

"She's a nut but she's smart," Jasper returned, defending his girl.

Layne gave him the honesty. "You wanna keep her safe you keep her *far* away from this guy. Do you get what I'm sayin' to you?"

Jasper stared at him, the blood running from his face, a muscle ticked in his cheek, and he nodded.

Layne looked to Tripp. "Do you get it, Tripp?"

"He's a bad guy," Tripp whispered, the excitement now out of his eyes and those eyes were wide.

"I don't know but I've learned to listen to my gut, and on this my gut is tellin' me whatever is happening there is not good. And I don't know what he's doin' but my gut tells me he likes doin' it, he's got a sweet gig goin' and he's not gonna want anyone to make him stop. Not anyone. Not a cop and not a high school kid. That means you gotta go in there and be smart. You feel somethin's not right for you, you get the fuck out. You feel safe, you listen, you watch and you got two missions to start with. One, you get close to the girl Rocky tells you to get close to. You make friends with her and you do it in a way that, when this is done, you're still friends with her. You get her to talk to you and you do that smart too. You wanna know about Youth Group. You wanna get involved. You wanna be a part of it all. You wanna be her friend. But you find out everything you can about what they do and where they're doin' it. What you see. What they'll let you get involved in. But, mostly, what they *won't*. The other part is you get me something he's touched. A can of pop, a pen. I don't give a fuck what it is. You do your best not to touch it too much and I'll give you a bag to put it in. I want to pull his prints off it and run them. We gotta know who this guy is and who we're goin' up against. He's in the system, this goes quick. He's not, we gotta find another way. You think you can you do that?"

Tripp nodded.

"Good," Layne told him and then he gave Rocky another squeeze, dipped his head and said close to her ear, "Who'd you pick for Tripp, baby?"

She nodded too and Layne lifted his head as she said, "You have three choices, Tripp. Giselle Speakmon, Sabrina Tilley or Darcy Cassini."

"Giselle Speakmon," Jasper said immediately.

"Why?" Devin entered the conversation on a bark that made Jasper, Tripp *and* Rocky jump.

"'Cause she's hot," Jasper replied.

"She's out," Devin shot back. "Next."

"She's hot *and* she's shy. Freakin' shy, like, it's *painful*. She's a freshman too, like Tripp," Jasper continued, his eyes steady on Devin. "Sabrina is nice and she's okay lookin', at a push, but she's a junior and Tripp would be outta her league if she wasn't just okay lookin' and, like I said, that's *at a push*. So, actually, *she's* outta *his* league. Darcy's nice too, but she's a sophomore and she's big as a boat. It'd look funny, he got friendly with either of them. He wouldn't have any reason to do that. This guy's a predator like you think he is then he'll cotton on to Tripp's game, he gets close to one of those chicks. Everyone knows who Tripp is and everyone knows what Dad does." Jasper's eyes went to his old man. "No one would question Tripp gettin' friendly with Giselle. She's hot and girls like Tripp, think he's cute. Tripp would have to work it 'cause she's so shy, but, if anyone could get Giselle talkin', it'd be Tripp and Tripp could play it like he's there *just* to get Giselle to talk to him. That's the way I'd play it. And he'll be cool. He'll work it, no one will know why he's there and he'll get what you need."

In that moment, there was a lot happening at that island for Tanner Layne. So much it was too much for Layne to process. The first part of it being the fact that he'd gone beyond vastly underestimating Jasper. The second part was that Devin was staring at his oldest son with blatant respect, something Devin very rarely did. The third part of it being the fact that Raquel Merrick was standing, unresisting, in his arms with her fingers curled tight, holding on to him. The last part of it was Tripp looking at his brother with unashamed love shining from his eyes.

Layne had seen a lot of things in his life, the woman he held in his arms being the most beautiful. Or she was until Layne saw Tripp look at his brother like that.

"Then it's Giselle," Layne declared, heard his voice was gruff and he knew Rocky heard it too because her fingers gave his arm a squeeze. Layne cleared his throat and went on, "Youth Group meets tomorrow night, Tripp, seven thirty. You start then."

Tripp nodded at Layne again.

"I'll take him and go with him the first night," Jasper offered.

"That works, but no Keira," Layne replied.

"No Keira," Jasper agreed.

"How do you know he likes girls?" Rocky put in, and Jasper looked at her when she continued. "Have you seen this man?"

"Yeah, he's everywhere, at the games, at Reggie's after games, at the Senior Follies last year around about the time he first got to town. He's a good-lookin' guy and there's always a bunch of girls around him. He acts all holy and sometimes even carries a Bible, but I think that's so parents won't freak. There's boys in that Youth Group, but there's only about ten of them. They go to be around the girls, but they stay because they say this guy is the shit. They say he's funny as all get out, makes religion cool."

"You got friends who go there?" Layne asked.

"Not friends but I know some of the kids," Jasper answered.

"Then that's your job. You get them talkin' in school. Learn what you can and let me know," Layne ordered and Jasper nodded.

"Does Keira know this guy?" Rocky suddenly asked, and Layne's arms tightened around her.

"Don't know but I reckon," Jasper answered. "Everyone does."

"Do you think you could get Keira to point him out to me at Friday's game?"

"It's away. He won't be there," Jasper answered.

"Any game then, without her knowing why she's pointing him out," Rocky pushed.

"Roc, what the fuck?" Layne asked.

She let him go, turned in his arms and looked up at him. "I want to talk to him."

"Why?"

"And I want to get his picture and give it to Merry."

"That I can see, and that *I'll* do, sweetcheeks, but you aren't talkin' to this guy."

"I want to feel him out," she returned.

"Rocky—"

"I work around kids every day and around adults who work around kids. I'll know just by seeing him around the kids if he's right or not," she explained.

"You can use your gut for a lotta things, baby, but far's I know, havin' a bad feelin' about someone isn't cause for police to instigate a full-blown investigation, even if one of 'em is your brother. They gotta justify their use of limited resources, Rocky, and if Drew could pull that off, he'd be doin' this job himself," Layne told her.

Her face changed, the fire ignited in her eyes, Layne braced when he saw it, and she didn't disappoint.

"Okay, then I want to walk up to him, friendly-like, and, just as friendly-like, give him the indication that I'm not liking what I'm hearing at school. I'm paying attention. And I'm watching. And, oh, by the way, my boyfriend happens to be the town's badass private investigator. I'll do it just enough to make him be careful and maybe cool off what he's doing so Tripp can do his work, and in the meantime no one will get hurt, or *more* hurt, but not enough to make him run."

Yes, Rocky was a nut.

"Did you catch the part I said to Tripp about not wanting anyone to make him stop?" Layne asked.

"Yes, *Layne*, I caught that part. But I still want to make him stop, at least until we catch him," she shot back.

"Sweetcheeks, you're not getting involved."

"I'm already involved."

"Okay, then you're not getting *more* involved."

"Layne—"

"We're not gonna discuss this."

"Layne!"

Layne lifted his hands to rest on her jaws and he tipped her head back further as his face got into hers. "Jasper was right when he used the word predator. Anytime kids are involved, it's about predators. And predators are dangerous. Best case scenario, this is about drugs. Worst case scenario, baby, *you do not wanna know*. Either way, you are not gettin' *near* this guy. No lip, no discussion."

"These are my kids," Rocky snapped, pulling her jaw from his hands and stepping back.

"I get that," Layne replied, putting his hands on her neck and pulling her right back.

"Someone has to keep them safe."

"That'd be Tripp, but like I said today, Rocky, it's gonna take time. Give him time."

"And until then?"

"Until then, you keep your eyes and ears open. Jas does the same. Tripp does the same. You trust me and we fuckin' hope."

"That isn't good enough, Layne."

"It sucks, baby, and I know that, but that's all you got." Layne watched her eyes flash and he pulled her even closer, put his thumbs under her jaws to tilt her head back and put his forehead to hers. "I know this is frustrating and it's killin' you, baby, but stick with me on this and do *not* make it worse by puttin' yourself out there for this guy."

She stared into his eyes a beat until hers closed. Then she pulled in breath through her nose and let it out the same way.

She opened her eyes and whispered, "All right."

"I like her," Devin declared, and Layne and Rocky's heads turned his way. "Bet even with those fancy-ass duds, she don't live in no development with an HOA."

Layne turned to Devin, positioning Rocky in front of him at the counter and pinning her in again as he replied, "She lives in a luxury apartment complex."

"Okay then, I bet she don't *care* what her luxury apartment complex rules tell her what she can and can't do with her car," Devin returned.

"You're right. I don't care. But with the rent I'm paying, Devin, I should be able to park my car right next to the swimming pool if I've a mind to do it," Rocky put in.

"You got a swimmin' pool?" Devin asked.

"Yes," Rocky answered.

"Any lovelies who sunbathe there?" Devin went on.

"I just moved in a couple of weeks ago, Dev. It's October in Indiana so I haven't scoped it out yet and won't get that chance until next summer," Rocky told him.

"Well, I'll be back next summer. I'll help you scope it out," Devin offered and Layne heard Rocky's soft giggle.

His eyes went to his sons and both of them were looking at Rocky and smiling.

Then he looked at his watch and back to Jasper. "Too late to get started on pasta bake, bud. It's Keira time."

Jasper's body jolted. He looked to the clock over the microwave and hissed, "Fuck!" Then he held his hand out and wiggled his fingers. "Devin, keys."

"Don't care about no HOA," Dev grunted.

"You care about it or you go back to my office and sleep on my couch," Layne stated and Devin gave him a stubborn look.

"Devin! Keys!" Jasper fairly shouted, desperate not to be late for Keira.

"Just go, Jasper. I'll move Devin's car and start the pasta," Rocky said, slipping out from in front of Layne and heading to the stove.

"Thanks, Rocky, you're the shit," Jasper muttered then bolted to and out the door.

"You're not movin' my car either, girlie," Devin declared. "No woman drives the Calais, don't care how pretty she is."

Rocky turned her head and aimed the dimple at him, saying, "We'll see." Then she moved a pot to the faucet and started to fill it with water.

Layne reclaimed his forgotten beer and took a slug, his eyes on Devin.

When he dropped his beer to the counter, he muttered, "My money's on Roc."

Devin grunted.

Ten minutes later, the pasta was on, the hamburger was browning and the Calais was in the drive in the spot behind Rocky's Mercedes.

Layne found this hilariously funny for two reasons.

One, Devin wasn't lying when he said he didn't let women drive his car and he'd let Rocky drive his car. It was just the turn into the drive, but he'd let her do it.

And two, Rocky had pinned her own vehicle in for the night.

Layne sat at a chair at his outside table, a burning smoke between two fingers, the other three wrapped around a beer, his eyes on the dark, small wood behind his house.

That wood was one of the reasons he picked this place. His front faced houses, he had to drive through a sea of them to get home, but he walked out on his back patio and saw nature. It wasn't a lot of it but it was something.

Devin sat across from him with a stoagie between his lips.

"I know who she is, boy," Devin said quietly around his cigar.

"I know you know," Layne replied quietly back, lifted his beer and took a pull.

They'd spent a lot of time together and they didn't talk a lot, but both of them had talked and Devin knew all about Raquel.

Devin fell silent for a long while. Then he pulled his cigar out of his mouth, blew out smoke and whispered, "Look at that."

Layne looked at Devin to see Devin looking over his shoulder into the house so Layne twisted and looked into the house too.

The kids and Rocky were playing a game, girls against boys.

Keira was up on her feet, jumping up and down, her long, dark hair flying everywhere, her hands straight up in the air.

Jasper was sitting back in an armchair, his arms crossed on his chest, pretending to scowl, but his eyes were glued to Keira and far more than a scowl could be read from his expression and none of it was bad.

Layne couldn't see Tripp because he was sitting on the floor.

Rocky was on the couch, her head was to the back of it, her hands were up in front of her clapping and he could hear her laughter mingled with Keira's shouts of triumph.

Blondie, being a female but mostly being a canine, was jumping around Keira and sharing in what appeared to be a feminine victory by barking repeatedly.

Keira bent and he lost sight of everything but her behind as she gave Blondie a rubdown.

Layne turned back to the night.

"You lose hold of that again, boy, *any* a' that, I'll hunt you down and shoot you. Understood?" Dev declared.

"So that shit you handed me about the HOA is just that? Shit?"

"Fuck, Tanner, when I was your age, I'd *join* the fuckin' HOA patrol if it meant I could come home to that," Devin answered.

Layne didn't reply. He fell silent, took the last drag of his cigarette, stubbed it out in the ashtray on the table and sipped his beer while Devin enjoyed his stoagie.

Eventually, he said, "I need you to go to bed early, soon as Keira leaves."

"Why?" Devin asked.

"'Cause you're sleepin' on the couch. I wanna talk to Rocky and if you're on the couch the only place to do it is upstairs."

And Layne wasn't talking about the weight room.

"Gotcha," Devin said instantly, knowing Layne wasn't talking about the weight room.

Layne kept speaking.

"I know I briefed you yesterday, but I'll repeat that we need more than the tail Astley's been chasin' to make him come to heel. I told you Rocky was in a luxury apartment complex, but I didn't tell you I talked her into signin' the lease and I did it at a time when I thought she was far from hurtin'. With him cuttin' her off, she's gonna be hurtin'. I'm not in the position with her yet that I think she'll take help from me. Her brother doesn't have it, neither does her Dad. Short-term, maybe. Long-term, negative. That means time is against us, Dev. I don't want her worried more than she already is. We need somethin' on this guy that'll make him take the pressure off Rocky fast and then we need something that'll make him go away almost as fast. The dirtier, the uglier, the better."

"If this is time sensitive, I can make him dirty," Devin offered quietly.

"I'll let you know if it comes to that, but humiliation only comes on the heels of bein' outed for shit you did yourself. I don't only want him cowed, I want him brought low. You make shit up, with this guy, we'll be treated to righteous indignation and that doesn't help us and might even hurt."

"And if there isn't anything to find?"

"There's somethin' to find. This guy is an asshole. You just need to find it."

"You said he's investigating you," Devin noted.

"Got nothin' I've done I'm not proud of outside of walkin' away from those boys and everyone knows about that."

"Nope, you're right, Tanner. You haven't. But the shit you've done could be made to *look* dirty. This guy isn't afraid of not playin' fair, you gotta be ready for that to happen," Dev returned.

"Not worried about that either, Dev. People in this town, includin' my boys and Roc, know me and what kind of man I am, and, not includin' my boys but definitely Roc, know him and what kind of man he is."

"Yep, boy," Devin said softly. "That girl knows what kind of man you are."

His tone made Layne turn his head to look at Devin. "What's that mean?"

Devin kept peering into the night, puffing on his stoagie.

"Dev," Layne prompted.

Devin didn't turn his head when he replied, "You don't wanna know."

"You're wrong," Layne returned. He wanted to know and this was communicated further to Devin because Layne's voice was rumbling.

Devin looked at him. "Okay, then, you're not *ready* to know."

Layne straightened from his slouch in the chair. "Not in the mood for a mystery, Dev."

They stared at each other across the table before Devin asked, "You want her back?"

Instead of answering outright, Layne said, "You spent the evening with her."

"You want her back," Devin stated.

"Dev—"

Devin straightened, pulled the cigar out of his mouth and leaned toward Layne. "Tanner, that girl knows *exactly* what kind of man you are," he repeated and finished, "And you scare *the snot* out of her."

Layne felt the muscles in his neck get tight and he said, low and curt, "I'd never hurt her, old man."

"That ain't what scares her," Devin shot back.

"Come again?"

"How'd this start?" Devin suddenly asked.

"How'd what start?" Layne asked back.

"You and her. Why's she back in your life?"

"She had some stupid ass scheme…" Layne started then stopped. It hit him. It hit him so hard it suddenly all became clear.

He turned away from Devin and looked out into the night.

"Boy," Dev prompted.

"She came to the hospital when I got shot," Layne answered quietly.

"Right," Dev whispered.

Layne closed his eyes and muttered, "Fuck."

"Right," Dev whispered again.

Layne opened his eyes and whispered into the night, "Jesus."

"You're as domesticated as I suspect you're gonna get, dog, kids, house in a small town, office over a coffee shop. That don't mean you don't got dark and wild in you, boy. You got dark and wild in you, ain't no gettin' it out. Trust me, I know. A woman can see dark and wild. She can be attracted to it. She can want it. She can even fall in love with it. That don't mean she can live with it."

Layne stayed silent.

Dev sat back in his chair, put his stoagie to his lips and puffed.

Then he took it out and spoke. "Far's I can see, you got a lotta shit you gotta deal with. Her soon-to-be ex, whatever's happenin' at that church. But the biggest mission you got on your plate is to convince her that comin' home to dark and wild is a good thing, and more, convincin' her to *be* home and take a chance on the fact that that dark and wild may mean one day you *won't* be comin' home."

"Nothin's gonna happen to me, Dev."

"I know that. You know that. Your girl, she *don't* know that. So she's gotta think it's worth the risk."

"Her father was a cop," Layne pointed out. "Anyone knows the score, it's Rocky."

"A cop who got shot," Devin said, and Layne turned his head to look at his friend.

"What?"

Devin turned his head too. "A cop who got shot. I remember her story, boy."

"So she knows the score."

"And, I'll repeat, Tanner, that don't mean she can live with it."

"She's close with her dad. She's close with her brother. She's fine."

"Wild dreams," Devin replied.

Now the old man was just irritating him and he let it show when he said, "Dev, that doesn't make sense."

"You told me she shared your wild dreams. You went huntin' for yours. She ever leave this town?"

Layne stared at him then answered, "No."

"Somethin' means the world to you, you think one day you'll lose it, you got two choices. You cut yourself off from it so, when you lose it, that don't destroy you. Or you hold it so close, it can't ever go away. But if it does, you got as many precious memories as you can bag. Thinkin' about your girl, do either of those sound familiar?"

Layne suddenly found he was struggling to get enough oxygen in his lungs.

"Well, Tanner? Do they?"

"You know they do, Dev."

"So what you gonna do?"

Layne reached for his smokes and looked to the night.

"Two cigarettes, that's tellin'," Devin muttered.

"Shut up, Dev," Layne muttered back.

Devin shut up. Then he stubbed his stoagie out in the ashtray and got up. He moved around the table and stood behind Layne's chair as Layne fired up a cigarette.

On Layne's exhale, Devin said, "I'll leave you to your smoke."

"Obliged," Layne murmured.

Devin moved to the door and Layne knew there'd be a parting shot even before he heard Dev hesitate in sliding it open.

"Grab hold, Tanner," he whispered into the night then Layne heard the door open.

"Fuck," Layne whispered one second after he heard it close.

Twelve

TOOTHBRUSH

Rocky's warmth was pressed against him, her head on his chest, her arm heavy on his stomach, her knee resting on his thigh—pinning him to his back in the bed.

Her head shifted, her arm tightened around him and she slid up so her lips were against the underside of his jaw.

"You need to wake me up, baby. I need to get to work," she whispered.

Layne's eyes opened and he saw dark.

But what he felt was Rocky's warmth pressed against him, her head on his chest, her arm heavy on his stomach, her knee resting on his thigh—pinning him to his back in the bed.

Layne stared into the darkness and let penetrate the smell of her, the feel of her, the warmth, the softness, Rocky pressed close, pinning him to the bed for the first time in eighteen years.

He closed his eyes and focused on those sensations and the golden trail they left.

Then he opened his eyes and smiled.

The night before, after Layne sat outside brooding in the dark through his second cigarette and to the end of his beer, he entered the house to find Jasper and Keira preparing to leave and Rocky and Tripp in the kitchen putting the finishing touches on cleaning it.

Layne's eyes went to his watch and he saw that Jas had half an hour before Keira's curfew and Keira lived at most a ten minute drive away. So either his son was trying to ingratiate himself with Cal and Violet by taking her safely home with time to spare or he was going to take Keira somewhere so he could make out with her.

Layne was guessing the latter.

"Be back, Dad," Jasper called from the front door, his hand in Keira's.

"Thanks for dinner, Mr. Layne," Keira called after Jasper was done.

"Any time, Keira," Layne called back and they disappeared.

Layne looked at Devin who was standing at the front of the couch, already had his arms stretched over his head and was faking a huge yawn.

Then he heard Rocky announce in a firm, school teacher voice, "Layne, I need to talk to you."

Surprised at her tone, his eyes cut to her, she gave him a look and then strutted to the steps and up them, still wearing her heels, her ass swaying with every step.

Layne stood there and watched because he liked the show, but also because she was heading up the stairs and he hadn't had to make a complicated play to get her up there.

He heard Devin chuckle and he looked to his friend, saw his eyes shining and Layne grinned at him.

"Got some homework to do, Dad," Tripp informed him and Layne's gaze went to his son.

"Do me a favor and do it down here," Layne replied.

Tripp's eyes went in the direction of the stairs he couldn't see from his place in the kitchen. They came back to his old man, he grinned then he nodded.

Layne headed up the stairs.

The light over the desk was on when he got there but Rocky was standing in the middle of the set up, her head moving slowly, her eyes taking in the exercise equipment. When he arrived, they shot to him and he knew something was up. Rocky was *not* happy.

Jesus, how long was he outside?

She glanced at the open double doors to his room then back at him.

"Private," she said in a low voice, turned on her high heel and strutted into his room.

Layne stared after her a second then dropped his head and grinned at his boots while he followed her. He walked in, closed the door, wiped the grin off his face and looked at Raquel standing in his room.

Melody had come out after Layne had closed on the house. Melody had also chosen every stick of furniture and most of the homewares in that house. This included Layne's bedroom furniture, burgundy sheets and dark gray comforter. This also meant all of it was expensive, masculine, in good taste and of excellent quality. She'd bought him (using his money) three sets of sheets because she knew his aversion to laundry. Layne hadn't changed the sheets Rocky had slept in for over a week because it took that long for him not to smell her perfume. This could have been his imagination but he didn't fucking care.

"Do you work out?" Rocky asked, taking him out of his thoughts, and his eyes sliced to her because her tone was angry, and from her question, he couldn't fathom why.

"Come again?" he asked.

She jabbed a finger at the doors behind him. "Do you *work out?*"

"Uh…yeah," he answered.

She threw up both hands. "Layne, you got *shot* two months ago."

It was then, he got it.

He took two steps into the room, cautiously saying, "Yeah, sweetcheeks, I remember, I was there."

She crossed her arms on her chest. "You shouldn't be working out."

"Why not?" he asked.

She leaned toward him and hissed, "You were *shot* two months ago!"

Layne crossed his arms on his chest as well and replied softly, "Yeah, baby, I was shot, but it was *over* two months ago."

"You aren't recovered enough to work out," she declared.

"You in on my doctor's appointments?" Layne returned.

"No," Rocky snapped then glared at him.

Layne studied her, wondering how to play this, especially knowing what he now knew about Raquel Merrick.

Then he asked quietly, "You called me up here to tell me I shouldn't be working out?"

She kept glaring at him, trying to slip into a stare down, but he started toward her and she dropped her head, turning it slightly to the side to look at the floor as well as hide from him.

He got close and put his hands to her hips.

"Baby, look at me," he ordered gently, saw her chest expand and then, slowly, her eyes came to his. "I'm takin' it easy, yeah? I'm okay and I'll only get back to one hundred percent if I work on it. I'm not doin' my normal routine, I'm takin' it slow but steady and I'm bein' smart. Swear." She kept her eyes locked to his and he finished, "Now, tell me what's really buggin' you."

She bit her lip then pulled from his hands and walked across the room to look out the window. Layne watched as she tucked behind her ear that fall of hair that never stayed secured in the holders, clips and pins at the back of her head, and she stared into the dark night.

It took several seconds but she finally spoke to the window. "It isn't my place to say, Layne, he's not my son, but I'm having second thoughts about this Tripp business."

And that was when Layne knew it, seeing Rocky standing in his bedroom in her sexy getup and sexier high heels, her hair tucked behind her ear, her arms crossed on her chest, her concern for his son evident in her profile—Layne knew he was in love with her. Not only that, he'd never stopped loving her. Not once, not for a second, not for twenty-one years.

Fuck him.

It took a lot out of him but Layne stayed where he was, separated from her by ten feet in his bedroom.

"He'll be fine, Roc," Layne assured, and her eyes went away from the window, coming to him, her neck twisting to do it.

"I don't know. If this guy's a predator..." She shook her head. "Tripp's a fourteen-year-old boy," she reminded him.

"He's a smart kid," Layne told her.

"I know, Layne."

"He goin' in with his eyes open. He knows this is important. He won't jack it up and he won't put himself in danger."

Her brows shot up. "You sure about that?"

Finally, Layne allowed himself to walk to her. He got close but he didn't touch her.

"I been gone awhile but me and Tripp, we've stayed close all that time. I know my kid and I know him better now, bein' home. He'll be fine, Rocky, and if I didn't think he would, no way in hell I'd send him in there."

She turned to him, her body giving a small jolt as she did it. "I didn't mean to infer that you—"

"I know you didn't."

"I'm just worried," she shared.

"I know you are," he replied. "But I have faith in him and I'll have his back, so will Jas. He'll be fine."

Layne watched her eyes get warm, her mouth go soft and fought the urge to touch her. After she spoke again, he had to fight the urge to pick her up, throw her on his bed and cover her body with his.

"You're a good dad, Layne. Those boys love you."

He beat back the impulse and returned, "Tripp, yeah. Jas, not so sure."

She gave him the dimple after he stopped speaking, her eyes now warm *and* knowing, so he asked, "What?"

"Jasper is a cool, badass senior now, Layne, but when he was fourteen, he was a lot like Tripp. And, trust me, everyone in that high school knew all about you before you moved back home, and they did because Jasper frequently bragged about his badass, super-cool dad."

Layne turned his head and stared out the window, her words sliding across his skin light as a feather, but the sensations they made him feel were anything but light.

"Fucked up with those kids," Layne told the window.

"I hear a lot about what goes down at home and I see the consequences in my classroom and in those halls and you may not have made all the right choices, I know you went away, but you didn't turn your back on them. I don't know enough about it to know if you made mistakes, but I know enough about kids to know whatever mistakes you made, they weren't bad ones. Therefore, my professional opinion is, you didn't fuck up."

His eyes cut back to hers.

"At least not royally," she finished, giving him another dimple.

Christ, she didn't shut up, he was going to rip that soft sweater and tight skirt off her body and take her under the window.

Therefore, Layne didn't weigh his words or pick his time to announce, "You're spending the night."

She blinked and asked, "What?"

"You're spending the night," he repeated.

She looked to the door then to him. "Why?"

"'Cause your doors and security haven't been changed and 'cause you're my woman. A man and a woman together don't sleep at separate houses, not every night, even if kids are involved," he explained. "We want folks to think this is real, we gotta make it look real and the way you look, sweetcheeks, no man is gonna believe I got hold of somethin' like that and she doesn't sleep in my bed." He paused before he finished, "Regularly."

She was staring up at him, lips parted, eyes wide, off-balance.

She shook it off and reminded him, "Devin is sleeping on your couch."

"Yeah," Layne replied.

"So, where are you going to sleep? With one of the boys?"

"I'm gonna sleep here," he jerked his head to the bed.

"So, where am *I* going to sleep? On your weight bench?"

"No, you're gonna sleep here." He jerked his head to the bed again and she took a step back.

"What?" she whispered.

"We gotta make this look real," he repeated.

"Layne!" She threw her hands up. "No one can see *in* the house!"

"So?" he asked.

"So?" she repeated irately then looked around the room and back at him where her eyes narrowed. "What's going on?" she asked.

"You been in on it the whole time, Roc. You know what's going on," he answered.

Rocky crossed her arms on her chest and stated, "Two days ago we were at each other's throats. Now we're..." She hesitated, looked to the door again and back at him before she said in a heavy voice, "*Not.*"

"Two days ago was not good. The night before that, Rocky, when Melody was here, was worse. I can't take that, and what's more, I'm not gonna put *you* through that. We got a lotta shit goin' down around us and we don't need to be tearin' into each other while it happens. When this started, you and me, that night you came to dinner, that night of the game, it was good. We're goin' back to that."

"I'm not sure—" she started.

"I'm not askin' if you're sure. That's what we're doin'," he told her. Her eyes narrowed again and he went on, "You think we can convince people we're together, that this is real, if behind the scenes we're like that?" He shook his head. "We can't and too much is at stake. We gotta live this like it's real, Rocky, and that's what we're doin', out there," he pointed to the doors and then down at the floor, "and in here."

She stared at him then clipped, "Okay, Layne, agreed, but we're not sleeping in the same bed."

"You had a photographer takin' pictures in your house. You want someone, *anyone* seein' me sleepin' on your couch, wonderin' why and talkin' about it?"

"I'll get blinds," she shot back.

"All right, but you don't have them now," he returned.

She clamped her teeth together. Then she said, "Then I'll sleep here but I'll—"

Layne cut her off. "Sleep in my bed."

"Layne—"

"You're sleepin' in my bed."

"Layne!"

"Rocky, for fuck's sake, it's a big bed. Look at it. What do you think is gonna happen?"

Her head turned and she looked at the bed. He could tell she was thinking, and he felt no guilt at all for lying by implication that nothing was going to happen because he knew something was going to happen, and he knew exactly what that was going to be because he was going to be doing it…to her.

Then her head jerked back so she could look out the window and she muttered, "This is ridiculous."

"This is real. They gotta see it out there so we gotta live it in here," Layne returned and her eyes cut to him. It was totally lame, complete bullshit, and he knew it, but he sensed she was buying it.

Then she bought it.

"Perhaps we can start tomorrow," she suggested, and he beat back a grin.

Then he walked to his dresser, opened a drawer and pulled out a tee. He took two long strides back to her, tossed the tee at her and she caught it at her chest.

"Get changed and climb in, sweetcheeks," he ordered and watched her face pale. "I'll be back in five. We got stuff to talk about, we'll talk, we'll watch TV then we'll sleep."

"Layne," she whispered, but he didn't answer. He turned and walked out of the room.

He was in the kitchen clearing out the coffeemaker to get it ready for coffee the next morning when he heard her heels hit the tiles. His neck twisted and his eyes hit her, hers hit him, she gave him a scorching glare as she walked up to him, snatched her purse from the counter by the coffeemaker, turned smartly then started to walk back to the stairs.

Tripp was at the coffee table in the living room with his books. Devin was on the couch with his beer.

Before Rocky turned the corner, Layne announced loudly, "Boys, Roc and I are hittin' the sack."

Her body jerked and she tossed her head, but other than that, her heels on the tiles didn't miss a beat.

From his place on the floor, Tripp looked at his old man over the back of the couch and Devin did it from his place on the couch.

Then Tripp called, "'Night, Rocky," like he'd been saying goodnight to her while she walked to his father's bed since he could talk.

"Goodnight, Tripp." Layne heard Rocky call back from the stairs.

"Donuts tomorrow, darlin'," Dev added.

"Right, Dev. Goodnight." Rocky's voice was fading.

Tripp dropped his head and grinned at his books. Devin didn't move and grinned at Layne. Layne prepared the coffee for the next morning and he prepared it so it'd make a big pot.

Then he walked to his cell phone on the counter and called Jasper.

Not surprisingly, it rang four times before Jasper answered with an impatient, "Yeah Dad?"

"Do me a favor, on the way home from droppin' off Keira, stop at the store and pick up a toothbrush for Roc," Layne told him.

There was a beat of silence then, impatience gone, a smile in his voice, Jasper replied, "Gotcha."

"Be smart," Layne said as good-bye and disconnected, placed the phone on the counter and called goodnight to his son and Devin as he walked up the stairs.

When he arrived in his room, Rocky was in his t-shirt and in his bed. She was sitting cross-legged, the covers pulled up over her lap. She had the remote in her hand resting on her thigh, her eyes on the TV and her hair was out of the twist but it was now back in a ponytail, the ponytail full and wild from her hair being twisted up all day.

Her eyes came to him instantly and just as instantly she asked on a snap, "What do we need to talk about?"

Layne closed the doors behind him and walked to the dresser saying, "Jesus, sweetcheeks, give me a minute."

"I'm tired," she announced.

He pulled out a pair of pajama bottoms, looked to his watch, turned to her and said, "It's ten to ten."

"I go to sleep at ten o'clock every night, no fail, or I'm crabby in the morning."

She was so full of shit. He believed she went to bed at ten. She'd done that when she was with him. Rocky was early to bed and early to rise. But she was a morning person, always woke up in a good mood, even if she'd gone to bed late because she was studying or they were out.

"Give me a minute," Layne repeated, turning to head into the bathroom.

"Is this going to take long?" she called after him.

"It will if you don't give me a minute," Layne called back then turned and stood in the large archway that led to the bathroom. "Though, I could change in here."

Her eyes shot to the TV as she mumbled, "I'll give you a minute."

Layne pressed his lips together to bite back his smile, walked through the bathroom and into the walk-in closet. Well out of Rocky's sight, he pulled off his clothes, threw them in the direction of the laundry hamper Melody bought him, a hamper you couldn't see because of the clothes piled on and around it, then he pulled up his pajamas. He went to the bathroom, brushed his teeth and walked into his room.

Rocky's eyes stayed glued to the TV as he rounded the bed and got in. Shoving up the pillows, he settled with his back to them on the headboard, his body on top of the covers, legs stretched out in front of him and ankles crossed.

Even after he was in, Rocky didn't tear her eyes from the TV.

"Can you mute that, sweetcheeks?" he requested.

It took her a second to comply, and when she did, her head turned to him but her body stayed facing the TV across the room from the foot of the bed.

She lifted her brows.

Layne smiled at her.

"Well?" she prompted.

"I need your help with something," he told her.

"What?"

He slid down, rolled to his side toward her and put his head in his hand, his elbow in the pillows. Her body tensed as he did this and didn't relax until he stopped moving.

"It's about Gabby," Layne told her and Rocky's eyes got wide then, almost immediately, they blanked.

"What about Gabby?"

That's when Layne told her about Stew and about Gabby, most everything about Stew and also a lot about Gabby. He didn't leave much out including the fact that Gabrielle was living blind and acting desperate to keep hold of a shitheel of a man.

When he was done talking, she'd shifted so she had her body turned toward him, the remote in the bed beside her and her hands held loosely together in her lap. Her face had also grown soft and her eyes had grown warm.

"Poor Gabby," she whispered.

"Yeah," Layne whispered back.

"So what do you need my help with?" she asked.

"I gotta know how to play this," Layne answered, and her head tilted to the side in confusion.

"How to play it? Layne, you do what that Ryker guy said and make him pay through the nose and then get him behind bars."

"I'm not Gabby's favorite person, baby. She isn't gonna thank me for getting involved."

"She'll understand especially when she *understands*. She's a good mom, Layne. She'll want to make sure her boys are safe from that."

"She might eventually understand, Roc, but we got Jas and Tripp in the middle of this, and, like I said, I'm not her favorite person and she's gonna be pissed in order to hide the hurt and humiliation, and she's gonna take it out on me. When she gets pissed at me, sweetcheeks, she doesn't do it privately. Jas and Tripp are gonna hear it, see it and they're not gonna like it. They'll feel it. They'll feel for her. Jas already knows I'm steppin' up for his mom, he's glad I'm doin' it. Tripp'll feel the same. So they'll get caught in the middle and it's my job to try to cushion them from that shit."

Layne watched as she took in a deep breath, and while letting it out, she fell to her side, stretched out and settled with her head in her hand, elbow in the pillow, facing Layne.

"You think you can keep your part in this whole thing quiet?" she asked.

"I can try, but Gabby's got a way of finding shit out. Tripp's not in the know about me workin' this but he's also not dumb. Not to mention he's learnin' cool, but he's got a ways to go so he can run his mouth. He loves his mom. He loves his old man. He'll be happy I'm lookin' out for her and he won't get it that she won't be happy. Shit happens and I gotta plan accordingly."

She studied him a moment before she said softly, "Then you're going to have to suck it up, Layne."

Layne's brows knitted. "Come again?"

"Earlier tonight, you told me you fucked up with your boys. Now, Gabrielle has done it. Everyone knows Stew's a jerk. She knows it too, deep down. She knows she's fucked up, bringing Stew into her sons' lives not to mention bringing him into *hers*. I don't want to sound like a bitch, but all this boils down to her and the decisions she's made. She's the kind of person who has to take that out on someone, even if it's unreasonable because that someone was only trying to look out for her and their kids, then that someone, namely *you*, is going to have to suck it up."

He grinned at her. "Not sure you got much of a flair for reassurance, sweetcheeks."

Rocky grinned back. "Sorry, did I miss that part of my job description?"

"Skipped right by it, baby."

"I'll take time tomorrow to review it," she told him.

"That'd be appreciated."

The grin changed to the point he got the dimple, and Layne gave himself a moment to enjoy lying in bed facing Rocky and her dimple before he said softly, "I watch Letterman, baby, you gonna be able to sleep through that?"

The dimple faded and her face changed, showing him a hint of fear before she got her shields up and nodded, and if she hadn't changed, she wasn't lying. She went to bed at ten but Layne didn't so it was more accurate to say she went to *sleep* at ten because most of the time she was stretched out on the couch with Layne watching TV and she fell asleep while he kept watching it. If she was really out, he'd carry her to bed. But most of the time, when he moved, she woke up enough to stumble to their room, pull off her clothes, tug on one of his tees, collapse into bed and fall straight back to sleep.

"Pass me the remote," Layne ordered, and she rolled. Coming back to him, she handed him the remote.

Then she stayed where she was, head in hand but her eyes directed down her body toward the TV. Layne rolled to his back and sat up, lifting his legs, whipping the covers out from under him and settling back against the headboard.

Layne changed the channel finding a crime drama. He watched it then watched the news and finally watched Letterman.

Jas was home five minutes into the drama.

Tripp hit his bedroom fifteen minutes into it, Jasper following him half an hour later.

Rocky was asleep after ten minutes of the drama.

Layne fell asleep after trying to find it for half an hour after Letterman.

Now he was awake to find Rocky had moved during the night and she'd pinned him to the bed.

They'd both set a record. It took him one night to get used to it and it took her one night to break out of sleeping in her tight guarded ball and sprawl.

He turned his head to the side to look at the clock and he saw that his dream Rocky had given him plenty of time.

So Layne turned into his real Rocky. Wrapping his arms around her, he pulled her up his body. She released a sleepy mew and Layne lifted his head then buried his face in her neck.

He could smell a hint of her perfume.

He kissed her neck and then touched it with his tongue, sliding it up to right under her ear, liking the taste of her.

Her body started to come alert in his arms, so he touched his tongue to her earlobe then moved his lips along her jaw then up, to her mouth.

Her head tipped back and her voice was drowsy when she whispered, "Layne?"

That was when Layne slanted his head and kissed her. He started soft until he felt her hands light on the skin of his chest. Then he touched his tongue to her lips and her hands slid up to curl on his shoulders. He touched his tongue to her lips again, her mouth opened. Layne slid his tongue inside, and the tips of her fingers dug into his shoulders as she made another mew, this one not sleepy.

At the sound of it, the feel of it against his tongue, what it meant and what it was doing to his body, he rolled her to her back and then he *kissed* her.

Rocky tied herself up with him instantly, tangling her legs with his, winding her arms around his shoulders, one hand sifting in his hair, the other one drifting down his back and she let him kiss her, her back arching, her mouth unbelievably generous.

His hands moved, up her t-shirt and in, skin on skin, her body warm from his and being cocooned in his bed, her skin soft. She pressed up into him and moved one arm down, shoving it under his so she could reach more of his back and she did, her fingers trailing. Layne's hand went down to her ass, cupping her and pulling her into his hard cock and her fingers trailing the skin of his back became nails dragging against it.

Hot.

He stopped kissing her to mutter, "Yeah, baby," against her mouth and her reply was simply a breathy, "Layne."

For some reason, hearing her say his name like that, in that voice, her body soft and warm under him, Layne suddenly lost control. His hands in her shirt pulled it up and he didn't even notice her arms were already lifted by the time he got it over her head.

He tossed it aside and went back to her, kissing her harder, taking more and he got it, she gave it to him, and he knew Rocky had lost control too. He knew this because her hands were urgent on his skin, both of them, moving, pressing in, fingers, nails, then down, sliding inside the waistband of his pajamas, across, then up, down, inside, and the fingers of both her hands curled into the muscles of his ass as her hips pushed up, her back arching, her soft tits pressing into his chest.

"Fuck," he muttered against her mouth then moved down her chest. Not taking his time, his hands slid up her sides and he palmed one of her breasts then cupped it, lifted it. His mouth fastened around it, he took a second to swirl his tongue around her rock hard nipple before he sucked it deep.

Her back left the bed and she fed herself deeper into his mouth as he heard a low, deep moan glide up her throat.

Fucking hell. Beautiful.

His other hand cupped her other breast, thumb sliding across the nipple then tweaking, rolling as he pulled hard with his mouth on the other and Rocky's hands roamed on him, searching, clearly desperate. One moved around the front and curled tight around his cock.

That felt so good, Layne groaned against her nipple and her back arched again. Her hand tightening, she stroked him and pulled him closer at the same time, telling him she wanted more.

He let her go and pulled himself up her body, one arm wrapping around her hips, the other hand trailing down her belly. She stroked his cock and his mouth hit hers.

"You ready?" he asked and she arched her neck. "Baby?" he called, his fingertips sliding into the top of her panties, happy to find out for himself when her body locked, her hand left his cock and shot to his wrist, wrapping around.

"No," she whispered. She tucked her chin down and pulled his hand up her belly. "I'm sorry."

He tugged his wrist from her fingers and slid it along her waist, rolling her with him to take them to their sides.

"That's okay, honey."

She tucked her face into his throat and nestled into his body, repeating on a whisper, "Shit, I'm so sorry."

"Rocky, baby, that's okay."

Both her hands were on his chest and he felt her fingers curl in so they were held in light fists against his skin.

He kept one arm wrapped tight around her, her body close, and his other hand slid into her hair. The ponytail holder still in it, he gently yanked it out, tossed it to the bed and started to run his fingers through her hair.

When her fists didn't loosen, he asked gently, "You all right?"

"I'm sorry, Layne," she repeated.

"Baby, I said it's okay."

She pressed her face into his throat and then said so softly he barely heard her, "I'm on my period."

His hand cupped her head, his arm gave her a squeeze and he understood.

She grew up with two men and no mom at one of those times when a girl *really* needed her mom. She had therefore guarded that fact of nature from the men in her house like it was a state secret. She did the same when she'd first moved in with Layne. Clearly, she'd not moved beyond this which, he had to admit, caused him some uneasiness because she was now thirty-eight years old, she'd spent ten years living with a medical doctor and it was a goddamned fact of nature.

On the other hand, he was fucking thrilled she'd stopped the proceedings because she was on her period and not because she didn't want them to continue. Not to mention the fact that she'd cuddled into him afterward instead of throwing a conniption fit, bolting from bed, getting dressed and stomping from the house.

Layne didn't respond and started sifting his fingers through her hair again. He did this until her fists uncurled and her hands rested flat against his chest.

Finally, he whispered, "You gotta get up, Rocky."

"Yeah," she whispered back.

"Jas bought you a toothbrush. I'll bring it up."

For some reason, her body locked and her hands moved quickly to his shoulders, fingers pressing in as her head tipped back, taking her face out of his throat.

"Jasper bought me a toothbrush?" she asked.

"Yeah," Layne answered.

Her voice had changed a lot when she said, "Layne."

He grinned in the dark and replied, "I'll go get it."

Her fingers curled deeper and she repeated, "Layne."

"Rocky, you need to get a move on."

He started to roll away from her but she rolled with him. Coming up on an elbow in the bed, she planted the other hand firm in his chest and he saw her shadow looming over at him.

"You asked your *son* to buy me a *toothbrush*?" she snapped, sounding hilariously disgusted.

"He was out so…yeah," Layne answered.

She lifted her hand and smacked his shoulder with it, saying on a quiet shout, "Layne!"

He knifed up to sitting and his arms went around her. He twisted and took her down to her back, his torso pinning her to the bed.

When he got her in position, he informed her, "Sweetcheeks, everyone needs a toothbrush."

"I can't believe you," she hissed.

"Am I wrong?"

"You are not to be believed!"

"Baby," he murmured, sounding only slightly less amused then he actually was.

"Layne," she snapped back, sounding probably just as pissed as she actually was.

Even though he couldn't see her clearly in the dark, they went into stare down. He let this go on for a while before he used option two, bent his head and kissed her hard.

She resisted, he persisted, and the minute he got his tongue in her mouth, her body relaxed under his.

He took his fill and enjoyed doing it, almost too much, before he lifted his head and ordered, "Get yourself sorted out, sweetcheeks. I'll be back with your toothbrush."

Then he intentionally squeezed the breath out of her so she couldn't get a shot in by rolling his bodyweight over her, getting out of bed on her side, lighting the lamp on the nightstand and aiming a grin at her lying on her back but up on one elbow, the other hand holding the covers to her chest, glaring at him before he walked out of the room to get her toothbrush.

When Layne hit the kitchen, he saw Devin sitting at a stool in his wife beater and boxer shorts, a mug of steaming coffee in his hand, his eyes on the news playing low on the TV. They cut to Layne when he appeared and they watched Layne walk to the toothbrush sitting on the island.

The toothbrush Jasper bought Rocky was white and pink. Yes, his son was sharp. As a tack.

Also on the island were two big white baker's boxes opened and stuffed full with Hilligoss donuts.

Layne stopped and looked at Devin. "Please tell me you put on your pants when you went to the bakery."

"Of course, boy, it's cold out there."

Thank fuck.

Layne turned to the cupboard with the mugs, making a note to move them to the one over the coffeemaker, and he did this in an effort not to think about why in *the fuck* Devin took *off* his pants when he arrived home from the bakery, when Devin went on, his tone mulish, "Calais is at the curb."

"That's good," Layne returned, walking his mug to the coffeemaker. "'Cause Rocky's gonna blow through here in about five minutes and she's probably gonna take out the garage door when she goes and it'd be a cryin' shame she damages the Calais, seein' as you put so much effort into keepin' it in pristine condition for twenty-five years."

Without missing a beat, Dev muttered, "Better put my pants on then."

Layne poured a cup of coffee, spooned in two sugars and was stirring it when he turned and saw Devin sauntering back to the island in wife beater and slacks.

"Remember a time when they left your room in the mornin' with a smile on their face, boy. You must be losin' your touch," Devin remarked.

"Figure you'll be in town for a while, old man, it might be good to brace," Layne advised, dropped the spoon on the counter and took a sip of joe.

Devin's eyes locked on Layne's. "We gonna have fireworks?"

Layne dropped his hand holding the mug but held Dev's gaze. "How easy do you think it is for a man to talk a woman into takin' a risk on dark and wild?"

"Lotta women not worth that effort," Dev returned. "Though, the one you got on your hands, boy, it is and it is 'cause it's not gonna be easy *at all* and that means...*kaboom*!"

Layne walked to the toothbrush and tagged it, saying, "Like I said, brace."

Then he turned and walked up the stairs and into his room. He found Rocky in the bathroom in her bra, her back to him, zipping up the back of her skirt.

"Toothbrush, sweetcheeks," he said, and she whirled, one arm going to her middle, one arm covering her breasts, but not before he saw her bra, too, was deep pink and made entirely of lace.

Christ.

"A moment of privacy, *Layne*," she snapped, her eyes full of fire.

Her hair was back in a ponytail and Layne tossed the toothbrush on the bathroom counter, set his mug down and walked up to her. He reached around, wrapped his fist around her ponytail, tugged her head gently back and kissed her hard and closed-mouthed.

When he lifted his head, he kept his hand at her ponytail so she couldn't move.

Therefore, she had to fight her fight verbally. "What was *that*?" she hissed up at him and he grinned down at her.

"Hot piece of ass in my bathroom wearin' nothin' but a sexy bra and a tight skirt after she spent the night pinnin' me down to the bed, I walk in on her, I'm gonna kiss her." He gave her ponytail a playful tug. "Just keepin' it real, sweetcheeks."

"Don't call me a piece of ass," she snapped, definitely pissed.

"Baby," he replied, not pissed at all.

"And will you *stop* calling me *sweetcheeks*?" she asked on a demand.

"No," he answered.

She glared at him then stated, "I did not pin you down to the bed."

"Rocky, you were all over me."

"Was not."

"You were."

"Was not!" Her voice was rising.

"Why do you think you got the wakeup call you got, Roc?" he lied through his teeth. "Man wakes up with a woman wrapped around him, he acts on instinct."

She tugged her hair from his hand and stepped back. Forgetting she was only wearing a bra and skirt, she planted her hands on her hips.

"I see us sleeping together is *not* going to *work*," she declared.

"I don't know." He grinned. "Worked for me."

She leaned back. "You do know, every cop on the force thinks of me like a sister? It's highly unlikely they'll arrest me for assault and battery."

Layne couldn't take it anymore. He tipped back his head and laughed, and since he didn't have to fight the urge, his arm shot out and hooked her around the waist, yanking her forward roughly so her body slammed into his. He tilted his head and shoved his face in her neck so he could laugh there.

"Layne," she called, her hands on his abs pushing.

"Give me a second, sweetcheeks, I'm tryin' not to bust a gut here."

"Layne!" she shouted.

His head came up and he smiled down at her. Then he kept smiling down at her as he wrapped his other arm around her shoulder blades and pulled her closer, trapping her hands between them.

Then he dipped his face close to hers and he whispered, "You're cute as hell when you get pissed. You always were cute as hell when you got pissed. I used to piss you off just to see you get pissed, I liked it so much."

Her hands stopped pushing and her lips parted as the fire died out and she gazed up at him with that intensity in her eyes.

He dropped his head so his forehead was resting against hers. "And, baby, I don't like it any less now," he whispered.

He heard her suck in a soft breath but he ignored it, touched his mouth to hers and let her go.

Turning, he nabbed his coffee mug and didn't look at her as he walked out of the room, saying, "Dev went to Hilligoss. There's two dozen donuts downstairs. You better get down there before the boys do, sweetcheeks, or you're gonna be disappointed."

Then he walked out of the room.

Thirteen

My Kind of Partner

The security beep sounded and Layne, sitting at his desk in his office, turned to look at the monitor.

Colt was walking up the steps.

Layne glanced at his watch and clenched his jaw. He was late. He was supposed to go over to Rocky's for a quick dinner before they went to the boys' game. But that afternoon, a bitter wind started to whip through the 'burg and he needed to go home and get a sweater. To get to Rocky's he should have left ten minutes ago. To get home and then get to Rocky's he should have left twenty minutes ago.

He heard the front office door open and close and he reached out to the desk to pick up his cell. He started to engage it when Colt's tall frame filled the doorway and his thumb on his phone stopped when he saw Colt's expression.

"Have a minute?" Colt asked.

"I didn't until I saw your face," Layne answered.

Colt walked in, sat down in one of the two chairs facing Layne's desk and didn't say a word or take his eyes from Layne.

"Give me a second, I gotta call Rocky. I'm already late for dinner," Layne told him and Colt nodded.

Layne scrolled down to Raquel's number as he watched Colt lean forward and tag a yellow legal pad from Layne's desk then he nabbed a pen.

He sat back and started writing on the pad while Layne put the phone to his ear.

It rang once then, "Hey, Layne!"

Layne blinked and his eyes unfocused so much Colt was there but he'd disappeared.

She sounded excited and happy, excited and happy to hear from him.

It had been two days since Keira, pasta bake and Rocky spending the night in his bed.

After that, Rocky had put her shields up but it wasn't the same game as she'd been playing. It was friendlier, more open but she was still on guard. He let her have that play and backed off, not because he intended actually to back off, but because he wanted to soften her up, get her guard down, take her off-balance before he made *his* next play.

Not to mention, he had to wait until she was done with her fucking period.

They'd slept together both nights in his bed. Both nights she started with her back to him and both nights he'd woken with her pinning him to the bed. Each morning, Layne woke before Rocky, waited until she did and also waited while she slid carefully away and exited the bed. Layne never let on that he was awake before her and Rocky never spoke of it. He didn't know if she knew he was awake and she didn't share.

They'd also had dinner at his house both nights. The first night was Wednesday before the Youth Group meeting.

When the boys were gone, Rocky had been as jumpy as a cat waiting for Tripp and Jasper to get home. Luckily, Devin was there and entertained her with his own particular blend of cantankerous, flirtatious and hilarious.

When the boys got home, though, Raquel interrogated them like she'd been trained by the CIA. Even so, they didn't have much, it was a Church Youth Group and the boys were getting the lay of the land. But Jasper decided to go to the Saturday afternoon meeting as well before he left Tripp to it. They didn't try to bag anything with a print. The other kids were surprised to see them there, the Layne boys weren't Church Youth Group kind of guys. Their turning up caused a minor sensation and his sons, rightly, didn't make any rash moves.

The second night was Thursday, and after dinner, he made Rocky stretch out on the couch with him and watch TV while Tripp took one armchair, Devin the other and Jasper talked on the phone with Keira upstairs while he was supposed to be doing his homework.

Rocky didn't like it but she didn't fight it, likely because Tripp and Devin were there. She fell asleep with her back to the couch, her cheek to his chest, her arm resting on his abs and her legs tangled with his. And just like eighteen years ago, when he moved after Letterman, she woke, groggy, and he helped her stumble up the stairs. She disappeared in the walk-in closet while he gave her time to change, came out wearing his tee, collapsed in bed and was out in seconds.

But for two days she didn't give him an in and she didn't let her guard down for him to knock her off-balance. She played the part, but every word, look and step she executed with extreme caution.

And now she was greeting him, excited and happy.

"Hey, sweetcheeks," he greeted back.

"We're having hot beef sandwiches for dinner," she informed him and then finished, "with cheese."

"Sounds good, Roc, but I'm gonna be late."

There was silence then a disappointed, "Oh."

Fuck. He liked Rocky excited and happy. He was not a big fan of Rocky disappointed.

"Colt came by, we need to talk," he explained.

"Um...okay. Are you going to be long?" she asked, and Colt moved. Layne looked at him and saw he was leaning forward.

Colt dropped the legal pad in front of Layne and the words, "Do you sweep?" were written on it.

Layne's eyes went to Colt. He wasn't talking about the floors. He was talking about bugs.

"Might be a while," Layne said to Rocky, but his eyes never left Colt as he nodded his head.

Colt sat back and held Layne's gaze.

Rocky hesitated then replied, "I'll wrap them up. We'll take them with us and eat on the road."

"Perfect, baby," he murmured. "Gotta go."

"Okay, Layne. Tell Colt I said hi."

"Will do, Roc. Later."

"Bye."

He disconnected and Colt didn't hesitate before saying, "It's clean?"

"It's clean," Layne replied, moving the phone in his hand, sliding it between his fingers, end to end, then flipping it around and doing the same. "What's up?"

"We got a situation," Colt replied.

"That being?" Layne asked.

"Sean's sister," Colt told him and Layne's brows went up.

"Sean's sister?"

"She's got a tumor on her pituitary gland," Colt answered.

That sucked. Sean was a good man, a good cop. A newer detective in the department, he was young, his sister younger, but it would suck that anyone was sick. That said, Colt didn't need to give him this information and therefore Colt had another reason for giving him this information.

"You're tellin' me this because…?" Layne prompted.

"I'm tellin' you this because it's benign, it won't kill her, but it messes with her hormones. She's gotta have replacement therapy her whole life or she'll feel like shit. She got diagnosed, had neurosurgery where they got most of the tumor, but before they got the tumor, it damaged the gland. That's not unusual, Sean says the damn thing is the size of a pea and it's not easy, maneuvering up there. They go through the freaking nose." He shook his head then went on, "But the gland doesn't work right and she's not feelin' better. She's got two kids, an asswipe of a husband who bagged on her when she started to get sick, before she was even diagnosed. He's gone and not comin' back. Now they're tellin' her she has to have an injection, she has to take it every day and they say it'll help her get back on her feet, feel more like herself. She can't work but part-time, doesn't have the energy, quality of life is shit. She needs this injection."

"Okay, Colt, now you're tellin' me *this* because…?" Layne repeated.

"Because, with part-time work, her insurance won't cover the entirety of the injection and it's expensive."

"You takin' a collection?" Layne asked, but he knew he wasn't.

"They say sometimes it takes as long as six months for it to really kick in. She's got a good job, pay's all right, but part-time isn't gonna cut it. Until she gets back on her feet, goes back to full-time, gets decent insurance, she's gonna need help and that help's gonna be expensive."

Layne stared at Colt and Colt stared back.

Then Layne whispered, "He's vulnerable."

He meant Sean. Sean wanted his sister to feel better and her kids' life to get better.

Which meant he needed money to do it, a lot of it, more than a cop made unless that cop was dirty.

"Someone's recruiting," Colt whispered back.

Colt knew about Rutledge. This didn't surprise Layne. Not much got by Colt and Rutledge's slipshod police work would definitely not be lost on Colt.

Colt also knew about Layne, and more than likely, Merry. This also didn't surprise Layne.

"I have to let that cool down," Layne said quietly.

"I get you, that doesn't mean it's not still hot," Colt replied. "You gotta know what you're workin' and who you're up against."

"You gonna let Sean go down?" Layne asked and this *did* surprise Layne. Those boys took care of their own, like they were blood brothers. And even if they didn't, Colt being Colt, wouldn't let Sean go down.

"You aren't the only one lookin' into this," Colt returned. He was ticked. Not angry, irritated that Layne would even think that. "I understand why Merry didn't go to the captain because, bein' how the captain is, that's not a great play and that's the reason I'm not makin' that play either. I've never seen this shit before but I've heard of it. That small of a department, this small of a town, that shit leaks out, we're all tarred with the same brush and cap will fuck it up and it'll be sure to leak. If we take care of this internal, private, that doesn't happen. But it's gotta be taken care of."

"Colt, I was shot because of this shit," Layne said.

"Yeah, Layne, I remember," Colt returned.

"This is dangerous. You and Feb got a young son," Layne reminded him.

"And you got two older ones," Colt shot back.

Layne shook his head. "Let me work this."

"My department."

"Colt, I'm tellin' you, let me work this."

"Sean'll go down. This shit with his sister, it's been goin' on a long time. It's not good, the whole family's strugglin'."

Layne stared at Colt and got an idea.

"Rocky," he said.

Colt shook his head. "I gotta hope you know what you're doin', sendin' her in there, her gettin' close to—"

Colt had noticed that too.

"Not my choice," Layne cut him off firmly. "She wants to do something, there's no talking her out of it. I got her back, so does Merry. What you see with their little chats is as close as she's gonna get. It makes her feel like she's doin' something and I'm givin' her that. But that's all she's doin'."

"Then what do you mean, 'Rocky?'" Colt asked.

"What I mean is, she does those charity gigs. She helps set them up. I tell her about this, she'll be all over it. Something else to focus on, not that piece of shit in the department."

Colt grinned. "Cop's sister goin' all out for a cop's sister."

Layne grinned back. "All in the family."

"It'd be good around about this time, that dirt in the office gettin' up in his face, Sean's reminded about family."

"Yeah, it'd be good," Layne agreed.

Colt's grin turned into a smile. "Hear she's raised a fuckwad of cake."

Layne had no idea. He knew she did them because he'd heard about it in passing. He didn't know how successful she was at it. Though, this was Rocky, if she could talk the School Board into letting her kids listen to rock 'n' roll for a week in English Lit class, she could probably raise millions.

"I'll talk to her, get her to talk to Sean," Layne replied.

"Like that idea, Tanner," Colt said and Layne nodded. Then Colt's brows went up at the same time the ends of his lips tipped up and he asked, "What's for dinner?"

"Hot beef sandwiches," Layne answered then smiled. "With cheese."

"I don't even know what the fuck that is and it sounds good," Colt returned.

It did and Rocky had cooked both nights at his house. She'd come to his place Wednesday night with enough grocery bags in her car to feed twelve for Thanksgiving dinner. The first night was roast chicken with stuffing, mashed potatoes and gravy. The second night was pork roast with fried potatoes and fresh baked rolls.

Gabby wasn't much of a cook, she hated doing it and her food tasted like she hated doing it. Devin had been single since his third wife took off with his baseball card collection fifteen years ago and he'd been that way because he was the kind of man who missed his baseball card collection more than his wife. Devin could pour a helluva mixed drink, but he wouldn't know a spatula from a frying pan. Jasper, Tripp and Devin were in ecstasy because Rocky loved to cook and she made roast chicken and pork taste like heaven on a plate.

Layne sure as fuck liked her food but he liked her cooking in his kitchen for him and his boys better.

And her being around meant the boys didn't bitch when they had to clean up.

Yes, Layne was looking forward to hot beef sandwiches with cheese. But he was hoping that he'd have them with a Rocky, happy and excited to see him.

"I gotta get to Rocky, brother," Layne told Colt.

Colt straightened from the chair saying, "Yeah. See you at the game?"

Layne palmed his phone and stood too, replying, "Yeah. You goin' to an away game?"

Colt smiled at him. "Cal came over yesterday. Over what sounded to be a much-needed bourbon, he told me he was takin' Keira and Heather because she's fired up to support her new boyfriend while he plays ball, and since she's had three fender benders since she got her license, Vi isn't letting her drive outside the city limits and Vi doesn't trust Heather's driving any more than Keirry's. If Cal didn't say he'd take her, he'd be forced to put duct tape on her mouth and tie her to a chair because she wouldn't shut up about it. He didn't think Vi would like that overly much, so he said yes. I'm goin' for moral support."

That was about a quarter of the reason Colt was going. Colt was a 'dogs fan too. He'd played for them years ago and was good enough to get a partial ride to Purdue. That team did good things for him and he remained loyal to the end.

But the reason Cal told Colt he'd said yes was total bullshit. Joe Callahan was a pushover for that girl. He'd kill for her, her sister and her mother. Layne knew this because Cal got that chance, he pulled the trigger and didn't blink.

Layne walked Colt to the door where they shook hands and clapped each other on the arm before Colt took off. Then Layne closed down the office and left, setting the security alarms as he went. He drove home and lifted the garage door, didn't pull inside and walked through the garage and into the house.

Blondie greeted him, and if his son's dog could cross her legs, she would. So Layne unarmed the alarm and let her out back. Then he turned and jogged up the stairs.

Going direct to his drawers, he pulled out a thermal and then went to the walk-in closet, flipping on light switches as he went. He unbuttoned his shirt and shrugged it off, throwing it without looking in the direction of the mound of dirty clothes. He pulled on the thermal, yanked a sweater off the built-in shelves in the closet and tugged it on. He grabbed the scarf his mother bought him for Christmas last year and his leather jacket and headed back to the bedroom, putting them on, and stopped dead, staring at the bed.

It was made. Not like Layne "made" it, yanking up the covers and letting them fall. The comforter was smoothed, the sheet and comforter folded over at the base of the pillows. The four pillows stacked neatly on top of each other, two by two.

He turned and looked at the long, double-basin bathroom counter. Next to his toothbrush, Rocky's pink and white one was in the holder Melody bought that was on Layne's side of the sink. Also on Layne's side of the sink was a makeup bag that had exploded. Tubes, bottles and tubs everywhere, applicator brushes, a stick of deodorant, a fancy bottle of perfume, a comb and a bunch of hairpins scattered around.

That morning, Layne had left before Rocky because he had to get to Indy to follow a man to work, a new case. The man didn't go straight to work, as suspected. Rocky had brought a bag with her on Thursday night but Layne hadn't paid much attention to it except the fact that he liked that she brought it. Clearly, Rocky had gotten ready at his place, standing at his basin doing her makeup and hair.

A memory tugged at him and Layne walked to the bed. He lifted the pillows on his side and found his pajamas folded neatly under it. Then he walked around the bed to Rocky's side, lifted the pillows and found his tee that she'd been wearing folded under those. She'd done that, every morning, when they were living together.

Every morning.

He dropped the pillows and drew in breath through his nose, smelling the indistinct scent her perfume.

It was faint but it was still there.

Then he smiled to himself, turned out the lights, walked swiftly from the room and jogged down the stairs. He let Blondie in, secured the sliding glass door and gave Blondie a rubdown that lasted a lot less time than she liked. He set the alarm at the garage door and jogged to his SUV.

He swung in and drove to Rocky's.

He was two steps from the landing to her door when the door was thrown open and she was out of it. He was one step from the landing when she turned to him, eyes bright, giving him the dimple. He stopped dead at the sight of her and she lifted both of her hands and slapped them, hard, on his chest just under his shoulders. So hard, he was glad he was wearing three layers, and she left her hands where they were.

"You will not *believe* what happened!" she cried.

On his step, eye to eye with her, the dimple appearing to be a permanent fixture, Layne smiled. "What?"

"*I* don't even believe it!" she said on a near shout.

Layne put his hands to her hips and repeated, "Roc, what?"

Her head suddenly turned sharply to the side and then she looked back to him and exclaimed, "Oh! We have to go!"

Then she tore from his hands, turned so quickly her ponytail whipped across his face and flew into the apartment.

Layne followed her and closed the door, saying, "Rocky."

But when he got into the apartment, she was already at the kitchen counter, pulling on a velvet jacket that was another berry color, this time blackberry. It fit her snug over her matching deep purple turtleneck. She buttoned the jacket with one hand and grabbed the handles of a bag that was on the counter.

"I've wrapped up the sandwiches. We'll eat in the car. I've got drinks in the bag too." She hefted up the bag and handed it to him, ordering, "You carry that."

He took it, and considering he thought it contained sandwiches and drinks, its weight surprised him. His arm jerked down with it, she saw it and her shining eyes came to his.

"I made cookies. Chocolate chip. You get two. The rest are for Devin and the boys," she announced then turned back to the counter, nabbed a scarf and her purse and started winding the scarf around her neck with one hand, the other one hooking the strap of her purse on her arm at the same time she started shooting around the apartment turning off lights.

"Sweetcheeks, this bag weighs a ton. How many cookies did you make?" Layne asked as he watched her move in her velvet jacket, tight dark gray cords and high-heeled black boots.

"Three dozen," she answered, switching off the last light then heading toward the door, Layne following.

"Three dozen and I only get two?" Layne asked when she'd pulled open the door.

She whipped her head around again, her ponytail flying to land over her shoulder and curl around the scarf at her neck, and she smiled up at him. "Okay, you can have three."

He smiled down at her and muttered, "Thanks, baby."

Her smile brightened even further, the dimple firmly in place, then she exited the house. Layne moved out behind her, she turned and locked the door, and they headed down the stairs.

"All right, Roc, you wanna tell me what's goin' on?" Layne asked.

"In the car, we need to get going," she answered, hoofing it to his Suburban.

Layne bleeped the locks. Rocky climbed in and he handed her the bag which she set between her legs on the floor as he shut her door. Layne rounded the back and when he swung in his side, she was already buckled up but straining the belt because she was bent forward and digging in the bag. She pulled out what appeared to be a huge, oval, foil wrapped sand-wich while Layne pulled out of the parking spot.

"You gonna talk?" he asked when they were out of the complex, on the road and she seemed intent on unwrapping the sandwich. A sandwich that, as she unwrapped it, subsequently filled the cab with a mouth-watering scent of fresh roast beef.

"Get this," she started, handing him the sandwich that had its foil-over-greaseproof paper unwrapped enough for him to eat, wrapped enough so that he could eat it without the gargantuan portion of warm beef and melted cheese stuffed in a hoagie roll dripping all over his jeans. "I called my attorneys this morning because, well…" She paused. "I told you about Jarrod playing dirty but I didn't tell you *how* and he cut me off, money-wise. Rent is due at the end of next week and things will be…" She paused again. "Well, you know, I told you about it."

"Yeah?" Layne prompted through a mouth full of succulent, warm roast beef and tangy melted cheese when she stopped speaking.

"So, I called my attorneys to see if anything was happening with that. They promised to call Jarrod's attorneys, and this afternoon, I had a text to phone them back urgently."

Layne had a feeling he knew where this was going. He'd been letting Devin do his work and hadn't asked for a status report since that first night. Layne was the only man Devin had worked with in his career, post-CIA, so Devin was used to working alone, doing his own thing and not reporting in or asking for instructions. Therefore, Layne's feeling was that Devin had done his own thing.

"Did you phone them back?" Layne asked Rocky and glanced her way.

She yanked open a bag of chips and set it between the two seats, the opening of the bag facing Layne.

"Oh yeah, I phoned them back," she told him. Going back to the bag and digging, she pulled out a can of cola and snapped it open. "And guess what?"

"What?" he asked as she put it in his cup holder.

"Fifty thousand dollars is what!" she announced then started digging in her bag again.

"Come again?" Layne asked.

She came up with a can of diet orange, which she popped open while saying, "Fifty thousand dollars, Layne. He's transferring it into my new account on Monday."

Yep, Devin had done his own thing.

Layne smiled and said, "Good news, sweetcheeks."

She placed her pop in her holder and went back to the bag. "No, Layne, not good news. *Great* news! I was freaking *out!*" she declared and Layne's smile died. "My attorneys told me they called his attorneys and they phoned back in, like, thirty minutes. He offered ten K at first but my attorneys pushed it and got *fifty!*" He glanced at her to see she had her own sandwich in her hand. She sat back, wiping the fingers of her other hand on her brow and emitting an adorable yet annoying due to its cause, "Shoo!"

That fucking jackass. Ten K? He should give her fifty times that. He had it and she'd lived with his bullshit for ten years so she'd earned it. Not to mention, she'd lived a week with the worry she couldn't make her rent.

Right before she took a huge bite of her sandwich, she said, "I wonder what happened."

Layne knew what happened. Devin Glover and Natalie Ulrich happened.

"Maybe he isn't so stupid," Layne replied.

"Or maybe he's moving on," Rocky suggested through a mouth full of sandwich he knew she swallowed before she went on, "That would work for me, maybe he'll settle and this will be done and I can get *on* with my *life*."

Layne glanced at her before his eyes went back to the road, knowing one way or the other, Dr. Jarrod Astley would settle so Rocky could get on with her life.

"Beginning of the end, baby," he muttered.

"I hope so," she replied.

Layne ate and drove and when he heard Rocky's hand crinkling the chip bag, he spoke.

"Need you to think about doin' somethin' for me."

"What?" she asked, and he heard crunching chips.

"You know Sean O'Leary?"

"Of course," she replied, reaching for her orange soda.

"His sister's in a bad way."

She took a slug, put the pop back, and Layne heard the foil move on her sandwich as he peeled back more on his.

"I know," she said softly. "Meghan's had it tough. She was having symptoms for ages and no one knew what was going on. It took five years to diagnose her. Can you believe that?"

Jesus, five years?

"There's a treatment that they think can help," Layne told her. "Colt stopped by, told me about it." Layne took another bite of sandwich and said while chewing. "It's expensive."

"Most of them are," Rocky murmured, and he heard her moving foil.

Layne put his sandwich in his hand at the steering wheel and dug into the bag of chips. "She can't afford it and I thought you could do your magic."

He knew she'd turned to face him when she asked, "My magic?"

He shoved the chips in his mouth, chewed, swallowed, glanced at her and saw she was looking at him. "Yeah, baby, your charity magic. Raise some money for her. Help her out."

He glanced back out the windshield and reached for his pop as she whispered, "Shit."

Layne took a slug and put the soda back as he said, "Roc, your plate is full, you don't have to—"

"It's not that, it's just that Halloween is just around the corner. A charity haunted house would be *the bomb*. We did that three years ago, ran it for the whole month of October and we raised a fortune. But now, I don't have enough time to pull it off, and to rake in the dough, we need it to run awhile." She paused for several long beats before she muttered, "I'll have to think about this."

Layne smiled before he ate the last bite of sandwich and asked, "So you'll do it?"

He was balling the foil and grease paper in his fist when he saw her hand reach out in front of him to take it. He gave it to her as she said, "Yes, Layne, I'll do it. Sean's a neat guy and Meghan's lovely. I'll be happy to help."

He reached out, curled his fingers around her upper thigh and squeezed. It was high enough that it was far more intimate than a squeeze on the knee, low enough not to be too forward.

"Thanks, baby," he whispered.

She didn't answer. Instead, surprising him, her fingers curled around his on her thigh. Not to pry them away, but to give them a squeeze.

She let his hand go and asked, "Do you want a cookie?"

"Yeah," he answered, and she immediately leaned forward and started digging in the bag again.

By the time they made it to the field at the high school two towns over where the game was, he had his three cookies, she'd had *her* three cookies and she'd cleared everything but the pops away. He parked and met her at the rear of the SUV, getting close and sliding his arm around her shoulders. She reciprocated, her arm gliding along his waist under his jacket, her hand curling in at the side. There were others heading toward the gate and Layne knew the ones from the 'burg because they were watching Layne and Rocky walk to the field like they were two movie stars in the middle of filming a romantic comedy.

He paid and they made their way to the away team's bleachers, Layne spying Colt and Cal standing at their normal spot at the fence. Keira was standing with them and with her was a red-haired, freckle-faced girl who could do Irish Spring commercials.

"Hey, Ms. Merrick!" Keira shouted as they approached.

"Hey, Keira, Heather," Rocky greeted back, showing no reaction to being referred to by her maiden name then she smiled at Colt and Cal. "Hi, guys."

"Rocky," Colt smiled at her and Cal smiled as well but didn't verbalize his greeting. He just lifted his chin.

Rocky looked up into the stands and scanned. Layne's eyes followed hers and he felt her move, looked down at her to see her waving at someone and he looked back into the bleachers to see Dave sitting with Spike and Ernie. He gave them a chin lift, got them in return and felt Rocky turn into him. He dipped his chin to look at her as she tipped her head back.

"You want coffee?" she asked.

He shook his head. "No, I'm good."

"I'm going to go say hi to Dad."

"All right, sweetcheeks."

She grinned at him and then, surprising him again, she got up on her toes and touched her mouth briefly to his. Apparently lip touches weren't restricted in her contract. Or maybe they were allowed when the school activity was on another school's property.

Good to know.

"Be back," she whispered and then moved away.

He watched her strut through the crowd and kept watching her doing it as she climbed the bleachers and scooted in to sit by her dad. He also kept watching as she burrowed under her father's arm until it moved around her shoulders and she stayed close, turned to her old man, smiling up at him.

"Gotta say, Tanner, your woman can strut," Cal noted on a rumble, and Layne tore his eyes from Rocky and looked at Cal.

"Rocky started strutting when she was three years old," Colt remarked.

"She'd need to start then considering she's perfected the art," Cal returned.

"What are you talkin' about, Joe?" Keira asked Cal, her head tipped back to look up at her stepfather. When she did, he hooked her with an arm around her upper chest and pulled her in front of him, muttering through a grin, "Nothin', girl."

Layne chuckled and took his place at the fence. Jasper and Seth, the captains of the team, were out in the middle of the field for the coin toss. It was almost time to roll.

Then Layne stood in the bitter cold with Colt and Cal through the first quarter and two minutes into the second before he was done standing with Colt and Cal in the bitter cold. The 'dogs were holding their own, zero to zero, this being the score because their defense kicked ass but their offense sucked.

Layne being done meant, when the 'dogs tried and failed to kick a desperate-to-get-on-the-board field goal that was well beyond the capabilities of their sophomore kicker, who was good, but who wasn't playing for the Colts, and the ball was changing sides, Layne turned and looked up at Rocky to see she was still cuddled into her dad. He put his tongue to his teeth and gave a loud, sharp whistle. Raquel's eyes went from the field to him and he lifted his hand and crooked a finger at her.

It was night and she wasn't exactly close, but the field was bright and he could see her roll her eyes. She gave her father a peck on the cheek, reached out to squeeze Spike and Ernie's hands then she scooted back along the front of the other spectators to the aisle and made her way down to him.

"You called?" she asked when she got to him.

He hooked her with an arm around her neck, turned her, pulled her back to his front and wrapped his arm around her upper chest, his other arm around her ribs. Positioning her in front of him at the fence, he dipped his head, and in her ear, whispered, "I'm cold, sweetcheeks. Need somethin' to keep me warm."

Her body had grown stiff when he'd taken hold of her and stayed that way for three seconds. Then she relaxed on an annoyed sigh, but both her hands came up to wrap around his forearm at her chest before she muttered, "At your service."

Layne lifted his head, grinned and turned his eyes to the field.

He kept her close the rest of the quarter and it happened thirty seconds to half-time.

The 'dogs were fifteen yards out from their goal line. It was fourth down and for some asinine reason, Cosgrove kept his kicker on the bench and called a passing play. All the eligible receivers scrambled, Jasper got open, but the QB ignored him and threw toward Cosgrove's heavily defended son in the end zone. This time, Seth Cosgrove didn't intentionally blow the play. He went all out, it was plain to see, but with three defenders, he was no match for it and was intercepted. Seth didn't hesitate. He bore down on the opposing player, deflected a block and made a diving tackle, wrapping his arms around the player's legs, taking him down on the five yard line.

Visibly and justifiably angry, Seth tore his chin guard down and ripped off his helmet as he jogged to the sidelines. Five feet into the field, his father was there to greet him and he greeted him with a vicious, open-palmed tag to the side of the head, making his boy lurch two steps to the side.

"What the fuck was that?" Cosgrove shouted, bearing down on him again and then he brought both hands up in fists and sent them crashing down on his son's shoulder pads so hard, the boy's knees buckled and he almost went down, his father still shouting, "Hunh? Seth? What the fuck was that!" Another crash, this one more brutal, the sound of his fists hitting the pads cracking through the suddenly silent night. Then came another.

Rocky had frozen in his arms but Layne didn't hesitate. He set her aside, put two hands on the top of the chain link fence and pushed himself up, throwing his legs over. Colt was doing the same as Cal followed, but Layne's gaze was riveted to the coach and his boy as Cosgrove landed another open-palmed blow to the side of his son's head, sending Seth stumbling down on a knee.

Jasper was closer and got there before Layne, Cal and Colt, even though they were all three sprinting.

"Coach!" Jasper yelled, using both his hands to wrap around Cosgrove's raised arm and Cosgrove turned, hard, yanking back his arm and he caught Jasper in the chest with his elbow causing Jasper to stagger back into two other players and another coach, all who were close.

"Sit your ass down, Layne!" Cosgrove bellowed at Jasper as Layne, Colt and Cal hit the scene. Cosgrove's eyes shot to Layne. "Parents off the field!"

"Locker room," Layne growled. Cosgrove's face went pale when he caught the look on Layne's, but then his chest puffed out as an official jogged up.

"You can't call me out in the middle of a fuckin' game!" Cosgrove roared as the whistle blew.

"Unsportsmanlike conduct," the ref shouted, his arms straight out, palms down, his shout scratchy because he was pissed. "Fifteen yards!" Then he leaned into Cosgrove, stuck a pointed finger in his face and clipped, "Get a handle on it, Cosgrove, or you're off the field and I'm only lettin' you stay on it 'cause this is the last thirty seconds of your last game. Do *not* even *think* of comin' back after half-time." He leaned in further and hissed, "And by God, you better brace man, because after that shit, I'll see to it you're suspended *permanently*."

"Locker room," Colt repeated Layne's words and the referee and Cosgrove's eyes went to Colt. "Hand off to Fullerton and get your ass off the field." Cosgrove opened his mouth to speak and Colt leaned in and warned, "You got one second, man, before you're in cuffs."

Cosgrove took that second to save face and glare at Colt before he yelled, "Fullerton!" tore his whistle from around his neck and tossed it to one of the assistant coaches. Without further hesitation, head down, he started to jog off the field.

When he did, both sets of bleachers burst out in a loud standing ovation that rocked the field, but Layne went to Seth who was still down on a knee, his face pale, his eyes on his departing father.

Layne reached a hand to him and called, "Seth."

Seth's eyes sliced to him then down to Layne's hand. He put his gloved hand in Layne's and Layne hauled him up.

"Head back in the game, man, but, after, you need a place to crash, you got one," Layne said quietly, wrapped his fingers around Seth's neck, gave him a squeeze with a tug then turned, gave Jasper a head jerk indicating Seth. Jas jerked his chin up in return, moved toward Seth and Layne jogged back to the fence. He put his hands to it and cleared it.

Rocky was there within seconds, her hands at his abs, she moved in close.

"Sweetheart?" she whispered, and his eyes tipped to hers.

"It's okay," Layne told her, curling the fingers of both his hands around her neck.

"Seth?" she asked.

"It's okay, Roc. He'll be okay."

"Jasper?"

"It's all good, baby," Layne whispered.

Her eyes searched his then she leaned into him and put her forehead to his chest. One of his hands moved to the back of her neck and gave her a squeeze as his eyes went to find both his sons on the field.

They moved the ball fifteen yards and play resumed.

Even with the penalty, the opposing team didn't manage to translate their turnover to points on the board by half-time.

The second half Layne watched with Rocky at his side, snuggled into him with both arms around his middle, her head most of the time resting on his shoulder. With Fullerton calling the plays, Jasper seeing the ball and Tripp taking turns with Seth, the 'dogs won twenty-one to three.

With a variety of other parents, fans, Colt, Cal, Keira, Heather, Dave, Spike, Ernie and Rocky, Layne waited after the game to watch the boys load up in the bus.

When they filed out, Cosgrove was not among them.

When his boys came into view, Layne saw this time Tripp was crowding Jasper and Jasper was crowding Seth. His sons were supposed to go to their mother's that night after pizza on the town. It was the beginning of her week. But Jasper had heard Layne's invitation and he'd talk to Seth about taking Layne up on it if he got the vibe that Seth wouldn't be safe at home. Therefore, Layne wondered where he'd put another body in his house. He should have bought one of the four bedroom floorplans.

When Tripp saw him he waved, though he was clearly learning cool, his wave was a flick of a hand. Jasper noticed his brother and his eyes came to Layne and, king of cool, he jerked up his chin but no more except another chin jerk to Keira before they hustled into the bus.

"Is he going to be okay, Mr. Layne?" He heard Keira ask and his eyes dropped to see she was staring at the bus looking worried.

"Yeah, Keira, he'll be fine," Layne answered. She looked up at him and she didn't seem any less worried.

So she turned to Cal. "Joe, if Jasper isn't up to pizza, can he come over to our house and watch a movie?"

Proving Layne's earlier theory correct, Cal didn't hesitate to reply, "Sure, honey."

Keira leaned into him and whispered, "Thanks," as her eyes went back to the bus. Cal's arm curled around her shoulders and he pulled her closer.

"You good?" Cal asked him and Layne nodded.

He was good because Rocky was leaned into him the same way and had been since they took their places outside the locker rooms. This meant he could deal even though his sons had survived another game-time drama and Gabby was standing alone twenty feet away, no Stew, and when she wasn't craning her neck to look for her boys, she was staring at Layne and Rocky. Layne felt this was progress considering she was staring and not glaring.

Layne forced his mind off Gabrielle and his eyes went to Colt. "Roc's gonna see what she can do for Meghan."

Colt nodded and he looked at Rocky. "Cool, Rocky, thanks. Sean will appreciate that."

She smiled up at him but didn't reply and it was then that Layne realized that the game was over, the latest drama was over, his kids were likely gone for the night, Rocky was likely done with her period, and therefore it was time to go home.

"We're outta here," Layne mumbled and led Rocky away.

They got a variety of good-byes and Layne a clap on the shoulder from Dave as they stopped at him so Rocky could give her dad's cheek a kiss. Then they walked away.

They were nearing the Suburban when Layne heard the pipes. His head turned and he saw Ryker sitting a Harley, bald head open to the elements, leather biker jacket undoubtedly covering another tank top. When Layne's eyes hit him, the pipes roared for a second, which Layne decided was Ryker's way of telling him he wanted a chat.

Layne stopped Rocky and dug into his pocket for the keys.

He handed them to her and ordered, "Open it up and climb in, honey. You're cold, turn her on. Yeah? I'll be right back." Her eyes shot up to him and she opened her mouth to speak, but he got there before she did. "Not now, sweetcheeks. That's Ryker on the bike. Just get in the truck."

She looked over her shoulder at Ryker, back at him, nodded and then again got on her toes to give him a mouth touch before she swiftly walked to the SUV.

Layne walked to the bike.

He stopped at Ryker's side noticing Ryker's eyes had followed Rocky and not Layne.

"Eyes on me," Layne demanded, keeping his voice as low as he could and still be heard over the pipes, and Ryker looked at him.

"That your woman?" he asked.

"Yep," Layne answered.

"Jesus, sport, traded up, didn't you?" His eyes slid back to Layne's truck before they came again to Layne. "*Way* up."

Layne didn't have time for this. Rocky was feeling affectionate and her guard was down. He had other, better things to do.

"You got somethin' for me?" Layne prompted.

"Jumped the fence," Ryker stated, talking at the same time studying Layne. "Didn't hesitate. He clipped his boy and you were over the fence. Saw your face as you sprinted up to that mess, thought you were gonna lay that motherfucker out." He gave Layne a head to toe to head again and went on, "That look on your face, sport, figure I underestimated you."

"Did you call me over to flatter me, Ryker? 'Cause, as you can see, I got another date and she's prettier than you," Layne told him and Ryker grinned.

"In a hurry?" Ryker asked. Layne didn't respond so Ryker's grin got bigger and uglier. "*I'd* be in a hurry, that piece was in my truck waitin' on me to take her home."

Layne turned to leave, muttering, "A waste of my fuckin' time."

"Sport," Ryker called. Layne looked at him and Ryker continued, "Action. Stew. Tonight."

Fuck. That was what Layne was worried he'd say.

"When?"

"Meet me at the bar at eleven o'clock."

Shit. That would give him just enough time to drop Rocky off, grab his camera and get to the bar, and he'd still be late.

"Just tell me when and where. I'll take care of it."

"Comin' with," Ryker stated.

"No, you aren't. I work alone."

"This ain't a one man deal."

"Since when?"

"Since Stew's workin' with a crew tonight, bro, and, you get tagged, you'll need backup. Colt can't back you on this without makin' a lotta arrests and where's that gonna get your ex?"

Fuck! This was not getting any better.

"I can take care of myself," Layne told Ryker.

"'Spect you can, but I know this crew. The smarter move would be to go in with backup." Layne knew he was right, in any uncertain situation it was smarter to go in with backup. That didn't mean he wanted Ryker to *be* that backup. "You got a permit to carry concealed or you don't, don't give a fuck, you come carryin'. Yeah?" Ryker continued.

"I can see you're eager to pop someone's cherry, Ryker, so I hate to tell you this isn't my first time."

Ryker grinned again. "Bummed, bro."

"Can you explain why you're all of a sudden my BFF?" Layne asked, not about to walk into the bar he met Ryker in at eleven o'clock at night to meet Ryker, a guy he did not know, he did not trust and he wasn't sure he liked.

"Thought you were gonna lay that motherfucker out," was Ryker's explanation.

Layne didn't feel that was enough of an explanation so he prompted, "And?"

"And that motherfucker thought you were gonna lay him out too."

Layne crossed his arms on his chest and repeated, "And?"

Ryker watched him a full five beats then leaned in. "And I know, by that look on your face, you didn't have two bleachers full of people, kids on two football teams, coaches, refs and your woman lookin' on, you woulda laid that motherfucker out. No hesitation. No holdin' back. That guy would be breathin' through a tube just about now. Am I right?"

He was right.

Layne stayed silent.

"Not even your kid this time," Ryker went on.

Layne remained silent.

"You got control and you understand my vision of justice." He leaned back and smiled his ugly smile. "My kind of partner."

"Great," Layne muttered and Ryker added an ugly laugh to his ugly smile.

Then he said, "Eleven," and shot off on his bike.

Layne watched him go before he whispered, "Fuck."

Fourteen

SCARED OF THE DARK

Layne let Rocky into the house and Blondie assaulted them both at the same time.

Rocky took control and forced the dog into the kitchen with her hands and legs, giving Blondie scratches behind the ears as she did it.

Layne saw a note on the island and didn't pick it up to read it seeing as the big black scrawl could be read from across a room.

"Out," was all Devin had written.

Layne smiled at the note as he moved to the sliding glass door, disarmed the alarm, which was always set for doors and windows since the dog would trip it if they used the sensors in the house. He pulled out the steel rod at the door and slid it open. Blondie immediately lost interest in Rocky and raced out the door.

"Tell me again why, when you're working, I shouldn't just sleep at home?" Layne heard Rocky ask.

Layne slid the door to and turned to her.

They'd had this conversation in the car. He thought he'd convinced her. Clearly, Rocky remained unconvinced.

"Because enough people in town saw what went down tonight, which means that most the rest of the town will hear about it before sun up tomorrow. After that shit went down with me and Jasper involved, they'd expect my woman to show her support, not sleep in her own bed," Layne reiterated the point he'd made on the way home.

Again, he knew this was lame.

And again, she appeared to be buying it, if hesitantly.

She bit her lip, let it go and remarked, "But my car is at my house, they won't know."

Layne thought about Natalie and then he thought about Natalie's big mouth.

"They'll know," he replied.

She visibly got nervous and cried, "Layne! They aren't watching that closely!"

He shook his head. "You're wrong, baby."

She stared at him. He held her stare.

Then he said softly, "Get ready for bed, Roc."

"Layne—"

"Bed, sweetcheeks, I've got to go."

She stared at him some more. Then she bought it and Layne knew this because she sighed, loudly and heavily, and strutted to the stairs and up them.

Layne watched until she rounded the top and disappeared. Then he followed.

By the time he got up the stairs, Rocky had vanished into his room. Layne turned on the light over his desk and grabbed a digital camera from a drawer. He checked the battery and memory card then grabbed an extra one of both.

He opened the drawer with the key to one of the cabinets in the unit taped to the bottom, yanked it off, unlocked the cabinet and took off his leather jacket, swinging it around the back of the chair. He pulled the shoulder holster with the .22 out, checked its load and hooked it around his shoulders. Then he pulled the holster with the .38 out and clipped it to his belt. Devin had taught him you could never be too careful and one part of careful equaled firepower. Since Devin taught him that, Layne had learned that Devin was right and life had proved that Layne was lucky to have learned it prior to learning it the hard way.

Layne locked the cabinet, replaced the key, shrugged his coat on, dropped the battery and memory card in his pocket and walked into the bedroom.

Rocky was moving out of the bathroom wearing his tee.

Layne didn't hesitate. It was preview time. She was getting her guard back up and his job was to tear it right down.

He got in her space, wrapped an arm around her waist and pulled her to his body.

She tipped her head back and put her hands on his chest. "Layne."

His other hand went into her ponytail. He tagged the holder, slid it out and tossed it across the room toward his dresser where it skidded across the top and over the back to disappear, probably forever, or until he moved.

A good place for it to be.

"Layne!" Rocky snapped and shoved at his shoulders.

He looked down at her, her hair around her face and shoulders, her eyes igniting. Then he bunched her hair in his palm as he cupped the back of her head, tilted it to the side and his mouth came down on hers. She'd opened it, possibly to snap his name again, which was not a good move.

Layne took advantage, slid his tongue right inside her sweet mouth and he kissed her, deep, wet, hard and for a very long time. It had been a few days, he needed his fix. So he took it and kissed her long enough that he was losing his motivation for this mission. Long enough that her fingers had curled around the edges of his jacket and she was holding on *and* holding him to her.

He thought that should just about do it. For now.

He lifted his head and saw her eyes were unfocused, gazing up at him.

She was off-balance, guard down, perfect.

He lifted his hand to cup her jaw and ran his thumb along her cheekbone as he whispered, "Sleep tight, sweetcheeks."

His thumb moved to her lips so he felt as well as heard her breathy, "Okay."

He grinned at her, turned and left the room, grabbing his camera before he went down the stairs. He let Blondie in, secured the door, set the alarm and headed out of his house.

When Layne arrived at the bar he saw Ryker wasn't in the mood to have a drink and socialize. He was standing outside the front door, shoulders and the sole of one boot to the wall, biker jacket opened and Layne was right, another black tank was stretched across his massive chest. He was enjoying a smoke, but flicked it in a wide arc when he saw the Suburban swing into the lot. He pushed away from the wall and Layne slid the truck to a halt in front of the doors.

Layne looked at the clock on his dash as Ryker folded his huge frame into the passenger seat. It was eleven oh seven.

Ryker slammed the door and instantly reached between his legs to push the seat back the two centimeters it had to give and then he adjusted the seatback so it was nearly in full-on recline as if he was preparing to cruise with his homies.

"You're late," Ryker noted on a grunt once he'd settled in and Layne accelerated to turn around in the lot.

"Needed time to say goodnight to my woman," Layne replied.

"I'll accept that excuse," Ryker muttered.

It was nuts but Layne couldn't help it. He was beginning to like this guy.

As Layne drove, Ryker gave him directions and he also gave him information. They hit the storage units in Speedway and Layne knew instantly why this was the pay point. Easy to get to at the same time off the beaten track. Neighborhood not close, also not great and the lighting was shit, which meant rent on the units was either low or the people who rented there were stupid. No one around to hear or see and the light was so dim, if someone was around, they couldn't be sure what they were seeing.

Layne cut the lights, parked behind a unit, they got out and Ryker guided them to their position.

When Ryker exited his SUV, Layne had noted he had a .45 shoved in the back of his jeans and he wasn't hiding the huge-ass knife clipped to his belt. He might be beginning to like Ryker but he still didn't trust him, so he kept to Ryker's back.

Ryker didn't seem to mind.

The temperature had dropped and the bitter wind had not died down. It was fucking freezing, he was in Speedway, in the dark, with a man he didn't trust who was a little nuts, crouching beside a big garbage container, and Rocky's soft, warm body was at home, in his tee, in his bed.

Definitely he needed a new job.

They waited twenty minutes and conversation was scarce, as in non-existent, which meant it was a long twenty minutes. Then the guy walked up.

Five foot six, maybe seven, slight, he had half a head of hair, the top so bald it shone in the dim lights lighting the storage unit. Wearing a navy windbreaker that probably wasn't doing shit to break the wind. Company logo on the chest. Chinos. Visibly nervous. Layne pegged him as IT or an accountant. Probably IT.

Looking at the guy, Layne hoped he had the money. He needed Stew out of his sons' and Gabby's lives but he didn't want to watch Stew working this guy over. He didn't particularly want to watch Stew working anyone over, but especially not this guy.

Stew and his crew of three arrived ten minutes later. The guy was wired by the time they got there and the minute he saw them, he became jittery.

Shit, he didn't have the money.

Layne assessed the scene. Stew did not need a crew to deal with this guy. Especially not this crew of thugs. He brought one because he was an asshole.

Layne lifted the camera, quickly and expertly adjusted the telephoto and started shooting.

Stew no sooner made it to him than the guy handed over an envelope. Stew took it, bent his head to it, thumbed through what was inside, handed it to a lackey at his back and then turned and hammered the guy, fist to cheekbone.

There it was. The envelope was light.

Layne shoved back the instinct to move in and kept taking shots as Stew whaled on IT guy with his fists until he was down and then kicked him in the ribs with his boot four times after he was down.

The guy was curled in a ball on the pavement, whining, loudly and shrilly, "It's all I've got!" when Stew stopped, bent over, said something to the guy that Layne couldn't hear, his finger in his face. He lifted up, kicked him one more time and then stood over the guy, staring down.

It was at that point when Layne would understand why Ryker said Stew had a special flair.

The guy was down, cowed and beaten, bleeding from the face and likely had one or more broken ribs. The message had been delivered, and by the look of him, the guy would talk his grandma into selling her plasma so the next payment wouldn't be light.

Stew still pulled a gun out of his jeans and drilled a round in the prone man's thigh. The guy cried out in agony and curled into himself deeper, cradling his thigh.

Flesh wound, it'd bleed like a motherfucker and hurt worse, but it was way over the top.

Then Stew kicked him again, this time in the spine, turned, jerked his head at his crew and they all disappeared.

Layne tensed to move toward the guy but Ryker curled a meaty hand around Layne's shoulder.

"Focus, bro," he whispered. "Tonight you're a hero for your boys, not this guy. Let's go. Baranski's not done."

Layne clenched his jaw, knowing Ryker was right. It would be the right thing to do, but being seen would also jeopardize the mission. People talked even if you told them to keep their traps shut. He didn't need his and Ryker's attendance at the festivities getting out.

Though Ryker was right and Layne was pissed about it, he still moved through the shadows with Ryker to the Suburban. Once they were in the cab, they still had eyes on the guy and Layne waited with Ryker, both of them silent, until the guy crawled to his feet, arm wrapped around his ribs, bent nearly double with his other hand at his thigh, blood oozing between his fingers, and he scuttled into the night dragging his bad leg.

When they lost sight of him, Ryker muttered, "Bet that dipshit lost the urge to visit the track anytime soon."

Layne turned to Ryker, not in the mood for a breakdown. "Stew has another collection?"

Ryker shook his head. Layne felt his eyes on him in the dark and he didn't get a good feeling when he saw the white of Ryker's smile. "Nope. After he's done a job, he gets horny."

"Come again?" Layne asked.

"Your ex ain't gonna like those photos you just took but he's got her hooked deep and he knows it. You wanna be certain to get a woman to set a man out, you show her pictures of that man porkin' another woman. Even Baranski isn't stupid enough for you to show him those kinds of shots and not know his time in Big Momma's House o' the Free Ride is up."

This just got worse and worse.

Jesus.

"You know where he'll be?" Layne asked, but he knew Ryker knew.

"Yeah," Ryker sounded like he was laughing. "Sorry, bro, 'bout to show you the only thing that'll put you off that piece you got waitin' for you at home."

"Great," Layne muttered and started the SUV through Ryker's chuckle.

Ryker led him to a trailer park just out of the 'burg. Negotiating it, Layne knew that Stew's other woman might not carry extra baggage like Gabby, on her body and through two boys fathered by another man, but she wasn't a supermodel either.

Layne cut the lights when Ryker told him they were rolling close, parked where Ryker instructed and they both walked through the cold, silent dark of the trailer park. When they got to the trailer Ryker indicated, one end was lit, the curtains opened. Ryker stayed clear and kept lookout as Layne approached the trailer.

When he got there, Layne saw that Stew was already celebrating, and Ryker's information already proved legit, became even more so. She was naked on her hands and knees, she was absolutely no supermodel, Stew was naked behind her and he was going through the back door. Not pretty.

Layne's mouth filled with saliva and he swallowed it down.

Jesus.

He *definitely* needed a new job.

He wasted no time and didn't try to hide. He'd done this often enough. Even with him right at the window, they weren't going to spot him. They were both concentrating on other things. Layne got his shots, moved from the window, crouched with his back to the trailer and scrolled through what he had viewing the screen on the back of his camera. He decided he had enough at the same time he decided, once those shots were printed, he was going to destroy the memory card *and* the camera.

His eyes went to Ryker and he nodded. Ryker nodded back and they moved to the SUV.

When they were underway, Ryker said, "Drop me by my babe's."

"You got it."

Ryker directed him to a neighborhood in the 'burg. Lower middle class, neat but tiny houses that people took care of. Layne pulled into the drive that Ryker indicated and no sooner had he stopped when the outside light came on. There was a black flag by the door with an orange pumpkin on it and three carved jack-o'-lanterns lining the front steps. Layne was mildly surprised that Ryker bagged a babe who lived in a tidy neighborhood, had a pumpkin flag flying at her door and jack-o'-lanterns on her steps.

He was more surprised when the front door opened, a leggy woman with a mass of curly red hair stood in it, her thin, short robe not hiding much of her phenomenal figure, but it also wasn't putting it on show either. She was peering at the truck, looking awake but ready for bed and whatever might happen there. She'd waited up for her man.

Layne looked at Ryker and noted, "Not bad."

At Layne's words, Ryker turned to him and shared, "She makes pumpkin bread that should win awards and the same can be said for the way she gives head. Seriously, bro, every time she goes down on me, every single time, I swear my dick's gonna explode. She's that good."

Layne shook his head. "I already got Stew goin' at his piece burned in my brain, Ryker, now you're just bein' cruel."

Ryker shot him his ugly smile, opened his door and folded out of the cab. Layne put the SUV in reverse, pulled out but caught sight of Ryker entering the house, his huge frame hiding his woman but he had an arm around her, his neck bent to look down at her, shuffling her back. Ryker kicked the door closed and Layne's eyes went back to the road.

He drove home and noted no Calais on the curb or in the drive, and when the garage door went up, no Charger. Seth apparently decided to brave the homefront and Layne hoped he hadn't made the wrong decision.

Layne entered the house and Blondie moseyed up to him, prepared to give a greeting but tuckered out. He gave her a quick rubdown then moved beyond her, up the stairs, Blondie following and they separated at the top, Blondie heading to Jasper's opened door. He shrugged his jacket off and swung it around the back of his desk chair. Then he secured his guns and the camera in the locked cabinet and walked into his room.

He stopped at his side of the bed. Moonlight was shining through all three of the windows, the curtains opened, Rocky on her side of the bed curled tight into a ball. He reached under his pillows, got his pajamas and didn't bother going to the walk-in to change, he did it right there. Then he walked to the windows and started to close the curtains. He was on window three when he heard Rocky.

"What are you doing?"

He turned to her and replied softly, "Closin' us in, baby."

He watched, the moonlight from the window he hadn't shut off to outside illuminating her as she threw back the covers and got out of bed.

She went to one of the windows he'd done and threw open the curtains.

What the fuck?

"Roc—"

She turned to him and whispered, "It's too dark."

Okay, again…what the *fuck*?

She'd never been scared of the dark.

"Rocky, we need the curtains closed."

She shook her head and moved to the window next to the one he was at. "No."

He walked to her as she threw one side of the curtains open and asked what was on his mind. "Baby, what the fuck?"

"It's too dark," she repeated.

"We don't need people seein' in, Roc, and there are people out there who'll be lookin'."

"It's too dark," she said yet again.

She moved to pass him to get to the other side of the drapes and he caught her by hooking an arm around her belly. She stopped and looked up at him.

"Rocky—"

"I need them open, Layne." She tried to pull from him but he tightened his arm, sliding it around her to bring her up against his front.

"We can't sleep with them open, Roc, too much exposure."

"I need them open," she repeated.

"Sorry, sweetcheeks, that's not gonna happen," he told her, felt her body get tight, not with anger, with something else. Something that started seeping into the room. Something not good and not right.

"I need them open," she whispered, her voice suddenly trembling.

Layne heard it and treaded cautiously when he reminded her, "Baby, you've slept with them closed the last three nights."

"Yes," she was still whispering, "but you were here."

Layne's body went solid at her words and whatever was coming from Rocky started filling the room, pressing into them. He sensed that whatever it was, she didn't have it in her to beat it back. Whatever it was, he needed to beat it back for her.

"You scared of the dark?" he asked gently.

She didn't answer. Instead she said, "I need the light."

"You scared of the dark, Rocky?"

"I need the light," she repeated, now her body was trembling.

"You weren't scared of the dark twenty years ago, honey."

"No, I wasn't," she whispered again. "Because *you* were there."

Fucking hell.

His hands went to the sides of her head and he turned her, moving her backward toward the bed.

"What scares you?" he asked. She didn't answer except to shake her head in his hands. "What scares you, baby?" No answer, her legs hit bed and he stopped, thinking he knew, so he explained, "Tonight wasn't dangerous, Rocky." She tried to look away but he kept her head tipped toward him and his face got close to hers. "It wasn't dangerous and I had backup."

She lifted her hands and curled them around his wrists, whispering, "Layne."

"I'm good at what I do," he told her, and she shook her head in his hands again so he gave her a gentle squeeze and moved even closer. "Swear, I'm good at what I do."

She stared in his eyes through the dark, and suddenly, she lifted up on her toes half an inch and her mouth was on his.

He didn't know what was happening with her and it more than concerned him, but even so, Layne didn't hesitate. He accepted her invitation by slanting his head to the side, his hands moved from her head to her waist, curling around her back, trapping her in his arms, and he kissed her.

After all those dreams, Layne was ready for what was about to happen and had been ready for a long fucking time, and Rocky showed him she felt the same. She gave with her mouth and took with her hands. Greedy, hungry, she was all over him, pressing into him, communicating need.

He understood her need. Her need was in his blood, blood that was now coursing through his body and making his cock hard.

He put his hands to her pits and lifted her up high. His mouth disengaging from hers, he growled, "Knees," and she knew what he was saying. She kicked her calves back and he set her on her knees in the bed.

His hands went to the hem of his tee she was wearing and he nearly growled again when, without delay, her arms went straight up to help him. He yanked off the tee, tossed it aside and one hand went to the middle of her back, pushing in and up, arching her back. He bent and used his other hand to lift her breast, he took it with his mouth and sucked deep.

Her fingers slid into his hair and she moaned, arching her back further, holding him fast. He pulled hard then swirled with his tongue, pulled hard again and then moved to the other side to do the same. When he was done, she was clenching his hair in her fists and she pulled him up, his mouth to hers, and he took it, the kiss deeper, wilder, out of control as she pressed her bared tits tight to his chest and one of her hands went into his pajamas to curl into his ass. The other one went in the front to wrap around his hard cock and she pulled him to her.

Christ, she was primed already.

He tore his mouth from hers and she stroked his cock before gently tugging him toward her again, and he shook his head. "Unh-unh, baby. I'm hungry."

He listened to her breath catch and he knew she remembered. He'd say that to her when he wanted to go down on her, whenever he wanted to go down on her. He'd walk up behind her as she was doing the dishes. He'd whisper it in her ear when she was curled into him on the couch. When he'd wake her up in the middle of the night or when he woke up in the morning wanting the taste of her. It got to the point if he said it because he was hungry for food, her eyes would go half-mast, her mouth would get soft, and he knew what she was thinking and would have to fight against going hard.

And she knew now. He knew she knew because she let him go and moved to her back. He moved in. Sliding his fingers into her panties, he yanked them roughly down her legs and tossed them aside. She pulled herself up on the bed and was opening her legs before he got a knee to the mattress.

She wanted it, his Rocky, fuck, she was magnificent.

Hands to the soft skin of her inner thighs, he spread her wider and put his mouth to her. Her hips jerked and she gave him another mew. That coupled with the taste of her, having it back after so long meant he didn't go slow. He didn't take it easy. He just took. Her feet went into the bed and she lifted her hips to offer more, rubbing herself against him.

Christ, amazing.

He took and she gave and he listened as her excitement increased, became feverish, his cock so hard it was aching by the time her hands slid into his hair, her hips surged up, she cried out and he heard and felt her come.

He left her still moaning, going up and over her, hooking the back of her knee with one hand to pull it up as he pulled his cock out of pajamas, guided the tip to her slick pussy and drove in.

No, he'd been wrong. *This* was amazing.

"Layne," she breathed, her pussy still convulsing with her orgasm.

"Take me, baby," he grunted, driving in, hard, deep, fast.

"Yes," she whispered, lifting her other knee, holding him tight at his sides with her thighs, her arms wrapping around his shoulders.

He buried his face in her neck and kept driving. "Christ, you feel beautiful."

"Baby," she gasped, and he heard it. Fuck, he heard it.

She was going to come again.

"That's it." He kept thrusting, her arms tightening around him, he pushed deeper.

"Oh my God."

Shit, he was close. She sounded just as close and he hoped to God she was.

He moved his lips up her throat to take her mouth in a kiss as she took his driving cock and she panted through his kiss then sucked his tongue deep with her orgasm.

When she did, Layne let go and joined her, groaning into her mouth as he buried himself to the root and his world erased of everything but his cock and Raquel and the beauty only she could give him.

When he was done, he stayed rooted but moved his face into her neck and listened to her heavy breathing as he fought to control his own. He let minutes pass before, one by one, he moved her legs so her calves were swung in and she was wrapped all around him.

Her head turned so her lips were at his ear. "I think that's about as real as it gets," she whispered.

Oh yeah, that was about as real as it got, and about as good.

He lifted his head and grinned down at her in the shadows. "You're right about that, sweetcheeks."

He felt her body tighten around him even as she moved a hand to lay it against his jaw.

"Layne—" she started.

Oh no. *Fuck* no.

He pulled out of her, righted his pajamas then moved off her and up. He took her with him, planting her on her feet beside the bed. He found the tee and she stood there, motionless, as he pulled the neck of his tee over her head and she shoved her arms through.

He put his lips to hers and whispered, "Get cleaned up, baby."

She remained immobile, her head tilted back to look at him, but she whispered so softly it was hard to hear, "You remembered."

He remembered.

He remembered she didn't like to sleep naked. She might fall asleep that way but she always got up and put something on. She also liked to clean up after they were done. Even if they'd go for a second or third round, she'd clean up after each time. Sometimes he'd do it for her.

Yes, he remembered. He remembered everything.

And she should know that.

Kristen Ashley

His fingers curled around her neck and he put his forehead to hers before sharing, "I remember, Rocky. I remember everything. I remember every...*fucking*...thing."

Her fingers curved into his at her neck and she breathed, "Layne—"

He cut her off by ordering, "Get cleaned up and come back to me."

"Sweetheart—"

"Go, baby, and come back to me."

She hesitated a second before nodding. He let her go and she moved away. He closed the curtains and got into bed on her side. He was in the middle waiting for her when she returned and slid in the bed then instantly moved into him.

"You want your panties?" he asked.

"Do you know where they are?" she asked back.

"No fuckin' clue," he answered and heard her soft giggle, liked it, so he slid one hand down her back, pulled up the tee then cupped the soft, generous cheek of her ass.

"No," she said softly when his fingers curled into her. "I don't think I want my panties."

"Good," he whispered and pulled her deeper into his body as her arm stole under his and around his waist.

He fell silent and so did Rocky, until she called tentatively, "Layne."

He knew by her tone where she was going.

"No, Roc," he replied.

"Baby," she whispered. "This was a mistake."

His hand tightened on her ass, his arm tightened around her back and his voice was a rumble when he returned, "Made a lotta mistakes in my life, didn't know about them until later. Sayin' that, sweetcheeks, I know deep in my gut this was no mistake."

"But—"

"It wasn't, Rocky."

"I think—"

His hand and arm gave her a squeeze and she stopped speaking.

"We'll talk tomorrow," he told her.

"But Layne—"

He interrupted her. "It's dark."

282

She paused before she asked, "What?"

"It's dark, baby. You scared?"

Silence and then a soft, "No."

She hadn't even noticed he closed the curtains.

So he made his point by repeating, "This was no mistake."

"Okay," she whispered.

He held her in the dark. It was late and he'd just fucked Rocky for the first time in eighteen years. He'd come hard, after months of dreaming about her, each dream hot, but having her was far, *far* hotter.

He was sated, relaxed, tired and close to sleep when she whispered, "Layne?"

"Yeah, baby."

He heard her hair move on the pillow before she snuggled closer, and still whispering, she said, "I'm hungry."

Layne suddenly wasn't tired anymore. He rolled to his back, pulling her over him and he found her mouth with his.

"Feel free to take as much as you like," he invited on a mutter against her lips, felt her lips smile then she slowly made her way down his body and she took as much as she liked.

Then Layne took as much as he liked.

After, Rocky got up. Pulling the tee back on, she cleaned up, came back and pinned him to the bed.

Fifteen

LIVE IT WITH ME

*L*ayne's body jolted awake when the doorbell went and kept going, a long continuous set of very annoying peals.

What the fuck?

Rocky moved. The weight of her head coming off his shoulder, her arm around his abs sliding to become a hand at his gut, she went up to an elbow and, in a drowsy voice, started to say, "What—?"

She stopped speaking because the bell stopped and then it started right up again.

"*Fuck!*" he hissed, sliding from under Rocky, *not* happy that his first morning waking up with Rocky after getting back together started with the goddamned doorbell. Also *not* happy that his first morning waking up with Rocky after getting back together started with the first thing he did was get out of bed. Finally, *not* happy the next thing he was going to do was rip someone's fucking throat out.

"Layne, are you expect—?" Rocky started to ask as he rounded the bed, looking for his pajama bottoms.

She stopped again because the doorbell also stopped again then it started right back up.

"Baby, where'd you throw my pajamas?" he asked over the bell.

"What?" she asked back and he looked at her. She was out of bed, standing at his side of it, her hair tousled, looking adorably mystified as her eyes scanned the floor in the weak light coming through the curtains. "I don't know, um…"

Layne saw them in a fold of the comforter, yanked them free, spied her panties also caught in the bedclothes, freed them and tossed them to Rocky who caught them.

He tugged on his pajamas as he heard from below, "Jesus Fuckin' Christ, keep your goddamned pants on!"

Devin. Great.

He heard a loud bark.

Blondie. Even better.

Devin would probably shoot whoever was at the door and Blondie would likely lick the wounds clean.

He moved to the bedroom doors, Rocky moving behind him and he was three steps down the stairs when he heard a shrieked, "*Oh my God!* Who are you? What are you doing in my son's house? *And why do you have a gun*!?"

Fuck, fuck, *fucking hell.*

Vera Layne had come calling.

And, as suspected, Devin had answered the door with his gun.

Blondie started barking.

Layne moved faster down the stairs, turned the corner and saw Devin in a wife beater and boxer shorts, carrying his nine millimeter and standing three feet from the front door just to the side, scowling. Layne's mother was just in the doors looking pissed. And Blondie was prancing between both of them wondering who was going to let her out.

Vera's eyes came to Layne, her face started to gentle, then her eyes went beyond Layne and her face went instantly hard.

"*I knew it*!" she shrieked, her hand shooting up and she pointed at Rocky. "Flo told me and I *knew it*!" she went on, dropping her hand, stomping in four feet then stopping and rocking back. "You're not back home a few months and there she is!" She exaggerated and threw her hands out to the sides in apparent disgust.

Layne scratched Aunt Flo on the top of his mental shit list before he started, "Ma—"

Vera's eyes narrowed on Rocky. "Didn't you do enough damage the first time around?"

"Ma—"

"And aren't you *married?*" she shouted at Rocky.

"Ma," Layne clipped. "Shut it."

Her narrowed eyes went to Layne. "Do not tell me to shut it, Tanner Preston Layne! Do *not!*"

"Maybe I should—" Rocky whispered from behind him, and Layne turned to see her edging back along his wood floor in her bare feet. Her hair down and mussed. Her face free of makeup. Her body covered by his big, maroon t-shirt. And he remembered, not long ago, Rocky walking in his house for the first time, hair perfect, makeup perfect, outfit perfect, her high heels sounding on his floors.

Now she'd cooked in his kitchen. She'd watched TV with him on his couch. She'd let out his dog. She'd laughed with his sons. She'd toasted with the only man who was even close to being a father to him. She'd slept in his bed. He'd gone down on her, she'd returned the favor and he'd fucked her twice.

All in this house. His house.

Rocky, his Rocky, was back and in his house.

And she was not going to be made uncomfortable there. Not even, as much as he loved her, by his mother.

"Roc, come here," he ordered, and her eyes flew to his.

"Layne, I think I should probably—"

He cut her off on a growl. "Sweetcheeks, get over here."

Her eyes held his and then, slowly, she moved to him. When she entered his reach, he tagged her around the waist and pulled her into his side, turning them both to his mother.

"Maybe you'd like to try this again, Ma." His voice was still a growl. "This time, you might wanna start over by welcoming Rocky back."

"I will *not* welcome *that woman* back into *my son's life,*" Vera announced.

Blondie barked.

Layne turned to Devin. "Do me a favor, Dev, put your pants on, put down your gun and let the dog out. Not in that order."

"She escape from an asylum?" Dev asked instead of doing what Layne requested, and he asked it with a tilt of his head to Layne's mother.

Layne closed his eyes.

286

"Well!" Vera huffed. "Who are *you?*"

Layne opened his eyes.

"Devin Glover, friend of your boy's, retired PI and good judge of character," Devin shot back then turned away and started walking to the back door, making his point by saying on a huge smile to Rocky, "Mornin' darlin', hope you slept okay."

"I did. Thanks Dev. Hope you did too," Rocky replied quietly, her body as tight as a bow.

"Couch sucks," Devin muttered as he kept moving, Blondie crowding him. "Too soft."

"Hello!" Vera called loudly. "I came all the way from Florida to stop my son from making a grave mistake, *again*. Anyone?"

Layne's eyes sliced to her. "Ma, seriously, no more of that shit."

"Are you kidding?" she returned then crossed her arms on her chest and finished, "Seriously."

Rocky started to pull away, murmuring, "Layne, I really think I—"

"His name is *Tanner*," Vera spat out and Rocky stopped moving. "*Tanner*. It isn't hard to say. It isn't hard to remember. I would *never* understand why you always called him *Layne*. Before, I didn't mind, because I liked you. Now, *I do not like you*."

"She calls me Layne because you told me when I was seven that my father named me Tanner," Layne put in. Vera's back shot straight and her eyes shot to her son. "I don't hate the name, I don't like it. But anytime someone says it, it reminds me it was the only thing he gave me and it wasn't worth much."

Vera's eyes had grown wide and her voice grew soft when she said, "You never told me that."

"I never told anyone except Rocky," Layne replied. "She used to call me Tanner until I told her that. After I told her, she never said it again. I didn't ask her to call me Layne. She just did."

Vera's eyes moved to Rocky for a beat then came back to Layne and Layne kept talking.

"Now, Ma, I'm happy to see you. The boys'll love it that you're here. It's even cool why you're here, comin' home to look after your boy. But you don't know what's going on, you don't know what *went* on and you're not gonna know. All you gotta know is, what you see is the way it is. You don't like it, I don't care. You'll have to learn to hide it. You can't learn to hide it and keep actin' like that, I hate to say it because I love you, but I'll show you the door. Is that clear?"

Vera's hand went to her throat and Rocky went solid beside him.

"Layne," Rocky whispered.

"You're choosin' her over me?" Vera asked on a breath.

"No, you're choosin' to hold on to something that isn't there over Rocky. You never had a daughter, you told me when I hooked up with her you were glad I gave you a good one. Look close, Ma. She's back."

"She—" Vera started.

"I know, Ma. It happened *to me*. It's over. We're movin' on. That's all you're gonna get because that's all you need," Layne stated.

Vera's eyes moved back to Rocky then to Layne.

"I just—" Vera began.

Layne cut her off. "I know, now you can just cool it."

Vera stayed silent. Rocky remained unmoving against his side.

Devin closed the sliding glass door and called, "Anyone gonna go get donuts?"

"I'll go get donuts," Rocky said instantly.

"No, *I'll* go get donuts," Vera returned.

"Fuck me," Layne muttered.

"Jesus, *I'll* go get donuts," Devin stated and Layne heard a belt buckle clink.

"Then I'll go get dressed," Rocky whispered.

"Excellent idea," Vera retorted.

"Ma," Layne said warningly and then looked down at Rocky. "Make coffee, yeah?"

She looked back at him and replied, "Sure, but I'll get dressed first."

"It's Saturday and there's a law that on Saturday, you don't get dressed until at least noon," Layne told her.

She bit her lip, let it go, and said, "Layne—"

"Make coffee."

"Layne—"

His arm gave her a squeeze. "Sweetcheeks. Make. *Coffee*."

"Someone make coffee. I'll be back in ten with donuts," Devin declared, and without looking at a soul, he walked through the bodies around the front door and out of it. While the door was opened, Layne saw he'd parked at the curb.

Fucking Devin.

"*I'll* make coffee," Vera declared, stomped into the house and rounded the corner into the kitchen.

Rocky watched her, going so far as to twist her neck to look over her shoulder.

"Baby," Layne called gently, and Rocky's eyes snapped to his.

"I need to go home," she whispered, and he turned her full frontal into him and wrapped both arms around her.

"You don't need to go home," he replied.

"I need to go home," she repeated.

"Okay, well, you're not *goin'* home and you can't get home anyway, you don't have a car."

"I'll walk," she returned.

Layne grinned and dropped his face close to hers.

"You think, after last night, I'm letting you out of my sight until you have to leave Monday morning to go to school, think again, sweetcheeks," he murmured.

Pink came into her cheeks and her body shifted into his even as her hands came up to his biceps and gripped.

"You said we'd talk," she told him and his grin turned into a smile.

"Well, that's not gonna happen with Ma here, Devin here and donuts comin'."

Her fingers gripped harder even as her body pressed closer. "Layne, we need to talk."

He dipped his face closer, veered to the side and whispered in her ear, "I'll talk and I'll use my mouth, but what I say won't be words and how I use my mouth, baby, I know you're gonna like."

"Layne," she breathed and his cock twitched.

Christ, he liked it when she breathed his name like that. That was new. That was this Rocky in his arms. She didn't do that before. She might moan his name, but that sweet, breathy hunger he'd never heard.

And, fuck, but he liked it.

He lifted his head and his hands. Gathering her hair in both palms, he held it loosely behind her head, resting his forearms gently on her shoulders and went on, "Live this with me, just live it. Whatever happens. However it happens. Live it with me for two days. It doesn't go the way you like, we'll talk Monday night. It goes the way you like, we live it real and ride it out. Will you give me that, honey?"

Her brows drew together. "Live it with you?"

"Live it with me, Roc. Live it here, with me. Make it real, as real as it can get for two days."

"Make it real," she whispered.

Layne nodded. "For two days."

She stared up at him and he knew he had her when her fingers uncurled on his biceps and her hands moved to his chest.

She confirmed it by saying, "Okay. Two days."

"Promise," he pushed. She hesitated, so he tugged gently at her hair and repeated, "Promise."

She gazed into his eyes and then whispered, "Promise."

He dropped his forehead to hers, ran her hair between his hands, his hands traveled down her back then he wrapped his arms tight around her and trapped her close.

"Thanks, baby," he whispered.

"Coffee's brewing!" Vera shouted.

Rocky jumped.

Layne grinned.

Then he heard the garage door go up. His forehead left hers, he turned his head and listened.

Only he and Jasper had a garage door opener. Devin had the key to the front door. And Jasper had no reason to be there.

Shit.

"Is that—?" Rocky started and Vera appeared around the corner. She'd lost her antagonism, her face was beaming.

"I think the boys are here!" Vera shouted.

"Now I definitely need to get dressed," Rocky murmured and it sucked but she was right. At this juncture, Rocky wandering around his house on a

Saturday morning in his tee was not cool when both his sons were getting used to a new woman in his life as well as the fact that they both went to her school. It'd take a while before it was cool.

He decided he'd give it a month.

They heard the back door open and Rocky shot out of his arms, her bare feet sounding on the floors as she dashed to the stairs, turned and disappeared while Vera threw both her arms up and yelled, "My babies!"

"Grandma!" Tripp shouted, and Layne saw his son connect with his grandmother. His tenuous hold on cool slipping, he threw himself in her arms and gave her a big hug.

Layne moved toward the kitchen and saw Jasper hanging back, his eyes on his grandmother, a smile on his face.

"Come here, handsome," Vera ordered, and Jasper moved forward.

His hold on cool, firm and strong, he muttered, "Hey, Gram," and kissed her cheek while she still had hold of Tripp.

"What're you doin' here?" Tripp asked, stepping back and looking down at Vera.

"You've grown, like, seventeen inches since the Fourth of July," Vera noted, giving Tripp a head to toe, skipping past the visit she'd made two months ago when Layne was shot and not answering his question.

"What're you doin' here, Gram?" Jas repeated Tripp's question.

Vera looked up at her older grandson and Layne could see she was searching for a lie.

She found it and it was lame.

"Surprise!" she shouted.

"Cool!" Tripp didn't think it was lame.

"Surprise?" Jasper saw right through it.

"Surprise," Vera repeated. "Can't a mama and grandma surprise her boys?"

"Totally! Anytime!" Tripp replied enthusiastically but Jasper's eyes cut to his old man.

Layne gave his son a "later" shake of his head and Jasper gave him a chin lift.

Vera cupped Tripp's cheek, smiled big at him then walked into the kitchen and went to the cupboard over the coffeemaker, saying, "That

Devin man is going to get donuts. I hope he's smart enough to get them at Hilligoss and not a grocery store. The grocery store donuts are okay, but nothing beats Hilligoss." She opened the cupboard, looked in it, appeared confused for a second then shut it, moving across the kitchen, muttering, "I forgot. You keep your mugs across the kitchen. Crazy. Mugs should be close to the coffeemaker."

Layne tipped his head back and looked at the ceiling not knowing whether to laugh or shout.

He righted his head and looked at Jasper. "Family reunion over, boys, what're *you* doin' here?"

Tripp looked at Layne, at Jasper then he ducked his head and moved to the door. "Gotta let Blondie in."

Layne's eyes sliced to Jasper and Jasper jerked his head indicating upstairs. Layne nodded and Tripp slid open the door. Blondie bounded in then ran back and forth between Tripp and Jasper, jumping up on both of them but not giving either of them time to greet her before she pushed off and headed back to the other one. All this company and all her boys home equaled heaven in the form of a house in sea of similar houses in a small town in Indiana and she didn't know what to do with herself.

"Hey, where's Rocky?" Tripp asked, sliding the door shut, crouching and capturing Blondie with both hands to give her a rubdown.

Vera's eyes shot to Layne and her face set straight to disapproval.

Layne ignored his mother and answered his son. "Upstairs, gettin' dressed." He moved to the stairs and ordered, "Feed Blondie, pal, okay? Jas and I gotta have a chat."

"Sure Dad," Tripp replied, straightening and heading to the kitchen.

Layne ignored Vera now giving him an assessing stare as he turned and headed upstairs and to Jasper's room.

Jasper followed and closed the door behind him. Layne surveyed the room and tried not to breathe too deeply before he turned to his son.

"Do me a favor, bud, take some time and pick up in here, change your sheets, vacuum and open a window to air this shit out. It smells like a fuckin' locker room in here," Layne said to his boy.

"Smells okay to me," Jasper returned.

"Yeah, well, you eventually wanna study with Keira in here, it won't smell okay to her," Layne replied. Jasper held his eyes then he nodded and Layne realized Keira being Jas's girl was going to make life a little easier on Jasper's old man. "Now, tell me what you two are doin' here," Layne ordered.

Jasper pulled in breath before he said, "Mom's workin'. She wasn't supposed to but someone called in sick." Layne nodded and Jasper went on, "Stew's home and I didn't want to be around Stew today and didn't want Tripp around him."

The muscles in Layne's neck contracted as he asked sharply, "Why?"

Jasper didn't delay in answering. "Stew got home late last night. He does that a lot. Sometimes Mom is cool with it, sometimes they fight. Last night they fought. It wasn't good. It's never good but last night it *really* wasn't good. I think he's steppin' out on her."

He'd be right.

"So you're here to hang rather than bein' there and hangin'," Layne stated.

"No, we gotta go to the school and swim with the team and then we gotta go to Youth Group. There's another reason why we're here," Jasper replied. Layne was silent and Jasper continued, "When they were shoutin' last night, in the middle of it, Mom freaked. Said somethin' about blood on Stew's clothes."

Layne took in a deep breath and let it out.

He wasn't surprised that there was blood on Stew's clothes. He'd beat the shit out of someone and then shot him at close range. The blood splatter was bound to hit him.

Gabby was cottoning on. Layne didn't have much time.

"You say Stew is home?" Layne asked. Jasper nodded and Layne carried on, "And your mom is out?" Jasper nodded again. "How long's Stew stay home on a Saturday?"

Jasper shrugged. "Stew doesn't have a schedule but he got home late and they fought, like, for-freakin'-ever. I reckon he'll sleep in."

Layne nodded. "Good call, comin' here, bud. It's showtime. I'll do my thing today."

"What do I do?" Jasper asked.

293

"Keep your phone close. Once I'm done, I'll give you a brief."

Jasper nodded as he said, "You got it, Dad."

Layne looked at his son and made a decision.

Therefore, he shared, "You remember I told you Rocky didn't know it wasn't fake anymore?"

Layne watched his son's eyes grow intense before Jas said, "Yeah."

"Well, she knows it isn't fake anymore," Layne finished, and Jasper grinned instantly, his grin huge.

"Cool," he murmured.

"Your grandma isn't here as a surprise. She's here because she heard about Rocky bein' back in my life. She and Rocky used to be tight. She loved her like a daughter. She was not happy when Rocky took off, mostly because of what it did to me but also because she missed her. So that means she's not happy that Rocky's back. I need your help with that," Layne told him.

"How?" Jasper asked.

"Roll with it and make whatever plays you feel you need to make. I trust you to make the right ones. But Rocky's ridin' the edge of this reconciliation. It's good, she knows it, but somethin' isn't right. Until I know what that is and sort her head out, we all gotta tread cautiously. She gets an excuse, she's gonna make a break for it, from me, from you and Tripp. And when Roc breaks, she breaks hard."

"It's her dad," Jasper stated and Layne stared at him.

"Come again?" he asked.

"Everyone knows her story. Everyone at school. Everyone thinks she's cool because she's cool. Everyone thinks she's cooler now because she's with you. But everyone likes her because she's how she is even though she went through what she went through. She's hot. She dresses nice. She smells good. She smiles a lot. She takes care of the kids, and not just the ones in her classroom. She knows everyone. She talks to 'em. Gives a shit. She's totally got it together. Lotta people who went through what she went through wouldn't be like that. But that's what she shows the kids. I see the way she looks at you. It's the way Mom always looks at you when you don't know she's lookin', but it's more. She likes you but you're like her dad, like Merry. Doctors don't get shot at, Dad."

Layne stared at his son for a beat before he said quietly, "I ever tell you you're sharp?"

Jasper stared at his old man for a beat before he replied quietly, "No."

"As a tack, bud," Layne whispered.

Jasper swallowed, but his son, being his son but also being all Jasper, didn't look away.

And because he didn't, Layne walked up to him and put both hands to his son's neck, giving it a firm squeeze. He looked him in the eyes and whispered, "Fucked up with you, know it, but you're a fuckin' good kid despite that, and even though I didn't have much to do with it, I'm proud of you." He gave his son's neck a gentle jerk and finished, "Love you, bud."

Jasper swallowed again but didn't take his eyes from his dad.

He also didn't pull away or slide into his asshole teenage kid attitude.

Layne let that golden trail sweep through him before he went on.

"You got time before swimmin', clean up this room, yeah?"

"Yeah," Jasper whispered.

"I'm gonna be doin' somethin' at the computer in a minute. You keep Tripp downstairs. Got me?"

Jasper nodded.

Layne gave him another squeeze and walked out of the room. He went to his room and found the bed made and Rocky at his sink, her ass in her gray cords tipped back, her torso bent over the counter, a makeup brush in her hand, bristles at her cheek. She was wearing her cords and a deep purple bra. This bra was satin and lace, mostly lace. There was a wet towel on the rack. He'd heard it and knew she'd taken a quick shower. He lived any other life, he'd be in that shower with her and they'd probably still be in it.

Another time and he was looking forward to that time.

She hadn't washed her hair and it was up in a messy knot secured by a band at the top of her head. Seeing it, he determined, when her clothes hung in his closet and her shit was in the drawers under that counter, when she was at work, he was going to take scissors to every one of those fucking bands, melt down her pins and snap her clips.

Now, he took advantage of it.

She stayed bent over the basin but her eyes came to him as he approached. He moved in behind her, ran his hand across her ribs just under her tits and pulled her up.

"Layne," she whispered as his head went down and his lips went to the skin on her neck. "Layne," she breathed, and when she did, he wrapped his other arm around her belly. He pulled her deeper into his body as he ran his tongue up her neck to behind her ear. "Baby," she whispered.

His head came up and he looked at her in the mirror.

Eyes half-mast, mouth soft, beautiful.

"Like this bra," he murmured in her ear and his thumb slid along the satin at the underside of the curve of her breast.

"Thanks," she murmured as his thumb slid back and he felt a tremor glide through her body.

"Hate to say this, sweetcheeks, but the boys bein' home means my mornin' just got more complicated," he told her.

She held his gaze in the mirror but she lost that look as she did it. The instant it was gone, he missed it.

"Seth?" she guessed.

"Stew," he replied, and she bit her lip but nodded. "Need to give this my attention. Have some work to do here then I gotta go but I'll be back as soon as I can. I'll talk to Devin, ask him to take you home so you can pack up some shit, enough for the weekend and to get to work on Monday. That cool with you?"

She nodded.

"Ignore Ma," Layne went on. Rocky bit her lip again and Layne's arms gave her a squeeze. "Ignore her, Roc. She spends time with you, she'll come around."

"Okay," she whispered, but he could tell she wasn't buying it.

"Stay strong for me, two days, you promised," he reminded her.

She held his gaze again then she nodded and said, "I promised."

"Good," he muttered, bent his head and kissed her neck before he let her go and said, "I gotta get dressed."

He saw her eyes follow him then she bent over the basin again and went back to her makeup.

Layne went out to the weight room and turned on his computer and printer at his desk. Then he went back to his room and Rocky had her face so close to the mirror she could kiss it as she applied mascara. Her ass was tipped way back, her neck bent, her back arched and, seeing her like that, Layne loved his boys, he loved his ma and he loved Devin, but he wished they were all on another planet.

He shook off his thoughts, pulled on clothes, crowded Rocky as he brushed his teeth and then walked to his desk. He was sitting down and transferring the images from the memory card to the hard drive when Rocky walked out of his room wearing her turtleneck, her hair still in a bunch at the top of her head, her arms full of dirty towels.

Layne looked at the towels then at her.

"You seriously need to do laundry," she announced, and didn't wait for his reply, she walked down the stairs.

Layne turned and grinned at his computer.

Playing this real meant, for Rocky, having free rein to do his laundry.

Bonus. Big time.

He was printing images on photo paper and saving them to a data stick he would put in his safe at the office when he heard her come back. He was busy and didn't turn to her until he saw a mug of coffee slide onto his desktop, scrunched next to it was a Hilligoss cinnamon roll wrapped in a paper napkin, his favorite. He bent his neck back to look up at her and saw her hands wrapped around a mug, her eyes were on the computer screen and her face was perfectly blank.

He looked to the screen and it displayed a picture of Stew landing a kick on his mark. Seeing it, and knowing Rocky saw it, Layne had to make a decision. Protect her from his work or let her in and help her to understand and cope.

So he made his decision.

He wrapped an arm around her hips, swiveling his chair toward her, and guided her carefully into his lap. She didn't resist and settled in as he bent forward and grabbed his mug.

"Wasn't pretty, baby," he muttered against the rim before taking a sip.

She slid her mug on the desk and reached out to grab the photos from the printer tray. He watched her bend her neck to look down at them and fought the urge to take them from her hands and protect her from what she'd see as she shuffled through them.

297

"Stew's an asshole," she whispered, her eyes scanning the photos.

"Yep," Layne agreed, watching her face and, unfortunately, not paying attention to the photos so when she sucked in breath and her body got tight, he wasn't sure why.

He assumed it was a shot of Stew drilling a round into the man's thigh.

It wasn't. It was a shot of Stew drilling something else.

Layne put his mug down and tugged the photos out of her hands. He turned them face down, dropped them to his desk and looked up at Rocky to see her eyes wide, her face pale and her lips parted.

Then she whispered a hilariously disgusted, "Gross."

She was okay. Thank God.

Layne smiled and remarked, "That about sums it up, sweetcheeks."

Her eyes caught his. "That wasn't Gabrielle," she informed him of something he already knew.

"Nope," he agreed.

"Women put up with a lot of shit," she noted.

"Yep," Layne agreed again.

"Not many would put up with that," she went on.

"You're gettin' it, baby."

Her eyes slid to the pictures and then back to him.

Then she said, "I bet that wasn't fun."

"You'd win that bet."

She held his gaze for a moment then her hand came to his jaw and she dipped her head and touched her mouth to his.

She moved away an inch and said softly, "She won't agree but she's lucky you're looking out for her, Layne. This isn't fun but it's the right thing to do."

Yes, she was all right. More than all right. Thank fuck.

"Thanks, baby," he said softly back, giving her waist a squeeze.

"I'll leave you to it," she muttered, turning away to nab her coffee mug and then moving out of his lap.

He didn't want her to leave him, but if she did, he could get this done and then it'd be over so he could concentrate on the other thousand things happening in his life. So he had to let her leave him to it.

He felt Rocky's presence glide away as she moved down the stairs. He pulled out the data stick and slipped in another one. One was for his safe, insurance. One was for Colt, retribution. He'd make another one and give it to Devin, more insurance.

He did his work, ate his cinnamon roll, called good-bye to his sons when they went swimming and hoped to God Devin could play peacemaker downstairs between Rocky and his mother.

Then he shut down his computer, locked two of the data sticks in his cupboard and put the photos in a folder. He went to his room and pulled on socks and boots, went back to his chair and tagged his leather jacket and walked down the stairs.

He gave the data stick to Devin.

He gave his mother a kiss on the cheek.

He gave Rocky a touch of the lips.

Then he went out the door, swung into his truck and drove to his ex-wife's house.

Sixteen

REAL

$\mathcal{S}$tew handed Layne the envelope and, just by the feel of it, Layne knew it wasn't light.

Even so, he counted every bill and took his time doing it. Ten thousand dollars. He'd come up with the cash in less than an hour, which was the amount of time Layne had given him to do it.

Their earlier conversation hadn't gone well, mostly because Stew was an asshole. But even if he was an asshole, apparently Stew wasn't as stupid as Layne thought because after he treated Layne to a fuckload of bullshit bluster, he'd agreed to meet Layne in the alley behind J&J's Saloon, which also happened to be behind his office.

Layne tucked the flap in the envelope, shoved it into the inside pocket of his leather jacket and looked at Stew.

"Good," Layne muttered. "Now get to Gabby's and get your shit. You're out before she gets home from work."

Stew glared at him then grunted, "No skin off my nose. Bitch is a pain in the ass."

"Excellent, then I won't have to worry about you cryin' while eatin' chocolate and watchin' soap operas."

Stew's eyes narrowed right before he got stupid and hissed, "Fuck you, motherfucker." Then he got more stupid, leaned in and threatened, "You'll regret this."

300

Layne moved instantly and he moved fast. He pulled up a forearm and caught Stew under the chin with it, knocking his teeth together and jerking his head back. Then Layne went for Stew's exposed throat. Wrapping his fingers around it tight, he shoved Stew hard into his Suburban, pushed him back and bent over him to get in his face.

"You even fuckin' *breathe* in my direction, Jasper's, Tripp's, Gabby's or Rocky's, I swear to God, you're dead. Swear to *God.*" He squeezed tighter and Stew's feet scuffled against the pavement as his hand pushed against Layne's wrist. He forced his arm between their bodies and shoved up, but Layne didn't move, using only his hand on Stew's throat to bend him further backward until a gurgling noise came from Stew's throat. "You think to get smart, your ass is in jail and those photos are all over the Internet so, when you get out, everyone in the 'burg will know why you're such an asshole considering you like it so much."

"Fuck you!" Stew hissed, spittle coming out of his mouth, his face turning purple.

"I need to know you get me," Layne pushed, squeezing harder.

"Get off me!" Stew choked.

"I *need*," Layne squeezed harder, laying all his weight into his hand, "to *know* you *get me.*"

"I get you! Get the fuck off!" Stew wheezed.

Layne pushed off, took a step back, and Stew righted himself from the car. Bending over, he put his hand to his throat.

"Gabby's," Layne ordered and turned to his SUV, swung in and, still choking, Stew had to jump out of the way as Layne drove out of the alley.

He headed to Gabrielle's grocery store to do something that he was looking forward to only slightly more than dealing with Stew Baranski. But she'd find out eventually and Rocky was right, Layne had to suck it up. He might as well take the shit she was going to lay on him now rather than enduring a surprise attack when she found out.

He found her at the customer service desk and her eyes came to him when he was five feet away.

"You're takin' a break," he informed her when he made it to the desk. He ignored the customers in line and finished, "Now."

Gabby stared at him a second, turned to someone with her and said, "Give me a minute." Then she moved from behind the desk and Layne followed as she led him to the back, through a door, down a hall and into the break room.

Two employees were sitting there. One, a zit-faced kid who really needed an appointment with a dermatologist, the other a blonde who really needed to lay off the eyeliner or learn how to put it on better.

"We need privacy," Layne announced when he and Gabby walked in. He watched them both start then freeze, so he ordered, "Now."

They moved then and shot to the door.

The minute it closed behind them, Gabrielle turned to him. "Jas—?" she started.

Layne shook his head and cut her off. "Boys are good." He reached into his pocket, pulled out the envelope and handed it to her.

She took it, bent her head to it, opened the flap, and even with her head bent, Layne saw her mouth drop open.

Her head shot back, her eyes bright and hopeful. "What?"

Fuck. She thought he was bailing her out.

"That's not from me," Layne told her, the hope died and she looked confused and wary. "It's from Stew. He's gone. You go home tonight, he's left a pair of tighty whiteys, I wanna know."

Her face started getting red before she snapped, "What'd you do?"

He gave it to her straight and didn't waste time.

"Stew's an enforcer for a guy called Carlito. He doesn't owe him shit. He works for him and gets paid big. He's been playin' you, Gabby, but he's not playin' you anymore."

Her torso jerked back.

"That's...that's impossible," she stated, but he knew by the look on her face, her anger dying, understanding dawning, she knew that was a lie.

"Well then, I watched his twin beat the shit outta some guy last night while I was takin' pictures. Then I watched him celebrate with a chick he keeps at the trailer park on the southwest of town."

Layne watched the blood drain out of her face. She was a bitch and he didn't much like her, but she was the mother of his sons and he fucking hated doing this to her. But he had to. She'd given him no choice.

"He's bad news, Gabby," Layne went on. "We don't need our boys around that and I don't need my boys' mom around that. You deserve better. So I made it so he did right by you with that money," he tipped his head to the envelope, "and now he's gone."

She stared at him and then her hand clenched the envelope. "Tanner—"

He shook his head and interrupted her again, "We don't need to process this. It's done. The boys stay with me this week and you go stay with Brandy. The whole week. You put two K of that in your account and you use that, your pay and what I pay you to take care of your bills. When you buy groceries or anything else that takes cash, you use that money. You put no more than two K of that in your account, Gabrielle. The rest of that money stays under the radar. Are you clear on all that?"

"Yes," she whispered.

"I'll keep an eye on your house and get a quiet word out to the boys to do the same. Jas will be checkin' in with you regular. You got problems, you say, 'I'm fine, honey, everything is *just* fine,' and he'll know it's not and he'll know to get in touch with me." At these words, her face went completely white, but Layne kept on. "You wanna say you're okay, you use other words, not those. Can you remember that?"

"Are the boys in danger?" she asked.

"No," Layne answered.

"Am I?"

"No," Layne repeated. "That doesn't mean we aren't gonna move forward smart."

Some color came back into her face and her eyes started to get squinty. "Did you bring Jasper into this?"

"Yeah, I did. He's seventeen, he's fuckin' smart and he doesn't like his mom gettin' walked on. I didn't take care of this shit, there would come a time when he'd feel the need to step in. I stepped in before that time came. And if you think Tripp doesn't know somethin's goin' down, you're wrong. He's as smart as Jasper and just as worried about his mom."

She pressed her lips together and couldn't hold his eyes so hers went to the floor.

"I need to know you're clear on all this before I go, Gabrielle," Layne prompted, and she forced her eyes to his before she nodded.

"Good. You go home tonight, check things out then get your ass to Brandy's. And find time next week to change the locks," Layne finished and turned to leave.

"Tanner," she called. Layne turned back, bracing because he knew she was going to hit him with it and he froze when he saw standing across the room a Gabrielle Weil Layne had never seen before in his life.

"I'm sorry," she whispered and, fuck him, he knew she was about to cry. Shit.

He'd never seen her cry except tears of being extremely pissed off.

He turned to face her but didn't walk back into the room.

"You fucked up," he said gently. "I fucked up so I know it doesn't feel good when you figure out you did it. But it's done. It's over. Now you move on."

She blinked her eyes rapidly and he knew she was struggling against the tears.

Fucking shit.

"Gabby," he called and she blinked again but kept her eyes open and nodded. "We didn't have a lot of good times, but when you forgot to be pissed off at me and the world, you could be funny. You've never been sweet, but, fuck, woman, you could be funny. When you took care of yourself, there was a lot to look at and all of it was good."

He watched her mouth slowly open. She stared at him and he kept going.

"You look around you and see you got a good job, a nice home and two great boys, all of which you worked hard at and created all on your own, you might realize that you've got a better than average life and you built that all by yourself. You learn to be funny again and spend time takin' care of yourself rather than takin' care of some asshole who doesn't deserve your time, you don't wanna be lonely, you won't be and you'll be spendin' your time with someone who's worth havin' it."

She kept staring at him and Layne finished.

"And, Gabby, when you forget to be pissed off and act like a bitch, your time is worth havin'."

With that, he left her staring after him and walked out of the room, through the store and to his truck. He folded in and drove to her house, idling in the alley out back and waiting until he saw Stew come out with a box full of shit.

Then he pulled out his cell and called Jasper.

He watched Stew walk back into the house and got Jasper's voicemail. "Minute you get this, bud, you call me. It's all good but we gotta brief."

He disconnected, sat in his truck and waited until he saw Stew come out with an overstuffed, beat up workout bag that had to be his. Gabby might not be rolling in it or working out herself, but she kitted the boys out better than that. When Stew re-entered the back gate, Layne put the Suburban into gear and drove down the alley. Then he drove home.

He rolled down his street to see both the Mercedes and the Calais at the curb in front of his house along with his mother's rental car.

He was sitting waiting for the garage door to slide up when he saw the door to the utility room open and Rocky stood there. Seeing her, he had added evidence she'd been to her apartment because now she was wearing jeans and a long-sleeved green tee that had a high neckline that was wide and showed some skin at her shoulders. She also had her hair in what he knew was a clip because a spray of it could be seen at the top of her head. He also knew she was seriously pissed about something. He knew this because her arms were crossed on her chest, her hip was hitched, one foot was out, she was tapping her toe and she was wearing a face like thunder.

Fuck.

He pulled in and she watched him until he switched off the ignition. She was standing at his door when he cleared the car.

He'd barely slammed it when she announced, "I'm going to *kill* Adrian Cosgrove."

Oh shit. That was not what he was expecting to hear.

It was worse.

"Why?" Layne asked.

"You'll see," she shot back, turned on her bare foot and stomped into the house.

Layne followed, looking at his boots and contemplating vacation spots.

He hit the kitchen, took one look at Paige Cosgrove sitting at a stool at his island, her left eye blue and nearly swollen shut, her lower left lip split and he froze, keeping his body still in an effort to control the burning rage that suddenly engulfed his system.

Then he barked, "*Where's your boy?*"

She started and he knew he should have gentled his tone but he didn't have it in him.

Paige pulled in a breath and whispered, "Swimming with the team."

"Cosgrove?" Layne asked.

She shook her head. "Don't know, he...after..." Her eyes went to the island and she whispered, "He took off."

"Seth look like you?" Layne demanded to know.

"No, I...he'd already planned to spend the night at his friend Jamie's."

Layne yanked his phone out of back pocket, tossed it to Dev, who was standing beside the island next to Vera, who was sitting close to Paige, and he ordered, "Call Jas. Tell him to get his, Tripp's and Seth's asses home immediately." Then he looked at Rocky and growled, "Upstairs."

He prowled by her and felt her hot on his heels as he took the stairs two at a time and she ran up them. He went directly to his room but stopped at the door, his hand on it. When she cleared it, he slammed it behind her.

She turned to him, he saw her anger was gone, at that point she was all about controlling his and he knew this because she said immediately, "Breathe, Layne."

"I'm breathin'," he bit out.

"No, sweetheart, you're spitting fire." She walked up to him and placed her hands on his chest. "*Breathe*, baby."

Layne stared down at her and sucked in breath. The fire inside died down but didn't go out.

"I see I should have warned you," she whispered.

Shit yeah, she should have warned him.

"Talk to me," he ordered.

"This isn't the first time, for her or, last night, for Seth."

"No shit?" Layne asked with biting sarcasm. He knew what kind of man Cosgrove was. He watched Rocky flinch and take a step back, her hands falling away from his chest. "Not pissed at you, Rocky," he told her.

"I know," she said quietly and watched him closely.

"What's she doin' here?"

"Her family's from Valparaiso. She's got friends but she doesn't want…" Rocky trailed off and then said, "I think she thinks you'll make her and Seth safe."

"She give you a reason she didn't go to the cops?" he asked.

"She did. She called last night after he left. I called Merry after she told her story. Merry says they're looking for him, but until they find him, there's nothing they can do."

That was what sucked about being a cop and it was precisely the reason Layne wasn't one anymore. He could play by the rules but he wasn't a big fan of doing it with his hands tied. There were too many times when good people were in trouble, you wanted to help and you could, but most the time you couldn't do all you needed to do because you didn't have the resources.

"Layne," Rocky called and he focused on her. "She said it was worse last night than normal."

"Yeah," Layne returned. "You know how you know that, baby?" he asked, and she shook her head. He knew by the expression on her face she didn't want to know but she was going to listen all the same. "Man like Cosgrove doesn't make his marks seen. He's got a place in this community and that'd fuck with his cred, people knowin' he's a fuckin' asshole rather than just suspecting it and talkin' behind his back. So he does it invisible. Last night, he lost control, made it visible. That's how you know it was worse."

"Okay, Layne," she whispered then her head tipped to the side. "Are you going to help?"

"What do you think?" he asked and he saw her mouth twitch.

"I think you're going to help," she answered.

"Fuck," he muttered, turned, opened the door, walked out of the room and down the stairs, Rocky again right at his heels.

"Phone," he growled at Devin who threw his cell to him immediately. Layne caught it and engaged it as he avoided the eyes on him.

"Your boy's on his way home," Devin informed him.

Layne nodded as he scrolled down, found the number and hit go.

He put a hand on his hip, his eyes to his boots, his phone to his ear and he listened to it ring.

Cal answered on the third ring. "Yo."

"You sell your house yet?" Layne asked.

"Nope," Cal answered, his voice no longer casual but alert.

"It furnished?" Layne went on.

"Nope," Cal repeated.

"Utilities on? Security system installed?"

"Yeah and yeah. What's up?"

"Paige and Seth Cosgrove need a place to stay."

Silence then a mumbled, "Fuck."

"Right," Layne confirmed what he knew Cal knew. "Feel like new neighbors?" he asked.

"Send 'em over," Cal replied immediately.

"Need you to keep an eye—" Layne started.

"Done," Cal stated before Layne could finish.

"Brief Colt," Layne told him.

"Done," Cal repeated.

"Activate Vi, Feb and their posse. They need beds and shit until they get sorted."

"Got it."

"Cosgrove's got a warrant out on him," Layne explained.

"She went to the cops?" Cal asked.

"Yep."

"Good," Cal muttered then asked, "Her or her boy?"

"Her, last night, both otherwise."

"Fuckin' dick," Cal clipped.

"I'll wait until Seth gets here and then I'm bringing them over myself."

"We're home," Cal returned.

"Thanks, man," Layne murmured.

"You didn't provoke this, Tanner, you know that, yeah? Dick just has it in him." Cal stated.

"I know it," Layne replied.

"Get them over here," Cal finished.

"Later," Layne said.

"Later."

Layne flipped his phone closed and looked into the room to see he was right. All eyes were on him.

He looked at Paige. "Until we know you and Seth are safe, you're movin' in next door to Joe Callahan."

She nodded.

"Cal and Colt'll keep an eye on you," Layne continued.

She kept nodding.

"You see Cosgrove, you call the cops first, me second," Layne went on.

Paige was still nodding.

"Has Doc seen you?" he asked.

"Paramedics checked me out last night."

This time, Layne nodded before he kept going. "Seth see you like that?"

Paige looked away.

"Eyes on me, Paige," Layne ordered gently and her eyes slowly moved back to him. "This time, has he seen you this time?"

"No," she whispered.

"I'll talk to him before he walks in here," Layne told her.

Tears filled her eyes and started falling down her cheeks before she whispered, "Thank you, Tanner."

Vera moved in on one side, sliding an arm around her waist and Rocky moved in on Paige's other side, wrapping both arms around her shoulders. The women's heads bent to her and Paige pressed her cheek against Rocky's breastbone as Vera clucked softly in Paige's ear and Paige kept silently crying.

Layne's eyes went to Devin, who was looking at the women, his mouth tight, his eyes hard and glittering. He felt Layne's eyes on him and looked to Layne. Layne jerked his head to the door and moved to it, Devin following. He waited until they were both in the garage, the garage door still open, before he spoke.

"You feel like multitasking?" Layne asked.

"You want a busted lip for askin' a stupid question?" Dev answered.

Layne smiled. Devin would get the goods on Coach Adrian Cosgrove. Even if Paige pressed charges, if he did any time at all, it wouldn't be much. She needed leverage and Devin would get it for her.

Layne got close and his voice got quiet. "Even if you have to make shit up."

Devin grinned. "I like playin' dirty."

It was then they heard the grumbling roar of the Charger and they turned to watch Jasper pull into the garage. Then they watched the boys pile out of the car. Layne kept his eyes on Seth and Seth didn't peel his from Layne. He knew what was happening. Layne didn't have to say a word to Seth Cosgrove about what he'd find inside Layne's house.

But he had to warn his boys.

"What's up, Dad?" Tripp asked as they got close.

Layne tore his eyes from Seth and looked at his youngest son then at his oldest and back to Tripp.

"You're gonna walk into the kitchen and see shit and hear shit and everything you see and hear stays in that house. You don't talk to friends about it. You don't pray to God about it. You keep your mouth shut. Get me, pal?"

Tripp stared at him and nodded.

Layne kept talking. "It's not gonna be pretty but you play it cool when you get in there. Be smart and be yourself, except, like I said, cool." He smiled at his son to take the bite out of his words and Tripp smiled back. It was small, it didn't reach his eyes but he smiled.

Layne's eyes went to Seth. "You know?"

Seth nodded, face pale, jaw tight then he hissed, *"Fuck!* I shoulda gone home."

"Put it away, son," Devin said firmly. "Ain't no goin' back, only movin' forward. You learn that, you learn it fast and you learn it now. What's done is done. Now you go in there and see to your mother."

Seth had no idea who Devin was but he still nodded to him before he looked at the door to the utility room and closed his eyes. Layne hoped he'd beat it back but he knew the kid was struggling. He was nearly a man but this shit wore you down. Layne wouldn't be surprised at tears and he hoped his sons would get it that their friend wasn't weak, he was just powerless.

But Seth beat it back, opened his eyes and walked straight to and through the door.

Jasper moved to follow but Layne put a hand on his chest and looked to Tripp.

"Get your grandma to make everyone lunch," he ordered.

Tripp nodded and then hurried after Seth.

Devin gave Layne and Jasper a look before he followed Tripp.

Layne took his hand out of Jasper's chest and said, "We gotta be quick and you gotta get down everything I say." Jasper nodded and Layne laid it out for him. What happened with Stew. What the gig was with Gabby. And what his role was with Seth. "You get that?" he asked when he was done.

"Got it," Jasper answered.

"You think you need to bag on Youth Group?" Layne asked.

"Naw, we gotta keep on that too," Jasper replied.

Shit, Jasper was a good kid. But he'd told him that once today and once was enough, so Layne just nodded.

"Check in with her regular," he repeated.

"I said I got it," Jasper returned.

"Rocky and me'll take Paige. You follow with Seth in the Charger. We go to their house first, help them get their shit, then we go to Cal's."

Jasper nodded.

"Control Keira," Layne ordered. "The woman in our house is humiliated enough. We don't need Keira sayin' anything or doin' anything nutty."

Jasper's chest expanded. "She'll be cool."

Layne lifted his chin. "I reckon she will." Jasper relaxed, Layne turned and moved to the door, muttering, "Let's get lunch and get this done."

He had a hand on the handle when he heard Jasper call, "Dad?"

He looked to his boy. "Yeah?"

Jasper stared at him, expression hidden except a muscle ticking in his cheek.

Finally, he spoke and the words seemed forced out of him. "I'm glad you're proud of me." Layne jerked his chin up and started to turn the handle on the door when Jasper finished, "'Cause I'm proud of you too."

A new burn ignited, just in his chest. So hot, he was finding it hard to breathe.

His voice was hoarse and low when he said, "Good to have you back, bud."

He saw Jasper's chest was moving like Layne knew his was moving and he knew his son had the same burn inside him so he left him alone to beat it back, turned the handle and walked into the house.

Layne hit the button on the remote and the TV flicked off.

He looked down at Rocky's head resting heavily in the middle of his chest.

Vera was upstairs in Tripp's bed. Tripp was on an air mattress in Jasper's room, Jasper in his bed. Gabby had called in to Jas and she was safe at Brandy's. Stew was wherever Stew was but none of his shit was at Gabby's. Paige and Seth were at Cal's old house.

Devin was out, whereabouts unknown, but he was either at J&J's getting hammered or he was talking a bookie into doing him a favor and laying a fake trail of Coach Cosgrove betting on high school football games as well as giving insider information on when he'd be throwing them. Layne thought this because that was what Layne would do and Devin had taught him everything he hadn't learned in the field. So if Dev felt like playing dirty, Layne reckoned that was how he'd play it.

And Layne was on his back on the couch with a sleeping Raquel, her body half on his, half tucked into the seat of the couch at the back. Her knee was cocked, thigh resting over both of his, her pelvis snug in his hip, her arm was slung along his waist and she'd been out for the last hour.

He moved and her head instantly came up.

"Time for bed, baby," he whispered and her eyes came to his.

He watched her blink, look around the room and he started to curl up, his arm around her back tensing to take her with him when she pressed into him and her gaze came back to his.

He settled back when she moved her body so it was mostly on his, only partly in the couch and she crossed her arms on his chest and put her chin on her hands. He'd pulled the clip out of her hair hours ago, so it was down, falling around her shoulders and on his chest.

Now she was studying him, sleep still in her eyes, something he couldn't read with it.

"You know," she started softly, "I promised I'd live it real."

"Yeah?" Layne asked when she said no more.

"Well, I'm thinking about going back on that promise," she told him and his arm around her squeezed.

"Roc—"

One side of her mouth she couldn't control twitched up and she said, "Layne, if this is your real, I think we should live it fake for Sunday. I'll wear an apron and make a pot roast and you can put on loafers and we can pretend to be Ozzie and Harriet without seeing disgusting pornographic pictures starring Stew 'Ick' Baranski, shaking anyone down, setting up safe houses for victims of domestic violence or sending teenage kids on undercover assignments at Church Youth Groups."

He used his arm around her to pull her up his chest, her chin came off her hands, her face came level with his and he gathered her hair in his other hand as he fought back a smile and told her, "Don't own loafers, sweetcheeks."

"We'll go to the mall," she offered. "I don't own an apron either. We'll pick one of those up too."

"Not a big fan of shopping," he informed her.

"That's okay, you can swing by and get me a coffee. I'll do all the grunt work."

He used her hair to bring her mouth to his and he kissed her lightly. He did it lightly because she put pressure on his hand and pulled back a little and he watched her eyes move over his face then her hand came up and he felt her fingers at his jaw. She watched as they glided feather light along his jaw, his lips and then over his cheekbone before her fingers slid into his hair at the side of his head, curling around the back and her eyes came back to his.

"I know about you," she whispered.

"What do you know?" he whispered back.

"You help people." She was still whispering.

"Rocky—"

She interrupted him. "I know about Kim Kempler."

"Roc—"

"And I know about Winona Jakobi."

"Baby—"

"Mostly women, right Layne?" she asked softly and he felt his body get tight.

"It isn't—"

"Women with kids but on their own," she cut him off. "Women like your mom who struggle going it alone."

"Ma did all right," Layne reminded her.

"Yeah, because her son got a paper route the minute he could and got a job the minute he could get that. Couldn't play football, even though you were good, as good as Alec Colton, if not better, because you had to quit when you were fifteen and work after school to help out at home."

Layne tried to lighten the mood. "I don't have amnesia, sweetcheeks."

Rocky didn't feel like lightening the mood. Her eyes had grown intense and her hand moved out of his hair so she could run the backs of her knuckles against his jaw. She flattened her hand on his cheek and her eyes held his.

"What am I going to do with you, Tanner Layne?" she whispered.

"If you're open to suggestions, I got a few," Layne whispered back.

"Do you want real?" she asked suddenly and he didn't understand the question.

Still, he answered, "Yeah, I want real."

"How real?" she asked quickly back.

"Lay it on me, Rocky," Layne invited.

"I didn't love him," she returned and his body got tight under hers again. "I talked myself into thinking I loved him, but I didn't. I liked him. I admired him. He's brilliant at what he does. He's passionate about it. I wanted to love him. I tried. But I never did."

"What I'm hearin', Roc, he wasn't an easy man to love," Layne replied.

"He treated me like shit," Rocky announced and his arm automatically squeezed her as his hand holding her hair balled into a fist. "That's why I couldn't love him, I guess. Because he treated me like shit. For ten years. Even before we were married. And I took that, Layne. I took ten years of it. I took it."

"You goin' somewhere with this?" he asked.

"Do you think *we're* going somewhere?" she asked back.

"We *are* goin' somewhere," he returned.

She nodded. "Then you need to know what kind of woman I've become."

Layne stared at her a second and he fought it, he really did, but he couldn't help it and he burst out laughing.

"Layne!" she snapped after he'd been laughing awhile and he rolled so she was on her back in the couch and he was mostly on top of her. When he got her in that position and kept laughing, she repeated, "Layne!"

"Give me a minute, sweetcheeks, that was fuckin' funny."

"I wasn't trying to be funny," she hissed.

"Well you were," he said through waning laughter.

She glared at him then announced, "He's bad in bed." Layne burst out laughing again and Rocky slapped his arm. "Stop laughing, that's not funny!"

"No, baby, you're right, it isn't, *for you*. For me, I find it hilarious," Layne returned.

"I put up with that too," she declared stubbornly then went back on it. "Well, I did then I didn't so I guess it's no surprise he went looking elsewhere because…well…"

Layne's body was shaking and his side hurt, so he said, "Please, Roc, you're killin' me."

She fell silent. Layne got control of his hilarity and when he did he saw she was staring at him, serious as a heart attack.

"It's interesting you think the last ten years of my life are amusing," she noted, and Layne sobered instantly and just as instantly gave it to her straight.

"I'm not glad he treated you like shit and I'm not glad he was shit in bed, but at the same time I am. I'm glad you didn't move onto anything better than what we had because I didn't. Not in bed and not out of it. Not ever. Not once. Not even close. It would suck if you did because that would kill and these last eighteen years without you were bad enough. These last eighteen years thinkin' you'd gone onto somethin' good, somethin' solid, somethin' that made you happy cut straight to the bone, Rocky. Knowin' you didn't is a relief. You should know that and I don't give a fuck what you think about it. That's how I feel."

When he was done, she was still staring at him but her face had changed, her lips were parted and her eyes were intense. But she didn't speak so he took that at his cue to continue.

"Somethin' else, sweetcheeks," he went on. "I know what kind of woman you are, you can't hide it. So you made shitty decisions. I got blotto a week after you left me, fucked the first woman who came along that night who reminded me of you, the condom broke and she got pregnant. I was drunk but that's no excuse. It was a shitty decision. I was pissed and in pain, made that decision and bore the consequences. I lucked out and got Jasper and Tripp outta that. You, if you play your cards right, can take his ass to the cleaners and make it so you'll never worry about money. That's what you'll get out of yours."

"I think, don't you, that I should just cut my losses and move on. There's no reason to make Jarrod pay for me not loving him," Rocky replied.

"Oh yeah...yeah there is," Layne returned.

"Really? What?"

His face dipped close. "Because he could have made you happy. It was me, you gave me a shot, I'd tie myself into knots to make you happy. He didn't do that. He treated you like shit, made you feel small and fucked around on you. You *think* you played him, but you didn't. He might not be any good at fuckin' but he's the master at fuckin' you over and he should pay for that."

"Layne—" she started, her mouth had gone soft, her eyes had gone half-mast, but he was on a roll.

She wanted to talk? They were going to talk.

"Why were you in my hospital room?"

Her body went solid underneath him and she repeated, "Layne."

His arms gave her a rough squeeze. "Answer me, Rocky. Why?" She closed her eyes and he gave her another squeeze on a warning, "Roc."

She opened her eyes and whispered, "You know why, Layne."

And that was when Layne watched the tears fill her eyes and one slid out the side, down her temple, into her hair and there it was. He knew it, or he had wanted to know it but he couldn't be sure. But there it was, the proof leaking from Rocky's eyes.

He lifted his hand, slid his fingers into her hair and used his thumb to wipe the wetness away.

"Yeah, baby," he said gently. "I know why and now that I've reminded you, can we get past this shit?"

Apparently they couldn't, not yet.

"You were drunk when you slept with her?"

"Yeah."

She stared up at him and took in a deep breath then another one until her eyes cleared and she asked, "Why do men do that?"

"Baby, I did it and *I* don't even know why I did it."

She studied his face and then nodded and he felt her body ease under his. Something he knew wouldn't last long because he had to ask, so he was going to ask.

"Why'd you leave me?"

Her eyes held his, Layne held his breath and she surprised the fuck out of him when she answered.

"I did it," she stopped and licked her lips, "and I don't know why I did it."

He closed his eyes and turned his head away because that was pure and complete bullshit. Such bullshit, when he was being straight with her, that it pissed him right the fuck off. So he started to knife away but stopped when he felt her fingers curl around his neck.

His eyes went back to her.

"You know, right after I left you, two days I stayed in my room at Dad's house and I don't remember a second. I don't remember eating or sleeping or going to the bathroom. I just remember getting up on the third day, all my stuff from our house in boxes and suitcases jammed into my room. I walked down and Dad was eating cereal. He looked at me and said, 'Want me to take you back to Tanner?' and I said, 'Never,' and that was it. I don't know why. I know…"

She closed her eyes and Layne held his breath again until she opened them and went on in a whisper.

"I know it hurt. I know every day I struggled with it. I know every day I wondered why I was struggling. I know how it felt when you'd call, come over, I'd hear you arguing with Dad or Merry. I know how all of that felt. I remember all of that. I know it didn't feel good and I knew then that the only way to make it better was to go back to you. I just don't know why I couldn't."

The tears came back into her eyes, shimmering for a second before falling and she lifted her head, closed her eyes, pressed her forehead to his and finished.

317

"Until you got shot." She opened her eyes and, close up, they locked on his. "Eighteen years, every day I struggled against finding a way to connect with you but I couldn't fight it anymore when you got shot."

His hand sifted into her hair at the side and he slanted his head and touched his mouth to hers, muttering, "Baby."

She shook her head and her arms slid around his shoulders. She buried her face in his neck and her body trembled with her tears as she kept talking, her voice rough and thick, difficult to hear and not because her words were hard to make out.

"Every day for eighteen years, Layne, every *fucking* day. I missed you every day. I'd wake up next to Jarrod and wish it was you. I'd go to sleep next to him and wish it was you." She pulled her face out of his neck and her eyes hit his, but hers were so wet he knew she couldn't focus on him when she said, "That's why he said that at the restaurant. He knew. He threw you in my face all the time. We fought about it, *God*, all the time. Once," she pulled her hand through her hair then swiped at her cheeks in agitation, "we were making love and he asked me, right in the middle of it, 'Who do you see, Rocky? Do you see me or is Tanner fucking you?'"

Layne had been holding his tongue.

Until then.

Then, he growled, "You are fuckin' shitting me."

"No!" she cried and flopped back on the couch, covering her face with her hands. "I don't blame him." Her head was shaking side to side. "I don't blame him."

"Baby," Layne's hands went to her wrists to pull hers away from her face but they moved suddenly, turned to frame his and they held on tight.

"Merry called," she whispered. "He called me and told me to get to the hospital. He couldn't go. He was dealing with..." She shook her head. "He told me. He told me you'd been shot. When I got there, Gabrielle was there with the boys. She was so pissed when she saw me. Jasper and Tripp, they were in a fog. They didn't even know I was there. But Gabrielle, she was pissed. And I didn't care. I just sat there until the boys left you and I could get into your room and I sat there until you woke up and I knew you were okay. And that was it. I couldn't fight it anymore, whatever it was and now…" She stared up at him. "Now…" Her eyeballs went side to side, "Well, now I'm here."

"Now you're here," Layne repeated, her eyes came to his and her hands slid from his face and down to rest on his chest.

"Now, I'm here," she whispered.

"You play me?" Layne asked and he felt pressure at her hands at his chest before they went away, one folding around the other and she rested them on her chest.

"Play you?" She was still whispering.

"Sweetcheeks, leg of lamb?"

Light dawned and Layne watched her face close down but not before he saw the pain knife through her eyes. "No, Layne," she said softly. "I didn't play you."

Then she shifted as if to slide out from under him, but he gave her all his weight, pressing her into the couch and he framed her face with his hands.

"You played me," he murmured, looking into her eyes.

"I didn't." She bucked her back to try to throw him off.

"You played me, just didn't know you were doing it."

She stilled under him, held his gaze and announced, "I think I'm sleeping at home tonight."

He grinned. "Oh no you're fuckin' not."

"I am."

"You're not."

"Layne, *I am* so *get off*," she demanded, bucking again.

His thumb slid over her cheek and down to rest on her lips and his face got close. "No, Roc, you're not gonna go home. You're gonna go upstairs and you're gonna get naked and climb into my bed and then you're gonna let me do what I want to your body. Whatever I want for as long as I want, and when I make you come, you're gonna hafta be quiet about it so you don't wake up Ma and my boys."

"Get off," she whispered but there was no fire to it and his grin turned to a smile. He dropped his head and whispered in her ear.

"First I'm gonna suck your tits and finger fuck you 'til you come. Then I'm gonna go down on you 'til you come. Then I'm gonna fuck you hard 'til

I come." He lifted his head and looked at her face, eyes half-mast, mouth soft, and she was already breathing heavily. "You're up to it, you can come when I fuck you too. We'll see how I do."

That got him the breathy, "Layne."

He had her. He not only had her, pretty soon he was going to *have her.* Thank fuck.

He put his mouth to hers and whispered, "I gotta turn the lights out and secure the house. Go upstairs and get naked for me, baby."

"I don't know if I can—"

"Sweetcheeks. Go upstairs and get naked for me."

"Layne."

"Do it."

She pressed her head back into the couch and whispered, "But...I don't think I can be quiet."

Layne grinned again.

She probably couldn't. She was a moaner eighteen years ago and she was again last night. She was great at giving head, mostly because she liked doing it and it helped when she moaned how much she liked it around his cock.

"We'll get creative," he promised and her eyes got round. "Go upstairs, honey, and get naked for me."

"Okay," she whispered.

He rolled to the side. She shot off the couch but strutted up the stairs.

Layne took his time as he secured the house, turned out the lights and followed her.

He found her naked in his bed.

He got naked and joined her.

Then he did everything he promised and then some.

And he just managed to muffle her moans with his hand the first time she came, his mouth the third time and she muffled them in a pillow the second.

With Rocky dead to the world and pinning him to the bed, Layne stared at the dark ceiling and remembered his dream.

"Do you get it?" Rocky whispered in his ear.

"Get what, baby?" he whispered back.

"Why I left you?"

He didn't get it. She'd finally explained it and he still didn't get it.

That wasn't a scene she acted out on his couch. That was real.

Fuck, *Rocky* didn't even fucking get it.

Which made Layne wonder why she left him? Why she took everything from their house, jammed it into her room, and lost two days. Why she spent every day for eighteen years struggling against connecting with him. Why she spent the last months since he'd been shot losing that struggle but grasping at it.

Why was she so afraid of the fucking dark?

And what was that he felt coming off of her, seeping in the room so strong it even pressed against him, reeking of a fear that was more than fear of the fucking dark?

He knew one thing. That fear wasn't a fear of dark and wild. That fear was dark but it wasn't fear of him. It was a fear of something sinister.

Layne had no answers to these questions.

But he knew who did.

Seventeen

FIGHTING TO WIN

*L*ayne felt her moving against him, over him, her hair sliding on his shoulder, her lips at his throat, she shifted astride him, he felt her knees at his sides, her bottom settle into his crotch, her breasts against his chest.

His hands went to span Rocky's hips.

He opened his eyes.

Layne saw dark ceiling.

Rocky was astride him, her lips moving from his throat to the hinge of his jaw, her hips in his hands.

She wasn't a dream.

Now, *this* was how he wanted to wake up yesterday.

"Baby," he murmured, her lips left his jaw and he saw her head come up, her hair falling down to frame both of their faces.

"Morning," she whispered, that soft, sweet word said with her warm body on top of his drove into his mouth, down his throat, burning a golden trail through his chest, his gut, straight to his cock.

She tilted her head and her lips hit his.

The moment of impact, his hands slid in, his arms going around her waist, one slanting up, his fingers gripped her hair. She opened her mouth, his tongue slid in as he growled and rolled her to her back.

⌒⟶

Layne was at the bar doing pull-ups wearing nothing but shorts, ankle socks and running shoes.

He'd pulled up when one of the double doors to his bedroom swung open. Rocky walked out and stopped dead.

He dropped down and hung there, staring at her.

She had her hair wrapped in a towel, a huge bundle of dirty laundry piled in her arms and her body wrapped in his plaid, flannel robe.

Jesus, where'd she find that fucking robe?

He'd had it since he was seventeen and he had no idea why he kept hold of it. His mother bought it for him it to take to Ball State. He'd skipped a grade, going from sixth to eighth and therefore graduated from high school early. He remembered she'd given him that robe with tears in her eyes, distraught. She'd told him that her baby, not even a man, was going away. He remembered it had annoyed him immensely because he thought he *was* a man. He'd worn it sometimes during his freshman year in the dorms when he had to walk the corridors to get to the bathrooms and then never wore it again.

He'd had it when he was with Rocky, obviously, but she'd never worn it. She'd had her own robe but mostly she strutted around in his tees. So she wasn't the reason he kept it.

He had no clue why he kept it. He just did.

Looking at her now, Layne was glad he kept it and he was equally glad Rocky had dug through his shit to find it. She looked adorable in that old robe.

"Hey, sweetcheeks," he greeted, and she stared at him as he pulled himself up, chin over the bar, then slowly lowered himself down.

"Is that taking it easy?" she asked in a tone that stated clearly any answer other than "no" and any future action other than him letting go of the bar and hitting the shower was unacceptable.

"Yep," he replied and pulled himself back up.

She glared at him as he slowly let himself down and continued to glare at him as he pulled himself back up. Then she stomped to the stairs.

She returned as he was hooking his ankles under the bar at the weight bench he'd declined, and he was about to roll back to do sit ups. He twisted to watch her glare at him as she walked back to his room, one hand holding the handle of a coffee mug, the other hand precariously balancing a pile of his folded clothes under which, hooked on her fingers, were hangers on which hung his ironed shirts.

"Your mother re-ironed everything I ironed yesterday," she told him in mid-strut, tone now displeased. "She says I don't do it right."

She didn't wait for him to respond, not that he had a response. She walked into his bedroom and kicked the door closed.

Layne twisted back and rolled down, grinning.

"Pancakes!" Vera shouted from downstairs, and three seconds later Tripp tore through his bedroom door, racing down the hall to the bathroom.

Tripp was a big fan of his grandma's pancakes and there was a reason why. Her pancakes were the shit.

Not twenty seconds later, Jasper came out of his room and, with his back to the bench, Layne looked at his mostly upside down son who was staring down the hall at the closed bathroom door.

Jas's eyes came to his dad. "Tripp in the bathroom?"

Layne grunted, "Yep," as he curled up.

"I'll use the one downstairs," Jas mumbled and Layne heard his footfalls on the stairs.

Proof that Vera's pancakes were the bomb. It was Sunday morning, his sons were both teenagers, it was just eight o'clock and they both were out of bed.

Layne rolled back to the weight bench, again grinning.

Layne was standing outside with hair wet from his shower wearing thick socks, track pants and a freshly laundered, white, long-sleeved thermal. He bent down to pick up the tennis ball Blondie had just dropped at his feet, tipped his head back to see she'd inched back, front legs out and sprawled, chest to the cement patio, behind in the air, tail wagging and her eyes were riveted to the ball.

Layne tossed it and she went racing after it.

Then he straightened, turned to the table, picked up his coffee mug steaming in the cold air, sipped at it and turned back to Blondie who was dropping the tennis ball again at his feet. He repeated his actions, she raced away and Layne reached to the table and grabbed his cell.

By the time it was ringing in his ear, he'd thrown the ball for Blondie three more times.

He heard the connect then, "You've reached Lieutenant Garrett Merrick. I'm unable to take your call but leave a message and I'll get back to you."

After the beep, Layne said, "Merry. Layne. Call me when you get this."

Then he disconnected, tossed the phone on the table, bent and threw the ball for Blondie and turned to the table to get his mug. Something caught his peripheral vision; he twisted his neck to look through the sliding glass doors and froze.

Rocky was walking down the stairs.

Not even ten minutes ago he'd left her in the bathroom. After he'd finished his workout, he got in the shower when she was blow-drying her hair. When he got out of the shower, she was still blow-drying her hair.

He could see this. His woman had a lot of hair.

After he'd dressed, he'd left her bent over the basin applying mascara.

Now she was strutting down the stairs wearing a tight, dark brown skirt, a blue sweater with one of those cowl necks—the one on Rocky's sweater hanging deep, past her tits and showing skin at her chest, the rest of the sweater skintight—and a pair of dark blue pumps with a high, thin heel, a closed toe and a thin, sexy ankle strap. Her makeup was done full-on. Her hair was back and he couldn't tell how she'd pulled it back this time, but he thought it was a waste of all that effort with the blow-dryer to pull it back and he'd be pulling it down about two seconds after he found out what in *the fuck* she was up to, dressed like that on Sunday morning.

He grabbed his phone and was nearly to the door when Blondie caught him and dropped the ball at his feet. He transferred his phone to his hand carrying the mug, bent, grabbed the ball and tossed it side arm as he straightened. She dashed after it and Layne slid open the door and walked into the house.

Rocky was now at the island transferring shit from one purse to another. Vera was at the sink, doing dishes. His boys were both camped out on the couch watching TV and he couldn't see but parts of their bodies as they were lounging.

"We don't usually dress to watch the Colts play, sweetcheeks," he remarked after he slid the door closed.

He thought it was telling that she didn't lift her head when she answered and he knew why with what she said.

"I'm going to church."

Layne stopped dead and felt his eyes narrow. Vera turned slowly from the sink and her surprised eyes hit Rocky. Both his boys' heads popped up over the couch.

"Come again?" Layne asked quietly, but he couldn't keep the rumble out of his tone.

Rocky lifted a compact at the same time she unscrewed the lid of a tube of lip gloss and her eyes skidded across him before she flipped the compact open, her eyes going to it and she repeated, "I'm going to church."

Then she calmly slid the applicator across her lips, transferring a glimmering, peachy gloss to them as Layne watched and wondered if counting to ten actually worked.

Then he decided, fuck it.

He walked to the island and stood at the end of it next to where she was at the front, put his mug and cell down and asked, "You're going to church?"

She rubbed her lips together, shoved the applicator in the tube and snapped the compact closed, taking this time, he knew, to pluck up the courage to meet his eyes.

Then she met his eyes. "Yes. I'm going to church."

"When's the last time you went to church?" Layne returned.

She pulled in breath and shrugged.

It was then, Layne was done.

"You're not goin' to church," he stated firmly but his voice was pitched low.

"Yes I am," she replied firmly but her voice was pitched a little high.

"No, Roc, you aren't."

"Yes, Layne, I am."

"Why?" Layne asked sharply.

"I feel in the mood for fellowship," she answered, and Layne heard both Tripp and Jasper laugh. Tripp's was louder and Jasper's was more a chuckle.

"Roc—" Layne started, wondering if his mother and sons would find it inappropriate if he threw her over his shoulder and carried her up the stairs, knowing at least his mother would, and then wondering if he gave a fuck.

He was cut off by Vera. "That's an excellent idea. Let me check my hair. I'll go with you."

Rocky's startled eyes turned to Vera, who was definitely not Rocky's best friend and she'd made this clear beyond yesterday morning. Re-ironing Layne's shirts was just the continuation of it. They'd been in détente during the Paige drama but Vera laid it on after they got back from Cal's. When they'd arrived home, Vera had been in mid-October spring-clean of the house, which now, top to bottom, was sparkling. And after Layne had brought in the cookies that Rocky made and his sons devoured them like they'd never tasted anything but sawdust in their lives, Vera had demanded to make dinner then demanded to clean up after dinner. She also practically raced Rocky to the washing machine any time Rocky looked to be heading that way, and therefore, they'd engaged in a hostile tag team to do Layne's laundry. Through this, Vera was making clear whose house this was and who was welcome to make themselves at home in it and clear whose it wasn't, and that person was Rocky.

Vera rounded the stairs and by the time Rocky's head turned back to him, she'd realized the advantages to Vera's unexpected alliance and she smiled smugly up at him.

He stared down at her wondering if her lip gloss tasted like peaches at the same time wondering if she'd attack him again after he spanked her fucking ass.

"I'm goin' too!" Tripp shouted and catapulted himself over the back of the couch.

Layne watched his son race up the stairs then Jasper rolled off the couch, muttering, "I'm not gonna miss this," and he followed his brother.

Layne's eyes went back to Rocky and she was dropping her compact and lip gloss in her bag and, incidentally, failing miserably at hiding her smile.

"Sweetcheeks," he called.

Her smile vanished, her head came up tilted to the side, her eyes alight, and she mumbled, "Hmm?"

"What're you doin'?" he asked quietly.

"Didn't you hear?" she asked back. "We're *all* going to church."

"What're you doin'?" Layne repeated.

Her eyes locked with his and she went into stare down.

He was pissed and she knew it so she couldn't hold it and whispered, "Layne."

"I told you, you're not on this guy's radar."

"Layne—"

"I told you, this guy is a predator."

"But—"

"Jas has been datin' Keira for a few weeks and he's keepin' her clear of this guy. You think, what you mean to me, eighteen years I finally got that back, I'm not gonna do what I gotta do to keep you clear?"

Her eyes went hooded a half second after they went intense, her mouth got soft then she swallowed before she ran the tip of her tongue along her bottom lip, then her teeth sank into it. It sucked he was so fucking pissed at her because, that look on her face, he *really* wanted to see if her lips tasted like peaches.

She held his eyes and they went back into stare down.

She broke it again by saying softly, "Then you better get dressed to go to church, sweetheart."

He stared at her.

He should have known. It'd been too easy to talk her down that night when she'd come up with her fool plan to confront the fake TJ Gaines. When Rocky got something in her head, she never let it go. She'd been waiting for her opportunity and here it was. He was cornered. With his mother and boys in the house, they couldn't have the showdown he needed to stop her.

He should have known.

Shit, he was out of practice. He was going to have to step it up.

Layne leaned in and she braced as he did but held her ground.

"I'll get changed but, baby, fair warning. You're gonna pay for pullin' this shit."

He watched her eyes get wide right before he turned and walked up the stairs.

The parking lot to the Christian Church was jammed by the time Layne and his family arrived, so he let them off at the door, twisting his neck toward the backseat as he did, giving Jasper a look that communicated his responsibility was keeping Rocky out of trouble. Jasper read this loud and clear if his grin was anything to go by. He nodded and Layne watched him stick close to Rocky as they walked in the door.

By the time he parked and made it to the crowded vestibule, he found Rocky, Vera and the boys deep in conversation with a short, squat woman with a dark helmet of hair and very large tits. So large, the blouse she was wearing opened at the buttons, exposing her bra.

He moved in beside Rocky, sliding his arm around her shoulders and Rocky looked up at him with a smile as the woman exclaimed, "Oh my goodness! There you are!" and Layne's eyes moved to her. When they did, hers shot to Rocky. "Oh Rocky, the girls in the office are right! He's even more handsome close up! You *lucky duck*!" she cried loudly.

At that, Layne watched Rocky's dimple come out.

"Sharon, let me introduce you to Tanner Layne." Rocky kept smiling at the woman and then turned that smile to Layne. "Layne, this is *Sharon Reynolds*."

She emphasized the "Sharon Reynolds." Layne found that name in his memory banks and looked back at the church office lady.

"Sharon," he greeted.

"So nice to meet you and *so nice* to have you and your mom back at church." Sharon turned to his sons. "They used to come here all the time, a long time ago, I remember. Or," she paused, "at least, your grandma did before she moved away to Florida." Her eyes went to Vera. "We sure missed your weekly contributions, I can tell you that." Then her antennae, obviously always active and working overdrive, dinged, her head suddenly jerked and her eyes focused on someone. "Oh! There's Gray Lacey," she announced and everyone turned to look where she was looking. "His offering has been light the last two weeks. He usually gives a hundred dollars and now he's only giving fifty. This is probably because his wife Donna has been hitting the wine or, I should say," she paused again to lean in, her eyes never leaving her target, and confided, "hitting it *more than usual.* I need to go speak to him." She turned back to them explaining, "Fifty dollars *is* fifty dollars and a member of this flock shouldn't be spending that fifty dollars on *booze.*"

She bustled away as they all watched her.

Layne's arm gave Rocky a squeeze and her eyes came to him.

"Definitely the church needs a new office lady," he murmured.

"She's harmless," Rocky replied.

"I think, sweetcheeks, weekly offerings are confidential. I also think that it's not a law not to gossip but it *is* a commandment and we're standin' in a building where God pays a fair amount of attention." Rocky pressed her lips together but her eyes were dancing and she didn't reply so Layne went on, "Probably coulda asked her for the personnel file and she would have handed it over."

He heard Rocky's quiet giggle then they all heard, "Rocky!" and Layne turned to see Josie Judd bearing down on them.

"Hey, Josie," Rocky smiled, moving out of Layne's arm to give her friend a hug and get one in return.

When they stepped away from each other, Josie's eyes surveyed the group and went back to Rocky.

"Jeez, you're a miracle worker, honey," Josie noted. "I left Chip in his underpants on the couch counting down the minutes to when he can crack open a beer. And the kids are all still in bed doin' their zombie act, which they only do on Sunday mornings or on days when they have tests at school. How'd you get these boys all dressed up and to church?"

Layne looked at his sons. Jasper was wearing a pair of chinos and a blue shirt under the leather jacket his mom bought him last Christmas. Tripp was wearing the same except his shirt was maroon and he had a navy sweater pulled over it. Layne was wearing another suit and shirt that he'd never worn before that Melody had given him.

"Um…" Rocky mumbled and Josie waved her hand between them and kept talking.

"You can share your secrets without an audience and *with* a bottle of wine," she stated. "And also when we sit down and talk about the bachelor auction. I had a gab with her and Heidi's in. Did you talk to Feb and Vi?"

"Bachelor auction?" Layne asked.

Rocky ignored him and answered Josie, "I had a word with Vi yesterday. She's in and she said she'd talk with Feb, Cheryl and Jackie."

"Bachelor auction?" Layne repeated.

"This is going to be *so fun!*" Josie exclaimed. "I *love* it!"

Layne claimed Rocky with an arm around her shoulders again, turned her into his side, dipped his head and asked yet again, "Sweetcheeks, bachelor auction?"

"We're doing a bachelor auction for Meghan Reilly," Josie answered before Rocky could and Layne looked at her. "Gettin' all the single boys at the police department and fire station to volunteer. Havin' a fancy dinner, a band, a casino and sellin' stuff in silent auctions. Rocky called me yesterday, it was her idea and it'll be a hoot."

"Cool!" Tripp entered the conversation.

"You should invite kids. I could talk to some of the football team. They'd go up for auction," Jasper put in.

Josie swung to him and clapped her hands. "What a *great* idea! The more the merrier."

"What's this?" Vera asked, and Layne looked to his mother.

"Meghan Reilly, she's sick and can't afford her medication," Josie answered. "Things are not good. She's gettin' behind and Rocky does charity gigs, usually it's for hospitals and clinics and stuff, but this time she's doin' it just for Meghan."

Vera's eyes hit Rocky but before she could say more, Tripp butted in.

"You go up for auction, Jas, you better get Keira to save up her allowance," Tripp advised Jasper.

"My woman'll take care of me, Tripp-o-matic," Jasper returned arrogantly, and Layne's eyes rolled to the ceiling.

"You could go up for sale too, Dad," Tripp went on and Layne's eyes rolled back to his boy. "You'd get top dollar."

"Think I'm off the market, pal," Layne said quietly and felt Rocky's body go tight before it relaxed against his side just as Josie's eyes shot to him and a huge smile spread on her face.

"Yeah, Dad, but you aren't actually *off the market* and Roc's loaded. I reckon she'd pay a whack for you," Tripp went on and every pair of eyes in their huddle turned to him, including Rocky's.

Fuck, but he was *not* going up for auction. Firstly, because Rocky wasn't loaded. She had a nest egg but she didn't need to be depleting it bidding on him. And secondly, because he was *not* going up for auction.

"We'll talk about it later," he muttered. Josie giggled softly. Vera gave him a stare. And Rocky looked down at her shoes, that fall of hair that wasn't tied back in the ponytail at the nape of her neck not succeeding in hiding her smile.

Vera saved him by announcing, "We should probably find a pew."

"Good idea," Rocky murmured and looked at Josie. "Sit with us?"

"You bet," Josie replied, and they all moved into the sanctuary.

They were there approximately thirty seconds when Rocky and Layne spied him at the same time.

He was at the front of the church, wearing about the same outfit as Jasper except he had dark blue pants. Even so, it was plain to see it wasn't the same quality. Both Layne's boys cared about their appearance and their clothes, it was essential to the high school experience, and Jasper mostly, but Tripp also, had a role amongst their peers to lead the pack of high school cool. Layne knew exactly how expensive their clothes were since he'd paid for them.

The man at the front of the church's clothes were of lower quality, but that was a deception, something Rutledge had not yet learned. Layne knew this was a deception because the man at the front of the church had more shit in his hair than Tripp and a haircut that he didn't get at a barber. He

332

also had a tan that wasn't from the sun or from an olive skin tone. It was October in Indiana and unless someone was fresh from vacation, no one had a tan.

And he was extremely good-looking, out of a magazine good-looking, and he had an easy, very white smile that he was shining on the flock of girls surrounding him.

Bleached teeth, carefully crafted tanning-bed tan and a fifty dollar haircut.

Definitely not a Youth Minister.

"Excuse me," Rocky murmured and slid away from him before he could catch her.

She wasn't three strutting strides away before Layne ordered a simple, "Tripp."

"On it," Tripp muttered and moved to follow Rocky.

Rocky strutted naturally but Layne watched and learned something new about his woman. When she meant business, her strut changed. It became subtly more suggestive and a fuckuva lot more watchable. She captured TJ Gaines's attention ten pews from the front and she kept it. He had teenage girls hanging on his every word and practically hanging off his every limb. But, for Gaines, they'd vanished. Gaines was watching Rocky and even standing at the front of a church, his look was openly carnal.

Nope, definitely not a Youth Minister.

Rocky rounded the front, hips swaying, ass swinging, and didn't even glance at him but smiled brightly at someone in the second pew back. She stopped and greeted an old woman Layne didn't know, going so far as to put a knee to the vacant front pew to lean in, take the old woman's hand and have a chat. This also meant that tight skirt, which Layne had noticed had a slit up the back, stretched across her hips, thighs and an ass which was now pointed straight out.

Gaines's eyes locked on her ass and his look kept the carnal but added hungry.

Fuck.

Rocky just hit his radar with a big, fucking *ping*.

"Shit, Dad, she's good," Jasper muttered from beside him.

Layne felt his jaw tighten and he held himself back as Rocky's attention was caught by a couple of the girls, as she knew it would be. She squeezed the old lady's hand and turned to the girls and Gaines. He saw her head move around as she greeted Gaines's entourage and then, even though her back was to Layne, he knew the second her eyes met Gaines's because he arranged his features to hide the hunger, but they didn't change to kindly Youth Minister. Instead, they changed to blatant interest. An interest she was meant to see, read and, Gaines hoped, act on.

Layne tensed to move when Gaines held out his hand and Rocky's lifted hers to take it but Layne stopped when Tripp did his thing.

He'd been talking to one of the girls, but the minute Rocky's hand touched Gaines's, Tripp didn't hesitate. He turned toward Layne and called, "Okay, Dad, we're comin'!" even though Layne hadn't said a word.

Then Tripp leaned in, grabbed Rocky's hand, said a few words to Gaines and the girls around him, turned and tugged Rocky behind him as he led the way back to Layne, Jasper, Vera and Josie, dragging Rocky behind him.

Layne grinned as his son and his woman moved. Tripp grinned back. Rocky didn't grin. Rocky looked displeased.

Tripp didn't let Rocky's hand go until Layne's arm slid around her shoulders, he pulled her front to his and tipped his chin up at Tripp who stepped away.

Then he dipped his chin down to look at Rocky.

"Not fair," she whispered before he could speak. "Reinforcements."

"Baby," he replied on a smile.

"We should sit," Vera announced abruptly. Rocky's head turned to her, Layne let Rocky go with a sigh and they all slid into the pew.

Without telling his son to do it, Jasper worked with Layne to engineer the seating arrangement to pin Rocky between them so that Tripp went in first, then Vera, Jas, Rocky, Layne, and finally Josie.

The service started and they did a lot of standing, sitting and singing, though Layne didn't sing. While people's eyes were to their hymnbooks, Layne's eyes were locked on Gaines, who was sitting in a pew three rows back and to the side. He had a very pretty, very young blonde girl on one side and a very pretty, very young, redhead on his other side. His entire pew was taken with girls, some pretty, some not-so-pretty, but all of them were young. Layne guessed freshman, at most sophomores.

Two seconds after the sermon started, Rocky turned into him and her lips went to his ear.

"He's not right," she whispered.

"I know, baby," he whispered back.

"He's *really* not right." She kept whispering.

Layne turned his head to her, her lips went away from his ear but he put his face close to hers, held her eyes and whispered back, "Baby, *I know.*"

She gazed at him a second, worry open in her eyes then she nodded and turned to face the front.

Layne glanced back at Gaines and his followers, and he felt his gut squeeze.

At that, he made a decision.

He leaned in front of Rocky, caught Jasper's attention, and Jasper leaned in front of Rocky too.

"You just went active duty," Layne murmured.

Jasper's eyes sliced across the church to the third pew then back to Layne.

"Gotcha," he returned quietly and sat back.

Layne sat back too, glanced at Rocky and saw she was smiling.

After the sermon, Layne walked back into the vestibule holding Rocky's hand and they stopped when one of his mother's friends called her name and Vera broke off to greet her.

Five seconds later, Layne felt Rocky's hand squeeze his tightly. He looked down at her to see her eyes directed across the vestibule and his eyes followed hers.

Gaines was again tending his flock, but the very pretty, very young redhead was close to him and had a hand resting on his chest. She couldn't be more than fourteen but she rested her hand on his chest the way Rocky would rest hers on Layne's.

Layne's stomach roiled.

This wasn't about God, Jesus and religion. It also wasn't about drugs. This was what he'd suspected it was, but hoped it wasn't. It was about something else. Something far worse than drugs.

But what Layne didn't get was that the guy wasn't hiding it. It was like he had carte blanche to cultivate his underage harem right in the vestibule of the church. And, if he was into young girls, how could he also be so blatantly into Rocky?

Layne scanned the crowd and he saw some adults had their eyes on the group, their manner watchful and uncomfortable. Parents who had concerns but who were not stepping in.

Layne looked back at Gaines, whose hand was dropping from doing something around the redhead's ear.

Dedication.

Those girls were devoted, not to their faith in Jesus, but to their worship of TJ Gaines. These parents had had words and the girls had gone teenage-girl berserk. The parents were either lazy and didn't want the headache of dealing with pissed-off teenage girls in the throes of a very sick crush or they had nothing to go on but speculation they *really* hoped wasn't accurate.

In the 'burg, it was undoubtedly the latter.

Layne looked at his sons. "Jas, Tripp, shut that shit down," he growled.

Both his boys nodded and wove through the crowd.

"Layne?" Rocky called on a whisper and Layne looked down at her.

"New plan, sweetcheeks," he replied.

"That would be?" she prompted.

"Steppin' it up," Layne returned.

"Stepping it up?" she asked, and he bent to her.

"That man needs competition," he whispered.

"I thought you said he wouldn't like anyone, even high school boys, cutting into his action."

"He won't," Layne stated.

"So?"

"So, I'm hopin' that he'll act to defend his territory and fuck up or he'll realize he's blown and get outta town."

"I thought you wanted to take him down," Rocky noted.

"I did. Don't like the idea of him movin' on to other prey. But right now, seein' that shit with my own eyes, I don't like that his prey are my people. We can't take him down, I want him outta the 'burg."

She stared up at him a second before she gave him the dimple and moved closer.

When she got close, she tipped her head way back and whispered, "You probably shouldn't say the f-word in a church, Layne."

"Think God's got bigger concerns in His house than me droppin' the f-bomb, sweetcheeks."

The dimple depressed deeper, her hand lifted to curl her fingers around his neck and she got up on her toes to touch her mouth to his.

"Uh…" They heard Josie mumble from close and both of them turned their heads to her. "You wanna let me in on what you two are whispering about?"

"Not really," Layne replied and Rocky giggled.

"We're just discussing what we're going to have for dinner," Rocky lied.

"Right," Josie returned, her eyes sharp and intelligent. "You two have been on Code Red Alert since you entered the sanctuary." Her eyes locked on Layne. "What gives?"

Before he could answer, or in this case *not* answer, Rocky suddenly called, "Harry!" Her head swung to Josie and she said, "I'll call you later, honey. Okay?" And before Josie could answer or Layne could get his eyes on what had her attention, she moved away from him and toward Harrison Rutledge.

Layne's body locked as he watched Rocky greet Rutledge by putting her hand on his shoulder and kissing his cheek.

Considering Layne spent a fair amount of time following Rutledge, he knew that Rutledge rarely missed Sunday church. He'd never understood why a man who wasn't smart enough to hide he was on the take went to church, but he suspected it was precisely that. An effort to hide he was on the take.

He'd forgotten about Rutledge but Rocky hadn't.

She knew he'd be there.

Shit, she'd orchestrated one helluva a play. Two birds with one stone.

"Excuse me," Layne muttered to Josie and followed Rocky.

"You'd *so* do me a favor if you could help out." He heard Rocky saying as he got close and Rutledge's eyes moved to him and went wary.

"Rutledge," Layne greeted as he hit them, and he slid an arm around Rocky's waist, pulling her away from Rutledge and tucking her into his side.

"Tanner," Rutledge greeted back.

Rocky looked up at Layne. "I've asked him to go up for auction. He'd be perfect!" She looked back at Rutledge and lied, "The women will be at each other's throats for you."

Harrison Rutledge wasn't exactly ugly, but at five foot ten with light brown hair that was quickly thinning and a gut that was equally quickly forming, he wasn't exactly calendar man material either.

"I don't know, Rocky," Rutledge muttered.

"Oh you have to do it," Rocky urged. "Layne won't because he's with me, Colt is taken and we need as many hot guys as we can get."

"Have you talked to Mike?" Rutledge asked.

"He's on my list!" Rocky answered enthusiastically, Rutledge looked unconvinced and she leaned forward, grabbed his hand and gave it a squeeze. "Just think about it, Harry," she asked and dropped his hand but tilted her head. "For me?"

Rutledge stared at her, smiled and said, "All right, Rocky, I'll think about it."

She clapped her hands and cried, "Great!" before looking at Layne and saying, "Isn't that great, sweetheart?"

"Yeah, baby, great," Layne muttered to her and looked at Rutledge. "It'd help out a lot, man. Sean would be grateful."

Rutledge's eyes went from wary to guarded. He watched Layne a beat then nodded. "I'd do anything for Sean."

Fucking lying sack of shit.

"Perfect!" Rocky exclaimed with a little jump and Rutledge's eyes shot to her tits to watch them bounce.

Sack of *shit*.

Layne was done, and he communicated this by giving Rocky a squeeze and saying, "I missed out on pancakes, sweetcheeks. We need to get home. I'm starved."

She looked up at him and slid an arm around his waist. "Right, of course." Her gaze went to Rutledge. "See you later?"

"Later, Rocky." He nodded to Layne. "Tanner."

"Later," Layne grunted and moved Rocky away.

When they'd taken five steps, she muttered under her breath, "That went well."

"Do me a favor," Layne muttered back.

"What?" she asked.

"Don't jump around that asshole."

She stopped and looked up at him, confused. "Why?"

He looked down at her. "Baby, you got a great rack. Gonna have to put up with everyone noticing it, but don't wanna have to put up with that assclown's eyes locked on it."

Understanding flooded her face, understanding and disgust.

"Oh," she whispered.

"Oh," Layne repeated.

"Okay, I won't jump," she relented immediately.

"Appreciate it," Layne replied.

Vera approached. "I've decided on pork chops and au gratin potatoes for dinner," she announced and then went on, "And I'm making my Milky Way cake." After this, Layne felt Rocky go completely solid at his side. "We need to get home. I need to get to the store."

Layne suspected that Vera just pulled out the big guns. Pork chops, au gratin potatoes and Milky Way cake were his favorite and Rocky knew it because *she* was the one who'd made him his first Milky Way cake on the first birthday he'd celebrated with her, and Vera had been there. Milky Way cake wasn't Vera's, it was Rocky's. Except the fact that Vera had a variety of occasions in the last eighteen years to make it for him and Rocky had not. Layne wasn't hip on chick war tactics, but he suspected his mother just escalated hostilities.

"Ma—" Layne started to warn but Vera cut him off.

"We need to go," she stated. "I'll go get the boys." Then she hustled in the direction of Jasper and Tripp, who'd managed to pry a throng of girls from TJ Gaines's snare and were shining their football stud light on them.

Layne's eyes went to Rocky to see her eyes on his mother.

"Roc—"

"That's *my* cake," she whispered, her eyes still on his mother.

Layne sighed, then repeated, "Roc—"

Her gaze shot to his. "She can't have that cake."

"Just let her do what she thinks she has to do."

Rocky glared at him then her eyes changed, and Layne's neck contracted when they did because he didn't like what he saw, before she hid it by looking away from him.

"Rocky?" he called.

She looked at him again. "You know, I haven't made that cake in years. Not for Dad, not for Merry, even when they asked for it, and *not* for Jarrod."

He understood the look, both his hands went to her hips and he murmured, "Baby."

"That's *my* cake," she repeated, back to whispering. "And she knows it."

Then she pulled from his hands and strutted away.

Yep, he was right, an escalation in hostilities.

He took in a deep breath through his nose, looked to see his mother corralling his sons and when they started to walk his way, Layne turned and followed Rocky to the car.

When they hit the house, Rocky was still pissed at Vera, and wordlessly she marched through the house and up the stairs.

Layne followed her, not because she was pissed. She'd made that bed by leaving him and she had to deal with his mother her way. He'd said his piece. Vera had ignored it. Rocky clearly wasn't going to bolt because of Vera's antics. So now he wasn't getting involved.

No, he followed her because *he* was pissed. She'd made her play and got her way and Layne didn't like how she went about it. It didn't matter that she was right—putting that shit with Gaines under his nose so he'd intensify the operation. Because, in doing it, she'd also put herself out there and that, coupled with how she'd made her play, pissed him off.

It was time to teach Rocky a lesson.

She was halfway across his bedroom when he made it to the door and closed it loudly behind him. The instant he did, she stopped and whirled.

"I'll be needing to have words with your mother," she announced.

"Later," Layne returned, moving toward her.

"No, in about two minutes, *before* she goes to the grocery store and comes back and *steals my cake.*"

"Got things bigger than cakes to talk about, sweetcheeks," Layne replied, still advancing on her. Her face cleared. She got a good look at him, she read him and astutely started backing up.

"Layne—" she started, her hand coming up and Layne didn't stop moving, but his eyes went to her hand then back to hers.

"Not wearin' your bandage," he remarked.

She kept edging backward, her hand still up, and she asked, "What?"

"Bandage, baby, for your wrist." Layne kept moving forward, she hit the edge of the archway to the bathroom and righted herself instantly, moving backwards into the bathroom.

"Um...it doesn't hurt anymore," she replied.

"Doc say you can take it off?" Layne asked as they moved through the bathroom and into walk-in.

"No, Layne, um...what are you doing?"

"I'm talkin' about your wrist and then, in about two seconds, I'm gonna carry you to my bed, turn you over my knee and slap that sweet ass of yours."

Her eyes grew round just as she hit the wall of the walk-in.

"Layne—"

He got deep into her space. Her hand hit his chest and he kept going, forcing her arm to bend at the elbow and trapping it between them as he put his hands on the wall on either side of her.

"Played me, sweetcheeks."

"I know." She surprised him by instantly copping to it. "But it was important."

"It's important, we talk about it. You don't fuck me."

She stared up at him and rested her free hand at his waist. "I didn't fuck you, Layne," she whispered.

"Oh yeah you did, baby, now," his head dipped and he got in her face, "I fuck you."

"Layne," she breathed, her eyes glued to his and hearing that, he lost it.

His hands moved from the wall to her jaws. He tipped her head back further and pulled her up as his mouth slammed down on hers.

She opened it immediately. His tongue slid inside, her arms glided around his shoulders and she pressed herself into him.

He kissed her hard, demanding, wet, and she gave it to him, everything he took from her. Her fingers moving to his jacket to pull it off his shoulders, he released her face, dropped his arms and let it fall. His hands went directly to her ass, pulling her hips tight against his hardening cock and her hands went to his shirt, pulling it out of his pants, going in, her fingers trailing his skin.

His mouth released hers and traveled down her neck.

She turned her head and whispered, "Baby," in his ear and his hand went under her sweater, up, and he cupped her breast. She strained into it and repeated her whispered, "Baby."

She smelled good, she tasted good and her nipple was hard against his palm. She was wearing one of her tight skirts and high heels and Layne liked all of that. He'd been liking it for a while and he was about to like it a lot more.

"You want it?" he growled in her ear.

"I—" she started and abruptly he pulled away, turned her to facing the wall and moved into her.

"Put your hands to the wall and don't move them," he ordered.

"Layne."

"Do it. Now."

"Layne."

He pressed his hard cock into her ass. "Now, sweetcheeks."

She put her hands to the wall. He pulled her tight skirt up her thighs and heard her suck in breath as he looked down.

Fuck, she was wearing lace-topped thigh highs and satin-backed, dark blue panties that showed a fuckuva lot of cheek.

Christ, hot.

"Layne," she repeated on a breath.

He got her skirt around her waist and one hand went down, in the front of her panties and the other hand went up, yanking her sweater over her tits, then he jerked down her bra and his fingers tugged her nipple.

That got him another gasp. His finger hit her clit, her hips jerked and she whispered, "Oh my God," and moved to press back into him.

"Keep your hands on the wall," he growled in her ear, working her clit and nipple at the same time.

Her head fell back on his shoulder and her breath got heavy.

"Oh my God," she repeated, turning so her forehead was pressed to his neck. Her back arched into his hand and her hips ground down into his fingers.

"You like this?" he asked, even though he knew she did. He wanted to make her say it.

"Yes," she breathed.

He stopped playing with her clit, thrust two fingers into her drenched pussy and turned his head to watch her neck arch, pressing her head against his shoulder, her lips parted. She pushed back against him, losing concentration, her hands slipping down the wall.

"Hands to the wall, Rocky," he ordered, and her hips jerked as his fingers moved in and out of her and his other hand worked her tit.

"You," she breathed urgently after he'd worked her for a while.

"You'll get me, baby," he promised, watching her face. "Fuck yourself on my fingers."

She instantly did as she was told. Rocky, his Rocky, Jesus, so fucking hot. She took herself close, so close, she was reaching for it, it was going to be good and watching her he nearly came in his pants.

When she was almost there, he moved away. She gasped and started to turn.

"Hands to the wall," he demanded. She kept her hands to the wall but twisted her neck to look at him, her eyes unfocused, her face filled with need and he hooked her panties with his thumb and tore them down her legs. "Step outta those." She did as ordered again. Layne freed his cock from his pants and went on, "Spread your legs." She again did what she was told, tipping her ass to him, ready for it, nonverbally begging for it. "That's it," he growled, bent his knees and thrust into her.

Fucking bliss.

"Oh God," she whimpered and he drove into her. One arm wrapped around her belly, he moved his hand from her breast and covered her mouth as the moans came.

"Take me, Rocky," he grunted as he drove harder, faster, and listened as her stifled moans got deeper.

He kept at her, knowing it was building in her as it built in him until her head shot back, colliding with his shoulder, and he felt her mouth open against his palm as her pussy tightened around his cock.

Beautiful.

He let go, drove in deep and exploded.

Fucking beautiful.

Christ, but he loved her.

He rode her gently as he came down then rooted himself and used his hand at her jaw to twist her neck so he could take her mouth in a kiss. Her tongue danced with his before he pulled out, turned her back to the wall and kissed her again while he shoved the skirt back down her hips.

His mouth left hers but their eyes locked, her arms wrapped around his back, one of his hands at her neck, the other one righting his pants as they stared at each other.

She dropped her eyes, pressed in and kissed his throat.

Her lips stayed there and he felt them move when she said, "Today is starting *a lot* better than yesterday."

He grinned, his hand moving to her jaw to tip her head back so he could look at her.

"It ain't Ozzie and Harriet, sweetcheeks," he remarked.

"Poor Ozzie and Harriet," she replied.

His grin turned into a smile before he got serious.

"Don't play me again, Roc. You want something, we talk about it."

Rocky didn't feel like getting serious.

"I'm not sure that was a deterrent, baby, more like an incentive."

"I'm bein' serious," he informed her.

"So am I," she shot back.

He looked down at her face and it hit him that she looked happy. She hadn't looked happy any of the times he'd seen her since he'd been home and now she looked happy. And he knew it was only part just having an orgasm against the wall in his closet. It was mostly being with Layne in his closet.

His irritation slid away as that look on her face settled deep in his soul. He slid his thumb along her cheekbone and softly asked her the same question she'd asked him last night.

"What am I gonna do with you, Raquel Merrick?"

Her expression shifted. He couldn't quite read it but it looked like she was scared. It was not exactly fear. Instead she looked anxious and maybe even timid before her quiet words explained her look.

"Anything you want, Layne, as long as you're with me when you do it."

There it was. Thank fuck, there it was.

Rocky was going to take a chance again on dark and wild.

Layne felt another golden trail burn through him, but he asked just to confirm.

"I take it that means we don't need to have a conversation tomorrow night."

Rocky studied him only a beat before she nodded.

Layne grinned.

Then he dipped his face close and whispered, "Go get cleaned up, sweetcheeks."

"Okay," she whispered back, touched her mouth to his and slid out from in front of him.

She started to walk away but turned back suddenly, dropped to a knees-closed crouch, nabbed her panties and tossed them into the mostly empty but still partly filled hamper. Then she threw him a satisfied grin and walked into the bathroom.

Layne looked at her panties knowing exactly what they said.

Vera could have Milky Way cake and Layne's laundry, but Rocky had her panties *in* that laundry, panties he'd torn down her legs before he fucked her.

It was a dirty play, a hit below the belt, but it made her point irrevocably.

His hands went to the buttons of his shirt and he smiled.

His mother was a contender, but Rocky was definitely fighting to win.

Eighteen

THE LIFE AND TIMES OF TANNER LAYNE

*L*ayne grabbed his smokes, his cell and headed outside in an effort not to kill his mother.

He slid the door back, stepped outside, slid it to and sat at the table. Shaking out a smoke, he fired it up.

Vera had spent the afternoon and evening taking a trip down memory lane and dragging Layne, Jasper and Tripp along with her.

She'd asked them if they remembered when Layne flew them all to Sedona for Spring Break and the boys had gone horseback riding.

She'd asked them if they remembered when Layne flew them all out to Colorado for Christmas, they'd driven up to Winter Park and the boys had gone skiing.

She'd asked them if they remembered coming down to Florida four years ago and "your father met that lovely Cassie woman and stayed out *all night.*"

And she'd asked them, while serving Milky Way cake, if they remembered going to LA for his birthday two years ago, and she'd taught "that sweet Melody" how to make Layne's favorite cake.

At first, these stories completely deflected off of Rocky and the boys had joined in with their grandmother. Rocky was too busy rooting for the Colts, eating junk food and bumping fists with Tripp anytime the Colts made a great play to cotton on to Vera's new dirty game.

Then, after the never-ending stories, it started to wear on Rocky and she ate less and got quieter. Jasper noted it at this point and stopped joining in and started paying more attention to texting Keira than his grandmother or football.

Then, when Vera brought up Cassie, Tripp got silent and became so engrossed in the game it was as if he'd be asked to re-enact it play for play.

Rocky had been stretched out in front of Layne on the couch, and when Cassie was brought up, Rocky went still as Layne went solid. She waited ten minutes, rolled off the couch and went to the bathroom. When she returned, she curled up in the side of the couch by his feet, her knees tucked to her chest, her elbow to the arm rest, her head in her hand, her eyes on the game, and Rocky locked herself right in her head.

She'd accepted a piece of cake then set it aside after two bites, which was approximately ten seconds after Vera announced she'd taught Melody how to make it.

Which was approximately five seconds after Layne's cake plate hit the table with a crash. Vera jumped. Tripp's shoulders slumped. Jasper's concentration on his phone became visibly acute. But Rocky didn't move her eyes from the TV.

Layne moved. He rolled off the couch, got his cigarettes and cell and went outside.

He took a drag and on the exhale, called Merry.

"You've reached Lieutenant Garrett Merrick. I'm unable to take your call but leave a message and I'll get back to you." He heard in his hear.

"This is the third time I've called today, Merry, you get this, call me back," Layne growled into the phone, flipped it closed, took another drag, and on the exhale, he called Dave.

"Hello?" Dave answered.

"Dave. Layne."

"Tanner, son, how are you?"

"Been better, Dave," Layne answered honestly. An answer he wouldn't have thought he'd give after he woke up that morning and after what transpired in his closet that day, but, fuck him, there he was, giving it. "Listen, I've been tryin' to get hold of Merry. You know where he is?"

"He's on call this weekend, Tanner, probably busy," Dave replied.

This wasn't an excuse for Merry not to take his calls. Merry always took his calls.

"He got anything else goin' this weekend?" Layne pushed.

"Not that I know of. He had a hot date last night but then he's always got a hot date. Boy needs to settle down. He's too old for this shit. I don't know what was wrong with Mia. Never could get that."

Layne couldn't either. He hadn't been around when Merry hooked up with Mia, but he knew her before he left town. She was a seriously pretty, petite redhead with a temper that matched her hair but a wicked sense of humor and a smile that rivaled Rocky's, falling short because she didn't have a dimple and Layne had never been in love with her. Word was Merry fell and fell hard, then broke loose for no reason.

Seemed the Merrick kids shared a particular trait.

Fuck, he *really* needed to talk to Merry.

"Dave, can you tell him if you see him or hear from him that I need to talk to him?" Layne asked. "As soon as he can."

"Sure, son, no problems." Dave paused then asked, "How's Roc?"

"We're back together," Layne announced without preamble and this was met with utter silence.

Layne let the silence stretch and waited for Dave's response as he took a drag and exhaled.

Finally, Dave whispered, "Sorry?"

"We're back together, Dave," Layne repeated. "Things changed on Friday and we talked it through last night."

"You talked it through?" Dave repeated.

"Yep," Layne replied and waited.

"You been separated for closin' on twenty years and you talked it through," Dave said.

"Yep," Layne returned.

"How is she?" Dave asked, this question giving Layne nothing.

"She would be fine but Ma's here and not Roc's biggest fan, so let's say it's not goin' as smooth as I'd like it to go."

"Vera's there?"

"Yep."

"Oh boy," Dave muttered, knowing Vera and living in the same town as Vera until Vera moved to Florida five years ago. Vera hadn't just decided to hate Rocky for breaking Layne's heart. She became an equal opportunity Merrick hater, blaming them all. The only person Vera hated more than Rocky and her family was Gabby and that was only because Gabby wasn't just a bitch to Layne. She was a bitch to his mother too, and such a far cry from what Vera had when she had Rocky, it dug that particular knife in deeper.

"You need me to come over, even out the numbers?" Dave offered.

"I'll take care of Roc," Layne replied.

There was more silence then, "Tanner, I'm happy for you. I'm happy for Rocky, if this is the right thing, but…" He hesitated before he went on, "Doesn't this seem sudden?"

Sudden? Jesus.

"Don't know, Dave," Layne returned. "Been wanting her back for eighteen years. She's felt the same. We've been together for a month, both of us strugglin' to hold it back. Friday it broke through. That doesn't seem sudden to me."

"Right," Dave whispered.

"You got anything to give me?" Layne asked.

"Anything to give you?" Dave asked back.

"Yeah, anything to give me," Layne repeated.

"Like what?" Dave asked.

"*Anything*," Layne returned, losing patience.

Dave was silent.

Layne lost patience.

"Dave—"

Dave cut him off. "I'll give you this, Tanner. I'll tell you I lost faith in God the night He took Cecilia from me, but, if I'd believed in Him, I woulda prayed for this to happen. So now that it's happened, it's made me think maybe He's finally kickin' back in."

This statement made Layne go silent.

"Happy for you, son, happy for Rocky. It's about damned time," Dave whispered and Layne heard the disconnect.

He dropped his phone, took a drag from his cigarette and turned to look into the house to see Vera sitting back in her armchair, a smug smile

on her face. He couldn't see Tripp but Jasper was staring at his grandmother, his profile not happy and Rocky was strutting up the stairs.

Fuck, she'd said something else.

Layne crushed out his cigarette and entered the house just as Rocky
disappeared around the top of the stairs, heading to his room.

Layne moved after her.

"Tanner," Vera said. "You shouldn't smoke. Not even one a—"

She stopped talking when her mouth clamped shut after Layne's eyes
hit her and she read what was in them.

Layne took the stairs two at a time.

He found Rocky in his bed, back to the headboard, knees up, an arm
around her calves, pillow sandwiched between her chest and thighs, cheek
to her knee and an arm outstretched to point the remote at the TV.

Her head came up when he walked in.

"Hey," she said softly.

"Hey," he replied, walked direct to the bed and climbed in.

She watched him do this, her face blank, clearly locked in her head.
When he settled, she went back to the remote, flipping channels on the TV.

"I'm footballed out," she mumbled her fictitious excuse to leave the
living room.

Layne leaned forward, pulled the remote out of her hand, switched
the TV off, tossed the remote to the foot of the bed and then gripped the
pillow Rocky was cradling and tugged it out. Her head came up and he
shoved the pillow behind his back at the headboard and then he went after
her. Grabbing a hand, he yanked her forward until she came off-balance
and landed with a hand to his chest, her body to his side and her head to
his shoulder.

Her head went up and back and she started to pull away while looking
at him.

"Layne—" she began.

He interrupted her. "Don't lock yourself in your head, sweetcheeks.
Talk to me."

Her head tipped to the side. "About what?"

"Cassie was a one night stand," he told her straight out.

Her eyes got wide then shut down. Layne ignored it and kept talking.

"Ma was takin' the boys to Disneyworld. I'm not a Disneyworld type of guy so I wasn't goin' with them. They were gonna leave at oh dark thirty and I went out the night before to meet a friend of mine who lives down in Florida now. I met Cassie while we were out. I came home as they were leavin' and Ma's not stupid. But Cassie knew my friend, he gave her my number, she called my cell while we were still there and Ma picked it up. Ma never even met her and I only saw her that once."

"You don't have to explain this to me, Layne."

"Yeah, Roc, I do."

The blank went out of her eyes as they started to ignite then she said, "Okay, then I don't *want* you to explain this to me, Layne."

"I know you don't, but you need me to."

"I don't think so."

"I do."

"Why?"

"'Cause I had a life for eighteen years and you're gonna hear about it, and when you get upset or your feelings hurt, I want you to talk to me about it and not lock yourself in your head."

"I lock myself in my head to sort things out," she told him.

"Yeah, baby, but once you locked yourself in your head and locked *me* out."

She froze against him then started to pull away, but he yanked her right back and when she struggled, he rolled so she was on her back and his weight was on her.

She stilled and glared up at him.

"Why am I always asking you to get off me?" she snapped.

"I don't know, probably because you're always tryin' to take off when I'm not done talkin' to you." he clipped.

"Get off me," she bit out.

"We're not done talkin'," he shot back.

"We are," she informed him. "See, you just threw that in my face, which tells me you're not past it and it also tells me you're not going to *get* past it so maybe all this was a bad idea."

"I didn't throw it in your face, sweetcheeks."

"You damn well did!"

Layne cupped her cheek in his hand and dipped his face into hers. "You're pissed at Ma, takin' it out on me and I'm tryin' to smooth it out. I'm not throwing anything in your face. I'm tryin' to get you to talk."

"Well, maybe I don't want to talk."

"I had a life, Rocky."

"I know."

"There were women in it."

"Trust me, *Layne*, I *know*."

"None of them was you," he went on.

"I know that too," she snapped.

"So, except for the one I married 'cause I got her pregnant, none of them even so much as had a toothbrush at my place."

She snapped her mouth shut and stared at him.

Then she asked, "Really?"

"Really."

"Not even a toothbrush?"

"I was seeing Melody for four years and she tried to leave at least three toothbrushes, a box of tampons and pair of underwear at my place. I found 'em and I put 'em in her purse. She eventually got the message and quit trying."

Rocky stared up at him with her lips parted.

Then she asked, "Why?"

"Why?" Layne repeated.

"Yeah, why?"

Layne took his hand from her cheek, pulled in an impatient breath and tipped his head back to look at the wall before looking down at her and explaining, "Baby, 'cause she wasn't *you*."

Rocky stared at him. Then the fire in her eyes went out.

"Poor Melody," she whispered and she didn't know the half of it.

Layne knew Melody was in deep with him. He even tried to find it in her. He just couldn't but she never pulled away. She kept trying, kept hoping one day she'd get in. She never did. He should have cut her loose ages ago, but even if she wasn't Rocky, she was the closest he'd had.

"It's over with her," Layne stated and Rocky's body relaxed beneath him.

"Does she know how to make Milky Way cake?" she asked softly.

"Ma taught her but Melody is not a kitchen person. Melody is a get dressed up, wait at the bar for an hour and half for a table and then eat a fifty dollar meal person."

"That doesn't seem your style," Rocky noted.

"It isn't."

"I like to get dressed up," she informed him. "Um…every once in a while."

"Baby, you wear that dress you wore the other night, I'll take you out where you can get dressed up every fuckin' night."

She grinned. "That's not even my best dress."

Jesus.

"Seriously?" Layne asked.

"Seriously," Rocky answered. "I have this one. It's clingier and shorter and—"

Layne's brows shot up. "Clingier?"

"Yeah."

"And *shorter*?"

"Uh…yeah."

He rolled to his back, his arm over his eyes, muttering, "Shit. You're killin' me."

She rolled into him, put her hand on his chest and called, "Layne." He dropped his arm and looked at her. "How am I killing you?"

"Because Rutledge stares at your tits, Gaines stares at your ass, and every other man who lays eyes on you finds somethin' to stare at. This does not exactly make me happy."

"Baby," she whispered. "If I wear that dress, it's just for you."

He looked up at her and her eyes were hooded, her mouth soft and he liked that look so much, that look directed at him again, finally, after all these years, that he lifted his hand to her jaw and ran his thumb along her cheekbone.

She turned her face into his hand, looked at his chest and kept whispering. "I wasn't in my head because of Cassie and Melody." Her eyes came back to his. "It was because I fucked up and your mom talking made me realize just how badly I did it."

"Rocky—"

She shook her head and kept talking. "I missed those birthdays and Christmases and horseback rides. I tried to remind myself while she was talking that if I didn't, Jasper and Tripp wouldn't be in that room but it didn't make me feel much better."

Layne rolled into her, putting his arms around her and settling them both on their sides.

"Roc, honey, I don't know what to say." And he didn't because she was right. With her, there would be no Jasper and no Tripp, and Layne couldn't imagine that. Without her he had them and he knew he was lucky, no matter how fucked up it got along the way.

"There's nothing *to* say. I just need to lock myself in my head and sort it out."

"I know how it is to fuck up and miss birthdays and Christmases with people you care about, baby. And I fucked up bigger than you because I didn't miss just one person's, but three."

"Layne—"

"Don't go into your head. Let me in and maybe I can help you out. Yeah?"

She stared into his eyes for a beat that led into three and then she whispered, "Yeah."

Layne smiled at her and leaned in to touch his mouth to hers, but her head suddenly moved back and he stopped.

"Just that…" She hesitated. "Can I ask that that's the last we talk about the Cassies and Melodys in the life and times of Tanner Layne?"

He was still smiling when he rolled her to her back, slanted his head, and with his lips on hers, he muttered, "Yeah, baby."

Then he kissed her and Rocky kissed him back.

⟵⟶

"Is Roc okay, Dad?" Jasper called out when Layne was walking down the stairs, leaving Rocky in his bed because she wanted a minute to "get presentable," which he figured meant she needed a minute to shore her defenses before she faced Vera again.

Not to mention she needed a minute to right her clothes considering Layne not only made out with her, he felt her up.

Layne hadn't even made it to the middle of the stairs before Jas asked his question and by the time he hit the bottom, Vera and Tripp's eyes were on him.

"She's good, bud," Layne answered.

"She got quiet," Tripp noted as Layne walked to the couch.

"She gets that way when her feelings get hurt," Layne replied, and Jas and Tripp both looked at Vera.

Vera looked at the television.

"What hurt her feelings?" Jasper asked after Layne had stretched out on his back on the couch, head to the armrest, and his eyes went to his boy.

As usual, Layne gave it to him straight.

"She lost her mom when she was fourteen so pretty much every memory for her is fucked. The birthdays and Christmases before her mom died have bitter mixed in with sweet 'cause she had birthdays and Christmases after her mom died that weren't so good because her mom wasn't there, and she remembered them bein' better when she was. So, talkin' about that shit today made her realize she missed your old man during those times while we were apart and she got upset about it. 'Cause of what happened with her mom, she doesn't deal with getting upset like other people do. She gets quiet first then she shuts down."

Jasper's eyes went back to his grandmother but Tripp asked, "But she's good now?"

"She's good, Tripp."

Tripp nodded then muttered, "I got homework," and he got to his feet and went to the stairs, avoiding looking at his grandmother.

"You got homework, Jas?" Layne asked.

"Yeah," Jasper answered.

"It done?" Layne asked.

"No," Jasper answered.

"Boy…" Layne said low, and Jasper looked at his grandmother then to Layne.

"I was wondering if Rocky could help me. It's English Comp. We're diagramming sentences and it's stupid. I try to get it but it just doesn't make sense to me. My teacher is a dork and when I asked her after class if she'd give me some time, she made *me* feel like a dork because I didn't get it."

"Who's your teacher?" Layne asked.

"Mrs. Reiger."

Layne didn't know Mrs. Reiger. What Layne did know was that diagramming sentences *was* stupid and the only person in that house who probably wouldn't agree was Rocky.

"*Roc!*" he shouted.

There was a beat of silence then the "*What?*" of Rocky shouting back.

"Jas needs your help with his homework!" Layne yelled.

There was another beat of silence and Layne and Jasper stared at each other as this became prolonged. Then Layne heard quiet footfalls on the stairs.

"What are you studying, Jas?" He heard Rocky ask from the stairs.

Layne grinned at his boy and Jasper's lips twitched, but he said to Rocky, "Diagramming sentences."

"Get your books, honey. We'll work at the island," Rocky invited.

Jasper moved and Layne looked at the television set wondering if Jasper actually needed help diagramming sentences or if he'd just played his grandmother and Rocky.

Probably both.

"You shouldn't say the f-word in front of the boys," Vera murmured and Layne twisted his neck to look at his mother.

She caught his eye and tried to hold it but eventually looked back to the TV.

"Ma," he called when she did, and her gaze slid hesitantly back to his. "Don't pull that shit again," he whispered.

She pressed her lips together and glared at him for about a second before he saw the shimmer of tears in her eyes and she looked back to the TV.

Layne sighed.

The front door opened and Blondie, who'd been flat out on her side napping in front of the television, shot up to her feet, barked and galloped to the door.

"Damn mutt," Devin grumbled.

"She's pure bred, Dev," Jasper informed him.

"She's still a mutt," Devin returned. "Please God, Jesus, Mary and Joseph, tell me you have whisky." Layne heard Devin call.

Layne didn't bother lifting his head from the armrest when he replied, "What do you think?"

"Cupboard over the coffeemaker," Jas answered.

"Thank fuck," Devin muttered and Vera's eyes shot to him. She had the tears under control and her eyebrows flew up.

Layne ignored his mother, leaned forward, nabbed the remote from the coffee table and found another football game.

Layne walked into a mostly dark house. He dropped his keys onto the kitchen counter and saw Dev's head turn to look at him over the couch. He was watching TV which was, with light coming from upstairs, the only light in the room.

"Get anything?" Dev asked.

Layne had explained to Dev about TJ Gaines and his teenage harem. He'd also gone to the church to see if he could tag Gaines and follow him home after evening service.

Gaines didn't attend evening service.

"Nope," Layne answered walking into the house. "Everything in his personnel file is bogus. I'm workin' cold on this. Until I tag his vehicle and follow him home, I'm operating blind."

Dev nodded.

"Jas and Tripp are gonna ask questions tomorrow at school. See if they can get a make and model and an address," Layne went on.

Dev nodded again.

"Where is everyone?" Layne asked.

"Boys are upstairs bickerin' 'cause Tripp's studyin' and Jasper's supposed to be studyin' but he's textin' Keira. Your ma 'retired early,' her words. Rocky went up just after your ma."

Layne twisted and looked at the clock over the microwave. It was barely nine.

This meant Vera was feeling guilty. Jas and Tripp likely both did have homework. Rocky was a wildcard.

Layne shrugged off his leather jacket and was about to say goodnight to Dev and turn to the stairs when Dev said, "Need a brief, boy."

Layne's eyes went to the old man, saw his face was serious and nodded. He tossed his jacket on the back of the couch, walked to an armchair, pivoted it to face Dev and lounged back, aiming his gaze at his friend.

"Hit me."

"Got the goods on her ex-asshole, need to know how you want me to play it," Dev replied.

Layne didn't get a good feeling about the fact Devin was asking. Dev wouldn't normally ask. Dev would normally play it whatever way he wanted to play it.

"What is it?" Layne asked.

"Campaign contributions that, if taken public, would make him and the Republican Party a bit uncomfortable," Dev answered.

Jesus, Rocky married a Republican. She must have worked hard on convincing herself she was in love with the dick. Both Dave and Merry were staunch Republicans, but Rocky had followed in her mother's footsteps and voted straight ticket Democrat. Thus a variety of heated political discussions ensued over the dinner table, that heat mainly emanating from Rocky, and Layne had learned to keep his political opinions to himself.

"Over the limit?" Layne asked and Dev shook his head.

"Shell companies set up for the sole purpose of feedin' into the current Governor havin' his bed at the Governor's mansion. Far's I can tell, Republican Committee knew all about it because Astley sits on it. So do a good number of his buds, all of 'em paid their dues, but Astley was the mastermind."

"Use it," Layne ordered, still not understanding why Dev was discussing this with him.

"This hits, it puts him out there," Dev replied.

"It won't hit, he'll back down," Layne returned.

"Guy's an asshole, boy, I get that you get that, but I don't think you get how much of an asshole he is. Thinks he's untouchable."

"He isn't, no one is."

"He calls your bluff, you got no choice but to put this out there. You put this out there, first, you make a fuckload of enemies and not the HOA. We're talkin' local power brokers here. Second, it'll be a media circus."

Layne now understood why Devin was hesitating.

"Roc's clear of him, Dev," Layne assured.

"It ain't Rocky I'm worried about," Devin returned and Layne shook his head.

"Got markers I can call," Layne reminded him quietly. "Even if it gets hot and I get on power players' radar, got markers I can call, markers with people who can trump anything he's got and you know it."

"Ain't you I'm worried about either," Dev replied.

Layne was losing patience and therefore asked, "We gonna play twenty questions?"

That was when Devin gave it to him. "Worried about Marissa Gibbons."

"Who the fuck is that?" Layne asked.

"Rocky's replacement," Devin answered and Layne's brows shot up.

"And I care about that bitch because...?" he prompted when Devin said no more.

Dev leaned toward Layne, put his elbows on his knees and his eyes got intense as his voice dropped low.

"You care about that bitch because her dad was a drug dealer. He pimped out her mom until she bit it due to an overdose, Social Services cottoned on and Marissa went into foster care. Bounced around awhile, managed to get a high school degree, no idea how except a sheer miracle because she followed in Mom's footsteps and fell in with the wrong crowd. And when I say that, boy, I mean it was *the wrong crowd*. Saw with my own two eyes the results of her acting career. She wasn't no star but she was good. Even I was convinced she was lovin' every second of it when she took a huge fuckin' cock so far down her throat it proved positive she has no gag reflex *whatsoever*."

Layne felt his neck muscles contract.

"Porn?" he whispered.

"Three films, none of them starring roles. She did them under false names, different colored hair, carryin' an extra twenty pounds, hadn't yet had her boob job, was underage and looks it. But no denyin' it's her."

Layne grinned, not because Marissa Gibbons's life clearly sucked but because he fucking *loved* it that Astley was fucking a porn star. No doubt he was still shit in bed, but at least she'd have the skills to convince him he wasn't

Devin watched him grin and shook his head, leaning even closer.

"She pulled herself outta that shit, Tanner. Don't know how she did it, but she did. She's goin' to IUPUI, studyin' to be a social worker. She's turned her life around. This shit hits, no matter how big the names are around hers, she's the face of it for...fuckin'...ever. History books, boy. Online encyclopedias. Google her name and she could cure world hunger but that's the first thing you'd see. No more Pacemate, the squad will dump her. She'll quit school. She'll go back to what she knows. You tip Astley, you destroy *her* life. We both know it wasn't a good choice for her to hook her star to his or how she did it, but now we know why she did it. You want me to use it, I'll use it. I'll even use all of it, which means he'll set her out before he takes you on, whatever way that comes about. But he doesn't bite, you go the distance, you take her down. She's not a good woman because she's had no role models, but even so, she's tryin' like hell to learn how to be one. You do this, you set her back in that task, I'm guessin' irrevocably." Devin sat back and finished, "That said, your call."

Layne stared at Devin and made a decision.

"Lean on 'em both," he ordered.

Devin's brows shot up. "What?"

"Go to her, tell her what you got on him and what you got on her. Porn past or not, she can do better. Fuck, *anyone* can do better," Layne explained. "I'm guessin' here, but what they got is no love match so we're doin' her a favor. She leans on him one way, we lean on him the other. We partner up, coach her, play it right, he pays her off, settles with Rocky and they both get on with their lives with him not in it but his cash in their accounts."

Layne leaned forward and continued.

"He still doesn't play, you go one by one through the Republican Committee. I'll lay money down that one of 'em will buckle and I'll lay more down on it bein' the first one you talk to, especially seein' as this isn't blackmail, you're sellin' quiet cheap. They won't have to dish out anything but a little pressure. Astley may think he's untouchable from me, from Roc, but those boys can convince him a fuckuva lot different."

Devin smiled and leaned back, saying, "Like the way you think, boy."

Layne pushed up out of the armchair, replying, "You should, you taught me how to think." He moved to the side of the couch, stopped and looked down at his friend. "Losin' your touch, old man, you'da called that five years ago."

"Lucky for me, I had the foresight to train my replacement before the dementia kicked in," Devin shot back.

Layne bit back his smile and shook his head, muttering, "Goin' to bed."

"Don't blame you," Dev muttered back, his eyes moving to the TV.

Layne hesitated then asked, "Ma all right with Roc while I was gone?"

Devin didn't look away from the TV. "Seein' as both your boys threw down on Rocky's side, then yeah." He turned his head to Layne. "They're good judges of character, like me."

That didn't sound good.

"They both threw down?" Layne asked.

"Not a word spoken, but blind, deaf and dumb would know that to them it's warm as the waters of the Caribbean with Rocky, frosty arctic with your Ma."

Dev's eyes turned intense again before he went on.

"You didn't ask my advice but I'm givin' it. I don't know what went down when I wasn't here, but I know by the aftermath it wasn't good. So you better tell that woman to get her head outta her ass. They love her but they're your boys. They see that soft spot Rocky's got and, like you, they're movin' in to protect it. Not only that, she makes you happy in a way your ma cleanin' your house and makin' cake ain't *ever* gonna make you happy and they want that for you. It's a fight she ain't ever gonna win and she better get smart before she loses a lot more than she'd ever expect."

"Roc's stronger than you think, Dev," Layne said quietly.

"You think that, you better look closer, Tanner, because she sure as fuck ain't," Dev returned, just as quietly, and those muscles in Layne's neck went tight again. "I can see you hangin' back and lettin' the women battle this out, and normally I'd agree with that play. But not here. You're skatin' on thin ice, boy, and you better be careful with every stroke of those blades because, you fall through, those waters are bitter cold and you know it 'cause you been livin' in 'em a long time. You don't want those waters to close over you again, Tanner, you have a word with your ma."

Layne sighed then he nodded, knowing after his mother's behavior that day Dev spoke the truth but wanting to have a word with his mother about as much as he wanted to talk to Gabby yesterday.

Dev gave him a stare and then looked back at the TV.

"'Night, old man," Layne muttered as he turned to the stairs.

"'Night, boy." He heard Dev mutter back.

Layne was halfway up the stairs when he heard Tripp say, "Jeez, Jas, you're gonna go over your limit of texts and Dad's gonna be pissed."

He hit the top of the stairs to see Tripp at the desk and Jasper with his back to the weight bench, knees bent, soles of his feet to the bench, his cell phone held over his face as he replied, "Dad'll be cool. He gets it about takin' care of your babe."

"True enough, Jas," Layne put in, and Tripp swiveled around to look at him as Jasper's head turned and his eyes focused on Layne. "Still, you go over your limit, I'll be pissed."

"She's hot, Dad. Gotta keep her hooked so no one moves in," Jasper explained.

"Boy, why do you think I bought you that goddamned car?" Layne asked. He stopped and crossed his arms on his chest. "Right about now, when you're feelin' like that, you stop playin' it cool and her ass is here or your ass is there, you stake your claim and you don't do it through fuckin' texts."

Jasper sat up, dropping his feet to straddle the bench. "You cool with Keirry bein' here when you're not?"

"Just as long as I don't have to set up a crib in the corner of your bedroom. That is, if I win at hand to hand combat defendin' my son against a gonzo Joe Callahan," Layne answered.

Jasper grinned and crossed his cell phone over his heart before he lifted it in the air, "Swear. Gentleman. Totally."

Layne stared at his son then looked to Tripp who was also grinning at him and who decided to add, "Giselle Speakmon's parents are totally devout. When I get in there and we hook up, there won't be any cribs for me either, Dad, because I reckon they'll make her wear one of those chastity belts, knowin' Jas is my brother and all."

Layne felt his brows go up and he beat down any thoughts of his youngest being sexually active. Jasper was the firstborn boy, his leap to manhood Layne took in stride. Tripp was still just a kid in his eyes. Layne was not ready to go there, not by a long fucking shot.

Still, he asked, "You like her?"

Tripp nodded. "Got her talkin' to me and she's cool and she can be funny, in a quiet way that's kinda awesome."

"She at church today?" Layne asked and Tripp nodded again, his smile getting bigger.

"Yeah, she was the blonde who sat next to TJ in church."

Layne felt his body lock as he looked at his boy. "Right next to him?" he asked quietly.

Tripp's grin faded at his father's tone and he answered quietly back, "Yeah."

"She's here after school too or you're there. Jasper will be your ride," Layne ordered instantly.

"Her parents won't—" Tripp started and Layne cut him off.

"Then you call in Rocky. Even if her family's religious, they won't question Roc. They know she's here, they'll know Giselle is good. I'm not here and Roc's not here but at her apartment, you're over there with Giselle and I'll talk to Rocky."

"Dad," Tripp's voice was still muted. "She's cool. She's there because she's religious. I don't even think she likes TJ."

Layne felt his gut squeeze. "She was sitting right next to him, pal."

"She doesn't like him but he way likes her," Tripp replied and Layne's gut twisted.

"She's here or you're there. You tie her up one way or another, Tripp, you get me?" Layne asked and Tripp's face got pale.

"Do you think—?" Tripp started to ask, and Layne interrupted him again.

"I don't think, Tripp, you don't either. This is now, we move on from here and you tie Giselle up and you're glued to her at Youth Group meetings." Layne stared at his son and finished, "Now, do you get me?"

"I get you," Tripp whispered.

"She got a cell phone?" Layne asked and Tripp nodded. "Got her number?" Layne went on and Tripp nodded again, so Layne nodded back. "Go text her now."

Tripp slid from the chair and whispered, "Got it," then walked to Jasper's room.

Layne looked at Jas to see his son's focus was intent on him and he ordered, "You have his back."

"Giselle's a favorite, Dad," Jasper muttered.

"You have his fuckin' back," Layne returned. Jas stared him in the eyes and nodded. "I want an address or the make, model and color of his car by tomorrow, bud," Layne ordered low.

"You'll have it," Jasper assured him and Layne walked close to look down at his boy.

"We've passed finesse," Layne told him quietly. "We're goin' forward hard."

Jasper nodded up to him and Layne continued.

"You don't gotta be cool about this. He cottons on, I don't give a fuck except you and your brother are in the middle of this shit. *That* you play cool, you play smart, you have Tripp's back, you listen to your gut and you *communicate with me*. You walk down the halls, you know who's walkin' behind you. You have a chat with a Youth Group kid, you pay attention to what's goin' on on their face, not what's comin' outta their mouths. You also pay attention to who might be listenin' in. You drive down the road, you check your rearview mirrors. You see a car more than once on your ass, you get a plate. You with me?"

"Yeah, Dad," Jasper whispered.

"You're in this house, alarm is armed. At all times, Jas."

"Right."

"Roc's on his radar and Tripp laid claim to her today. Because of that, when light dawns, he'll know where she sits with this. That means, I'm not around, you have her back too."

"Gotcha."

"He got any other favorites?" Layne asked and Jasper nodded.

"Alexis McGraw."

"The redhead today?"

"Yep."

"Any ideas how to keep her clear?"

Jasper shook his head. "She's in deep. She thinks he's the shit. They're always together."

"Fuck," Layne whispered.

"I'll think about it. She used to have a thing for Seth. Maybe—"

Layne cut him off. "Seth's got enough to deal with."

"Yeah, which means, I figure, takin' his mind off of that shit will do him good," Jasper returned. "We've talked about this, before Tripp and me started undercover, and Seth thinks it's creepy as all get out too. I reckon he'd come on board and he'd be cool, Dad. After yesterday, he'd do just about anything for you and Rocky. Alexis is a freshman and Seth is a senior, but she's cute and it isn't unheard of. Jamie's a senior and he's datin' a freshman and Seth and Jamie are tight."

Layne nodded and asked, "Any bright ideas of how to shut the rest of it down?"

"Yeah," Jasper whispered and stood, clearing the weight bench and bringing him close to his old man. "We don't have to play it cool anymore, I start a campaign. Kids think it's weird, teachers think it's weird, but no one's talkin' out about it. It's all real quiet. Whispers. I talk out about it. Make like I'm goin' as a joke. Get Seth and some of the team to go with me. Start fuckin' around at Youth Group, and at school, make it uncool other than to go for shits and giggles. A place to fuck around and pick up girls."

"I don't know, Jas, bold play but could have the opposite effect, make the devoted more so and make it popular for kids to go, even if they're fuckin' around, which might put more girls on the line. It also puts Tripp out there if Giselle is religious. She'll want to think he's into that too and her family will definitely want to think that if he wants to spend time with her."

"Just because Giselle's family is religious doesn't mean she has to go to Youth Group," Jasper replied. "Tripp can play her, and in the end, she's still a shy girl who's got a chance at the only freshman on the football team. She pushes it that she prefers to be with Tripp, her parents'll cave. The other shit, leave it to me."

Layne smiled and asked, "Lots of parents cave?"

Jasper smiled back. "Totally. Especially the girls. How do you think I hit so many? Before Keira that is."

"Jasper Layne, football stud," Layne muttered, still smiling.

"Off the market stud," Jasper muttered back, also still smiling. "Just like his dad."

Layne chuckled as he lifted a hand and curled it around his boy's neck, pulled him in and gently bumped foreheads with him before he let him go.

"All right, bud, you play it how you feel it but you communicate with me. Okay?"

"Okay."

"You call your mom today?" Layne asked.

"Yeah, twice," Jas answered.

"Good man," Layne murmured. "Homework done and tomorrow thank your gram for cleanin' your room. She deserves it especially since, for most humans, it was a no go zone and I reckon Keira will be spendin' time in it and we won't want to rush her to the hospital after she's exposed to the fumes."

Jasper shook his head, grinning. "It wasn't that bad."

"Boy," was Layne's only reply as he turned to walk away but he thought better of it and turned back. "Did you get your sentences diagrammed?"

Jasper's grin died and he looked confused. "What?"

"Your sentences. Did Roc help you get them diagrammed?"

"Oh, yeah. Sure," Jasper mumbled.

"Jas?" Layne called his son's attention to him. "Did you have sentences to diagram?"

"Yeah," Jas answered, and Layne stared at him so Jasper's eyes went to the double doors. He walked the two feet Layne had moved away and he whispered, "Two weeks ago. I got a C on the assignment. Next time, I'll ask Roc to help *before* I get the final grade."

Layne swallowed down laughter before he muttered, "Good call."

Then Layne turned back to his room and walked to it as he heard Jasper say, "'Night, Dad."

"'Night, bud," Layne replied and opened the doors.

Rocky was diagonal on the bed, on her stomach, papers spread in front of her, pen in her hand, bare feet swinging in the air. Layne knew Jasper didn't have to whisper his secret because she had earphones in her ears, an MP3 player on the bed and between the sound and her concentration on the papers, she hadn't noticed he came in.

He rounded the bed wide until he got to her side and then moved in. He put a knee to the bed and was dropping forward with a hand on either side of her when she cried out, jumped and started to turn, but his torso hit her back and he pinned her to the bed.

She popped an earphone out, he heard the music through it, and she twisted her neck to say, "Layne, you scared the beejeezus out of me."

He didn't reply. He smiled at her before he leaned around her, putting his mouth to the opposite side of her neck at the same time his hand went into her hair and he tugged out her goddamned ponytail. He'd left her and her hair was down which was how he liked it, so now it was going to be down again.

"Would you *quit* pulling out my ponytails?" she asked, sounding annoyed and trying to roll. But he moved his lips up her neck and then nipped her ear with his teeth and she quit trying to roll.

"Don't like 'em," he whispered in her ear.

"I don't care," she replied. "I do."

"I don't care." He ran his tongue along the curve of her ear and her body froze. "I don't," he finished.

"Layne."

There it was. Breathy. Needy. Beautiful.

"You're either gonna have to wait, baby, or let me gag you or fuck you in the closet again. The boys are usin' the weight room to study and fuck around," he said softly in her ear.

"I'll wait," she whispered, his head came up and she twisted her neck to look at him. "Do they stay up late?"

He grinned at her then leaned in and touched his mouth to hers before he suggested, "We could take a shower."

"Hmm," she mumbled and her eyes dropped to his mouth.

He liked her eyes on his mouth, so much, if he did something about it, they wouldn't make it to the shower. So his eyes dropped to her papers thinking he'd be seeing homework assignments, but they weren't.

"What are you doing?" he asked as he studied the papers.

Her head moved and he saw she'd looked down too.

"Lesson plans," she answered and then twisted her neck to face him again. "Next week is *To Kill a Mockingbird* week. It's my favorite week of the semester."

He got that. It was her favorite book. He'd read it in high school, thought it was pretty good, but didn't think much of it until she'd gone on about it. Because she'd loved it so much, he'd read it again and he'd appreciated it a fuckuva lot more. His favorite book was *Slaughterhouse Five*, then and now, but *To Kill a Mockingbird* was a close second.

Looking at her face, suddenly he realized he'd pay money to watch her teaching it.

"You nearly done?" he asked.

"Nearly," she answered. "I was about to finish up."

"Good," he muttered, pulled her hair away from her neck, kissed the skin there again and then looked at her. "I'm gonna go make coffee and secure the house. Meet you in the shower."

He started to knife away from her but she caught him by saying, "Okay, but you can't get my hair wet."

He stared in her eyes before he asked, "Come again?"

"You can't get my hair wet because if you do I'll have to blow it out before going to bed and that'll take forever and—"

He cut her off. "Baby, your hair's gonna get wet."

"Layne—"

"Blow it out tomorrow."

"I can't, it'll be—"

Layne rolled off her, pulled her on top of him and then rolled her to her back, Layne on top of her. Then he kissed her until her arms were tight around his back, her leg had hooked around his hip and she was mewing in his mouth.

He lifted his head and whispered, "Your hair is gonna get wet and your gonna blow it out tomorrow, yeah?"

"Yeah," she whispered back immediately, eyes hooded, arms locked tight around him.

Christ she was cute *and* she was hot.

"Look at me like that a second longer, sweetcheeks, I won't give a fuck my boys hear you moan," he warned, her eyes got wide and he grinned before he brushed his mouth against hers and ordered, "Finish then shower."

"Right," she murmured.

Layne knifed away and Rocky rolled to her stomach.

Then he walked downstairs, let the dog out one last time, got the coffeepot ready for the morning, let the dog in and secured the house. He said a last round of goodnights, went to his room, and heard the shower going.

He met his woman there, her hair got wet and he made certain other parts of her got wetter.

In the end, the water didn't have to drown out her moans since Layne performed that chore with his mouth.

After, he watched the news, shoulders against the headboard with a sleeping Rocky's wet, tangled hair splayed over his chest as she pinned him to the bed.

Nineteen

Wisdom, Compassion and Strength

"Hi, Tanner! You here to see Rocky?"

Sharon Reynolds had seen him when he walked in the front doors of the school and she'd hightailed it away from her desk to greet him before he even hit the office door.

Layne smiled at her. "Sharon. Yeah. She free?" he asked, but he knew she wasn't.

"Nope, she's teaching in the auditorium," Sharon answered.

"Need to talk to her, it's kind of important. Can you get a message to her?"

She waved her hand in front of her face. "Oh no, don't worry about that. I'm sure the kids won't mind *you* interrupting." She leaned in and gave him a wink. "Just go on to the auditorium. You know where it is, don't you?"

"Yeah, do I need to sign in?"

She smiled big at him. "I'll do it for you. Just promise to stop by to visit the girls in the office and sign out, okay?"

Layne smiled back at her, just as big, and her eyes locked on his mouth. "Promise. Thanks, Sharon."

"Right," she whispered, still staring at his mouth and Layne didn't hesitate, he turned and walked down the hall.

It was Wednesday and it was *To Kill a Mockingbird* week. Between working his cases, both paid and unpaid, talking to his mother, keeping an eye on

Gabby's place as well as Stew, hosting two teenage girls at his house every night and trying to fit in catching up with Rocky, the week had already been staggeringly busy. He hadn't had time to sneak in and watch Rocky teach.

Luckily, Sharon Reynolds made the sneaking in part easy.

The rest of it hadn't been so easy.

Layne spoke to her, but apparently Vera wasn't ready to lay down her weapons. At least now, her shots were fired wide rather than Vera gutting Rocky with the bayonet.

Jasper had got Layne the make, model and color of TJ Gaines's car but no address. As far as Jasper could gather the intel, no one knew where he lived and no one had been there. Layne had cruised the church a dozen times in two and a half days and never saw a blue Honda sedan in the lot in order to stake it out and follow him home. He'd also cruised by the teenage kids' hangouts, and still no go with the Honda. This meant Layne was on duty that night to wait for Gaines to leave Youth Group and follow him from there.

Layne found out that Jasper wasn't wrong and Keira *was* a nut *and* she liked boy bands and Jasper liked her enough to let her play boy band music in the house and do it loud. Layne did not see good things in the future because Tripp didn't like boy bands, Vera definitely didn't like boy bands, Devin *seriously* didn't like boy bands, and Rocky detested them nearly as much as Layne did. Jasper was going to have to shut that shit down soon or there was going to be all out war.

And Monday night Layne discovered Giselle Speakmon *was* the pretty blonde sitting next to TJ Gaines. She also clearly thought of Raquel Merrick as her idol and her parents did too seeing as Giselle's younger sister had some kind of very shitty cancer that was far shittier than cancer was on the whole, and Roc had done some charity event that made money for a house for parents to stay in close to the hospital. The house was about to be closed down and Rocky's event had saved it. Giselle's parents didn't live far but what amounted to a two-hour trip every day for months was a burden they couldn't bear on top of having a really sick kid as well as a healthy one at home. That house was next door to the hospital and one or the other got to stay in it for six months while their daughter had inpatient treatments, which made life a whole lot easier and they fully credited Rocky with this saving grace.

The sister was now in remission and the Speakmon family was in awe of Saint Rocky.

Therefore, because Rocky was there, their sweet, very quiet, painfully shy daughter was allowed to hang with Tripp at Tripp's house. The parents dropped her off and Rocky took her home.

Monday night, she'd been silent except she spoke a little to Rocky and a little to Keira. She gave Vera a wide berth, probably because Vera was trying too hard with Giselle at the same aiming bullets at Rocky. Jasper, Layne and Devin openly scared the shit out of her. But she seemed at her most comfortable huddled with Tripp and Layne knew why. Tripp made her laugh and there was something about the kid, something that made Layne's gut get tight, because seeing her laugh he suspected she didn't do it often, as in, *at all.*

Tuesday night, she started coming out of herself, letting Vera in, but Layne knew for the rest of them it was going to be a painful process.

With a house full of kids, his mother and Devin, Layne and Rocky didn't find much time to connect, at least not the way he wanted to connect. They had zero chance to talk alone and by the time they hit the sack, she was out within minutes. Luckily, his dream Rocky hadn't abandoned him. She woke him in plenty of time for Layne to turn to his real Rocky and wake her with his hands and mouth. It wasn't as much as he wanted, but it was always great, it kept getting better and it was a whole lot more than nothing, so he wasn't going to complain.

Stew, at least, was keeping his distance, and Gabby, at least, was doing what she was told. She'd deposited the two K and she was laying low with her friend Brandy.

Layne turned right at the end of the wide front hall and walked down the corridor to the auditorium. Quietly, he opened the door, entered and kept his hand on it so it would just as quietly close behind him.

Then he stood at the back and watched Rocky do her thing.

She was sitting on the edge of the stage, her ankles crossed, her kids in the auditorium seats in front of her, one of them talking.

"You think Atticus Finch is hot, Ms. Merrick?" the girl asked, and Rocky smiled at her and rested back, her palms on the stage.

"Oh yeah," Rocky answered, Layne grinned, leaned a shoulder against the wall of the entryway to the auditorium, settled in and listened.

"He doesn't even have a woman," a boy called out.

"A man doesn't need to have a woman to be hot, Dylan. He just has to be *a man*," Rocky replied.

"Yeah, I can see it," another boy put in. "He shot that dog. That's *all* man."

"No," Rocky shook her head. "That wasn't. But *why* he shot the dog was."

The kids were silent, waiting for Roc to impart wisdom, and she didn't disappoint.

"You see, I read this book when I was young. I'd read it before I even *had* to read it, like I'm making you do," she told them. "When I read it the first time, it was all about Boo."

"Boo's cool!" a girl cried out. "I *love* Boo."

"Lots to love," Rocky said. "Boo's pure all the way through."

"What do you mean pure?" another kid shouted.

"What do you think I mean?" Rocky asked.

"He's a good guy?" the kid asked back.

"Yep," Rocky answered.

"He's kind," a girl yelled.

"Right," Rocky stated.

"He's shut up in that house but he still cares about Jem and Scout. He lives his life through them," a boy called out and Rocky nodded. "He looks out for them, keeps them safe."

"All kids need folks to look out for them," she told her class. "But motherless kids, well, they can have a great dad and they can have a great brother, but in the end, Jem and Scout were lucky they had Boo."

At her words, Layne felt his chest seize and the auditorium got deathly quiet. She hadn't talked about that when she was telling him why she loved *To Kill a Mockingbird* twenty years ago.

"Did you..." A girl started then paused, calling up the courage to go on, "Did you have a Boo, Ms. Merrick?"

The auditorium grew silent again. This time it was uncomfortable because it was a personal question, asking too much.

But Rocky didn't hesitate with her response. "No, Brittany, I never had a Boo. That's why, when I first read *To Kill a Mockingbird*, it was all about Boo." She leaned forward and put her forearms on her thighs. "See, that's the beauty of books. We get to take what we want out of them and it can be different for everyone. You get a good one, you may even find what you need. I needed Boo when I read that book the first time and I got him. So, in a way, I *did* have a Boo. *The* Boo. The second time, I needed my mind opened. The third time, I needed Atticus. That's why this is such a brilliant book. Firstly, because it *is* brilliant. Secondly, because every time you read it, you get something new out of it."

"You needed your mind opened?" a boy yelled.

"Yep," Rocky answered. "You taste injustice, even if it's fictional, really *taste* it, it has a way of doing that. Sometimes, you can never put the shoe on the other foot. We can't go back in time and know what it was like to be a black person then."

Her eyes scanned the all white faces of her class and she went on.

"Even today, when things are supposed to be so much better, not one of you can understand what it's like to be black, to live with the knowledge of what happened to your ancestry and still face injustice. But that book makes us taste it, and reading it we know how bitter that taste is and we know we don't like it. But that bitter wakes you up. And when you wake up, you open your mind to things in this world. You make yourself think. Then you'll decide you don't like the taste of injustice, not for you and not for anyone, and you'll understand that, even though all the battles can't be won, that doesn't mean you won't fight."

"Like Atticus," a girl called out.

"Like Atticus," Rocky repeated on a smile and sat straight. "Atticus Finch is the most beautiful man I've ever met in print. He's a good dad and he does what's right, not what's safe, not what's popular. What's right. He's gentle. He's smart. He's strong. He's decisive and he's willing to follow through with his decisions, no matter what the odds. Even if it means doing something heinous, like walking into a street and putting down a rabid dog. Taking the life of another being to put it out of its misery and make people safe. If you only read that one scene, you'd know the beauty that is Atticus Finch. Lucky for us, we had that whole book to get to know him."

"Is that why you think he's hot?" a boy asked.

"Yes, Zach, that's why I think he's hot," Rocky answered.

"I liked it when he sat outside the police station and faced down the crowd," another boy called out.

"That's good too," Rocky told him on a smile.

"I liked the courtroom scenes," a girl shouted. "They *rocked!*"

"Yes, Luanne, they did. Except for the verdict, they definitely rocked," Rocky agreed.

"The verdict sucked," a boy yelled.

"Did it make you angry?" Rocky asked him.

"Well, yeah," he answered.

"How angry?" Rocky asked.

"It ticked me off," the kid returned. "I had to quit reading for a while."

Rocky smiled at him and asked, "And why did it tick you off?"

"Because it was wrong," he replied.

"It was more than wrong, Will. It was injustice." Rocky jumped off the stage, the movement liquid, landing gracefully on her high heels and she walked to stand close to the class. "Open your minds and learn from this tale. Do not stand still for injustice. If you know something isn't right, find your strength and stand against it. I'm not going to kid you that it's easy, it's not. If you think Atticus Finch went home at night and slept easy because he knew he was doing the right thing, you're wrong. He worried. He worried for his children. He worried for himself. He worried for his town. He worried for the world he lived in and his children were growing up in. He worried for the man he was trying to defend. And he knew he was going to lose. He knew it. But that didn't stop him. Because even one voice in a wilderness of ignorance is a voice that is heard by someone. Because every woman and man, no matter their color or their religion, is entitled to a good defense. And because Jem and Scout would grow up to be like their father, spreading his wisdom, understanding his compassion and sharing his strength, which are the only, the *only* weapons we have against injustice." She walked along the front of the class but her eyes scanned the kids while she did it and her gaze was focused, piercing every last kid. "If you're nothing else in this life, be wise, be compassionate and be strong, because those three things are *everything*."

There was utter silence until the boy named Dylan shouted, "I'm strong, Ms. Merrick. I can bench press two fifty."

The other kids hissed, called insults, some threw wads of paper at him and one yelled, "You're so full of it, Dylan, you can't bench press a Barbie."

Rocky was standing in front of the class, arms crossed on her chest and a smile was on her face.

"Dylan," she called and the kid yelled back, "Yo!"

"Hard not to see you're ripped," Rocky commented, and Dylan immediately stood and cut some poses, flexing his muscles while more wads of paper were thrown at him and comments were shouted. Dylan ignored them, kept posing and Rocky spoke over them. "That kind of strength, I bet any bully you saw in the halls doing stuff and saying stuff they shouldn't, you called them on it, they'd stop. That's strength *and* compassion." She grinned. "Now you just have to pass my midterm and maybe you'll add wisdom to that."

The class burst into laughter, Dylan grinned back at Rocky, sat down and another kid called out, "Don't hold your breath, Ms. Merrick!"

The bell rang and Rocky held up her hands. "All right, more Jem, Scout, Boo and Atticus tomorrow and Friday because we're watching the movie and I'm introducing you to Gregory Peck, so be prepared to get your socks knocked off. But remember, Friday, I want you all to bring in the title of your favorite song. We're talking lyrics, not music, people. And if one of you brings in the title to a boy band song, automatic detention," she threatened. There was more laughter and she turned toward the stage, saying, "Dismissed."

The kids shot up and filed out and as they did, Layne realized that every one of them had read the damned book. There was mass participation, but even though he barely tore his eyes off Rocky, he'd noticed even the kids who hadn't called out comments or questions had been totally engaged.

He stepped into the auditorium from the entryway, the kids saw him and some of them stared, some grinned, some nudged others and avoided his eyes.

But when Dylan saw him, he turned back and shouted helpfully, "Mr. Layne is here, Ms. Merrick!" and a bunch of girls giggled when he did.

Rocky had been picking up her papers but she whirled at Dylan's comment, scanned the back and her eyes locked on Layne as he strode forward. She dropped her papers and started up the aisle toward him, meeting him halfway with a smile.

"Hey," she said softly through her smile.

"Hey," he replied and tore his gaze off her dimple to look in her eyes.

"What are you doing here?" she asked, tilting her head to the side.

"Wanted to watch you do your thing," Layne answered.

The smile faded but her lips parted and she stared up at him with something in her eyes he couldn't quite read.

So he guessed.

"Baby, I was only there for ten minutes. I didn't—" he started to explain but she cut him off on a whisper.

"You wanted to watch me do my thing?"

Layne studied her face, still couldn't read it, so he kept explaining. "You made me want to reread that book and the way you did it made me appreciate it in a way I wouldn't have if you hadn't loved it so much. You told me you were teaching it and…" Layne stopped talking when she looked down and to the side. He lifted a hand to curl it around her neck. "Roc."

Her head twisted back, her eyes locked on his and she whispered, "Jarrod didn't discuss my kids, my work, none of it. He had zero interest. None. And you're spread so thin it's a wonder you aren't transparent and you find the time…"

She suddenly trailed off, bent to the side, dislodging his hand and looked around him as he heard the sounds of kids entering the auditorium.

"Up front, center, first three rows," she called to the kids. "Kayla, do me a favor and tell folks when they come in, Mr. Layne and I need a minute."

"Sure, Ms. Merrick," Kayla called back and Layne wasn't sure what was going on in Rocky's head, even though he figured it was good, but he was fucking thrilled the "Ms. Merrick" thing had caught on.

Rocky grabbed his hand, her fingers wrapping strong around his and she tugged him down the aisle and along the front of the seats. She kept hold of his hand as she led him up the steps at the side of the stage and then ducked backstage with him.

When they were out of eyesight, she stopped, kept hold of his hand and stepped into him so their bodies were nearly brushing.

"Okay, well, it goes without saying if a hot private investigator can't make out with me at a football game, I can't lay one on a hot private investigator *in* the school with my class assembling fifty feet away. So you'll just have to make do with the knowledge I really, *really* want to make out with you right now, Tanner Layne," she announced, and he grinned as he stifled a laugh.

He dropped her hand and put both of his to her hips, bringing her the inch forward he needed for their bodies actually to be brushing while he murmured, "Sweetcheeks."

She rested her hands on his chest and asked, "Was it okay?"

"Was what okay?"

"The lesson. There's just so much to say with that book, you can't get to it all so I have to melt it down. I mean, we could talk about it for a month and not—"

Layne cut her off. "It was okay."

She stared into his eyes. "You sure?"

He dipped his face closer to hers and whispered, "Baby, they were eatin' it up."

She instantly blew off his compliment. "It's a good class. Those kids are bright."

"No, Roc, you're a good teacher. Those kids might be bright, but *you* make it interesting and I reckon you changed a few lives in there today. Or at least the way they look at things."

"You think?" she whispered.

"Oh yeah," Layne whispered back.

She smiled, eyes bright with dimple and, fuck, but he wanted to kiss her.

"You need to negotiate a new contract, sweetcheeks," Layne informed her and she burst out laughing then tilted her head down and pressed the top into his chest above her hands before she leaned back and looked up at him.

"Guess what?" she asked, the laughter still playing about her lips.

"What?" he asked back, watching her mouth.

"Adrian Cosgrove called in sick Monday and yesterday," she stated and his eyes went to hers.

"Yeah, you told me."

"Well, he didn't call in sick today."

Layne's brows shot up. "No shit?"

She shook her head. "No shit. You haven't heard?"

"Been busy, baby."

"Then you should call Colt or Merry and get the lowdown because he barely stepped in the door when the principal called him into his office. Then, about five seconds after Principal Klausen suspended him, Chris Renicki and Marty Fink arrested him for assault and battery."

Layne grinned. "Day's lookin' up."

Rocky grinned back. "Definitely." Then her grin faded and she stated, "He'll make bail."

Layne shook his head. "Don't worry, Roc. Paige and Seth will stay where they are until they're safe. They'll be covered."

She nodded and asked, "Did Jas call you during lunch?"

"Nope," Layne answered. "Everything okay?"

She nodded again and said, "Yeah. Apparently Tripp negotiated a double date."

"Come again?"

"He asked Giselle if she'd ask her parents if it was okay, after football practice but before Youth Group, if Giselle could go out with Jas, Keira and him for pizza and then Jasper could take her home. They said yes."

Layne smiled. Jas was right. Religious or not, the parents had caved.

"Why are you smiling?" Rocky asked.

"Nothin', sweetcheeks."

She let it go and announced, "That means I'm heading home tonight."

Layne's smile died. "Why?"

"The boys won't be at your place, you told me you have to work late and then you're staking out Gaines's car so *you* won't be there. And as much as I like Devin, without you and Jasper and Tripp running interference, I don't know if I could take a night of mostly full-on Vera while waiting for you to come home."

It was definitely time to have another chat with his mother.

"Roc—"

"Anyway," she interrupted him. "It feels like I haven't been home in ages so it'll be good to go through mail, make sure no lab experiments are fermenting in my fridge and watch something other than football and cop shows."

"There's something other than football and cop shows?" Layne asked and she smiled.

"Yes, celebrity dance contests," she answered. Layne tipped his head back to look at the ceiling and tipped it down when he felt her press close. "I'm kidding, sweetheart. I hate those shows. I much prefer football."

His hands gave her hips a squeeze, the bell rang and her head turned to the side.

"Key," he said quickly and she looked back at him.

"Sorry?"

"Drop your extra key at my house or in the mail slot in the door to my office. Text me where you put it. I'll come over when I'm done and spend the night at your place tonight."

She looked to the side again as the noise the kids were making unsupervised got louder and then back to him.

"You sure?" she asked.

"Yeah."

"What about Jasper and Tripp?"

"They're not kids anymore, sweetcheeks, and anyway, Vera and Devin are there. Devin can have a bed. He'll be fuckin' thrilled."

She looked to the side again and whispered, "I have to go."

"Roc. Key," he ordered on a squeeze of his hands at her hips and she looked at him.

"Mail slot at your office. Just in case Devin isn't home when I stop by."

Yep. He definitely needed another chat with his mother.

"Right," he said.

She made to move away from him, repeating, "I have to go," and Layne released her.

"Baby," he called when she'd walked three feet away, and she turned back. "You owe me a make out session."

She grinned. Then she disappeared.

Layne found the backstage door and headed down the side hall to the corridor and then to the office where he signed out and made nice with all the office ladies, keeping them sweet because he figured, with Rocky working there, one day he'd need it.

Layne was headed out the front doors when he heard his name called and he turned to see Nick Fullerton jogging down the hall toward him.

"Heard you were in the school. Glad I caught you," Nick said when he made it to Layne.

"Hey, Nick, everything all right?" Layne asked and Nick grinned.

"Yeah, got promoted officially to head coach today," Nick answered.

Layne shook his hand and clapped him on the shoulder. "Congratulations. Way you called the second half of the game Friday, they made the right choice."

"Thanks, man." Nick was still grinning. "Anyway, been spendin' the last coupla days in Adrian's office, goin' through stuff. Just wondered if there's a reason Jas isn't talkin' to the scouts. He decide he's not goin' to college or something?"

Layne felt the muscles in his neck contract. "What?"

"Scouts," Nick said. "From Ohio State, Illinois and Ball State. They're interested in Jasper. They know he's got the goods even if he isn't handling the ball. He'll make all-county and, he performs under me, maybe all-state. He doesn't have great grades, but he's scored high on the SATs and he's a class officer."

Layne felt a muscle jump in his cheek before he said low, "Nick, far's I know, Jasper hasn't heard word that any scouts have come forward and declared interest. We knew they were scoutin' but nothin' after that."

Nick stared at him hard.

Then he said, "I'll return some calls."

"Obliged," Layne murmured, Nick nodded and turned to jog back down the hall.

Layne watched him for three beats until his neck relaxed and his temper was under control.

Then he turned and walked out the door.

"Merry, you been dodgin' me for three days. You get this, you call me. I don't hear from you by tomorrow, I hunt you down," Layne growled into his phone and snapped it shut.

No sooner had he closed it when it chimed in his hand and he looked to see he had a text from Rocky. He opened his phone and read it.

Going to bed early. Have a headache. You don't need to come over. See you tomorrow?

Layne clenched his teeth and hit the reply button with his thumb.

I'll be over.

He hit send, turned the phone off, tossed it on the seat beside him and looked out the windshield of his truck toward the side doors of the church.

Youth Group should be out any minute now.

He wanted to get this done. He wanted to shut Gaines down. Find a way to make Adrian Cosgrove pay for beating his wife and son and fucking with Jasper's future. Rest in the knowledge his ex-wife was safe in her own home. Take down Rutledge and whoever was pulling his strings. Bring Jarrod Astley low so he'd be out of Roc's life. Talk his mother into getting her shit together or getting her ass back to Florida. And he wanted to talk to Merry so he could sort Rocky out.

Then he wanted to go on vacation.

With Rocky.

And maybe his boys.

His phone chimed, he looked at it sitting in the seat, its screen lit and he picked it up. Another text from Raquel.

Okay, baby. You have dinner?

He smiled at the phone, his earlier irritation evaporating, and texted back.

No, but I'm good.

He sent the text and started upending and twisting the phone in his fingers as he looked back at the doors to see kids coming out.

Youth Group met in the old sanctuary, the church that had stood there for fifty years before they built on the new, modern sanctuary, which was four times the size, and the new build included a Fellowship Hall, kitchens and offices. They still used the old sanctuary for church business, like Youth Group, and rented it out.

The new church wasn't new, as such. It had been built when Layne was a kid. But it didn't resemble the old church at all, even if it was attached to it. The new church was attractive but the old church had charm, it fit the 'burg. Even when he was a kid and his mother took him there, Layne never understood why they built it that way. The two buildings were attached but they didn't match. Two different styles, two different eras and the new church, even though it dwarfed the old one, never seemed like it belonged.

He watched Jasper, Giselle and Tripp leave the building and head to the Charger. He also watched Tripp say something that made Jasper throw his head back and laugh and Giselle turned hers to smile a big smile at his son. Then he watched Tripp take advantage of the smile and grab her hand. She couldn't hide being startled by the contact, but she didn't pull away either and walked to the Charger holding Tripp's hand.

Layne's lips tipped up. Tripp was definitely learning cool.

His phone chimed and he had another text from Rocky.

There's a plate in the oven. Remember to turn it off, will you?

Got it. Go to sleep. Layne texted back, turned off the phone and tossed it back to the seat.

He watched the kids drive away in their cars or with their parents who had come to pick them up. Then he waited for Gaines to leave. The Honda and a red Ford Focus were the only cars left in the lot.

Then he waited longer.

Then he waited even longer.

Finally, he saw the lights streaming through the stained glass windows of the old sanctuary go out, and five minutes later, Gaines walked out with a young girl. Pretty. Tall. Thin. Dark, long hair, so healthy it gleamed in the lights of the parking lot. Layne knew she was sixteen since she could drive, maybe seventeen. But she didn't have the confidence of a senior. She didn't hold her body in that way that hinted at the woman she'd become. She still had girl in her.

Which made their farewell turn Layne's stomach.

They were right under an overhead light but she still placed her hand on Gaines's chest and got up on her toes and he bent his head, put his hand to her waist and kissed her neck.

"Son of a bitch," Layne hissed at his windshield.

So much shit was going down, he was off his game. He should have had a camera ready mainly because he'd promised Rocky he'd get a photo of Gaines to Merry, but now because if Layne had shots of it, that kiss would make the Youth Minister need to answer uncomfortable questions. He had one in the glove compartment but he didn't have it out.

Even so, he would never have imagined Gaines would stand in the parking lot of the fucking church and kiss a teenager's neck for any driver in any passing car to see.

This guy was bold, which meant he thought he was untouchable.

There had to be a reason for that. There had to be leverage. He had to have something.

Layne pulled out his camera and took shots and watched as Gaines smiled at her all the while she waved as she went to her car. She got in and took off and Gaines got in his Honda and left the lot. Layne waited while Gaines turned right on Green then he tossed his camera to the passenger seat, rolled out of the secluded, tree-shrouded, unlit back area of the lot and kept his eyes on the Honda, flipping on his headlights and turning right with three cars between them.

Gaines turned right again on 56 and so did one of the three cars between them. Layne followed.

And he followed him straight to The Brendel where Gaines turned right into the entrance and Layne had no choice but to turn right with him.

Jesus. He either lived at The Brendel or he was visiting someone there at ten at night.

Layne slid through the gate Gaines opened and Gaines took the first right while Layne went left, toward Rocky's place. He parked in one of her spots, grabbed his smokes from the glove compartment, his small digital camera from the seat and got out of the car. He walked into the road, tucking the camera in his inside jacket pocket and looked toward where Gaines turned.

No Honda in sight.

Layne took a swift moment to survey the area. Muted lighting but it was good. It didn't invite strangers. There weren't many dark corners. The streets were well-lit so you could make your way. Someone came there wanting to do something they shouldn't, they'd think twice because there was nowhere to hide and it was easy to see.

Good for the tenants. Bad for Layne.

He shook out a cigarette and walked to the sidewalk in front of Rocky's unit. Then he lit it and took a stroll. A man outside having a smoke and a walk, he moved past the unit next to Rocky's and jogged across the wide entrance road to the complex. Then he hit the sidewalk on the other side. Four units in, just around a curve, he found the Honda parked next to a sporty red Mazda.

Unit K.

Apartment one, lights out. Apartment two, lights on behind blinds. Lights on in apartment three, up the stairs and facing the small field that separated The Brendel from the next development, wide windows and a long balcony, twice the size of Rocky's but without the two-story windows. No curtains or blinds closed but Layne had no reason to stand there and watch.

"Fuck," he whispered, lifting his smoke, taking a drag and exhaling as he dropped his hand, staring at the license plates on the cars and memorizing them. To save time so he didn't have to do it in the morning, he was considering jogging quickly to the parking spaces to check their apartment number with the hope no one spotted him when he glanced back to the window and saw him.

Gaines at the window to close the blinds. Jacket off. Shirt untucked. Bottle of beer in his hand. He was home or at least in for the night.

He lived at The Brendel.

No Youth Minister could afford The Brendel.

The blinds started swinging closed and Layne made his way back to Rocky's.

Tomorrow, unit K, apartment three officially went on radar.

Layne flicked the butt in a drain in the street ten feet from Rocky's stairs. As he jogged up them he pulled out his keys. He'd already put Rocky's on his ring.

He let himself in. A light by the couch lit. The under cabinet lights in the kitchen lit. Soft but welcoming. The smell of something in the air, fruity, like berries. One of her candles she'd put out but the smell lingered.

He took off his jacket and threw it on the armchair. Then he went to the fridge, saw bottles of Bud and smiled. He took one out, twisted off the cap, took a slug and then pulled open the door to the oven. Homemade macaroni and cheese with bits of hotdog.

At the sight, his smile got big. When they were living together she'd made it her mission to make the best homemade macaroni and cheese on the planet and she mostly did this because he loved her first try and told her, so she twisted herself in knots to make it better. It was fucking tasty by the time she left him. It was probably heaven on a plate if Astley stooped low enough to eat mac and cheese with cut up hotdogs.

Layne stood in the kitchen, hips against the counter, eating it and drinking beer. He was about to go to the fridge to see if she had leftovers he could nuke for a second helping when the loud knock came at the door.

"Rocky, open the fucking door!" Layne heard Jarrod Astley shout.

Layne stood in the kitchen with his empty plate in one hand, the fork resting on top, his bottle of beer in his other hand. He stared at the door and decided to count to ten.

He got to three when the knock came back and he heard, "I know he's in there too, you stupid slut! Open the fucking door!"

Layne's beer hit the counter with a thud and his plate with a crash and he was at the door in less time than it took him to count to three.

He pulled it open and filled its frame.

"What the fuck?" he asked an openly furious Jarrod Astley.

Astley barreled forward, hitting Layne in the chest with his shoulder and shoving him to the side all the while saying loudly, "Get out of my way, asshole."

Layne stepped away from him, threw the door to and turned to see Astley in the middle of the open space between kitchen and living room, looking around him. Then Astley shouted toward the stairs, "Rocky! Get your ass down here!"

Layne moved. Going direct to him and gripping his upper arm, he yanked him around.

"You got two seconds to leave, you don't, I'm puttin' you out," Layne clipped low.

"*Fuck you!*" Astley bellowed.

"Roc's got a headache," Layne ground out. "You got somethin' to say to her, you wait until she's feelin' better or you say it through your attorneys. You do *not* come bustin' into her home fuckin' shoutin'."

Astley pulled sharply at his arm, demanding. "Take your hand off me!"

Layne yanked him forcefully in the direction of the door. Astley stumbled but righted himself and Layne ordered, "Get out."

"*Take your goddamned hand off me!*" Astley roared, twisting his arm, lifting a hand and shoving it in Layne's chest.

Layne braced so Astley's shove only rocked him back and then he pressed forward, turning to crowd Astley and force him to the door when they heard from the stairs. "Jarrod?"

Both of them froze and looked to the stairs.

Rocky was at the middle, hair down and around her shoulders, a King's Island nightshirt could be seen, the closed banister hiding the rest of her. Her face was pale and she looked visibly hazy, not from surprise or upset.

This wasn't a headache. This was one of her *headaches*.

Fuck.

"Baby, go to bed. I'll deal with this," Layne called to her.

"Fuck that and fuck you!" Astley yelled and yanked his arm free, skirting Layne and taking two steps toward Rocky, which were two steps to Layne's three. Layne rounded him to stand in front of him and stood firm to block his way, bringing Astley up short.

"Get out," Layne ordered.

Astley ignored him and kept his eyes pinned on Roc.

"Get your ass down here, you bitch!" At that, Layne put a hand to his chest, wishing he could put a fist to his face, and Astley's eyes sliced to him. "Do not *touch* me!" he shouted. "I know what *she*," he jabbed a finger at Rocky, "put you up to. I *know*!"

Devin clearly had been busy.

"You need to go someplace and calm the fuck down," Layne warned quietly.

"And *you* need to go fuck yourself!" Astley shouted then looked at Rocky. "You're with him a month. A *month* and it's like you spent ten minutes with me. You're back to nothing. A piece of *shit*."

Layne's mouth got dry but his palms got prickly and he took two quick steps forward, forcing Astley back with his hand and his body.

"Layne," Rocky called, and Layne stopped and pushed Astley back another step with his hand but didn't step back himself.

Astley glared at him, angry and stupid enough to stay in Layne's space, and Layne felt Rocky come up to his side and her hand curled around his bicep.

"What are you talking about?" she asked softly, her voice as hazy as her expression and pinched with pain.

Layne's patience, already strained, slipped.

"Blackmail," Astley spit out.

"Blackmail?" Rocky whispered, her hand clenching spasmodically on Layne's arm.

"Yes, Rocky, *blackmail*. Don't pretend you don't know," Astley returned.

"She doesn't," Layne put in and Astley's eyes shot to his as he felt Rocky's hit him. "That was all me."

"Bullshit," Astley snapped.

"It's true. She has no fuckin' clue," Layne replied. "Now, seein' as you're a doctor and all, and considerin' you spent the last ten years with her, I reckon you can take one look at her and know she's not in a good way so, I'll tell you again, get...the fuck...*out*."

"And I'll tell you again...fuck *you*!" Astley bellowed.

And then Rocky wasn't there. Layne turned and watched her racing up the stairs with her hand over her mouth.

Shit, she was going to be sick. The pain was so bad she was nauseous because of it.

And her ex-asshole was shouting.

Layne locked eyes with Astley then followed her, taking the steps three at a time.

He found her in the hall bathroom, on her knees in front of the toilet, one arm on the seat, one hand clenched in her hair to pull it back, head in the bowl, retching.

He grabbed a washcloth folded in a triangle over a towel on the rod and tossed it in the sink. Drenching it with cold water, he wrung it out and crouched beside her.

He gathered her hair in one fist, gently pulling it from her hand, then set the cool cloth on her neck and murmured, "Baby."

She spit then moved to rest her forehead on her arm as her back bowed with the effort to hold back her gags and Layne reached out and flushed the toilet.

"I hate this," she whispered on a heavy breath.

"I know, honey." Layne held her hair and pressed lightly on the cloth at her neck then she moved back over the toilet and heaved again.

She was back to resting her forehead on her arm, her back bowing and arching with the deep breaths she was taking when Layne heard Astley's voice.

"Has she taken a pill?"

Layne looked to the door to see him standing in it, staring down at them, his face cleared of anger, something Layne didn't have the focus to read replacing it.

Roc didn't move.

"Her pill?" Layne asked.

"I took it," Rocky whispered into the toilet.

"When?" Astley asked.

"Not too..." big breath, "not too long ago," she answered. "I thought I could fight it."

Astley sighed loudly before he said, "I'm always telling you Rocky—"

"I know," she whispered.

"Where are they?" Astley asked.

"Bathroom in my bedroom," she answered and Astley disappeared.

Layne looked down at Raquel. "Baby, what pill?"

She took in a deep breath and sat back on her calves. He let go of her hair, flushed the toilet again and she looked up at him.

"There's a pill I have now. Jarrod knew about it. It works, if I take it in time. Sometimes even when I don't take it in time, if it doesn't end up in the toilet, like that one did."

Layne took in this information and moved the cloth from her neck to her face, wiping her brow and sliding it down to clean her mouth last.

"Thanks," she whispered, her eyes still foggy but pointed at him.

"Anytime, sweetcheeks," he grinned at her, "you know that."

Her mouth got soft and her lips parted right before her eyes slid from him and he looked over his shoulder to see Astley at the door, watching them. He had a glass of water in one hand, the other hand balled in a fist. He took one step into the bathroom and put the glass on the basin of the sink and dropped a light blue tablet next to it.

"Give her that. She keeps it down, she'll be better in an hour," he stated then he walked out of the room.

Layne listened while he helped Rocky to her feet but he didn't hear the door downstairs close. He kept listening as he gave Roc the tablet and handed her the glass. She gulped it down. He took the glass from her, set it on the basin and led her into her room knowing Astley still hadn't left.

She went direct to the master bath off her bedroom and he leaned against the doorjamb and watched while she quickly brushed her teeth. Then he stepped aside as she wandered in her pain-fueled fog to the bed, gingerly entered it and just as gingerly laid down on her side, curled her knees into her belly and pressed her head into the pillow.

He walked to her, pulled the covers over her and let them drop lightly on her. Then he leaned in and shifted her hair off her neck. He wanted to kiss her but if it was as bad as it seemed, she wouldn't want that. So he left her in the room and closed the door behind him.

He found Astley standing and staring sightlessly out her huge windows.

"Astley—" he started.

Astley cut him off. "Tell her to tell her attorneys what she wants. I'll consider it and counter if it's inappropriate."

Fuck, he was caving.

"You're gonna settle?" Layne asked.

Astley turned and gazed at him.

He did this for a while and Layne held his gaze, waiting. Then Astley looked away and walked to the front door.

Hand on the knob, he turned to Layne. "I want *you* to know it's not because of your antics." His eyes slid to the stairs then back to Layne. "It's because of her." He stared at Layne a beat that fed into five. Then he whispered, "You're not the only one who can love her, you know."

Layne felt his body lock, his temper flare and his patience ebb. "Fuckin' strange way of showin' it, man."

"You think that then you've never loved someone so much, wanted someone's attention so badly, you'd do anything to get it," Astley shot back. "You think I'm an asshole. She's been cheating on me for twelve years, since our first date, sitting across the table from me and wishing I was you."

His chest got tight at Astley's words but he still returned, "You're wrong. She wanted to love you."

Astley shook his head and looked back to the stairs.

Eyes on the stairs, he whispered, "I didn't stand a chance."

Then he opened the door, stepped through and was careful to close it quietly.

Layne didn't hesitate and walked across the room to turn the lock and flip the latch.

He stood with his hand still on the latch not thinking about Astley's final words. He wasn't giving headspace to that asshole. Instead he was thinking one down, half a dozen to go.

Then he walked to the fridge to find Roc's leftovers.

Forty-five minutes later Layne quietly entered Rocky's bedroom.

"I'm awake and I'm better," she said softly from the bed.

Layne walked to her side and sat on it. She was still curled into a ball, her back to him and she didn't move. This wasn't unusual. He remembered, after she'd battled the pain, she wasn't herself. Not in a fog, but she'd lose a hint of lucidity.

He leaned over her and put a forearm into the bed in front of her.

"You need anything?" he asked.

"I'm good," she answered.

"That pill obviously works wonders, sweetcheeks, I remember sometimes it'd be hours and it was only sleep that brought you peace."

"Yep, it's the wonder pill," she whispered.

"So why do you wait to take it?"

"Because I'm an idiot?"

She was joking and he laughed softly, leaned in and kissed her forehead. Then he moved away from her, rounded the bed, closed the curtains she'd left open, pulled off his clothes and joined her.

He reached out, gathered her in his arms and she snuggled closer.

"All right, Roc, no jokin' around. Why do you wait to take it?" Layne repeated his question and she sighed.

Then she answered, "Hope springs eternal. I hate those headaches and they don't come very often so, in between times, I tell myself I'm done with them, I've had the last one. Then, when they start, I tell myself it isn't one of those. It's just a headache because I don't want to believe they've come back. Then, well…they come back."

"You need to take the pill, Rocky."

"Taking the pill is admitting defeat, Layne."

He rolled into her, taking her to her back, lifted up and looked down at her shadowed face.

"Any battle worth winnin' is worth using every weapon available," he informed her.

"Right, like blackmailing Jarrod?" she returned and Layne got quiet. When he didn't speak, she asked, "*Did* you blackmail him?"

"*I* didn't," Layne answered somewhat honestly.

She was silent. Then she whispered, "Dev."

Layne didn't reply.

"What'd you get on him?" she asked.

"Dirty campaign contributions," Layne partially answered.

"I can believe that," she said softly. "Especially considering he was so pissed. He loves being one of the good ole boys. He can get pissy but that was off the charts."

Layne reckoned Jarrod Astley didn't like losing, especially not something as important as Rocky. And he also reckoned the man didn't like any time when he couldn't do what he damn well pleased.

But he doubted that anger was about campaign contributions.

That kind of anger was about love or money and not money spent on politics.

Devin had pulled the Marissa card and Astley was facing paying out twice and losing hold of Rocky, even the sick hold he had that was essentially just yanking her chain.

So it was both. Love and money.

"He's settling," Layne announced and felt Rocky's body still.

"Sorry?"

"He's settling, baby," Layne told her. "He says for you to tell your attorneys what you want, if he's not happy with it he'll counter."

"Seriously?" she breathed.

"Seriously."

She was motionless and silent a moment before she lifted her hand and curled it around his neck then she lifted her head and touched her mouth to his.

Then she said, "Thank you, baby."

Thank Christ, she wasn't pissed, she was grateful.

So he took advantage. "This means you owe me and what you owe me is promising me you'll take that pill the minute a headache comes on."

"Layne—"

"Non-negotiable."

"Layne—"

"I love your hair, sweetcheeks, and my fingers in it, but it isn't my favorite thing to do, holding it back while you puke."

Rocky fell silent.

"You with me on this?" Layne prompted.

"Yes," she gave in softly.

"Promise," he pushed.

"I promise," she stated.

That's when he grinned and bent his head to brush her lips with his.

As he was lifting his head, she asked, "Did you find out where Gaines lived?"

"Five guesses," Layne replied. "And if one of them isn't The Brendel, you lose."

Rocky gasped then asked, "The Brendel?"

"Yep." Layne fell to his side and she rolled into him, pushing him to his back with her body and lifting her head and shoulders up but her hand was still at his neck.

"I don't believe it."

"Believe it. He either lives here or he's visiting his girlfriend who's got cabbage. He drove straight here, knew the gate code, and I took a stroll, found his car and saw him close the blinds, a beer in his hand."

She was silent a moment before she said, "He doesn't have a girlfriend. Women can be pretty blind, Layne, especially when a man is that attractive, but if she goes to church and sees the way he is with those girls—"

Layne interrupted her. "You think he's attractive?"

"Well…yeah," she answered.

"Roc, evidence is suggesting this guy is into some sick shit. I saw him kiss a sixteen year old's neck as his way of sayin' good-bye." He felt her body get stiff as he went on, "That shit's not right."

"I'm not saying he's attractive, as in, if I didn't lay claim to the hottest guy in the 'burg, I'd go for it. I'm just saying, you know, technically he's attractive in an 'euw, gross, he's into sick shit which is too bad because he's cute' kind of way."

Layne burst out laughing, his arms went around her and he rolled her again to her back.

This time he covered her torso with his, buried his face in her neck and asked, "You lay claim to the hottest guy in the 'burg? Who's that then?"

She slapped his arm lightly and whispered, "Shut up."

He lifted his head and smiled at her shadowed face, "No really, I wanna know."

"Stop fishing for compliments."

He bent his neck and rubbed the side of his nose against hers, whispering, "You think I'm hot."

"You *know* you're hot, you always did," she stated and he lifted his head.

"Yeah, and you always did too. That's why you strutted back and forth to the window at Fulsham's Custard Stand five times while I was sitting there eatin' my cone the first time I saw you. 'Cause you wanted some of this and got it by swinging your ass in my face."

She gasped again. "I did not!"

"Sweetcheeks, you so did."

"If I recall, I needed a napkin," she shot back.

"*Five* of them?"

"It was a hot day! My cone was melting too fast for me to eat it."

"Baby, when you weren't struttin', you were lickin' and you took your time because that got my attention too."

"I forgot how full of yourself you could be," Rocky snapped.

"And I forgot about you lickin' that cone," Layne returned. "We're goin' to Fulsham's tomorrow after dinner."

"It's closed for the winter," she retorted.

"Then I'm buyin' ice cream and cones at Kroger's."

"And I'm arranging to be fed intravenously until the end of my days."

Layne burst out laughing again and rolled to his back, taking Rocky with him so she was on top. He knew she wasn't seriously pissed and they were playing at bickering when she scooted down and settled with her cheek to his chest and her arm around him. He lifted a hand and slid it through her hair, then again, and repeat.

"Baby," he called and she mumbled, "Mm?"

"The third time, you said, you needed Atticus," he stated and her head and hand came up but only so she could rest her chin on her hand in his chest and look at him.

"What?"

"In class today, you said the third time you read *To Kill a Mockingbird*, you needed Atticus." He felt her body get tight and he pushed, "When was that?"

"Layne—"

"When was that?"

"I don't—"

His hand twisted in her hair and his other arm went around her, pulling her up his chest so they were face to face.

"When was that?" he repeated.

She was silent and this silence spread.

Then she whispered, "When I lost my real-life version of him."

"Jesus," Layne whispered back instantly.

She'd said, *Atticus Finch is the most beautiful man I've ever met in print. He's a good dad and he does what's right, not what's safe, not what's popular. What's right. He's gentle. He's smart. He's strong. He's decisive and he's willing to follow through with his decisions, no matter what the odds.*

"Jesus," he repeated, still whispering.

Rocky took advantage of his immobility and moved, making her point by brushing her lips lightly against the scar beneath his shoulder then putting her cheek there, her arm around his abs, pinning him to the bed.

"You aren't the same as him, of course. Atticus wasn't a badass, or, if he was, he was a quiet one. But Atticus was about doing what was right and you were too and still are. And I missed you, so when I read it again, because I was missing you and I figured I'd never have anything like that again, it was all about Atticus. Because if I couldn't have it, it felt good to be able to spend time with it in my head."

She stopped speaking. Layne stared at the dark ceiling and Rocky's arm tightened around him.

"You have it again."

That came from Layne, his voice thick.

"Weird," she whispered. "I thought it was perfect. But somehow it's better this time around."

At her words, Layne was done and he communicated this by rolling her to her back, covering her with his body and kissing her hard and deep.

Rocky kissed him back. Then she did other things to him, he did other things to her, and she ended up sliding out of bed, finding her nightshirt, going to the bathroom, cleaning up, coming back to bed where she pinned him and fell instantly to sleep.

Layne didn't.

Layne wanted to believe but he couldn't. He'd believed before and his beautiful life was torn from him.

So tomorrow, he was talking to Garret Merrick even if he had to hunt the man down.

Twenty

GOOD GIRL

"Dave, I'm bein' serious here, it takes much longer for him to contact me, it won't be good." Layne, in his chair behind his desk, swiveled to look out the window toward Main as he growled in his phone.

"I hear what you're sayin', Tanner, and all I got for you is work it out with Roc," Rocky's father replied.

"Bullshit," Layne hissed. "And that's the same bullshit Merry fed me."

"Are things not good?" Dave asked.

"They're fuckin' great," Layne answered.

"So maybe *you'll* explain to *me* what your fuckin' problem is," Dave suggested, losing patience, just like Layne.

"They were fuckin' great before too," Layne reminded him.

"She's not a girl anymore, Tanner."

"Yeah, Dave, I lived and aged those eighteen years right along with Rocky. And a week ago, I also held her in my arms in the dark while she was beggin' me to let in the light and felt a fear so disturbing, swear to God, I still feel it on my skin."

Dave was silent and this silence was loaded.

Layne filled the silence. "I need to know what that shit is."

Dave didn't reply.

"I also need to know why both your kids hooked up with people they instantly knew they wanted to spend the rest of their lives with and then dropped them, without a word, without a reason, and didn't look back," Layne went on.

"Roc looked back, son, you're together," Dave argued.

"I think you catch my point," Layne shot back.

"You need to work this out with Roc," Dave repeated.

"Jesus Christ, what's the big fuckin' secret?" Layne exploded.

Dave changed the subject by shifting blame. "Last time, you let her get away."

"Bullshit," Layne clipped. With that incendiary comment, his anger, already primed, was about to detonate.

"You let her get away," Dave reiterated.

"Wait, wasn't that you who barred the door the fifty fuckin' times I came over, wanting to talk to her?" Layne's voice was sarcastic.

"Why are we talking about this? It's water under the bridge. You both have moved on and found each other again," Dave informed him, again shifting the point.

Layne brought it back. "Whatever that was that I felt comin' from Roc was not history. It was real, it was now and it fuckin' terrified her. She's your daughter, man, does this not worry the fuck outta you?"

"No," Dave stated instantly. "No, it doesn't. Not anymore. Now that she's got you."

"Godammit, Dave," Layne ground out.

"Can you explain to me why *you* won't talk to her about this?" Dave asked.

"Are you serious?" Layne asked back.

"Deadly," Dave snapped.

"All right, I lost her once and I do not get why, even though she explained it I'll repeat, I do not get why. This time my boys are in the mix. They like her. They think she's the shit. The longer they're around her, the more they're gonna like her. Then they'll fall for her, like their old man, hook, line and sinker. The fact that I lost her once and the way you and Merry are actin' tells me I gotta tread cautiously. You know the landmines you're dodgin'. I have no fuckin' clue and you're not givin' me shit. I'm walkin' that minefield blindfolded and any second I can step on one of those mines. I'm stuck, Dave, I can't move. I move, I could fuck this up.

You think I'd do anything, *anything*, to fuck this up? To fuck this for me, for my boys, for *Rocky*?"

When Layne finished talking, he listened to silence.

So he prompted, "Dave…"

"Give me time," Dave said quietly.

"What?" Layne asked.

"I need to think," Dave stated.

"Jesus, about what?"

"About if this goes bad, I tell you and fuck it up with my daughter, how I'll play that because, son, I don't have eighteen years."

Layne's neck muscles got tight and he opened his mouth to speak but he heard Dave disconnect at the same he heard the beep that indicated someone walked through the door to the street.

Layne turned his head and looked at the monitor.

"Fuck me," he whispered, tossing his phone down on his desk and watching Astley's girl toy, Marissa Gibbons walk up his steps.

He straightened from his chair and was two feet in the reception office when she opened the door and stopped, hand on the handle, staring at him.

Layne crossed his arms on his chest.

Marissa Gibbons swallowed then said, "Uh…hey."

"Hey," Layne replied with clipped courtesy.

"Uh…can we talk?" she asked.

"Talk," he invited and didn't move.

She stared at him, looked out in the hall, stepped into the office and closed the door. Then she turned back to him, her eyes skidding to the door to the inner office and back to his.

"Could we, uh…sit down?" she requested.

"No," he denied.

She hesitated, glanced to the floor then back to him and asked, "Can I buy you a cup of coffee at Mimi's?"

"No," Layne repeated.

She stared at him and this lasted a while.

Finally, she whispered, "You think I'm a slut."

"Is that what you came to talk about?" Layne asked.

"Uh…" she began then faltered and stopped.

"Listen, Ms. Gibbons, I don't think anything about you. You came here with somethin' to say, say it. No disrespect, but I'm a busy man."

"I had to do it," she stated.

"Had to do what?" Layne asked, confused at her words, having started his day in Rocky's bed and moving on to handing the photos of Stew over to Colt, which meant Stew's days of being a free man able to wear something other than a jumpsuit became severely limited. Then having this brilliant start diminish when he couldn't find Merry anywhere and when he went back to The Brendel to see there were window cleaners *and* the gardeners raking leaves, which meant he couldn't stake out TJ Gaines's apartment so he could find a safe time to break in. He was still pissed about his conversation with Dave and therefore he had zero patience left.

"The movies, I had to do them. I was—" she started to explain.

Layne cut her off. "Listen, I don't give a shit about that. I been in this business a long time, people do shit, shit they gotta do. I get that. You didn't have to fuck my woman's husband though, not ever but especially not for the reasons you did it. That's not cool."

Her eyes brightened and she took three steps forward, saying, "But, I've heard about you and her, in the 'burg people talk about it. If it wasn't for me, you wouldn't have had the chance—"

"Maybe you're right," he cut her off again, and the way he spoke, she stopped moving. "But you made her feel like garbage. You made her the chump. You caused her pain. I'm glad she's rid of that asshole but I'm not down with that."

"Then why?" Marissa asked. "I don't get it."

"Why what?" Layne asked back.

"Why didn't you...why did you...?" She stopped and started again. "I got two hundred thousand dollars from him and he let me keep the 'vette. Mr. Glover told me what to say, how to play it. He helped me get it."

"Mr. Glover's got a soft spot for people who're tryin' to turn their lives around," Layne returned.

She stared at him, and as she did it, her stare turned shrewd.

Then she whispered, "You do too."

"Come again?"

"You have a soft spot too."

Layne took a deep breath into his nose then exhaled. What he didn't do was reply.

Marissa Gibbons took the hint, nodded, turned and walked to the door. She had it opened when she turned back and locked eyes with him.

"I didn't tell Social Services, but he pimped me out too," she announced and Layne felt his stomach turn and his chest squeeze, but she couldn't know that so she went on to say more shit he really did not want to hear. "Never—back then, when someone was pumping away at me and I didn't know anything but that it hurt so bad, it hurt *so bad* that was all I could think about—never did I think I'd have soft sheets and a fancy car and beautiful clothes and live in a house right on a lake. I got that shot and you're right, I didn't think about her. I jumped at it. And you know what?" she finished on a question.

"What?" Layne prompted when she didn't go on, why he did *not* know.

"It was the same thing. Some guy I didn't like pumping away at me, just in soft sheets. And it didn't hurt so bad because I've long since discovered the wonders of lube."

"Ms. Gibbons—" Layne started.

"One day," Marissa said over him, "I was suckin' cock while someone was filmin' and thinkin' about this social worker I had. She was young. She was pretty. She had a big, honkin' engagement ring on her finger. And she was nice, she cared. She got me in a good foster home that I stayed in until they moved out of state and I got lost in the system again because that social worker got married and changed jobs and I was fucked…again. And I was suckin' cock and thinkin' I'd rather be sitting at a desk, wearin' an engagement ring and makin' sure girls like me didn't end up suckin' cock. I started to find the path then lost my way." She held his eyes and finished, "Then you and Mr. Glover helped me find it again."

"Marissa," Layne murmured and she lifted a hand and flipped her hair over her shoulder.

"You know anyone that wants a nearly new 'vette, I'm sellin'," she declared, turned and walked out, closing the door behind her.

One second elapsed, Layne muttered, "Fuck," then he dropped his arms and followed her.

When he was standing on the landing outside the door he called, "Marissa."

She was mostly down the stairs, but on hearing her name, hand on the banister, she turned and looked up at him.

"Don't lose your way again," he warned and her face, which had filled with expectation, closed off.

"Right," she muttered and started to turn away but stopped when Layne spoke.

"You start thinkin' of goin' that way, I'm not goin' anywhere for a while. You find me. I'll buy you a Mimi's and talk you out of it."

And that's when Layne witnessed it. What Astley saw in her. What he wanted. It wasn't the hair, the similar features. It was her mouth getting soft, in doing so it changed everything about her. She didn't speak with her eyes like Rocky did but it was close to what Rocky could give with just one look, and it was nice.

"Soft spot," she whispered, turned and part walked, part skipped down the rest of the steps and out the front door.

The door didn't close all the way before a hand was on it, pulling it open, and Layne saw Vera move into the doorframe, her head turned to watch Marissa walk away.

Layne looked to the ceiling and implored on a mutter, "Kill me."

"Hi, honey!" Vera called.

Layne looked down at his mother. "What are you doin' here?"

"I'm so glad I caught you in the office," she stated, walking up the stairs, carrying a white cup with brown cardboard wrapped around it. She stopped, looked at her cup and then looked up at him. "Do you want a coffee? I just stopped in to get one and then decided to try your office and—"

"Ma, what are you doin' here?"

She started walking again, muttering, "Yeesh. Someone's in a bad mood even after having a meeting with a pretty girl."

Jesus. That shit was going to hit Rocky next.

"She's an ex-porn movie bit player who just fleeced Jarrod Astley for two hundred K. She's pretty but she's not my type," Layne informed her, his mother stopped two stairs down from him and her mouth was hanging open.

Then she whispered, "Porn?"

"Ex-porn. She's straight now. So, now that we got that sorted, I'll repeat, what the fuck are you doin' here?"

"You say the f-word too much, Tanner Layne," Vera snapped.

"Ma," Layne growled.

She looked at the door then to him. "Can we go in your office?"

"Will that make you tell me what you're doin' here?" Layne countered.

"Yes," she answered.

Layne sighed. Then he walked into his office and his mother followed. He went straight to the reception desk and sat on it. She went straight to the couch and settled in like they were going to shoot the shit for the next hour.

"Ma," Layne prompted.

"I've had *the best* idea," Vera announced.

Layne suspected he wouldn't think it was the best.

"You gonna share?" he asked when she said no more.

"I'm going to sell my condo in Florida, come home and be your receptionist!" she declared with a little bounce on the couch. "Isn't that *great*? You won't have to pay me much and I'll get to—"

Layne interrupted her. "That's not gonna happen."

Her face grew confused. "What? Why?"

"How many reasons do you want?" Layne asked.

"*All* of them," she shot back.

"Okay, first, the shit I do, see, photograph and investigate, you do not wanna know, you do not wanna see. If you can't handle the f-word, you can't handle my job. Second, I'm done with your shit in regards to Rocky. I told you when you came home that you didn't learn to hide your attitude, which you haven't, I'd show you the door. I've been patient and I'm letting you know, now, straight out, I'm not gonna be patient anymore. You pull one more stunt with Rocky, I'm done. You're out."

"Tanner," she whispered.

"I'm bein' straight with you. No joke, do not push me on that, you won't like the consequences. And if you do it when I'm not around, but Jas and Tripp are, I'm tellin' you straight about that too. You won't like the consequences of that either."

403

"They're my grandsons!" she protested. "She's known them all of a month."

"Yeah, and they're my sons. I fell in love with her in three weeks, *twice*. You do the math."

She snapped her mouth shut, looked away and sucked back some coffee.

Then she told the wall, "She's going to hurt you again."

"Yes, she is," Layne agreed, and Vera's eyes shot to him.

"What?" she whispered.

"She's got somethin' in her, Ma. Somethin' not right and I gotta help her get it out, but I don't know what the fuck it is. I don't even think *Roc* knows what it is. It made her leave me eighteen years ago and I know in my bones it's gonna happen again, unless I sort that shit out, and all three of us are gonna lose her. Now, you can play your games and piss me off, piss off my boys, and cause a rift in this family because you're bein' stubborn. Or you can fuckin' help me, 'cause, Ma, she makes me happy. I love her. I don't want to lose her again. And I need all the help I can get."

He watched his mother's eyes change and she looked the way she looked when he was eleven and took that huge header on his bike, walked home with blood running from his knees, his forearms and his temple and she cleaned it up with a hot, soapy towel then wiped it with alcohol, blowing in between each stroke.

And the way she looked at him, just months ago, when he was in the hospital after getting shot.

"She's got something in her?" Vera asked quietly.

"She's shit scared of the dark unless I'm there," Layne shared.

"Is this new?"

"No, I don't think so, but it's new to me. She wasn't that way before but she said it was because I was there. And she isn't that way now when I'm there. But if I'm not there, and it's night, the curtains are open and she cannot handle them closed, and when I say that, she *seriously* cannot handle them closed."

"Did you ask what scares her?"

"Yeah, but she didn't answer. She just started shakin' and then I felt something comin' from her and I won't go into details, Ma, but I been in

404

some serious situations and been in the presence of some serious people, and I've never, not in my life, felt anything as nasty as that."

She put her hand to her mouth and took a breath before dropping it and asking, "Why do you think she didn't answer?"

"I don't know. She just wouldn't go there."

"What do Dave and Merry say?" Vera asked.

"They don't. They won't talk about it."

"What?"

"They won't talk about it, Ma. At all. They say if they do, she'll cut them out like she cut me out."

"My God," Vera whispered. "What on earth—?"

Layne cut her off. "I don't know. I know two things. She's scared of the dark, *really* scared, and she won't go there to understand why. And I suspect one thing, whatever this is ties up with why she left me."

"Did she explain that?" Vera asked softly.

"Yes and no," Layne answered honestly.

Vera's eyebrows shot up. "What?"

"She explained it but she says even she doesn't know why she did it. She just knows it hurt. She wanted that connection back. She fought against it and missed me for eighteen years. Me gettin' shot broke through."

"That doesn't make sense," Vera observed.

"No shit?" Layne asked.

Vera's back got straight. "Do you want me to talk to her?"

Oh Christ.

Layne shook his head and stated firmly, "Fuck no."

"What?" Vera snapped. "Why not?"

"Ma, seriously?" And his mother had the grace to look as guilty as she was.

"Okay," she said. "So I won't meet her after school and invite her to manicures and confessions of the soul. I'll um...win her back and then... um..."

"How about you work Dave, I'll work Merry, and one or the other of us maybe will figure out what the fuck is goin' on and find a way to get past it," Layne suggested.

"Dave isn't my best friend," his mother reminded him.

"Yeah, you did that too. But you go over there, wavin' the white flag while carryin' one of your pistachio bunt cakes with that kickass icing that he always liked so much, and *maybe* he won't shoot you."

Vera grinned then her grin wavered and her eyes got bright with wet.

"One big happy family," she whispered.

"One big happy family," Layne whispered back.

"Again," she finished, now trying to force her smile.

"You missed her," Layne said softly.

"She made you happy," Vera bullshitted.

"Bullshit," Layne called her on it. "You missed her."

She took in a deep breath then she spoke.

"You know, Tanner, I was once head over heels in love," she told him. "Blind with it. Blind. Then he walked out on me just like she walked out on you."

Fuck. Jesus. *Fuck!*

Layne hadn't thought of it like that.

"Ma—"

"Then I had to watch it happen to you *and* feel it again because yes, I loved her and when she left, I missed her. But she wasn't gone, like your father, and every time I saw her, it hurt even more."

Layne stared at his mother.

Then he ordered, "Come here, Ma."

She shook her head. "No. If I do, you're gonna be my sweet boy and make me cry and I don't have waterproof mascara on."

"Come here, Ma," Layne repeated.

"Tanner."

"Get over here."

She sighed, set her cup on the arm of the couch, got up and walked to him. When she got close, Layne jumped from the desk and folded his mother in his arms.

He knew she was crying even with her voice muffled by his chest when he heard her say, "You know, you haven't hugged me since I got home."

Layne bent and kissed the top of her head and then said there, "I'm a shit son."

Her head tilted back and her wet eyes hit him, mascara running down, before she whispered, "No, not that. Never that, honey. Never."

"Love you, Ma," he whispered back. She grinned and lifted her hand, patting him on the side of the neck twice before her fingers curled around.

Then her smile got bigger and she stated, "I'm glad we got this sorted out. Being mean is exhausting. Especially when, at the same time, you're over the moon that your eldest grandchild has finally sorted out his head and your son is with a woman who cheers on the Colts, helps his boy with his homework and falls asleep on his chest. And not one that screeches her nonsense at the top of her lungs at every available opportunity. So, I'll warn you now, if you ever think of reuniting with Gabrielle, I will not offer to be your receptionist. I'll have you committed."

Layne smiled down at her. "Not thinkin' that's in the cards, Ma."

"Thank God," she breathed, still smiling.

She took her hand away and smeared her mascara across her face.

"Maybe you need a mirror," he suggested, and she jumped from his arms.

"I knew it!" she cried, whirled and rushed into the bathroom.

Layne looked at the closed bathroom door while counting them down. That was two problems covered, his Ma and Astley. Then he walked back into his office thinking, his mother wanted to help out, he'd let her. She could do the books. He had checks to cash, invoices to send and bills to be paid. He was going to spend Monday doing it. Now, Vera could spend Friday doing it.

He didn't make it to his desk when he heard the beep, looked to the monitor and saw Ryker walking up the stairs.

"What the fuck?" he whispered to himself, quickly rounded the desk, pulled his nine millimeter out of a drawer and shoved it in the waistband of his jeans at his hip.

He was back in the outer office by the time Ryker came through the door.

"Yo, bro," Ryker greeted.

"Ryker," Layne returned, hoping his mother was adding a whole new layer of makeup.

Ryker looked around the office then back at Layne. "Dig the digs," he commented.

"Thrilled you approve," Layne replied.

Ryker's eyes dropped to Layne's gun then went back to his and he smiled his big, ugly smile. "Nine millimeter? Take that as a compliment, bro."

Layne cut to the chase. "You here for a reason?"

Without delay, Ryker walked in, skirted Layne and went into his office. Layne stood where he was, eyes on the bathroom door, counting to ten.

He found this didn't work and he followed Ryker into his office to see him lounging in one of the two chairs in front of Layne's desk.

Layne rounded the desk, pulled out his gun and set it on the desktop, close, as he sat down.

"Well?" he prompted.

"Thought we could go out, get a beer, play some pool," Ryker replied and Layne stared.

Then he asked, "Come again?"

"Pool. Beer. Women. We both got hot babes but that don't mean we can't look."

"Not sure what keeps you in motorcycle boots and leather jackets but it's four o'clock in the afternoon and I got two growin' boys so I gotta work for a living," Layne replied.

Ryker smiled his big, ugly smile again and stated, "Yeah, been askin' 'round about you. You're like King Dick. The top of the Private Dick Heap. What you charge, bro, you could work three hours a day and still feed those two powerhouses."

"I worked three hours a day, Ryker, wouldn't have clients to pay those fees," Layne returned.

Ryker shrugged, "Suit yourself." Then he leaned forward and asked, "So what we workin'?"

Oh shit.

"We?" Layne asked back.

"Yeah," Ryker lounged back in his seat. "We."

"I think I told you already I work alone."

"Now you work with me."

"I skipped a part," Layne informed him. "How'd that happen?"

"Baranski's out of your *old* old lady's house. That happened because of me. You think I do somethin' for nothin'?"

Fuck.

"And payback is we partner up?" Layne asked.

Ryker shrugged again. "Sure, when I'm bored and I'm bored," he answered. "So what we workin'?"

Layne heard the bathroom door open and Ryker shot out of his chair. His hand going behind his back, he pulled out his .45.

Fuck!

"Honey?" Vera called.

"In here, Ma," Layne called back and then said low to Ryker, "Stand down."

Ryker relaxed and shoved his gun back right before Vera hit the door. She looked up at Ryker and her mouth dropped open.

"My," she breathed, "you're a big boy."

"Ma, this is Ryker. Ryker, Vera Layne," Layne introduced.

Ryker grinned his ugly grin and stuck out a meaty hand. "Ma'am."

Vera took it and shook it, placing her other hand on top, saying, "Ryker. Is that your first name or your last?"

"Both," Ryker replied and her eyebrows shot up.

"Both? You're a one name man?" she asked and Ryker let go of her hand.

"Yep," Ryker answered and Vera's eyes shot to Layne.

"How neat!" she exclaimed. "I've never met a one name person before!"

Ryker turned his ugly smile to Layne.

Layne sighed.

Then he suggested, "Ma, how 'bout you get your coffee, get your ass to the grocery store and buy a beef tenderloin for dinner."

Vera stared at him and then stated firmly, "Beef tenderloin is for special occasions, Tanner. You know that."

"Like you makin' up for bein' a bitch to Roc for the last week, an occasion like that?" Layne replied. "It's her favorite, or when *you* used to make it, it was."

Vera was silent before she whispered, "Oh, right."

Layne smiled at her to take the bite out of his earlier words. "Don't forget the horseradish sauce and you can come in tomorrow and do my books."

He watched his mother's face light up. "Really?"

Jesus, only his mother, the nutcase CPA, would be excited about doing books.

"Yeah," Layne said.

"Fantastic!" she cried then turned to Ryker and announced, "It was a pleasure to meet you," she leaned in, grinned and said like she and Ryker shared an in-joke, "*Ryker.*"

Then she disappeared.

Layne looked to the monitors to watch his mother walk down the stairs as Ryker resumed his seat.

"Your Ma was a bitch to your babe?" Ryker asked and Layne's eyes cut to him.

"Long story," Layne mumbled.

"Bro," Ryker grinned.

You understand my vision of justice, Ryker had said.

Layne stared at him but he didn't spend much time doing it before he made a decision.

"You know TJ Gaines?" Layne asked.

"Who?" Ryker asked back.

"Youth Minister at the Christian Church," Layne answered and the grin faded from Ryker's face and Layne watched it go scary.

"Don't know what that is," Ryker said quietly, his voice lethal. "Just know that shit ain't right."

"Have you heard something?" Layne asked.

"Everyone in the 'burg is whisperin' about it," Ryker responded. "No one likes it but no one's got a handle on it."

"Well, I'm lookin' into it and now you are too."

Ryker's grin came back. "What you got?" he asked.

"Nothin'. Just an apartment at The Brendel. Don't know if he lives there or if he visits someone there. Unit K. Apartment three. I need to know when I can get in so I need someone watching it. You need to get me intel on who the occupants are, how many there are, when they come, when they go and when I can get in to do a clean sweep. I don't wanna toss the place. I need time to do it right but I gotta know when that time'll be."

"Brendel's the 'burg's Fort Knox. Even pads on The Heritage don't have that kind of security. And even if I manage to hang out and take notes, which, bro, I don't know if you noticed but I'm not exactly the kinda guy who fades into the woodwork, especially at a place like The Brendel, ain't no way you'd get in."

"They sensor the windows not the doors," Layne replied.

"Hunh?"

"If they fucked the security at Gaines's place like they fucked the security at Roc's place, they sensored the windows on his balcony, not the doors."

"Roc?"

"My woman."

"Her name is Roc?" Ryker shook his head. "Bro, I got a good look at her and she don't look like no rock to me. Nothin' hard on her, all curves and soft."

"Her name's Raquel, and just a heads up, maybe after I have a few beers and a game of pool, I might be okay with you talkin' about my woman like that but…" Layne hesitated and gave him a look. "Wait, no, I'll *never* be okay with you talkin' about my woman like that," Layne warned.

Ryker grinned again.

Layne lost patience.

"Are you in?" he demanded.

"Never done a stakeout."

"Today's your day," Layne told him.

His cell on the desk rang as Ryker replied, "I'm on it."

Layne looked at the display to see it said, "Tripp calling".

His brows drew together. Tripp should be at football practice.

He gave Ryker a one-minute finger, took the call and put the phone to his ear.

"Hey, pal, what's up?"

"Dad," Tripp whispered and Layne's back went straight at his tone.

"Tripp, what's up?"

"I told Coach Fullerton I had to use the john," Tripp told him.

"You're callin' me to tell me—"

Tripp cut him off. "It's Rocky, Dad."

411

Layne stood instantly and walked to the monitor to switch it off, asking, "What's Rocky?"

"She'd be mad," Tripp said. "I didn't know if I should tell you, but I reckon I should tell you and this is the first chance I had to call."

"Tripp," Layne bit out.

Tripp started talking in a hurry. "I think she's gonna do somethin'. I went to her classroom after school, you know, just to say 'hi' and 'see you tonight' but I didn't go in because I heard her talkin' to Mrs. Judd."

Shit. His woman was a nut. This could be leading anywhere and with Raquel it was a crapshoot as the various degrees of bad it could be leading.

"What was she saying?" Layne asked, his eyes slicing through Ryker who was sitting, watching him, reading Layne's tone and body language and therefore on alert. Layne walked to his desk, dumped the nine millimeter in the drawer, locked the desk and grabbed his jacket from the chair.

"I don't know for sure," Tripp answered. "But it sounded like they were makin' plans to break into the management office at The Brendel for some reason."

Shit! Where it was leading was bad considering it was felonious.

Layne cocked his head to hold his phone between ear and shoulder and swung his coat over an arm.

"You did good tellin' me, pal," he told his son.

"You won't tell Roc I snitched?" Tripp asked.

"No, Tripp, our secret. I'll take care of it. See you tonight," Layne answered, taking his phone out of his shoulder and shrugging on the other side of his coat.

"Okay, cool. Later, Dad."

"Later, pal."

Layne disconnected and Ryker barked, "*What?*"

Layne headed to the door saying, "Gotta go, brother, just got word my woman is plannin' on committing a felony."

Ryker immediately unfolded his big body from the chair and followed Layne. "Shit, things aren't borin' for *you*."

"I'd pay for boring," Layne informed him of the God's honest truth.

"Trust me, bro, you wouldn't," Ryker replied as Layne opened the outer door and Ryker strode through.

Layne punched in the code to the alarm thinking that Ryker was *way* wrong.

⌣───➤

On his Harley, Ryker trailed Layne through the gates of The Brendel and then through the grounds as Layne followed the signs to the management office.

When they made it there, Layne's jaw got tight as he saw the operation was already in full swing. Josie Judd was standing outside with two young, attractive women wearing expensive suits. One was the blonde who showed Rocky her apartment. Josie was gesturing wildly with her arms toward a Jeep that was parked in front of the offices and she looked in full snit.

Layne parked outside the management office three spaces down from the Jeep that Josie and the women were standing on the sidewalk in front of, Ryker pulling up on Layne's side.

Layne got out and heard Josie shout, "Who's gonna pay for that? Hunh? I got that nail in my tire *here*! Innocently visiting my friend and the next thing I know I have a flat! I have kids to take to school! I have errands to run! I have bills to pay that *don't* include a patch job I should *not* have to get on my tire!"

Josie, apparently, was providing distraction.

Layne's eyes sliced to Ryker. "You shut that shit down in there." He jerked his head to the management office where Roc, no doubt, was breaking into file cabinets. "I'll deal with this." And he jerked his thumb toward Josie.

"Shouldn't that be the other way around?" Ryker asked and Layne gave him a look that Ryker read. If he went inside and caught his woman doing whatever she was doing, hell would be paid. It was going to be paid anyway, it just wouldn't be as bad if he had to go inside and drag her ass out.

Therefore Ryker grinned, muttered, "Gotcha," and loped off.

Layne rounded the hood of his car and approached Josie and the women and neither of the women looked his way because they were both staring at Josie who was still shouting. She did this until her eyes came to him and she didn't let on that she knew from one look at him that her best friend had just bought herself a world of pain. Instead, she approached him.

"Tanner! I'm so glad you're here!" she exclaimed, wrapping her fingers around his bicep and giving it a squeeze. "These *women*," she flung an arm out toward the women, "say there's no construction on The Brendel but *I* had no nail in my tire when I visited Rocky last night and *I* had one in my tire this mornin' *and* it was flat! I saw it my damn self when they showed me the tire so I know it wasn't an imaginary nail!"

She was good. He knew Josie didn't visit Rocky last night and he knew she had no nail in her tire but even he was half-convinced she did the first and had the second.

"Josie," Layne said but got no more out. Josie let his arm go and turned back to the women.

"The rent here is outlandish. With that kind of dough, you can *at least* sweep the streets. *At least!*" she shouted.

"I'm sorry, ma'am, but The Brendel can't take responsibility for your vehicle. We have no construction on site and you can't prove you picked up that nail on the premises. You could have picked it up anywhere," one of the women put in.

"But I didn't pick it up *anywhere*. I picked it up *here*," Josie lied and she did it loudly.

"We're sorry for your troubles but we really can't do anything to help," the woman who showed Rocky her apartment stated.

"This is outrageous!" Josie shouted.

"Josie, let's go," Layne said and grabbed her arm, pulling her to her car.

She looked up at him, giving him a swift, short shake of her head indicating she felt Rocky needed more time. Layne looked down at her, giving her a swift, short nod of his head indicting Rocky's time was definitely up. Her eyes got big and Layne's narrowed. Then she gave in.

"You haven't heard the last of this!" Josie threatened as she stomped to her car, Layne's hand still on her arm.

"I'll meet you at Roc's," he murmured after he let her go and she yanked open her car door with apparent fury.

"She's—" Josie started to whisper but Layne interrupted her.

"I'll meet you at Roc's," he repeated.

Her eyes went beyond him, they got wide again and her lips parted. Layne turned to see both the women still standing on the sidewalk outside the office watching them and rounding the building was Rocky with Ryker. Ryker's arm was draped casually around Rocky's shoulders. Rocky was wearing a face like thunder.

When Ryker and Rocky got close to the women, they both started and stared as his woman and his...whatever, walked past them.

"Yo," Ryker said to them as they stared up at him.

"Uh..." one mumbled and, in the face of all that was Ryker, the blonde who showed Rocky's apartment didn't have it together enough to speak.

Ryker's eyes cut to Layne. "She on the back of my bike or in your truck?"

"I'll go with Josie," Rocky snapped.

"Truck," Layne clipped.

Rocky glared.

Ryker led her firmly to the passenger side of Layne's truck. Layne bleeped the locks and looked back at Josie who was folding herself in her car. She bit her lip and looked up at him before she closed her door. Layne turned, nodded to the women who were looking back and forth between the four of them appearing both confused and slightly freaked out. But Layne ignored that and walked to his SUV. Ryker was "helping" Rocky into her seat while she now glared at him. When she cleared the door, Ryker shut it, turned his head to Layne and grinned his ugly grin.

"Where do we meet?" Ryker muttered when Layne got close.

"Rocky lives here, unit E, apartment three."

Ryker nodded, rounded the back of the Suburban and headed to his bike. Layne rounded the hood and got in the driver's side.

"How'd you know?" Rocky snapped the minute he cleared the frame and he knew she was pissed.

He slammed his door and turned to her, resting his forearm on the wheel and locking eyes with her.

Yep, definitely pissed.

"Sweetcheeks, advice," he stated. "Take the two minutes you got while we drive back to your place to shut down that attitude. Yeah?"

She leaned in and hissed, "Layne! You can't just—"

"Shut it down," Layne repeated.

"I don't believe you!" she shot back and his hand snaked out and hooked her around the back of the neck. He pulled her to him as he leaned in.

"Shut it down," he growled. "You do not know what you're doin'. I do this shit for a living, I know what I'm doin'. I do not need you runnin' wild, actin' like a nut, gettin' yourself into trouble. You let me handle this."

"I was trying to help," she bit out.

"If there's a time you can help, *I'll* tell you when that time is *and* what you'll be doin'. You do not go off on your own draggin' your best friend into this shit. You got caught, she got caught, you'd both be arrested."

"My brother's a cop, Layne," she reminded him.

"Yeah, sweetcheeks, but just because your brother's a cop doesn't mean you have comprehensive immunity to do any fuckin' thing you want. You do the crime, he can't do shit for you and, by the way, breaking and entering is a crime."

"I didn't *break*, I just *jimmied* and entered," she returned.

Layne let her go, looked to the gearshift and took in a deep breath.

"Layne—"

His head shot up, he pierced her with a look and she clamped her mouth shut.

Then Layne asked, "How much does Josie know?"

Rocky's eyes slid to the dashboard but her face stayed turned to him.

"Roc," he prompted and her eyes slid back.

"I let her in on the whole operation," she whispered.

"Fuck," he clipped low.

"*She* was the one who talked to *me* about it!" Rocky defended herself hotly. "She's heard things about TJ Gaines too. She saw us at church on Sunday and she figured we were up to something and she's been calling, like, every day to find out what's going on. She guessed and offered to help. I couldn't say no."

"Yeah," Layne replied quietly. "Yeah, you could say no."

"She's my best friend!" Rocky cried.

"Well, that's good. Least she'd be there to have your back when some rough chick in lockdown made the move to make you her bitch and you'd be able to return the favor."

Rocky rolled her eyes. "That would hardly—"

"Sweetcheeks," Layne growled, she shut up and glared at him but didn't say more.

The silence lengthened as they went into stare down.

Layne didn't have time for it so he broke it by saying softly, "You earned a spanking with this shit, baby." He watched her lids lower and her mouth get soft and he liked it but he was too pissed to let it penetrate so he went on, "No, Roc, seriously, this shit means I'm gonna tan your ass."

Her soft look disappeared and she whispered, "You do that, Layne, we have problems."

"Sweetcheeks, we *already* have problems," he pointed out the obvious, turned to the wheel, slid in his key and started the truck.

Rocky was silent as he backed out of his spot and drove to her apartment. Josie's Jeep was in one of Rocky's slots, Roc's Merc in another and Layne pulled in between them. Ryker's Harley was not in sight, which likely meant that, since he'd breached The Brendel's outer fortress, he was scouting the lay of the land.

Rocky was out of the SUV before he switched it off and she was hoofing it across the street toward the stairs. Josie was standing at the top, waiting for them. Layne took his time following his woman and he did this in an effort at gathering patience. Rocky and Josie were both in the apartment by the time he entered.

"Do you want a drink?" He heard Rocky asking Josie.

"Love one, hon, but you know Chip's a dinner-on-the-table-at-five-thirty-sharp type of guy. I gotta get home and start cookin'," Josie answered then asked, "You find anything?"

During this exchange, Layne took off his jacket and threw it on the armchair. By the time he turned, Josie was finished speaking and Rocky was standing in the kitchen.

Her eyes flashed to him as she answered her friend, "*No*, I was *interrupted*."

"So all that was for nothing?" Josie asked and while she did, she turned to pin him with an angry woman glare too.

Layne crossed his arms on his chest. "Tell me, Cagney and Lacey, what were you looking for?"

"Rental agreements," Rocky returned instantly.

"On what?" Layne shot back.

"On an apartment, *Layne*," Rocky retorted with deep sarcasm.

"What apartment?" Layne asked and Rocky's head jerked slightly.

"Sorry?"

"What apartment, sweetcheeks? I didn't tell you which unit he was in and I already told you he's got nothin' in the name of TJ Gaines in this 'burg. So how, exactly, were you gonna find an agreement when you didn't know what fuckin' agreement you were lookin' for?" He watched her glare turn even angrier as he pointed out her incompetence. He ignored it and continued. "There's fifteen units in this complex, forty-five apartments, not counting the twenty townhomes. Every unit occupied. Were you gonna copy them all?"

"I would have thought of something," she replied sharply. "Except I barely got through the window before Scary Biker Bob interrupted the proceedings."

"Count yourself lucky Ryker was with me, Roc. He thinks this is amusing. *I* do *not*."

Rocky gave him a long, last glare then turned to Josie. "You know how I was telling you the other day that getting back together with Layne was like someone had answered my prayers?" she asked conversationally and Layne's chest froze.

"Unh-hunh," Josie answered on a mumble, her eyes darting back and forth between Rocky and Layne.

"Well, I take that back," Rocky snapped.

Layne looked at his boots as Josie asked, "Do I need to take Rocky into protective custody?"

Layne looked at Josie. "It'd be smart, but I'm not gonna let you do it."

Josie studied Layne awhile then she grinned. "I expect punishment won't be too harsh."

She probably wasn't wrong about that.

Probably.

"Anyhoots!" Josie suddenly cried. "I gotta go." She hitched her purse more firmly on her shoulder. "Even though the operation was a bust, it was fun anyway since The Brendel didn't hire Chip to do their security and brought in a firm outside the 'burg, which is *way* uncool and meant I couldn't have that trip to Hawaii I was planning after he put in his bid." She started to the door but she did it with her torso twisted to Rocky. "See you at the game tomorrow?"

"Maybe," Rocky replied. "I'll want to see Tripp and Jas play but I won't want to be anywhere *near* their father so I'm undecided as to my plans tomorrow night."

Layne's neck got tight but Josie smiled like she was trying not to laugh and replied, "Okay, see you at the game then."

At any other time, Layne would have laughed. At that time, Layne didn't laugh.

Josie had the door opened and was standing in it when she delivered her parting shot and she did it to Layne.

"She's worried," Josie stated quietly. "They're young girls and she's worried. Yeah?"

She finished on a question but didn't wait for his answer. She knew she'd driven her point home. She just stepped through the door and closed it behind her.

Layne's eyes cut to Rocky who was moving around the kitchen but she wasn't ignoring him. He knew this when she spoke.

"I have things to do tonight. Go to the grocery store, grade papers, make some calls about the bachelor auction, stuff like that." She pulled the coffeepot out of the coffeemaker and went to the sink to rinse it. "I'll give your house a miss again."

"Roc," he called and she picked up some plastic thing filled with yellow dish liquid and swirled its sponge around the pot. What she didn't do was respond.

"Roc," he called again and she rinsed the soap out of the pot and upended it in the dish drainer.

Layne walked to the bar separating the kitchen from the living room.

"Sweetcheeks, eyes to me," he ordered quietly.

She turned off the sink, leaned to the side, grabbed a dish towel and turned, drying her hands with the towel. Her eyes hit him and her brows went up.

Layne spoke. "Cosgrove got word from three colleges they wanted to talk to Jasper. He didn't pass on those messages."

Her brows lowered, her lips parted, and she started to look concerned as she tossed the towel on the counter behind her.

Layne continued, "It's time I started focusing on Rutledge again but I don't have that time because I gotta work to pay my bills. I also gotta keep an eye on Stew and Gabby's house. It's likely that fuckwad is gone and Colt's lookin' into shit, but she goes home tomorrow and my boys go back to her tomorrow so I can't lose track of what's goin' on there. I gotta keep sharp about Cosgrove because he's thrown down, fucked with Jas and he's the kinda man who won't see his shortcomings and understand he brought all this shit on himself. He'll make someone pay. I reckon that'll be Paige and Seth, Jasper or you. And I got nothin' on Gaines except I know what he drives, I know where he went last night, and I know he's gotta be shut down. Both my boys are out there on this and somehow, Rutledge, a dirty cop who's makin' the department look bad enough that pretty soon the chief's gonna get his head outta his ass and figure out what's goin' on. He's gonna step in and he's gonna fuck it all up because he got to be chief not by bein' a good cop but by bein' good at playin' politics. But my boys and my woman come first. You want Gaines, and Tripp and Jas are seriously tied up in *all* this shit and I gotta have their backs."

She stared at him and he knew she was no longer pissed but she wasn't ready to let it go either.

So Layne went on, his voice soft.

"I love you, baby, and part of why I love you is because you're worried and you'd do something about it. Any other time this shit you pulled would be cute. Now it isn't because I don't have time to have *your* back *and* my boys' *and* get the shit I need done, done. I was gonna run Gaines's plates this afternoon but I couldn't because I'm here." Her face had changed completely, eyes half-mast, mouth soft and Layne knew he'd gotten to her. "So, help me out in a way that actually helps me out. Be there for me and be smart. Those are the only two things you gotta do, easy enough for you, but they'd mean a lot to me."

The instant he was done talking, Rocky spoke. "You love me?"

Layne's head moved to the side. "What?"

"You said you love me," she told him.

Layne stared at her and replied, "Well...yeah."

"You love me," she whispered, her eyes still hooded but they were intense and Layne felt his chest freeze again.

"Baby, what do you think we're doin' here?" he whispered back.

She shook her head.

"You ever fall out of love with me?" he asked softly.

"No," she whispered and it sounded like she struggled to get that one word out. But Layne didn't care, that one word meant everything to him.

"That feeling is definitely mutual, honey."

She held his gaze one beat, two, three then she sucked in breath, her eyes filled with tears and she looked down and to the side.

Layne moved around the bar, walked to her and pulled her into his arms. Rocky didn't resist, slid her arms around his waist and held on, twisting her neck and pressing her cheek in his chest.

He dipped his chin and put his lips to her hair. "This," he said there, "this right now answered more than just your prayers, Rocky."

He heard her breath hitch as her body jolted with a fresh wave of tears and she held on tighter with her arms and pressed her body deep into his.

He lifted a hand and pulled her ponytail holder out of her hair then ran his fingers through its length and he kept doing it as he listened to her cry.

When her tears quieted, he whispered, "Ma's making beef tenderloin tonight."

Her head jerked back and his lifted up as she looked at him with wet eyes that apparently were ringed with lashes coated with waterproof mascara. They were spiky with wet but her cheeks weren't streaming with black.

"Beef tenderloin?" she asked quietly, knowing exactly what that meant. Layne liked Vera's beef tenderloin but Rocky loved it. She knew Vera wouldn't make it if things weren't good.

"We had a chat," Layne answered, she melted even deeper into him, dropped her chin and rested her forehead against his chest.

"I like Vera's tenderloin," she whispered there.

"I'm bringin' home cones and ice cream."

Rocky's head jerked back again. She looked startled a second then she let out a little giggle.

"You're impossible." She was still whispering and he grinned.

"Promise me you're done with this shit, I'll take watchin' you eat a cone and then, later, watchin' you wrap your hand around my cock and lickin' it as payback for savin' your ass instead of tannin' it." The softness went out of her face and she started to pull back but his hand went out of her hair and both his arms got tight around her. "Promise me, Rocky."

She tried to go into stare down but he knew she didn't have it in her when she muttered, "Oh, all right."

"Is that a promise?" Layne pushed.

"Yes," she snapped.

"All of it?"

Her head tipped to the side. "What?"

"No more stupid shit."

She pulled her arms from around him and put her hands on his chest but she replied, "No more stupid shit."

"And you eat dessert tonight," he pressed.

"Fine," she snapped.

"Then you eat me later."

"Fine!" she repeated, still snapping and still not meaning it, and he smiled.

"Don't pretend you don't like it as much as me, sweetcheeks."

"Um, I think you like it more than me, Layne."

She wasn't wrong about that.

He didn't confirm, he ordered, "Now kiss me good-bye. I gotta get back to the office and run those plates and you need to get your ass to my house so Ma can get a headstart on makin' amends."

"You missed one more thing *you* need to do and that's quit bossing me around."

He kept smiling. "Baby, what in all that isn't good for you?"

"The part where you boss me around, that's the part not good for me."

Layne still kept smiling. "Quit bitchin' and kiss me."

"Layne—"

"Sweetcheeks, kiss me."

"If you're so busy, maybe you should—"

Layne shut her up by kissing her.

Rocky was nursing a snit but still…she kissed him back.

⌒⟶

Layne's shoulders were to the headboard, his legs were spread, knees bent to the ceiling, his hands were in Rocky's hair and his eyes were glued to her mouth working his cock.

Damn, but he liked her mouth.

But he didn't want to come in her mouth. He wanted to come in her pussy.

"Baby, get up here," he growled and her eyes went to him but her mouth stayed where it was, her fingers wrapped tight around him and he watched her swirl the tip with her tongue.

Fuck. Beautiful. Everything about it. Her hand, her tongue, her hair framing her face and all over his lap, and her eyes telling him exactly how turned on she was.

"Get up here," he repeated and she bent to him, taking him deep one last time and sucking hard as she slid back up.

Jesus. Fucking beautiful.

Layne closed his eyes and gritted his teeth.

Rocky's mouth released his cock, he opened his eyes and watched as she crawled up his body to straddling him and pressed her tits to his chest, her face to his neck and he felt her tongue there.

"Climb on, baby," he grunted, needing to be inside her and she didn't hesitate.

She reached between them, wrapped him again with her fist and guided him inside, sitting up and filling herself, her head dropping back, her back arching, her nails dragging his chest and she moaned.

Heaven.

One of his hands went to her hip, the other one cupped her breast as he ordered in a thick voice, "Ride me."

She needed no coaxing. She moved, not slow—fast, hard. She was primed, so fucking hot, so wet, taking him deep as he rolled her nipple between his fingers and watched his woman drive herself down on his cock over and over.

When he was close and she was closer, he sat up, both his arms going around her, and he demanded, "Mouth on mine, baby."

She tipped her head down and did as she was told, moving on him and breathing into his mouth, "Layne, baby, you feel so good."

"Faster, Rocky," he urged and she did as he asked, the noises coming from her throat telling him where she was at.

One of his arms slid up her back and his fingers tangled in her hair, fisting. He held her mouth to his as his other arm moved and then he smacked her, hard, on the ass.

Her body jerked and her head jolted against his hold but he kept it stationary.

"You gonna be my good girl?" he whispered.

"Layne," she breathed and he liked that, fuck, he liked that. It went straight to his cock.

He smacked her ass again, her body jerked again and then she started riding him harder. She liked this, his Rocky.

"You gonna be my good girl?" he repeated and smacked her ass again.

Rocky moaned into his mouth, her hand slid to his neck, fingers digging in, her other arm around his back, and she started fucking him hot and hard and really fucking fast.

He smacked her ass again. "Rocky—"

"Yes," she breathed into his mouth. "Yes, Layne, I'll be your good girl."

Then she slammed down on his cock, ground into him and her head shot back so fiercely it took his hand with it and she moaned deep as her pussy convulsed around him.

He whipped her to her back and drove into her, his mouth on hers, taking her moans and whimpers while she absorbed his grunts, riding her until his world exploded and he poured himself into Rocky.

After he came down, he stayed rooted inside her and ran his nose, his lips and his tongue along her neck, ear and jaw, and she held him safe, wrapped tight in all four of her limbs.

When he had his face in her neck, she turned her head, and in his ear, whispered, "Love you, Layne."

Layne stayed where he was, still and unmoving as he let the golden trail of her words glide through him. Then he lifted his head and looked at Raquel, her hair spread out on his bed, her face gentle, her pussy still hot and wet, her body soft under his and he whispered back, "Love you too, baby."

He dipped his head and kissed her, not hard, but long, his tongue sliding in her mouth, tasting her, so sweet, and she gave, even sweeter, until he broke off the kiss, sliding his nose alongside hers.

"I gotta go clean up," she whispered.

"I'll be here," he replied, pulled out and rolled off her.

He watched her move gracefully from the bed, find his tee, and she tugged it on as she moved to the bathroom.

Layne got under the covers and rested against the headboard, listening to Rocky in his bathroom. He was thinking they could move the entirety of her living room furniture in his room, when she walked out and wandered to his bed, her strut fluid and lazy and he liked it more knowing the laziness came from the orgasm he just gave her.

She pulled back the covers and climbed in, scooting over until she settled with her cheek to his chest, her arm around him, she tangled a leg with his. He pushed his arm under her, pulled up her tee and cupped her bared ass with his hand.

That was new too. If he fucked her, she slept without underwear. She didn't used to do that.

He liked it.

He moved and turned out the lamp on the nightstand, plunging the room into blackness but she didn't make a noise.

He settled back and ran his hand over the cheek of her ass. "Did I hit you too hard?" he murmured.

She shook her head slightly against his chest, her arm getting tight a second and she mumbled, "Unh-unh."

He grinned in the dark. "You liked it."

It was a statement.

She didn't respond except to curl deeper into him which *was* her response. She liked it.

"I dream of you," he told her and *that* caused a response. Her head came up and she looked at him through the dark.

"What?" she asked.

"After you came to visit me in the hospital, I started dreaming of you. Every night. Even when I was in the hospital, I dreamed of you. I still do."

"Really?" she whispered.

"Yep," he replied.

"Wow," she breathed and his hand moved to find her face. Cupping her jaw, he pulled her up as his neck bent. Then he touched his lips to hers.

After, he said softly, "Yeah, wow. More than wow, sweetcheeks. In my dreams, we're almost always fucking."

Her head moved back an inch and her hand slid up his chest to curl her fingers where his shoulder met his neck.

"Really?" she repeated.

"Oh yeah," he whispered.

"Is it good?" she asked.

"Yeah, it's good. As good as what we just did, not by a long shot, but it's good. I haven't dreamed of us having sex since you came back, but I still dream of you. You talk to me."

Her body got tight and she asked, "Talk to you?"

"Yeah."

"What do I say?"

"You wake me up. Tell me you need to get to work. The two times I was at your place, you told me to get home to my boys."

"That's it?"

"Yep."

She relaxed then asked, "Why?"

"What?"

"Why?" Rocky repeated. "Why are you dreaming of me?"

"No clue," Layne answered. "But I like havin' you here and there." He pulled her face to his until their lips were touching. "Best of both worlds."

He felt her smile then he kissed her lightly, released her jaw and she moved down to rest against his chest again.

"So, you going to tell me what you learned with your search?" she prompted.

After he'd kissed her at her place, he'd rendezvoused with Ryker, who was waiting by Layne's truck. Ryker had told Layne he'd scoped out unit K, apartment three and assured him he was "on the job" then took off on his Harley. Layne went to the office, ran his searches, ran more because of the results and got home in time for his mother to lecture him on punctuality and courtesy. Since dinner was ready, Keira was there again and Devin was home and visibly salivating to tuck into beef tenderloin, Layne hadn't had a chance to brief Rocky.

He did get the chance to watch her eat an ice cream cone and therefore they went to bed early.

"Both cars are registered to a woman," Layne told her. "Victoria Aubry."

"Victoria Aubry," Rocky whispered.

"You heard that name?" Layne asked and she shook her head against his chest, so he went on. "She rents the apartment too. She's also married to a man named Baxter Aubry."

Her head came up and he felt her eyes on him through the dark. "Who's that?"

"Driver's license picture in the system shows he's TJ Gaines."

"Oh my," she breathed.

"Yep," he replied.

"What else?" she prompted.

"Nothin'," Layne said and Rocky was silent.

Then she asked, "Nothing?"

"Not one fuckin' thing. Both of them came into existence about nine months ago. I've run every check there is, couldn't find anything. They got credit cards, bank accounts, own their cars outright, pay their insurance, rent, utilities on time, except they do it with cash. Only thing they pay with check is the credit cards which, even though they live high, are cleared every month."

"What does this tell you?" she asked.

"Well, seein' as I dug deeper and found Victoria Aubry died of a stroke at age eighty-two six years ago and her husband Baxter Aubry died a year and a half later of emphysema, it tells me the least those two are guilty of is identity theft."

"Shit," she whispered.

"Other than that, not much else," Layne finished.

"What's next?"

"What's next is, we need a fuckin' print. For both of 'em."

"Right," she said softly.

"Baby," he called and her arm squeezed him in response. "Goes without sayin' it won't be you gettin' those prints."

Rocky's body tensed and her voice was terse when she said, "Of course."

Layne slid down into the bed, taking her with him and rolling them both to their sides so they were face to face, but his hand didn't leave her ass and he gripped it when he murmured, "Just makin' sure you stay my good girl."

He felt her body give a small jerk before she relaxed into him and kissed his throat.

"I'm still your good girl," she whispered there.

"Good," he whispered back.

Her face came out of his throat and her head settled on the pillow. "Isn't that enough?" she asked. "Identity theft is bad, even if people are dead. Can't you hand it over to Merry now, get him away from those girls?"

"Yep," Layne answered.

"Are you going to do that?"

"Yep, Merry or Colt or Sully or Mike, whoever I get to first."

"Excellent," she replied quietly.

"One problem with that, sweetcheeks," Layne told her.

"What?"

"There's somethin' bigger here, somethin' we don't know. They got a shitload of money in the bank. They live high. She's got a nice car. His is less than a year old, middle of the road but top of the line of its model. She's either into somethin' or they're bankrolled."

"So?"

"So, a weed grows, you don't pull off its leaves, you yank out the root. My gut tells me there's a big man pullin' their strings and that man's gotta go down so this stops. Not only here but everywhere."

"But the girls—"

"I'll take care of the girls," Layne assured her.

"How?"

"People like this, they got one allegiance. It isn't to the head honcho. It isn't even to money. It's to themselves. If they know they're fucked, they'll play."

"Sorry?"

"We turn 'em."

"Layne, I'm not getting—"

"We get to them, get them to make a deal. In exchange for reduced jail time, they give us the big man, and in the meantime, stop whatever shit they're doin' with the girls."

She was silent a second before she said, "Oh." Then she shared her news. "Rumor in the halls is Seth is taking Alexis McGraw out for pizza after the game tomorrow."

Layne grinned.

Rocky continued, "And word today was Youth Group attendance spiked last night. It's become the hot, in thing to go and see what the Layne boys are up to. Apparently, Jasper, Seth and their friend Mitch didn't disappoint, and TJ-slash-Baxter had his hands full attempting to explain how there could be dinosaurs *and* Adam and Eve. Not to mention, since half the football team was there, it's becoming the hot spot to see and be seen, pick up chicks and socialize. It sounded to me like Wednesday's Youth Group meeting was half single's club and half philosophical debate on religion, both of which TJ-slash-Baxter didn't have the tools to deal with."

Layne's grin turned into a smile. He'd seen himself the number of kids who'd walked out, and it wasn't sixty. It was more like eighty or higher. Jasper had been at work, which was good. Part of Gaines's advantage was that there were concerns voiced in whispers but no action. The more attention Youth Group had, the more parents would start waking up and asking questions and not in whispers, especially when Christian Youth Group became a single's club for teenagers and an opportunity to jack around. It would be hard to recruit young girls for whatever he needed them for when they were more interested in the football team and when your attention was diverted by questions about creationism to which you probably didn't have the answers and with angry parents breathing down your neck.

"Ryker's surveilling the apartment," Layne told Rocky. "We'll see what he gets and if he can find a time when I can get in there. I'll get prints, get someone at the station to run them and have a sit down with the boys." He gave her a squeeze and murmured, "This'll be over soon, baby."

Rocky burrowed into him and murmured back, "I hope so, Layne."

"It will. Swear," he promised.

She didn't respond and Layne was about to roll to his back so she could pin him to the bed when she called softly, "Layne?"

"Yeah, sweetcheeks."

He heard her hair move on the pillow.

"In your dreams..." she started then trailed off.

"Yeah?" he prompted.

"You said it's good?"

Layne knew where this was going and he grinned.

"Yeah, it's good."

"What..." she paused. "What do we do?"

Layne didn't hesitate. He rolled into her so he was on top of her.

"Layne?"

He found her mouth with his. "Show you," he muttered, his hands sliding up her sides, taking the tee with it. She lifted her arms. He pulled it off and tossed it away. Then his mouth went back to hers. "Hold on to the slats in the headboard and don't let go."

"What?" she breathed.

"Hold on to the slats in the headboard and don't let go, no matter what."

"No matter what?"

"No matter what. Promise."

"Layne."

Breathy. Beautiful. Jesus, he just came and his cock was already starting to get hard.

"Hands to the slats, baby, keep them there, no matter what." She hesitated only a moment before she moved. Her arms lifting, she grabbed onto the headboard. "That's my good girl," he muttered against her mouth. "Promise to hold on."

"I promise," she whispered and he kissed her.

Then Layne experienced the best of both worlds at the same time.

And it was unbelievably sweet.

Twenty-One

DON'T GET DEAD

She moved against him, he felt her sliding up and both his arms went around her.

He turned his head just in time for her lips to hit his.

But she didn't kiss him.

Instead, she whispered, "This is the beginning."

His eyes opened, looking into hers.

"Yeah, baby," he whispered back and watched her eyes darken, sorrow and fear mixing in them before she went on.

"The beginning of the end."

Then his arms were empty.

She was gone.

⌒

Layne's eyes opened, his body tense, and he stared at the ceiling.

Rocky was dead asleep against him, her arm a heavy weight on his gut, her knee cocked, thigh on his, he could feel her hair on his chest.

It was a dream.

"Christ," he whispered, his hand moving up her back, fingers sliding in her thick, soft hair.

She didn't rouse, didn't even move, didn't make a noise. She was out.

He turned his head to the side and looked at the clock. It was six twenty-nine. She didn't wake him early this time.

He was still looking at the clock when the digits changed and the buzzer sounded loud. Rocky's body twitched then she pulled up to an elbow, her other hand going to her hair and moving it from her face.

"An alarm," she whispered into the dark room. "God, I forgot what that sounded like." Then she plopped back down, landing on his chest, her arm going back around him and curling tight as Layne's arm moved out to hit the off button. "Can we snooze?"

Layne hit the snooze button instead, the buzzer died and he replied, "Yeah, baby, when do you need to get up?"

"Quarter to," she muttered, snuggling into him.

Layne was surprised. She was always out of bed early, considering it took her an age to get ready. Maybe she had a late start today.

"Quarter to seven?" he asked, just to be sure.

"Six," she mumbled.

"Baby, it's already six thirty," he replied and her body tensed.

She shot back up to her elbow and peered at the clock.

"*Fuck!*" she hissed, threw the covers back and crawled over him. "Fuck!" she repeated and darted from the bed.

"Roc," he called as she raced across his room.

"I'm late!" she cried, the bathroom light went on and she disappeared.

Layne didn't move. He lay in bed trying to shake off the dream.

It was nothing, he told himself. Just a dream. It wasn't surprising he had it. Things were good. Rocky was back. He was happy. But he'd had that before and it had gone bad before. He knew that subconsciously just as much as consciously. It would fuck with his head and it was. He had to find a way to sort her out, and until then he just had to deal.

He was out of bed and tugging on a pair of pajama bottoms when he heard the faucet go on in the bathroom and he headed that way.

Rocky was in his tee, her hair in a messy knot at the top of her head, standing at his sink brushing her teeth.

He leaned against the arched doorway, her neck twisted and her eyes came to his.

"Do me a favor?" he asked. Her eyebrows went up but she kept brushing and he went on, "Kiss me before you leave my bed."

She took the toothbrush out of her mouth as her brows drew together. "Wha'? Why?" she asked, her mouth full of foam.

"Just do me that favor," he answered.

She stared at him a second, bent and spit then looked back at him. "You okay?"

He gave it to her honest. "My dream wasn't so good this morning."

Layne watched some of the color run out of her face. "What?"

"My dream, about you, it wasn't so good this morning."

Her gaze didn't leave him for three beats then she turned, bent over the faucet, rinsed out her mouth, turned off the faucet and grabbed the towel from the holder. She wiped her mouth and dried her hand then came to him. She put a hand on his chest and leaned in.

"What happened?" she asked.

"Sweetcheeks, you're late," he reminded her.

"Yeah," she replied but didn't move except to fit herself to his front and curl the fingers of her other hand at his waist. "What happened?"

Layne put both hands to her hips. "You gotta get a move on."

"In a minute, tell me about the dream."

"It's just a dream."

"Tell me about it."

"Rocky."

"Layne."

He looked down at her seeing she was prepared to go into stare down if she had to. Therefore his arms curved around her, one staying at her waist, the other one drifting up her back, her exposed neck, to glide his fingers in her pulled up hair.

"You woke me up, in the dream, to tell me it was the beginning of the end," he told her.

Her eyes stayed locked to his then her chin dipped and she pressed her forehead against his chest.

His hand cupped the back of her head. "It's just a dream."

"I did that," she told his chest.

"What?"

She tipped her head back again and repeated, "I did that."

"Did what?"

Instead of answering his question, she informed him, "That freaked you out."

"Like I said, Roc, it's just a dream."

"Right," she whispered, her hand at his waist curling around his back and her hand at his chest sliding up so she could wrap her fingers around his neck. "Just a dream that made you get that look you've got right now and tell me to kiss you before I get out of bed."

"Not an odd request, sweetcheeks."

"I've been waking up next to you awhile, Layne. You've not made it before."

"Until this morning, I didn't need to." And this was true. He'd fucked her every morning she'd been back in his bed for real, and the one he'd woken up in hers, excepting the morning his mother had come calling.

She held his eyes and didn't respond. Then she lifted up on her toes and touched her mouth to his.

She moved back barely an inch to whisper, "I'll kiss you before I leave your bed, sweetheart. Promise."

"Thanks, baby," he whispered back.

Her arm and hand gave him a squeeze, she lifted up to touch her mouth to his again then she pulled away and moved to the faucet.

Layne watched her start to wash her face, his eyes moving around the basin, seeing all her stuff scattered there. All of her stuff around *his* sink. She didn't claim the other one, she used his.

Or you hold it so close, it can't ever go away. But, if it does, you got as many precious memories as you can bag. Devin had said.

You hold it so close...

You hold it so close...

Rocky rinsed her face, Layne still watching, knowing, using his sink instead of claiming her own, it was one of the ways Rocky was holding him close. Being at his sink, around his shit, just his toothbrush, his razor, but she was holding him close, even with little shit like that.

Holding him close.

He let that settle, and doing it, he let the after-effects of the troubling dream slide away. He moved in behind her and kissed the skin at the nape of her neck.

Then he went to the toilet.

⟋⟍

He opened the door to the Suburban just as his phone rang. He jumped down and held the door for Blondie to trundle out behind him as he pulled the phone out of his pocket, looked at the display, took the call and put the phone to his ear.

"Hey, sweetcheeks," he greeted.

It was third period time. She had it free so she could make calls. Even so, he was mildly surprised to get one since this was the first time she'd called since that day he'd visited her at the school to tell her what he found out about Gaines.

"Hey, baby," she whispered back in a breathy voice.

Hearing it, Layne decided that the next favor he was going to ask of her was that she call him on her free period every day.

But he'd do it later. Now, he wanted to know why she was calling.

He slammed the door to his truck and, with Blondie beside him, he walked up the sidewalk toward Mimi's.

"What's up?" he asked.

"Just wanted to tell you that the girls are having a Bachelor Auction Powwow tomorrow afternoon at my apartment. Is that cool with you?"

"Yeah, you comin' over after?"

"No, I thought I'd make you dinner at my place and you can stay the night with me."

He smiled into the phone as he opened the door to Mimi's and walked in, leaving Blondie outside. "Works for me."

"Anything special you want?" she asked.

"Surprise me," he answered.

"I can do that," she replied.

"Just a sec, sweetcheeks," Layne said into the phone then ordered from one of Mimi's employees, a kid with three piercings in her bottom lip, two in her nose, one in her eyebrow and she had pink hair.

Layne didn't understand piercing nor did he find it attractive and it went without saying that pink hair was not his gig. But this kid had made him coffee before and she was even better at it than Meems, which was saying something. She also had a great smile and she learned his name early and used it whenever she had occasion to do so, making him feel a member of the Mimi's Coffee House Family. This was a nice touch and the way she did it was real, not ingratiating. Therefore, he found he liked her hair and didn't mind the piercings because under all that shit was a genuine person, not one who wanted attention. Just one who got off on that shit.

To each their own.

He went back to Rocky after he got his, "What'll it be this time, Tanner?" he'd placed his order and as he pulled out his wallet to pay.

"You get to work on time?" he asked Raquel.

"Ten minutes late but no one noticed since Adrian was in and cleaning out his office with Principal Klausen and Nick Fullerton in attendance, so everyone was jabbering about that."

"You see him?" Layne asked.

"No, Sharon told me about it then I went to my room. I'm thinking avoiding Adrian Cosgrove is a good strategy."

There she was, his good girl.

"You'd be right," he told her.

"Did you set a meeting with one of the boys?"

He had, with Colt. Merry still wasn't returning his calls even though the subject of his messages had changed. Dave now also wasn't picking up, even on the home phone which didn't have caller ID and this meant he was making it his mission to avoid Layne. So it was Colt and it was also a study in patience not to hunt the Merrick men down and get in their faces.

"Colt, he's comin' to my office in half an hour," Layne answered.

"Good," Rocky replied.

Layne had paid and was standing at the other end of the counter waiting for his coffee when he heard Blondie bark three times and his head turned to the door to see Ryker come in. And it was a Ryker with a serious look on his face, and this look was aimed with pinpoint precision at Layne.

Layne held Ryker's eyes as Ryker stalked through the coffee shop toward him.

"Baby, gotta go," Layne said into the phone. "Ryker's here."

"Oh, okay," she replied. "Are we still going to the game tonight?"

"Yeah," Layne answered. "I'll pick you up. Get a snack, sweetcheeks, we're havin' pizza and beer at your place after."

"Oh, okay," she repeated, this time softer, breathy again. She remembered weeks ago. She liked what they shared weeks ago. She wanted it back and she wanted it to have a different ending, just like him.

"We gotta talk," Ryker growled.

He'd made it to Layne, he was impatient and Layne nodded.

"Be at your place at seven," Layne said to Rocky.

"All right, sweetheart, see you then," Rocky replied.

"Later, baby."

"Later."

He shoved his phone in his pocket and asked Ryker, "You want a coffee?"

"We gotta talk," Ryker repeated.

Layne studied him until his coffee was up. He grabbed it and led the way out of Mimi's. Blondie barked at Ryker again but followed close to Layne the short distance to his office, not taking her eyes off Ryker and not leaving her man. She didn't know what to make of Ryker and she wasn't sure what she was reading from Layne, but she did know what she was reading from Ryker, so she was being vigilant.

Layne let them into his office and he'd barely taken off his coat and settled in his chair, Blondie sitting sentry beside his desk, when Ryker spoke.

He was sitting across from Layne and his posture wasn't lazy. It was alert to the point of being wired.

"You used to be a cop," Ryker stated bizarrely, this not being the opening Layne expected, not that he knew what to expect.

"Yeah," Layne returned guardedly.

"On the 'burg's PD," Ryker growled and Layne studied him a moment before he nodded. "Still close with those pigs?" he asked and Layne's neck muscles contracted.

"Yeah, Ryker, I am and you already know that. I gave that comment a pass once, but heads up now that I'm not a big fan of my boys bein' called pigs and I'm not likely gonna give that comment a pass again," Layne replied softly.

"They're pigs," Ryker shot back, and Layne leaned forward, not a deep lean, enough to show Ryker he, too, was on alert and he was losing patience.

"I get you're a badass, Ryker, but this is my place, my office. You show respect here. Do you get me?"

Ryker didn't hesitate before he went on, "One of 'em in particular."

Layne stared at him, understanding, and he went hyper-alert.

Then he growled, "Stop fuckin' around. What's got you tweaked?"

"My babe's got a daughter," he stated.

"And?" Layne prompted.

"Name's Alexis," Ryker told him.

Holy fuck.

It was Ryker's turn to study him and he did, then he nodded. "I think you get why I was willin' to be all over that shit."

"Talk to me," Layne ordered low.

"Yesterday, last night, this mornin', I was all over that shit," Ryker said.

"What'd you get?"

"Man and woman, comin' and goin', no schedule, but they're both busy. The Youth Minister and his woman. Though, not sure she's his woman. They walked to their cars together, no touchin', just talkin'. He's either whipped or she's the one with the balls. He's not the big man with her. She was the one with the 'tude. She threw a stick and told him to fetch, he'd run."

When he stopped talking, Layne urged, "Keep goin'."

"Late night visit, bro, around eleven thirty, one of the tenants of The Brendel took a walk."

Layne's entire body got tight but he didn't say a word.

He didn't have to. He knew it when Ryker stated, "You get me."

He got him. Rutledge.

Rutledge went to church every Sunday. Rutledge lived at The Brendel. Gaines acted like he was untouchable because he was. He had a dirty cop in his pocket, or, more to the point, whoever the woman was, she did.

Ryker leaned forward. "You tell your boys at the pig factory about this shit, you got problems…with me. This shit *we* work, you and me." He lifted a big hand and motioned between the two of them. "The cops aren't in this."

"Only dirty cop in that department is the one you saw."

"You sure about that?" Ryker asked.

"Yeah," Layne answered.

"Well, I'm not," Ryker returned. "My guess, that shit comes down from the top."

"The captain?" Layne asked.

"He's so dirty, he stinks."

"He's not dirty, Ryker. He's ambitious, blinded by it."

"Like I said, dirty," Ryker retorted.

Layne rolled his chair to the desk, leaned his forearms into it and laid it out.

"This is my investigation. I don't like partners, especially partners who keep shit from me, like their woman's daughter bein' a favorite of the guy I'm investigating. That said, I'll work with one when it suits me. Even though it's uncool you kept that shit from me, workin' with you suits me. Needless to say, seein' as I don't like partners, I don't like men takin' over my investigations. I got shit invested in this. I got a plan. We're workin' this my way."

"You got a girl who's got that assclown under her skin?" Ryker shot back and before Layne could answer, Ryker did it for him. "No, you don't. My babe's worried but she don't wanna upset Alexis. Alexis' dad is a dickhead. Always cancelin' on his weekends, breaks Alexis' heart. He pays child support about once every six months, if Lissa's lucky. She don't have a lot and she can't give Alexis a lot, but she works her ass off to give her what she can and that means Alexis don't see her mom much either. Alexis likes this Youth Group. She likes this guy and has friends there. Alexis hasn't found much she likes. Lissa wants her to have what she wants. We been talkin' 'bout that shit and she's been callin' me down, but I been meanin' to look into it for a while. Now, I'm lookin' into it."

Layne got where Ryker's woman Lissa was coming from and also where Ryker was coming from.

Even so, it didn't matter. "You shouldn't have hesitated. Now it's too late, the wheels are in motion, both my boys are caught up in it and I'm not gonna have you jack them up."

Ryker stared at him then sat back and whispered, "Cosgrove."

"Come again?" Layne asked.

"Alexis has a date tonight, her first, with Seth Cosgrove. You set that up?"

Layne didn't answer.

"Only thing would get her out from under that fuckwad is Cosgrove. Alexis won't shut up about him. She thinks that Youth Minister is the shit but she thinks the sun shines outta Seth Cosgrove's ass," Ryker told him.

"Lissa religious?" Layne asked.

"She prays but she don't pray to a God in a house that let a jackal in," Ryker answered.

"Then she needs to suck it up. You and I both know that is not a good place for Alexis to be. Alexis freaks, she freaks. But get your woman to pull her daughter's ass outta there," Layne advised.

"That ain't gonna work. Alexis is a handful."

"Then you step in."

"Not my place."

"You bangin' her mom?" Layne asked and Ryker's jaw got tight.

"Not my place," Ryker repeated.

"How long you been bangin' her mom?" Layne pushed.

"Bro," Ryker leaned in warningly, "not my place."

Layne held his angry gaze and said quietly, "Don't give me that badass bullshit. You care about this kid, you didn't, you wouldn't have spent the time you spent surveilling Gaines's apartment. What you're doin' isn't for Lissa so much as it's for Alexis. You know it. I know it. You deny it, I'm tellin' you that's bullshit. She doesn't have a dad? Be a true badass, Ryker, and give her one by protectin' her from what you and I both know is some seriously bad shit."

Ryker glared at him but didn't answer.

So Layne continued, "I call the moves on this investigation. You make the moves I call. You don't then you go it alone. But I'm tellin' you right now, you fuck up what I got goin' on and you put my boys' asses further out there than they already are, we got problems." Layne paused then whispered, "I'm not someone you mess with, Ryker. I think you already get that and my guess is that you don't want a demonstration of why. Do not make me demonstrate why. Clear?"

Ryker kept glaring at him but still didn't answer.

"I got a meet with Colt in about fifteen minutes. Girls are on the line, and we got no choice but to go in hard at every angle we can manage. Colt isn't stupid and he knows what's happening in his department. He'll take care of that. Now, you got two jobs. One is to do what I tell you to do and the other one is to get your woman's daughter outta that mess. You with me?" Ryker didn't respond so Layne prompted, "I need to know you're with me."

Ryker hesitated only a beat before he grunted, "I'm with you."

"Then you stay for the meet with Colt. You need to know all that's goin' down but you're gonna hear shit that doesn't leave this office. I find out it leaves this office then I'll know who shared and that is not gonna make me happy."

"Think I'm done with you threatenin' me, bro," Ryker growled.

"Got two boys, a woman, a dog and nearly three months ago I took three bullets because of this shit," Layne said softly and Ryker's brows went up. "Yeah, you heard about it. Two and two are makin' four and I mean that for both of us. Now, you think I'm gonna go through that again, put my boys and woman through that again, you think wrong. I'll do what I gotta do to prevent that. So, boilin' that down, big man, I'm not makin' threats."

Ryker stared at him. Layne sat back, grabbed his coffee off the desk and took a sip.

When he put the coffee back to his desk, Ryker spoke.

"One thing," he said.

"Yeah?" Layne asked when he said no more.

"Cosgrove better be into her. This is just a mission and he leaves her crushed—"

Layne interrupted him and fought back a grin. He couldn't have been sure Ryker was doing what he was doing for Alexis rather than the best head he ever had that he got from her mom. Now he knew this was for Alexis.

He also knew what kind of man Ryker was.

"My boys understand there's no collateral damage. They'll have briefed Seth. Jasper would have found another way to steer her clear if he thought Seth wasn't into her. That means Seth is into her."

"He better be," Ryker returned.

"Relax, brother, he is."

Ryker glared at him some more. Then he nodded.

When he did, Layne said, "You got just about enough time to get a coffee from Mimi before Colt gets here."

"Don't drink that fancy-ass shit," Ryker stated.

Layne took another sip.

"You're missin' out," he muttered after his sip.

Ryker looked at Blondie. "Fuck me, bro, a badass who drinks sissy coffee and owns a yellow lab." His eyes came back to Layne, his attitude shut down and he grinned his ugly grin. "Gotta say, impressed you could pull that off."

Layne put his cup down and pulled his phone out of his pocket, suggesting, "Maybe you should get Alexis a puppy."

Ryker sat back and stretched his legs out in front of him, still grinning. The showdown was over, Layne was again his bud and Layne relaxed in his chair.

"They already got three cats and two hamsters. Don't need no dog," Ryker told him.

Layne activated his phone, scrolled down to Devin, hit go and looked at Ryker, muttering, "Your call."

"What?" Devin answered in his ear.

"Give me Marissa Gibbon's cell number," Layne replied.

"Why?" Devin barked.

"Just do it, old man. I'll brief you later," Layne told him.

Devin sighed then gave him the number, which Layne wrote down on a legal pad on his desk.

"Boys are with Gabby for the week and I'm at Roc's the next two nights," Layne told his friend.

"I'll inform the President," Devin replied then disconnected.

Layne grinned at his desk then punched Marissa Gibbon's number in his phone.

"Marissa Gibbons?" Ryker asked as Layne's thumb hit the buttons.

"I'll tell you later," Layne murmured and put his phone to his ear.

⌒⟶

"This is the last time we meet," Layne said to Colt, who was sitting by Ryker in his office, his fingers toying with the flash drive with Gaines's pictures that Layne gave him. "If they haven't already, Rutledge, Gaines and the woman are gonna start bein' more vigilant and they don't need to see you comin' and goin' from my office."

Colt nodded and leaned forward. "Copy that, but I gotta know, man, why am I here and Merry isn't?"

"Merry and I got family issues," Layne answered. Colt's brows went up and Layne felt Ryker's gaze grow intense.

"Rocky?" Colt asked.

"Yep," Layne answered.

"Somethin' I can do?" Colt offered.

"Can you pry Merry or Dave's heads outta their asses?"

Colt smiled. "Probably not."

"Then no, there's nothin' you can do," Layne answered.

Colt leaned back but kept Layne's gaze. "We're goin' hard means you're swingin' your ass back out there again."

"Had the heads up to beat all heads up on that, brother. This time, also got backup," Layne replied, jerking his head to Ryker.

Colt didn't even look at Ryker. Colt was undecided about how he felt about Ryker.

Therefore he said, "Stay sharp."

Then he stood, glanced through Ryker and walked out the door.

Layne stood too. Picking his keys up from the desk, he walked to his storage room, Blondie following him.

"You think he's gonna be able to keep his shit quiet?" Ryker asked Layne's back as Layne unlocked the storage room door.

"You live in this 'burg," Layne said by way of response.

Ryker didn't like that response and told him. "Was that an answer?"

443

Layne opened the door and turned to Ryker. "This is a small town but shit goes down in a small town just like in the big cities. It might not be as relentless, but people steal, people deal, people rape, people beat their wives and kids. Colt and his woman caught the attention of a sick fuck who obsessed on both of them since high school and ended up hackin' through people in four states. He took that guy down and saved three lives. He knows his shit. I think he can keep our investigation of a dirty cop quiet."

Ryker nodded.

Layne walked into the storage closet, turned on the light and started sorting through his collection of bugs while Blondie sniffed the corners.

"Have you *seen* this fuckin' guy?" Devin asked in his ear.

Layne was standing outside Conesco Fieldhouse in Indianapolis, his dog sitting next to him breathing heavy, her tongue hanging out, her nose pointing in the direction of anyone who walked by. He was leaning against his truck that was parked three cars down from a yellow Corvette.

"You can trust him," Layne told Devin, referring to Ryker.

Layne had talked to Ryker and given him the equipment. Then he'd called Devin and briefed him about what he was going to be doing that day. He had not, however, shared much about who he was doing it with.

"This is a delicate operation and this guy is a fuckin' bull, as big as one and I bet he snorts like one too. He has no idea what he's doin'. And, I'll repeat, he's a *fuckin' bull*. I'd rather go in alone than go in with this guy takin' my back," Dev replied.

"You can trust him," Layne repeated.

"He's gonna blow the whole thing. It's impossible for this guy to be invisible."

"The Brendel has twenty-four-seven security, guards patrolling, cameras, and he managed to surveil the place for seventeen hours without raisin' alarms. I think you're good," Layne assured.

"I work alone" Devin returned.

"So do I. But twice I trusted him and twice he's not let me down."

"I don't like it," Dev clipped.

"I don't care. He's takin' your back."

"Boy—"

Layne pulled out the heavy artillery. "His woman's girl is a favorite of Gaines's."

Devin was silent.

Layne kept going. "I want ears in there and I want them in there today. Plant the bugs, get me a goddamned print for them both, get anything else you can get and get the fuck out. He'll cover you however he's gotta do that, but trust me, old man, he'll do it."

There was a moment of silence then, "He doesn't, you get the blame," Devin returned then disconnected.

Layne leaned to the side to give Blondie's head a rub as he shoved his phone in his pocket.

He was waiting for Marissa Gibbons to finish Pacemate practice. She told him to meet her there. He didn't like it, it was too open. He didn't want people to see them together the day after people could have seen her walk out of his office. But she wasn't going to miss practice and he didn't have time to wait, so he was meeting her there. Tonight, he'd tell Rocky about her. He'd wanted to avoid doing that, for Roc *and* for Marissa, but now he had no choice. If Astley hadn't called off the dogs, that asshole would use anything to get back in with Roc and Layne had to head him off.

The girls came out, all wearing varying degrees of tight workout gear, but Marissa came out scanning for him. She saw him, said something to her girls then broke off as the rest of them eyed him. When Blondie saw Marissa was on approach, she got up to all fours and her body went in full wag.

"Cute dog," Marissa remarked when she arrived, bending to give Blondie a rubdown.

Layne didn't reply. He kept his gaze to her girls who were finding reasons to hang so they could watch Marissa with who they wrongly assumed was Astley's replacement.

"Get them to go," Layne ordered and Marissa straightened.

"What?" she asked.

"Your friends. Get them to go. Now."

"They'll eventually—" she started and Layne's eyes sliced to her.

"I told you over the phone the shit I gotta talk to you about is important. But it's shit you do not want them to hear. Get them to go."

"We'll get in your truck," she suggested.

"Woman, your ass is not in my truck," Layne returned. "Ever."

Her head tilted to the side and she smiled at him. Flirting. Fuck.

It didn't take much to make her want to wander off her chosen path.

"Why?" she asked.

"Do not play with me," he whispered his warning. "I am not a man who likes to be played. Get...them...to...*go*."

She stared at him. She read him. Then she nodded and turned to her girls. "See you guys later!" she shouted.

The women went from curious to confused as Marissa didn't get in his truck, didn't touch Layne, Layne didn't touch her and she hinted that they should take off. All of them were used to a lot more attention, the kind they wanted and getting it exactly when they wanted it. This confusion turned to concern and they didn't move.

"Marissa," Layne growled.

"It's cool!" she shouted instantly. "This is my cousin's boyfriend. I'm watching his dog while they go on vacation!"

The women looked at him then at each other and one shouted, "Right, Riss! See you!"

"See you!" Marissa shouted back. There were some waves, more yells and the women headed to their cars.

When the last one slammed her door, Layne turned to Marissa and he didn't fuck around.

"I need information from your former life," he announced and he watched her body get tight so he continued, "I would not ask you if it wasn't important."

Her face had changed. Today's flirty gone. Yesterday's attempt at friendly a memory. She was pissed.

"I see. You find out I sucked dick for the cameras, you got that on me, now I got no choice but to be your rat," she snapped.

"That's not the way it is," Layne told her.

"Looks it to me, asshole," she shot back.

Layne kept his position, back to the truck, and kept his eyes locked to hers. "You read me yesterday, you read me right. Listen to your gut, woman. Like I said, this is important."

"Yeah, and in a couple weeks, it'll be important again and then a month later it'll be important again and I'll live that shit over and over because you bought yourself a sneak. Well, I'm not a rat and that isn't my life anymore so you can go fuck yourself."

She turned to leave and Layne spoke.

"My guess is, there's a racket in the 'burg, fourteen, fifteen year old girls, modeling or filming." She stopped and turned back to him. "It's either happening now or it's gonna happen. One thing I know for certain is they're recruitin' through the church."

Marissa stared at him.

"You know anyone into that shit?" Layne asked.

Marissa didn't speak.

Layne pushed away from the truck but didn't move toward her.

His voice got soft when he said, "Marissa, I haven't seen your work, don't want to, but Dev says you were underage. Who do you know that's into that shit?"

She looked away but she still didn't speak.

"A woman," Layne prompted. "A woman who runs the show."

Marissa's eyes snapped back to him. Her face had bleached entirely of color and Layne took a step toward her to get into her space.

"They're recruitin' from a Youth Group, Marissa. You got anything, you gotta give it to me."

"I can't," she whispered.

"You can, you don't want girls travelin' down that road you were forced to take," he replied.

"She's..." Marissa swallowed and leaned into him. "She's a nasty piece of work, Tanner. Listen to me, do *not* go there."

"Let those girls swing?" Layne growled, glaring at her.

"No." She shook her head and did it hard. "She'll have a front, a guy, probably not too smart, definitely hot. He lines 'em up, pulls 'em in. You take him down, she'll move on."

"Not too far considerin' you know her," Layne noted. "Means she's worked Indy at least, what? Ten years?"

"You want your reunion with your sweetheart to last more than a coupla weeks, you steer clear and let the next place she hits deal with her."

"What do you know about her?" Layne pressed.

"She's a nasty piece of work," Marissa repeated.

"What do you know?" Layne pushed it.

"I know you do not want to go there." She wasn't giving him anything.

"Goddammit, Marissa, what do you know?" Layne bit out.

"I know she's got two markets but only one she takes real good care of. That one, the girls are fresh and young. *Fresh* and young. She didn't want me for that. She wanted me for somethin' else. I did not like it but I did not do shit about it because I learned early how to stay in one piece. Another girl with me who was in her stable, she wasn't so smart. This bitch cut that girl up, Tanner, cut her up on the *inside*. Cut her up so bad, nothin'll feel good down there. Ever. Not in her life. She did it herself. She didn't get one of her boys to do it. She did it herself. The girl was thirteen, and even after she sliced her, she pimped her."

"Jesus," Layne whispered.

"You do not want to go there," Marissa reiterated.

"How'd you get out?" Layne asked.

"She worked the foster home angle then. Got me through that then I hit sixteen, too old for her clientele," Marissa answered. "I made no trouble. I did my job. I didn't complain. I gave good head. I did as I was told and she let me loose when she couldn't use me anymore. Let me loose as in sold me, Tanner. She sold me to the producers who'd work me until I was eighteen. And I got outta that because I give great head. I've had enough practice and a lotta men get stupid when they get great head. I wanted a boob job. I asked right before I made him come, I got a boob job. When I wanted to move on, I asked right before I made him come, I got to move on. Then I took off some weight, changed my hair, gave more head to get a new identity...exit Anita Dewmeyer, enter Marissa Gibbons."

Layne looked over her head and he did this in an effort not to touch her. It wasn't his place. He didn't know her. That was not where their relationship could ever go. But he reckoned she'd never been held in an act of kindness, not in her life. And knowing a lot more about her life than he ever wanted to know, none of it good, all of it the worst it could be, he felt compelled to kindness.

He beat back the urge and looked at her.

"I'm sorry, honey," he whispered. He meant his words and her torso lurched like he'd punched her, sock to the gut.

Nope, Marissa Gibbons hadn't experienced much kindness.

Layne ignored the look in her eyes that seeped into her face and went on, "If you gave me names, would your ass be out there?"

She sucked in breath and answered quietly, "They found out it was me, my ass would be in the White River."

"Then get the fuck out of here, now," Layne returned just as quietly and her look intensified.

"What?" she whispered.

"Go, now. And you let it be known to someone who talks that all you got from me is coachin' to fuck over Astley. What you do not know is dick about what's goin' on in the 'burg."

"You..." She paused, took in another breath then asked, "You're gonna leave it at that?"

"Right now, I'm spread thin. I don't have the resources to watch your back, not in the short-term and not in the long-term should something blow back on you and anyone else in that business thinks to fuck with you. So, yeah, I'm gonna leave it at that."

She held his gaze and she did it too long.

"Go," he ordered then turned toward his truck.

"Nicolette Towers," she called, and Layne's head turned to her.

Fuck.

"No more, Marissa," he warned.

"She'll be usin' another name. Her rap sheet, though, will be under Nicolette Towers."

"Go," he ordered.

"She likes to play," Marissa went on, and Layne turned to her as his stomach churned.

"Go," he repeated.

"That's how you'll get her. She lets her boy enlist but she's hands on, Tanner. As hands on as she can get."

"Honey," Layne whispered. "Go."

"She buys immunity from local cops. Keeps 'em happy with money but gets them under her thumb because they like to watch her play. She gets that shit on them, they'll do anything. But she keeps them fat and sassy by puttin' them on payroll *and* givin' them as much of their kink as they can stand. Just for that, they'd do anything for her."

Layne swallowed the saliva that filled his mouth and growled, "No more, woman, go."

"She's got muscle and she's got firepower. She even *thinks* you're gettin' close, she does damage but she likes a first warning. It's about power, control. Someone thinks to fuck with her, she likes knowin' they're livin' and knowin' she got the best of 'em. They come back after her, they'll go down."

Jesus fucking Christ.

"How do you know this shit?" Layne asked.

"I did my job. I didn't complain. I wasn't fresh but I was a favorite. She knew I was a survivalist. She knew I would never do what I'm doin' right now. So she didn't hide her business from me when she was of a mind to keep me close. And, bein' a survivalist, I learned to keep quiet and listen. So I did."

Layne stared at her.

Then he made a decision.

"How tied to Indianapolis are you?" he asked.

"What?" she asked back.

"How do you feel about LA?"

Her lips parted and she stared back.

"Dev's got a job today," Layne said. "Tonight, he's got another one. You make contact. You make a meet. You pick up your new identity tomorrow from Dev. You sell that fuckin' car and you get your ass to LA. I got a friend out there, he'll help you get set up and he'll watch your back until he knows no shit is gonna blow west. You do not check in direct. You check in with him, he'll get word to me."

"I got school here," she stated.

"They got universities in LA," he returned.

"The Pacemates—"

"Are a memory. You are no longer visible. You do not veer from your path. This shit gets done, you find a decent guy, you give him great head, you get him hooked, you settle and you keep that shit from him. You put your ass on the line for me just now so in return, I'll give it to you straight. Do not share with him, no matter how decent he is, about Anita Dewmeyer or Marissa Gibbons. You were in the system. You lived a shit life. You had a social worker who showed you the way, but other than that, you don't wanna talk about it. Ever. You wanna look ahead, never behind. You keep him facin' forward, Marissa, don't you and don't let him ever look back. But you find you need to talk about that, work things out after this is over, you contact me or Dev. You do not lay that shit on your man. Yeah?"

"If I disappear, especially from the Pacemates, they'll know—"

Layne cut her off. "I told you, I got a guy who'll watch your back."

"He got twelve eyes? Because they can come from all directions," she returned.

He knew that even better than she did. He got hit with three bullets and each of those bullets came from different guns. Ambush. The only things Marissa had given him were who was behind it and why they didn't drill a round in his head after he went down.

"You trusted me to do the right thing with that shit you just shared. Now trust me to do the right thing by you," Layne told her.

"I've been takin' care of my—"

He stepped back into her space and she clamped her mouth shut.

"I know you have, Marissa, so I know this won't be easy, since no one has ever looked out for you. But I'm not like the trash that's been twistin' around you your whole life. You know it. This guy knows what he's doin' and if I didn't think he did then I wouldn't send you out there."

She'd closed down. He could see it. She was giving him nothing and she wasn't buying one word he said. That was how terrified she was of what she'd just done. And fear could make you do some seriously stupid shit.

So Layne pushed, "Your life just changed. You had an opportunity to turn your back on a bunch of girls you don't know who're either livin' nightmares or goin' to. You didn't do that. You did the right thing. Now you leave the wrong life behind and look...the fuck...forward to an entirely new experience."

She gazed up at him and he knew she was undecided.

So he decided for her.

"Dev doesn't get a call, you make me hunt you down, which I'll do, Marissa, no fuckin' joke, that'll piss me off. But I got too much to worry about to worry about you and if something happens to you, I'm not livin' with that on my conscience. So you make me take time out to take you to LA and make you safe, like I said, that'll piss me off. You don't wanna piss me off. So, tonight, pick up the phone and *call Dev*."

He didn't know how he got to her but he got to her and he knew that when she whispered, "I'll call Dev."

"Eyes and ears open until you reach LA. You don't turn that 'vette, just leave it," Layne pressed.

She nodded.

"Until you're with my man, you get a bad feeling, you call Dev."

She nodded again.

"You got friends. They're not your friends anymore. You'll make new friends in LA."

She swallowed then she nodded again.

Layne examined her face then he toned it down. "You did the right thing."

"Right," she whispered, and Layne knew she didn't believe him but instead wished she could turn back time and keep her mouth shut.

"Before it turned shit for you, how would you feel if some woman saved you from that life?"

"They'll never know it was me," she returned.

"You wouldn't have either, but you also wouldn't have had that life. Isn't knowin' that enough?"

She pulled her lips between her teeth and pressed her teeth together. Then she nodded again.

"You did the right thing," he repeated.

She nodded yet again then her teeth released her lips so she could say, "Do me a favor?"

"What?" Layne asked.

Her face changed, she gave him that look with her mouth going soft, and Layne hoped for her that she'd direct that look to the right guy. A guy who would show her the life she should have had.

"Don't get dead," she replied on a whisper, bent and gave Blondie a quick rub and then without looking at him again, she turned and jogged away.

Blondie woofed her excited good-bye.

In case they had an audience, Layne didn't watch her go. He immediately opened the door to his truck. Blondie jumped in. He slammed it, rounded the hood, folded into the driver's side and pulled out of his spot. He scanned the area as he did so and he drove home with his eyes on his mirrors just as much as they were on the road.

He'd wait until the planned meet later with Devin and Ryker to give Devin his next assignment.

Layne was sitting in Merry's armchair in his living room, facing his front door as Merry walked in.

"You're a hard man to get hold of," Layne remarked.

Merry turned quickly, his hand going into his jacket toward his gun before he saw Layne and stopped.

"Jesus, fuck, shit, Tanner, what the fuck?" Merry clipped.

"Been callin' you, brother," Layne reminded him.

"Yeah, so, I'm busy and you break into my goddamned house?" Merry asked, coming into the room shrugging off his leather jacket and throwing it on the back of the couch.

"You're busy?" Layne asked, not making the slightest move in his chair except to raise his eyebrows.

"Yeah, *brother*, busy," Merry bit off then asked, "How'd you get in here?"

"Picked the lock," Layne answered.

"You're tellin' me you picked the lock of a cop's apartment?"

"Nope, I'm tellin' you I picked the lock of the apartment of the man who's supposed to be my partner in an operation, one that got my ass shot. He's also the man who's supposed to be my goddamned friend and he knows I got all sorts of shit goin' down, some of it with my boys on the line. He's also the man who's brother to my woman, who—"

Merry lifted a hand and interrupted. "I get it."

"You do? I don't think so. See, if you did, you'd return my goddamned phone calls."

"I've been busy, all right?" Merry lied.

"That's fuckin' lame and you fuckin' know it," Layne growled, having trouble keeping his seat.

Merry moved straight off the defensive to take the offensive. "You been busy too, brother."

"Yeah, I have," Layne agreed.

"So, let me help you with that. Lay off Dad," Merry returned.

Layne stood and Merry tensed.

Then Layne spoke.

"Rutledge is providing safe haven to a Caucasian female in her mid-forties named Nicolette Towers. The shit goin' down at Youth Group is her game. She likes girls, she likes pimpin' 'em any way she can and she just plain likes 'em."

Layne ignored Merry's face twisting with disgust and continued.

"Colt's in on this as is a guy named Ryker, who I 'spect you know. Ryker and me, we've partnered up and my man Devin is workin' this too. We're goin' in hard, her boy is goin' down, Rutledge is goin' down and Towers is goin' down. Of that cast of characters, the one with the most to lose is Rutledge. She's got dirt on him and it's not just dirt. It's filth. Only thing the boys in the hole hate worse than a cop is a pedophile. He's both and he's fucked."

Layne crossed his arms on his chest, kept his eyes locked on Merry and kept going.

"I got intel that says what we suspected, that ambush was a warning. If they meant to kill me, they'd have done it. They won't give me a second warning. That said, I'm not pussyfooting around with this shit. I want Rutledge scared, I want Gaines freaked and I want Towers on alert. And all that shit is gonna come from me, not you, not Colt. Me. Colt's workin' it but he's not swingin' his ass out there. I am. What I don't want is any of them to run. They run, we're fucked. They'll go out of your jurisdiction and they'll do it after they drill a round in my skull. This operation is gonna require skill and it's gonna require teamwork and I gotta know right now if you're out, because you disappear off radar like you did this week, I'm dead."

"I'm not out," Merry clipped.

"Good, welcome back to the team," Layne returned.

Merry scowled at him then asked, "You done?"

"Nope," Layne answered. "I'm guessin' you know Roc and I are back together."

"Yeah, forgot to send my congratulations bouquet," Merry retorted sarcastically and Layne pulled in breath.

They watched each other and Layne waited. Merry couldn't take a stare down, didn't have enough control, therefore he broke the silence first.

"I figure, since you aren't movin' toward the door, you got more to say," he prompted.

"No, I'm not movin' to the door because I'm waitin' to hear what *you* have to say," Layne replied.

"Think we had this conversation before, brother," Merry reminded him.

"And I think I made it pretty clear I didn't like the way that one went," Layne shot back.

"Seems you liked it enough, since my sister's keepin' you warm at night again."

"Don't piss me off," Layne whispered his warning.

"You aren't already pissed?" Merry returned.

"Good you could read that, Garrett."

"Not hard, Tanner."

"Okay, then I'll keep makin' it easy for you. You and your dad, you're scared shitless of whatever the hell it is your scared shitless of that would make Rocky cut you out if one or the other of you grows a pair and pulls your head outta your ass—"

"Okay, now you're pissin' me off," Merry growled.

"I'm not done," Layne told him. "To finish, I find out you sat on somethin', somethin' that kept her from me when I wanted her and she wanted me. Somethin' that meant we lost eighteen years. Somethin' that kept her livin' in fear, led her to a dickhead who treated her like shit. Then you better stop worryin' about her cuttin' you out and start worryin' about me. Because, brother, there is nothin' that is gonna tear us apart, not again. She's mine until she dies. And I find that shit out, I hold a mean grudge and, God's honest truth, Garrett, you'll lose us all and not one of us is ever comin' back. Do you get me?"

Merry smiled and it was nasty. "Don't play that game, Tanner. You pit yourself against me and Dad, when it comes to Rocky, I promise you, you'll lose."

"You seem sure."

"That's because I am."

"She's thirty-eight and still embarrassed about her periods and scared shitless of the dark. Tell me, Garrett, you two handled her with care, how can that be?"

Merry's face changed and Layne couldn't read it before he hid it.

So Layne bluffed, "That's what I thought. You're not so fuckin' sure, are you?"

Layne won his bluff, he knew it when Merry whispered, "Fuck you."

He looked at his watch and back to Merry. "You got fifteen minutes before I gotta go pick her up for the game. You got anything for me?"

Merry was silent and Layne waited.

Then Layne warned quietly, "This is the last time I'll ask you, brother. You got anything for me?"

Merry kept his silence.

Layne nodded and whispered, "Right."

Then, without looking at his friend and without another word, Layne walked right past him and out the door.

"Oh my God," Rocky whispered, her face white, she was staring at him.

Layne was at one end of her couch, his feet on her coffee table, the mostly empty pizza box and several bottles of beer scattered on it. Rocky was at the opposite end of the couch, her feet were in his lap and he'd just told her Marissa Gibbon's entire story.

"Sorry, sweetcheeks," Layne said softly. "I woulda kept that from you, but if Astley still has someone watchin', he could have been takin' pictures and that could get back to you. Forced my hand. You needed to know."

"I don't know what to say." She was still whispering.

"Nothin' to say except try to find the silver lining and that is that Marissa Gibbons learned how to be a good woman today. She tried it on and it fit. You know Devin called me when we were at the game. She set the meet. Now she gets to move on, leave this shit behind and maybe find a good life."

Her eyes stayed glued to him until her mouth got soft, her lids lowered then she pulled her feet out of his lap, twisted her hips in the couch and crawled on all fours until she had her hands on his shoulders and she was face to face and chest to chest with him.

"You're a good man, Tanner Layne," she said quietly then her eyes dropped to his mouth.

His arms went around her but he pulled his head back an inch and her eyes went back to his.

"Want your mouth on mine, honey, but we're not done talkin'," he murmured.

"I don't like the look on your face," she replied, losing her look, that look he liked so much, and Layne would be seriously fucking happy when all this shit was over and life was just life.

So he didn't waste time. Wasting time would mean a delay in getting to the good part of the evening, and he didn't want that for him or for Roc.

He'd briefed her about the day's events, all except his chat with her brother, but he still had a few things he needed to make clear. So he set about making them clear.

"We got a lot done today. Devin, Ryker and me are gonna be takin' turns listenin' to the bugs. We know who she is and Dev's got prints from the apartment that an independent lab is runnin'. We'll have results tomorrow, so we'll know who he is and hopefully get confirmation on her. We know whose pocket Rutledge is in. This means it's gonna get hotter. I told Jasper and I'll tell you. You keep sharp. You stay smart. You don't talk to Josie, Violet, Feb, anyone about this shit. You lock your doors when you're in your car and you drive with your eyes on your mirrors. You see the same car more than once, you call me immediately. Tomorrow, I take you to the office and get you a panic button and you carry that with you everywhere. You don't go anywhere unless someone knows you're goin', where you're goin' and when you're expected to get there. You don't sleep alone. I'm not home, you stay awake. I'm not in this apartment, you're not in this apartment. Those vultures live close and my security system at home is solid, they still haven't fixed this one."

"But, the girls are coming over tomorrow to—"

"Yeah, and I'll leave when they get here and come back before they're gone. Colt's wife and Cal's wife will both be here. Someone might be dumb enough to fuck with you, and, baby, that's the truth even if I can see it freaks you out. But no one would be dumb enough to fuck with the three of you."

He stopped speaking and she didn't say anything, just held his eyes so his arms gave her a squeeze.

"You get all that?" he asked.

Rocky nodded.

"You freaked?" he went on.

Rocky kept nodding.

"You think I'd ever let anything hurt you?"

Rocky stopped nodding, her mouth got soft, her lids lowered and she shook her head.

"All right, baby," he whispered, his hand traveling up her back, her neck to cup her head. "I'm gonna clean this shit up," he told her quietly, tipping his head to the table. "You go upstairs and get ready because I'm hungry."

"Layne," she breathed, her tits pressing deeper into his chest and his cock started getting hard.

"Go get ready for me," he growled.

"I have to ask you something first," she said, her hands moving up his neck, her fingers sliding into his hair and curling around at the back.

"Yeah?" he prompted when she said no more.

"That night, after that first game we went to together, do you remember?"

"It was only a month ago, sweetcheeks."

458

"So you remember," she pushed.

"Yeah, Roc," his arms tightened, "I remember every second."

She smiled. She'd liked that night but she liked that he liked it too. Then she shared, "I didn't want you to leave."

"I know."

Rocky kept smiling and she kept sharing, "Before Merry came, I was going to make a move on you."

Layne smiled back. "Yeah, I know."

Her smile got even brighter before her face went strange, uncertain, and she started, "Would you have...um," she pulled in a breath, "caught my move or deflected it?"

Layne felt his smile fading and he answered honestly, "I don't know, baby."

She nodded, her eyes slid away and he used his hand on her head to bring her attention back to him.

"It didn't happen and I don't know what I would have done if it did. But I do know that it would have killed to turn you down." She studied his face and he repeated, "It would have killed, Rocky. I wanted you to make that move and even thinkin' then that we'd never again be where we are right now, I wanted you and I wanted you to want me."

One of her hands came out of his hair to cup his jaw.

Then she said, "You know, one of the reasons I fell in love with you was because you were always honest. With everyone, including me. I loved that. It made me feel safe. I still love that about you, especially knowing it takes courage to be honest. Your courage, I love that about you too."

And he loved her words, fucking loved every one of them. What he didn't love was what they might mean.

And he had to know what they might mean.

"In your life, was someone not honest with you?"

She pulled back an inch and her hand dropped to his chest. "What?"

"What you said made me think that maybe you meant that it was refreshing, someone being honest because you had someone not honest in your life."

Her eyes drifted over his shoulder but she wasn't hiding from him, she was thinking.

Still, he ordered, "Roc, eyes on me," and her eyes came back.

"I don't know," she replied. "I don't think so but…" She trailed off, her face going unfocused, she was still thinking.

Fuck.

He knew, looking at her, he was standing in a field full of mines. He'd put himself there. And now he had to find a way to get the fuck out or purposely jump on a mine that might cause damage, but do it with the hope his body didn't blow to smithereens taking Rocky with it.

"Sweetcheeks," Layne called and she focused on him. "Did your dad ever talk to you about the facts of life?"

A startled giggle erupted out of her and she asked, "What?"

"Sex. How men's bodies work. How women's bodies work. That kinda shit?"

"I learned most of that in school, Layne." She was still smiling.

"So he didn't," Layne surmised.

"Well, no, not exactly. He did say when I told him you asked me out, and he knew who you were and how old you were, and after we fought when he said I was *not* going out with you and I told him I *was*, that if you laid a hand on me, he'd rip your heart out. After he cut your hands off, that is. But, other than that, he pretty much steered clear of the facts of life."

Layne had heard that story, not only from Rocky but also from Dave and Merry. After they started living together, it was a favorite tale for the three of them to cackle over.

It was also not where he was leading her.

"So, he left you to it," Layne stated.

Rocky cocked her head to the side. "Left me to it?"

"To learn that shit yourself."

"Well," she whispered as her hand started to fiddle with the collar of his shirt. "I did, relatively young, find myself a good teacher."

Automatically, Layne's arms gave her a squeeze but he stayed on target. "What about your period?"

Her eyes shot to his and her fingers arrested mid-fiddle. "What?"

"Who taught you about that?"

Her body started to tense and edge away so his arms got tighter. Rocky read his message and gave up.

"Who?" he pushed.

"I learned that in Sex Education in Health class in junior high," she answered.

"When did you start your period?" Layne asked.

For some reason, her eyes saturated with fear, Layne braced, and she asked back, "Why are we talking about this?"

"I wanna know everything about you," he answered. It was lame but he hoped it would get them where they needed to go.

"Well, I don't remember," she lied, every girl remembered.

"Was it before your mom died or after?"

Her body locked.

Fuck.

"Baby, was it before your mom died or after?"

"I don't get why you want to know," she whispered.

"Tell me, Rocky. Was it before your mom died or after?"

"Who cares?" Her voice was pitching higher and the fear was stark on her face.

Fuck!

"Why won't you answer?" he asked gently, pushing carefully but unfortunately not treading cautiously.

"Because I don't get why you care," she answered. "And anyway, it's private."

"Nothing is private between you and me."

"*That's* private," she returned.

"It isn't."

"It is."

"Baby, I've had my mouth down there. I know you there better than *you* know you there. I know how you taste, how you feel, how you look—"

"Stop it," she whispered.

"Why?" he asked.

She shook her head, both her hands going to his chest and she tried to push away. Layne locked his arms, trapping her torso just as he shifted and threw a leg over hers, trapping her lower limbs.

"Why?" he repeated. "Why do you want me to stop?"

She looked across the room, still putting steady pressure on his chest, that fear on her face.

So Layne called up the courage she loved in order to explore something that had been festering insidiously in his brain since the secrets started and he asked, "Baby, what happened that night?"

"Layne, let go."

"Did Carson Fisher get to you?"

Her eyes cut to his and Layne's chest seized at the look of terror on her face as she started fighting him.

Fuck. Fuck. Jesus, fuck, no.

"Did he get to you?" Layne pushed even though he really didn't want to know. He had to know. But more importantly, Rocky had to face it.

"Let me go," she whispered.

"You didn't tell the cops. It's not in the report. I pulled it and I read it. But you told your brother and he told your dad. He got to you, didn't he? He got to you and he hurt you."

It was then, she heaved at the same time she let out a grunt and made it to her feet. Layne was up right after her, he caught her at the waist before she could run and he turned her into his arms. She pulled back at the same time she pushed at his chest with her hands.

"Layne!" she shouted, "Let me *go*!"

"You can tell me, baby, honest to God, you can tell me. It changes nothing. Not one fuckin' thing."

"No!" she yelled. "No! He didn't get to me. Do you think my mother would *ever* let him get to me? No! I didn't even see him."

"Swear it," Layne pushed.

"I swear," she hissed. "And I started my period *after* Mom died. The *week* after Mom died. Dad was in the hospital and I couldn't ask Merry, so Gram took me to the grocery store and she helped me pick what I needed and she was sweet about it, but I didn't want her there. I wanted Mom there. I could talk to Mom about that shit. Mom would have known what to do, what to say. The cramps hurt so goddamned much and I bled a lot, it lasted *a day*. It scared the *fucking shit* out of me. I didn't want a lifetime of *that*. Gram tried, but she wasn't Mom. She'd never be Mom. I couldn't talk to her about it, ask her questions. I couldn't talk to *anyone* about it except my mom and she was *dead.* Until I was thirty, my periods were the worst. They made me feel like shit, they brought on a lot of pain and I bled out fast. I *hated* them so much I *dreaded* them. They're still not my favorite things to have nor are they my favorite things to talk about. But there you go. The story of my fertility. Happy?"

"Yes," Layne replied honestly, her body jerked with surprise at his answer then went still in his arms.

"Yes?" she asked.

He dipped his chin and put his face close to hers. "I'm a guy. A guy who grew up without a dad. Shit happens to you, you want someone to talk about it with. So, I get what you're sayin' more than pretty much anyone would get what you're sayin'. You needed your mom and she died the week before you needed her. That would suck, baby. What I need you to know is, growin' up without a dad, *I get it* and that means you can talk about it with me."

She stared him in the eye for long moments before her body relaxed and she whispered, "Layne."

"You don't have to hide anything or be embarrassed about anything, not with me. Yeah?" Layne stated.

"Yeah." She was still whispering.

Layne took in a breath. Then he let it out.

Then he realized he'd made it through the minefield without getting blown to pieces, Rocky was safe and in one piece in his arms, and he relaxed.

When he did, he noticed Rocky watching him with a look he couldn't read on her face.

"You okay, baby?" he asked.

"I don't really need to process my period anymore, Layne," she said softly. "I'm kind of used to it by now."

"You get embarrassed," he told her honestly.

"I lived with two men, one of them a teenager. They avoided any of my period paraphernalia like the plague. And, newsflash, sweetheart," she put her hand to his jaw, "you're also a man."

"Yeah," Layne smiled. "But I don't have any hang ups about that shit. *I* grew up alone in a house with a woman."

Her mouth got soft.

"And I just want you to know you're safe with me, always safe with me, with anything," he told her.

Her lids lowered but not to half-mast. They closed and when they opened, her face was openly troubled.

"You're worried I'm going to leave you," she whispered, surprising Layne by taking it right to the point.

"Yeah," he whispered back, his arms getting tighter around her, her hand slid from his jaw and both her arms closed around his neck.

She pressed into him and she did this deep, getting up on her toes so her face was close to his. He looked in her eyes and there was an intensity there, so strong it felt like her eyes were burning into his.

"Don't let me leave you," she whispered so quietly he almost didn't hear her.

But he heard her. He not only heard her, he understood what she was saying and his chest seized, his gut twisted but his arms got even tighter.

"I won't," he whispered back, his voice was quiet too and thick.

"No matter what." She was still talking low.

"No matter what," he replied.

"Promise."

"I promise, baby."

She held his gaze then she asked softly, "Can I ask you something?"

"Anything."

"You told Marissa, when she found another man not to tell him about her past."

Oh fuck.

He wasn't out of that minefield yet.

"Yeah," he answered carefully.

"Honestly? Do you think, even if she finds a good guy, a *really* good guy, she shouldn't tell him?"

"What are you really askin', baby?"

"I'm asking about Marissa."

"Then, if you're askin' about Marissa, yes."

Her head moved back half an inch. "Because you think he'd think less of her? Judge her?"

"No, because she deserves to be loved for who she should have been, who she'll be, not despite what was forced on her."

He heard Rocky suck in breath and her eyes went back to intense and seeing it, he decided he'd managed not to get blown to bits yet again, he'd managed to hold her together and she'd made him promise never to let her go. He could do that. He could make her stay. He had her permission. Whatever it was, when they finally faced it, he had her permission to do what he had to do to make her stay.

Thank Christ that was done.

He also decided she'd had enough for one night, so had he, and it was time to move...the fuck...on.

So he lowered his head to take her mouth but her head went back another half inch and he stopped.

When he did, his eyebrows went up and Rocky whispered, "I need to go upstairs and get ready. My man's hungry."

And before he could say a word, she pulled out of his arms but she did it with both her hands trailing along his neck and down his chest before she turned and strutted up the stairs.

Layne watched until she was out of sight, going so far as to move to the foot of the stairs to enjoy the whole show.

Then he cleared away the pizza and beer, checked that the apartment was secured, turned out the lights, went upstairs and ate dessert.

Twenty-Two

NOTHING MEANS EVERYTHING

"*L*ayne," she whispered, pressing into him, her fingers digging into his neck.

Layne opened his eyes, dipped his chin and saw her staring up at him, her eyes burning.

"Tripp." She kept whispering, her body pushing into his hard, like she wanted him to absorb her, her fingers digging into his tense neck so hard he felt pain. "Tripp," she repeated, her voice scared.

Layne's eyes opened and he heard his cell phone.

Rocky shifted and then came up on an elbow.

Another dream. Another fucking, shitty, fucking dream.

"Baby," Roc whispered. "Your phone."

Layne rolled. Putting a hand to the floor, reaching out with the other one, he yanked his jeans toward the bed and pulled his cell out. He pushed off the floor, rolling again to his back as his eyes slid across Rocky's clock to see it was ten after eight.

They'd seriously slept in.

The phone stopped ringing by the time he settled back. He engaged it and looked at his received calls, Rocky moving into him again.

Tripp. Tripp at eight o'clock on a Saturday morning. The boys had to be at the pool with the team but not this early.

Fuck.

"Who was it?" Rocky asked.

"Tripp," Layne answered, scrolling down to his son's phone number in his contact list, he hit go.

Rocky pressed closer as Layne listened to it ring, his body tense because of the time and because of a phone call from his son at that time and because of his fucking dream.

It rang twice before Layne heard Tripp saying in his usual Tripp way, "Yo, Dad!"

Layne pulled in breath.

Then he let it out while replying, "Yo, pal. You called. What's up?"

"I was actually calling Rocky but she wasn't picking up. I thought you might be with her."

Rocky's phone was likely in Rocky's purse, which was downstairs on the bar in the kitchen.

"Why'd you want Roc?" Layne asked, shoving an arm under Rocky, his forearm going up, his fingers beginning to play with her hair.

"Need to check somethin'," Tripp answered.

"What?" Layne asked.

"Girl stuff," Tripp answered.

Layne looked down at Rocky, who was gazing up at him.

"Girl stuff?" he repeated and he watched his woman's lips form a small smile.

"Yeah, see, she's a girl and I need to ask her girl stuff," Tripp said.

"What kind of girl stuff?" Layne asked.

"The kind where she'd tell me why Giselle wasn't out for pizza last night and why she isn't textin' me. That kind. I figure she's playin' hard to get. She's shy but she goes out for pizza, everyone does. I used to see her there all the time and we've been hangin' the last coupla Fridays. She wasn't out last night and she always returns my texts and she isn't, so…is Rocky there?"

While his son spoke, Layne's body, which had relaxed, got tense then he sat up, taking Roc with him. She got tense against him and her arm didn't leave his gut as she pressed tight against his side.

"Yeah, Tripp, Roc's here but I wanna know about Giselle. When's the last time you saw her?" Layne asked.

Tripp was silent and Layne felt Rocky's body go still.

"Tripp," Layne said carefully. "When was the last time you saw her?"

"At school yesterday," Tripp stated quietly.

"Was she at the game last night?" Layne pushed.

"Don't know," Tripp answered and Layne looked at Rocky.

"You see Giselle at the game last night, baby?"

Rocky stared him in the eyes then shook her head.

Layne went back to Tripp. "You talk to her at school yesterday?"

Tripp hesitated a beat then answered, "No, she was bein' weird. Kinda closed off. Avoiding me. I thought—"

Layne cut him off. "Text me her home number."

"Dad, do you think—?"

"Do it, pal, now, yeah?"

"Yeah," Tripp whispered.

"I got this covered, Tripp, okay?" Layne assured gently. "Me and Roc got this covered. It'll be okay. I'll call you, but before you hang up I wanna know you know your old man has this covered."

"I know." Tripp was still whispering.

"It'll be okay."

"Okay, Dad."

"Text me the number."

"Right."

"Talk to you soon, yeah?"

"Yeah. Later, Dad." He was talking quickly, in a hurry to get the number to Layne.

So Layne said without delay, "Later, pal."

He disengaged and Rocky moved slightly away from him, but when he looked at her, her eyes were drilling into him.

"What?" she asked sharply.

"Get dressed, baby. I need you to call Giselle Speakmon's parents. Find out if she's actin' okay."

"Why?" Her voice was still sharp.

"She's cut Tripp out. Sudden. She—" Layne started to explain but didn't finish because Rocky was on the move. She threw the covers back, jumped out of bed and ran to the bathroom.

Layne's phone chimed in his hand. He saw Tripp sent him Giselle's home number and cell number.

Layne got out of bed, grabbed his jeans, tugged them on and then followed Rocky to the bathroom only for her to come out before he got there. She skirted him and went directly to her underwear on the floor.

Layne turned to face her while he advised, "Sweetcheeks, brush your teeth, wash your face, make coffee. Settle. Sort your head out before you make the call."

"They got to her," Rocky hissed while she tugged on her panties under her big nightshirt. Then her head flew back and her blue eyes pierced him. "We waited too long."

"We don't know that," Layne replied and Rocky glared at him so he went on, "Settle, Roc, you need your shit together to make this call."

"We waited too long," she repeated, her face so filled with worry it was twisted.

"Raquel, *settle*," Layne ordered low.

She stared at him. Then she walked to him, around him and back into the bathroom. He went to stand in the doorway and he watched her preparing her toothbrush.

"What do I say?" she asked then shoved the toothbrush in her mouth.

"In this scenario, you're not Ms. Merrick, high school Lit teacher. You're Rocky, Tripp's dad's girlfriend. Tripp's your boy and your boy likes their girl, their girl likes your boy. You're equals. You're makin' a special dinner for a special occasion. It's a surprise and you want Giselle there."

She pulled the brush from her mouth and through the foam demanded to know, "What special occasion?"

"Doesn't matter. Make it up. Anniversary. Birthday. They don't know and won't care. Then you lead the conversation another way, is Giselle okay? She was actin' funny at school yesterday. You didn't see her at the game last night. She and Tripp are tight, you and her are tight, but you've noticed a difference."

She nodded, bent, spit, rinsed and wiped. Then she walked to him, snatched his phone from his hand and walked out.

Layne used the toilet, brushed his teeth with the toothbrush she'd given him the morning after the night Astley came to visit, then he walked down to the kitchen to see the coffeepot filling and Rocky getting down mugs.

She didn't even look at him when she whispered, "I want this done, Layne, all of this done. I want it to be you and me and the boys and Blondie, and the worst thing that could happen is Jas burns the pasta bake."

"I get that, sweetcheeks."

Her neck twisted fast, her hair, that she hadn't taken the time to put up, flying over her shoulder.

"You need to make that so, Layne," she ordered.

He grinned at her because she was cute when she was bossy, because he loved it that her concern ran that deep about a kid she didn't know all that well and it ran deeper because that kid meant something to his boy, and because she ordered it because she knew deep down he could do it and that meant she believed in him.

"Aye, aye, captain," he muttered. Her eyes narrowed and she opened her mouth, probably to yell, but he lunged toward her, hooking her with an arm around her waist and stepped back, pulling her into his body. She tilted her head back and he looked down, speaking before she could get a word out. "It'll be okay," he assured her softly.

"They hurt her, I'll kill them," she whispered fiercely.

"It'll be okay," Layne repeated.

"It better be," she snapped.

"If it isn't, it will be, baby. Shit happens, you know that better than anyone, and people deal. We just gotta move now to make certain, if it's already happened, nothin' more happens." She opened her mouth to speak but Layne kept talking. "I've given you a job, Roc. Quit fuckin' around and do it."

She went stiff in his arm before she nodded.

Then she turned toward the coffeepot.

"Hello, Adele?" Rocky said into her phone. She was tense and she'd taken three big breaths before she'd dialed the number.

Layne was sitting on the counter, holding a mug. Rocky was standing on the floor, her waist pressed to his knee, her hand resting lightly on his thigh.

Then it squeezed as Layne watched her face go pale and her eyes go unfocused.

"What?" she whispered. "Yes, sorry, of course, I'll let you go. If you need anything…" She trailed off and Layne put a hand to her chin. Gripping it between thumb and finger, he forced her eyes to his and he sucked in breath at what he saw. "I'm…yes, I'm with him. He's right here. You want to talk to him?"

Shit, shit, fucking *shit*.

"Just hang on one second, okay?" Rocky said into the phone.

She took her phone from her ear and wrapped her other hand around it.

"Giselle was supposed to go to the game last night. They live close to the school. She walked there but her friends say she never showed and she never came home," Rocky whispered, her eyes bright, the tears not forming but they were threatening.

This was unexpected and definitely unwanted. Withdrawal was one thing, missing another.

Layne put his mug down, jumped off the counter, grabbed the phone she was holding out to him and put it to his ear.

"Adele?" Layne said into the phone.

"No, Tanner, you've got Wade, Wade Speakmon," Giselle's father spoke back and his voice was tight.

"Wade, Rocky told me Giselle didn't come home last night," Layne said.

"The cops know, we called them already. They've been here. Still, I know what you do, I want you to look for her and I'll pay you. I'll pay you whatever you want. You come over right now, I'll give you a thousand dollars."

He had called the cops but Layne didn't get a call.

A young girl from Youth Group missing, Merry would hear or Colt, Layne would get a call.

Fuck.

"That won't be necessary," Layne stated quickly and carried on, "Which uniforms did you get?"

"Sorry?"

"Who were the cops who came out on the call?"

"He didn't wear a uniform. They sent a detective. I figured they weren't messing around, seeing as she's a…" He stopped talking and Layne visualized him swallowing, struggling to keep it together and Layne struggled with him, trying to keep his patience. Then Wade continued. "They sent a detective right off."

Fuck!

Layne looked at Rocky then he was on the move, moving swiftly toward the stairs, speaking and walking. "What was the detective's name?"

"Rutledge. Harry Rutledge," Wade answered.

Fuck!

Layne took the stairs two at a time.

"Only Rutledge?" he asked.

"Sorry?" Wade answered.

"Was it only one detective? Did they only send Rutledge?"

"Yes."

"I want the names and phone numbers of all her friends. Every one. You get your wife to write them down. You call the police, you talk to Garrett Merrick, Alec Colton, Patrick Sullivan, Mike Haines or Drew Mangold. You don't talk to anyone but one of those men and you absolutely do *not* talk to Harrison Rutledge."

"Why?"

"No time to explain. I'm hanging up now. Do it. Someone will be over to get that list."

"Okay," Wade Speakmon whispered.

"Don't worry Wade, I'll find your girl," Layne promised then disconnected.

He was in Rocky's room and he bent to pick up his t-shirt as he again engaged his phone.

"Layne," Rocky called and his neck went back to see her standing in the door, face pale, dark hair framing it, she was holding her body carefully.

"Not now, baby," he whispered, straightened, pulled his shirt over his head then he scrolled down to Ryker in his phone and hit go.

It rang once then Ryker answered with a, "Yo."

"You listening?" Layne asked.

"Yep, to nothin'," Ryker replied. "Relieved Dev, who, by the way, is a pain in the ass."

Layne was moving while bent, grabbing his boots and socks. "Dev get anything?"

"Nope, that's why he's a pain in the ass. Pissed and left while bitchin' about spendin' all night listenin' to nothin'. Don't think they're even there. Silence."

"I want Gaines," Layne stated. Sitting on the edge of the bed, he put the phone between ear and shoulder and Ryker finally read his tone.

"What?"

"You got any clue where he'd be?"

"Why?"

"Speakmon girl is missin' and has been since last night. She left to go to the game, never made it there, never made it home. I want Gaines. You leave my office, you get on your bike and you find that fucker. You got friends, you get on the phone, you mobilize their asses and they find that fucker. I want him in my office."

"Blows your operation, bro," Ryker said softly.

"We'll worry about that later. Find that fucker," Layne replied, yanking on a boot.

"Blows everything, you take him," Ryker returned.

"Find. That. Fucker," Layne repeated, disconnected and yanked on his other boot.

"Layne," Rocky whispered and Layne didn't look at her.

He called Devin.

"What?" Devin clipped, Layne stood and moved to Rocky.

"Giselle is missing," Layne answered.

"I'm on it," Devin declared and disconnected.

Layne stopped at Roc and finally looked down at her.

"It'll be okay," he whispered.

Her hands came to his tee at his sides and fisted.

"Layne," she whispered.

He wrapped his hand around the back of her head, pulled her to him and kissed the top of her hair.

Then, his lips still there, he whispered, "It'll be okay. Get to my house. Now."

He felt her head nod.

Then he let her go, pulled gently away and took off.

He was out of the gate and on the road when his mind cleared of everything except trying to shut it off from thinking he waited too long.

He was trying but he was failing.

The door to the reverend's house opened and Layne looked at Pastor Knox.

"Well, Tanner Layne!" He smiled big. "What a surprise, you here, you and your ma back at church, bringin' your boys and Raquel into the fold—"

Layne didn't smile and cut him off. "I need the whereabouts of TJ Gaines and I need them right now."

Pastor Knox's smile faded, his brows drew together in confusion, and he asked softly, "What?"

"Your Youth Minister, TJ Gaines, is not a Youth Minister. He's the recruiting agent for an underage sex racket," Layne laid it out and Pastor Knox's face went as white as his hair. "Giselle Speakmon went missing last night and I need Gaines."

"That can't be," Pastor Knox whispered.

"It is," Layne returned. "Now I got a girl missin' and I don't have time to convince you this is true. You know where he is, where he might be or how I can get in contact with him, you need to tell me and you need to do it right now."

"I...we...we check out all of our employees. He checked out."

"TJ Gaines checked out, sure. But the man you got workin' for you is not TJ Gaines."

"I—"

"Reverend, you can freak out later, "Layne cut in impatiently. "Now, I need everything you can tell me about TJ Gaines."

Pastor Knox stared at him then he stepped back from the door, turning sideways, and Layne didn't hesitate. He walked right in.

⟲

Layne's boots made noises on the tile around the high school swimming pool but no one could hear it because all the noise the boys were making while swimming their laps was reverberating around the huge room.

But Nick Fullerton saw him. He pulled his whistle out of his mouth, smiled big and walked to Layne.

"Tanner," he called while walking. "Jas tell you? He picked up another one last night. Purdue." His smile turned huge but it would, Nick Fullerton was a Boilermaker. "They're real interested."

Again, Layne didn't smile back.

Instead, when Nick stopped close to him, he ordered, "I need my boys out of the pool, showered and their asses in Jas's car. Giselle Speakmon went missin' last night."

Fullerton's eyes got wide and he whispered, "No shit?"

"No shit. Tripp and Jas know Giselle. I need my boys."

"Dad!" Tripp yelled. He was out of the pool and running as best he could on the grips on the tile toward Layne and Fullerton.

Layne glanced at his son then his eyes went back to Fullerton. "Any boys want to help find her, it would be appreciated. They find anything, they call me. Tripp and Jas have my number. She isn't alone, they don't go in, they stay clear and they call me. No one else. Not the cops. *Me.*"

"Dad," Tripp repeated but Layne didn't look at him. He lifted his hand and curled it around his son's wet shoulder but he didn't take his eyes from Fullerton.

"That understood?" Layne demanded.

"What do you mean, she's not alone?" Fullerton asked.

"Someone might have her," Layne answered.

"This someone dangerous?" Fullerton asked.

"Absolutely," Layne answered.

"Shit," Fullerton muttered.

"Dad!" Tripp yelled and grabbed his father's forearm so Layne looked to him to see Jasper was at his back, Seth, Jamie and Mitch at Jasper's back.

"I can't send high school students on a girl hunt if it's dangerous, Tanner," Fullerton said, calling Layne's attention back to him.

"Then don't. But my boys are huntin'," Layne returned and his eyes went to Jasper. "Shower. Charger. You go to Giselle's house, you get a list from her mom and dad I asked them to make, you call and you visit every one of her friends. You make those girls talk. They heard anything from Giselle, *anything*, you report it back to me."

"Right," Jasper said instantly.

"You see TJ Gaines or his car while you're out, you report it to me. You don't go in. You don't follow him. You get the fuck out of there, call and report where you saw him or his car, get me?" Layne went on.

"Got you," Jasper replied.

"I fucked up," Tripp whispered and Layne's eyes cut to his youngest.

"Get that outta your head," he ordered.

Tripp shook his head, taking a step back, pulling from Layne's hand but running into his brother so he stopped. "I fucked up. I was bein' stupid. Selfish. I thought she was playin' games with me. I shoulda said something. I thought she was—"

Layne hooked his son behind the neck and pulled him forward, bending slightly to get in his face. "*I* fucked up, Tripp. *I* did it. *I* knew better than to finesse this. You're fourteen years old and you were doin' what you were told. You did good, you did right, and now you gotta keep your shit together and help me find your girl."

Tripp didn't believe him. Tripp liked this girl. Tripp was scared as shit. Layne knew it and seeing it in his boy's eyes, it tore him up.

But he couldn't dwell. He needed to move.

He gave Tripp's neck a squeeze, straightened and looked at Jasper.

"Shower. Charger," he ordered, his eyes sliced through Fullerton, he turned and he walked out of the natatorium.

Layne was in his Suburban, making his fourth pass around the Christian Church when his phone rang. His neck was tight, he was pissed he had so little intel on Gaines he had no clue where to look.

He grabbed the phone off the passenger seat, looked at the display and put it to his ear.

"What you got for me, Dev?"

"Cell number the reverend gave you binged. We got his location. Ryker rendezvoused at the office to report in, he was here when I locked on the GPS signal and we moved out. On our way now. Ryker says ETA is ten minutes."

"Give me a location," Layne ordered.

Devin gave him the location and the location surprised him, since it was on Colt and Cal's street. Not only on their street, next door to Cal, directly across the street from Colt. Then Dev stated, "We're not waitin'."

"Don't," Layne returned, cutting through the parking lot to do a uey to the alley so he could hit Main and back up Devin and Ryker. "I'm five minutes behind. See you there."

"Copy that. Out," Devin grunted and Layne heard the disconnect.

He was in the process of tossing his phone to his passenger seat when it rang. He twisted it in his hand, looked at the display, took the call and put it to his ear.

"Sweetcheeks, now is not a good time," he said into the phone.

"Your mom and me are on our way to Giselle," Rocky said back and Layne's chest seized.

"No you're not," he growled.

"Yes, we are, Layne," she shot back. "I've been calling her all morning, leaving messages. She picked one up and she called me back. She says she's alone, hiding out, scared to death. She says she only wants me. No one else but me."

Good news was, Giselle was alive and able to make calls on her phone. Bad news was, Layne's woman was a nut.

"Where is she?" Layne asked.

"Two two three Rosemary Avenue. A girlfriend's house. I know this girl, her parents took her out of school. Her grandma's sick and not going to make it. They all flew to Florida to be with her, their house is empty."

Two two three Rosemary Avenue was not where Devin and Ryker were heading.

"You know this is where this girl lives?" Layne asked.

"No, but that's where Giselle says she is and we're headed there," Rocky answered.

Fuck.

"Where is it?" Layne asked.

"The Sunny Hills development, toward Clermont."

Layne knew it.

"I'll go, you go back to the house," Layne ordered.

"She told me not to tell anyone. She's scared to death, Layne. She told me she'll only open the door to me."

"I'll go, you go back to the house," Layne repeated, clipped this time.

"She's terrified, Layne!"

"What did I tell you about doin' stupid shit?" Layne bit out.

"She's alone and she's scared," Rocky snapped back.

"You think, maybe, she isn't alone? You think maybe she's sayin' somethin' someone's tellin' her to say?" Layne gritted through his teeth.

Rocky was silent.

Then she said, "We won't approach. We'll recon the area and stop at a side road. Your mom's driving because my car is a two seater. They won't know the car even if they see it. You go in first. She's not alone, that's yours. She is, I come in and that's mine. Deal?"

Recon the area? Jesus.

"Deal," Layne replied because he had no time to talk her out of something she was determined to do, and making matters worse, Vera was acting sidekick which meant Layne had zero chance of talking *both* of them down.

He was rethinking his maneuver of reuniting his ma with Roc when he called Dev.

When he disengaged on the call to Dev, he called Merry.

"You don't have backup," Rocky whispered through the window.

"Merry's on his way, not five minutes out," Layne said back, glanced at Vera then his eyes went back to Rocky. "It's all good, I'll take it slow and won't take chances."

"Layne—" Rocky whispered.

"Keep your phone in your hand, your eyes peeled." His gaze went to his mother. "Car on, Mom, hand on the gearshift, anything goes down, you're gone."

Vera, eyes wide and lips pressed together, nodded.

"Layne—" Rocky repeated, still whispering.

Layne locked eyes with her.

"Be back, sweetcheeks," he whispered back, turned away and started to move through backyards.

It was broad daylight but it was cold, overcast, the air heavy with an impending rain that was going to be chilly—no one was out barbequing, mowing their lawn, gardening, playing with their dogs. That didn't mean no one saw him. It was doubtful if they did they'd confront him. They'd call the police. Layne was counting on that. Confrontation would be bad, a waste of time. Cops he could handle.

He counted down the house numbers and as he did he thanked God that no one in this development had put up fences, undoubtedly an HOA restriction, open space was attractive, a variety of fencing not so much. Rosemary Avenue's numbers started on the opposite end of the street, Rocky and Vera had done a drive through and reported they ended in house number two thirty-five. Two twenty-three was seven houses in, no cars in the drive and no movement they could see when they drove by.

Layne approached two twenty-three keeping out of sight behind a big pine tree. He skirted the tree and looked in the windows. Blinds and curtains pulled.

Fuck.

He waited seconds and did so as he watched for movement, the blinds flipping up or the curtains pulled back for someone to look out.

Nothing.

He moved around the tree and quickly to the house. Back to it then he ran bent double under the windows to the French doors that led to a low patio.

Curtains pulled on the doors. He moved to them and silently tried the doorknob.

Locked.

He crouched. Pulling his kit out of his back jeans pocket, he picked the lock.

The owners needed a new lock. It took him less than thirty seconds.

He put the kit back in his jeans and pulled his gun out of the holster at his belt.

The flashback hit him and it hit him hard.

Ambush.

When he got shot, he'd infiltrated one of Rutledge's crime scenes. He was looking for evidence Rutledge missed in his report. Merry said the work had been shoddy, every cop in that department knew it, but none of them could go back to the scene to follow up on Rutledge's work without Rutledge knowing he'd been made.

Rutledge set him up. Fucked up the case because he knew someone would feed it to Layne and Layne would be looking.

This could be the same thing, but with Giselle Speakmon caught in the crossfire.

Fuck.

He flipped off the safety on his gun, sucked in breath, slowly turned the handle and opened the door just enough for him to get through.

Nothing. No alarm, no sound, no movement.

He slid in, swiftly and silently closed the door and crouched low.

Still nothing.

Quietly, he moved through the family room into the living room seeing they were clear, through to the front, across the foyer into the dining room. Clear. Back into the kitchen. Clear.

No noise. No movement.

Back through the family room, living room and into the foyer, putting his back against the wall, gun up, eyes up, he crept up the stairs.

He made it to the top, doors all around, all of them closed. Sitting duck.

Fuck.

A door opened slightly, Layne's gut squeezed and he pointed his gun to it, crouched low and moved to the opposite side of the landing, shoulder to wall.

He waited.

Nothing.

Then it flew open and Giselle Speakmon darted out of it. She ran straight to him then tried to get around him. His arm went out and he caught her at the waist. She screamed and he straightened, picking her up clean off her feet. He strode to the door closest to him, opened it, entered gun up, then he slammed the door, went down to the ground. Giselle in front of him still screaming, he rolled over her and came up, scanned the room, eyes and gun pointed at each corner.

Empty.

Giselle was on the move behind him, he turned and grabbed her, pulling her to him.

"*No!*" she shrieked.

"Giselle, honey, it's me. Mr. Layne. You here alone?"

She was struggling against his grip and he was having trouble controlling her because he didn't want to drop his gun.

She got free, planted a foot to run but he caught her forearm, pulled her to him and got in her face. "Giselle, calm down. Are you here alone?"

"I won't do it again!" she cried, shaking her head, twisting her arm against his grip.

Shit.

"Honey, calm down. You're safe. Your dad sent me."

"I won't do it again! I won't! *I won't!*"

Layne yanked her close, wrapped an arm around her and backed up, keeping her close and pulling her away from the door.

"You don't have to do it again, honey. You never have to do it again. I promise. It's over. Never again," he whispered.

He heard movement in the hall and so did Giselle. Her head whipped toward the door and Layne pushed her behind him and trained his gun on the door.

Slowly the door opened, Layne aimed, the door opened further then he saw Merry's head jump in view as he cased the room before it disappeared.

It came back and Merry slid into the room, closing the door.

Giselle pressed into his back.

Layne dropped his gun and whispered, "Got Giselle. We need to check the upstairs is clear."

Merry nodded.

"I'm alone," Giselle whispered from behind him and Layne turned, dropped into a crouch and got close to her face.

"You're alone?" he asked.

She nodded.

"Why are you here alone, Giselle?" Layne asked.

She shook her head, stepped back and ran into the bed. Her body got still and she stared at him.

"Rocky," she whispered.

"I'll call Roc," Merry murmured and Layne stood.

"No, Merry, we gotta check the house. I want to make sure it's clear before Rocky gets here."

Merry nodded.

"I'm alone," Giselle repeated and Layne looked down at her.

"We're just going to check," Layne said as he heard Merry moving through the room, opening the closet doors. "You stay here, keep that door closed, don't go anywhere, stay quiet, yeah?"

She nodded.

Layne's eyes moved to Merry then they moved out.

"I want eyes on this door, Merry," Layne whispered after they closed it. "She could make a break for it."

"Why?"

"Don't know. Somethin' tweaked her."

Merry nodded. "I already checked down."

"I did too."

"You in or out?"

"In, you're on the door."

Merry nodded again and Layne nodded back.

Layne opened doors and Merry didn't leave the landing. He entered the rooms, checked closets and bathrooms and came back out.

"Clear," he said after the last one. "Call Roc. Then call Colt."

Merry nodded, holstered his weapon and reached for his phone.

Layne went to Giselle.

"He's in your office," Devin said into Layne's ear.

Devin and Ryker picked up TJ Gaines.

"Good," Layne replied, his eyes on Rocky who was crouched in front of Giselle and Giselle was sitting on the bed in the room he'd taken her to. He was standing with Merry and Vera out on the landing, his mother slightly removed. She was talking to Wade and Adele Speakmon, telling them their girl was safe.

Layne couldn't hear anything from the room. All he could see was Giselle whispering and Rocky nodding.

"You get her?" Layne asked Devin.

"Not her. He was with another her. He was gettin' a blowjob from some woman Ryker says is named Tina Blackstone. You know her?"

Tina Blackstone. Shit. Everyone knew her and everyone knew to avoid her.

But Tina Blackstone wasn't Giselle's age. Tina was older than Rocky.

"You sure it was Tina Blackstone?" Layne asked.

"Don't know her, boy, but Ryker does. He called her that. She answered to it. So, yeah, sure enough."

"Tina Blackstone's got a big fuckin' mouth, Dev," Layne told him.

"And your boy Ryker has a persuasive way about him, Tanner. Trust me, the bitch won't talk."

Well, at least that was good.

"You want us to sit on him or you want us to get him to talk?" Devin asked.

"Sit on him. Let me see what's happenin' here," Layne answered. "But forward thinkin, if you need to make him talk, use Ryker. Let him loose. No rules. Scare the piss out of him. He needs to be more afraid of us than that bitch he works for. But no visible marks," Layne instructed.

"Tanner," Merry whispered and Layne's eyes cut to him.

"You didn't hear that," Layne whispered back.

"We makin' a double agent here?" Devin asked but he knew. He was clarifying.

"That bitch know we got him?" Layne asked.

"Far's I know, no," Devin answered.

"I'll call when I know more. He may walk out of there in cuffs or we may need him. We need him and you can't break him, again, he walks out of there in cuffs. You can, he's just switched sides."

"Oh," Devin whispered. "We'll break him."

Disconnect.

Layne pulled his phone from his ear.

"Brother," Merry murmured and Layne looked at him.

"We rush this, we take him down and him alone. We turn him, we get her and Rutledge."

Merry got close. "This may have escaped you, Tanner, but we got a tweaked teenage girl in there. Her parents are gonna blow this and you do not want your end messy."

"I know her parents are gonna blow this, Merry, that's because it's blown. But if I make a mess, you gotta do what you gotta do to clean it up and you gotta keep a close eye on Rutledge if he hasn't already disappeared. He intercepted the missing person call last night. Went to the Speakmons' house alone then sat on it."

Merry's brows went up.

"Yeah, you haven't heard about it means he didn't share. You got a teenage girl missin' in this 'burg, every cop in the department will know and every one of them would be on the hunt. Whatever happened, they thought she was gonna blow them. He intercepted that call means he knew the Speakmons would call it in. That means he was waitin' for it. That means somethin' happened last night with at least Gaines, maybe the woman. He can't hide his shit anymore, Merry. That proves he's linked to at least Gaines. We got them both. Gaines comes in limpin', that's the least of your worries."

Merry got closer, "I want Rutledge out now."

"I got no problem with her losin' her protection," Layne returned. "But you call it out now, you have to open an investigation. You got dirt, he'll need to explain, boys'll be lookin' over their shoulders, whisperin', but that shit takes a long time, Merry. And he'll bolt but, like I said, he could have already bolted. You hold out, we get what she's got on him, he's never seen again."

"Then no investigation. I'm just swingin' my ass out on this right alongside yours, brother. I want him just as tweaked as that girl is in there." Layne studied him and Merry nodded. "Yeah, brother, I heard her." He leaned in closer and his voice dropped lower. "I fuckin' *heard* her."

"Means you could get dead and I could get dead," Layne whispered back.

"His desk is beside mine," Merry hissed.

Jesus, the Merricks.

"Patience, Garrett." Layne kept whispering.

"She said, 'I won't do it again.'" Merry reminded him.

"Patience, brother. We're close."

"I want this done," Merry repeated his sister's words of that morning.

Layne leaned to an inch away from his friend. "I do to, Merry, but cool it. Let's see what she has to say. *Then* we'll decide the way to play it."

Merry stared in his eyes then he nodded.

Vera approached. "Parents are coming over now," she whispered.

Layne nodded to his mother and wrapped an arm around her.

"I don't think I want to be your receptionist anymore, honey," she said when she rested her weight into his side.

"Didn't think so," Layne murmured, giving her a squeeze then going alert when Rocky stood. She rested a hand on the side of Giselle's head and slid it down to cup her cheek. Then she bent low, said something, turned and walked out of the room.

"Vera, would you—?" Rocky didn't finish. Layne's mother hustled into the room toward Giselle.

Rocky's eyes went to Layne then to her brother then she walked down the stairs.

Layne and Merry followed her.

She was in the kitchen and they barely got close to her before she started whispering.

"He came after her last night, when she was walking to the game. Gaines. Said he'd give her a ride. She said no. He stopped and got out of the car. She said no again. He made a grab for her and she took off. At first, she hid. Then she waited. Then she came here thinking he might go to her house. She broke in through a window."

"Why didn't she call her parents?" Layne asked and Rocky locked eyes with him.

"They took pictures of her."

Layne's stomach pitched and Merry jerked away, probably looking for something to throw. Rocky moved forward, her hand curling around her brother's bicep and he stilled.

"Not like that, but it still wasn't good and she didn't like it," Rocky whispered quickly then her eyes went back to Layne. "She said they were pictures with her clothes on. She says they told her they were recruiting models. She'd go to New York City. She'd be in magazine ads. She did it with Alexis and another girl. Tiffany Emmerson. She didn't say anything about the pictures because Alexis and Tiffany were excited about it, talked her into keeping quiet, but she still didn't like it. But him being alone, making a grab for her, that's what freaked her out. She said even a Youth Minister should know not to offer a ride to a girl alone and definitely not push it when she declines."

Smart girl, thank fuck.

"Tiffany Emmerson sixteen, long, dark hair?" Layne asked and Rocky's eyes got wide.

"Yes," she answered.

"Drive a red Ford Focus?" Layne went on.

"I don't know. Why?" Rocky answered.

"Hunch," Layne muttered, knowing exactly who Tiffany Emmerson was. Too old but up for it except she didn't know what "it" was. Fuck. He looked at Merry. "That's a blonde, a redhead and a brunette."

"Collecting types," Merry murmured and Layne nodded.

Layne looked back at Rocky. "She place the woman there?"

Rocky nodded to Layne. "Yes. Said she was touchy."

Layne bet she was.

Jesus.

"Said she gave her the creeps," Rocky continued and got closer to Layne. "She said she didn't have a problem with Gaines until he took her to that woman and she definitely has a problem with him after last night. He was just the Youth Minister and she didn't really think much of him, except he was the Youth Minister and he was cute. But she didn't like that woman."

"Was the touching inappropriate?" Layne asked and Rocky shook her head.

"No, just familiar and frequent. She played with their hair, positioned their bodies for the photos, put makeup on them. But it was all normal photo shoot stuff as far as Giselle knew. Except Giselle said it was a lot of makeup and Giselle didn't like the poses."

Christ.

"So why didn't she call her parents to come and get her?" Layne asked and Rocky shook her head again.

"I don't know, sweetheart. She's fourteen and she was freaked. She said if her parents knew she did the photo shoot, they'd be angry. They're over-protective, especially after her sister got sick. That's why she didn't phone them. She thought she'd be in trouble if they found out. She wasn't thinking straight, just got scared and hid. Tripp called and texted, and her parents called and texted, and the more they called the more scared she got. But she got my call and she thought she could trust me so she called me back."

She paused, Layne nodded, and Rocky continued.

"The photo shoot was about a month ago but nothing after that even though Gaines offered it. Giselle wouldn't do it and she doesn't think Alexis or Tiffany did either, but they were trying to talk her into it. They'd made a girl pact. It was an all or nothing thing. Then she said Gaines spent a lot of time with her after that, talked to her a lot, tried to make friends, and she felt weird about it because he was pushing another shoot. She said she'd swear she'd sometimes see him, when she left school, in his car outside her house, but she'd look again and he wasn't there so she thought she was see-ing things. But last night, she wasn't seeing things."

No, she wasn't seeing things.

Ryker needed this intel. If they were doing it to Giselle, they could be doing it to Alexis.

"This happened last night, why'd she cut Tripp out at school yester-day?" Layne asked.

Rocky's expression cleared and her lips twitched. "Alexis's advice. Told her she was making it too easy on Tripp. Told her to play hard to get. That was nothing to do with Gaines or any of this. She's almost more worried that Tripp is going to be mad at her than she is about her parents or Gaines."

Jesus, teenagers playing games. Starting young. It felt like Layne had a lifetime of that and he sure as fuck was glad that shit was over.

"They change clothes?" Layne asked and Rocky's face grew confused.

"Change clothes?" she repeated and Layne moved close to her, putting his hand to her neck.

"Change clothes, Roc, at the photo shoot. Even alone, if they did it, they could have had cameras on them," Layne explained and Rocky swallowed.

"I didn't ask," Rocky whispered.

Layne jerked his head toward the ceiling and whispered back, "Ask, baby, hurry before her folks get here."

"Shit," she muttered, looked at her brother then walked out of the room.

Merry moved to Layne.

"So, what's the play, brother?"

"He's out," Layne stated instantly, looking at Merry. "I outed him to the reverend as exactly what he is. He doesn't know it yet but he doesn't have a job anymore. Pastor Knox would not let him work undercover and we're not workin' that angle with that perv. No more recruiting. This model business is out too. We tell the Speakmons, we tell Ryker, who's seein' Alexis McGraw's mother, and we tell the Emmersons."

"Then they'll flee, they're outed and got no way to recruit."

"Maybe and maybe not. We turn Gaines, we may be able to get him to talk them into trying to play it another way. They're dug in, set up. They spent a lot of time on this and they were goin' in for the kill. They got a lot invested, and because of that, there's a lot to keep them here. They need to dismantle the operation, they lose big. We turn Gaines, we get him to get them to cool it, convince them he's still got the girls, he leads us to them and we take them all down."

"Rutledge?"

"We don't get what she's got on him, we find him, you're gonna hafta flip Rutledge in the interrogation room."

Merry smiled.

Layne didn't return his smile. He pulled out his phone and called Ryker.

"Yo," Ryker answered on the first ring.

"Alexis safe?" Layne asked.

"Yeah," Ryker answered.

"How sure are you of that?" Layne asked.

"Sure enough, since I been callin' my babe probably every fifteen minutes since I heard that girl was missin'. Alexis is at home. Ticked. She's grounded because she mouthed off bad when Lissa cut her off from Youth Group."

Every fifteen minutes and cut off from Youth Group. Layne believed it. Proof Ryker was the man Layne thought he was.

"Right, they're keepin' an eye on the girls. Don't know why but they're followin' them. You need to brief your babe and you got a friend you can trust, you put a man on her house."

"Shit," Ryker muttered then said, "Roger that."

"Gaines sweating?"

"He's tied to a chair watchin' your man clean his gun. He's findin' it fascinatin', bro."

Layne didn't laugh.

"All right, Ryker, I need you to get me four things from this guy. One, why'd he go after Giselle last night? Two, are Towers and Rutledge still in town? Three, are they lookin' for Giselle? And four, if they are, why's he gettin' a blowjob from Tina Blackstone?"

"You got it," Ryker replied.

"I'll want more later. Start with that and anything else you wanna know."

"Ditto on the 'you got it,'" Ryker repeated.

"Keep listening to the apartment. If he's gettin' head from Tina because they're not tweaked by Giselle running then the woman might go back to the apartment. We'll need to hear what she has to say."

"Devin's all over that," Ryker told him.

"Right," Layne replied. "Tell Devin he's on clean up. He needs to make sure the Reverend doesn't talk. Youth Group is suspended for the time being, no explanation, that's it. Nothin' else leaks."

"I'll tell 'im."

"Later." He disconnected and called Jasper.

Jasper answered on the second ring.

"What's up, Dad?"

"We have Giselle. She's fine. *Totally* fine. Tripp with you?"

"Yeah."

"Tell him now."

He listened to Jasper say, "Dad's found Giselle. She's cool, Tripp-o-matic. It's all good."

"Where is she?" Layne heard Tripp ask.

"Her parents are coming to pick her up." Layne answered, but didn't wait until Jas relayed this information before continuing. "You boys finish gathering intel from Giselle's friends. We need everything we can get on Gaines. When you're done, you can go home to your mom's. And Jasper, I need you to locate Tiffany Emmerson. If you don't have her number, find someone who does. I want you to call in to me when you know she's safe then I want one of your boys glued to her until I can get to her parents."

"Another favorite," Jasper muttered.

"You got it, bud," Layne muttered back. "Closin' ranks, son."

"Gotcha," Jasper replied. "Later."

"Later, Jas." Layne flipped his phone shut and looked at Merry. "I need your dad. We're spread thin and I gotta have ears on that apartment. Can you call him and get him to the office?"

Merry nodded, pulled out his phone and stepped away.

Then Rocky walked into the room.

"They didn't change clothes," she announced when she got close. "They told them what to wear to the shoot. It was skimpy and Giselle doesn't do skimpy. Alexis told her she could borrow something, but Giselle wouldn't do it. She told me Alexis and Tiffany did, but the woman, the photographer and Gaines didn't make a big deal out of it that Giselle didn't."

"Good kid," Layne muttered.

Rocky got close and slid an arm around his waist so he slid his around her shoulders.

"She's feeling a bit foolish, sweetheart, thinks she made a big deal out of nothing. Worried her parents are going to be angry, Tripp…I didn't know what to say."

Layne had looked down at her while she was talking and when she stopped, he asked, "What did you say?"

"I said always go with your gut. You get a bad feeling, you get safe and then you find someone you trust, which was what she did. I didn't get into Gaines. I just told her she did the right thing and everyone would understand."

Layne squeezed her shoulder and muttered, "Good answer, sweetcheeks."

"Probably be a good idea you get Tripp to text her, say he heard she's all right, he's glad and she should give him a call when she can." Rocky pressed closer and whispered, "She likes him, baby, like, *a lot*."

Merry moved back to them. He was off the phone, his head tilted to listen to the car pulling into the drive and then he looked at Layne. "Parents," he murmured then started to the front door.

"You call him, Roc. He'll like to hear that from you," Layne told her and she nodded, smiled up at him and her arm got tight around him.

Then her head turned to the door they heard Merry opening.

"We better talk to Adele and Wade," she whispered, eyes still pointing in the direction of the door.

"Yeah," Layne sighed and he kept his arm around his woman as he led her to the door.

When Layne arrived at his office, Dev met him at the outer door.

"You got here just in time for the good part," Dev whispered on a scary smile.

"He talkin'?" Layne asked.

"Yeah and I'm wonderin' 'bout her now, she picked this guy," Devin answered. "First, that boy is stupid as shit. I reckon he got by on his looks his whole life and that worked for him so he uses about a quarter of the eleven percent of the brain that other people use. Second, he's scared of her. He's scared of us. He's scared of everything. Last, he don't care who he works or who he works for, he just wants to stay pretty."

"Pretty isn't gonna serve him very well in the hole," Layne observed.

"Yeah, I explained that to him. That's one of the reasons why he's scared of us," Dev replied.

491

"You get my answers?" Layne asked and Devin nodded.

"First, the woman is gettin' impatient. She's got clients all lined up, a party, big money. They need those girls but can't get a lock on 'em because of Giselle. The girls have made it clear they move as a unit and Giselle's doesn't feel like movin'. Towers is unhappy as in un...hap...*pee*," Devin answered then grinned at Layne. "This is not only 'cause Giselle doesn't want shit to do with them, but also because Giselle found herself a boy-friend and they couldn't find any time with her away from Tripp."

At that, Layne grinned back. It was a small grin but it was a grin because Tripp had done good and because his son would be pleased he did his part to keep Giselle safe.

Devin continued, "Now she's runnin' outta excuses for her clients who are chompin' at the bit after seein' the girls' photos. The two other girls are good to go, his words. Words, I'll add, that made your boy Ryker go a bit scary, Tanner, and when I say that, I mean he scared *me*, he got so fuckin' scary."

"He cares about Alexis," Layne muttered.

"Well, that's plain to see," Devin muttered back then kept talking. "Anyway, Giselle was muckin' up the works. Towers was puttin' on the pressure and he was gettin' desperate, started followin' her and acted on his own. He found his opportunity, Giselle alone without Tripp at her side, and he took it. When she bolted, he freaked, told Rutledge. According to Gaines, Rutledge is nearly as scared of this bitch as Gaines is. Told him he'd take care of it and keep it quiet. The woman doesn't know shit. Gaines, bein' what I know now of Gaines, shrugged his shoulders. Once he handed off to Rutledge, he went his merry way and his way is paved with all things merry. Apparently, when he isn't spreading the word of God while workin' at settin' up teenagers to get gang raped, he's been bangin' this Tina person for months, amongst others."

Layne nodded, thinking briefly of Tina Blackstone. Tina would open her legs for anyone but she'd make a world record of it if that someone was good-looking. And she didn't care who they were or what they did. He seriously doubted Tina would blink if she learned she was getting hit by a guy who was recruiting for a child prostitution racket. To be fair, she might shiver a bit, but then she'd shake it off and move on.

Devin got out of his way and Layne set aside thoughts of Tina and walked into his office. Dev followed him and Layne saw TJ Gaines, or as Layne knew him now from the phone call he'd made getting his identity from his prints, Jeremy Goulding, tied to one of his office chairs and looking about ready to piss his pants.

"You," he whispered when he looked from Ryker sitting in Layne's desk chair and cleaning his fingernails with his huge, freaking knife, to Layne.

"How's it goin', Jeremy?" Layne asked, walking to his desk and leaning on it.

Jeremy's head jerked.

"Yeah," Layne said softly. "I know who you are. Got solid evidence you're guilty in the State of Indiana of identity theft and know you got a warrant out on you in Tennessee too."

Jeremy's eyes slid beyond Layne to Ryker then to the side to take in Devin then they shot back to Layne.

"Big step up," Layne remarked, "Movin' from small time cons, all women, to child prostitution."

Jeremy's pale face turned gray. "That isn't part of my deal."

Layne's brows went up. "No?"

Jeremy shook his head.

"Saw you kiss Tiffany Emmerson's neck. Saw Alexis McGraw put her hand on you. Heard you shared gum with Alexis, mouth to mouth, after it had been chewed," Layne noted and he felt the sudden wall of rage coming off Ryker slam into his back, just as he'd intended.

Jeremy felt it too and he bucked his body, scooting his chair back, his eyes locked on Ryker.

"Sit still, Jeremy," Layne said quietly as Dev moved in behind Jeremy.

Jeremy's eyes didn't move from Ryker, but he did as he was told.

"I didn't...I didn't," he stammered, "I didn't do that."

"You callin' Alexis a liar?" Layne asked.

Jeremy's eyes darted to Layne. "No!" he cried.

"So you *did* share gum with her," Layne pressed.

"I...no, she shared gum with me," Jeremy amended.

"Okay," Layne said then lied, "I see the difference."

"It's just a job," Jeremy explained quickly as Layne heard and felt Ryker move behind him. "I didn't like it. I'm not into girls. I'm into women, you know, like your lady." Layne's back straightened and his face changed and Jeremy's body bucked again. "No! No! I mean, she's pretty. I'm complimenting her. I'm just saying I'm not into girls. But that was my part of the job. And Nic said she'd take care of the girls, she said she always takes care of the girls."

"Takes care of them how?" Layne asked.

"Every way. Money, clothes, attention. Girls love that shit and Nic loves them. She's good with them. It isn't as creepy as you think," Jeremy explained and Layne had trouble controlling his sneer and the urge to open up the flesh of Jeremy's face with his fist.

"You're wrong," Layne whispered. "You are *way* wrong. It's as creepy as I think. Fuck, Jeremy, it's *creepier.*"

"They're not as young as you think either," Jeremy quickly went on.

"Sorry, man, but you're wrong about that too. Giselle's datin' my son and she's fourteen. She's exactly as young as I think," Layne told him.

"Yes, I mean with Giselle, yes, she's...she...I'm sorry about her, okay? She wasn't the right one. Nic told me who to pick and I knew Giselle wasn't the right one but I had to do what Nic said. But the other two, they're fourteen and sixteen goin' on thirty," Jeremy replied.

Ryker moved again. Layne knew he'd been standing. Now he was making his way around the desk.

"Ryker, stand down, brother, he can't talk if he's got a broken jaw," Layne said quietly not taking his eyes off Jeremy who was staring, eyes-wide, body inert, at Ryker.

"That's my girl," Ryker growled.

"I...I know, but you gotta know what she's like," Jeremy replied, proving just how stupid he was because that wave of rage burst out of Ryker again and Layne stood.

Layne turned to Ryker and whispered, "Focus, brother. This guy is not our end game."

Ryker's eyes didn't move from Jeremy and Ryker's body also didn't move. He held it taut. He was struggling. And Devin was right. Ryker pissed was pretty fucking scary.

494

Finally, his gaze slid to Layne and Layne watched as Ryker forced his body to relax.

Time to move on.

Layne turned back to Jeremy.

"You're goin' down," he informed him and Jeremy's eyes cut swiftly to Layne. "Now, though, now you gotta decide how far down you're goin'."

"I—" Jeremy started but Layne cut him off.

"I'm not done talkin'." Jeremy snapped his mouth shut and nodded. "We're workin' with the cops on this and now you're workin' with them too."

Layne watched Jeremy gulp and he kept at him.

"You're gonna leave this office and you're gonna convince Towers and Rutledge that everything is just fine. You're gonna tell them you're close, Giselle is breaking, they gotta give you some time. A week, they don't go for that, a few days. In the meantime, you gotta know, you're blown. Pastor Knox is changin' the locks on the church as we speak. The Speakmon and Emmerson families know what you did and they've both agreed to hold fire and wait for Towers and Rutledge to go down. You're blown, but you convince your partners you're not even though you don't get near any of those girls, any kids from Youth Group or anyone under the age of eighteen in this town or out of it. You work with us, you don't go down all on your own and trust me, man, Towers and Rutledge get a whiff that their scheme is goin' south, they'll bolt and they'll leave you to swing."

"What...what do you want me to do?" Jeremy asked.

"You get me what she's got on Rutledge and in about fifteen minutes, you and Ryker are gonna take a ride. At the end of that ride, there's gonna be a cop. You're gonna tell him everything you know about Rutledge and Towers. Then, we're gonna let you go. You get them talking in the apartment about what you're doin', where you're doin' it and when it's gonna go down."

"I...they're...she's not stupid. She's—"

"I don't give a fuck what she is. You're not a good actor, now you got an hour to learn to be one and you stay in character all the time. When you get up, when you go to bed, when you eat, when you take a shit, when you're fuckin' sleepin'. All the time. Towers gets tweaked, we'll take it out on you."

Jeremy didn't move, didn't nod, didn't blink. He just stared at Layne.

Layne continued, "What you gotta know is, we let you go, you try to disappear, we'll find you. We find you, we're not cops, we don't have rules and when we find you, we'll do you a favor. We'll make it so you won't be so attractive, and we'll make that permanent. So when you do time you won't be instantly made into somebody's bitch."

"I—" Jeremy started, that one syllable a squeak, but he stopped when Layne bent over him, getting in his face.

"You're good, we'll talk to the cops, see what we can do since you cooperated. You're not, Towers and Rutledge disappear, this gets fucked in *any* way, our sole focus, our only reason for living, is to find you and fuck you over so bad, Jeremy, swear to God, you'll regret bein' born. You get me?"

Jeremy didn't answer. He just stared into Layne's eyes, his Adam's apple bobbing.

"You played with girls, young girls. You fucked with their heads. You freaked them out. You betrayed their trust. You took advantage and you did it through *a church*," Layne whispered. "Young girls who should be worried about a pop quiz or if some boy is into them, not worried about bein' caught up in the shitty, creepy, fucked up games you've been playin'. That's some fucked up shit, you asshole, and you're gonna pay for that. But I'm givin' you a break. A break you don't deserve. And *you* get to decide how much you're gonna pay. Now, I asked you, do you get me?"

"I get you," Jeremy whispered.

Layne straightened away from him but looked down at him as he crossed his arms on his chest. "I'm glad to hear that, Jeremy. Now, I know you're not too bright but I want you to concentrate real close on what I'm sayin'. We got you covered. We know your every move. We know where you live, what you drive, where you hang and who you fuck." Part of this was, of course, a lie, but the look on Jeremy's face said he bought it. "So, just to repeat and make sure you get it, you are on our radar and there is no hope of camouflage. You're playin' our game now."

"Right," Jeremy was still whispering.

Layne stared at him a second then he cut his eyes to Devin and Ryker and walked out of the room.

On the landing outside his office, he turned to both men when the door closed behind Ryker.

"Find out everything you can from him," Layne ordered Devin. "Dave Merrick should be here soon. He's going to be listening to the bugs and he's got two friends by the names of Ernie and Spike who are gonna be helping him. They're all ex-cops, they know what they're doin' and they've been briefed." Devin nodded and Layne carried on, "And I want a device on his car. You'll find them in the storage room."

"Key," was Devin's answer and Layne dug his keys out of his pocket, twisted the key to the storage room off his ring and gave it to Devin.

Then his eyes went to Ryker. "You're gonna get a call from Garrett Merrick in about five minutes. He'll tell you where to meet him. You take Jeremy there. You don't have to handle him with care. He falls down half a flight of stairs, shit happens." Layne watched Ryker smile his ugly smile and kept talking. "He's scared but I want him shit scared. You stay while he talks with Garrett then you take him back to his car and turn him loose."

Ryker nodded.

"Game on, men," Layne whispered.

"Fuckin' A, bro," Ryker grunted.

Devin just stared at him then nodded.

Layne turned away and walked down the stairs. The Bachelor Auction Powwow would be done soon, which meant Rocky would be alone soon and he needed to get to his woman.

⟨⟩

"How together are you?" Layne, standing outside on Rocky's balcony, his phone to his ear, asked his youngest son.

"Today freaked me, Dad, but I'm cool," Tripp replied. "I did what Rocky said, texted Giselle to tell her I was glad she was all right. Giselle called me back and Giselle's parents are lettin' me go over there tomorrow to watch football then have dinner. It's all good."

Layne scanned the landscape as he repeated to his son, "How together are you?"

Tripp was silent, then he asked, "I don't know what you're askin', Dad."

497

"You're fourteen, pal, and I got somethin' I wanna tell you. But I gotta know you can take it."

"Is it bad?"

"It could have been."

More silence then, softly, Tripp said, "He was gonna hurt her."

"Yes," Layne answered. "But he didn't and part of the reason why he didn't was because you made it impossible for him to get to her. That's the part I wanted you to know."

Complete silence.

"You did good, pal."

More utter silence.

"You took care of your girl."

Another beat of silence then, "Thanks, Dad."

"Nope, Tripp, I gotta thank you. This is all gonna be over soon and you and Jasper made that happen."

"Cool," Tripp whispered but he didn't sound like he thought it was cool. The word was heavy. He'd felt the weight of what could have gone down, and even though that weight was lifted, the memory of it was fresh.

The door opened, Roc stuck her head out and said, "Sorry, sweetheart, dinner's almost ready. Do you want me to put it to warm?"

"I'll let you go," Tripp, obviously hearing Rocky, said in his ear.

"Give me a minute, Roc," Layne said to Rocky, she smiled and closed the door.

Layne watched her strut through the living room and into the kitchen as he asked Tripp, "You okay, pal?"

"I'm good, Dad."

"This shit starts fuckin' with your head, you call me, yeah?"

"Yeah."

"Good," Layne muttered.

"Dad?" Tripp called.

"Yeah?"

"Jas told me you and Roc aren't fake anymore," Tripp informed him and Layne pulled in a deep, silent breath.

Then he replied, "Thought you figured that out yourself."

"I did. Jas just confirmed it, said you told him it wasn't."

"Well, it isn't," Layne confirmed it again.

Another beat of silence then, quietly, "I'm glad."

He knew that but it was still good to hear it.

"That's good, pal," Layne said quietly back, then, "I gotta go eat dinner."

"Wish I was eatin' Rocky's food," Tripp muttered, Layne knew that too and he grinned.

"Next week, Tripp."

"Okay," Tripp replied then called again, "Dad?"

"Right here, buddy."

"I don't know how to say this," Tripp told him and the muscles in Layne's neck got tight because Tripp sounded like he didn't know how to say whatever he had to say, but also that he didn't want to say it.

"You can be straight with me on anything, you know that," Layne returned.

"Well, it's gonna sound stupid."

"Nothin' you say sounds stupid."

"This will," Tripp shot back.

"No, Tripp, it won't. What's on your mind?"

"It's just..." He paused. "Rocky."

Layne's entire body got tight. "What about her?"

"I'm glad you got her back," Tripp said on a rush and the tightness left Layne's body but it stayed completely still as Tripp kept talking. "For you, 'cause you're my dad but mostly for her."

Layne was silent.

Tripp filled the silence. "Is that weird? I mean, you're my dad and I should—"

Layne cut him off. "It's not weird."

"I mean, I'm glad for you, but Rocky—" Tripp was still talking fast.

"I get it, pal," Layne whispered.

"Is she..." Tripp hesitated. "Is she going to be okay?"

"Why do you ask?"

"Because...well, I don't know but when I talked with Giselle today, at first she was bein' weird and then I realized she thought I was mad at her and I felt bad because she felt bad, and I didn't want her to feel bad because she didn't do anything wrong. And that got me to thinking that maybe Rocky, because of what happened with you guys a long time ago, would feel bad because she thought you were mad at her, but that was big. Bigger than what happened with Giselle and that…that kind of thing…well, I guess I just think it would be hard to let that go."

Christ, but his kid was sharp.

"I've let it go, pal," Layne assured him.

"Has she?"

"We're workin' on it."

"Good," Tripp whispered.

"Got anything else on your mind?" Layne asked.

"No," Tripp answered.

"World peace? Starving nations? The state of the economy?"

He heard Tripp's laugh then, "No, Dad, jeez."

"That shit starts weighin' on you, boy, I'm only a phone call away."

"Right, I'll call when I start worryin' about world peace," Tripp returned.

"I gotta eat," Layne told his son through a smile.

"All right, see you later."

"Later," Layne said then called, "Tripp?"

"Yeah, Dad?"

"Love you, pal."

"Love you too."

"Later."

"Later."

Layne flipped his phone shut and turned to the door. He opened it and was assaulted with the fumes he'd left behind ten minutes ago. Chicken tacos. Rocky had been stewing the meat all day, anxious about Giselle and turning her mind to cooking rather than worrying so she'd put it on that morning before she headed over to his place. This was another recipe she'd perfected in their kitchen years ago. Stewing in the crockpot all day meant the meat would be tender and shredded and after cooking in its spices for the last hour, full of flavor.

Rocky was at the counter, her back to him, and she didn't turn when she asked, "You need a fresh beer, baby?"

"I'll get it," Layne replied but he didn't get it. He walked up to her back, fitted his front to it and slid his arms along her belly, looking over her shoulder to see she was grating cheese.

She didn't stop grating when she noted, "Don't keep beer in my stomach fridge, Layne."

"Mm," Layne replied through a smile, dropped his head and kissed her neck.

Then he lifted a hand, yanked her ponytail holder out and her hair tumbled to her shoulders.

She stopped grating and her neck twisted so she could glare at him. "Seriously, stop doing that."

Layne was still smiling when he replied, "Seriously, no."

Her eyes narrowed then she went smack into stare down. Layne held her stare as his other arm wound around her again and when he was done with the stare down, his arms tightened and he tickled the sensitive skin at her sides.

Her body jerked and twisted as her head shot back, her hands dropped the cheese and the grater, went to his wrists and put pressure on as she shouted through annoyed laughter, "Stop it, Layne!"

"Nope," Layne returned.

"Stop!" she yelled, still twisting in his arms, putting pressure on his wrists and now she was giggling.

Layne was relentless and he kept at her because he missed this. He knew he missed it but having it back, hearing Rocky's laughter, feeling her body against his, doing something normal like preparing to eat dinner together, he realized he didn't miss it, he *missed it*.

And when that feeling threatened to overwhelm him, he stopped tickling her, his arms went around her tight and hard, and he buried his face in the hair at her neck.

When he didn't speak and after she controlled her body and laughter, she called, "Layne?"

"Right here, baby," Layne said into her neck, not lifting his head but giving her a squeeze.

"Are you okay?"

"Oh yeah," he replied.

Her body relaxed but her hands tightened on his wrists.

Then she asked, "Is Tripp okay?"

"Yeah."

Her hands at his wrists slid along his arms so they were crossed on his. "What are you doing?" she whispered.

He lifted his mouth to her ear and answered, "Nothin', which means everything. I forgot that. I forgot how nothing meant everything."

"Layne," she breathed.

"Love you, baby."

Her hands squeezed his arms. "Love you too, sweetheart." She was quiet then she said, "But Layne?"

He lifted his head. "What?"

"New rule. You can't make me cry into grated cheese again."

He turned her around to face him and saw the tracks her silent tears left on her face. His hands moved to her jaws and he used his thumbs to wipe away the wetness.

"Or any foodstuffs," she went on and his eyes went from his thumbs to hers.

"Right," he whispered. "No making you cry into...*foodstuffs*."

She grinned up at him, put her hands to his jaws, lifted up on tiptoe and touched his mouth with hers.

She didn't take her mouth from his when she whispered, "Tacos."

Then she pulled gently away and opened the cupboard to take out the flour tortillas.

Layne went to the fridge and got himself a beer. He got her a fancy-ass one. Then he sat in front of the TV with his woman leaned up against him and ate heaven, Mexican style.

Twenty-Three

ENOUGH?

*H*er hand came up to his jaw, her lips at his ear, Rocky whispered urgently, "Jasper."

Layne's eyes opened and he saw dark.

His cell phone on Rocky's nightstand was ringing but Rocky didn't move. She was out and it was the dead of night.

Layne's neck twisted and he reached for his cell as his eyes took in Rocky's alarm clock. It was one oh seven in the morning.

Fuck.

He looked at the display on his phone and quickly took the call while Rocky stirred at his side.

"Everything okay, bud?" Layne asked Jasper.

"Dad," Jasper replied, and the tone of that one word made Layne squeeze Rocky then swiftly slide out from under her.

"Talk to me," Layne ordered, coming to his feet at the side of the bed.

"It's Keira," Jasper whispered, sounding freaked out.

Fuck!

"What's Keira?" Layne asked. He was moving through the dark room to get clothes. In between the office and Rocky's, he'd gone home and

503

packed a bag. He found it and started pawing through it as he heard Rocky moving in the bed.

"I don't know. She's out. She's in my car and she's out, Dad. Passed out. I've been drivin' around, tryin' to get her to wake up, talk to me. I can't take her back to Mr. and Mrs. Callahan like this. They'll freak. But it's way past her curfew and they're gonna freak anyway. I don't know what to do."

"Break it down for me, bud," Layne demanded. His phone between ear and shoulder, he tugged up his jeans. The light came on, Rocky was out of bed.

"We went to a party. Dad…shit, okay…*shit*," Jas hissed and stopped speaking.

"Jasper, listen to me, boy, you need to give me information right now. Do not worry about getting in trouble. Focus."

There was a pause then, "Okay, well, there was beer and we had some."

Layne pulled a tee out of his bag and yanked it on, keeping his phone to his ear as best he could as Rocky disappeared into the walk-in closet.

"Right," he prompted when Jasper said no more.

"It wasn't that much, Dad, swear. *Swear.* I had one or two because I was drivin'. Keira didn't have much more. I swear, Dad. No way she should be passed out, not like this."

"Keep talking." Layne had grabbed his boots and Rocky was out of the closet wearing unzipped jeans and carrying a sweater.

"She was fine one second, not drunk or anything, and then the next she started stumbling around, acting funny, totally out of it. It didn't take long, minutes, just minutes, Dad, and she passed out. I carried her to the car and started drivin' around. I didn't know what else to do."

"Has she been sick?"

"No, no way. She wasn't that drunk."

"She breathin' okay?"

"Yeah, totally fine. Sometimes she mumbles, moves around. She's just passed out."

"How long ago was this?"

"We were gettin' ready to leave. Her curfew is midnight. So, an hour and a half at most."

Layne was sitting on the bed. His socks on, he was pulling on his boots.

"She ever out of your sight?" he asked.

"What?"

"Keira, at the party, was she ever out of your sight?"

"Yes," Jasper answered. "Once. She went to the bathroom right before she started acting funny."

"The beer, was it bottles, cans, keg?"

"Keg," Jasper replied.

"You get her beers or did someone else?"

"Uh…me, mostly, I think. I don't know."

"It's important, bud, did anyone give her a drink?"

Jasper was silent. Then he bit out, "*Shit!*"

"Someone got her a drink?" Layne pushed.

"No, I don't know, maybe. Some people were doin' shots, Dad, but Keirry and me weren't. At least she wasn't when she was with me. But now I get it. She's not passed out, someone gave her a drink and they slipped her something."

"That's what I'm thinkin'," Layne said. He was up and moving toward the door, Rocky right with him. "Where are you?"

"In the parking lot of Shanghai Salon, in the back."

"Roc and me'll be there in ten. Hang tight and do not leave her."

"Gotcha," Jasper muttered and disconnected.

Layne took his phone from his ear as he moved down the stairs.

"Keira's been slipped something?" Rocky asked his back.

He made it to the bottom and went to his coat on the armchair. Nabbing it, he shrugged it on.

"Yeah, they were at a party, drinkin' beer," Layne answered as he turned to see she was at the bar, grabbing the coat she'd thrown on a stool in front of it. "He says she's totally out."

Rocky's eyes came to him. She was pulling on her coat. "Vi and Cal are gonna freak," she noted softly.

Vi and Cal had been through enough. They were gonna freak, absolutely.

Layne walked to the bar and tagged his keys. "On your phone, sweetcheeks, they're probably worried. Tell them Keira's safe. She was slipped something at a party, Jasper's been takin' care of her and we'll get her home within half an hour."

Rocky nodded, grabbed her purse and dug for her cell as they walked out. Layne locked up and they both hoofed it to the Suburban.

Rocky called Vi and Cal in the car, and listening to her, he knew she got Cal and further he knew she got an unhappy Cal. Layne drove to Shanghai Salon then around it, finding the Charger parked in the dimly lit back. He parked close and got out as Jasper and Rocky got out, Rocky going directly to the passenger seat of the Charger, Layne leaving her to it and going to his boy.

"We're gonna take her home," Layne said to his son without preamble. "You're drivin' Keira, I got your back. You own up to the beer and take what Cal dishes out." Jasper nodded and Layne asked, "You know who would do this to her?" Jasper shook his head. "You know anyone who does this shit?" Jasper shook his head again. "Anyone at the party actin' funny, watchful?"

"Nope," Jasper replied then went on honestly. "But I wouldn't really know, Dad. We were havin' fun. I wasn't payin' much attention."

Layne nodded. "She got admirers?"

"Yeah," Jasper answered. "She's hot."

"Any one of those give you a bad vibe?" Layne asked.

"All of 'em, Dad, she's my babe. Not big on her havin' admirers."

Jesus, uncanny, Jasper was so fucking like him.

"All right, you think about that shit on your way to Violet and Cal because Cal's gonna be askin' these same questions and it's gonna go better for you, you have answers."

Jasper nodded and Rocky walked up to them.

"In the car, bud, let's go," Layne ordered and was about to move away but stopped when he saw Rocky's hand reach out. She grabbed Jasper's and gave it a visible squeeze. Jasper looked to her, his son's face a mixture of extremely pissed off and seriously anxious, and her squeeze did nothing to alleviate this. Raquel saw that, but still, she gave him a sweet, understanding smile, another hand squeeze with a shake then she let his hand go and walked silently to the passenger seat of the Suburban.

The buzzing started, it was loud, and it didn't stop.

Layne's eyes opened as Rocky came up to an elbow at his side.

"Jesus, fuck, what the fuck is that?" Layne mumbled, moving his head on the pillow to look at her.

"Someone's at the gate," Rocky mumbled back. "You can get them on the phone."

Layne turned to the nightstand, saw it was six forty-three and he felt his jaw get tight.

He nabbed the phone and put it to his ear, "Yeah?"

"Figured you'd be there," Gabby snapped back. "Let me in."

Fuck.

"Gabby, it's early. We're not doin' this," Layne told her.

"Let…me…in or I swear to God, swear to *God*, Tanner, I'll sit out here all *fucking* day and I won't do it quiet," Gabby bit out.

She'd do that. Gabrielle in a snit, she'd do anything.

Layne's eyes went to Rocky and he asked, "It's Gabby. How do I let her in?"

He watched Rocky's eyes get big then she answered, "Hit three."

Layne hit three, put the phone down then rolled from bed.

"What's she doing here?" Rocky asked as he heard her rolling out behind him.

Layne grabbed his jeans off the floor and turned to her. She'd confiscated his t-shirt last night after they got home from talking Cal down from kicking the shit out of Jasper. He'd pulled the shirt off and barely got it over his head when she yanked it out of his hand, pulled it on and collapsed into bed.

"Stay up here, sweetcheeks. I'll deal with her," Layne ordered instead of answering her question, and Rocky locked eyes with him.

"Why'd you let her in?"

"Because she wanted in, she was diggin' in, she's a bitch, and she doesn't get what she wants, she's more of a bitch. So I've learned to let her blow it out, get it over with and then move on."

Rocky nodded then she clipped, "Fine, but this is my house and I'm not staying up here."

"Roc," Layne started, buttoning his jeans. "Seriously, honey, trust me on this. Stay up here."

"No," Rocky returned, standing at the side of the bed not moving and not getting dressed.

Fuck. Now Rocky was digging in.

He loved her. He was happy as all hell to have her back. But in that moment, with his ex-wife heading to the apartment and Rocky dug in in front of him, Layne allowed himself half a second to reflect on what life would be like with an adult Giselle-type woman—shy, quiet and sweet, a woman who got worried when he got pissed.

Then he realized that would probably bore him stiff.

That was when he gave in.

"Right, then give me my tee," Layne ordered.

"No," Rocky repeated and Layne stared at her.

"Sweetcheeks, give me my tee."

"No, Layne, it's not even seven o'clock, it's Sunday, and for weeks you've been busting your ass for her and half of the 'burg. Vera told me about her so I know what this is. She doesn't get to come here and throw a tantrum when you've been putting your ass on the line for half the 'burg and, I'll repeat, *for her.* But, since she's come here to throw a tantrum, obviously she's got a point to make so I've got a point to make too. And that point will be made by her walking into *my* house, *early* on a *Sunday morning*, pulling *my man* from *my bed* and she'll see me *wearing his tee.*"

Shit, she was staking her claim, staking it with Gabby of all fucking people.

He'd forgotten this about her. Soft, sweet, cute, funny, loving, touchy, hot in bed, but she was also a Merrick. You didn't cross a Merrick.

Layne moved close and put his hands to her neck. "Baby, listen to me. She is no threat," he said softly.

"I know that and now she's going to know it too," Rocky returned.

Her eyes were bright and hard, flashing, she was pissed.

Seeing that, Layne instantly thought this whole thing was funny instead of a pain in the ass. He thought this mainly because Rocky was cute pissed but also because Gabby could be a bitch and he reckoned she was about to meet her match. He had to admit, his ex had busted his balls for so long, he was looking forward to the show.

He swallowed his laughter, successfully fought back a smile, let her go and turned from her to pick up the dirty t-shirt he wore yesterday.

He was straightening when the doorbell went and the tee was yanked from his hand.

His eyes went to Roc. "Sweetcheeks—"

"Nope," she snapped, turned on her foot and marched out of the room still carrying his tee.

Apparently her point would be made further by Gabby being confronted with a bare-chested Layne.

Layne followed her, eyes to his feet, allowing himself a smile until he hit the stairs and he wiped his expression blank.

He hit the bottom step as Rocky, no longer carrying his tee, which had mysteriously disappeared because Layne couldn't see it anywhere, opened the door.

Gabby didn't hesitate even a second before she fired the opening shot. "You didn't have time to put on clothes?" she snapped, cottoning right on to Rocky's play.

"It's Sunday," Rocky shot back, stepping aside for Gabby to enter. "After you leave, Layne and I are going straight back to bed. I'm not wasting my time getting dressed only for Layne to undress me again."

Jesus. Below the belt straight off the bat. He knew it but this knowledge was fortified by Gabby's face getting red at the same time it twisted.

"Well, don't let me put you out, you can go right back to bed," Gabby returned, not moving into the apartment. "Anyway, I'd rather you not be here while Tanner and I talk about *our sons*."

Direct hit and Rocky's eyes narrowed when it connected.

"I'm afraid you can't tell me what to do in my house. You want a private conversation, you act like a normal human being, call Layne at a decent hour, set up a time to meet over coffee and talk like civil people. You want a drama, right here and right now, you're going to have to act it out with an audience."

"Suit yourself," Gabby muttered and her eyes went to Layne who was standing, watching and keeping his mouth shut.

"Get in the apartment," Rocky demanded when Gabby opened her mouth to address Layne and Gabby's eyes sliced back to her.

"Don't tell me what to do," Gabby snapped.

"You are not going to throw your tantrum outside my apartment. Come inside," Rocky returned.

"I'm not stepping foot in your house," Gabby retorted.

"You have two seconds to come inside. You don't, you'll find the door shut in your face, I'll call security and they'll remove you from the premises," Rocky warned.

"Good," Gabby hissed, leaning forward. "I'll tell Jas and Tripp that you had me removed by security and they might not like Saint Rocky so goddamned much anymore."

"They might not. Then again, they might wonder why you're on my doorstep before seven o'clock, forcing a confrontation," Rocky shot back, and Layne's mouth twitched because his boys loved their mother but they also knew her, Gabby knew that, therefore Rocky had Gabby there.

"*You think this is funny?*" Gabby squealed, taking five quick steps into the house and Rocky closed the door behind her. He'd been looking at Roc. He missed Gabrielle's eyes coming to him.

"Yep," Layne replied.

"This is not funny." Gabby's voice was rising, indicating she was going to lose what little hold she had on her control and that was never pretty.

This meant Layne was done enjoying the show. "Why are you here?"

"My son got home after two o'clock in the morning," Gabby answered without hesitation. "I dragged his ass out of bed an hour ago and he told me what happened last night. He did not call and tell me he was going to miss his curfew. He did not call me when he was in trouble. He came home and went to bed like he lives in a fucking hotel and his mother isn't tossing and turning, waiting up for him and worried out of her brain."

"You're tellin' me this because…" Layne prompted.

"I'm tellin' you this because *you* should have told me what was happening and if you didn't, since *you* were with Jas last night, *you* should have advised *him* to share the minute he got home," Gabrielle returned.

"We had it covered," Layne replied.

"I'm his mother!" Gabby shouted.

"Jesus, Gabby, keep it down," Layne ordered.

"Fuck you," she shot back.

Layne uncrossed his arms and put his hands to his hips. "All right, woman, you're his mother and he fucked up last night. He had a couple of beers. He let his girl have a couple of beers. He's seventeen, that shit is gonna happen. I did it. You did it. Everyone does it. It wasn't right, but he was bein' smart, he didn't get drunk because he was drivin'. But his girl got slipped a mickey and it freaked him out. He cares about her. He didn't know what to do. So, if I didn't advise him and he didn't decide to let you in on that shit, it's his call. He had enough to deal with considering his girl got drugged against her will on his watch and her stepdad was pretty fuckin' displeased. If he didn't feel like puttin' up with your shit after that, I don't fuckin' blame him."

"He doesn't *get* to decide if he gets to put up with my shit, Tanner," Gabby returned. "I'm his mother, he's seventeen. You treat him like he's thirty-five."

"He's a smart kid," Layne replied.

"Yeah, he is, he's smart, but he's still seventeen. He's still a kid." She threw her arms out and her eyes shot fire. "You let them curse, both of them and Tripp's only fourteen. You think that shit doesn't leak to *my* house? Tripp told me straight out you let them cuss!"

Shit, but Tripp sometimes had a big mouth.

Gabby carried on, "And this business with the Youth Group, I don't know what's happening with that. All I know is, neither of my sons have found Jesus. It's not like I haven't heard people talking about that so it makes me think I *should* know what they're doing there because my guess is you're involved somehow. It's dangerous, and no seventeen and fourteen-year-old-boy should be involved in one of your operations."

He skirted right around Youth Group, a topic that would make Gabby's head explode, and he had to admit, rightfully so, and he focused on something that might not. "Gabrielle, they cuss at school, they cuss with their friends. Who gives a fuck if they cuss?"

"I do!" she yelled.

"That's ridiculous," Layne returned.

"It's being a good parent, Tanner," she snapped back.

"Do not go there, Gabby," Layne warned. "I'm a good dad."

She nodded and crossed her arms on her chest. "Oh yeah. Yeah you are. The best dad ever. The *coolest* dad in the world. News flash, Tanner, you didn't have one so let me educate you." she announced bitingly. "Bein' a good dad does not mean bein' a *cool* dad. It means bein' *a dad.*"

Layne took two steps toward her, and as he did it he watched her brace, which he figured was a good call on her part, considering he'd lost patience and didn't hide it.

"I know my boys, I know what they're capable of and we communicate. They're both almost men and they gotta learn how to be good ones," Layne told her, his voice low, rumbling. He was pissed. "You made it clear from the beginning, even before we got divorced, that we were both in this parent thing on our own. We never agreed. You never compromised. So, you do it your way, I'll do it my way, but since you made that decision, you don't get to get in my face and tell me to do it your way. I'll raise my boys as I see fit."

"Right, so it's okay they curse, fuck this and shit that. And it's okay your fourteen-year-old son is *already dating* and he can't even *drive*. And it's okay that your seventeen year old son is fucking his way through five different high schools. That's all okay because," she stepped back and flung an arm toward Rocky, "that's the kind of man *you* are and that's the kind of man *you're* teaching them to be."

"What's that mean?" Rocky entered the conversation on a hiss.

Gabby swung to her. "You don't have children, Saint Rocky, so you won't get this, but it is *not* okay and does *not* teach good lessons to have Dad banging the high school Literature teacher right under their noses."

Before Layne could speak, Rocky did.

"You know that's not right," she whispered, but she was whispering in order not to yell.

"I do?" Gabby flung back.

"You know it's not right," Rocky repeated.

"You know what's not right? Someone like you, who has it all, who's *always* had it all, taking more. Taking more and more and more," Gabby snapped, striding to Rocky, and Layne moved with her so he was at Rocky's back. Gabby didn't even look at him when she stopped two feet from Roc. "You don't have enough with your clothes and car and mansion, you need my kids too?"

"You don't care about your kids, Gabrielle," Rocky said quietly. "You care about Layne."

Gabrielle's torso shot back and she pushed out a puff of air. "Please."

"You want him, you've *always* wanted him," Rocky replied.

"Had that," Gabby stated, her mouth a sneer, not glancing at Layne. "Got rid of it."

Layne rolled his eyes to the ceiling but Rocky laughed, and it was laughter without humor so he rolled his eyes back to his woman.

"You are so full of it, Gabrielle, completely full of shit," Rocky said quietly.

"Trust me, honey, you ever stick around long enough to get his ring on your finger, you'll throw it back too," Gabby stated.

Layne went still but Rocky went solid.

That didn't mean Rocky didn't speak. She did, to say, "Right, so, to get his ring on my finger, what's your advice, Gabrielle? Should I quit taking birth control and get him drunk?"

"Bitch," Gabby hissed on a forward lean.

"Oh wait," Rocky threw down. "*I* don't *have* to get him drunk for him to want to fuck *me*."

Fucking hell.

"Women," Layne growled.

Both ignored him.

"Go to hell," Gabby snapped.

"See, full of shit." Rocky went back to her earlier theme.

"What's full of shit is you bein' Tripp's guide to all things girl and you playin' matchmaker to get Jas what he wants. Yeah, I know. I hear Tripp on the phone. I saw you with Keira Winters at the game. Then, *poof*," her hand flicked out, "Jasper's dating the most popular girl in school. Shit, you've crawled so far up their asses, it's a wonder they can walk!" She ended on a shout.

"Tone it down, Gabby," Layne warned, but Rocky spoke over him.

"Um…let me educate *you*, Gabrielle," she said. "I'm a teacher. I see it year after year, Keira's the most popular girl and Jasper's the most popular boy. That shit happens, the most popular boy and the most popular girl hooking up. It was going to happen one way or another. But, just so you know, I didn't work Keira, Keira worked *Jas*."

"Right, Keira hasn't been to *my* house for dinner," Gabrielle retorted.

"Then ask her," Rocky shot back.

"This is goin' nowhere," Layne cut in and his eyes locked on Gabby. "And this is not cool. You said your piece, and as usual, we don't agree. Now we move on."

"Oh no, no we don't," Gabby told him, her eyes still shooting fire and he knew from experience, by the look on her face, she was about to step way over the line.

And she did.

"You want to know what isn't cool? What isn't cool is you two teamin' up to take away the only things I got left, my boys. And what's also not cool is *you*," she jabbed a finger at Layne, "lettin' them do what they damn well want to do whenever they want to do it. I leave here only if we have an agreement and that's gonna be that *she*," she jabbed her finger at Rocky, "doesn't stay at your house when the boys are there and *you*," she jabbed her finger again at Layne, "learn how to suck it up and be a decent father!"

Layne clenched his teeth and started counting to ten even though he knew that didn't work. He had to try something so he didn't lay his hands on the mother of his children.

Rocky didn't count to ten.

She marched to the door, opened it and ordered, "Get out."

"No way, Saint Rocky, you wanted me in, the drama happens here," Gabrielle retorted, pointing to the floor at her feet.

"Get out," Rocky repeated.

"You horned your way in on this discussion, you see it out," Gabby retorted.

"I didn't *horn* my way into anything, Gabrielle, this is *my* living room!" Rocky's voice was close to a shout.

"Enough," Layne clipped and both women's eyes came to him, but his eyes were on Gabrielle. "I've put up with your shit for a long time, penance for fuckin' up with my boys, but that's done. I'm warnin' you right now, Gabby, that's done. You fucked up and I straightened your shit out. I'll remind you of somethin' you forgot and it sucks I gotta throw it in your face, I wanted to avoid that but you forced my hand. But woman, you no longer have the high ground. You obviously didn't pay even a little attention to me the last time we talked so you've again made a choice. The wrong one, but it's your choice."

He moved into her space, looked down at her and dropped his voice.

"You do not tell me how to raise my boys. You do not tell me when my woman can sleep in my bed. You do not bring drama to my doorstep or her doorstep at six forty-five in the morning or at *any time*. You get your support payments and we share sons. You exist for me only as their mother and that's it. The bridge has been smoldering a long time, woman, but you just burned it to the ground. We...are...done."

"That's not going to work," she shot back, leaning in and getting up on her toes to get in his face. "I know you hate it Tanner, but I'm their mother and you don't have a choice but to deal with me."

"Jas is in college next year, Tripp's three years behind him. They're nearly gone, Gabby. It's gonna work because I'm gonna make it work."

"Then we'll see what the court has to say about you fucking Saint Rocky with the boys in the house," she returned.

"Yeah, they'll probably not like that, you know, a single man havin' a girlfriend. They probably never heard of that. But, a single woman havin' a live-in boyfriend who's also an enforcer for a loan shark, they'll like that you reckon?"

Her face paled. She'd made a faulty play, she knew it then. She knew he had her but Gabby, being Gabby, didn't give it to him. She went into stare down. She wasn't as good at it as Rocky mainly because she did it with her face twisted and bitter instead of full of adorable attitude. It wasn't nice to look at and it wasn't fun at all.

Layne stepped back, ready to move things on, but Rocky spoke and she did it softly.

"It's almost sad," she said and Gabby's eyes and body swung to face her. "How much you want him and what lengths you'll go to for his attention."

And Rocky sounded sad. She looked it too. Her eyes were no longer flashing, they were filled with understanding.

But Layne didn't process that mainly because his gut squeezed and his eyes moved to Gabby whose face had lost all of its color and she looked like she'd been struck.

Jasper had said it but Layne hadn't really heard it.

I see the way she looks at you. It's the way Mom always looks at you when you don't know she's lookin', but it's more.

Jesus fucking Christ. It was Jarrod Astley, Gabby-style.

"Gabby," he murmured and her gaze shot to him then over his shoulder.

"Screw you," she whispered to his shoulder then turned to Rocky. "Screw you too." She walked to the door, stopped, turned back and swept them both with a glance that didn't really connect with either one of them. "You have it all, do what you want, you always had it all and did what you wanted. I should have known that would never change."

"You think that, Gabby, you haven't been payin' attention," Layne said quietly as he moved to stand behind Rocky.

Gabby looked at him. Her eyes moved to Rocky then down them both and back to Layne.

"Screw you," she repeated, turned, walked out the door and disappeared down the stairs.

Rocky threw the door to and turned to look up at Layne.

"Last Sunday started a whole lot better," she noted.

Layne looked into her eyes a beat that led into two.

Then he burst out laughing.

Rocky pressed into him, her hand going over his mouth, hissing, "Layne, she might hear you!"

"Don't care," Layne said from under her hand.

"I do. It's mean!"

One of Layne's arms went to span her waist, the other hand went to her wrist and he pulled hers away from his mouth and down then he pressed it against his chest.

"Live by the sword, die by the sword," he muttered.

"She's mother to your sons."

"She's a bitch."

"Layne!"

"What?"

She stared at him then shook her head but didn't answer.

It was, again, time to move on.

"All right, sweetcheeks, my guess is, we got about ten minutes before the next trauma. We can brush our teeth, make coffee and barricade the door with your couch or we can go back to bed. Your choice."

"Can I suggest an alternate scenario where we barricade the door, start the coffee, go back to bed then brush our teeth and have a cup of joe?"

"That'll take more than ten minutes."

Her eyebrows went up, her body pressed closer and her arm wound around his waist. "Are you saying you aren't up for the challenge?"

He dropped his head so his face was close to hers and whispered, "No, I'm sayin' I'm hungry and I don't like to be rushed when I eat."

Her body melted full into his but it did this while she shivered.

"Bed it is, then," she whispered back.

Layne grinned.

⌒

"Uh...Layne?" Rocky called hesitantly. She was sitting next to him while he drove her Mercedes, which, even though Astley got it for her, Layne had to admit was a sweet ride.

"Yeah, sweetcheeks," Layne answered.

The next trauma hadn't happened. In fact, he'd enjoyed Rocky, Rocky had enjoyed him. Then she'd walked downstairs to start coffee, came back upstairs and joined him in the shower. They both enjoyed that then he sat on the counter in her kitchen while she made poached eggs on toast and hash browns. He kept sitting there, beside Rocky, when they ate poached eggs on toast and hash browns. Then Rocky had taken approximately half a year to blow out her hair and put on makeup while Layne called a variety of people to check on a variety of things. All that done, they headed to his office.

He'd been unable to outfit her with a panic button the day before and he'd learned from Dave that Ernie was on duty listening to the bugs. He figured he should take his turn, even though he wanted to do this about as much as he wanted to endure water torture, but he might as well do it with Rocky hanging with him part of the time. She was going grocery shopping and had a few places to target for silent auction items for the charity gig, but in between times she was going to hit the office. She'd be able to get him Mimi's and lunch, and he was pretty sure he could make out with her on his couch and still pay enough attention to the bugs to hear if anything was going down.

Though, the last part, he was only *pretty* sure about.

"Um…I'm not entirely certain how to say this," she cut into his thoughts, still talking hesitantly. "But, I guess we'd get to this point eventually since you do have two sons and it would seem I'm going to be in your life for a while."

Layne didn't know where she was heading with this, but he still grinned at the windshield and muttered, "Yeah, baby, you're gonna be in my life for a while."

She was silent a moment then she said, "Okay, well then, um…she could have chosen a more diplomatic way to make her point but her point was valid."

Layne was confused, therefore he asked, "Come again?"

"Gabrielle."

Oh shit.

"Rocky—"

"Okay," she said swiftly, and he knew she'd turned to face him and a glance in her direction proved this true. "I'm in your life and they're your sons so they're in *my* life, but that said, most of the time, promise, sweetheart, I won't wade in unless you want me to. This time, I mean, I've seen Gabrielle around a lot over the years with the boys, and it seems to me she's a good mom. Being a good mom, regardless if Jasper is a boy or not, she probably worried about him last night just as much as Vi and Cal did about Keira. I know you're a man and he's your son, a boy, and you know how boys are so you won't get this, but I know she worried and," she sucked in an audible breath, "you should have phoned her to let her know he was all right."

"Sorry, were you not there a couple hours ago?" Layne asked.

"Yes, but—"

Layne talked over her. "I try to avoid communication with Gabrielle."

"Well, I can see that too, but—"

"She's a bitch."

"Um…yes, but—"

Layne turned on Main and lucked out, in Rocky's Mercedes, with a double spot open in front of the office, he could pull right in rather than needing to use all of his attention to steer the Suburban behemoth.

Therefore he was able to continue talking over Rocky as he parked. "She isn't a bitch to the boys, but she's a hard mom. She's strict. She's in their business. I'm not down with that." He put the car in neutral, set the parking brake, switched off the ignition and turned to face Rocky. "That's her choice. We discussed it when they were young, we discussed it throughout the time I was away and we discussed it when I came back. That wasn't the first conversation I've had like that with her, Roc, but it was the last."

Rocky looked directly into his eyes but she spoke quietly when she asked, "Do you at least see where I'm coming from?"

"Yeah, I see where *you're* comin' from. You're the woman who got up without a word, without a judgment, got in the car and went with me to take care of my boy. You're the woman I saw grab hold of Jas's hand last night when he was freaked and pissed, and his girl was passed out in his car and he was gearin' up to face Joe Callahan. You think Gabby would do any of that shit?"

"Um—"

"No, she wouldn't. She'd lose it. That's why Jas called me. That is also why he avoided her last night and went to bed."

"But, Layne, he shouldn't be underage drinking."

"You did," Layne returned, and he knew she did. She didn't do it with him, but she called him twice when she was out with friends and got hammered. He'd come to pick her and her girls up to take them home.

"It wasn't right when I did it either," she replied softly.

"So, I get in his face about it next time he fucks up, and there'll be a next time, Roc, he didn't like the consequences of him mannin' up and callin' me, he goes it alone. Like Gabby said, he's seventeen. He didn't know what to do last night. What happens when he doesn't know what to do but he feels compelled to go it alone because he doesn't wanna put up with the grief he'll get by comin' forward and bein' honest?"

As he spoke, Rocky's face changed and when he was done, she whispered, "I hadn't thought of it like that."

Layne reached out a hand and curled it around her neck, leaning forward as he pulled her to him.

When they were close, he said gently, "I tried the lecture gig with Jas, it doesn't go over, as in, it doesn't go over *at all*. He's a learn by doin' type of kid and he'll make mistakes. My only hope is, he fucks up royally, he'll call me in for guidance. Last night he fucked up, not royally, but he called me in for guidance. It was the right thing to do." She nodded and he squeezed her neck. "And Gabby earned what she got last night. That's the kind of parent she wanted to be, that's what she gets. She's too hard on 'em. That's my opinion. I can't say it hasn't worked because they're good kids. I can say I don't agree with all the ways she goes about it. We never found a middle ground. I was willin' to give, she was not. This is what's left of that."

"Okay," Rocky whispered.

"Somethin' else, sweetcheeks," Layne went on.

"What?" She was still whispering.

"You're in my life, I'm in yours. I come with them. You wanna talk to me about them, about my decisions regarding my boys, about anything, you don't hesitate. You got somethin' to say to them, you say it. If I don't agree, we'll talk about it later. But this is your life now and I think you know, bein' a teacher, when it comes to kids, you can't hesitate."

Her eyes went intense as her lids lowered, her mouth softened and she leaned in. Veering to the side, she kissed his jaw.

Then she shifted her lips to his ear and said, "All right, sweetheart."

His hand flexed on her neck and then slid up into her hair.

"Sweet kiss, baby, but it's not enough," he muttered.

Her lips moved and she kissed his cheek.

"Enough?" she asked this with her lips moving against his skin.

"Nope."

She moved again and her lips brushed his, her eyes looking into his, she repeated, "Enough?"

"Quit fuckin' around, Roc," he ordered.

He watched up close as her eyes smiled.

Then they closed.

Her head tilted.

And she gave him more than enough.

Layne had his feet up on the desk. He was eating the Reuben Rocky bought him, his mouth over a square Styrofoam container held up almost to his chin.

Rocky was sitting on his desk, dipping a curly fry into ketchup next to her half-eaten French dip. They were listening to nothing but Layne hadn't heard only nothing. Layne had heard a showdown between Towers and Jeremy. Jeremy had won, talking Towers down, earning a few more days to swing Giselle around. Clearly, they'd motivated him appropriately the day before. He'd handled it like a pro. Then both of them had left and now silence.

Rocky had been in and out twice. After he spelled Ernie, she'd gone to get him a Mimi's, hung out with him awhile and then she'd headed out to hit the jewelry store on Main for a donation (and scored herself a gold and amethyst bracelet, it wasn't fit for a queen but it wasn't shabby either). Then she'd gone grocery shopping, taken it back to her apartment and come back with lunch.

"When does Spike come to relieve you?" she asked, popping the fry into her mouth.

"Three," Layne answered.

She moved her Styrofoam container from one hand to the other and looked at her watch. Then her nose scrunched.

"That's nearly two hours away," she muttered, picking up her sandwich and shoving it into her little plastic container of au jus. "I've never done it, but I'm pretty certain watching paint dry is more interesting. At least it changes colors. So, maybe it just darkens a shade but that's *something*."

Layne grinned at his Reuben.

"Told you this investigation shit is mostly boring," Layne muttered back, her eyes slid to him and he took a huge bite of one of many of Frank's Restaurant's freaking fantastic sandwiches and watched his woman smile.

Layne's phone rang, her eyes dropped to it on his desk and then narrowed.

"Cal," she whispered as Layne pulled his feet from the desk and reached for the phone.

He took the call and put the phone to his ear. "Yo, Cal."

"You at a place where you can move quick?"

Layne's back went straight.

"Maybe, why?"

"'Cause Keira just came shooting out of her bedroom. Even though she's grounded and Vi told her no phone calls or texts for a week, she found a way to take one from Jasper. Apparently, he's been on a mission today. He found out what happened last night and he's meanin' to do somethin' about it."

Oh fuck.

Layne put his lunch down and stood, reaching for his jacket. "She tell you what he found out?"

"Yep. He heard from someone who witnessed it that Keirry took a shot from a kid named Tyler Berger. Keira says she doesn't remember it but if she did it that was the only drink she had that Jasper himself didn't hand her. Jasper learned she took it after usin' the bathroom right before they were gonna leave, so the timing fits. According to Keira, Jasper is not a big fan of Tyler Berger mainly because, while he was playin' it cool and textin' her, Tyler asked Keira out. She didn't go but this made Tyler pretty fuckin' unpopular to Jasper. Jasper told Keirry that he reckons this kid slipped her the drug and he's itchin' for payback for last night and for Tyler tryin' to move on his territory. That said, Keira says Tyler's a slimeball and she doesn't put this shit past him. She says his parents are out of town and it was his party they were at last night. Jasper is headin' that way and so am I."

He had his jacket on and his eyes glued to Rocky. "Where is it?"

"The Heritage. Don't have the house number but Keira says it's the second left in the development, at the end of the street. I figure I'll see Jasper's Charger parked out front."

"I'll be there in ten," Layne stated.

"Good. I'll be there in five, I'll deal with what I find and you take it from there," Cal replied.

"He was pissed, Cal, and he's protective. What you find may be messy," Layne warned.

"Yeah, why'd you think I went easy on him last night? He was more torn up about what happened to Keirry than Vi and I were, and man, I gotta tell you, your girl gets slipped a date rape drug, it tears you up. But Keira is on a mission to live her high school years to their fullest and is definitely not immune to fucking up, as in taking a shot from a known slimeball and downin' it."

This was not in doubt. The Layne family had learned Keira was a nut and it was further indication his son was just like his old man.

"I hear you, brother, but I'm on duty in the office. I gotta brief Roc before I leave so she can take over. I gotta go," Layne replied.

"Gotcha, see you in ten," Cal said and Layne heard the disconnect.

His eyes were still on Rocky so he spoke. "Jasper found out who slipped Keira the drug. He's bearin' down on him now. Cal's five minutes out, I gotta get to my boy."

"Go, baby," she whispered.

"You take notes you hear anything important, see the numbers on the screen?" he asked. She glanced at the screen and nodded, "Write down timings. I can scroll back and listen. You hear something big, something that freaks you, you take note of the time and call Merry then you call me. Yeah?"

"Yeah," she nodded, "Go."

He leaned in quickly to kiss her forehead that she helpfully tipped back for him and he took off.

Jasper's Charger and Cal's truck were in front of an enormous house that took up the entirety of a secluded cul de sac at the end of a street on The Heritage. The house was set back from the road and surrounded by trees. Its front yard was also littered with cans, bottles, chip bags and used plastic cups.

Layne parked behind Cal's truck and jogged to the front door, which was partially ajar. He slipped through and saw the house was like the yard, except a lot worse. The place was a disaster and it smelled like vomit and stale beer. And there wasn't one keg in the wide entryway, there were three.

He heard the voices from upstairs; Jasper's pissed, Cal's a murmur, another boy's sounding scared.

Layne took the stairs two at a time, moved down the hall and walked into a bedroom that was a mess, not from the party, but from a teenage kid living in it. And it was enormous. It had a queen-sized bed, heavy, expensive furniture and it was stuffed full of everything a kid could want. State-of-the-art stereo, computer, TV, PlayStation, shelves full of DVDs, CDs and games, handheld video games, digital picture frames, expensive cell phone and an MP3 player scattering the surface of the desk and chest of drawers. Tangles of clothes everywhere.

All three pairs of eyes came to him when he entered the room and Layne saw Cal had Jasper held back with a hand in his chest. Jasper was keeping it in check but that didn't mean he wasn't straining.

Another boy, three inches shorter and definitely slighter than his son, his hair a sandy blond mop on his head, a bedhead, Layne had no doubt when he primped it was styled past Tripp's best efforts, had pressed himself against a wall. His eyes were bloodshot and his skin was gray because he was hungover. His lower lip was already swelling fat and a trickle of blood was seeping from his nose because Jasper had time to get a few in before Cal arrived.

Layne's eyes went to his son. "You cool?"

"No," Jasper bit out, his eyes never leaving the other kid.

Layne looked at Cal and Cal shook his head.

Layne looked back to Jas. "Stand down," he said low.

"Slipped it to her, Dad," Jasper growled, his gaze piercing the other boy.

"Stand down," Layne repeated.

"Drugged her, drugged my babe, made her pass out. I wasn't there—"

Layne got close to his son as Jasper spoke and demanded quietly, "Jasper, cool it."

Jasper scowled at Tyler Berger and he did this for a while as everyone waited, tense. Then he took a step back from Cal's hand and Layne watched him force his body to relax.

Cal studied Jasper then dropped his hand and looked at Tyler. "You do it?"

Tyler's frightened eyes went from Jasper to Cal. Then he realized, with two adults in the room, things had changed. One look at his room and

Layne knew that Tyler Berger played the adults in his life and he was really good at it.

This was proved true when he jutted out his fat lip and grunted, "No."

"You did it," Jasper said softly.

"You see me do it?" Tyler shot back.

"Nope, but Justin did," Jasper replied.

"Justin's an asswipe," Tyler returned.

"Justin's got no reason to lie," Jasper retorted.

"Maybe *he* did it," Tyler suggested.

"Yeah, right, he did it," Jasper said sarcastically. "He's Keirry's lab partner in Biology, they're friends. *And* he's dating Heather and thinks he's gonna get in there. You think he's gonna fuck that up by drugging Heather's best friend?"

Tyler shrugged.

Layne entered the conversation. "Advise you to come clean, boy."

Tyler's eyes came to his and they were belligerent. "I didn't do anything."

"Then you better be a whole lot more convincing than you are right now," Layne told him. "'Cause Cal and me, we can control what happens in this room. We cannot control what happens at school. You get me?"

Tyler straightened and stated, "No. I don't *get* you. What I get is that I'm gonna tell my parents that you and him and your kid broke into my house and he hit me. They're gonna call their lawyers and we're gonna see if the Great Jasper Layne plays ball for Purdue after my parents' lawyers get done with him."

Layne clenched his teeth.

"My future doesn't hinge on a full ride," Cal remarked and all eyes went to him.

"What?" Tyler asked when no one spoke.

"Carried my girl to her bed last night. Her boy here says she had three or four beers and she was out. She's probably a lightweight but she was *out*. You're young. You don't know how a man feels when life proves to him how vulnerable his girl is when she's not under his watch. Not a good feelin', boy," Cal said.

"I'm so sorry for you," Tyler sneered.

"Thinkin' you better get smart pretty fuckin' soon or I'll make it so you feel a whole lot sorrier," Cal whispered, and Tyler's eyes widened before he quickly pulled his asshole teenage-kid cloak back into place.

"My parents will hear that too," he snapped. "You threatening me."

"Won't be able to do shit," Cal returned. "You don't play this smart right fuckin' now, I can guarantee you Jasper is gonna make your days a livin' hell and I'm gonna make it my mission to make the rest of your life a livin' hell. Now, do you get *me*?"

"You can't threaten me." Tyler's voice was rising.

"Sure I can," Cal replied casually. "Can fuck with you too and you don't cop to what you did, I will. That's a promise."

Tyler looked to the floor, muttering, "This is bullshit."

"I see you don't feel like gettin' smart so we're done here," Cal stated, moving to Jasper, putting his hand on his back and starting the both of them toward the door, he finished with, "It's on."

Cal and Jasper kept moving, but Layne kept his eyes on Tyler as Tyler's narrowed on Cal. He was scrambling. He knew he was fucked, he just couldn't find a way out.

So he took the only way out he knew.

"He can't come in here and hit me and you can't come in here and threaten me!" Tyler was beginning to shout. "And you can't fuck with me! My dad's CEO of Wyler Pharmaceuticals."

Cal stopped, turned and looked at him, brows up. "He is? Well, fuck me, that's impressive." Cal put his hands to his hips and went on, "It's impressive but what it isn't is frightening. What's he gonna do, come to my house and throw pills at me?"

"Shut up," Tyler whispered.

"Still not bein' smart," Cal muttered, shaking his head.

"Tyler," Layne called and Tyler's angry eyes came to Layne. "Do you know what I do?"

Tyler glared at him a beat then jerked his chin up in an affirmative.

"Then you know I'll follow the trail and I'll find evidence you had the drug," Layne stated and Tyler's face started to pale. "So, you can spend the rest of the day cleanin' this house but you're gonna miss somethin'. Or, what I saw downstairs, somethin' was likely damaged or missin' and my guess is what's missin' is the contents of your parents' liquor cabinet. Your parents are gonna know you threw a party and it's likely they're not gonna be happy about it. But they'll probably let it slide because I reckon they let a lot slide with you, considering you're a punk and a boy isn't born a punk, he's made that way."

"Go to hell," Tyler whispered, his cheeks getting red.

Layne kept talking. "What I also would guess is, they're not gonna let it slide when I prove you drugged Keira Winters. They're not gonna let it slide because Cal isn't gonna let it slide. I get the evidence, they'll press charges, and trust me, a punk like you, juvie isn't gonna be a whole helluva lot of fun."

The red bleached out of Tyler's face, it went white and his mouth dropped slightly open.

Layne kept at him. "They can have a lot of money, hire great lawyers, but I'll tie you so tight to that shit you can't get loose. And Keira Winters is famous in this 'burg. I don't reckon you'll find a judge who'll look kindly on you druggin' a girl whose father and uncle were murdered and whose mother was stalked and kidnapped. I reckon a judge will think Keira Winters has suffered enough in her short life, her mother has too, and I reckon a judge will look at your parents' expensive attorneys and take in your punk attitude and know you need a lesson. I also reckon he'll smile when he gets to be the one to give it to you."

Tyler swallowed.

Layne continued, "So, right now, you got a choice to keep bein' a punk or man the fuck up. Admit what you did, explain why you did it, apologize to Cal and Jasper and we'll all move on. That's your choice. You got one second to make it before we move out."

"I—" Tyler started.

"No joke, Tyler, one second," Layne warned.

"Coach Cosgrove gave it to me!" Tyler blurted and the entire room went wired.

Everyone was silent for long tense moments until Layne broke it by asking, "Come again?"

"He gave me a hundred bucks, told me to slip it to Keira and keep her from Jasper," Tyler told them, his eyes darting between the three males in the room, and Layne knew he was giving it to them straight but there was something missing. "It wasn't even me, really. I just put it in the shot and gave it to her. It was Coach Cosgrove."

Layne was frozen, so when Jasper moved, Layne couldn't do a thing about it, but Cal got hold of him and shoved him back.

"Stay cool," Cal growled at Jasper and Jasper must have gotten himself under control because Cal turned back to Tyler. "No shit?"

"No shit. Freaked me out, he showed at the party about five minutes after *they* showed," he pointed at Jasper.

"Tell me exactly what he said," Layne demanded and Tyler looked at him, his body alert, his mind still scrambling.

"He didn't say much of anything. He just said give her the drug, keep her away from Jasper and let it play out however it played out. Problem was, she was with Jasper all night and I couldn't get to her. I didn't know they were leaving when I gave it to her. No one has a midnight curfew, that's crazy," Tyler replied.

Layne felt Cal's eyes on him but he didn't take his from Tyler. "So, you're tellin' me the coach of the football team was settin' Keira Winters up to get hurt."

"I don't know what he wanted. Just know what he said," Tyler answered then continued, "She sticks to him like glue." His eyes slid to Jasper and he couldn't hide the jealousy, it was stark on his face. Then they slid back to Layne, "Couldn't keep her from him after she took the shot so she went funny when she was with him." That jealousy took hold and his voice took on the thread of a whine when he went on, "Then he picks her up like he's in some stupid romance movie, carries her to his car while all the girls watch like he's some kind of fuckin' movie star, and then they were gone. There was nothing I could do."

"Cosgrove come back?" Layne asked.

"No," Tyler answered.

"You didn't see him at all?" Layne pressed.

"No, not at all," Tyler replied.

"Has he called you?" Layne pushed.

"No, nothing. Haven't seen or heard from him at all," Tyler said.

"That doesn't make sense, Tyler," Layne noted. The kid was hiding something.

Tyler jutted up his chin, digging in. "Well that's what happened."

Layne studied him a beat then asked, "How old are you?"

"Seventeen," Tyler answered.

Shit, as Layne suspected, he was underage.

"When do your parents get home?" Layne went on.

"Tonight," Tyler replied.

"Where are they?"

"Chicago. Mom's shoppin'. Dad's got some conference," Tyler told him.

"On the phone," Layne ordered, walking to the kid's desk and tagging his cell. "Tell them they're coming home now." He turned and tossed the phone to Tyler who fumbled and dropped it.

Tyler squatted to the phone but his head was tipped back to stare at Layne. "What? Why?" His voice was shrill.

"Because I'm callin' the cops and they can't talk to you unless a parent or guardian is present," Layne explained. "And I reckon it'll be better for you to call them now than wait and have the cops call them and tell them they've got you at the station."

Tyler nabbed his phone and straightened like a shot. "But you said—"

"I thought you were fuckin' around. I didn't know Cosgrove was involved."

"But I can't—" Tyler tried.

"You can and you will," Layne demanded.

"I can't! Everyone will know! Coach Cosgrove will be pissed!" He was freaked right the fuck out.

Definitely hiding something.

"All right, this has escaped you but this is not about you anymore. This is about Cosgrove. You owned up to it, got smart and you were honest. You fucked up. You took a coupla hits and manned up. Now, if you keep your shit together and cooperate, it'll look good for you. You go back to bein' a punk, this time a *sissy* punk, it won't look so good and you're in that hole you were in five minutes ago with Jas and Cal both happy to ride your ass until you beg for mercy and me workin' with all I got to make you pay for what you did to Keira. Again, kid, you got a choice. Make it but make it now," Layne ordered.

Tyler stared at him.

Then he asked, "I won't get in trouble?"

"Can't tell the future," Layne replied. "Your folks'll probably be pissed. Girls and their parents know you aren't afraid of usin' a date rape drug, you won't get a date until you go to college. As for the cops, you cooperate, they might feel generous."

Tyler hesitated so Cal entered the conversation.

"Best deal you're gonna get, boy," he growled.

"God!" Tyler, backed into a corner, for once in his life without his daddy's money or hotshot CEO bluster to hide behind to keep him safe, exclaimed, "This is jacked up!"

"Yeah, it is," Jasper told him. "It's totally jacked, Tyler. So, maybe, take a second to think about this shit and do right, you freakin' moron."

Cal cut his eyes to Layne and Layne watched his friend's lips twitch while he pressed his own together.

Then Layne looked to Tyler. "What's it gonna be?"

Tyler stared at him again before his eyes did a sweep of Cal and Jasper.

Then he looked to his phone, pressed a few buttons, put it to his ear, and after a few beats, said, "Mom?"

⟻⟶

Colt and Sully left the interrogation room, both their jaws tight, their faces hard.

They left behind Tyler Berger and his father Travis.

Travis Berger was probably an inch shorter than Layne but no less fit. But whereas Layne worked at being lean and strong, Travis Berger worked at bulk and intimidation. The man was a brute in a suit and his son was definitely a mama's boy. Layne reckoned Tyler got to be a punk because Dad worked long hours, Mom was a pushover and Dad wasn't all that thrilled with the results of his inattention, but his priorities were fucked.

One look at those two and it was evident that career was definitely more important than family. Watching them for half an hour, it wasn't only evident, it was definite. Travis Berger barely knew his boy and what he knew he didn't like much.

Cal and Layne were both in the observation room and the air was thick and volatile. They'd watched Colt and Sully work the kid and they'd done it in silence. The silence was because even a word could spark the invisible fuse in the room, and when it did, that fuse was short and, once lit, the room would explode.

Travis had let Colt and Sully go all out on his boy, he hadn't intervened once. He was now standing in the corner, staring down his nose at his son, legs planted wide, arms crossed on his barrel chest, face a mask of pissed way the fuck off.

The door barely closed on Sully when Travis spoke. "What'd I say?"

Layne watched Tyler stare at the table in front of him, but he whispered, "Dad—"

"Three strikes," Travis cut him off. "I told you after you kept fuckin' around and didn't listen to me, you had three strikes left. Now, one was that pot I found in your room two weeks ago. Two was that fuckin' party, and I saw your mom's Royal Doulton smashed, Ty. To bits. She loves that shit. God knows what other damage was done. I work hard, Ty, I work fuckin' *hard* to give you and your mom nice things. I go away for work and come home and I get *this*?" He sucked in breath, his face twisted with rage, gearing up for the worst part and he continued. "And three is you *drugging* Joe fuckin' Callahan's daughter in order to *get in her pants*."

Layne had been right. Tyler had been hiding something and what he'd been hiding was that Cosgrove gave him the drug to frame Jasper. He was supposed to give it to Keira, lead her away, get her in a compromising position, "find her" and tell everyone, including the cops, he saw Jas do it. Considering he'd given her Rohypnol, even Keira wouldn't have known who slipped her the drug or what happened to her because she wouldn't have remembered. Jasper would have been fucked, his future ruined, his reputation destroyed and he'd lose his girl.

Cosgrove didn't go so far as to tell Tyler to compromise Keira, just to remove her shirt and undo her jeans. Under not-so-delicate pressure from Colt and we're-all-men-we-get-it bullshitting from Sully, Tyler had given up that he felt this was a golden opportunity he wasn't going to pass up. His intention was to take advantage of Keira who he suggested—lamely and by no means convincing anyone in that room—had a thing for him.

What he didn't plan on was that Jasper and Keira were as tight as they were and Keira wasn't big on leaving her boy's side, so she didn't, except to go to the bathroom, and on the way back accept an ill-advised shot after which she wasted no time in getting back to her boyfriend. He also didn't plan on Jasper turning the tables and enhancing his reputation by publicly taking care of his girl.

The door opened and Sully and Colt walked in but Cal and Layne didn't move. Cal probably couldn't move for fear he'd commit murder.

Tyler's head came up, "But Dad—"

Travis Berger leaned forward and roared, "*Shut the fuck up!* Jesus Christ, whose kid *are* you?" Tyler blanched and Travis threw his hands out then clenched them in fists. "You *drugged* a girl for fuck's sake! Who does that?"

"Dad, Coach Cosgrove said—"

"I don't give a fuck what that twat said. Jesus, Ty, Jesus. The man beats his wife and kid. Jesus. You see a man like that, that man hands you an illegal substance, you call the fuckin' cops. You do *not* take direction from him! Fuckin' shit." Travis shook his head but his eyes didn't leave his son. "Jesus fuckin' shit. What do I even do with you? I gotta deal with you and I don't even wanna *look* at you."

Tyler's face crumpled and Layne knew he was going to cry. He didn't need to see that shit so he forced his eyes away, reached out to flip the switch to shut off the audio and looked at Colt.

"You thinkin' what I'm thinkin'?" he asked and Colt nodded.

"Yeah, man, but you don't know what I know," Colt replied and Layne felt Cal move to position himself at Layne's side.

"What do you know?" Cal growled, and Colt and Sully looked at him.

"Hendrick's County Hospital had seven admissions last night, six females, one male. All unconscious or incoherent on admission for reasons unknown until the test results came back and all of them had been roofied. Last, all of them had been drinkin' at J&J's Saloon," Sully answered.

Layne shook his head. Cal planted his fists on his hips.

"Was Cosgrove seen at J&J's?" Cal asked.

"Yep, Cheryl clocked him, pointed him out to Darryl and Darryl showed him the door. That said, it was Saturday, it was a madhouse as usual and Cheryl, Morrie who was also on, nor Darryl know how long he was there before Darryl chucked his ass out," Colt answered.

"So, Cosgrove is metin' out payback. I confronted him, Cal's providin' safe harbor for his wife and kid and you're both sittin' sentry, that the play?" Layne asked, but he knew, that fucking dick, he knew.

"That's my guess," Colt replied.

"Goes without sayin', I want his ass in a cell," Cal snarled.

"Goes without sayin'," Colt agreed.

"Also goes without sayin' I want that punk-ass piece of shit in that room to face some serious as fuck consequences," Cal went on, jerking a finger to the observation window.

"Goes without sayin'," Colt repeated.

"Good news on that is, it's pretty clear his dad's feelin' much the same way," Sully murmured.

"No, Sully, he's not. He's not feelin' the same thing I'm feelin' right... fuckin'...now." Cal's voice was a scary whisper.

"I get you, man," Sully whispered back but his whisper was conciliatory. "I'm just sayin' you won't have a battle on your hands on top of all this shit. He's not gonna fight his son's side 'cause he knows his son doesn't have a side. He didn't step in once when we were questioning him. He's gonna let that boy swing."

Cal was silent and so was the rest of the room, everyone stuck with pretty fucking unhappy thoughts.

Sully broke the silence. "Got shit to do. A bulletin to put out. Bar patrons to interview. Shit like that. Am I gonna be able to get down to that or am I gonna get a busted lip and split knuckles losin' my fight to lock down you three badasses?"

Layne and Colt instantly relaxed. Colt's lips even formed a small smile.

Cal didn't think anything was funny. Then again, Cal's stepdaughter narrowly missed getting raped the night before. It was going to take a while before Joe Callahan cracked a smile.

"We're good, Sul, do your work," Colt muttered.

Sully studied Cal, must have read what he wanted to read, he nodded and walked out.

Cal turned to Layne. "You straight with your kid?"

"Yep," Layne answered.

"You gonna share that shit?" he jerked a thumb at the observation window.

"Not sure about that," Layne replied because he wasn't sure. He shared what Tyler Berger and Adrian Cosgrove had planned, Jasper would be uncontrollable. He knew it because that shit happened to Layne, he'd be uncontrollable.

Cal nodded. "I'll talk to Vi. Keira's not only supposed to be off her phone, she's also grounded until next Monday, no studyin' at Jasper's house, no visits from Jasper, no dates. I'm thinkin' after what went down last night, it wouldn't be good to keep her from Jasper or Jasper from her. I'll talk Violet into lettin' Jasper come over."

Translation: *I've been reminded my girl is vulnerable and it's been proved your boy has her back so he's just been recruited to keep having her back indefinitely.*

"Be appreciated," Layne murmured.

Cal nodded and walked to the door. Before he opened it, he turned back.

"Lotta boys would do different, they got a hot, unconscious piece in their car. Lotta boys wouldn't even bother takin' her to their car much less makin' sure she's safe."

"Jasper's not a lotta boys," Layne replied.

Cal held Layne's eyes. Then he nodded. Then he left.

"You gotta be all kinds of stupid to fuck with Joe Callahan." Layne heard Colt mutter and he looked to him to see Colt staring into the interrogation room.

"He's seventeen, Colt, his brain is in his dick and you've seen Keira. That kid had no shot, and he's not used to not havin' what he wants and he's got no qualms about doin' whatever he feels like doin' to get what he wants. Cosgrove knows this kid. Cosgrove knew exactly what he was doin'. And Cosgrove's convinced himself after spendin' years cowing his wife and son that his balls are big enough he could take on a badass like Joe Callahan. Bad luck that Tyler threw that party and Jasper and Keira gave him his shot."

Colt turned to Layne. "You gotta be all kinds a stupid to fuck with Cal but Cal's retribution would be swift and painful. Yours, man, slow and lasting." When Layne's eyes met his friend's, Colt finished, "What I'm sayin' is, you're standin' here, so I'm guessin' you're takin' this a lot better than I expected."

"I started my day with Gabby in my face, spent most the rest of it listenin' to the masterminds behind a child prostitution ring havin' a twenty minute conversation and then a lot of nothin'. I got a good kid and he made the right decisions last night, which means right now we're dealin' with justice not tragedy. I'm feelin' pretty good about that and I've gotta hold on to the good because fuck knows what's gonna hit next."

Colt grinned. "What's next is, it all eventually goes away and you're left with wakin' up next to Raquel Merrick every day and goin' to sleep next to her every night."

Layne grinned back. "Yeah, that's the plan, except she was there when Gabby came over to throw down this morning and Rocky wasn't down with that. First time in two decades, brother, I took a moment to reflect on what it would be like to have a shy, retirin' woman sharin' my bed."

"How long'd that moment last?" Colt asked.

"About a nanosecond," Layne answered.

Colt's grin got wider as he laughed softly.

Then Colt quit laughing and his face got serious. "I had shy and retiring. Trust me, brother, it's not all it's cracked up to be."

Layne wasn't around when Colt was married to Melanie Seivers, who was painfully shy and retiring, but his mother was and the tragic, lost love of Alexander Colton and February Owens was 'burg lore. That meant Vera Layne and her cronies had spent a lot of time chewing over the fact that Alec Colton and Melanie Seivers were not a match made in heaven. Layne knew this because Vera knew Colt was a friend and she repeatedly shared her cronies' conclusions. No one was surprised by Colt and Melanie's divorce. And no one was surprised when Colt hooked back up with February, a woman who was not shy and retiring by any stretch of the imagination.

"So you got yours, I got mine, what the fuck are we standin' in a little room for?" Layne asked.

Colt's grin came back. "Fuck if I know."

"You got anything to brief me about that other shit?" Layne asked, moving toward the door.

"Nope," Colt answered, following him and they stopped. "Same as this mornin'. We talked to IMPD and they know all about Nicolette Towers. What they don't know is where she keeps her stable. We have boys on her tail at all times and she's steerin' clear of that location and Rutledge is steerin' clear of her. He doesn't leave the 'burg and he's been nowhere near her. We've clocked her with some of her muscle so we're puttin' names and faces to her crew, but she's not leadin' us to her girls and neither are they."

"She know she's been made?" Layne asked even though she gave no indication of that during her conversation with Jeremy that day.

"Nope," Colt shook his head. "Rutledge doesn't either considering he visited a known prostitute last night, took his twenty minutes, got his blow-job and went."

"Got a source that says she's hands on," Layne told him.

"Don't know what to say, Tanner. We can pull her in on identity theft and hold Jeremy Goulding over her, but she's gonna have to roll over we do that, and what I've read and what IMPD know, this bitch is made of steel. We're not gonna break her. We need evidence. You said your man didn't find the photo shoot photos at her apartment?"

"Dev found nothing. He had a good amount of time to look and it was clean, so he planted the bugs and got out."

"Even if he found 'em, not against the law to take pictures of teenage girls. It's not cool but we got nothin' messy to stick to her."

"Jeremy bought us a few more days," Layne told him. "Heard it when I was listenin' this morning."

"Well, let's hope she fucks up before he cracks. Read up on him too. Small time con, not too bright, stupid recruit for her but maybe not, since she's made him nearly the sole face of this shit so he's also the perfect fall guy. It's a miracle he hasn't disintegrated before now."

That was precisely what Layne was worried about.

Colt's voice dropped lower. "This shit moves a lot faster, your source comes out in the open."

"I told you, I told Merry, that can't happen," Layne replied just as low. "Tanner—"

"We still have no evidence. We don't have the location of her stable. We don't have a lock on her army. And we don't have anything to connect her to Rutledge, except the word of a small time con and whatever the fuck Ryker is and Ryker only saw Rutledge visit the apartment once. My girl would be swinging in the wind, and trust me, brother, you'd never hold Towers on the word of my source, and without any evidence, she wouldn't even go to trial. We need patience."

"We don't need patience, Tanner, we need time and I'm guessin' a coupla days isn't gonna get us shit. Goulding is gonna cave and she's gonna bolt."

"You got any bright ideas?" Layne asked.

"Only one I got is not bright, it makes my teeth hurt and leaves a bad taste in my mouth," Colt answered.

"Set up one of the girls," Layne muttered.

"Not gonna happen," Colt muttered back.

They shared unhappy silence until Layne broke it. "Patience."

"Prayer," Colt returned. "They used God. Let's hope He feels motivated to lend us a hand."

"I'll get Vera on that," Layne offered.

"Yeah," Colt replied, one side of his mouth up in half a grin.

Layne opened the door and walked out.

Colt followed.

Layne nodded to men he knew as he walked through the bullpen on his way to the back stairs. He pulled out his cell as he jogged down the stairs and was out the door and nearing the Mercedes when Rocky picked up his call.

"Hey, sweetheart," she answered.

"Hey, baby. Where are you?"

She'd called and told him that Spike had relieved her, she'd gone down to Mimi's, ran into Feb, and since she was rideless and Layne was busy, she and Feb were going to hang.

"At Vi's. Where are you?"

"On my way to Vi's," he replied, folding into her car.

He heard her soft laugh then it went away and she asked, "Everything okay?"

"It will be."

A pause and then, "That's not a great answer, Layne."

537

"Best I can do for now, sweetcheeks. I'll brief you when we get home. Is it your house or mine tonight?"

"Mine," she replied immediately.

"You don't like the toothbrush Jas bought you?"

She burst out laughing and Layne listened to it thinking Rocky's laughter made a day of good and bad turn mostly good again.

When she got it under control, she answered, "No. My house doesn't have Devin and Vera in it."

Oh shit.

"I thought you and Mom were cool."

There was nothing for a few beats and then he knew why when she spoke quietly. She'd been looking for privacy.

"Vera and I *are* cool. But not so cool I suspect she'll be happy to hear her son making me moan and I enjoy you, baby, but I don't want to court suffocation every time we have sex."

This meant Layne was going to get him some that night. This wasn't surprising. Eighteen years had done nothing to shear even a layer off Roc's sexual appetite, or Layne's. But that didn't mean the promise of it didn't feel fucking great.

Shit, it was almost over but the day kept getting better.

"Good call," Layne muttered and twisted the key in the ignition.

"See you soon," she replied.

"Absolutely."

Layne disconnected, put the Mercedes in gear and backed out of his parking spot.

Then he reengaged his phone, scrolled down to Jasper's number and told his son just enough so his boy would sleep in peace that night.

Twenty-Four

THE MAN YOU WOULD BECOME

onday, 5:12 a.m.

"Layne," Rocky breathed, one of her hands in his hair, cupping the back of his head tight, one of her arms caught under his body, her fingers curled into his ass.

"That's it, baby," Layne whispered, watching her face in the shadows as his fingers toyed with intent in the wetness between her legs.

"Oh God," she breathed, her back arching, she was close.

"Give it to me, Rocky," he ordered.

Her fingers clenched his ass.

"Come inside," she begged.

"After you come."

"Now, baby, please," she whispered.

"After."

Her hips ground into his hand. "I want your cock."

"You'll get it."

"Oh God."

"That's it."

"God, Layne."

"That's it, baby," he whispered, dropped his head, took her nipple between his lips and pulled hard.

That did it, her back left the bed and a ragged moan tore from her throat.

Layne's fingers left her pussy. He rolled over her, her legs spread wide for him even as she was coming, and his fucking cell phone rang.

"No," she whispered.

"Fuck, you gotta be fuckin' shittin' me," Layne growled, kept himself seated between her legs and reached out for the phone.

He turned it to face him, saw what was on the display and growled again, this time with no words.

Then he took the call and put the phone to his ear.

"This better be fuckin' good." He was still growling.

Rocky lifted her knees, pressed her thighs against his sides as her arms wound around his back, the tip of his cock slid through her wetness and Layne clenched his teeth.

"Did I wake you?" Sully asked.

"No," Layne grunted.

Silence then, "Oh."

"Sully," Layne rumbled.

"Right, okay, well, thought you'd want to know. Adrian Cosgrove is incarcerated. Chris Renicki and Marty Fink found him about two hours ago. He had enough Rohypnol on him to roofie the entire junior class. Possession of an illegal substance, conspiracy to commit a felony, violating his bond agreement—"

Layne cut him off. "I get it, he's fucked."

"He's fucked," Sully confirmed.

"Good. Can I go now?" Layne asked with only an edge of patience.

Layne heard Sully chuckle and he again clenched his teeth.

"Yep," Sully answered.

Layne disconnected, tossed his phone on the bed and bent his head toward Rocky.

"Is everything—?" she started.

"Fine," Layne gritted then he drove his cock inside her and her back left the bed again as a mew slid out of her throat.

Jesus. Heaven. All of it.

Then he bent his head further and kissed his woman at the same time he fucked her.

Hard.

⌣⟶

Layne laid on his back in bed, his head resting on his hands, and listened to Rocky in her bathroom.

His mind wasn't on the sweet orgasm he'd had or the one he'd given her. It also wasn't on the noises coming from the bathroom. It further wasn't on the million and freaking three things he had going on in his life.

His mind was on walking into Vi and Cal's house and seeing Raquel sitting cross-legged on the floor with Vi and Cal's baby daughter, Angela, bouncing on her little feet in Rocky's lap. Rocky was holding Angela's little hands and laughing in Angela's giggling face.

Back in the day, they'd planned to have three kids. They were both agreed on that, it was definite. Three. Layne had no siblings, he'd always wanted one and he'd wanted one more seeing how Roc was with her brother. Rocky had a brother and she loved him so she would have been happy to have another brother or a sister, she didn't care. Family meant everything to her, the bigger, the better. So they decided three, definitely three.

He had two.

Rocky had none.

Rocky walked out of the bathroom carrying a mug of coffee, her hair up in a twist at the back and she was wearing a dark green set of underwear, satin with a hint of dark gray lace. Layne had learned this meant she was wearing green somewhere on her body that day. Rocky had a lot of underwear in a lot of colors and she matched it to her outfits. This, too, was new and this, too, Layne liked. He liked it because, even if he didn't see her dress, he could make a fair guess at what she was wearing under her clothes.

And he liked that a lot.

"Baby, come here," he called and she looked his way.

"I have to get to work, sweetheart."

"Come here," he repeated. She stopped in the doorway to her closet, stared at him a second and walked to him.

When she got close, Layne did an ab curl, grabbed one of her wrists and took the mug of coffee from her other hand. He set it on the nightstand then, with a tug on her wrist, he laid back down and Rocky hit him full frontal.

"Layne!"

His arms moved around her, trapping her.

"I have to get to work," she repeated.

"I know but I have to ask you something."

She stopped pressing back when she paid attention to his face.

Then she whispered, "What?"

"You want kids?" Layne asked, straight out.

Her body jerked before she repeated, "What?" but it was breathy this time.

"You want kids?"

"I…um…" she stammered and her eyes slid to the pillow beside his head.

"Eyes to me, Roc," he ordered and her eyes shot back.

"Yes," she answered, that one word quick, forced out and openly scared. He knew this because she barely hissed out the "s" before her body braced.

He grinned at her and whispered, "Good, baby, how many you want? Two, three?"

She stared in his eyes, her body still, her eyes getting bright and her nostrils quivered. She was going to cry, and to fight it back, she served up attitude.

"What?" she whispered back. "Are you growing an army?"

Layne laughed, rolled her to her back, rolled right on top of her and buried his face in her neck.

"You didn't answer," he said into her neck.

"Layne, you're messing up my hair."

He lifted his head. "Sweetcheeks, answer my question."

She glared at him. Pure bullshit. He could see she was happy and his chest squeezed at the sight.

"One, if it's a boy. If it's a girl, two but only with the hopes of having another girl."

"Evening out the numbers?"

"No."

Layne's brows went up. "You don't like boys?"

"Little boy clothes aren't as cute as little girl clothes."

Layne stared at her and saw she was being serious, basing her desire of what gender child she wanted to have on shopping.

Then he muttered, "Jesus."

"They aren't," Rocky defended.

"Girls means I've got Cal's headaches and gotta pray every night they meet a boy like Jas, when Jas is into them, that is. Boys you just give condoms."

Her body locked under his and she snapped, "Layne!"

"It's true."

"Boys means I have to hope they don't pay a lot of attention to their badass dad and don't want a career where they sleep with a gun under their pillow."

He grinned. "You caught that?"

"Hard to miss when I put your pajamas on it, Layne."

His voice softened when he assured her, "It's just a precaution."

"Against your enemies or the pissed-off fathers of Jasper's pre-Keira escapades?"

He grinned again. "You caught that too?"

"Kids talk and, by the way, that's reason two, no boys."

"Why?"

"How many more reasons do you want?" she asked.

"Twelve," he answered.

"A girl…" She stopped, her eyes unfocused and her body got tight. When she spoke again, he knew into his soul, it wasn't to him. "A girl I can teach. I can tell her things. I can show her the way. I can explain the stuff that will happen in her life." Her eyes refocused and her body relaxed under his. "A girl I can give all that my mom never got the chance to give me."

"Girls it is then," Layne whispered instantly and he watched Rocky blink, her face startled before that surprise died, hope filled the space it left and she smiled.

"Is that a guarantee, Tanner Layne?" she whispered back.

"Nope, but I'll see what I can do."

Her hand came to his jaw, her thumb sweeping his cheek then his lips before it slid across to wrap around his chin, she lifted up and touched her mouth to his.

She dropped her head back to the bed and whispered, "I have to get to work, baby."

"Yeah," he replied then dropped his head to kiss her.

He did it a lot harder and a lot longer and Layne's kiss was wet.

Then he rolled off her, watched her roll off the bed and walk to the closet.

Girls.

The first one they'd name Cecilia.

Tuesday, 6:53 p.m.

Layne jogged up Rocky's steps, slid his key in her door and walked in to soft lighting, soft music and candles lit around the room.

He closed the door and turned toward the kitchen where Rocky was standing wearing a purple t-shirt with a snarling white bulldog on the front and she was looking at him.

"Sweetcheeks, I appreciate the effort, but I gotta tell you, I'm a sure thing."

She grinned but planted her hands on her hips. "A house doesn't always have to be filled with the sounds of shoulder pads crunching and grunting and the smell of stale beer," she returned.

"Nope," he agreed, shrugging off his jacket and walking to the armchair. "Sometimes it has to be filled with the sounds of shoes skidding on a court and whistles blowing and the smell of nacho cheese."

He tossed his jacket on the chair and turned just in time to brace because Rocky had run from the kitchen and was in the act of launching herself in his arms.

He caught her at the ass. She wrapped her arms and legs around him and dropped her head, her mouth hitting his, opening. His opened in return and her tongue slid inside.

He let her kiss him then he growled and took over the kiss until she mewed and then her head came up and she looked him in the eye.

"Catch any bad guys?" she whispered as he walked her to the kitchen.

"Unfortunately…no," he whispered back.

Her brows went up. "Any bad women?"

"Ditto on the no."

"Damn." She was still whispering and he set her ass on the counter. She kept her limbs tight around him so he moved in close and wrapped his arms around her.

Layne changed the subject. "What's for dinner?"

"Mushroom risotto."

It was Layne's turn to lift his brows. "Does that have meat in it?"

She smiled. "Um…no. It has mushrooms in it."

"Pepperoni?"

"No."

"Sausage?"

"No."

"Hamburger?"

She started giggling and forced out a "No."

"Baby," Layne whispered.

"You'll like it. It has lots of parmesan cheese in it and cheese makes everything awesome."

Christ.

Jasper had said that and she remembered. She remembered what his boy said.

Christ. He loved her.

He didn't tell her that, instead he asked, "Is this my welcome home every night?"

"Do you want it to be?"

"Yeah."

"Then yeah."

Fuck, he remembered this. This hadn't changed. Coming home to Rocky had always been the best part of the day. Always.

Shit yeah, he loved her.

"You gonna feed me or let me fuck you on the kitchen counter?"

545

Her mouth got soft, her eyelids lowered, but she asked, "Without food, do you have strength to fuck me on the kitchen counter?"

"Haven't had anything since breakfast."

Her lips tipped up. "Then I'm going to feed you."

"All right, then I'm gonna get a beer."

She didn't let him go and Layne didn't move.

"Sweetcheeks," he prompted as her limbs got tighter, her face got softer and her eyes dropped to his mouth.

She was changing her mind and Layne liked the direction it turned, so he slid his hands up her back.

Then she froze.

"I still don't have blinds," she whispered.

Shit.

"Right," Layne whispered back. She moved in, touched her mouth to his then released her limbs.

Layne got a beer. Rocky took another sip from her white wine before she pulled a pan out of the oven. Then she fed Layne mushroom risotto and it was pretty good.

But it could use meat.

Wednesday, 4:02 p.m.

Layne's cell rang. He looked from Dev sitting across from him in his office to his cell on the desk. He read the display, gave Devin a one minute finger, picked up his cell, took the call and put it to his ear.

"What's up, sweetcheeks?" he said by way of greeting.

"Something weird just happened," Rocky replied and Layne's eyes shot to Devin as the muscles in his neck got tight.

"What?"

"Um…a woman came up to me after school and talked to me like she knew me. Really chatty, really friendly and, Layne, she talked *for ages*. I've seen her around, not much but I've seen her around. Her name is Lissa McGraw. She's Alexis's mom."

"And," Layne prompted when she hesitated.

"Well, she said that you and her man are tight, you're partners and since you're partners, we should all get to know each other and to do that we should have dinner. So she kind of set a double date before the game on Friday and then said we could all go to the game together. I didn't know what to say. She was so friendly, I couldn't refuse. Um…do you have a partner?"

Layne relaxed, sat back and his eyes dropped to the desk as he grinned. "That's Ryker's woman."

"Ryker the big biker guy?"

"Yeah."

"Is he your partner?"

"No, he isn't my partner but I'm his."

"What?"

"Ryker and I view our relationship in different ways."

"Oh," she whispered then shared, "He's kind of scary."

"He can be," Layne agreed. "He also cares a lot about Lissa and her daughter."

There was a hesitation and then, "So, he's big and scary and looks somewhat like a raving lunatic but he's good people."

Layne's grin got bigger. "Yep, that's about it, sweetcheeks."

"Are we having dinner with them?"

"That isn't at the top of my list of things I wanna do but I get the sense that big, scary, raving lunatic Ryker does not have a lot of buds. And Ryker tells me Lissa spends a lotta her time working her ass off to give her girl a decent life, and likely, with Ryker her man and him looking like a raving lunatic, she doesn't have a lot of chicks of her own. So I reckon they're recruitin' a posse and we're pretty much the only candidates in the 'burg who wouldn't run a mile. Not to mention Alexis was a target and we made it so she was safe, so I'm guessin' Lissa feels grateful and friendship is a good gift to give when you don't have much else to offer."

"So," Rocky said, drawing out the word. "We're having dinner with them."

"Wouldn't kill us."

"You like him," she observed.

"He's solid," Layne replied.

"I liked her. She's nice and it was kind of sad because she also seemed desperate, which she shouldn't have to be because, well...she was so nice."

"Proves my point."

"Yeah," she whispered.

"He wants her to have a decent life, baby," Layne whispered back. "He's not a man who shares much, but what he says, she hasn't had it too good and he wants her to have good."

"He doesn't scare me anymore."

"He shouldn't. Can't say he'd lay down his life for you but you're my woman and if anyone hurt you, he wouldn't blink before huntin' them down and breakin' their neck just because he's built a connection to me, and that's his kind of justice. And I'm not sayin' that to say it, Roc. I mean he'd hunt them down and break their neck...literally."

He could tell she was smiling when she said, "Now, I'm beginning to like him."

Layne chuckled.

"Are you busy?" she asked.

"I'm always busy," he answered.

"I'll let you go."

"What's for dinner tonight?"

"Meat."

"Just meat?"

"Yep, a smorgasbord of meat."

"You're full of shit," he muttered through a smile.

"See you later," she replied through a giggle.

"Later, sweetcheeks."

He disconnected, looked at Devin and felt his neck muscles contract again when he caught the look on Devin's face.

"What?" Layne asked when Devin didn't speak.

Devin shook his head.

"What, old man?"

"Just thinkin', thinkin' about a man who'd walk out a door and never turn back. Thinkin' about where he went, what he did and how it could never be worth losin' what he left behind. Your father is a grade A, one hundred percent jackass, boy, turnin' his back and never knowin' the man you would become."

Layne didn't speak, his throat was burning, his chest was frozen and that golden trail was searing through his system.

Then he found his voice. "You gonna kiss me?"

Devin rolled his eyes.

"A hug?" Layne suggested.

Devin's eyes narrowed.

Layne stared into them. Then he said, "Thanks."

Devin replied with, "Right."

Moving on.

"I need you to get to Jeremy," Layne stated.

"We need more time," Dev surmised.

"We've run everyone in her crew and they own no property. Phone records show calls to her crew but she must use a disposable to talk to clients. She's not leadin' us anywhere. Merry interrogated Jeremy before we let him go and he doesn't know shit about her operation outside his part in it. She compartmentalizes. Everyone has their job and only their job. Even if we picked one of them up and they rolled, they couldn't give us anything. The location of the photo shoot was a day rental. Jeremy has been unable to find what she's got on Rutledge. Merry's chompin' at the bit to put pressure on Rutledge and he's stepped out. Confronted Rutledge about the missing person call for Giselle he didn't report he took on his own and then didn't follow procedure. Colt and Sully backed him up on that. All their asses are swinging out there now. Rutledge had a bullshit excuse and he's full of bravado. Merry and Colt thought he'd run scared but he's keepin' his shit together. We're not getting anything. We need time and we need Jeremy to dig, get her talking in the apartment, and to do that, he's gonna need a coach. That coach is you."

"I'll pick him up."

"You gotta play that smart, Dev. We want him scared but we don't want him to fuck up."

"Don't have to tell me that, boy."

Layne nodded. "I wanna know who her clients are, who she has lined up for the party. We pull one of them in, they'll probably roll over."

"You think she'll give that up to Jeremy?" Devin asked, his eyebrows up.

"No, but we gotta try."

"Desperate times," Devin muttered. "But even if we get one, the event hasn't taken place nor is it goin' to."

"Nope, but we could use them for a set up. They could act impatient enough to want *something*, even if it isn't fresh, and she's got a stable of girls, she could give it to them. They could at least lead us to that."

Devin nodded. Then he put his hands together in front of him in prayer position and pressed them against his lips as his eyes grew intense.

Layne knew what that meant.

"You've got a bad feeling," Layne noted.

Dev dropped his hands. "You don't?"

"I do."

"In my gut, boy. This is gonna go south and not them slippin' through our fingers. I can't shake the thought that we're missin' somethin'."

"Vigilance."

"Yeah."

They held each other's eyes then Devin stood as the beep came and both men looked at the monitors to see Vera walking up the stairs.

Devin's eyes came to Layne. "Like her a lot more, she's not bein' a bitch to Rocky."

"Someone made me the man I am."

Devin nodded his head but whispered, "True enough, to a point. Men like you aren't made, though, Tanner. Men like you just are." His eyes turned to the monitor as Vera nearly made the landing and he remarked, "But, gotta say, boy, your mother can fuckin' cook."

With that, he walked out of Layne's office as the outside door opened and Vera walked in.

"Devin!" Layne heard her cry. "I'm glad I ran into you. Flo and Helen are coming over tonight. I'm making my beef and noodles. You'll love it."

Oh shit. Vera was matchmaking.

His Aunt Flo and Vera's friend Helen were both single. And, unlike his mother, who got burned bad enough she never went there again, they were both on the market.

His Aunt Flo had been married but Layne's Uncle Gene died seven years ago. His mother's friend Helen had been married as many times as Devin.

Flo turned Dev's eye, he'd think he'd died and gone to heaven, good food, lots of attention, a listening ear and no questions asked about his activities.

Helen turned Dev's eye, he'd be in a world of hurt because she was seriously high maintenance.

Flo looked, acted and dressed like his mother, she was far from hard on the eyes, made an effort, had style, knew herself and was comfortable with who she was. Helen looked, acted and dressed like a woman who wanted attention and a lot of it. That said, she was a beautiful woman, even at the age of sixty-three.

If Layne had to place a bet on which one Dev would pick, it would be Helen.

"Don't know when I'll be home, woman," Devin said to Vera.

"Oh, even if you're late, we'll keep it warm for you," Vera replied.

"Right," Devin muttered and Layne knew he was leaving because he heard Vera call, "See you later!"

Devin made no reply.

Vera came into the office.

"Hi, honey," she greeted.

Layne stood as she rounded his desk and he bent so she could kiss his cheek.

"Hey, Ma," Layne murmured.

She squeezed his arm, turned and bustled away. Layne resumed his seat as she sat opposite him.

"I just got off the phone with Rocky. Tomorrow after she gets off work, we're going furniture shopping," she announced, plonking her purse on her lap.

"What?" Layne asked.

"You need a dining room table. You also need something for that front space. I'm thinking a reading area. Chaise lounge. An elegant table. A floor lamp."

Fucking hell.

"Ma—"

She cut him off. "I'll be in the office tomorrow during the day. I talked to Dave. He said you need listeners and I'm a good listener. I can do some office work while I'm at it."

He wasn't going to turn that down.

"Ma, the furniture—"

Vera looked him straight in the eye. "Is Rocky eventually going to move in?"

"Yeah," Layne answered.

"Then you need to give her a home to move into."

"It's already a home, Ma, and she hasn't complained."

"She moves in, are *you* going to go furniture shopping?"

"Fuck no."

She threw out a hand and announced, "No time like the present."

She had him there so Layne grinned.

"You're a nut," he muttered.

"Yep," she replied on a smile.

"You gonna stay in town much longer?"

She tipped her head to the side and shared, "Florida isn't all it's cracked up to be. They have hurricanes and they don't have Hilligoss donuts."

This was true and Hilligoss was worth moving back home. So was being close to her grandsons before they both moved off to educate themselves and start their lives, as well as being close to her son when he was happy, and last, being close to Rocky again.

"So you're moving back."

She answered with, "I can do your books."

That wasn't a receptionist but it was something.

"Thanks, Ma."

"You're welcome, Tanner."

"By the way, I'm not sure you'd be doin' Aunt Flo or Helen a favor, hookin' them up to Devin. He's not young but that doesn't mean he's not wild."

She cocked her head to the side again. "Hooking him up with Flo or Helen?"

"I know your game."

She smiled and it was a smile he'd never seen before in his life.

Then she suddenly stood, hitched her purse on her shoulder and walked to the door. In the door, she turned and leveled her gaze on his.

"It isn't Flo or Helen makin' him beef and noodles, Tanner."

Holy fuck.

Layne stared.

Then he started, "Ma—"

Her smile turned lazy and Layne didn't know what to do with that because he was a man and she was his mother, for fuck's sake. And as a man he knew what that smile communicated, and he hoped to all that was holy she never directed that smile at Devin. The man wouldn't stand a chance.

"All these years, after your father, never met a man who was worth the trouble because, except to get you, your father proved not worth the trouble," she remarked.

"Ma—"

"Until now."

Oh shit.

"Ma—"

"See you later, honey," she said cheerfully, turned and walked out.

Layne stared at the door. Then he shook his head.

He stopped shaking his head and started laughing as he reached for his phone to call Rocky.

⌐⌐⌐⌐

Thursday, 6:11 p.m.

His client lifted his eyes from the folder he was reading and noted, "This didn't take you long."

Layne sat across the client's desk from him. "He wasn't real smart with hiding it," Layne replied. "And he didn't try."

The man's face closed down. He was embarrassed, or more accurately, humiliated. And he should be. He had an employee who had been embezzling for over three years and he didn't cotton on until about a month before he hired Layne, which was only a few weeks ago.

Layne moved him past it.

"He's also got a ticket to Argentina. He leaves Sunday. So, my advice, pick up your phone and call the cops."

The man nodded, reaching for the phone.

Layne stood and moved from his office but stopped and turned when the man called his name.

"You ever need a reference, you can tell your potential clients to call me," the man stated.

"Obliged," Layne muttered and moved out of the office.

He was out of the building and nearing the Suburban when his cell rang. He pulled it out, looked at the display and took the call.

"Yo, sweetcheeks."

"You like oak?"

Layne bleeped the locks on the Suburban. "Come again?"

"Oak. The wood. For the dining room table," she explained. "See, I don't like oak. I mean, it's okay, but I prefer walnut or cherry. Also mahogany. But your mom and I found this awesome dining room table. Ladderback chairs. One beautifully carved, thick, center leg, with four clawed feet coming out at the bottom. It's amazing. Two leaves so it could sit ten. You could even squeeze twelve in, at a push. The perfect Thanksgiving dinner table."

By the time she was done talking, Layne had swung up in the cab and closed his door. "You like it, get it."

"Well, does it sound like something *you'd* like? I mean, oak...I'm not sure."

"You like it, get it," Layne repeated.

"Layne—"

"Roc, I really don't care about furniture. If it's there, I use it. I don't care what it looks like or what it's made of. So if you like it, get it."

She was silent.

When this lasted awhile, Layne called, "Roc?"

"You care," she said softly.

"What?"

"You care, Layne, and that's okay. You can be a badass and also have style. I mean, you dress really nice too."

Layne blinked at the steering wheel and repeated, "What?"

She laughed softly. "Sweetheart, it's okay if you give a shit about this stuff. It's not like it makes you any less of a man."

What the fuck?

"Uh...Rocky, what the fuck are you talkin' about?"

"Your clothes, your furniture, Layne, they're stylish, handsome. Your clothes make you look good, especially when you dress up. Definitely hot." He knew she said this through a smile but he was too busy concentrating on his neck muscles contracting to let that penetrate. "And your furniture is fantastic. I wouldn't have guessed you'd be able to put a house together like that, Layne, but it looks great. I mean, it's comfortable and manly, but it's still attractive. I love it and I wouldn't change a thing."

Shit.

"Roc—"

"So, baby, since you know what you're doing, in a badass interior decorator kind of way, tell me, do you like oak?"

"Roc—"

"Or do you want to come and look? Maybe we can swing in on Saturday."

Shopping.

Shit.

He pulled in a breath then he let it out and made a decision. And he made his decision because shit happened and if he didn't tell her, she'd eventually find out somehow. That shit had a way of making it to the light. Usually through Tripp.

"I didn't buy that furniture, baby," he said softly.

"Sorry?"

"Or most of my clothes."

Silence then, "Sorry?"

"Melody did."

He waited. She didn't speak.

Fucking *shit.*

"Rocky—"

"Um...I've gotta go."

"Roc—" he stopped speaking because he had dead air.

"*Shit!*" he hissed, tossed the phone on the passenger seat, started the truck and headed to her house.

He was standing out on her balcony an hour and a half later having a smoke when he watched her car drive up and swing into the spot beside his truck. She got out and moved from under the awning over her spaces, her eyes lifting to him. Then she dropped her head and walked to the sidewalk.

Layne moved to the little, black wrought iron table she'd had delivered from the Garden Center and he stubbed out his cigarette in the ashtray she left out for him.

He was inside when she came through the door.

"Rocky—" he started.

She didn't look at him when she shrugged off her coat and stated, "I need some alone time."

He crossed his arms on his chest and said softly, "Baby, you know that shit's not right."

She tossed her coat on a stool by the bar and turned to him. "I do?"

"We've had this discussion," he reminded her.

"Yes, you had women in your life, we've had this discussion," she agreed. "What you failed to mention during that discussion was that I was sleeping in *her* bed."

Fuck, he was getting pissed.

He controlled it and replied, "She picked it. I paid for it. I sleep in it. It's my bed, Roc."

"Did she sleep in it?" Rocky shot back.

"Don't do that shit," Layne returned.

"She slept in it," Rocky muttered, dropping her head and moving into the kitchen.

He followed her but kept his distance, stopping on the other side of the bar.

"Like I said a while ago, sweetcheeks, I wasn't in suspended animation when we were apart."

She was at the fridge and she'd pulled out a fancy-ass beer. She opened a drawer, popped the cap, tossed it and the opener on the counter and turned to face him, resting her waist on the edge of the counter, lifting the beer and taking a pull.

She dropped her hand, her eyes hit his and she said, "You know, I've been thinking."

What he knew was that was not good.

"Rocky, don't do this," he warned.

"And what I've been thinking is that, a while ago, you were right. I played you."

Layne was silent.

Rocky was not.

"You were right as well that I didn't know it, but thinking about it, I did. I played you."

"Where you goin' with this?" Layne asked even though he really did not want to know.

"So, I asked you the other night, if I made that pass, would you have accepted it and you said you didn't know. Which means no."

"You don't know what it means. I don't even fuckin' know what it means," Layne returned.

"It means no."

"Rocky, Goddammit."

"Because she was in your life."

Layne shook his head, barely controlling his temper and feeling his patience ebb. "I explained that too," he reminded her.

"How long was she in your life?"

"Point is, she isn't now."

"She thought she was, surprising you like she did."

"Honestly, you wanna process this?"

"I'm putting two and two together, Layne," she announced.

"And, sweetcheeks, you're comin' up with five."

"I'm not."

"Baby, you are."

"You wouldn't have done it," she stated in a way that he knew whatever the fuck she was referring to was important.

"Done what?"

"Made the play."

"Made *what* play?"

"For me."

Fuck!

"Roc—"

"You had your Melodys, your Cassies. You didn't need me and you wouldn't have made that play. Thinking about it, thinking about the way you spoke to me that first morning I came to your house, you had no intention of finding us again."

Layne clenched his teeth and when he won the battle for control, he reminded her, "Rocky, you were married and you still are."

Her eyes narrowed and she returned, "You knew it was over when we were sitting on Merry's couch, and you knew it had been over a long time. You knew it was bad. And you still walked away from me."

"Now I'm standin' right here so what the fuck does it matter?"

"It had to be me that made the play."

That was when he lost it.

"Yeah, Rocky, it had to be you because, sweetcheeks, *you* left *me*. I wasn't gonna swing myself out there again, not unless I knew I'd find a different ending this time."

"There it is," she announced. "You're throwing it in my face again.

"Jesus Christ," he muttered and his eyes locked on hers. "You're workin' for it. You want this. I'm givin' it to you, but warning Rocky, you told me last Friday not to let you do this shit and I'm not gonna let you do this shit. There is nothin' here for you to be pissed about. You're just pissed to be pissed because you're scared as shit."

"I'm not scared," she stated.

"Baby, you've spent two decades controlling everything in your life so you wouldn't feel what you feel right now with me. And I'm not stupid, I know why."

"Yeah? You do? Enlighten me, oh wise Layne. Why?" she asked with deep sarcasm and Layne's body got tight.

"Raquel, fair warning, I'm already pissed. Don't make me mad."

"*You're* pissed?" she asked, leaning forward, her words a hiss. "*You're* pissed? *You* fucked me in *her* bed. *You* fucked me in your closet wearing *her* clothes. And *you're* pissed?"

"I do not give a shit about furniture and clothes. You want, build a bonfire in my yard, toss it all on and replace it. I do *not* care. It means nothing to me."

"Melody meant something to you."

"Yeah, she did, and clue the fuck in, Roc. It wasn't enough or I wouldn't be here right now."

"You should have told me," she snapped.

"Yeah? When? When I had you against the wall moaning for me, do I whisper in your ear, 'By the way, baby, Melody bought me this suit.' Or, when you're locked in your head because of Ma's games and I had to talk you out of that shit, 'And since we're discussing Melody, you should know, she picked out this bed.' Jesus, Roc, seriously?"

It was then, Rocky went in for the kill.

"I've never had an orgasm, except with you and, obviously, self-induced. I've had two lovers. My husband and *you*. I've kissed two men in my life. I'm thirty-eight years old, Layne, and I've kissed *two men in my life*. One I married, the other was *you*."

He had no idea where she was going with that but it didn't mean she hadn't scored a direct hit.

"Baby—" he whispered.

"I've loved one man, and that was also *you*."

"Rocky—"

"You're beautiful and I see how women look at you. I also know what I did to you. You don't think *I* wonder, especially when you bring it up all the time, when you'll remember what I did to you and when you'll wonder if it isn't worth the risk. If you decide it isn't, I'll be right back there, Layne, without you, and now without Tripp and Jas. And you'll move on. You did before. You can have anyone you want. You'll move on. But I won't. I never did even though I got married, and you know it. But you did. Maybe not the same way, but you did. And you didn't make the play for me. You would have carried on and you wouldn't have to do it alone. *You* think *you* took a grave risk taking me back. What do you think *I'm* feeling? Knowing, any time, your head can turn to someone who'll know she's lucky to have you, who wouldn't do anything to rock that boat and you'll decide I'm not worth the worry and you'll be gone."

Layne stared at her, completely stunned that any of that shit was in her head.

Then he said quietly, "Baby, that's totally fucked up."

"It isn't," she declared.

"It is."

"No, Layne, it isn't."

"Come here," he ordered.

"No," she denied.

"Sweetcheeks, come here."

"I said no."

"Don't make me come there," he warned.

She shook her head. "Go home, Layne. I need to think."

"Nope," he replied. "No you don't. 'Cause you just told me what you've been thinking and every last bit of it is seriously jacked."

"I'm being honest!" she cried.

"Yeah, I get that, but that doesn't mean what's in your head isn't jacked."

"I'm telling you what I think."

"And I'm tellin' you it's jacked."

"Layne—"

Layne had had enough.

"Christ, Rocky, I'm in love with you!" he shouted, leaning forward and putting his hands on the bar. "I've kissed more than two women and I've fucked more too, but I've only ever loved you. You cut me up, baby, when you left me. You cut me up bad."

She winced but he kept talking.

"So, what's it say to you I'd take this risk? What's it tell you? You nearly destroyed me, Rocky, I loved you that much. Shit, I *love* you that much. I existed for eighteen years. Now I'm livin' again. And I like it. I like it so much, it's worth the risk. *You* are worth the risk. Yeah, you had to play me because I needed that statement from you. But, baby, I didn't make you work too hard and you fuckin' know it. You did that to me and you're back in my life. Think about *that*, Roc. Give *that* a second. What's that say about how I feel about you? Does that say I'm *ever* gonna let *anything* turn my head?"

"Layne—"

"Shut it, sweetcheeks, you walked in here full of attitude and you just spewed some seriously stupid shit. You need your head straightened out and you're gonna keep your mouth shut while I see to it."

Her eyes were big when she whispered, "Okay."

Layne went on, "Melody was in my house for maybe ten minutes at the most after you left. She called it. She knew it before I knew it. She knew who you were because she snooped and found the pictures I kept of you." Rocky's lips parted and Layne nodded. "Yeah, baby, I never let go of you. Never. I carried you with me *everywhere*."

"Layne—"

"You were so freaked out, you didn't see it, but after my preliminary shock and—somethin' else you didn't catch—anger at seein' a near naked woman in the house I share with my sons, she ceased to exist. It was all about you and your reaction. Melody caught it, you didn't. So now, cast your mind back, baby, and see it through her eyes. That's why she left because she knew why she never got in there and she knew it was because of you."

"Layne—"

"And she told me to be happy before she left. She told me she hoped you'd make me happy again. That's the woman who picked the bed you sleep in. She wasn't the one because *you are* but she's a good woman and she cared about me. I didn't have you, you don't love me enough to want me to have at least that?"

"You can stop talking now," Rocky whispered.

"If I can, then get your ass over here and show me your head is straight and that you've let go of this shit so I can fuckin' do it," Layne returned.

She put her beer on the counter immediately but she walked to him slowly. She wasn't working her strut, it was hesitant. She knew she'd pissed him off and she wasn't sure what she was going to get.

The minute she was in reach, he leaned forward, caught her wrist and yanked her into his body after which his arms wrapped tight around her, caging her to him.

Her hands at his chest, she tipped her head back. "Um…" she started.

He interrupted her. "Don't be cute. Cute's gonna piss me off."

"Oh, okay, I won't be…um…cute," she whispered uncertainly.

"Roc, you're bein' cute," he warned.

"Oh, well…okay. I'll stop." She was still whispering then she pressed her lips together, stared at him with big eyes and her look was incredibly cute.

"Fuck me," Layne muttered.

"You're still mad."

"Baby…uh, *yeah*."

Her hand slid up to his neck.

"Don't be mad, I have my head on straight."

"You gonna treat me to this shit again?"

"I'll try not to."

"That the best you got?"

"Uh…" Her teeth worried her lip then she went on, "Yes."

"I'll take it."

Rocky blinked. Then she whispered, "You will?"

"Pay attention, sweetcheeks, I'll take anything from you."

"Layne—"

Time again to move the fuck on.

"Did you buy the table?"

Her body jerked at his change of subject then she answered, "No."

"I'm not goin' to look at it."

"Okay."

"You like it, get it."

"Okay."

"You let my mother buy a chaise lounge for that front space, you earn a spanking."

Her body jerked again before it relaxed against him.

"Don't worry," she said softly. "I found this big corner sectional. It's like a couch but it's shaped in a square. You, me, Jasper and Tripp could all lounge on it and not touch. Not that we would do that, uh…but, uh…Vera and I tried it out. It's comfy."

"Get it."

"Okay," she whispered then called, "Layne?"

"Yeah?"

She pressed into him and kept whispering. "I'm sorry."

His temper slid away, Layne dipped his head and touched his mouth to hers. Moving only slightly away, he whispered back, "I know you are."

"I mean about tonight and..." Her eyes slid from his to over his shoulder and then he watched her force them back to him and her voice was barely audible when she said, "Back then."

Oh God. Jesus God. That felt good. Jesus, he needed that. He didn't know it, but having it, he knew he needed it.

"I know." His voice was barely audible too.

"I've always loved you."

"I know."

"And um...even though I was the one who did it to myself, um...you can ask Merry, I've never liked to share."

Layne stared at his woman a beat that fed into ten.

Then he burst out laughing.

Friday, 11:38 p.m.

"Fuck, baby, come here," Layne groaned.

She kept working his cock with her mouth. Her hand wrapped around the base, she was on her knees between his legs and he could see they were spread wide and her other hand was working her clit. And he knew she liked it, she was taking herself close because he could feel her moans vibrating against his aching, rock hard cock.

"Rocky, come here," he growled.

Her head kept moving, up and down, lips, tongue, suction, Jesus.

"Roc—"

Her mouth suddenly released him and he watched her head fly back, her lips parted, face flushed. She'd made herself come. Fucking beautiful.

He reached down, grasped her at her pits, yanked her up his body, rolled her, positioning between the legs she spread for him, he drove into her. Hard. Rough. No control.

"Layne," she breathed.

"Take me," he grunted.

"Yes, God, yes."

"Take me, Rocky."

"Harder, Layne."

He fucked her harder and her heels dug into the backs of his thighs as she lifted her hips to meet this.

"It's gonna happen again," she moaned.

"Let it."

"Layne, oh God." Her back and neck arched, her heels pressed deeper, her body locked, but her pussy contracted around his cock and a low, deep, *long* moan slid out of her throat.

Layne's hand went into her hair. He positioned her head and captured her mouth, absorbing the moan and then trading it for his as he thrust deep, to the root, planting himself in her and exploding.

When he was done, he started his strokes again, these slow, lazy, as his mouth explored her neck and throat. Her hand moved on his back, her other one gliding through his hair, her legs wrapped now around his waist.

He filled her and his lips moved up her neck, his teeth nipping her earlobe before he demanded, "Next time you make yourself come like that, you do it with my cock inside you."

"It was inside me," she whispered.

"I'm talkin' about an alternate location."

Her head turned and he felt her lips smile against his neck.

Then she said there, "Okay."

That was Rocky, his woman, up for anything.

"I need to get cleaned up," she whispered in his ear.

"No, I'm still hard."

"Layne—"

"You can get cleaned up when I'm not hard."

A beat of hesitation, then, "Okay," and then all four of her limbs got tight around him.

She held him close until he pulled out, rolled, and she kept rolling, moving off the bed. But she came back, put a knee in the bed by his hip, leaned into him, touched her mouth to his and whispered, "Love you, baby."

Before he could respond, she moved away, turned and walked to the bathroom naked.

When he lost sight of her, Layne moved under the covers, settling back, head to the pillows. Lifting his hands to his face, he swiped it hard.

Adrian Cosgrove was being held without bail.

Rocky and Vera were thick as thieves again.

Rocky's attorneys called that day to say that Astley had finally agreed on the settlement and they were proceeding, her divorce would be final in less than a month, and, at Layne's urging, she had, indeed, taken him to the cleaners. What was slightly disturbing was that Astley let her.

Layne did not dwell. He didn't give a fuck about Astley's motivations. All he cared about was that the papers would soon be signed, and the day they were, he was putting a huge, fucking rock on her finger. He'd seen the ring Astley had given her. It wasn't ostentatious but it made a statement.

Layne's was going to be bigger.

Stew had moved on, had been living with his piece in the trailer park, but word was he was moving, with her, into an apartment in the 'burg. He didn't mind Gabby knowing it either, since he paraded the skank in front of Gabby at the game that night five times (Layne hadn't paid attention, but Rocky had counted and shared this information). Gabby hadn't liked this and made the unfortunate play of letting that show. She didn't see the skank was a skank and Gabby was a better catch. But that was Gabby, always making the wrong decisions.

Layne and Rocky had dinner with Ryker and Lissa. In a social situation, Ryker was no less Ryker but Layne's woman was enough of a nut to find him charming (this was Rocky's word). She and Lissa had instantly formed a bond over some woman in the 'burg who gave manicures that were so good, both declared the manicurist an "artist." Before they left Frank's, the women had planned to have back-to-back manicures the next Saturday followed by lunch at The Station.

The Bulldogs had won again and Jasper and Layne had talked for half an hour on the phone before the game about which visits to universities he was going to accept. He only had so many and they were stacking up. Purdue had been added, as had IU and Michigan. Jasper was leaning toward Ball State. It was his dad's alma mater and it was a good school. It just wasn't Purdue.

Layne had allowed Ball State to be scratched on the list but the first visit was going to be to West Lafayette, Indiana. Jasper had agreed.

It was almost done, they were almost there. They just had to take down Rutledge and Towers and then life could be life.

His eyes turned to the bathroom when he caught movement there and his breath locked in his throat when he saw Rocky in a faded, red t-shirt with a peeling Ball State decal. It was the first one she'd confiscated from him twenty-one years ago. He remembered it because it was his favorite shirt and he'd known with an even deeper knowledge than he already had that he loved her when he gave it up without a fight.

She strutted to her side of the bed, pulled back the covers and slid in, her movements liquid. She shifted to him, reached across him and turned out the light.

Then she pinned him to the bed.

"Baby," he muttered, his voice thick.

"Yeah?"

"The tee."

She pressed closer.

"You weren't the only one who didn't let go," she whispered.

Layne's arm tightened around her, his hand giving her hip a rough squeeze, his other hand lifted and slid into her hair.

"Though, I should note, Jarrod wasn't a big fan of me wearing this to bed."

Layne's body went still.

"Which I did," she went on.

Layne stayed still and silent.

"A lot," she finished.

Layne didn't move nor speak.

Neither did Rocky.

Until she whispered, "I know it was a bitchy thing to do, Layne. But, I mean, he was a jerk and he kept throwing you in my face. So, I figured, since he didn't get over it and I never got over you, at least I should be honest."

Layne kept his silence.

"He deserved it," she muttered.

Layne's body finally moved but it was against his volition. It did this to shake with laughter.

Her head came up. "He did, Layne, seriously. He—"

"Baby," he forced out, his voice sounding choked.

"You think I'm a bitch," she wrongly surmised.

"Baby," he repeated but was unable to say more.

"Trust me, Layne, I'm not a bitch. He could get mean about you."

He rolled into her, his hand in her hair moving over her mouth. "Baby, shut up."

"Okay," she said under his hand.

Layne moved his hand, dropped his head and shoved his face in her neck where he kept laughing softly.

"Are you laughing?" she whispered, finally feeling the way his body was moving, not to mention hearing his laughter.

"Shit yeah," he replied.

"Oh."

"You wore my tee to his bed," Layne stated.

"I missed you," she whispered.

Layne went still again. Then his head tipped back and he roared with laughter.

"Layne!"

"You wore my tee to his bed," Layne choked.

"Okay, now I'm thinking it *was* bitchy."

"You wore my tee to his bed," Layne repeated, still choking on his hilarity.

"Stop laughing!"

"Wrapped yourself up in me and slipped into his bed," Layne went on, his body shaking so hard the bed was moving with it.

He loved this. He loved knowing it. He loved that she did it. He loved everything about it. And he didn't fucking care what that said about him or about her. He just loved it.

"Layne!" she cried. "Stop laughing!"

"Dad!" They both heard Jasper shout and they both went still. "We're home!"

"Right, bud," Layne shouted back. "Have a good night?"

"Yeah!" Jasper was still shouting.

"Hey, Dad!" Tripp yelled.

"Hey, pal," Layne yelled back.

"Hey, Rocky!" Tripp kept yelling.

"Hey, Tripp!" Rocky was now yelling.

"We're hittin' the sack!" Jasper shouted.

"Gotcha," Layne shouted back.

"See you in the morning!" Tripp yelled.

"Right, pal, goodnight," Layne yelled back.

"'Night, Dad. 'Night Rocky," Tripp kept yelling.

"'Night, Tripp," Rocky yelled back and Layne's body started shaking again.

"'Night, Roc!" Jasper shouted. "Later, Dad."

"'Night, Jas!" Rocky shouted and Layne's laughter became audible.

Still he managed to shout, "Later, bud."

He felt Rocky's eyes on him in the dark and then she said in a horrified whisper, "Jeez, we're the freaking Waltons."

At that, Layne roared with laughter yet again.

<hr />

Saturday, 2:32 a.m.

Tanner Layne slept with Raquel Merrick pinning him to the bed.

He was having good dreams.

<hr />

Rocky's eyes opened and she saw only dark.

Dark.

She felt it press into her, like it was physical, a weight, a heavy weight against her skin.

Her breath started to get heavy.

She saw only dark but she felt only Layne.

She let the heat from his body seep into her, feeling his strength under her arm, her cheek, her leg, down her torso.

She pulled in a deep, steady breath and stared into the dark, sucking in Layne's heat, his strength.

She used him to beat it back, closed her eyes and slept, pinning her man to the bed.

Twenty-Five

DARK

Saturday, 3:37 p.m.

They were losing her. Towers had followed Jeremy when he was supposed to be going to the church for Youth Group. He didn't realize he was being tailed, and when he didn't go to church but drove right past, she'd peeled off and gone back to The Brendel.

Colt had called Layne in. Emergency meeting. Jeremy hadn't been able to get the clients' names or the dirt on Rutledge and he'd fucked it up, went after it too hard, too desperate and she got curious as to why he wanted to know.

Now they were screwed.

Layne's phone rang. He pulled it out, looked at the display and saw it said, "Tripp Calling."

He took the call and started, "Yo—"

"Dad, somethin's wrong with Rocky," Tripp whispered.

Layne nearly drove off the road at the tone of his son's voice.

In order to get some work done, he'd left his family that morning with donuts and college football pre-game shows. They were having a special dinner that night and Rocky and Vera were planning the menu. Rocky had called the furniture store on Friday and ordered the furniture, paying extra for express delivery that day. Giselle was going to help them break in the table and Rocky had called Vi and talked her into letting Keira come, even

Kristen Ashley

though she was still grounded for two more days, just for the night, just for dinner.

Dave and Merry were coming too.

The whole family.

Rocky, wearing his robe, and Vera had been laughing about some woman shit and clicking through recipes on Jasper's laptop at the island when he left.

Now something was wrong.

Layne swiftly changed lanes and turned left to circle home.

"Talk to me, pal," Layne ordered while he drove.

"I don't know. The dudes got here with the furniture. They brought in the big couch and then the table. They tore all the shit away from the table and Rocky, she went funny. She stared at that table and she went funny. Then she took off running to your room. It was like Gram knew what was happening and she took off after her. Gram's in your room with her now and sometimes she shouts. Jasper is upstairs, standing outside your door. He won't leave it and he didn't have his phone. He told me to call you and then call Dev."

"Sometimes she shouts?" Layne asked.

"She doesn't even sound like her, Dad. It's..." His voice broke and Layne's stomach dropped hearing it. "Dad, it's freaking creepy."

Fuck.

Layne hooked another left. "What does she say?"

"Nothin' that makes sense."

"Tell me what she says, Tripp."

He was quiet a beat and then he said, "She says she can't make you do it."

"Can't make me do what?"

"I don't know, Dad. God!" He was getting agitated, or *more* agitated. "That's just what she says. Over and over again. 'I can't make him do it! I can't make Layne do it!"

Jesus fucking Christ.

"Do not let her leave," Layne ordered.

"Right."

"Tripp, listen to me. If she doesn't have her keys, find them and hide them. If she's got them, talk to Jasper and tell him to do what he's gotta do to get them away from her. She still tries to go, I don't care if you have to tackle her and pin her to the ground, do not hesitate, boy, and do not let her leave. Tell your brother."

"Right."

"I'm coming home right now."

"Right."

"Be there soon," he stated, disconnecte, scrolled down to Dave and hit go.

"Hey, Tanner," Dave answered.

"Rocky's turned," Layne announced and got silence. "Dave, did you hear me? Rocky's turned. Something's wrong. Tripp just called, said she's shouting at Ma about not making me do something and he says she doesn't sound like Rocky. He's freaked."

"I'm on my way," Dave replied urgently.

"No, no you are fuckin' not. Talk to me."

"She needs me."

"Talk to me, Dave."

"I'm at the tackle shop in Plainfield. I'll be there soon's I can."

"Dave—"

Dead air.

"*Fuck!*" Layne exploded, stopped at a red light and waited impatiently, adrenaline surging through his system, so much he could feel it. His hands were shaking, the muscles in his thighs quivering, he was staring at the no turn on red sign like he could make it designate with his eyes. "Fuck," he whispered.

He turned when he had his shot. The light still red, Layne went right and broke the speed limit by thirty miles an hour, overtaking two cars to make it home. He parked on the street and ran flat out to the front door. Opening it, he heard her instantly.

"*No!*" Rocky shrieked, her voice hoarse, guttural. Even as Layne moved to the stairs, he felt that voice send a shiver along his skin. "I've *got to go*! I have to be gone before he gets home!"

"Rocky, honey, just calm down, okay? Okay, honey?" Vera cooed.

Layne took the stairs three at a time and hit the top to see Tripp, Vera and Jasper had Rocky cornered in the weight room.

Her face was red, her body was wired, her hair was down and wild, like she'd been tearing her hands through it, a vein had popped out on her forehead, running down the middle to disappear at the bridge of her nose.

Her eyes came to his and hers were flooded with fear.

"Baby," he whispered and she moved, like a dart, shooting through his family, right at him.

She tried to dodge him at the last minute but he caught her, arm at the waist, swinging her up in front of him, her back to his front. Her legs kicked and her nails clawed at his arm but he turned and walked to his room even as she fought.

"Calm down, Rocky," he whispered in her ear. Her body bucked, her head colliding against his shoulder when he jerked his out of the way at the last second. "Calm down, baby."

"*Let me go!*" she screeched in that hideous voice.

He got into his room and she twisted violently in his arms. Her hand up, she scored his neck with her nails and the pain shot through him. His arms loosening, she yanked away from him and tried to get past him but he put a hand flat on her chest and gently pushed her back, feeling Vera, Tripp and Jasper moving in behind him to cut her off. She still made a run for it and Layne caught her again and pushed her back.

Her gaze swept Layne, his mother and his boys and she retreated, slowly stepping back, her eyes locking on Layne as he advanced.

"Don't," she warned, lifting a hand and stopping so Layne stopped too.

"Rocky, what's goin' on?" Layne asked softly.

"I can't make you do it," she told him and she began to pace, like an animal in a cage, side to side, her eyes flitting from him to Tripp to Vera to Jas to Layne and back as she repeated, "I can't make you do it."

"Do what?" Layne asked.

She shook her head, her eyes catching his. "I can't make you do it."

"Do what, baby?"

"Be with me," she said and then started chanting as she paced. "I can't make you be with me, I can't make you be with me, I can't make you be with me."

Jesus. *Jesus.*

"Rocky, baby," Layne whispered.

She started to shake her head and kept doing it, her eyes going to her feet. She was still pacing back and forth, "I didn't help her. I didn't help her. It was so dark."

"Oh my God," Vera breathed as Layne felt his chest squeeze.

"Rocky, what was dark?" he whispered.

She kept shaking her head. "It was so dark."

"What was dark, honey?"

"I hid. I hid. I hid when I should have helped her. I hid in the dark," Rocky whispered.

"You hid," Layne said quietly, inching toward her, "You hid when Carson Fisher came?"

She started nodding then, her head moving in a rhythm, uncontrolled, bobbing up and down. Rocky was gone. The woman she was was not there. She'd slid back twenty-four years.

Layne felt Devin's presence hit the room but he didn't turn and Rocky didn't notice him.

"Yes, when he came. She heard his car. She came to my room. She woke me up and told me to call 911. She told me to hide. She told me to hide." Her head jerked back and she stopped pacing, the look on her face searing into his soul when she whispered, "I did what I was told."

"Baby, you did what you were told. You called 911. You hid. You did the right thing."

"I should have helped her."

"You couldn't have helped her."

"She was shouting."

Layne was moving closer but stopped when Rocky noticed it, took a huge step back and started visibly trembling.

"Baby, you couldn't have helped her."

"He hurt her before he shot her," Rocky whispered.

Fuck, *fuck*. He knew that. He'd read the report. Carson Fisher had spent some time with Cecilia Merrick. Not much, he didn't have it. But he needed the evidence that Cecilia had so he tried torturing her to get it. He did a messy job of it in his haste and the results were unpleasant.

Cecilia had lived through it though, and died when she took a bullet to the face.

Layne just didn't know Rocky knew it.

Fuck.

"He hurt her and she was screaming."

"Honey, come here."

"I didn't help. I hid. I hid and it was so dark."

"Baby, please, come here."

"The eaves," she whispered. She was rocking her torso side to side, her arms sliding along her belly and holding tight, "Dad hated it when the birds got up there so he sealed it tight. I went out the little door to the eaves and it was so dark."

"Rocky, please, baby, come here."

"I went there, like a coward, and listened in the dark while she screamed."

"Rocky—"

"All alone."

"Rocky—"

"I left her all alone."

"Roc—"

Her hands suddenly went straight down, balled into fists and she shrieked, "*I left her all alone! He hurt her, I left her all alone! And she knew I could hear that! She died knowing I could hear that. She knew! My momma. Sheknewsheknewsheknew.*"

Layne moved forward fast, caught her in his arms, but she struggled, yanked free and ran to the corner. Pressing her side to it, she twisted to him, hand up, eyes on him.

"Don't touch me," she whispered and he watched her body tremble.

"Ma, call Doc," Layne ordered, not taking his eyes off Rocky. Vera didn't say a word but he knew she left the room, he saw Rocky's eyes follow her. "Rocky, baby, you aren't yourself," he told her, moving again slowly and her eyes shot back to him. "This is called post-traumatic stress, honey. You aren't yourself. This isn't then, this is now. You're safe."

She shook her head. "No, no I'm not."

"You're safe, baby, nothing is ever gonna hurt you."

"No, no, I'm not safe. You're not safe."

"I'm safe, Rocky."

"No," she kept shaking her head. "It isn't right. It could have been right but it isn't right now. Not now. It's worse than before. A lot worse. We could have had time but I fucked up."

"Honey—"

Her head still shaking she talked over him. "I can't make you do that."

She started sliding down the wall, her knees to her chest, her hand still lifted as if to fend him off.

"I can't make you do that," she repeated.

Layne crouched in front of her two feet away.

"Baby, can't make me do what?" he whispered.

"Lose me," she whispered back.

"You're not goin' anywhere," he told her.

"I'm going to die."

Layne's body froze.

Then he whispered, "What?"

"She was thirty-nine when she died. That's next year for me, Layne."

"Rocky—"

"That's what I'm going to get, for not helping her. I'm going to die when she died. I know. I've always known I'll never make it. I'll never make it. I knew what it would feel like to lose you and I knew you'd feel the same way if you lost me. Like Dad. You'd be like Dad. If we had the chance to have a life, I knew you'd never move on." Her hand dropped and she wrapped both arms around her legs but her eyes didn't leave his. They were burning into him and his chest was burning, his throat, and he could do nothing but hold her eyes. "I left you to give you a life, baby," she whispered, her voice hoarse, the tears hitting her eyes, sliding down, silent. "I wanted you to have a life."

"That's why you left me?" he asked quietly.

She nodded. "I didn't want you to hurt. I knew how bad it hurt. I felt it. Saw it in Merry. Saw it in Dad. I didn't want you to hurt."

"Rocky, come to me."

"We can't have a baby girl, she won't have a momma," Rocky whispered.

Layne's voice was rough when he begged, "Please, baby, come to me."

"I know what it's like to lose your momma."

"Baby, please."

"I can't sit at the table with the family, Layne. I let my family die, left her all alone to die, crouched like a coward in the dark and listened to her scream while I let her die."

"You didn't let her die, honey. Fisher killed her."

"I can't sit at the table when I let my family die."

Layne was done.

"I'm comin' to you, Roc."

She shook her head as the tears slid down her face, off her jaw to hit her sweater.

"Right now, baby, I'm coming to you."

She kept shaking her head as he moved to her and he braced for a fight but when he got to her, she surged into him, pressing in, deep and tight. He twisted and sat in the corner. She crawled into his lap, curling into a ball, her arms attached around his neck like she was never going to let him go and the tears came. Not tears. Great, wracking, body rocking sobs.

He held her close and looked up to see Devin, Tripp and Jasper had moved in.

"Dave's gonna get here and he'll have called Merry. They don't approach. I don't care what you do but I don't want them up here until Doc sees to her."

"Gotcha, son," Devin whispered.

"Go, close the door," Layne ordered.

Devin nodded. He turned but Jasper and Tripp didn't move. Their eyes were glued to their father.

"Go," Layne whispered.

Dev's arms came out and he hooked both Layne's boys, gently turning them and guiding them away.

Rocky shoved her face deeper into his neck. Layne dropped his head and spoke in her ear.

"We're gonna work this out of you, baby."

She shook her head.

"Swear, Roc, swear, I'm gonna take care of you. Yeah?"

She didn't answer, just pressed deeper.

Layne's arms got tight. "Love you, Raquel."

Another sob tore up her throat but, thank fuck, she held on.

Doc slid Rocky's hair off her neck then his eyes came to Layne.

"You can let her go, son, she's sleeping," Doc whispered.

"Get Ma," Layne ordered.

Doc looked into his eyes, took a breath in his nose and nodded. Then he walked out of the room.

Layne was in bed, shoulders to the headboard, Rocky curled asleep on top of him. Doc had administered the injection while she was still sobbing, Christ, so many tears. He didn't know a body had that many tears. She didn't struggle. She took the shot and slowly faded to quiet in his arms.

Now it was now and he knew both Dave and Merry were downstairs. He knew too that they had lost a wife, a mother.

And he didn't fucking care.

Vera slid into the room and her eyes went directly to him.

"Get in bed, Ma."

She nodded and hurried to Rocky's side of the bed. She sat like Layne was sitting and he turned Rocky into her outstretched arms. When Rocky's head settled on his mother's chest and Vera had pulled Rocky's arm around her belly, Layne slid out of bed.

"Don't let her go," Layne whispered.

"I won't, honey," Vera whispered back.

Layne walked to the door, closed it, and he should have taken a breath. He should have taken three.

He didn't.

He stalked down the stairs.

Everyone was in the kitchen, Dev, Tripp, Jas, Doc, Dave and Merry.

Dave was sitting at the island. Merry was standing beside it.

"How is—?" Dave started but stopped when Layne stalked straight to Merry.

Merry's face was ravaged with worry but that didn't penetrate the fury spiraling around Layne. What it did was bring Merry's guard down so he didn't move fast enough, which meant Layne got close, wrapped his hand tight around Merry's throat and he kept walking, pushing Merry back.

"Dad!" Tripp shouted.

Merry's hands came up to Layne's forearm as Layne squeezed.

"Tanner!" Dave yelled.

"Boy!" Devin yelled too, but Layne shoved Merry against the wall, pinned him there with his body and got in his face, still squeezing.

"Twenty-four years, you asshole, twenty-four years, you left that festering in her head."

"Boy, stand down," Devin ordered, his hand on Layne's back but Layne twitched his body, throwing off Devin's hand and he squeezed Merry's throat harder.

"You knew," Layne clipped as Merry choked. "You knew that's why she left me. You knew that was torturing her. And you left her to that agony."

"Tanner, son, please." Dave was close and Layne turned to him. His other arm shooting up, he pointed a finger right in Dave's face.

"You're not right here, old man, because you're an old man. You deserve worse," he growled and Dave's pale face grew paler.

"Brother," Merry choked.

Layne jerked his head around and got in Merry's face again. "I'm not your brother," he bit out.

Merry's eyes narrowed and he yanked on Layne's forearm. "You don't get it."

"I fuckin' well do. It leaked straight from her eyes into my skin, you asshole."

"You don't get it," Merry rasped.

"What didn't sink into my skin filled my head. She told me, Garrett. She *told* me."

"She made us promise, Tanner," Dave said behind him, his tone pleading.

Jasper got close and whispered, "Stand down, Dad."

Layne stayed in Merry's face and stared in his eyes. It didn't occur to him Merry wasn't struggling except to keep Layne's hand from squeezing the life out of him.

"Dad, stand down," Jasper repeated.

Layne's body locked before he pushed off, shoving Merry deeper into the wall as he took a step away.

"You aren't welcome in this house," he announced as both Merry's hands went to his throat.

"Please listen to me, son," Dave begged and Layne turned to him.

"You want me to listen now? Is that right? Now you want me to listen," Layne asked sarcastically.

"Devin told us it was bad up there," Dave said quietly.

"Yeah, Dave, I guess you could describe it as *bad*, watchin' my woman relive a nightmare where she heard her mother scream through torture. You could describe that as *bad*."

Dave flinched then his face got hard. "That's my wife you're talkin' about."

"No, Dave, that's *your daughter* I'm talkin' about."

Dave's jaw clenched.

"She made us promise, Tanner," Merry said softly and Layne turned to him.

"Yeah, she did? What'd she make you promise?" Layne asked.

"When she left you, she was out of it, like what you saw but worse. It lasted two days," Merry explained.

Two days. Rocky said she'd lost two days. She didn't remember it.

Fuck.

"And, what? You call Doc?" Layne's eyes cut to Doc. "They call you?"

"Nope," Doc answered, his eyes were sharp and he was pissed, Layne could tell. "Didn't get a call. Offered it, when she was fourteen and I knew this would play with her mind. But I didn't get a call Tanner, not at fourteen, or fifteen, or—"

"We could handle it in the family," Dave snapped.

"Right, see you did a fine job with that, Dave," Doc snapped back.

"This is none of your concern," Dave shot back.

"Was my concern when you brought her in with appendicitis. Was my concern when she had a chest infection. Was my concern when she dislocated her shoulder. The mind is a part of the body, Dave, and I've been her doctor for over three decades. It's my goldarned concern!" Doc returned.

Jesus, the old guy remembered all that? Fucking hell.

"We were handling it in the family," Dave repeated.

"And I wasn't family?" Layne asked and Dave's eyes shot to him.

"What?"

"Eighteen years ago, when she turned then, I wasn't family?"

Dave closed his eyes slowly.

"Answer me, Dave, wasn't I family?"

Dave's eyes opened. "Tanner—"

Layne leaned forward and roared, "*Wasn't I family?*"

"She made us promise, Tanner," Merry whispered and Layne swung around to face him. "You saw her. You saw the way she could be. Wouldn't you promise anything, *anything*, to stop her from being like that?"

"No," Layne shook his head. "No, I would not. What I'd do, no matter what she said, how she acted, what she threatened, was understand she needed some serious fucking help and *get it for her.*"

"Even if that meant losing her?" Merry shot back.

"Yes, *brother*, even if that meant losing her because even if I had to sleep at night without her, I'd know she wasn't tortured by her mother's dying screams. So, yes. Absolutely."

A muscle ticked in Merry's jaw, he turned his head and looked away.

"Losing Cecilia happened to all of us, Tanner," Dave noted and Layne looked at him.

"I've no idea, pray to God I never do. You all had it tough. But you didn't listen to her die, Dave, your daughter did. You didn't have the tools to deal with Rocky and you should have found someone who had those tools. You should have talked to Doc. You should have taken care of her."

"I did," Dave returned.

"No, Dave, you didn't. You didn't then, you didn't seven years later when she cut me out of her life and you knew, you and Merry, you both knew and don't bother denying it, you *knew* I was the only one who could heal those wounds and you let her cut me out. And you aren't now because you're standing there, in total denial and not admitting how huge a fuck up you perpetrated."

"I lost my wife!" Dave shouted.

"I'm sorry about that, Dave," Layne whispered. "But you didn't lose your life so that means it was your responsibility to get your head outta your fuckin' ass and take care of your daughter."

"Dad," Tripp called softly. "You're bein' too hard on Uncle Dave."

Layne turned to his son. "That's not my job, Tripp, lookin' out for Dave. That's my woman up there." He jerked his finger to the ceiling. "It's my job to look after *her.*" He turned back to Dave and swept through Merry with his glance. "It goes without sayin' you shoulda let me in on this shit eighteen years ago, but that's done. Then you had a second shot, both of you, I asked, I fuckin' begged, and you still kept this shit to yourself."

"This was coming back up for all of us, Tanner," Dave defended himself. "Knowing why she left you, knowing it might surface again, not only for her, but for all of us. This wasn't exactly easy."

"You have turns like that?" Layne asked.

"No, but I feel Fisher in my bones every time it rains," Dave returned.

"So, you think, maybe *all* of you might need some help to sort your shit out?" Layne suggested derisively. "So you could deal with that pain in your bones, Merry could get his head sorted after leavin' the only woman he's ever loved and Roc wouldn't have to endure another turn?"

"Dad and I talked and we thought, she had another episode, this time, we would have your back," Merry said and Layne's eyes locked on him.

"Well, you didn't, you weren't here. My boys and my mother had my back."

Merry stared at him a beat before he nodded.

Layne kept talking. "Rocky, she loves you, she'll always love you. Me, I'm feelin' a fuckuva lot different. She's in my house and she's under my watch now. I want you two gone. I know you'll be back and I know I'll have to deal, but right now, I want you two gone."

Dave puffed out his chest. "I want to see my daughter."

"You'll have to call her tomorrow," Layne replied.

"I want to see her now."

"She's sleepin' in my bed now, Dave, so, like I said, you're gonna have to wait until tomorrow."

"She's my daughter, Tanner," Dave hissed.

"Dad, let's go," Merry whispered.

"No, I'm not—" Dave started.

"Dad...let's...*go*," Merry clipped.

"He can't tell me when I can see my daughter," Dave shot back.

"Yeah, Dad, he can," Merry returned.

"He can't."

"Would you let someone see Mom, you're pissed as hell at them?" Merry retorted and Dave's torso jerked back. "Yeah, that's what this is. You know what this is. We're Merricks for fuck's sake. You're like that. I'm like that. Mom was like that. Rocky's like that. And you know Rocky's gonna find a man like that. So, Tanner's pissed and we need *to go.*"

Dave glared at his son. He turned his glare on Doc. Then he turned his glare on Layne. Finally, he turned on his foot and stalked to the front door.

Merry's eyes went to Layne. "We'll work this out, brother."

"I wouldn't hold your breath 'til that happens, Garrett."

Merry studied him then shook his head, a small, sad grin on his face.

Then he said, "You're pissed now but you love her. We'll work this out."

Merry was right but Layne sure as fuck wasn't going to give that to him. So he stayed silent and watched Merry walk out.

"I'll go to the office," Doc announced after the door closed behind Merry. "Get some names. Good counselors. I'll call you with numbers. She needs to find one she trusts and start right away."

Layne nodded.

"I didn't give her much, she won't be out long," Doc went on. "I'll leave some sleeping pills. She has trouble sleeping, you need to make her take them. If she wakes and she's still not well, exhibiting disorientation, any of the symptoms you saw, even amnesia, not remembering what happened today, I need to know."

"Right," Layne grunted.

Doc rounded the island and got close to Layne. "You need to make yourself safe harbor, Tanner. She needs to know she can lay this weight on you. It's heavy, son. You want her better, you learn to brace."

"She's safe now, Doc," Layne muttered and Doc's eyes searched his face.

Then he nodded and murmured, "I reckon so."

Doc's eyes swept the room, he nodded again then he turned to go but he stopped by the stairs and turned back.

His eyes locked on Layne and he spoke.

"Later, not now, later, you think about Rocky, how you feel about her, then how you'd feel learning that she was tortured then shot twice in the chest and once in the face." Layne's middle jerked back at Doc's words but he didn't break eye contact. "It happened to you, you might deal with it different. You might make better choices. But that man did what he could carrying the burden that he brought that on his wife and left his daughter with demons. A burden he's still carrying, Tanner. You're right to be angry but no good man can understand the burden Dave Merrick carries and hold a grudge."

With that successful parting shot, Doc turned away and disappeared.

Layne stood frozen for long moments after he left and only moved when he felt Tripp fit his body against Layne's side, his arms going around his dad's waist, his cheek to Layne's shoulder and his boy hugged him.

Layne's arm went around Tripp's shoulders and he gave him a squeeze.

Tripp stepped back from Layne and looked in his old man's eyes. "Can I go up and sit with Gram and Rocky?" he asked quietly.

God, Tripp was a good kid.

Layne lifted a hand, curled it around Tripp's neck and squeezed. "You okay after you saw that, pal?"

"Yeah, I'm just worried Roc's not okay."

"She'll be okay," Layne assured his son on another squeeze and a short tug.

"You think you can fix her?" Tripp asked.

"I know it," Layne answered.

Tripp smiled. It was wonky and halfhearted but he did it.

"Good thing is, I didn't have to tackle her," Tripp noted.

"Yeah, that's good," Layne replied.

"But I stole her keys out of her purse. They're in between Blondie's forty-first and forty-second food bowls," Tripp informed him and Layne returned his smile, figuring his was halfhearted too but at least it was a smile.

"Thanks, pal" Layne said on another squeeze.

"I'm gonna go up," Tripp whispered, Layne nodded and let him go.

Tripp gave him a long, last look, turned and ran up the stairs.

Layne felt cold on his arm and turned to see Jasper was holding a beer there.

"Think he needs whisky, boy," Devin grunted.

Layne took the beer from Jas, slapped him on the shoulder and said to Dev, "Not sure whisky's a good idea right now. Or, not as much as I want of it."

"Right." Devin was in the liquor cupboard. "You need your faculties about you. I, on the other hand, can get as drunk as I want."

Layne moved to the island and felt Jasper crowding him, like he did Tripp and Seth when Cosgrove abused them, and he turned to look at his son.

"I'm good, bud," he murmured.

"Okay, Dad," Jas murmured back but he didn't move away so Layne flung his arm around his boy's shoulders and pulled him, hard, into his side.

Jasper slid his arm around Layne's waist and held on.

Devin opened the bottle of whisky and turned to Layne.

"What'd I say?" Devin asked.

"About what?" Layne asked back.

Devin looked at him. Then he said, "*Kaboom!*" Then he put the whisky bottle to his lips, tipped his head far back and took a huge shot straight from the bottle.

Jasper turned his head and Layne did the same. They caught each other's eye and Jasper shook his head.

Layne looked back to Devin who was now staring at them, still holding the bottle by its neck.

"Also told you she's worth the effort."

"Already knew that, old man."

"Yeah, well, now you know it more." His eyes slid to Jas. "Seen a lot of things, done a lot of things. Wounds to the flesh hurt but they heal fast. Wounds to the soul never go away. It's how we cope with a pain that never dies that makes us the people we are. Daily, people demonstrate acts of courage just so they can get through to the night. That woman upstairs smiles and laughs and cooks and teaches and no one knew the pain she carried in her soul. In other words, there are warriors and then there are warriors. In your dad's bed lies a warrior. Learn from her, boy."

"Right," Jasper whispered.

"Your dad's gone, I'm gone, you or your brother have her back," Devin ordered.

"Right," Jasper repeated on another whisper.

"Until she's freed, she can turn at any time. One of us needs to catch her should she fall," Devin went on.

"Right," Jasper whispered again.

"Brief your brother," Devin demanded.

"Right," Jasper whispered yet again.

"Now," Devin announced, "I'm havin' a stoagie and gettin' drunk." His eyes hit Layne. "And that dog's been quarantined outside throughout this situation and I'm not lettin' her in yet so, goes without sayin', me outside with whisky and a stoagie and your fuckin' dog, tells you what you mean to me, boy."

Then he strode to the door, opened it, Blondie attacked him on his first step on the cement patio and he closed the door.

Layne squeezed Jasper's shoulder and stepped away.

"You good?" Layne asked.

"I'm good," Jasper answered.

"Ignore Dev, he can be dramatic."

"Seems pretty smart to me."

Layne looked into Jasper's eyes.

Then he asked, "Sure you're good?"

"Yeah, Dad."

"I was shot a while ago, bud, and—"

"I'm good, Dad."

"We haven't talked about that. I wanted to give you boys time."

"You don't need to give us time."

"Jas—"

"Dad, we know what you do for a living and we know why. It's jacked up, what happened to Roc's mom because she was a mom, not someone like you. It sucked, you gettin' shot, and I can't say that Tripp and me weren't scared. We were. But you're here. We're tight. So it's all good."

"You ever wanna talk," Layne said quietly.

Jasper grinned at him. "Yeah, but, I need to talk, I'll pick a time when Rocky's not sedated in your bedroom."

Layne grinned back. "Good call," he muttered then lifted the bottle in his hand. "You wanna beer?"

Jasper's brows shot up. "Seriously?"

"Fuck no," Layne replied.

Jasper chuckled.

Layne moved into his son, wrapped an arm around him and pulled him close, let him go, turned and walked up the stairs to Rocky.

Layne knew she was awake ten minutes before she stirred and lifted her head from his chest.

Her neck twisted and her eyes hit his.

"Faker," he whispered.

She blinked slowly.

Then she whispered back, "What?"

"Sweetcheeks, you've been fakin' sleep for ten minutes."

"Oh." She was still whispering and now pushing away.

So Layne's arm, already around her, tightened and he pulled her up his chest.

She put slight pressure on him, not too much but avoided his eyes.

"Baby, look at me," Layne ordered gently and her eyes came to his. "How you feelin'?"

"Weird," she answered.

"You remember?"

She pressed her lips together. Then she nodded.

"All of it?"

"What day is today?" she asked.

"Saturday," he answered.

"Then yes. All of it."

"How many days you lose to this shit?"

"Well, I've been lying there thinking about it and I'm guessing...two."

"That's my guess too," Layne told her. "So it never happened before?"

"Not that I know of."

"But you might not remember?"

586

"I'm thinking...no."

"Doc gave me some names and numbers of people you can call. We'll see it never happens again."

She stopped pressing against him and her weight hit his side.

Then she whispered, "Tripp and Jas saw—"

"Don't worry about it."

"I think—"

"Rocky, honey, you know they're good kids. This is life. I can't shield them from life forever. They've gotta learn how to deal. What happened was real. It needed to happen. You needed to get that shit out. You did it surrounded by people who care a lot about you. When that shit happens, that's the best place to be."

"It's embarrassing," she whispered.

"Baby," he whispered back, pulling her closer and wrapping his other arm around her. "Your mother died while you listened. That marked you. There is nothing embarrassing about that. You loved her, you lost her and it marked you. It's not embarrassing because there's beauty in that."

"Beauty?" she breathed.

"You loved her."

Her eyes grew bright with tears and she nodded.

"That's beautiful."

She dropped her head, planted her face in his chest and his hand came up and slid over her hair.

"You go to her grave," Layne whispered.

"I miss her," Rocky whispered back.

"She was a good mom," Layne stated.

"The best." She lifted her head and looked at him. "You would have liked her. She was funny."

"I remember her. You look like her."

She nodded. Then she sucked in breath.

"It was talking about having babies," she whispered. "After you said that, I started to get these thoughts."

Layne's arms gave her a squeeze. "I'm sorry, honey."

She shook her head. "Don't be. You can't guard against everything you say."

"No."

"Then it was the table." She shook her head again. "Mom always made us eat at the table. Every night. I have trouble eating at a table." Her eyes were intense on his. "It's been hard, since she's been gone, to sit at a table with family around. When we were together, I used to look at you. Something about looking at you made me settle."

Layne closed his eyes then opened them and wrapped his hand around her neck.

"I remember," he told her.

"It made me feel safe."

"Yeah?"

"I knew, you were around, you'd never let anything hurt me."

"Baby." His voice was hoarse and his arm at her back and hand at her neck gave her a tight squeeze.

"I'm scared a lot, Layne," she admitted quietly. "So often, I got used to it. It lives with me. It's in my skin."

"It gets to you, if it's dark."

She nodded. "You help me beat it back."

"Rocky—"

"Then and now."

"Baby—"

"I don't want to be scared anymore, Layne."

His fingers slid into her hair and he pulled her face to his, touching his mouth to hers, then he let her move back an inch.

"We'll see to that, yeah?"

"Yeah."

His thumb swept her cheek but his eyes didn't leave hers and then she dropped her head and rested her cheek to his chest, her arm wrapping around him.

"I ruined our dinner plans," she whispered to his chest.

"We'll do it next weekend."

"The boys won't be here," she reminded him.

"Jasper's got a car. They can be wherever they wanna be. They'll wanna be here."

"Gabrielle won't like that."

"Do I give a fuck?"

A startled giggle escaped her and she held on tighter.

Then she muttered, "I'm hungry."

"What you want, baby?"

She lifted her head. "Shanghai Salon?"

His brows went up. "Sesame chicken?"

Her mouth got soft and her lids lowered. "You remembered."

"How many times do I have to tell you, sweetcheeks? I remember everything."

"Thank you, Layne."

"For what?"

"For loving me like you do."

His arms tightened around her and they did it automatically.

"Christ, Roc," he muttered.

"Mom would have liked you too."

"Baby, stop it."

"Because you love me like you do."

"Rocky—"

"And 'cause you're hot."

He gave a startled bark of laughter and stared at her.

"Because I'm hot?"

"She used to point out all the cute boys to me. Say things like, 'Rocky, look at him. He's the perfect height for you.' And 'Rocky, he's cute, but he's blond. Blond boys can be cute but they'll always be cute. Cute dark boys will turn *gorgeous*.' Stuff like that."

He'd never heard her talk about her mother that way. Never.

He liked it.

"You're dark," she went on.

"Yeah, sweetcheeks, seen myself in the mirror."

She smiled at him. "And you're hot. Mom had a good eye for cute guys. Ergo, she'd like you."

"Ergo?" he teased.

"Shut up," she whispered.

He grinned at her, but his arms tightened in preparation.

Then he shouted, "Tripp!"

Rocky went still in his arms.

The door opened almost instantaneously and Tripp was there, which meant his boy was doing sentry duty close. When he arrived, Rocky's body jerked.

"Yeah, Dad?" he asked then his eyes slid to Rocky. "Hey, Roc," he said casually.

"Uh…hey, Tripp."

"You're awake, cool, can we eat?" Tripp asked.

"Shanghai Salon. Roc wants sesame chicken. I want Kung Pao shrimp. Get your brother, Gram and Devin's orders. Call it in. Delivery," Layne ordered.

"Cool!" Tripp shouted, his torso twisted and he yelled, "Jas! We're havin' Chinese."

"Awesome!" They heard Jasper's voice shout from far away.

"Chinese!" Vera shouted, also from far away. "I'll make tuna casserole."

"No way, Gram, we want Chinese!" Tripp yelled, turning from the door, he left it ajar and jogged away.

"I want lemon chicken, Tripp-o-matic," Jasper shouted.

Rocky settled into him, cheek back to his chest, arm tight around him.

"Okay, well, it appears they're not traumatized by my drama."

"No, sweetcheeks, but expect a lot of attention for a while. Tripp will likely talk your ear off and Jasper will stick to you like glue."

Her head came up. "Seriously?"

"Seriously."

"Why?"

"Because they care, because they want to know you're all right and because that's their way of making that so."

She lifted a hand to rest on his neck. "It's scary how much they're like you."

"I talk your ear off?"

"No, you want to make sure I'm all right and find a way to make it so."

Layne smiled at her.

Rocky kept talking. "Though, I have to ask, where did Tripp get his blond hair?"

"Fuck knows."

Her eyes unfocused and she said softly, "If he didn't have your exact body and your intensity, I would swear Gabrielle stepped out on you."

Layne started laughing. Roc's eyes focused on him then her face flushed. "I don't mean to intimate—"

"Baby," Layne said through his chuckles. "Tripp's my son and even if he wasn't by blood, he's still my son. That's all there is to it."

"He's your son, Layne, I know it."

"Yeah, me too."

"Dad!" Tripp yelled from downstairs. "I need your wallet!"

"Mine's in my purse on the counter, Tripp!" Rocky shouted back.

"You get Rocky's wallet, Tripp, you're grounded for a month. Come up here and get mine." Layne shouted after Rocky.

Her eyes shot to him. "I can pay for dinner, Layne."

"I know you can, you just aren't."

"Layne."

"Rocky."

"Layne."

"Roc."

Their stare down was interrupted by Tripp coming to get his wallet and Layne handing it over but Rocky's glare was intensified when his eyes returned to hers.

"Close the door, pal," Layne called, his eyes locked to Rocky.

"Right," Tripp muttered and Layne heard the door catch.

Then Layne chose option two to end a stare down. He rolled her to her back and kissed her, and when he was done, he shoved his face in her neck.

"Love you, baby," he whispered against her skin as his hands slid up her sides.

"Love you too, Layne," she whispered back and her arms got tight around him.

Layne's arms wrapped around her, his face still in her neck, he rolled them to their sides and he expelled a breath, a breath it felt like he'd been holding for decades.

And, Rocky in his bed, in his arms, her arms tight around him, it felt good to let that breath, finally, go.

Twenty-Six

MEANT TO BE

*L*ayne left his room, walked through the weight room, rounded the stairs and stopped dead when he looked down to see Vera and Devin sitting together three steps from the top.

When Vera sensed him, her neck twisted, her head went back and she put her finger to her lips.

"You have pictures?" Layne heard Tripp ask from downstairs and Layne's attention shifted to listen.

"Yeah, Tripp," Rocky answered.

It was Sunday morning, after Vera's pancakes, but the TV wasn't on. Layne couldn't be sure but he was guessing Tripp and Rocky were on the colossal, cushiony sectional that was a connected square that looked part-bed, part-couch and all comfortable and now sat in the corner by the front window taking up nearly the entirety of the front space.

"Was she pretty, like you?" Tripp asked and Layne pulled in a breath and his neck muscles got tight.

Tripp was asking about her mother.

Devin turned his head too and shook it at Layne.

"No," Rocky replied. "She was beautiful."

"So," Jasper put in, "like you."

Layne closed his eyes and his hand went to the top of the post at the stairs, his fingers curling around it, holding on.

592

"That's sweet, Jas," Rocky said softly.

"Yeah, I'm sweet. Keirry says so," Jasper returned arrogantly and Layne opened his eyes and smiled.

"You're also full of it," Tripp told him.

"Watch and learn, Tripp-o-matic, and you'll hook Giselle deep," Jasper noted.

"Giselle's already hooked deep, dude. She totally digs me," Tripp replied.

"That's because you're sweet too," Rocky said.

"Yeah?" Tripp asked, sounding like an affirmative answer meant everything in the world.

"Yeah," Rocky answered softly, with one soft word, giving his son the world.

There was silence then Tripp remarked, "I'm fourteen."

"I know, Tripp," Rocky replied.

"I turn fifteen next month," he told her.

"Yeah? What do you want for your birthday?" Rocky asked.

"Milky Way cake," Tripp answered.

"That can be arranged," Rocky stated.

"You were fourteen too," Tripp noted and Layne watched Vera's hand shoot out and clutch Devin's knee. She knew what he was referring to, they all did.

Layne's body went alert, ready to move in case this went bad.

"Sorry, honey?" Rocky asked.

"When it happened...uh, with your mom," Tripp answered.

"Tripp," Jasper said low, a warning.

"It's okay," Rocky whispered. "Yes, Tripp, I was fourteen."

"Dad was shot," Tripp announced and Layne started moving but Devin's head jerked around again. He shook it sharply as his arm went around Vera.

"I know," Rocky said softly.

"So, um...I just want you to know, uh...well, it wasn't the same, but...I know," Tripp stated and Layne, down two steps, dropped to sit on the landing mostly because, fuck him, his legs couldn't hold him up anymore.

"I guess you do," Rocky replied.

"It's not the same," Tripp told her something she already knew.

"Yes, that doesn't mean it wasn't bad," Rocky returned. "I was there and I saw you were worried. I know how that feels. My dad was shot too."

"You were there?" Jasper asked. "You were at the hospital when Dad was shot?"

"You didn't see me, but yes, I was there."

"Wow, totally missed that," Tripp muttered.

"Dad says that him getting shot tweaked you," Jasper remarked.

"Yes, Jas," Rocky confirmed and Layne could tell she was smiling. "It *tweaked* me."

"'Cause you were into him, even though, you know, you guys had broken up," Jasper stated.

"Yes, Jas, I was into him," Rocky confirmed.

"All these years, right?" Jasper pushed.

"Does that make you feel weird?" Rocky asked.

"No, it's cool. I'm a dude but girls say Dad's hot," Jasper answered. "So, I can see that'd make you stay into him."

"Yes, your father is hot and that's part of why I stayed into him." Rocky now sounded like she was trying not to laugh. "Though, just an FYI, Jas, you look like your father, you're very good-looking, but that isn't the reason why Keira likes you."

"It isn't?" Tripp asked.

"Nope," Roc answered.

"Why's she like him then?" Tripp asked.

"We already talked about it," Rocky answered. "Because he's sweet."

"No, she digs my six-pack," Jasper informed them and Layne pressed his lips together as he saw his mother's back go straight, and Devin's back start shaking with silent laughter.

"Jasper Layne, I do not want to think of why Keira Winters would know you have a six-pack," Rocky stated severely.

Jasper, always quick, replied, "She saw me at a pool party last summer."

This was not true. As far as Layne knew, Jasper didn't attend a pool party last summer.

"I hope that's it," Rocky muttered.

"What I don't get is," Tripp started, obviously helping his brother out changing the subject. "Shit happens for a reason."

"Sorry?" Rocky asked.

"Well, you and Dad had a thing and he, like, has photos of you. He showed us one. And, you know, it was kind of meant to be, you know?" Tripp said.

"I think so," Rocky responded hesitantly.

"What I'm sayin' is, like, see, Dad got shot which tweaked you, so that happened for a reason. I mean, it isn't good, you know, Dad having to get shot and you gettin' tweaked and all, but since you guys were meant to be, *something* had to happen for you guys to get back together and I reckon it had to be big," Tripp explained.

Layne felt his chest start burning and he noted his mother's head had fallen to Devin's shoulder, but this didn't penetrate as he listened to his son and his woman.

"Yes, honey, now I understand, so I guess you're right," Rocky replied.

"So, what I don't get…and, what really sucks…is your mom died for no reason," Tripp went on, Vera's head shot up, Layne's body shot up and so did Devin's.

Devin turned and shook his head at Layne and Layne scowled at him but held himself in check.

"Sometimes," Rocky said softly. "Sometimes, I guess, stuff happens for no reason."

"Our mom can be harsh," Tripp declared.

"Uh…okay," Rocky replied.

"But, it'd suck, losin' her," Tripp finished.

"She's a good mom and she loves you like crazy," Rocky told him.

"Yeah, that's why it'd suck," Tripp stated.

"You won't lose her," Rocky assured him. "So, you shouldn't think about that."

"I'm not thinkin' about that. I'm just thinkin', I'm sorry you lost yours," Tripp returned.

Layne closed his eyes again.

"I'm sorry too, Tripp," Rocky said.

"I am too, Roc," Jas put in. "You're the shit so I reckon your mom taught you to be the shit, so I bet she was cool."

Layne opened his eyes.

"Yep, Jas, she was super-cool," Rocky replied.

"Will you show us pictures of her?" Tripp asked.

"Sure, honey," Rocky answered.

"Cool," Tripp muttered.

There was silence and Layne started to move but something happened, something he couldn't see but it was something big and Layne stopped when Tripp spoke again.

"I gotta say somethin'," he announced.

"What, honey?" Rocky asked.

"You're gonna think I'm a dork," Tripp told her.

"It's impossible for you to be a dork. You're Tanner Layne's son and just like him, so there is no way you could be a dork," Rocky assured him.

"You think I'm just like Dad?" Tripp asked, his voice intense.

"Sure, a younger version of him, maybe, but yes."

"I don't look like him," Tripp noted.

"So?" Rocky prompted.

"Jas does," Tripp remarked.

"Yes, he does, but that doesn't mean Layne didn't give you both the best parts of him, and those have nothing to do with how hot he is," Rocky stated.

There was silence and then Tripp said quietly, "That right there is why I gotta say somethin' dorky."

"So say it, Tripp, jeez," Jasper prompted.

"Okay, Jas, but it's gonna sound stupid." Tripp was hesitant.

"Just say it, dude," Jasper pushed.

"Okay, well…yesterday sucked and I didn't like watchin' you go through that, Rocky, and I was thinkin' last night about it and thinkin' I didn't like watchin' that. But why wasn't because it sucked, you havin' to go through that, but because you were hurting and I didn't like watchin' you hurt so I reckon that means I love you," Tripp announced. That burn in Layne's chest deepened significantly and Tripp went on, "So, I know that's dorky, but your mom died and my dad got shot so I guess you should tell people how you feel so they know." He paused. "So see, stupid."

There was again silence before Layne heard Rocky reply. "Not stupid, baby, and thank you. That feeling is mutual…for both you guys."

"Cool," Tripp whispered.

"Yeah, cool," Jasper repeated, also on a whisper.

Layne was done, so he moved down the stairs, his head turned to the right and he caught sight of them the minute the stairwell opened up.

He was right. They were all on the big sectional. Rocky against the back, near the corner, legs curled up, facing Tripp who was sitting with his back to a cushion, his legs stretched out in front of him, feet crossed at the ankles. Jasper was lying full out on his back close to the foot of the couch with Blondie stretched out beside him, on her back, with all four of her legs hanging in the air.

Eyes came to him, including Blondie's, excluding Jasper's.

"Hey, Dad," Tripp called.

"Pal," Layne replied.

"Yo, Dad," Jasper said. He had a video game in his hands over his face and he didn't even look at his old man.

"Yo," Layne repeated, his eyes moving to Rocky who was watching him move, her lips smiling, giving him the dimple.

Layne stopped at the side of the sectional, put his hands on his hips and Blondie jerked, rolled to her belly and her neck twisted so she could stare at Layne, her dog eyes showing she was trying to understand his intent. Did his presence mean he was going to pet her, let her outside and go with her to throw her ball or was he there to give her dog treats?

"Good call, sweetcheeks, this couch." He tipped his head to the couch.

"It's comfy," Rocky replied.

"It is, Dad, totally comfy," Tripp agreed. "It's the shit. Giselle and I are gonna study here."

"No you're not, me and Keirry are," Jasper returned and Layne knew he was serious about staking this claim because he moved the video game from his face to pierce his brother with a stare.

"I called it!" Tripp shouted.

"So? I'm older than you," Jasper shot back.

"So?" Tripp returned, "That doesn't mean anything."

Layne moved to the other end, over Jasper's head, and he shifted his body into the couch. Claiming Rocky, he settled into the corner and she curled into his body and his arms as Blondie got up, walked over Jasper, got close and snuffled Layne's hand. The minute he started scratching her head, she dropped to her belly and rested her jaws on his abs just over Rocky's forearm.

Yeah, the couch was comfortable all right. Heaven on earth.

"It means everything," Jasper retorted to Tripp.

"Guys," Rocky put in, "I don't know if you noticed this but there are four people and a dog on this couch and none of us are touching, except, of course, me, your dad and the dog. I think you and your babes can share."

"Right," Tripp grinned at her, seeing Roc curled into his old man and visualizing something else entirely.

Fucking hell.

"I want privacy with my babe, Tripp-o-matic," Jasper started. "You and your babe take off."

Shit.

"Same here," Tripp shot back.

"Jesus," Layne muttered. Thinking of his two hormonal, teenage boys, he looked down at Roc. "Maybe this couch wasn't a good idea."

"They'll get used to it," Rocky muttered.

That was what he was afraid of.

"All right!" Vera shouted, pretending to walk down the stairs casually. "The Colts game starts at one and I'm making my Mexican layer dip. I need to go to the store. Does anyone want anything?"

"Mexican dip sounds *awesome*!" Tripp cried even though he'd downed five pancakes a half an hour earlier.

"I'm good, Gram," Jasper replied.

Vera disappeared into the kitchen, calling, "Rocky, honey?"

"I don't need anything, thanks, Vera," Rocky answered.

"Tanner?" his mother shouted.

"Nothin', Ma," Layne returned and Devin came down the stairs.

When he did, both Jas and Tripp went still and their eyes were riveted on Devin. Obviously having missed their ascent, they nevertheless cottoned on immediately to the fact that both Vera and Devin were upstairs, this was unusual, and they were up there together for reasons unknown and therefore suspect.

Devin made matters worse when he turned to the crew on the sectional and announced, "I'm goin' with Vera."

Vera rounded the corner hitching her purse on her shoulder and her eyes came to the couch. "Be back soon," she declared on a huge smile, and after securing her purse strap, she gave them a finger wave.

All the eyes on the couch, except Blondie's, watched Vera and Dev walk to the door, out of it and then they all looked through the window, Jasper even curling up and shifting to get a view, as Devin helped Vera into the Calais, Dev rounded it, got in and they drove off.

Rocky and Layne settled back in but Jasper and Tripp kept their eyes on the window even when Vera and Dev were out of view.

Then his boys' eyes came to him.

"What was *that*?" Tripp breathed and Rocky giggled.

"Yeah, I didn't think Dev even liked Gram and he, like, held her door for her," Jasper whispered.

"That's the gentlemanly thing to do, Jasper," Rocky advised him and Jasper's eyes cut to her.

"Dev's not gentlemanly."

Rocky giggled again.

"How about we let that play out how it plays out," Layne ordered through suggestion.

"Let *what* play out?" Tripp was still talking on a breath.

Rocky giggled again.

"Whatever," Layne muttered, confronted with the possibility of a Devin and Vera couple, live and in person, not knowing how he felt about it and deciding he was just not going to think about it at all.

However, Layne was not going to get this because Roc decided to educate the Layne men.

"A woman doesn't stop being a woman just because she becomes a grandmother."

"Roc," Layne said low as three sets of male eyes focused on her.

"It's true," Rocky returned and added, "I think they're cute."

"Euw," Tripp mumbled then Jasper and Tripp stared at her with identical expressions on their face that clearly stated, *gross*.

"Let's stop talking about this," Layne ordered.

"Why?" Roc asked with sham innocence.

"Because she's my mother, he's the finest man I know and I want them both to be happy. But I *still* don't know whether to slap him on the back, threaten him, punch him or vomit on his shoes," Layne answered.

Rocky's body started shaking but she managed to get out a strangled, "Okay, sweetheart, we'll quit talking about it."

"Obliged," Layne muttered.

"Dad," Jasper said in a quiet, guarded voice.

Layne's eyes went to his boy to see Jasper's were pointed to the window. Layne looked over Rocky's shoulder and both Dave and Merry's cars were pulling to a stop at the curb.

Shit.

"Cool, Dad and Merry are here," Rocky observed and Layne turned her to face him.

"Roc, I've got two seconds but I'm goin' out there, havin' a word with your dad and brother and no matter what you see, I want you to promise to stay here with my boys. Yeah?"

Her eyes widened and she stared at him as she asked, "Why?"

"Just promise and trust me, yeah?"

"Layne," she whispered.

"Two seconds are up, sweetcheeks. Do I have your promise?" She hesitated so he prompted, "Baby?"

"I promise," she whispered.

He touched his mouth to hers and moved swiftly off the sectional and to the door, giving both his boys a look full of meaning before he stepped out the door.

He met them both in the yard and Dave spoke instantly. "You aren't keepin' me from my girl."

"No, I'm not," Layne returned and Dave's body rocked back.

"You aren't?" Merry asked.

"I'm not," Layne answered. "That doesn't mean we aren't going to get a few things straight."

Both men tensed.

Layne spoke. "I was hard on you both last night. I had reason, I think you get that."

"We get that," Merry said quietly.

"You stepped over the line," Dave said antagonistically.

Layne's eyes cut to Dave. "No, Dave, I didn't and you know it."

"You threw a lot of shit in my face, Tanner, and kicked me out of your house without letting me see my daughter," Dave reminded him.

"Yeah, Dave, it was last night, I remember. I also remember watchin' Rocky have her episode and I remember it in a way I know I'll never forget so my guess is, even though it was eighteen years ago, your episode with Rocky lasted two days and it freaked you so you know exactly how I felt yesterday."

Dave pressed his lips together.

Layne's voice lost its animosity and he said softly, "You didn't do right by Rocky and you didn't do right by me, then and now."

"Are we gonna stand in your yard in the cold and go over last night's territory, Tanner, or are you gonna let me see my girl?" Dave asked tersely.

"I wasn't done," Layne replied.

"Then get to it," Dave ordered.

Layne sucked breath into his nose and then let it out.

"Okay Dave, I'll get to it. That said, that's done. This is now. We're movin' forward. Roc and me. Roc, Jasper, Tripp and me. And you're family so you're movin' forward with us."

"Sounds good," Merry stated cautiously.

"With conditions," Layne continued.

"Shit," Dave muttered.

"Cecilia existed," Layne told the old man and Dave winced then he cleared it and glared at Layne. "And she died a terrible death. That shit isn't under the carpet anymore. Rocky needs her mother and the only thing she has left is memories so she's going to be allowed to have them."

"I—" Dave started.

"She visits her grave," Layne cut him off and Dave's lips parted as Merry's body visibly went still. "When she needs her, she goes to her. I'm guessin' from your reaction you didn't know that."

"No," Merry whispered.

"Well she does," Layne returned, his eyes locked on Dave's and his voice got quiet. "I remember her, Dave. I remember that she was always smiling."

Dave closed his eyes. Layne ignored it and kept talking.

"She died and that was tragic, her missin' out on life, you losin' her, her kids losin' their mom. But Carson Fisher killed her, Dave." Dave's eyes shot open and he stared at Layne. "You didn't do it, you just were doin' your job. Rocky didn't do it by not putting herself in danger to help her mom. She did what her mother needed her to do and stayed safe and alive. Carson Fisher is solely responsible for what happened to your family. You have all got to learn to quit blamin' yourselves, feelin' guilt which means you cut out memories of Cecilia and connections with people you care about." His eyes shifted to Merry. "Start living again and bring Cecilia back where she fuckin' well should be."

"Why don't we focus on the matter at hand and you leave Mia out of this?" Merry suggested, his voice edging toward hostile.

"What makes you jump to the conclusion I'm talkin' about Mia, Merry?" Layne asked, and Merry's jaw got tight. "Okay then, just to confirm, that reaction right there means I'm talkin' about Mia, brother."

"Jesus," Merry clipped.

"You gonna heal all my family's wounds on your front lawn, boy?" Dave asked.

Layne's eyes sliced to him. "No, but I'm going to tell you when Merry told me Rocky was intending to put herself out there to out Harry Rutledge and I went to talk to her, she spoke about you and her mom. She did it with fierce pride, Dave, and that was pride instilled in her by her mother. Cecilia was proud of who you were, what you did and what you stood for, and she taught her daughter to feel the same way. You wore the white hat, Dave. Your son does it now. Your daughter is proud as hell of that. Now, I don't know, I'm not you, but I know my boys are proud of me and I know how it felt when Jasper told me that, straight out. So I get it, that wound runs deep, it'll never heal, but I can't imagine knowin' your wife felt that way and your daughter still feels it, that doesn't help, even a little bit."

Neither Merry nor Dave spoke, and Layne waited but they still didn't speak.

So he did. "Vera's out with Dev gettin' stuff for Mexican layer dip, we're gearin' up for the Colts so it's not noon but I'm havin' a fuckin' beer. You can come in if you want and you can stay as long as you like. Just understand, when Vera and Devin get back, I'm not discussin' the possibility that they're becomin' an item because it freaks me way the fuck out."

Both Merry and Dave's mouths dropped open.

Layne finished, "You can follow me and hang. You can come in and see Roc's all right, go away and plan my death. You can do what you want. But I'm havin' a beer."

With that, Layne turned and walked into the house.

The door didn't even begin to close on his back because Merry had his hand on it and he and his father were moving in right after Layne.

"Hey, Uncle Dave!" Tripp shouted. "Merry!"

Merry and Dave went to the sectional.

Layne went to the fridge.

It was halftime of the Colt's game, the Mexican layer dip was decimated so they'd moved on to crackers and cheese squirted from a can and Vera had whipped up an emergency batch of sour cream onion dip for chips. She'd put out some carrot sticks with the chips with more hope than realism. Blondie had stolen a carrot stick and then spat it out on the floor by the couch. No one else had touched them.

Merry, Devin, Dave, Blondie and Layne were outside.

Merry was sitting and smoking.

Dave was standing and tossing a ball for Blondie.

Devin was sitting and scowling at Dave and the dog.

Layne was sitting, drinking beer and looking over his shoulder into the living room.

He'd left the couch where Rocky was lying with her head on his thigh, her feet in her father's lap. Now, she was sitting between Tripp, who was turned toward her, his mouth moving, and Jasper, whose head was bent and his cell was in his hands. His boys had both moved from the floor to her before his and Dave's asses were out of the couch.

Vera was in the kitchen, likely assessing ingredients to concoct a dinner later, which would sit like a lead weight in his gut after all that junk food, but which his sons would burn off in approximately twelve minutes.

"Jig is up, brother," Merry muttered and Layne's eyes turned to Merry.

"We lost Towers," he surmised and felt Devin and Dave's attention shift to them.

"Yep, she's gone. Lost her tail and vanished. Even her army is laying low. The word is out they've been made and they're off the grid," Merry confirmed.

"Fuck," Layne whispered.

"Goulding?" Devin asked.

"Picked him up. Charged him with identity theft times two, Gaines and Aubry. Informed the authorities in Tennessee we've got him. We'll process him but he'll go down there first to answer to those charges. Don't expect we'll see him back in Indiana for a while," Merry answered.

It wasn't much but it was something.

Layne's eyes went to Devin and Devin nodded. Layne needed to tell his man in LA. Marissa didn't need to know, it was unlikely any of this shit would blow west, but his man needed a heads up, just in case.

"Colt, Sully and me went to the captain yesterday with what we have on Rutledge. He's called an investigation," Merry went on.

"Just like that?" Layne asked.

"Not exactly. Cap wasn't big on us keepin' this under our hats but he had his own suspicions. He said he didn't want to think that of a cop in his department which was why he didn't move on it himself. What he means was, he's too fuckin' lazy, not to mention worried what it'd say about him that a cop turned under his watch," Merry replied.

"Rutledge been picked up?" Layne asked.

"Yep, late afternoon yesterday. They were still talkin' to him after I got home from here last night," Merry answered.

"Did he roll over?" Layne asked.

"Investigation is off-limits to those officers not assigned to it, but since he went home last night, my guess is no," Merry answered.

"He bolted?" Layne asked.

"Not yet, got a man sittin' on The Brendel," Merry replied.

"He'll bolt," Layne stated.

"I know, the interesting thing will be, where will he bolt?" Merry returned and Layne's eyes went to his. "Goulding is stupid but Rutledge is a piss-ant. He's not gonna wanna go down for other people's shit."

"You think they can get him to inform?" Layne asked.

"No, I think he's gonna go lookin' for help outta this tough spot," Merry answered.

"Wanting to keep his job?"

"No way, wanting a lifetime guaranteed lounge chair in Brazil or wherever the fuck he intends to go."

"Shakedown," Layne muttered.

"Be my guess," Merry replied. "He's not keepin' whatever money he got from her in his accounts, we know that. It's probably in his mattress. But he lives at The Brendel. Roc tells me his clothes are nice. He drives a top of the line, Hyundai Genesis Coupe. He has a standard of living. He's the type of man who's gonna wanna keep it. He's not dumb, but he's just stupid enough to make that play."

"So we're not done yet, you reckon?" Layne asked.

"Nope," Merry answered.

Layne's eyes went to Devin. "Bugs."

"Can I finish the Colts game?" Devin asked.

Merry pulled out his phone. "Let me see where Rutledge is. He may be watchin' the Colts too. Obviously, I know nothing about illegal listening devices being planted in the home of an officer of the law. But I might be able to arrange to know when Rutledge leaves his apartment, where he's going, if it's safe for someone, say, theoretically, to plant illegal listening devices, and I might be able to arrange for that someone to know when Rutledge is on his way back."

Layne turned away from Merry and grinned at the mouth of his beer. Then he took a slug.

Merry ascertained that Rutledge was home and asked for updates on his activity. Devin and Dave wandered inside, taking Blondie with them. Merry shook another cigarette out of his pack.

"You might not wanna light that, brother, since I intend to talk to you about Mia," Layne told him and Merry's eyes cut to Layne.

"Don't go there," he warned.

"Sorry, I'm gonna," Layne returned.

"None of your business, Tanner."

"She cheat on you?" Layne asked.

"Tanner—"

That meant no.

"Bust your balls?" Layne cut him off.

Merry looked away and lit his cigarette.

"Was she shit in bed?"

Merry exhaled and then his jaw got tight.

That meant no too. A big no.

"You think about her when you fuck your other women?" Layne pushed and Merry's eyes sliced to him.

"Shut it, Tanner."

"You do," Layne murmured.

"Fuck off," Merry clipped.

"Not doin' any of those other women a favor, closin' your eyes and thinkin' of Mia," Layne remarked.

Merry was silent.

"You can fuck your way through the 'burg, you care about her and can't get her outta your head, you're never gonna find that again," Layne told him.

"Roc's had a tough weekend, brother, don't think she'll wanna rush out to your backyard and wade into a fistfight between her brother and her man," Merry threatened.

Layne ignored him and advised, "Get back in there."

Merry didn't respond.

"Look around and learn, Garrett, don't waste time."

Merry took a drag from his cigarette. "You did me a favor, brother. You took a chance and pushed me into makin' the right decision. Now, I'm returnin' that favor," Layne stated.

Merry wrapped three fingers around his bottle of beer, lifted it and took a pull.

"It's all around you, Garrett, wake the fuck up," Layne whispered and Merry didn't turn his head but his eyes slid to Layne.

"What?" he asked curtly.

"Colt and Feb, Cal and Vi, Roc and me. Jesus, just look at Cal. Fuck, what happened to him? Now I see him laughin'." When Merry made no comment, Layne went on, "I remember Mia had a wicked funny sense of humor."

Merry looked away.

"This is what I know," Layne started. "Life was what life was for me and after Rocky, it was never great. What sucks more is knowin' that Rocky led a life that also wasn't great. That sucks more, Merry." Layne stood and looked down at Merry who kept his eyes to Layne's yard and he fired his parting shot. "If Mia feels the way you feel, don't you wanna stop that?"

Merry closed his eyes and swallowed.

Layne turned and walked into the house.

〜

Layne's eyes shifted to Devin, who was sitting in an armchair, his head nodding. He needed the couch.

"Dev," he called and Devin's heard turned to him. "Try the sectional," Layne advised.

"Will do, you get your woman upstairs," Dev returned.

Layne looked down at Rocky who was stretched out with him on the couch, half on him, half off.

He curled up, taking her with him. Her head came up, she looked around, pulling her hair out of her face.

Her eyes semi-focused on Devin.

"Sorry," she whispered. "I fell asleep."

"No problem, girlie," Devin whispered back.

She looked at Layne then climbed over him, got to her feet and Layne rolled off the couch right behind her. She lurched toward the stairs. Layne got close and put his hands to her hips, guiding her while calling behind him, "'Night, Dev."

"'Night, boy."

They got to the stairs, Rocky bent double, mostly crawling on hands and feet up them while Layne tried not to laugh. She lifted up at the top and staggered into the bedroom. He let her go, closed the door and turned to see she was at her side, reaching under her pillowcase. He watched as she tugged her clothes off, put on his tee, threw back the covers and did a face plant in the bed.

Layne changed, joined her there and turned out the light.

Rocky shifted into him.

"Night, baby," she mumbled into his chest.

"Night, sweetcheeks."

Her arm tightened for half a second around his stomach and then she was out.

Layne stared at the dark ceiling while his hand moved, sifting into her hair. He pulled it out of her face, off her shoulder and neck, so it all fell down to the bed and on his arm.

Lying there, it occurred to him that life was now just life.

Therefore Tanner Layne smiled before he closed his eyes and fell asleep with his lips tipped up.

Twenty-Seven

SHEER EVIL

Saturday, 1:37 p.m., two weeks later
"I can't believe Gram's movin' back here, that is so cool," Tripp remarked from the back of the Suburban. He was sitting behind Layne, Keira was in the middle, Jasper behind Rocky.

They'd just seen Vera off at the airport. She was going home to put her condo on the market and sort her shit out. When she came back, she was taking over Rocky's rental because, even though The Brendel had a waiting list, they were not fond of letting people out of their rental agreements. To get out, Rocky would have to pay through the nose. The market was good in Vera's area but she wasn't going to wait it out. Just sort her shit, put the stuff she couldn't pack in at Rocky's in storage and she was going to take her time finding a place to settle in the 'burg. The Brendel's rent was a little steep, but Layne was going to help until the agreement ran its course and Vera was in her own space.

Rocky was moving in the minute Vera returned, sooner, if Layne could talk her into it. She, however, didn't want to move in until she'd signed the divorce papers, an event that was scheduled to happen late next week. He could see why she wanted that, which was why he was letting her make that play.

Layne's eyes went to the rearview mirror to look at Tripp then they looked out the back window to see the Calais peel off. Devin had followed

Kristen Ashley

Vera to return her rental car and driven her to the airport where Layne and his family met them, Vera checked in, they had a drink and they all waved her off as she headed through security. Now, they were still on I-465.

Layne had no idea where Devin was headed and he'd probably never know. Though it wasn't home to Ohio. Devin had stayed put on Layne's couch for the last two weeks and helped Layne with some of his cases. He seemed in no hurry to head back to Cleveland. Layne expected there would be a conversation later on down the line considering Vera and Devin had grown tight but he was glad that conversation had not yet happened. Things were settling. Roc was seeing a therapist twice a week. She liked her. The good life was shifting to beautiful and Layne didn't want anything to rock that boat, such as having his best friend and mother officially hooking up.

"Your Gram is cool," Keira noted. "One of my Grams is really shy. The other one is not very nice. But Joe's Aunt Theresa is totally awesome, a complete blast. When your Gram gets home, I should call Aunt Theresa and ask her to come down. They could have, like, a bake off or something."

Layne's eyes slid to Rocky to see she was smiling at the windshield.

"I thought girls weren't supposed to like to eat because they didn't want to get fat," Tripp stated, Layne rolled his eyes and Jasper exploded.

"Tripp, don't be a dick!"

"What?" Tripp asked.

"Joe says skinny girls don't do anything for him," Keira put in, obviously not offended in the slightest. "He says for a woman to be a woman, she's gotta have curves."

"Joe's right," Layne muttered and Rocky's hand shot out and she flicked his bicep with the backs of her knuckles.

"What'd you say, Dad?" Tripp asked.

"I said," Layne said louder. "Joe is right."

"Layne!" Rocky hissed.

"Baby, a woman without a great ass?" He shook his head.

The trio in the back laughed but he felt Rocky's glare.

"Don't know why you're pissed, sweetcheeks," Layne told her over their laughter. "That's precisely how you got your nickname."

"Layne!" Rocky repeated on a hiss.

"What was that, Dad?" Tripp asked.

Rocky's head whipped around to look in the backseat. "Nothing, Tripp. Your father is being tactless."

"What's tactless?" Tripp asked.

"Indiscreet," Rocky answered.

"Indiscreet?" Tripp sounded confused.

"*Rude*," Rocky said, putting great stress on that one word and Layne chuckled.

"Dad's never rude," Jasper put in. "He's just honest."

"I think boys think rude is honest and girls think rude is rude," Keira proposed.

"Exactly," Rocky muttered, turning to face forward again.

Layne found himself rethinking his desire to give Rocky a daughter because, by the time she reached Keira's age, his boys would be gone and he'd be outnumbered. He was still rethinking this when his cell phone rang.

He pulled it out of his inside jacket pocket, looked at the display and saw it said, "Ryker Calling." He took the call and put the phone to his ear.

"Yo," he answered.

"Alexis is gone," Ryker growled in his ear and Layne's neck muscles contracted.

"Come again?"

"Alexis. She's gone. Lissa had a half day shift at the restaurant, got home at one and Alexis was gone. No note, no nothin'. She's just gone."

"I take it she didn't have plans?" Layne asked.

"Yeah, her plans were to get her chores done, which means stayin' at home, cleanin' the house and then when her mom got home, they were goin' shoppin' and to a movie."

"She with a friend?"

"Negative. Lissa has called all her friends. No one has seen or heard from her."

"Her chores done?" Layne asked.

"Who cares?" Ryker answered.

"We care, brother," Layne said quietly. "We need to understand how long she's been gone. Now, are her chores done, and if they are, what time does she normally get up and how long does it take her to clean the house?"

"Don't know," Ryker answered. "But the house is cleaned."

"All right, talk to Lissa, let's get a time line here," Layne advised. "Once you talk to Lissa, you call Colt, I'll call Devin, but after you call Colt, you start knocking on doors. Did anyone see her leave? If they did, what time? Did she walk? Which direction? Was she with someone? Did she get in a car? If she got in a car, what kind of car was it? Did they see who was driving? Was anyone else in the car? Get a description. They probably didn't get a plate but they might have seen if it was Indiana plates or something else. Did you get that?"

"Got it," Ryker growled.

"You hear anything before I get there, report back," Layne ordered, disconnected and scrolled down to Devin.

"Layne," Rocky whispered and Layne felt the air in the car had changed from cheerful to tense.

"Tripp, on your phone, call Giselle. Yeah?" Layne ordered, ignoring Rocky.

"Right, Dad," Tripp replied.

He put his phone to his ear and heard Devin answer, "Miss me already?"

"Alexis McGraw is gone," Layne told Devin and heard the hiss of Rocky taking in a breath. "She's supposed to be shoppin' with her mother but Lissa came home and she's gone. No note. I've got Ryker started. I need to drop off Keira so I need you to get to him."

"Copy that, out," Devin said and disconnected.

"You can take me wherever you need to go, Mr. Layne. I can get Mom or Joe to come pick me up," Keira offered quietly from the back. "I'll call them now and they can meet me there."

"That'd be good, honey," Layne replied. "It's thirty-four Easton Street."

"Okay," she whispered and he heard her digging through her purse.

"Hey, Giselle, what's up?" Tripp said into his phone and Layne held his breath. "Oh, cool. Yeah, we got Gram off okay…" he went on and Layne let his breath go.

Rocky's hand came to his knee and squeezed. He covered hers with his and squeezed back. Then he drove carefully with precious cargo, the whole time his foot itching to press down the accelerator.

The minute they got to Lissa's house, doors opened, all of them on his truck and the front door of the house. Ryker prowled out first, followed by Devin, Colt, Sully and Merry, Lissa coming out last to stand on the little stoop. She didn't look good. She looked terrified out of her mind.

Rocky hustled Keira to Lissa. Layne, Jasper and Tripp went to the men, Jasper stopping a few feet away. He was on his phone, Layne didn't know why and he was focused on the matter at hand so he didn't pay attention.

"Around noon," Ryker stated before Layne even stopped. "A silver BMW. That bitch was behind the wheel."

Towers.

Fuck.

"Who saw?" Layne asked.

"Neighbor across the street. Bitch is nosy as hell, ugly too, but, swear, bro, her info helps, I'll fuckin' kiss her," Ryker answered. "Said she didn't think anything of it because Lexie walked right up to the car, seemed excited to see her, got in and they went."

"No one else in the car?" Layne asked.

"Nope," Ryker answered.

Layne's eyes slid through the group. "What else we got?"

"Not much, man," Colt muttered, his eyes on Ryker, his body alert for Ryker to blow. "Lissa's been calling Alexis's friends. No one knows about any plans. This is a sneak attack."

Layne's phone rang. He pulled it out and saw the display said, "Dave Calling." He took the call.

"Dave, I'm in the middle of—"

"Somethin's goin' down," Dave cut him off. "I'm on duty at your office, listenin' to Rutledge. He just had a conversation with someone, tellin' them it's too hot. He was freaked, though he didn't provide details. Whoever it was, they didn't listen. Now I got silence and I'm watchin' his car move. Looks like he may be headin' out of the 'burg."

Devin had planted the bugs and then Layne had planted a tracking device on Rutledge's car. Even though things had cooled down to the point they were ice cold, both were still monitored in the office 24/7.

"Where?" Layne asked.

"He's on Green and looks to me he's on his way to 74," Dave answered.

"Right, two hours ago, Alexis McGraw got in a car with Nicolette Towers," Layne told him.

"Shit!" Dave hissed.

"Keep an eye on him," Layne ordered. "Got some of the boys here, we'll get someone on his ass."

"Right, out," Dave said and disconnected.

Layne looked at Merry. "Was anyone sitting on Rutledge?"

"The investigation is ongoing but wrapping up since we don't have enough. Just shitty police work, so he's not gonna get a good performance evaluation, but it looks like he's gonna be cleared. He didn't bolt which looked good for him. Cap rescinded the unit on his tail," Merry explained.

"You need to call it in. He's headed to Indy, looks to hit 74. He needs to pick up a tail on his way. He just had a conversation with someone, tryin' to convince them it's too hot then he took off," Layne told them and Sully had his phone out before Layne was done speaking.

Sully stepped away and Layne heard Jasper's phone ringing behind him. He turned and swept his son with a glance to see Jasper was still hanging back, body partially turned away, eyes to the ground, focus intense.

Before he could ascertain what Jasper was doing, he sensed Ryker was on the move and he turned to see Ryker heading toward his bike.

"Ryker," Layne called, moving behind him.

"I'm headed to I-74," Ryker grunted.

"Ryker," Layne put a hand on his big arm, but Ryker shook it off and kept moving.

"Call me, you got info on where he's goin'," Ryker swung a leg over his bike, settling as he put his key to the ignition.

Layne's hand shot out and he yanked the keys from his friend.

Ryker's head turned to Layne and he had that scary look on his face.

"Not a bright idea, bro," he growled.

"Not a bright idea to get on your bike, pissed and lookin' to do damage. We can hope nothin's happened yet. It does, it doesn't, Alexis and Lissa are gonna need you right here, not have to find their time to visit you and talk to you through glass," Layne returned.

"She has my girl," Ryker growled.

"I know and it isn't helpin' matters, us spendin' time havin' this conversation. Get off your bike," Layne ordered.

Ryker glared at him.

"Dad," Jasper called.

Layne took a chance and turned his back on scary, pissed-off Ryker to see Jasper was jogging up to him.

"Tiffany's not answering her phone," Jasper told him when he got close.

Fuck!

"I got her number after the last thing and I've been callin' her. Know someone who's got some of her friends' numbers and her home number and they called. She's not at home. Parents said she was goin' to hang with some of her girls. None of her friends have heard from her and they didn't have plans."

"I'm on that," Colt muttered, pulling out his phone.

"Dad," Jasper called his attention.

"What, bud?"

Jasper looked funny and Layne knew that look. He hadn't seen it from Jas in years. It was hesitant, unsure, like Tripp looked when he had to say something he thought might sound stupid.

Jasper sucked it up and said softly, "Okay, Dad, stick with me, yeah?"

"I'm with you," Layne spoke softly back as he felt Ryker getting off his bike and Tripp, Devin and Merry got close.

"I know we don't have a lotta time, but will you let me talk this out?" Jasper asked and Layne nodded.

"Okay," Jasper whispered then took a big breath. "I've been thinkin' about all this stuff and somethin' never sat right with me 'cause that Youth Group guy has been around for ages, like, *months*, right?"

"Right," Layne agreed.

"So, I don't know how they think or how they work, but to work three girls, it doesn't seem like it would be worth that investment, takin' that long to do it," Jasper went on and Layne's eyes moved to Devin whose jaw was tight.

His eyes went back to his son. "Go on," Layne prompted.

"So, it just seemed funny to me but I don't know how they work so I didn't think about it much until you told us to go to Giselle's folks' house and get the list of her friends. We worked our way through that and none of her friends had much, but one of the names on it was Tara Murdoch. I thought that was weird 'cause Giselle doesn't hang with Tara, *no one* hangs with Tara. She's weird, a Goth, loads of piercings, black lipstick, total attitude and not the good kind. She's fourteen, Dad, and she's got tattoos."

Fuck.

Layne looked at Tripp. "Tara Murdoch a Goth last year?"

Tripp shook his head.

"She tight with Giselle last year?" Layne continued.

"Yeah, Dad," Tripp whispered. "They were best friends."

Fuck!

"Giselle tell you why she's not Tara's friend anymore?" Layne went on.

"We never talked about it but Tara went Goth. That's not Giselle's scene. That kinda thing happens with girls all the time. One day they're tight, the next day they're not," Tripp replied.

"You guys talk to her when you were doin' the rounds?" Layne asked Jasper.

"No, we went to her house and..." He shook his head. "She was there, standin' in the front window, watchin' us with this weird look on her face. Just standin' there watchin' us. We rang the bell and knocked, but she didn't move. Just stood there watchin' us. I thought it was some Goth shit and I knew she wasn't tight with Giselle so I figured she didn't have anything for us, so we walked away."

Layne nodded at Jasper. "You got anything else?"

Jasper nodded, sucked in breath and replied, "Summer Collins and Hannah Blair. Mitch had clocked both of them at a party, end of school last year. Giselle, Tara, Summer and Hannah were known to be the talent comin' up from junior high. All the guys knew about them. Giselle was shy. Tara turned Goth. Summer is more shy than Giselle, she doesn't go to games, doesn't go out for pizza, she just goes to school, doesn't have any friends that I know of, and she goes home. Sometimes she also doesn't wash her hair. Just kinda tries to fade, you know?" Jasper asked, but didn't wait for a response, he continued, "But it's Hannah. Hannah disappeared."

Layne turned to Merry. "You get a report on Hannah Blair goin' missin'?"

Merry shook his head but Tripp spoke. "She's in the hospital, Dad. Everyone knows about it. She wigged out this summer. Word is, she's, like, catatonic. Doesn't talk to anyone. Not her parents, her friends quit visiting her. She's just like…*gone.*"

Fuck, fuck, *fucking hell.* Devin was right. They'd missed something. Nicolette Towers had already thrown a party.

"They all go to Youth Group?" Layne asked Tripp.

"Don't know for sure but I think so. I know Tara did," Tripp answered.

"Brunette, blonde, redhead?" Layne asked.

"Tara was blonde, but now her hair's black," Tripp answered. "But yeah, Summer's got red hair and Hannah was dark."

Layne looked at Merry but he was already pulling out his phone, muttering, "Got it."

"I take it, it wasn't stupid," Jasper mumbled and Layne's eyes went to his boy to see he was not looking good. He was looking sick. He thought he fucked up.

"Jasper, shake that off. You couldn't save them but now they may be able to save Alexis and Tiffany. Focus on that. Yeah?"

"I should have said something." He was still mumbling but he was doing it looking sicker.

"Shake that off Jasper, I need you to think." His eyes cut to Tripp. "I need you both to think. Any other girls? A trio. Blonde, brunette, redhead. They were normal girls last year, attractive girls, and did an about-face over the summer. They could be freshman or sophomores. They went to Youth Group but they don't go now."

Tripp shook his head. Jasper was thinking.

"Jas," Layne prompted.

"No," he replied. "But to be sure, I'd need my yearbooks."

"Where are they, our place or your mom's?"

"Mom's," Jasper answered.

"You think of someone, you call Merry right away, not me, Merry. Yeah?" Jasper nodded and Layne looked at Devin. "Take the boys to their mom's." Devin nodded, moving to the Calais and Layne looked at Tripp. "You too, pal. Seventh and eighth grade last year, yeah?"

"Yeah," Tripp muttered and jogged after Jasper and Devin.

Merry and Sully came up to Ryker and Layne.

"Tennessee needs a call, Sul, they need to yank Goulding," Layne told him. "He held out on us. He delivered at least three girls to a party, maybe more. If he didn't deliver them, he primed them. We need to find out everything he knows. We need to know if there are more girls. We need him broken."

Sully nodded and again stepped away, looking down to his phone.

Merry said, "I gotta get to the station."

"Right," Layne replied, but Merry was already on the move.

"What're you thinkin' you can get from these girls?" Ryker asked low from Layne's side and Layne looked at him.

"Maybe a location, though I doubt she'll double up. Definitely cause for a warrant," Layne answered.

"Obviously none of them talked," Ryker noted.

"Probably too scared," Layne replied.

"So maybe they won't talk now," Ryker observed, his face and body tight. He was a man who liked to be on the move, in the thick of things. With Alexis on the line, this was killing him.

"Marissa Gibbons was hard as nails, Ryker, and she talked because she didn't want another girl to face what happened to her. They'll talk."

"It'll take time. They'll—" Ryker started.

"Patience, brother," Layne whispered and Ryker got scary again.

"Your girl isn't right now keepin' company with sheer evil, bro," he whispered back.

Layne held his gaze. "Stick with me, big man."

Ryker held his eyes and a muscle danced in his cheek. Then he looked to the house and muttered, "Gotta check on my babe."

Then he walked to the house.

Layne looked at his shoes, thinking, *fuck, we fucking missed something.*

He looked up when Joe Callahan slid his truck to a halt in front of the house, Vi's Mustang sliding in behind him. He watched Vi get out, she pushed back her seat to get to Angela's baby seat in the back. Cal jumped down and walked to Layne, his face intense.

He just made it to Layne when February Colton's VW Beetle slid up behind the Mustang.

That was the women of the 'burg. Trouble comes, they close ranks.

Cal stopped at him.

"Talk to me," he ordered.

Layne locked eyes with him and he talked.

Vi with Angela at her hip and Feb with her son Jack at hers rushed into the house.

When Layne could take no more, he tore his eyes from Tara Murdoch, her weeping mother, her stony-faced father, the softly-speaking Patrick Sullivan and the watchful child psychologist and he walked out of the observation room.

Cal moved with him.

Layne pulled his phone out of his jacket, scrolled down and hit go while he walked to the buzzing bullpen.

"What?" Ryker barked in his ear.

"Meet me at Towers's apartment at The Brendel," Layne ordered.

"I'll be there yesterday," Ryker replied and then dead air.

"Tanner," Cal murmured.

Layne stopped and turned to him.

"You can stay here or follow," Layne stated.

"I'm with you," Cal replied instantly.

"Tanner!" Sean O'Leary jogged up to him.

Layne checked his movement and looked to Sean.

"Yeah?"

"Bad news and kind of good news," Sean said, and when Layne did nothing but stare impatiently, Sean went on, "Rutledge didn't lead us to the location but he did lead us straight to four of her army. The cop on his tail called backup. They came in quick but cool and were there when Rutledge either pushed too hard or got impatient. Whatever reason, shots were fired, the boys moved in."

"Rutledge?" Layne asked.

"He went down. He's still alive, it's bad though, and he's on his way to hospital," Sean answered.

"Fuck, Sean, that is *not* good news," Layne clipped.

"No, the kind of good news is that Rutledge took down one of her army, the cops got the other three, they were all armed and, man, it is highly likely we'll get ballistic matches on the slugs they pulled outta you," Sean returned.

Sean was right, that was *kind of* good news.

"Any of her crew know where the party is located?" Layne asked.

"They're workin' them now," Sean answered.

Layne nodded and moved, Cal moving with him. They separated in the parking lot, both going to their trucks, Cal following close as Layne headed to The Brendel.

Ryker's bike was parked at the foot of the stairs leading up to Towers' apartment. Layne didn't bother finding a spot and neither did Cal, they parked at the curb. They both got out and started to jog up the stairs where Ryker was waiting.

"Bust it," Layne ordered, his head tipped back to look at Ryker, and Ryker didn't delay. He took a step back, lifted his big motorcycle boot and the apartment door crashed in.

The alarm immediately went off, Ryker and Layne ignored it, both of them moving into the space. Cal went to the alarm panel, ripped the face off, twisted some wires together and the alarm stopped.

"Shit, child's play," he muttered, his eyes slicing to Layne. "Rocky lives here. To do list, man."

Layne didn't have to think about Roc's security. Rocky was, that night, officially no longer living at The Fucking Brendel.

"What are we lookin' for?" Ryker asked.

"Anything," Layne answered. "Just look."

"Devin sifted through this place, bro, and I get the sense he's good at what he does," Ryker noted, pulling cushions off the couch.

Layne picked up a cushion Ryker pulled off, yanked his army knife out of his jeans and his eyes locked on Ryker.

"He had to go easy," Layne said softly. "We don't."

Then he ripped the cushion open with his knife.

Ryker smiled his ugly smile. It was without humor but filled with something else, which made it uglier and a fuckuva lot scarier.

Then he ripped a cushion clean in two with his bare hands.

⟨———⟩

Towers's apartment was clean so they moved to Rutledge's.

By the sounds of it, Cal and Ryker were tearing up the downstairs. Or, at least Ryker was.

Layne was working the bedroom when he flipped the mattress on the bed, his eyes glancing across the bottom of the mattress to go to the box springs then his eyes shot back.

Stitches.

Shit.

He walked on the mattress, crouched down to the stitches and carefully slid his knife in. Ripping the material away, he reached in and felt it. He found the edge, pulled out the manila envelope and also pulled in breath.

He knew he didn't want to see what was inside. Still, he opened the envelope carefully, shook out the eight by tens on the mattress and used his knife to move them around as his stomach churned.

Rutledge. Rutledge and Towers. Towers with girls with Rutledge in shot, watching. Rutledge with girls Layne had never seen. And Rutledge also with Tara Murdoch.

He stood, tearing his eyes away, looking at the wall, taking a moment to pull his shit together.

Then he pulled out his phone and called Merry.

"Hope this is good, big man, 'cause I'm—"

"I've just located evidence that Harrison Rutledge is a pedophile," Layne told him.

Silence then, "Where are you?"

"Rutledge's apartment."

"Man, we're still holding on the search warrant," Merry bit out.

"Good, then we've assisted the department in a time-saving measure," Layne shot back. "We'll finish up, leave visible what you need to see and move out. No one needs to know that you boys didn't make this mess."

"Fuck, Tanner," Merry hissed.

"Merry, suck it up and work with it," Layne advised.

"This is not your burden, brother, you didn't let those girls down," Merry said low.

"No, brother, we all did," Layne returned, disconnected and kept looking.

"This is bullshit!" Ryker barked. "Time is wastin'."

Cal's eyes cut to Layne. His phone to his ear, he moved out of Layne's office and into the reception area, closing the door. Cal was working through every number on Rutledge's cell phone bill. He had half the pile. Dave was sitting at the receptionist's desk with the other half. They'd taken pictures at the apartment of a number of hopefully useful documents and gone to Layne's office to print them out.

Ryker and Layne were going through credit card statements.

"Focus, Ryker," Layne advised.

"Every second we waste—" Ryker growled.

"You wanna hold hands and meditate and hope her location pops in one of our heads?" Layne growled back. "Or do you wanna investigate this fuckwad and hope he tripped up and leads us to your girl?"

Ryker glared at him. Layne held his glare then looked back to the statements.

His eyes shifted through the one in his hand, down and back up.

Then he stopped.

He had August's statement. August was the month when Tara Murdoch told Sully the party was held. It started with a photo shoot where they gave the girls champagne likely laced with Rohpynol or another fast-acting, date rape drug. She'd woken up blindfolded. A ball gag with a handkerchief stuffed in her mouth. She'd described what the gag felt like and he'd seen it. She'd been tied to the bed. She'd taken five men, none of whom she'd seen, one of whom he knew. She had no idea how much time each one had with her but she reported they took their time. However a girl enduring that, five minutes could seem like five hours.

When it was done, Towers had made her warnings and they were good ones. None of the girls talked for fear it would happen again. Each of them had a younger sister. Each of them was told, they talked, they'd come back and their sisters would be accompanying them. Alexis didn't fit this profile but Giselle and Tiffany did. The girls were told to tell their parents they were with each other. They did and held their secret until Tara spilled it in the interrogation room.

Hannah lost her mind. Summer faded into herself. And Tara built a wall.

And Harrison Rutledge had ordered himself a couple of drinks from the bar prior to his turn and the dumbfuck had paid for them on a credit card.

Layne stood, grabbing his jacket as he growled, "Let's go."

Ryker's head shot back then he was up with Layne. "What'd you get?"

Layne didn't answer. He had his cell phone out and he was out the door. Cal's eyes came to him when Layne put the cell phone to his ear. He jerked his head to the door, Cal took his cell from his ear and moved with them. Dave didn't miss a beat and kept talking into his phone.

Merry answered, "You got something, Tanner?"

"Get IMPD to get units to every exclusive hotel in Indy, starting with The Townsend. And tell them to go in soft," Layne ordered.

"On it," Merry replied and disconnected.

Layne led Ryker and Cal down the stairs.

"Stick with me," Layne murmured as he drove through the parking garage.

"We should get inside," Ryker hissed.

"Stick with me," Layne repeated.

"Shit, this is shit. This is bullshit," Ryker muttered.

"A woman like that is not gonna revisit the scene of her crime," Layne explained. "Rutledge had his sick fun at The Imperial. Second top spot in Indy is The Townsend. She's there and she's the kind of woman who can sense heat. She's gonna bolt. She's gotta go down, brother."

Then he saw it and braked.

Not the silver BMW, her sporty red Mazda.

He put the car in neutral, set the brake and turned to Ryker.

"Knife," he growled.

Ryker didn't hesitate; his hand went to his belt. He popped the button on his huge-ass knife, yanked it out and handed it over.

Layne opened his door, ordering, "Stay here."

He jogged quickly to the Mazda, motioning with flicks of his fingers, communicating to Cal. Cal nodded through his windshield and passed the Suburban.

Layne didn't watch to see where Cal went. He crouched by the back tire, thrusting Ryker's knife into the rubber. He moved forward and took out the front tire. He jogged around the car and did the same to the other side. Then he jogged back to his truck.

He swung in, handed the knife to Ryker, pulled out his cell, put the car in gear, released the brake, located the pedestrian entryway to the garage and scanned for a spot with good visibility all at the same time he scrolled on his phone.

He hit go and put it to his ear.

"Yo," Merry said quietly.

"You at The Townsend?" Layne asked. Seeing his spot, he started maneuvering the behemoth to reverse in while still talking.

"Yes, just got here. This is it, brother. Management says three weeks ago they had an unusual reservation. One day, big money, an entire floor of suites cleared. They had to juggle but they did it. I'm in the security room. They have cameras on the halls. She's got sentries. Two at the elevators. One outside each room. Three rooms. Two at the emergency exit. The hotel was told it was a VIP with stringent security and that they needed confidentiality and discretion, which the hotel assured them they could provide. So we got seven boys, from what I can see by the bulges in their jackets, heavily armed. We don't know if there are more in the rooms and the hotel didn't clock them, considering the promise of discretion and all. IMPD is pulling together a team to take the top without collateral damage."

"Three rooms?" Layne asked as he put the truck in neutral, set the brake and killed the ignition.

"Not good news, brother," Merry answered and Layne's neck got tight.

"What?"

"Wherever Tiffany went, she took her sister with her. She's thirteen, Tanner."

Jesus, Jesus, fuck.

He didn't want to ask with Ryker at his side but he had to ask.

"Have the parties started?"

"Ryker with you?" Merry asked back.

"Yeah," Layne answered.

"Then I'm not answering that question right now," Merry replied.

Layne clenched his teeth and his chest seized. Alexis McGraw had been to his house. Ryker and Lissa sat with Layne and Rocky at the dining room table drinking beer and shooting the shit while Alexis and Seth, Keira and Jasper and Tripp and Giselle all lounged on the sectional, doing kid shit. Alexis was chockfull of attitude, the good kind, though it had an edge. But underneath that, she was a sweet kid.

"You got eyes on her?" Layne asked.

Merry knew what Layne was asking. "Plainclothes everywhere, big man, but no one has seen Towers. Maybe she's in one of the rooms. They're scanning security footage now to see if she's entered the hotel."

"She's somewhere. I have eyes on her car. A red Mazda in the parking garage, not the hotel's, across the street and just south. I've disabled the car. We're on the third floor."

"I'll call that in."

"Merry, she's not getting away," Layne warned.

"You make a mess, Tanner, I'll clean it up," Merry replied.

Layne heard the disconnect and flipped his phone closed.

"Tell me," Ryker whispered and his tone was the tone of a man broken.

Layne's eyes went to him.

"Don't make me sorry you're at my side," Layne warned softly. Ryker stared at him and the air in the cab became suffocating. "I'll blow this to take you out," Layne whispered. "Do not mistake me, Ryker. I'll do what I have to do to keep you safe so you can take care of her because, brother, she needs you now. Do *not* fuck this up."

Ryker's breathing started to get visibly heavy, his huge chest moving with it.

"I can't lock this down, bro," he whispered.

"Yes you can."

"No, Tanner."

"Focus, brother."

"Lexie," he whispered.

"*Focus,*" Layne clipped.

"I can't."

"Be her hero, Ryker. Do not make her and her mother lose more than they've already lost today."

They held eyes and Ryker kept breathing heavy.

"Deep, Ryker, breathe deep, not shallow, suck in air, lock it down," Layne urged.

Ryker nodded and took in a deep breath, turned to face front, his eyes locked on the Mazda and his fists curled on his thighs.

Layne let out a breath, leaned over, pulled down the door to the glove compartment and yanked out his .38.

"She goes to the car, I go in. You call Merry. Cal provides cover. You're last resort. You got that?"

"What if she isn't alone?"

"Then you provide cover too, you got your .45?" he asked even though he knew. Ryker didn't go anywhere without his .45.

Ryker leaned forward and yanked out his .45. Then he nodded to Layne.

"This is not a shoot first and ask questions later, deal, Ryker. We are not officers of the law. We're skatin' on thin ice here, only so much Merry can cover for us. This is an incapacitate and incarcerate deal, yeah?" Layne ordered.

Ryker nodded again.

Layne called Cal.

"Yo," Cal answered. "I'm guessin' the Mazda is important."

"It's hers. You got eyes on it?"

"Yep."

"She approaches, I go in, you and Ryker are cover. Do you have a gun or do you need me to get you one?"

"My wife was kidnapped and nearly shot in the head, man. I got guns everywhere."

"I'll take that as a yes."

"Good call, since it was a yes."

"Right, we're done," Layne stated and flipped his phone closed.

Then he reached up, turned off the interior cab light, pulled the keys out of the ignition, tossed them to Ryker who caught them and his eyes went to the door to the stairs.

Layne was right, she felt the heat. They didn't wait five minutes before the door to the stairs opened and Nicolette Towers showed, wearing sick fuck, underage gang rape party hostess gear of fancy-ass dress and spike heels, her hair out to there, her face made up to perfection. She had a body-guard but, thank Christ, only one.

Ryker flipped open his phone and Layne didn't look at him. He opened his door, slid around it, didn't close it and ran quickly and silently, moving behind parked vehicles, keeping his eyes on Towers and her goon.

They were walking swiftly but engaged in intense conversation which was a mistake. At least the bodyguard should be vigilant. They must have clocked the intensity of the operation gearing up inside the hotel. She looked pissed. He looked tweaked.

Layne slid up the side of a Pathfinder, positioning at the hood. They were walking toward him. He bent with his body behind the vehicle, his gun aimed, arms resting on the hood.

"*Hands where I can see them,*" he barked when they were two cars away from the Mazda.

The goon didn't hesitate. He yanked a weapon out of his shoulder holster and started firing. Towers dashed to the Mazda.

Bullets slammed into the Pathfinder and ricocheted off. Layne returned fire almost blind then ducked. More fire coming his way but also from Cal shooting from the opposite direction.

The Pathfinder stopped taking hits and Layne bolted up, the goon was turned, returning Cal's fire. Layne aimed and fired, connected a bullet to his calf and the guy went down to his knee. Cal kept shooting and more gunfire entered play. Ryker had made his call and was in the game.

The Mazda reversed out of the spot, Towers cutting the wheel, riding the rims. She either didn't know or didn't care her man was down behind her because the Mazda slammed right into him. Layne wasn't in the position to see how she got him but he heard his howl of agony. She shifted into first and Layne moved out of cover, hunkered down and launched himself on the hood of her car.

Finding purchase on the lip of the hood by the windshield with one hand, his belly to the metal, their eyes locked.

She cut the wheel and Layne's body went sliding. She slammed into a car and skidded through it and the next, still moving.

Then she cut the wheel the other way to make the turn through the garage, the Mazda nearly uncontrollable, riding on rims, and Layne's body flew with the car. His hold slipped but held at his top knuckles.

She righted the car and he lifted his gun, taking aim at her shoulder.

He pulled the trigger just as she cut the wheel again, his shot went wide and so did his body. He was losing his grip. He wouldn't be able to hold on much longer. They skimmed down cars, metal against metal, sparks flying around his legs. Layne heaved himself back to full-on the hood, raised the gun and took aim when he heard sirens.

She cut the other way but Layne got off two shots through the windshield then let go, rolling with the movement of the car. He lucked out and rolled straight onto the hood of another vehicle rather than crashing to the ground and getting caught under her tires or smashed between the Mazda and another car.

He rolled up the windshield then down to his back. He did an ab curl just in time to see Towers drive through two empty spots, slam into the side of a car and stop.

Layne slid off the car and dropped to his feet, on the run the minute they touched the ground.

She threw open her door and fell out, crawling. He lifted his gun, took aim and shouted, "Freeze!"

She rolled to her back, lifting a .22 in his direction, blood staining the front of her dress.

Ryker came in from the right. Shoving his big body through the opening, he dropped down between floors, his tree trunk legs took the impact then he was up and he trained his .45 on her.

"Give me a reason," he growled.

Cal pounded up behind Layne then slowed, gun drawn, aimed, head cocked to the sight. He inched forward beside Layne.

Her eyes circled the men then her hand dropped. Not that she was giving up. She couldn't hold it up anymore. Layne knew this because her body dropped too, flat on her back on the pavement of a parking garage. A bubble of blood escaped her lips and slid down the side of her mouth.

They all approached slowly except Ryker who got there quick and kicked her gun out of her hand.

She was audibly wheezing then the blood gurgled in her throat.

Ryker crouched beside her and Layne and Cal tensed.

"Brother," Layne whispered as units came skidding around the parking garage, screeching to a halt, sirens blaring, lights flashing.

There was a lot of noise but, even so, Layne could hear as Ryker pulled the phlegm up his throat.

Then he bent and spit, the slimy, yellow hocker hitting her smack on the cheekbone, splashing into her eye.

"Cunt," he hissed then straightened.

"Stand down," a uniform ordered and all eyes moved to the advancing cops.

Layne dropped his gun hand, so did Cal. Ryker shoved his in his back waistband.

The cops must have got a heads up from Merry. They immediately lost interest in Layne, Cal and Ryker and trained their guns on Towers.

"Shit," Cal growled slow and Layne looked to him to see he was looking at Layne. Then he smiled just as slow. "You are one crazy motherfucker. Fuck me, you jumped on her car, man."

Ryker strolled close, his eyes locked on Layne.

Then he said two words.

"Epic, bro."

Layne, Cal and Ryker strode into the foyer of The Townsend as Merry was moving through it.

The minute Merry saw them he grinned huge, his gait quickened and that fist that had hold of Layne's chest loosened.

There was no reason to smile.

Unless a miracle happened.

"Word's spreadin', big man, remember us little people when you're baskin' in LA sunshine and the glow of superstardom," Merry remarked upon arrival.

"What?" Layne asked at this unexpected opening.

"Parking garage's got manned cameras, Tanner. That shit's flyin' 'round so fast—"

"You wanna cut the crap and tell me about my girl?" Ryker barked and Merry looked at him, his grin still in place.

"Yeah, man, I do," he said without hesitation. "They took the floor. Only blood shed was blood that deserved to leak. The team they put together was top notch. They got into the rooms and all the clients were inside. Champagne and hors d'oeuvres. The good news for you, brother, is that Alexis and the other girls had not yet regained consciousness. They're not only untouched; they don't even know where they are." Merry looked to Layne. "Apparently, they wait for them to be awake. Each suite had two bedrooms and a sitting room. In each suite, one bedroom had our girls in it, the sitting room had drinks and munchies, the last bedroom had girls from her stable. Previews for the final show but they didn't get the final show. Got some of 'em caught in the act. Pervs are fucked, every last one of them, pants down or not."

"She's okay?" Ryker growled.

"She's absolutely fine. She's with a female officer and still unconscious," Merry answered.

And that was when Ryker collapsed. One second he was standing, the next second his ass was to the floor, his knees bent to the ceiling, his forearms to his knees and his head was bowed between his legs. Merry, Cal and Layne all looked down at a big man brought low by a miracle.

When Ryker's shoulders started shaking, Cal stepped away, Merry looked to his boots but Layne crouched beside his friend.

He wrapped a hand around his thick neck and got close.

"Colt told me, since they used God, maybe He'd be motivated to help out." Layne murmured, put pressure on Ryker's neck and released him. "Apparently, He was motivated."

Ryker nodded to his lap.

Layne straightened and Merry and he moved two feet to Cal, giving Ryker time.

"Anything new?" Layne asked.

"Rutledge is still in surgery. Towers is bein' transported, no clue there but we've got her on identity theft, multiple counts of underage prostitution, multiple counts of statutory rape, blackmail, kidnapping, and any of her boys' guns match the bullets you took, brother, they roll and say she ordered the hit, conspiracy to commit murder. She lives after you drilled two into her chest, she'll never take another free breath."

"What about her other girls?" Layne asked.

"Too soon, they're bein' transported to the station to get questioned. Though, one gave up the location of at least one of her stables. They're puttin' together a raid now. There might be more. Each of those rooms had three or more girls in it, Tanner, and early info says these girls are not all she's got," Merry answered. "She left some behind."

"Jesus," Cal muttered, the word heavy with disgust. "It's this big, how can this be under IMPD's radar?"

Merry shook his head. "Don't know, outside the bitch was smart. But I reckon we'll find out."

"My source says she worked the foster care angle," Layne reminded Merry.

"Yeah, and we checked that out. She did that but, like Youth Group, she recruited through a front, a fall guy, or in that case, woman. The woman who acted as her agent is currently serving a nickel, but Towers never let her close enough. In fact, the woman never saw Towers. She handed over to a member of Towers' crew who disappeared after Social Services cottoned on and started their investigation and never was located. The girls were never recovered except to surface later as prostitutes, porn stars, bikers' bitches and equally limiting professions. That angle died seven years ago."

Ryker's presence hit their group.

"I wanna see Alexis," he announced.

Merry looked at him and nodded. He turned to a uniform who was standing with a plainclothes officer and whistled.

When he had the uniform's attention, he nodded his head to Ryker. "This guy is guardian to Alexis McGraw, the redheaded girl in room twelve oh three. He wants to see his girl."

The uniform swept his eyes top to toe on Ryker and then they narrowed on Merry. Ryker looked like guardian of the gates of hell, not guardian to a pretty, fourteen year old redhead.

"He's cool," Merry assured.

"Merry, are you gonna talk to the girls now or can they go home?" Layne asked and Merry turned to him as the uniform approached.

"They wake up, they'll be disoriented and since they were probably roofied, won't remember much. We can talk to them in the morning," Merry answered.

Ryker was moving away with the uniform, his hand in his motorcycle jacket but he called to Layne, "You're our ride, bro."

"I'm not goin' anywhere," Layne called back.

"I know, but you comin' or what?" Ryker returned.

Layne glanced through Merry and Cal, nodded and followed Ryker. It would seem big, scary, badass, looking-like-a raving-lunatic Ryker needed his BFF.

Fuck.

He heard Ryker on his phone when he stopped beside him at the elevator. "Liss, baby, she's okay. She's good. They found her. She's all right. I'm goin' to her now. We're gonna be home soon. It's all good."

The elevator opened and Colt with a variety of cops walked out. Colt clapped Ryker on the shoulder as they switched places but his hand came up to Layne. Layne took it and looked in Colt's eyes.

"Cal called, ran it down. Remember us when you're a big Hollywood action star," Colt remarked.

Layne let his hand go muttering, "Bite me," through his smile.

Then he moved to the elevator.

Layne pulled into Lissa McGraw's driveway and the front door of the house was opened before he came to a complete stop.

Lissa was running out, but Layne saw Jasper, Tripp, Keira and Seth Cosgrove standing in the yard, each with a can of pop in their hands.

Seth broke away and slowly approached the Suburban as Ryker hopped down. Layne exited the other side and watched Rocky wander out behind Lissa, Devin on her heels. By the time Layne rounded the hood, Ryker had Alexis in his arms. She was awake but not herself. She slid her thin arms around his huge shoulders just as Lissa collided with them. Her arms spanning them both, she burst into tears.

Rocky moved to him and took his hand.

"Somehow, Seth heard word. Paige is inside too. Jasper tried to get him to go but he wouldn't," she whispered, leaning in close.

"He's a good kid," Layne whispered back, eyes on Seth who was hanging back but his gaze was intense on Alexis.

"Lissa told us she's okay. Is she okay?" Rocky asked and Layne looked at her.

"She's good," Layne answered.

"Totally good?" Rocky pushed, her eyes as intense as Seth's and she was holding her body funny, guarded, alert.

"She's fine, baby, she woke up just when we got to her. She doesn't even know what happened but no one got a chance to touch her."

"Tiffany?"

"Tiffany too, it's all good." He leaned down and put his hand to her neck. "*Totally* good, Rocky."

Rocky nodded and her eyes moved to Ryker who was shuffling Lissa back while carrying Alexis to the house. Layne and Rocky moved with them. Layne nodded to Devin then his eyes cut to his sons.

Finally, he looked at Seth and stopped. "It's good you're here, Seth, but let me scope this out, yeah? Stay out here with Jas, Keira and Tripp."

Seth nodded. Layne nodded back, swept his eyes through his boys and he and Rocky went inside.

Vi, Feb, Josie and Paige were there. Coffee mugs were everywhere but Vi was collecting them. Angela was asleep in Paige's arms. Jack was sitting on his ass on the floor, sucking on something purple and edible that he'd gotten all over his face in a way that gave evidence to the fact it was sticky. Layne could see through a wide opening and Feb was in the tiny kitchen, doing something at the sink. Josie was wiping down counters. Lissa, Ryker and Alexis had disappeared, likely down the back hall.

Layne went to the mouth of the hall and waited.

Ryker came out five minutes later, walked to Layne and stopped.

"Your call, brother, you want company, they're here for the long haul. You don't, I'll get them gone," Layne offered.

Ryker stared at him, said not a word, then turned and disappeared in the room he came out of. Two minutes later, he was back.

"Liss likes to hear people in her house. Alexis is asking about Seth. Your crew is in for the long haul."

"Right." Layne nodded. "I'll call Reggie's and order pizza."

Layne turned to move into the living room but turned back when Ryker said, "Bro."

"Yeah?"

"She was wakin' up when we got to her."

"Yeah man, I was there."

"She was wakin' up when we got to her," Ryker repeated.

He had something to say so Layne waited for him to say it.

Ryker finally spoke. "She had less than an hour."

"Ryker—" Layne began.

"You hadn't called that location, bro..." He trailed off and stopped.

"Well, I did."

Ryker held his gaze.

Then he whispered, "Yeah, you did."

Then he turned around and disappeared back in the room.

Layne went to the living room, his eyes going to Rocky.

"Let the kids in. We need to order pizza," he said into the room.

Rocky's eyes locked with his.

Then she gave him the dimple.

Layne woke to his cell phone ringing and Rocky pinning him to the bed.

Instantly, her head came up.

He reached out to the phone, his eyes scanning his clock. It was three forty-two. He looked at the display, it said "Unknown Caller." He connected, putting the phone to his ear.

"Layne," he answered.

"Heard word from your man, it's safe to call you," a woman replied, it took him a minute to place the voice and then he did.

He scooted up in the bed and Rocky scooted with him.

"Marissa," he said on a squeeze of Rocky who gave him a squeeze back and pressed closer.

"She didn't make it," Marissa stated.

Marissa was right. Nicolette Towers was dead on arrival. Layne had no problem with this.

Jeremy Goulding had flipped and copped to Tara, Summer and Hannah, but there were no other girls from the 'burg. However, he did know of operations in other small town churches in two locations. Towers held these parties often and the girls went for top dollar. Jeremy withheld this information because he knew he was screwed and he didn't want to be more screwed. He thought, since the girls hadn't talked for months, this knowledge would never make the light of day. Fortunately, he was wrong.

Towers had two stables and recruited her other girls from out of state. Some were runaways. Some were sold into her operation. Some were clocked in juvie and picked up when they got out, their disappearance put down to running away, none of them missed. And none of them originally came from Indiana, thus flying under IMPD radar.

There were so many people involved, from pimps, to recruiters, to security, it would take the IMPD some serious time to dismantle the entire operation, but it was already disintegrating. Some of the men they picked up were heavy hitters, wealthy power brokers, also not all local. And they were all blabbing like old women.

Rutledge had survived and was currently handcuffed to a hospital bed. Cal and Ryker had uncovered where he hid his payoff cash in his apartment and they left it for the 'burg PD to find. It was highly unlikely he'd be offered bail. It was also highly unlikely he'd survive his prison term.

Ballistics matched on the three guns that shot Layne. Two put bullets in Rutledge, one was found beside the man Layne shot in the calf who then had Towers run over his legs. Since she did this driving on rims, one of his legs was cut clean off.

"No, she didn't make it," Layne confirmed and Roc gave him another squeeze.

"Heard from your man that you took her out."

"That's right."

There was silence.

Then, "Is it bad that I'm smiling right now?"

Layne felt his lips twitch. "No."

More silence then, "Glad you didn't get dead."

Before Layne could reply he had dead air.

He tossed his phone to the nightstand. Then he slid down into the bed, taking Rocky with him.

"She okay?" Rocky asked.

"Reckon so, considering she told me she's smiling."

Rocky shoved her face in his chest and he wasn't sure what this response meant until she lifted her head then shifted her body so it was on his, her face in his neck.

"Sweetcheeks," he murmured, his hand sliding in her hair.

Her lips went to his ear. "Never gave a hero a blowjob."

Layne started quietly laughing.

Her head moved and her mouth came to his.

"Or…maybe I have," she whispered.

"Well, baby, what are you waiting for? I'm not gonna stop you," he whispered back.

He felt her smile against his mouth.

Then she took her time, working her way down his body, before she gave him a really, fucking great, four o'clock in the morning blowjob.

Epilogue

A BEAUTIFUL LIFE

She moved, her lips sliding up his neck, over his jaw, to his mouth. His arm stole around her waist. His other hand went to her hip as her body moved on top of his.

"Thank you, baby," she whispered.

"For what?" he whispered back.

The side of her nose brushed his.

"A beautiful life."

⸺

Layne opened his eyes.

Rocky was pinning him to the bed.

He smiled at the ceiling.

Then he rolled into his woman.

⸺

Layne walked to the foot of the stairs.

"Sweetcheeks, get your ass down here!" he yelled.

"Coming!" she yelled back.

"Yeah, Roc, you said that ten minutes ago!" He was still yelling.

"Well, now I'm coming!" She was also still yelling. "You can put CeeCee in the car!"

That meant she actually was coming.

Layne turned to the playpen by the dining room table. Blondie was flat out on her side by the pen. Cecilia was in it, holding herself up, her baby fists around the bars, her big blue eyes staring up at her dad, a little tuft of dark hair in a mini-ponytail with a little purple bow sticking straight up on top of her head.

Layne approached and Blondie's head jerked up and twisted. The dog glared at him a second like she had no idea who he was then her tail started banging against the floor. Pretty much no one got near Cecilia unless they had Blondie's approval.

He reached into the pen and hefted up his daughter who immediately reached up, grabbed hold of his lower lip and tugged. Hard.

He knew what that meant so he dropped his head. She let his lip go and he buried his face in her neck and blew.

She giggled.

Layne pulled his face out of her neck, kissed her forehead then lifted a hand and gently tugged his daughter's fucking ponytail, *and* the goddamned bow, out of her hair.

He tossed it on the island, rounded it, nabbed his keys and walked his daughter out to the truck as she babbled at the same time she slapped his jaw repeatedly.

He strapped her into the seat and was just slamming the door when Rocky came out. She was carrying a pie plate in one hand, a huge, but stylish bag over her shoulder and she was wearing a short skirt, a sweet top that hugged her frame and her skin was tan. This was because Layne had a below ground pool put in because Rocky told him the winter before she'd always wanted one. The second the spring thaw came, the diggers were there.

"Told you I was coming," she informed him as she strutted to the truck.

"Get in the car, Roc," Layne replied, swinging in himself.

She rolled her eyes. He grinned.

She settled in, put the pie plate on her lap and buckled up as Layne pulled out. They were accelerating forward when Rocky turned and smiled at Cecilia.

Then he felt her eyes on him.

"Layne, where's her bow?"

"In the garbage disposal," Layne lied.

"Layne!" Rocky snapped. "It took me twenty minutes to get that looking right."

"So?"

She turned and faced forward. "I can't *believe* you."

Layne hit the button to roll down his window.

"What are you doing? Turn on the air con, that's too much wind for CeeCee," she ordered.

"You're cute when you're bossy, sweetcheeks," Layne replied, stopped at a stop sign and turned to his woman. His hand shot out, fingers fastening on the band in her hair. He pulled it out, tossed it out the window, checked the way was clear and turned left.

"Did you just do that?" she whispered irately as he rolled the window back up.

"Yep," Layne replied.

"I…I don't know what to say." She was still whispering irately.

"So don't say anything."

He felt her eyes on him and heard her twisting in her seat. "Last week, you pulled out my ponytail holder and took a knife to it *while I was making dinner* and *your mother and Devin were there.*"

"Yeah, Roc, I remember. I was there too," Layne returned. "Like I keep tellin' you, you quit wearin' 'em, I'll quit doin' shit like that."

She twisted back to face forward and crossed her arms on her chest.

Layne reached out a hand and slid it up her bare leg until she clamped her legs together and his fingers got stuck between her thighs.

"You're going to make me drop the pie," she snapped.

"So move the pie," Layne replied.

"You can't feel me up when I'm mad at you."

"Why not?"

She made a noise in her throat that made Layne chuckle. Then she moved the pie, wrapped her hand around his wrist and yanked it from between her legs. He twisted his wrist, caught her hand, curled his fingers around it and pulled it to his mouth.

He'd done as he'd intended. He'd given her a huge rock. A few months later, with his sons at his side and Josie Judd at hers, he'd slid a wide gold band at the base of it.

Right then, he kissed both.

Her fingers curled around his when he did and behind him he heard his daughter giggle. For some reason, Cecilia thought it was hilarious when Layne showed her mother affection.

His daughter laughed a lot.

"You know what's annoying?" she asked when he rested her hand on his thigh.

"Nope," he answered.

"When you're sweet when I'm angry at you."

"Right," he muttered.

"Stop doing that," she demanded.

"I'll get right on that."

He knew she'd turned her head to the side window when she murmured, "Big liar."

Layne burst out laughing.

Layne parked on the street outside Cal and Vi's house, a street that was lined with cars. One of those cars was Jasper's red Charger. Another one was Tripp's silver Camaro.

Layne released his grateful daughter from the confines of her carseat, Rocky grabbed her big bag and the pie, and he slid an arm around her shoulders as they walked up the side of the house between the garage and Cal and Vi's home and hit the backyard.

Violet had a way with flowers and her backyard was a showstopper. Now it was also filled with people, but even so, Layne clocked his sons immediately.

He stopped. Roc stopped with him, turned into him, got up on her toes and brushed her lips to his. Then she bent and brushed her lips to her daughter's head. After that, she turned toward the deck to take her pie to a table groaning with food.

Layne watched as Rocky climbed the steps and touched her cheek to the cheek of a smiling Violet who had a chubby infant attached to her hip. Eight months ago, Vi and Cal had added son Sam to their brood. Then Vi had declared she was done.

Cal was of another mind.

An epic battle had begun considering Cal kept dumping her birth control pills in the toilet and Vi kept bitching about this to her girlfriends, including Roc, at every available opportunity of which there where many. She also shared her strategies of waging war against Cal's determination to have another child. Apparently, from what Rocky told him, Cal was extremely determined and put a fair amount of effort into victory. Also, according to Roc, Vi enjoyed bitching about it but wasn't exactly fighting to win.

Layne turned from his woman and he and Cecilia made their way to his boys. To get to their destination, Layne had to dodge Jack chasing Angela through the thick, green grass. When the path was clear, his eyes focused on his sons.

Both were on their backs, side by side, legs straight out, ankles crossed, but up on their elbows. Giselle was sitting cross-legged close to Tripp, her knee resting on his hip. Keira was draped full down Jasper, her torso pressed to his side, one of her legs tangled with his, her arm resting on his abs, her cheek to his shoulder, but she was gabbing with Giselle.

Jasper and Keira had never stopped being inseparable. Like his dad, Jas knew exactly what he wanted when he found it, but unlike his dad, he was never going to let it go.

Keira followed Jas to Purdue and on more than one occasion at a variety of times during the day and night she answered Jas's cell or the phone in Jas's apartment. Layne knew what that meant as well as what their current intimate position stated and neither of them hid it. He had no problem with this and Cal, standing at the barbeque and not a stupid man by a long shot, didn't either. Both men knew the future would see Jas and Keira's children running through this grass.

Layne had no problem with that either. Keira had learned the hard way to take care of the people she loved while she had them. And there was no denying Keira Winters loved his son, she loved him deeply and she loved him in a way that Layne recognized would last a lifetime. Jasper was Jasper, he'd proven early he'd do anything for his girl and nothing had changed.

The minute he got close, his sons' eyes moved to him and he got identical smiles and nods.

Keira said, "Hey, Mr. Layne," and Layne greeted her back but Giselle didn't say a word. She just lifted her arms, instantly reaching for Cecilia.

Tripp and Giselle often babysat for Cecilia and Giselle doted on Layne and Rocky's daughter.

Tripp doted on Giselle.

She hadn't become less shy but she had become extremely tight with his son. They were as inseparable as Jasper and Keira but in a different way. Tripp's public displays of affection were limited to hand holding and sometimes when they were watching TV, Giselle would curl up at his feet and rest her head on his knee or curl on the seat of the couch and rest her head on this thigh.

Though once, Layne had started down the stairs and caught sight of them making out, hot and extremely heavy, on the sectional in a way that stated they did it often when they had no audience around. Not making a noise, Layne had retraced his steps, left them to it and hoped with his father, stepmother and baby sister all upstairs, making out was as far as Tripp was prepared to go.

But at all times, Tripp was gentle with Giselle and he was still the only person Layne had seen that could make her smile big or laugh hard, both unconsciously. She never liked attention but sometimes Rocky would nudge Layne, nod at Giselle and he'd see Giselle watching his son move through the kitchen or sit watching TV, and she'd do it with a look on her face that reminded Layne of Rocky. It wasn't the same but it was just as good. Tripp made her laugh, but he also made her feel safe and he made her feel special, three of the best gifts Tripp could give her, and her look made it clear she appreciated them.

He handed CeeCee to Giselle and dropped to the grass, stretching out like his sons.

"You and Roc missed the big announcement," Jas stated when Layne settled and Layne's eyes went to his boy, who was now no longer a boy in any sense of that word.

"Yeah?" he asked.

"Kate's gettin' married," Jas declared, Layne's eyes moved through the people and he located Kate Winters, Keira's sister and Vi's older daughter. Kate was just about to enter grad school and she was now leaning against a tall, lean but built, dark-haired man. She was also smiling happily and talking to Cal's Aunt Theresa and Uncle Vinnie.

"You know him?" Layne asked.

"Yeah, his name's Tony. He's a cop, Chicago PD," Jas answered, and Layne grinned, thinking the apple definitely does not fall far from the tree. Kate's dad was a cop on the Chicago PD. "He seems solid," Jasper finished.

"Good," Layne murmured and he looked at Keira. "You like him, Keirry?"

"Sure, he's hot," Keira replied. Jasper's eyes sliced to her, she grinned insolently at him then leaned in close to his face. "Not as hot as you, honey," she whispered, glanced over her shoulder at her sister and her man, then back to Jasper where she noted, "But no denying, the Winters women have *really good taste.*"

Jasper glared at his girl then looked at his old man. "You know, Dad, I woulda been happy with the gene you gave Tripp, the one that would lead me to a woman who wasn't a complete nut and also wasn't friggin' irritating all the time."

Keira, completely unoffended by this, burst out laughing. So did Tripp and, to a lesser extent, Giselle. Jasper did not.

Layne smiled at his son then he saw Cecilia straining away from Giselle, her arms stretched out to Tripp.

Tripp took one arm from under him as Giselle lost hold of a very determined CeeCee and she landed on Tripp's chest. His arm circled his sister's fat bottom. She reached up, latched on and pulled at his lip which made Tripp smile and instantly bend his head, heft her up his chest and blow into her neck.

Cecilia giggled.

The birth of Cecilia was an event that made a lot of people pretty fucking happy, including Layne's two boys. They loved their sister and CeeCee liked her mom and dad. She liked Vera and Devin. She liked Dave and Merry. She liked Keira and Giselle.

But she adored her brothers.

The person it didn't make happy was Gabrielle. Gabby detested her sons' devotion to Rocky and Layne's daughter and didn't mind letting that fact be known. She didn't say anything but it pissed her off, her sons preferring to be with their dad, Roc and their sister, and Gabby being Gabby, found her own, particular bitchy way to let this be known.

As usual, it wasn't a good play. Her boys didn't like it and she didn't let it go so she'd managed to alienate them both. Now, neither saw her very often. When Jas came home from Purdue, he was on the air mattress in his old room, now Tripp's room. And Tripp, more often than not, stopped taking his turns at Gabby's.

When this started, Gabby had threatened Layne with attorneys.

As he'd told her that morning at Rocky's apartment, Layne didn't respond because he never responded. She called, he didn't answer. She called him from a number he didn't recognize, he picked up, heard her voice then hung up. She left a message, he didn't return it. The buzzer beeped at his office and he saw her on the monitor, he walked to the outer door and locked it. She never came to the house because she tried that once, the door went unanswered and Tripp had pulled up while she was camped out on one of Rocky's Adirondack chairs on the front porch and this didn't go over very well with Tripp, as in at all, so she'd never tried that shit again.

Gabby didn't enter his or Roc's life except when he became annoyed when his sons' spoke of her bullshit bitter antics.

But Tripp had had a word with his mother, it was a word she didn't like, but whatever it was, it was also a word that made her back off. After that, Tripp went his own way and that way normally led him to his room at Layne and Roc's.

With time, Tripp had learned cool. He'd also learned to focus his intensity. And both made Tripp Layne a young man you didn't mess with, even if you were his mother.

Rocky had intervened on Gabby's behalf and she'd done this more than once, with both boys together and separate. She'd intervened but her efforts weren't successful.

Devin had been right, like their father, both Layne's sons saw Rocky's vulnerable spot even before she exposed it that Saturday afternoon, and her work at healing that wound hadn't stopped his sons' from militantly standing strong to protect against it, or anything causing her pain.

This wasn't because their old man loved Rocky. It was because they did. The addition of Cecilia just strengthened their connection with Layne's wife. That didn't mean they didn't love their mother that just meant she'd made an extremely stupid play. He knew his boys. They cared about Gabby. They'd find their way back. But when they did, they'd do it on their terms.

"Takin' Ellie down to Bloomington next week, Dad, she wants to scope out the campus," Tripp told him, his neck craning, dodging CeeCee's hand at the same time he was grinning at her and tickling her side with his fingers.

"All right," Layne replied.

"You go to IU, we won't be able to talk anymore," Keira told Giselle, dipping her head to rest her cheek back on Jas.

"They have a good med school," Giselle replied.

"So does IU...PU...I," Keira returned and Giselle shook her head, a small smile on her face.

It would be interesting to see if Giselle went to IU. She was determined to be a doctor and had the grades for it. She also had the diligence.

Tripp, however, had an uncertain future. It was uncertain, but it was bright.

He'd made the All-USA High School Football team and this meant he wasn't just a star in the 'burg, he was a star throughout the State of Indiana. With Giselle his girl, Rocky his stepmother and his head together, his grades were excellent. Because of this, Tripp had his choice of colleges. But considering his game kept improving and the high school team had seen two consecutive wins at State, both of these having a lot to do with Tripp, who excelled far beyond anyone's expectations, expectations that were already high, if he avoided injury it was highly likely after school he'd be drafted into the pros.

That said, Giselle might be quiet and shy, but she was also smart and knew what she wanted. If Tripp and Giselle went the distance through their upcoming senior year, it would be interesting to see who followed who.

Raquel speculated about it all the time. She figured Tripp would follow Giselle. Layne knew Tripp would do his own thing and if he wanted to keep connected with Giselle, even if they were apart, he'd make that so.

Layne's eyes moved from his son to his daughter seeing, at this point, not getting what she wanted from one brother, Cecilia was giving up on Tripp. She crawled across his chest, launching herself at Jasper who caught her with two hands, dropped to his back, disengaging from Keira. He threw Cecilia in the air and caught her as she giggled loudly.

Keira kept a hand on Jas's abs and watched, her face soft, her eyes longing.

Fuck.

Layne was thankfully taken from thoughts of imminent grandfatherhood when he felt cold on his arm and looked up to see Rocky holding a beer there.

"Beer, sweetheart," she whispered.

"Thanks, baby," he muttered through a smile and took the bottle.

She gave him the dimple before she dropped down beside him, her movement fluid, then she curled into him much like Keira had been curled into Jas except without her leg tangled with his or her cheek to his shoulder. But her torso was pressed to his side and her hand, holding a fancy-ass bottle of beer, was resting on his abs.

"So, how's Vi feeling about the engagement?" Layne asked her.

"Old," Rocky replied.

Layne grinned and looked at Vi.

She was now standing with Cal at the barbeque, Sam had been claimed by Keira's grandmother, Bea. Cal had his arm wrapped around Vi's shoulders and he'd pinned her to his chest, his head dipped down, his face close to hers. Vi looked pissed in a way Layne knew she didn't mean it and he knew this because Cal was grinning. What Vi didn't look was old. She looked tanned and healthy and full of attitude.

Layne took a slug from his beer, his eyes doing a scan, seeing Colt and Feb lounged in the grass much like Layne and Rocky. Angela was crawling all over Colt, Jack was chasing after her and Feb was holding on to her man. Colt was grinning down at Angela and Jack. Feb wasn't grinning. Feb's forehead was pressed to Colt's neck, her eyes had a faraway look in them and her face was, no other way to describe it, at peace.

Layne's eyes kept scanning and he saw Lexie with her latest boyfriend. Seth had gone to Ball State and Alexis had moved on, then again, and again, according to word from Rocky, Keira, Giselle and Lissa, all of whom kept close watch on Alexis's active love life.

Now she was dating Tripp's friend Shane and she was smitten because Shane was playing it cool. She'd finally met her match in the games-playing stakes but Lexie, *she* was fighting to win. Inside word from Tripp was that Shane was into her and she wouldn't have to fight too hard. Shane just didn't want to be a notch on Lexie's belt and he was setting about making that so.

His eyes kept scanning and he saw Lissa and Ryker who, after what went down, made their way in with this crowd then went about fixing themselves to it permanently. Immediately after it was over, Ryker had moved in with Lissa and her daughter. Not too long after that, Ryker had also officially adopted Alexis. Therefore Ryker's life was a living hell as new father to a spitfire and he bitched about it incessantly. But Layne knew he was full of shit. With the way Ryker did it, Layne knew he was loving every minute of it.

Ryker still partnered with Layne on occasion. Sometimes it was when Layne needed him, most of the time it was when Ryker was bored and needed something to do.

All other times, Ryker was just Ryker. Layne had long ago searched and found Ryker had been paroled two years after going down for grand theft auto. Once released, he'd stayed clean but he'd done this by staying off the grid and therefore Layne had no clue what he did to keep his Harley in fuel and his woman and daughter happy. Except for the fact he made it his business to be in everyone else's and information didn't come cheap. Layne had no problem with that either, since often in Layne's line of work, he needed information and Ryker gave him a discount.

His eyes continued scanning and he saw Devin chatting with Feb's father Jack and brother Morrie, Vera not too far away gabbing with Feb's mother Jackie.

Devin and Vera had officially hooked up, and six months ago in a small, private ceremony with Layne at Devin's side, his Aunt Flo at Vera's, and a single pew filled only with Rocky, a nearly newborn CeeCee in her arms, Jasper and Tripp, they'd taken vows.

Layne was no longer uncertain how he felt about this. Vera had her own life and liked living it so she did and let Dev go his own way. This left Dev free to go his own way without headache or constant nagging for an explanation, but with a good meal every night and a woman who put up with his bad attitude and more often than not gave as good as she got. Therefore, it worked for Devin in a way he'd never found before, the same for Layne's ma.

They were happy—Dev, cantankerously so, Vera deliriously so.

And this worked for Layne.

He felt Rocky's hand leave his abs and he watched her take a pull on her beer as she listened to Keira gabbing about something. She took the bottle from her mouth and smiled at Keira then laughed softly as Keira kept talking.

It was then it came to Layne that the sun was shining. The beer was cold. There were friends and family all around. Vi's backyard was beautiful. Layne's boys were close. His daughter was babbling happily at her brother. And his woman was pressed to his side, laughing softly.

Nothing.

He was lying in the grass with his boys, his girl and his woman doing nothing.

Which meant everything.

Layne felt that golden trail glide through him.

All this time, he'd never lost it. It was no longer as strong but it didn't need to be. It moved through him often, every day, sometimes more than once. He'd learned to savor it, not to take anything for granted, not even normal.

No, especially not normal.

Therefore, determined not to take anything for granted, his eyes glued to Raquel's profile, he lifted up. Her head turned. He twisted and locked an arm around her waist, pulling her up his chest.

"Layne—" she started but his head came down and he kissed his wife.

Hard.

He tasted her, smelled her, felt her soft body pressed to his and he loved all of that.

But what he heard was his daughter's giggle.

And he loved that too.

Layne laid the sleeping Cecilia on her belly in her crib in Tripp's old room.

He pulled the blanket up to her shoulders and let his hand rest on her bottom a second while he made certain she settled.

Then he moved out of the room, ignoring the excess decoration of pinks and purples and shooting stars. His wife could shop and she was thrilled beyond reason when she'd had a daughter, something Layne knew before she'd had her because Doc had told him, information Rocky had unusually not wanted to know until the day came.

Since her birth, Layne wasn't certain his daughter wore the same thing twice and he'd rarely gone into CeeCee's room and not found some new decoration or toy. Vera advised that he should curtail Rocky's tendency to spoil their daughter rotten. His mother had advised this but Layne had no intention of taking that advice. Layne intended to let Roc be whatever kind of mother she wanted to be and as the months slid past, he knew this was the right decision. This was mainly because Rocky was Rocky and it was also because she'd had two good teachers.

He heard his family downstairs and headed that way but stopped when his phone rang. He pulled it out, checked the display and put it to his ear.

"What's up, Sully?" Layne greeted.

"Got news, Tanner," Sully replied and this could mean anything.

Since it all went down, Layne's caseload hadn't lightened. Now that his mother did his books and he had a receptionist, his caseload had doubled. Thus, his daughter's room could be filled with girlie shit, his wife's closet filled with clingy dresses, his credit card statement filled with expensive dinners so he could eat while sitting across from his wife while she was wearing clingy dresses, his youngest son had a Camaro and his family had an underground pool.

Therefore, with a heavy caseload that often involved work with the 'burg's PD, Sully's news could mean anything.

"What?" Layne asked.

"Harrison Rutledge is dead, man. Happened yesterday. Shiv to the jugular. He bled out before the guards got to his body."

Well, that took longer than expected.

"World's not exactly a poorer place," Layne muttered.

"Yeah," Sully agreed. "But thought you'd wanna know."

"Thanks, Sul," Layne replied.

"One other thing," Sully stated.

"Yeah?"

"Stew Baranski's parole was denied."

Layne grinned.

"Not a model prisoner?" Layne asked.

"Guy's not only an asshole, apparently he's an asshole magnet. He and his crew aren't real popular with their fellow inmates *or* the guards. Dick's seen a lotta solitary. Why they even put him before the parole board is anyone's guess."

"Probably were hopin' to get rid of him. Not a good fix, turning him loose on an unsuspecting public, but at least he'd be outta their hair."

"Yeah," Sully muttered and Layne knew he was smiling. "That would be why."

Layne chuckled.

"That's all the news that's fit to print," Sully said then finished, "For now."

"Right, later," Layne returned.

"Later."

Layne took his phone from his ear and wiped his mind clean of Harrison Rutledge and Stewart Baranski. Those assholes had had enough of his time, his life, and Rutledge had been responsible for taking Layne's blood. They didn't deserve to be in Layne's house. Not ever but especially not now. Not when it was filled with the beautiful life, a place Harrison Rutledge, dead or alive, and Stew Baranski didn't deserve to be.

Layne walked down the stairs and saw through the sliding glass door that Devin was outside with a stoagie. Then he saw his boys and their girls were in the living room, Blondie sitting beside Jasper with her head in his lap, his fingers scratching behind her ears, her eyes closed in apparent dog ecstasy. Vera was in the kitchen looking like she was going to cook something even though they'd all just left the barbeque and they'd all eaten enough for a week. And Roc was sitting at the island, opening mail.

Layne went to Rocky, fitted his front to her back, swept her hair from her shoulder and dropped his head to kiss her neck.

"You could save a move if you let me wear my hair in a ponytail," she pointed out as she slit open an envelope.

"We'll leave that 'til I'm ninety and decrepit," Layne replied.

"Right," she whispered but he could tell she did it through a smile. "Like you're *ever* going to be decrepit." Layne straightened and Rocky asked softly, "She down?"

"And out," Layne answered.

"Good," Rocky whispered.

He started to move away when Rocky pulled something out of the envelope, studied it, twisted and asked him, "Do you know a Farrah Gerald or an Andre Washington?"

Layne's body went still and he looked down at the thick, embossed card in her hand.

"What?" he asked.

She flipped the card back and forth. "A Farrah Gerald or Andre Washington," she repeated. "This is their wedding announcement. I have no clue who they are but..." Her head turned, she flipped the thick cream envelope over and studied the address then looked back at Layne. "It's addressed to us." She went back to the card, flipped it over too and then twisted again to look at Layne. "And there's a note, sweetheart. It says," her eyes dropped to the card, "'Don't worry, he reminds me of you. He's a badass but he's got a soft spot too.'"

Layne stared at the card. Then he looked at Rocky who'd tipped her head back to look at him.

And he grinned.

Three blasts from the past in five minutes, one expected, one inconsequential, one unexpected, none unwelcome.

Layne got close and locked eyes with Rocky then he slid his hand up her back, under her hair, his fingers curling around her neck.

"Marissa Gibbons, baby," he whispered, watched her eyes grow wide then her head dropped and she stared down at the announcement.

When she did, he watched the dimple hit her cheek.

"Layne."

Breathy, beautiful. Fuck.

Layne kept driving his cock into his wife.

"Baby," she whispered into his ear through her pants.

"Don't hold back," Layne grunted into her ear, one of his forearms in the sectional, the other hand between them, finger at her clit.

"God, oh my God. Don't stop," she begged, lifting her hips for him, all her limbs wrapped around him, her wrists under her ankles, her fingers curled into his ass.

"Stop holding back, baby," Layne ordered.

She did as she was told, her hips surged up, her neck arched and a low moan slid from her throat as her pussy pulsed around his cock.

His finger left her clit, his hand went to her hip, he pulled her up to keep taking him as she kept coming underneath him and he thrust into her, hard, deep, fast and then his mouth found hers and he groaned down her throat as he exploded.

He came down and Rocky kept him trapped in her limbs as he kept stroking slowly through their combined wetness inside her. As he did this, his mouth explored her neck and hers returned the favor.

Then he rolled to his back, keeping their connection. He did an ab curl, grabbed the throw then laid back pulling it over his wife and his naked bodies.

"It's summer, Jas is home," Rocky said in his ear.

"Yep," Layne replied, not knowing where she was going with this.

She lifted her head and told him. "That means we have to stop fucking on the sectional, Layne,"

Layne fucked Rocky on the sectional a lot. It was comfortable, it was cozy and there was room to move. It wasn't as big as their bed but it felt like it was.

"They're all at a late movie, sweetcheeks," he reminded her.

"Yes, but—"

"They come home, we'd hear them."

"I wouldn't," she told him and he grinned.

"Well, I would."

"Hmm," she mumbled, her nose wrinkling and her eyes narrowing. "I thought I had your undivided attention when you're inside me."

"Yeah, well, they came home when I was inside you, that would be very bad timing," Layne remarked, her eyes got big and she burst out laughing.

Layne grinned but he didn't laugh with her. He savored the golden trail her laughter sent gliding through him, lifted his hands to pull her hair away from her face and he held it back as he watched.

She sobered but kept grinning at him. Then she caught the look on his face, and still grinning, she asked, "What's on your mind, sweetheart?"

He pulled her down to him, touched his mouth to hers then pushed her back an inch.

"Thank you, baby," he whispered.

"For what?" she whispered back.

"A beautiful life."

Her mouth got soft, her eyes went half-mast and her gaze grew intense.

Then she lifted a hand, laid it against his jaw, her thumb sweeping across his lips as her eyes watched it move.

Then they lifted to his and she gave him the dimple.

The 'Burg Series continues with *Games of the Heart.*

CPSIA information can be obtained
at www.ICGtesting.com
Printed in the USA
LVOW12s0051270917
550193LV00001B/61/P